Praise for *New York Times* Bestselling Author
Heather Graham

"Graham shines in this frightening tale. Paranormal
elements add zing to her trademark chilling suspense and
steamy romance, keeping the pages flying."
—*Romantic Times* on *Haunted*

"Graham's tight plotting, her keen sense of when to reveal
and when to tease…will keep fans turning the pages."
—*Publishers Weekly* on *Picture Me Dead*

"An incredible storyteller!"
—*Los Angeles Daily News*

"Demonstrating the skills that have made her
one of today's best storytellers, Ms. Graham delivers
one of this year's best books thus far."
—*Romantic Times* on *Hurricane Bay*

"A suspenseful, sexy thriller…
Graham builds jagged suspense that will keep readers
guessing up to the final pages."
—*Publishers Weekly* on *Hurricane Bay*

"A roller-coaster ride…fast-paced, thrilling…
Heather Graham will keep you in suspense
until the very end. Captivating."
—*Literary Times* on *Hurricane Bay*

"The talented Ms. Graham once again thrills us.
She delivers excitement [and] romance…that keep
the pages flipping quickly from beginning to end."
—*Romantic Times* on *Night of the Blackbird*

"With the name Heather Graham on the cover,
you are guaranteed a good read!"
—*Literary Times*

HEATHER GRAHAM

DEAD ON THE DANCE FLOOR

MIRA®

ISBN 0-7783-2137-1

DEAD ON THE DANCE FLOOR

Copyright © 2004 by Heather Graham Pozzessere.

All rights reserved. Except for use in any review, the reproduction or
utilization of this work in whole or in part in any form by any electronic,
mechanical or other means, now known or hereafter invented, including
xerography, photocopying and recording, or in any information storage or
retrieval system, is forbidden without the written permission of the publisher,
MIRA Books, 225 Duncan Mill Road, Don Mills, Ontario, Canada M3B 3K9.

All characters in this book have no existence outside the imagination of the
author and have no relation whatsoever to anyone bearing the same name
or names. They are not even distantly inspired by any individual known or
unknown to the author, and all incidents are pure invention.

MIRA and the Star Colophon are trademarks used under license and registered
in Australia, New Zealand, Philippines, United States Patent and Trademark
Office and in other countries.

www.MIRABooks.com

Printed in U.S.A.

For Ana and John,
with congratulations on their tremendous successes,
and best of luck, always, in the future!

For Shirley Johnson,
with the deepest thanks for all your instruction,
your smile—and the laughter!

For Vickie Regan,
eternally gorgeous, and of course our true reigning diva,
Honey Bunch.

And for Victor,
who always does me so much better than me!
But teaches so much and, with his work, gives to so many.

CHAPTER 1

There was always something to see on South Beach.

Always.

Glittering, balmy, radiant by virtue of the sun by day and neon by night. The rich and beautiful came and played, and everyone else came and watched. The beach sparkled, offering the most spectacular eye candy, gossip, scandal, traffic jams and more. Nearly bare bodies that were beautiful. Nearly bare bodies that were not so beautiful.

Models, rockers, skaters, bikers, would-be-surfers-were-there-only-some-surf, the MTV crowd, the very old, the very young.

But tonight there was even more.

One of the largest and most prestigious ballroom dance competitions in the world was taking place at one of the best-known hotels ever to grace the strip of sand called Miami Beach.

And with it came Lara Trudeau.

She spun, she twirled, she floated on air, a blur of crystal color and grace.

She was, quite simply, beauty in motion.

Lara demonstrated a grace and perfection of movement

that few could even begin to emulate. She had it all, a flair
to pin down the unique character of every dance, a face that
came alive to the music, a smile that never failed. Judges
were known to have said that it was difficult to look down
and judge her footwork, much less notice the other couples on the floor, because her smile and her face were so
engaging they almost forgot their duties. They had been
known to admit that they hadn't marked other couples as
accurately as they might have; Lara was simply so beautiful and spectacular and point-blank good that it was hard
to draw their eyes away from her.

Tonight was no exception.

Indeed, tonight Lara was more incredible than ever,
more seductive, alluring, and glorious. To watch her was
to feel that the senses were teased, stroked, awakened, caressed, excited and eased.

She was alone on the floor, or rather, alone with her partner, Jim Burke. During the cabaret routines, each of the
couples in the finals took the floor alone, so there she was,
her body a lithe example of feminine perfection in her
formfitting ball gown of a thousand colors. Jim, as talented
as he was, had become nothing more than an accessory.

Those who loved her watched in awe, while those who
despised her watched with envy.

Shannon Mackay, current manager of Moonlight
Sonata, the independent studio where Lara had long ago
begun her career and continued to coach, watched with
mixed feelings of wry amusement, not at all sure herself
whether she loved Lara or despised her. But there was no
denying her talent. Even among the spectacular performances by the best and most accomplished artists in the
world community of professional dance, Lara stood out.

"She is simply incredible," Shannon said aloud.

At her side, Ben Trudeau, Lara's ex, snorted. "Oh, yeah.
Just incredible."

Jane Ulrich, who had made it to the semifinals but been edged out at the end, as usual, by Lara, turned to Ben with a brilliant smile.

"Oh, Ben. You can't still be bitter. She's so good, it's as if she's not really of this earth."

Shannon smiled at Jane's compliment. Jane was stunning that night herself; her figure lean and trim, and her waltz gown, a deep crimson, set off her dark coloring in a blaze of glittering fire.

"I'd rather dance with you," Jane's partner, Sam Railey, said softly, giving her a squeeze. "You, my love, actually dance *with* someone. Lara uses her partner like a prop."

"But she *is* brilliant, just brilliant," Gordon Henson, owner of the studio, said. He was the one who had first taught Lara, and his pride was justified.

"Let's face it—she's a mean, ambitious bitch who'd walk over a friend's dead body to get where she wanted to go," said Justin Garcia, one of the studio's upcoming salsa specialists.

Next to him, Rhianna Markham, another contender, laughed delightedly. "C'mon, Justin, say what you really feel."

Shannon nudged Rhianna and said softly, "Careful. We're surrounded by our students." And they were, since the hotel was just north of the South Beach area where the studio was located. As a teaching institution, it was the envy of many a competitor, for not only was it located in the limelight of a varied and heavily populated area, it was situated right on top of a club that had turned into a true hot spot over the past few years, since it had been bought by charismatic young Latin American entrepreneur Gabriel Lopez—who had come this evening, as well, in support of his friends. Due to the proximity of the event, even a number of the studio's more casual students had come, entranced to see the very best of the best, competitors from all over the world.

"She's just gorgeous," Rhianna said loudly enough to be overheard, making a conspiratorial face at Shannon and lowering her head. Shannon had to grin.

But then Gordon whispered to her softly, "*You* should have been out there. You could have been more gorgeous."

She shook her head. "I like teaching, not competing."

"Chicken?"

She grinned. "I know when I'm outclassed."

"Never outclassed," he said, and squeezed her hand.

On the dance floor, Lara executed another perfect lift, spiraling down her partner's body in perfect unity with the music.

There was a tap on Shannon's shoulder. At first, she paid no attention to it. The crowd was massive, including students, teachers, amateurs, professionals, press and those who just liked to watch. A jostle meant nothing as everyone vied for space from which to watch the spectacle.

The tap came again. Frowning, Shannon half turned. The sides of the stage were dark, cast in shadow by the spotlights on the floor. She couldn't see the person summoning her, but it might have been the waiter behind her, a man dressed in tails. Strange, tonight the wait staff, some of the judges and many of the contenders were dressed almost alike.

"Yes?" she murmured, puzzled.

"You're next," he said.

"Next?" she queried. But the man, whose face she hadn't really seen, was already gone. He must have been mistaken. She wasn't competing.

"Ooh!" Jane said. "She's unbelievable!"

Shannon looked quickly back to the floor, forgetting the man who had been trying to reach her in a case of mistaken identity. She wasn't particularly concerned. Whoever was up next would know. They would already be waiting on the sidelines.

Waiting in a nerve-wracking situation. Following Lara would never be easy.

"Excellent," Ben admitted. "Every step perfectly executed."

From the crowd, a collective "Ahh!" arose.

And then, suddenly, Lara Trudeau went poetically still. Her hands, so elegant with their long, tapered fingers and polished nails, flew dramatically to her left breast. There was a moment of stillness, with the music still playing a Viennese waltz as sweet and lilting as the cool air.

Then, still graceful, she dropped.

Her fall was as elegant as any dance movement, a melting into the ground, a dip that was slow, supple….

Until her head fell to the dance floor in perfect complement to the length of her body and she did not move again.

"That wasn't in her routine," Gordon whispered to Shannon.

"No," Shannon murmured back, frowning. "Do you think it's something she added at the last minute for dramatic effect?"

"If so, she's milking it too far," Gordon replied, frowning as he stared at the floor.

At first, there was a hushed, expectant silence from the crowd. Then, as Jim Burke remained standing at her side, the room began to fill with the thunder of applause.

It ebbed awkwardly to a hollow clap here and there, then faded altogether, as those who knew dance and knew Lara began to frown, realizing that they hadn't witnessed a dramatic finale but that something was wrong.

A collective "What…?" rose from the crowd.

Shannon started to move forward, frowning, wondering if Lara hadn't decided to make use of a new ploy.

Gordon caught her arm.

"Something's wrong," he said. "I think she needs medical help."

That must have been apparent, because the first person to rush forward was Dr. Richard Long, a handsome young surgeon, as well as a student at Moonlight Sonata. He fell to his knees at Lara's side, felt deftly for a pulse. He raised his head, looking around stunned for a split second, then yelled out hoarsely, "Call an ambulance!" He quickly looked down again and began performing CPR.

The room was still for a second, as if the hundreds of people in it had become collectively paralyzed with shock. Then dozens of cell phones were suddenly whipped out from pockets and purses.

Whispers and murmurs rose from all around the dance floor, then went still.

Richard valiantly continued his efforts.

"My God, what on earth happened to her?" Gordon said, the tension in his eyes showing his inner debate on whether to rush up himself or not.

"Drugs?" Ben suggested.

"Lara? Never," Jane said vehemently.

"No," Shannon murmured, shaking her head.

"Yeah, right, no, never," Ben said with a sniff. "Let's see, drugs on South Beach? In Miami, Florida, gateway to South America? Right, never."

"Never for Lara Trudeau," Shannon snapped.

"There are different drugs," Justin said.

"Maybe," Gordon agreed ruefully. "She's been known to swallow a few Xanax when she's nervous."

"Or maybe alcohol?" Justin said worriedly.

"When she's dancing?" Rhianna protested, shaking her head.

"She truly considers her body a temple," Sam informed them with complete assurance. "But sometimes the temple needs a few offerings, she says," he added. "She must have taken something. I mean, look at her."

"I hope she's going to be all right. She's got to be all

right!" Shannon said, sharing Gordon's concern regarding whether or not she should step forward.

Gordon set his hand on Shannon's shoulders. "No," he said softly.

She stared at him, puzzled.

"It's too late," he told her.

"What?" Shannon said, disbelieving.

Yet even as she asked the question, Richard Long rose. "Clear the floor, please. I'm afraid it's too late," he said quietly.

"Too late?" came a shout.

"She's…gone," Richard said awkwardly, as if sorry that his words gave the final ring of reality to the unbelievable.

"Dead?" Someone in the crowd said.

Richard sighed, dismayed that he couldn't get his words to sink through the collective head of those surrounding him. "I'm afraid…yes."

The sound of sirens filled the night.

Seconds later the crowd parted and medical techs swept into the room. They added emergency equipment and a desperately administered injection to the CPR efforts.

But in the end, no matter how hard they tried, it was over. Those watching kept their distance but could not turn away.

Shannon stared at the uniformed men, frozen in disbelief, along with the others. And as she watched, unbidden, a strange whisper filtered back into her mind.

You're next.

Insane. Silly. Someone had mistaken her for the next dancer to compete, that was all. Everything was a mess, Lara had fallen, but would be all right in the end. The CPR would work. She would suddenly inhale and stand up, and soon they would all be talking about her again, saying that she would do anything to create the biggest impression of the evening. She meant to be remembered, to be immortal.

But no one lived forever.

As the crowd left the floor at last, still stunned, there were murmurs everywhere.

Lara Trudeau. Gone. Impossible. And yet, she had died as she had lived. Glorious, beautiful, graceful, and now... dead.

Dead on the dance floor.

CHAPTER 2

"Hey, Quinn, someone to see you."

Quinn O'Casey was startled to see Amber Larkin standing at the top of the ladder as he crawled his way up. He was in full dive gear, having spent the past forty-five minutes scraping barnacles from the hull of the *Twisted Time*, his boat.

To the best of his knowledge, Amber had been in Key Largo, at work at the office, where she should have been. He was on vacation. She wasn't.

He arched a brow, indicating that she should step back so he could come aboard. She did so, ignoring the look that also questioned her arrival when he should have been left the hell alone. So much for chasing a man down.

She backed up, giving him room, and when he stepped on deck, tossing down his flippers, pulling off his dive mask, he saw the reason she had come. His brother was standing behind her.

"Hey, Doug," he said, frowning at them both.

"You might have mentioned you were coming up. I wouldn't have had to drive down to Key Largo just to make Amber drive back up to Miami with me."

Maybe he should have mentioned his vacation time to his brother, but why drag him down? Doug had gone through the police academy less than a year ago. An enthusiastic and ambitious patrolman, he was a younger brother to be proud of, having survived his teen years and young adulthood without the growing pains that had plagued Quinn's younger years—and a few of his older ones, for that matter. But hell, that was why he was back in South Florida, despite the gut-wrenching work he'd found instead of the easy slide he'd expected at the beginning.

Quinn shook his head. He was glad to be back home in South Florida. It could be one hell of a great place to live.

It could also showcase the most blatant forms of man's inhumanity to his fellow man.

And thus, the vacation. It wasn't as if he felt shattered or anything like that. Hell, he knew he couldn't control the evils of the world, or even those of a single man. But who the hell had ever expected what had happened to Nell Durken? He should be glad that the scum who had killed her was under arrest and would either be put away for life or meet a date with death. Still, whatever Art Durken's sentence, Nell was gone. And maybe he did blame himself a little, wonder if he shouldn't have told her to get away from the man immediately. But she had just come in to hire Quinn for routine surveillance, so who the hell knew until it was too late just what kind of a hornet's nest they'd stirred up. Eventually he *had* suggested that she part from her husband, and he had assumed she meant to do so, armed with the information regarding the man that Quinn had been able to give her.

But she hadn't left fast enough. Art hadn't been abusive, not physically, though he had been sexually demanding of Nell while spending his own time in a number of places outside his own home—and with a number of women who had not been his wife.

Who the hell could have known the guy would suddenly become homicidal?

He should have—he should have suspected Nell could be in danger.

Today he felt something like the boat—his time on that particular case had caused a growth of barnacles over his skin. Some time off might help scrape off the festering scabs of surprise and bitterness.

Vacation. From work, from family, from friends.

Maybe especially family. Doug didn't deserve any of his foul mood or foul temper.

And also, he hadn't actually been up to spending time with Doug. His brother could be a royal pain in the ass, a nonstop barrage of questions and inquiries. Like an intern in an emergency room, ready to diagnose a malady in any tic of the body, Doug was ready to find evil in every off-the-wall movement in the people around him.

A tough way to be in Miami-Dade County, where more than half the inhabitants could be considered a bit off-the-wall.

Quinn didn't know whether to groan or be concerned. Doug wouldn't have hunted him down to ask hypothetical questions. A tinge of unease hit him suddenly.

"Mom?" Quinn said worriedly.

"Heart ticking like an industrial clock," Doug assured him quickly. "However, she did mention that you hadn't been by lately, and she enjoys it when you come around to dinner once a week. You might want to give her a call."

"I left her a message that I was fine, just kind of busy."

"Yeah, but she's a smart woman, you know. She reads the newspapers."

"Is that why you're here?" Quinn demanded, arching a brow.

"I have a case for you," Doug said, moving around his brother to grab the dive tank Quinn had just unbuckled.

"Guess what, baby bro? I don't need you to find cases for me. The agency does that very well—too well. Besides, I'm on vacation."

"Yeah, Amber told me. That's why I thought it would be a great time for you to take on something private I've been thinking about."

Quinn went ahead and groaned. "Dammit, Doug. You mean you want me to do a bunch of prying around for free." He glared at Amber.

"Hey, he's your brother," she said defensively. "And you know what? Now that we've found you, I think I'll let you two talk. I'm going over to Nick's for a hamburger." Tossing her long blond hair over her shoulder, she started off the boat, casting back a single glance so she could try to read Quinn's scowl and figure out just how annoyed he was with her.

Doug wore a rueful grin on his face. "Hey, I'll rinse your equipment for you," he said, as if offering some kind of an apology.

"Good. Go ahead. I'll be in the cabin."

Quinn took the two steps down to the *Twisted Time*'s head, stripped and stepped beneath a spray of fresh water for a moment, then wrapped a towel around his waist and dug a clean pair of cutoffs out of the wicker laundry basket on the bed of the main cabin. Barefoot and still damp, he returned to the main cabin area, pulled a Miller from the fridge in the galley and sat on the sofa just beyond it, waiting, fingers drumming, scowl still in place.

Doug came down the steps, nimble and quick, a grimace on his face as he, too, went to the fridge, helped himself to a beer and sat on the port-side sofa, facing Quinn.

"You want me to do something for free, right?" Quinn said, scowling.

"Well…sort of. Actually, it's going to cost you."

"What?"

"I need you to take dance lessons."

Quinn stared at his younger brother, stunned speechless for several seconds. "You're out of your mind," he told Doug.

"No, no, I'm not, and you'll understand in a few minutes."

"No, I won't."

"Yes, you will. It's about a death."

"Do you know how many people die everyday, Doug? Hey, you're the cop. If this was suspicious death, it was— or will be—investigated. And even if it was deemed natural or accidental, you must know someone in the department who can look into it."

Quinn shook his head. Looking at Doug was almost like seeing himself a number of years ago. There was an eight-year age gap between them. They looked something alike, identical in height at six-two, but Doug still had the lean, lanky strength of a young man in his early twenties, while Quinn himself had broadened out. Quinn's hair was dark, while Doug's was a wheaten color, but they both had their father's deep blue, wide-set eyes and hard-angled face. Sometimes they moved alike, using their hands when they spoke, as if words weren't quite enough, and folding them prayer fashion or tapping them against their chins when they were in deep thought. For a moment Quinn reflected on his irritation at being interrupted here, but Doug had always been a damned good brother, looking up to him, being there for him, never losing faith, even when Quinn had gone through his own rough times.

"I can't get anyone in the department interested in this," Doug admitted. "There's been too much going on in the county lately. They're hunting a serial rapist who's getting more violent with each victim, a guard was killed at a recent robbery…trust me, homicide is occupied. Too busy to get involved when it looks like an accidental death. There's no one who's free right now."

"No one?"

Doug made a face. "All right, there were a few suspicious factors, so there is a guy assigned to follow up. But he's an asshole, Quinn, really."

"Who?"

Sometimes guys just didn't like each other, so rumors went around about their capabilities. The metro department had endured its share of troubles through the years with a few bad cops, but for the most part, the officers were good men, underpaid and overworked.

Then again, sometimes they *were* just assholes.

"Pete Dixon."

Quinn frowned. "Old Pete's not that bad."

"Hell no. Give him a smoking gun in a guy's hand, and he can catch the perp every time."

"That from a rookie," Quinn muttered.

"Look, Dixon's not a ball of fire. And he's just following up on what the M.E. has ruled as an accidental death. He isn't going to go around looking under any carpets. He's not interested. He'll just do some desk work by rote. He doesn't care."

"And therefore I should? To the point of taking dance lessons? Like I said, bro, I think you've lost your mind," Quinn said flatly.

Doug smiled, reaching into the back pocket of his jeans. He pulled out his wallet and, from it, a carefully folded newspaper clipping. That was just like Doug. He was one of the most orderly human beings Quinn had ever come across. The clipping hadn't been ripped out but cut, then folded meticulously. He shook his head at the thought, knowing that his own organizational skills were lacking in comparison.

"What is it?" Quinn asked, taking the paper.

"Read."

Quinn unfolded it and looked at the headline. "'Diva

Lara Trudeau Dead on the Dance Floor at Thirty-eight.'"
He cocked his head toward his brother.

"Keep reading."

Quinn scanned the article. He'd never heard of Lara
Trudeau, but that didn't mean anything. He wouldn't have
recognized the name of any dancer, ballroom or otherwise. He could free-dive to nearly four hundred feet,
bench-press nearly four hundred pounds and rock climb
with the best of them. But in a salsa club, hell, he was best
as a bar support.

Puzzled, he scanned the article. Lara Trudeau, thirty-
eight, winner of countless dance championships, had died
as she had lived—on the dance floor. A combination of
tranquilizers and alcohol had caused a cardiac arrest.
Those closest to the dancer were distraught, and apparently
stunned that, despite her accomplishments, she had felt the
need for artificial calm.

Quinn looked back at his brother and shook his head.
"I don't get it. An aging beauty got nervous and took too
many pills. Tragic. But hardly diabolical."

"You're not reading between the lines," Doug said with
dismay.

Quinn suppressed a grin. "And I take it no one in the
homicide division 'read between the lines,' either?"

Doug smacked the article. "Quinn, a woman like Lara
Trudeau wouldn't take pills. She was a perfectionist. And
a winner. She would have taken the championship. She
had no reason to be nervous."

"Doug, are you even reading the lines yourself? We're
talking about something that no one can outrun—age.
Here's this Lara Trudeau—*thirty-eight*. With a horde of
twenty-somethings following in her wake. Hell, yes, she
was nervous."

"What, you think people keel over at thirty-eight?"
Doug said.

"When you're a quarterback, you're damn near retirement," Quinn said.

"She wasn't a quarterback."

Quinn let out an impatient sigh. "It's the same thing. Sports, dancing. People slow down with age."

"Some get better with age. *She* was still winning. And hell, in ballroom dance, people compete at all ages."

"And that's really great. More power to them. I just don't understand why you chased me down about this. According to the paper *and* everything you're telling me, the death was accidental. It's all here. She dropped dead in public on a ballroom floor, so naturally there was an autopsy, and the findings indicated nothing suspicious."

"Right. They found the physical cause of death. Cardiac arrest brought on by a mixture of alcohol and pills. How she happened to ingest that much isn't in the M.E.'s report."

Quinn groaned and pulled over the day's newspaper, flipping quickly to the local section. "'Mother and Two Children Found Shot to Death in North Miami Apartment,'" he read, glaring at his brother over the headlines. "'Body Found in Car Trunk at Mall,'" he continued. "Want me to go on? Violence is part of life in the big city, bro. You've been through the academy. There's a lot out there that's real bad. You know it, and I know it. Things that need to be questioned, and I'm sure the homicide guys are on them. But a drugged-out dancer drops dead, and you want to make something more out of it. You'll make detective soon enough. Give yourself time."

"Quinn, this is important to me."

"Why?"

"Because I'm afraid that someone else is going to die."

Quinn frowned, staring at his younger brother, wondering if he wasn't being overly dramatic. Doug looked dead calm and serious, though.

Quinn threw up his hands. "Is this based on anything, Doug? Was someone else threatened? If so, you're a cop. You know the guys in homicide, including Dixon. And he's not that bad. He knows the law, and on a paper chase, he's great."

"You know them better."

"*Knew* them better," Quinn corrected. "I was away a long time, before I started working with Dane down in the Keys. Anyway, we're getting away from my point. Doug, take a look at the facts. There was an autopsy, and the medical examiner was convinced that her death was accidental. The cops must see it that way, too, if all they're doing is a bit of follow-up investigation. So...? Did you hear someone threaten her before she died? Do you have any reason whatsoever to suspect murder? And if so, do you have any idea who might have wanted to kill her?"

Doug shrugged, contemplating his answer. "Several people, actually."

"And what makes you say that?"

"She could be the world's biggest bitch."

"And you know this for a fact?"

"Yes."

"How?"

Again Doug hesitated, then cocked his head to the side as he surveyed his brother. "I was sleeping with her."

Quinn groaned, set his beer on the table and pressed his temples between his palms. "You were sleeping with a woman more than ten years your senior?"

"There's something wrong with that?"

"I didn't say that."

"You sure as hell did."

"All right, it just seems a little strange to me, that's all."

"She was quite a woman."

"If you say so, Doug, I'm sure she was." He hesitated. "Were you emotionally involved, or was it more of a sexual thing?"

"I can't say that I thought I wanted to spend the rest of my life with her or anything like that. And I know damn well she didn't feel that way about me. But whether she could be a bitch or not, and whether or not we were meant for the ages, hell, yes, I cared about her."

"And are you asking me to look into this because your feelings are ruling your mind?" Quinn asked seriously.

Doug shook his head. "We weren't a 'thing,' by any means. And I wasn't the only one involved with her. She could play games. Or maybe, in her mind, she wasn't playing games. She kind of considered herself a free spirit." He shrugged, not looking at Quinn. "Kind of as if she was a gift to the world and the men in it, and she bestowed herself when she felt it was warranted, or when she was struck by whim, I guess. At any rate, I wasn't the only one she was sleeping with," Doug said flatly.

"Great. You know who else she was seeing?"

"I know who she might have been seeing—anyone around the studio."

"And how many people knew about your relationship?"

"I don't know," Doug admitted.

"This is pretty damn vague."

"It wouldn't need to be—if you would just agree to look into what happened."

Quinn surveyed his younger brother thoughtfully. He was caught up in this thing emotionally. And maybe that was why he didn't want it to have happened the way it appeared.

"Maybe you should make it a point to stay *away* from the homicide guys, Doug. If the police suspected someone of murder, you might be first in line."

"But I didn't kill her. I'm a cop. And even if I wasn't, I'd never murder anyone, Quinn. You know that."

"You had a relationship with the woman. If you convince people that she was killed, you could wind up under investigation yourself, you understand that?"

"Of course. But I'm innocent."

Quinn looked at the newspaper again. "She died because of an overdose of the prescription drug Xanax. The alcohol might have enhanced the drug, bringing on cardiac arrest."

"Yes," Doug said. "And the cop on the case is certain that in her pigheaded quest for eternal fame—my adjective, not his—she got nervous."

"Doug, I'm sorry to say it, but I've seen people do a lot of stupid things. It may be tragic, but it looks as if she got nervous, took the pills, then drank."

Doug groaned, shaking his head. "No."

"You don't think that's even possible?"

"No."

"The prescription was in her name. Her doctor was contacted. According to him, she'd been taking a few pills before performances for the past several years. It's in the article."

"That's right," Doug agreed calmly.

"Doug, unless you've got more to go on…I can't even understand what you think I can do for you."

"I've got more to go on. A hunch. A feeling. A certainty, actually," his brother said firmly. Quinn knew Doug. He was capable of being as steadfast as an oak. That was what had gotten him through school and into the academy, where he had graduated with honors. The kid was going to make a fine detective one day.

"There are times to hold and times to fold, you know," Quinn said quietly.

Doug suddenly looked as if he was about to lose it. "*I'll* pay you."

"We charge way too much," Quinn told him brusquely.

"Give me two weeks," Doug said. "Quinn, dammit, I need your help! Just come into the studio and see if you don't think people are behaving strangely, that people besides me believe she was murdered."

"They've told you this?"

"Not in so many words. In fact, those who knew her well all admit she took pills now and then. She had a drink here and there, too. And yeah, she was getting up there for a woman determined on maintaining her championships in both the smooth and rhythm categories, and in cabaret."

"Doug, you might as well be speaking a foreign language," Quinn said irritably.

"Rhythm is the faster dances, rumba, cha-cha, swing, hustle, merengue, West Coast swing, polka. Smooth is the fox-trot, waltz, tango. And cabaret is for partners and combines different things."

"All right, all right, never mind. I get the picture."

"So?"

"Doug..."

"Dammit, Quinn, there were plenty of people who hated her. Plenty of suspects. But if I push any further, someone will start investigating me. Will they ever be able to prove I caused her death? No, because I didn't. Can my career be ruined? Can people look at me with suspicion for the rest of my life? You bet, and you know it. Quinn, I'm not asking a lot. Just go and take a few dance lessons. It won't kill you."

It won't kill you. An odd sensation trickled down Quinn's spine. He wondered if he wouldn't come to remember those words.

"Doug, no one will believe I've come in for dance lessons. I can't dance to save my life."

"Why do you think guys take lessons?" Doug demanded.

"To pick up women at the salsa clubs on the beach," he said flatly.

"See? A side benefit. What are you going to do—hole up like a hermit for the rest of your life?"

"I haven't holed up like a hermit at all." Did he actually sound defensive?

His brother just stared at him. Quinn sat back and said, "Wait a minute—is this how you got into the whole thing to begin with? *Dance* lessons." He couldn't have been more surprised if he'd heard that Doug had taken up knitting. Doug had nearly gone the route of a pro athlete. He remained an exceptional golfer and once a week coached a Little League team.

"Yeah, I was taking lessons," Doug said.

"I see." He paused thoughtfully. "No, I don't see at all. Why did you decide to take dance lessons?"

Doug grinned sheepishly. "Randy Torres is getting married. I agreed to be his best man. He and his fiancée, Sheila, started taking lessons for the wedding. I figured, what the hell? I'd go with him a few times and be a good best man. There aren't nearly as many guys taking lessons as females. The place seemed to be a gold mine of really great looking women. The studio is on South Beach, right above one of the hottest salsa clubs out there. Nice place to go after classes and make use of what you've learned. So I started taking lessons."

"And wound up...dating an older diva?"

"That's the way it went. She wasn't actually a teacher there—she got paid big bucks to come in and coach now and then. So she wasn't really in on the teacher rules."

"What are the teacher rules?"

"Teachers aren't supposed to fraternize with students. A loose rule there, because everyone goes down to the salsa club now and then. Let me tell you, Moonlight Sonata has the best location in history for a dance studio. Sometimes couples come in, and they can dance with each other. But for singles...well, they're still nervous at first. So if you can go to a club and have a few drinks and have a teacher there to dance with you, make you look good—well, it's a nice setup. And hey, South Beach, you know. It's one of those places where rockers and movie stars stop in sometimes."

"So there are a lot of players hanging around. And, I imagine, drugs up the wazoo. What's the name of the club?"

"Suede."

Quinn arched a brow. "I know the name, and I never hang out on South Beach. I hate South Beach," he added. And he meant it. The place was plastic, at best. People never doing anything—just coming out to be seen. Trying to make the society pages by being in the right club when Madonna came by. Proving their worth by getting a doorman to let them into one of the new hot spots when the line was down the street.

The only good thing in his opinion was Lincoln Road, where some good foreign and independent films occasionally made it to the theater, a few of the restaurants were authentic and reasonable, and every canine maniac in the city felt free to walk a dog.

"Come on, the beach isn't really that bad. Okay, it's not as laid-back as your precious Keys, but still… And as for Suede, there was an investigation not long ago. A runaway-turned-prostitute was found about a block away, just lying on the sidewalk. Heroin overdose. So Narcotics did a sweep, but Suede came out clean. Hell, maybe the girl did get her drugs from someone at the bar. You know as well as I do that dealers don't have to look like bums. And there's money on the beach. Big money people pop in at Suede. But as for the management and the club itself, everything came out squeaky clean. In fact, they're known for enforcing the twenty-one-and-over law on drinking, and there was a big thing in the paper a few months ago when one of the bartenders threw out a rock star, said he wasn't serving him any more alcohol. It's a good club, and like I said, students and teachers see one another and dance, maybe have a drink or two—it gives the school a real edge, because people can use what they learn. But outside of that, teachers and students really aren't supposed to hang around together."

"Why?"

Doug sighed as if his brother had gotten old and dense. "Favoritism. Dance classes are expensive. Someone could get pissed if their teacher was seeing someone outside the studio and maybe giving that student extra attention. Still, it's a rule that gets broken. You need to come down there, Quinn. Could it really hurt you to take a few lessons, ask a few questions, make a few inquiries—get into it in a way I can't?" Doug asked.

Quinn winced. "Doug, one day, I'd like to take up skydiving. I'd like to up my scuba certification to a higher level. I'd like to speak Spanish better, and I kind of always wanted to go on safari in Africa. Never in my life have I wanted to take dance lessons."

"You might be surprised," Doug said. "Quinn, please."

Quinn looked down at his hands. He'd thought he would clean up the boat and head out to the Bahamas. Spend two weeks with nothing but fish, sea, sun and sand. Listening to calypso music and maybe some reggae. Listening to it. Not dancing to it.

But this seemed to matter to Doug. Really matter. And maybe something *had* been going on. Doug wouldn't be here if he didn't have a real feeling about it. Better he find it out before the police, because Doug would be a natural suspect.

He looked up at Doug, ready to agree that it wouldn't kill him just to check the place out and ask a few questions. Then he hesitated. "I need a break," he said honestly. "I'm not even sure you want me handling a case that means so much to you."

Doug shook his head angrily. "Quinn, you know better than to blame yourself for anything that's happened— lately. You do your best with what you've learned and what you know. And sometimes knowledge and laws work, and sometimes they don't. I still have faith in you—even if you've lost it in yourself."

"I haven't lost faith in myself," Quinn said. Shit. Beyond a doubt, he was sounding defensive.

"No?" Doug asked. "Good. Because I've got some news for you that I think will change your mind about this case—among other things."

Quinn looked at him questioningly.

"Your girl took lessons at the Moonlight Sonata studios. Right up until last November."

Quinn frowned. "My girl? My girl who?"

"Nell Durken. I managed to sneak a look in the file cabinet at Moonlight Sonata, and Nell Durken's name is there, right in the record books."

Quinn hadn't known a damn thing about Nell Durken's dance lessons. But then again, he hadn't known all that much about her, really. She had just hired him to find out what her husband spent his time doing.

So he had found out.

And the bastard had killed her.

"Actually," Doug continued, "Nell was one of their advanced students. Then, last November, she just quit going. Never mentioned it to you, I guess. Curious, though. The records indicate that she was gung ho—and then just gone. Makes you wonder, huh?"

"Fine," Quinn said flatly. "I'll do some checking. I'll take a few fucking dance lessons."

CHAPTER 3

"Hey, how's it going?"

Ella Rodriguez tapped on Shannon's half-open door, then walked the few feet to the desk and perched on the corner of it. Shannon sat back in her desk chair, contemplating a reply to her receptionist.

"I don't know. How do you think it's going? Personally, I think we should have shut down for the week," Shannon said.

"We shut down for three days," Ella reminded her. "That's about what most corporations are willing to give for members of the immediate family when someone has passed away."

"Her pictures are all over the walls," Shannon reminded Ella.

"Right. And teachers and really serious students are going to miss her—one way or another—for a long time. But you have some students who aren't all that serious, who never want to see a competition floor, and who are getting married in a matter of weeks, left feet and all. They need the studio open, Shannon." Ella had short, almost platinum hair, cut stylishly. She had a gamine's face, with incredible dark eyes and one of the world's best smiles. She considered herself the least talented employee in the studio, but whether she was right about that or not, her warmth and easy charm surely accounted for many of their students.

Except that now Ella made a face that was hardly warm or charming. "Shannon, I'm well aware you're not supposed to speak ill of the dead. But truth be told, I didn't like Lara. And I'm not the only one. There are even people who think that her dropping dead on the dance floor was a piece of poetic justice."

"Ella!"

"I know that sounds terrible, and I'm really sorry. I certainly didn't want anything to happen to her," Ella said. She stared at Shannon. "Come on, you've got admit it—she couldn't possibly have been your favorite person."

"Whether she was or wasn't, she was a dynamic force in our industry, and she started here. So this was her home, so to speak," Shannon said.

"We're all sorry, we know she was a professional wonder, and I don't think there's a soul out there who didn't respect her talent." Ella met Shannon's eyes. "Hey, I even said all that when the detective talked to me."

"You told him that you hadn't liked Lara?" Shannon asked.

"I was dead honest. Sorry, no pun intended. Oh, come on, he was just questioning us because he had to. You know—when someone dies that way, they have to do an autopsy, and they had to question a bunch of people, too, but hell, everyone saw what happened." Ella arched a brow. "Did you tell them you had adored her?"

"I was dead honest, as well—no pun intended," Shannon said dryly. "Well, for all of the four and a half minutes he questioned me."

Ella shook her head. "What did you expect? There's no

trick here. Her dance is on tape—her death is on tape." Ella shivered. "Creepy. Except Lara probably would have loved it. Even her demise was as dramatic as possible, captured on film for all eternity. She got carried away, and she died. A foolish waste. There's nothing anyone can do now. But you closed the studio in her honor. Now we're open again. And you've got a new student arriving in fifteen minutes."

"*I* have a new student?"

"Yeah, you."

Shannon frowned and said, "Wait, wait, wait, I'm not taking on any of the new students. Me being the studio manager and all? I have too much paperwork and too many administration duties, plus planning for the Gator Gala. Remember what we decided at the last meeting?"

"Of course I remember. But as I'm sure you've noticed, Jane isn't in yet. She has a dental appointment—which she announced at the same meeting. Rhianna couldn't change her weekly two-o'clock, because we don't open until then and her guy works nights. And this new guy is coming in because Doug bought him a guest pass. Actually, it's Doug's brother. Personally, I can't wait to see him."

"I keep telling you that you should go ahead and get your certification to teach," Shannon said. Ella had the natural ability to become an excellent teacher. But she had come to the studio two years ago looking for a clerical position and still shied away from anything else.

As for herself, at this particular time, Shannon just didn't want to teach, which was odd, because watching the growth of a student was something she truly enjoyed.

Everything, however, had seemed off-kilter since Lara had dropped dead. Naturally it had shaken the entire dance world. Sudden death was always traumatic.

But it was true as well that Lara Trudeau hadn't been her favorite person.

Championships—no matter how many—didn't guarantee a decent living, not in the States. Lara had coached to supplement her income. Gordon Henson had been her first ballroom instructor. He had maintained his pride in his prize student, and, to her credit, Lara had come to the Moonlight Sonata studio whenever he asked her, within reason. But after he had begun to groom Shannon to take over management of the studio, he had left the hiring of coaches to her.

And because Lara was excellent and a real draw for the students, Shannon had continued to bring her in. But unlike a number of the other coaches they hired, Lara was not averse to making fun of the students—or the teachers—after a coaching session.

Shannon also had other, more personal, reasons for disliking Lara. Even so, it still bothered her deeply that Lara had died. It might have been the simple fact that no one so young should perish. Or perhaps it was impossible to see anyone who was so much a part of one's life—liked or disliked—go so abruptly from it without feeling a sense of mourning and loss. Part of it was a sense of confusion, or of disbelief, that remained. Whatever the reasons, Shannon simply felt off, and it was difficult enough to maintain a working mentality to deal with the needs of the upcoming Gator Gala, much less consider teaching a beginner with a smile and the enthusiasm necessary to bring them into the family fold of the studio.

"She hasn't even been dead a week yet," Shannon said. "She hasn't even been buried yet." Because Lara's death had to be investigated, she had been taken to the county morgue until her body could be released by the medical examiner. But once his findings had been complete, Ben, Lara's ex, along with Gordon, had gotten together to make the arrangements. Lara had come to Miami for college almost twenty years ago, and sometime during the next few years, her parents had passed away. She'd never had children, and if she had any close relatives, they hadn't appeared in all the years. Because she was a celebrity, even after her death had officially been declared accidental, the two men had opted for a Saturday morning funeral.

"Shannon, she breezed through here to dance now and then, and yes, we knew her. She wasn't like a sister. We need to get past this," Ella insisted. "Honestly, if anyone really knew her, it was Gordon, and *he's* moving on."

Yes, their boss was definitely moving on, Shannon thought. He had spent yesterday in his office, giving great concern to swatches of fabric he had acquired, trying to determine which he liked best for the new drapes he was putting in his living room.

"I don't know about you," Ella said, shaking her head. "You were all upset when Nell Durken died, and she hadn't been in here in a year."

"Nell Durken didn't just die. Her husband killed her. He probably realized he was about to lose his meal ticket," Shannon said bitterly. Nell Durken had been one of the most amazing students to come through the door. Bubbly, beautiful and always full of life, she had been a ray of sunshine. She'd been friendly with all the students, wry about the fact that she couldn't drag her husband in, but determined to learn on her own. Hearing that the man had killed her had been horribly distressing.

"Jeez," Shannon breathed suddenly.

"What?" Ella said.

"It's just strange…isn't it?"

"What's strange?" Ella asked, shaking her head.

"Nell Durken died because her husband forced an overdose of sleeping pills down her throat."

"Yes? The guy was a bastard—we all thought that," Ella said. "No one realized he was a lethal bastard, but… anyway, the cops got him. He was having an affair, but Nell was the one with the trust fund. He probably thought he'd get away with forcing all those pills down her throat. It would look like an accident, and he'd get to keep the money," Ella said. "But they've got him. He could even get the death penalty—his motive was evident and his fingerprints were all over the bottle of pills."

"Have you been watching too many cop shows?" came a query from the open door. A look of amusement on his face, Gordon was staring in at the two women.

"No, Gordon," Ella said. "I'm just pointing out what happened to Nell Durken. And hoping the bastard will fry."

"Fry?" Gordon said.

"Okay, so now it's usually lethal injection. He was so mean to her, long before he killed her," Ella said, shaking her head.

Gordon frowned. "What brought up Nell Durken?"

"Talking about Lara," Ella said.

Gordon didn't seem to see the correlation. "We've lost Lara. That's that. She was kind of like Icarus, I guess, trying to fly too high. As to Nell…hell, we all knew she needed to leave that bastard. It's too bad she didn't. I wish she'd kept dancing."

"She stopped coming in when he planned that Caribbean vacation for her, remember?" Shannon said thoughtfully. "They were going on a second honeymoon. He was going to make everything up to her."

"And we all figured they got on great and things were lovey-dovey again, because she called in afterward saying that she wasn't going to schedule any more lessons for a while because they were going to be traveling. And, of course," Ella added pointedly, since Gordon was staring at her, his mouth open as if he were about to speak, "like a good receptionist, I followed up with calls, but I always got her answering machine, and then, I guess, after about six months, she kind of slipped off the 'things to do' list."

"It's horrible, though, isn't it?" Shannon murmured. "I hope we're not bad luck. I mean, an ex-student is murdered by her husband, and then…then Lara drops dead."

"You think we're jinxed?"

Shannon looked past Gordon's shoulder. Sam Railey was right behind Gordon, staring in.

"Jinxed?" Gordon protested. "Don't even suggest such a thing. Nell was long gone from here when she was murdered. And Lara…Lara is simply a tragedy." He held up three fingers. "The Broward studio lost two students and an instructor last year."

Shannon hid a smile, her brow quirking upward. "Gordon, the students were Mr. and Mrs. Hallsly, ninety and ninety three, respectively. It wasn't such a shock that they died with a few months of one another. And," she added softly, since she had been very fond of Dick Graft, the instructor who had died, "Dick had an aneurism."

"I'm pointing out the fact that people die and *we're* not jinxed," Gordon said.

"Man, I hope not," Sam said. "Because that would be two for us. And you know, things happen in threes."

"Sam!" Gordon said.

"Oh, man, sorry. Hey, don't worry, I'd never say anything like that in front of the students."

"I should hope not," Gordon admonished.

Gordon might have given the management over to Shannon, but if he were to decide that an instructor was detrimental to the studio, that teacher would be out in seconds flat.

"Hey," another voice chimed in. Justin Garcia, five-eight tops, slim, with an ability to move with perfect rhythm, was on his toes, trying to look over the shoulders of the others gathered at Shannon's door. "Psst." He stared at Ella, still perched on the desk. "New student out front. I'd try to start the lesson myself, but he's one big guy, and I think he'd cream me if I gave it a try."

"Doug's brother," Ella said, jumping up.

Doug was definitely one of their favorite new students. He'd come in to learn salsa for a friend's wedding and started out as stiff as a board, but within a week, he'd fallen in love with Cuban motion and wanted to learn everything.

He was a cop and he would laugh about the fact that his fellow officers teased him.

He was definitely appreciated by the studio's many female students—not to mention his teacher, Jane Ulrich. Jane loved the dramatic. With Doug, she could leap, spin and almost literally fly. She was an excellent dancer, and he had the strength to allow her to do any lift she wanted to do. He was tall, blond, blue eyed and ready to go, everything one could want in a student.

Ella pushed past the men, hurrying toward the front of the studio, where she could greet their new student and get him started on paperwork.

Shannon, rising, was startled when Ella burst her way back in almost instantly, her eyes wide. "Damn, is Jane going to be sorry she had that dental appointment. Get up! You gotta see this guy." Ella flew out again.

"Makes mincemeat out of me," Justin told Shannon with a shrug.

Curious, Shannon followed the group on out. By then, Ella was greeting the man politely, and the others were standing around, waiting to meet him.

They didn't usually circle around to greet their new clients.

Doug's brother. Yes, the resemblance was there. They were of a similar height. But where Doug had nice shoulders and a lithe build, this guy looked like he'd walked out of a barbarian movie. His hair was dark, his eyes a penetrating blue. Nice face, hard, but even lines. In a cartoon, he might have been labeled Joe, the truck driver.

Just before she could step forward, Sam placed his hands on her shoulders, pulling her back against him. He whispered teasingly to her, "Too bad it's against policy to fraternize with our students, huh?"

"Sam," she chastised with a soft, weary sigh. It was policy, yes, though Gordon had always preferred not to know what he didn't have to. She had maintained the same *Don't tell me what I don't need to know* attitude.

As she stepped away from him, she heard Justin whisper, "Policy? Like hell. For some of us, maybe, but not for others."

Even as she extended a hand to the Atlas standing before her, Shannon wondered just what his words meant.

Who, exactly, had been fraternizing with whom?

And why the hell did this simple question suddenly make her feel so uneasy?

She forced a smile. "So you're Doug's brother. We're delighted to have you. Doug is something of a special guy around here, you know." She hesitated slightly. "Did he drag you in by the ears?"

The man smiled. Dimple in his left cheek. "Something like that," he said. "He has a knack for coming up with just the right come-on." His handshake was firm. "I'm Quinn. Quinn O'Casey. I'm afraid that you're going to find me to be the brother with two left feet. You've got one hell of a challenge before you."

Her smile stayed in place, though the uneasy sense swept through her again.

One hell of a challenge.

She had a feeling that he was right. On more than one level.

What the hell was he really doing here? she wondered.

"Ella, could I get a chart for Mr. O'Casey, please?" she said aloud. "Come into our conference room, and we'll see what we can do for you."

The conference room wasn't really much of a room, just a little eight-by-eight enclosure. There was a round table in the middle that seated five at most, surrounded by a few shelves and a few displays. Some of the teachers' trophies were there, along with a few she had acquired herself, and several indicating that they had won in the division of best independent studio for the past two years.

Ella handed Shannon a chart, and the others, rather than discreetly going about their business, stared. Shannon arched a brow, which sent them scurrying off. Then she closed the door and indicated a chair to Quinn O'Casey.

"Have a seat."

"You learn to dance at a table?" he queried lightly as he sat.

"I learn a little bit about what sort of dancing you're interested in," she replied. Obviously, they were interested in selling dance lessons, and the conference room was sometimes referred to—jokingly—as the shark-attack haven; however, she'd never felt as if she were actually going into a hostile environment herself. She prided herself on offering the best and never forcing anyone into anything. Students didn't return if they didn't feel that they were getting the most for their money. And the students who came into it for the long haul were the ones who went into competition and kept them all afloat.

"So, Mr. O'Casey, just which dances do you want to learn?"

"Which dances?"

The dark-haired hunk across from Shannon lifted his brows, as if she had asked a dangerous question and was ready to suck him right in.

"We teach a lot of dances here, including country and western and polka. People usually have some kind of a plan in mind when they come in."

"Right, well, sorry, no real plan. Doug talked me into

this. Um, which dances. Well, I...I can't dance at all," he said. "So...uh, Doug said something about smooth, so that's what I want, I guess," he said.

"So you'd like a concentration on waltz, fox-trot and tango."

"Tango?"

"Yes, tango."

"That's what you call a smooth dance?"

"There are quick movements, yes, and sharpness of motion is an important characteristic, but it's considered a smooth dance. Do you want to skip the tango?"

He shrugged. "No, I haven't a thing in the world against tango." They might have been discussing a person. He flashed a dry smile, and she was startled by his electric appeal. He wasn't just built. He had strong, attractive facial features, and that dimple. His eyes appealed, too, the color very deep, his stare direct. Despite herself, she felt a little flush of heat surge through her. Simple chemistry. He was something. She was professional and mature and quite able to keep any reaction under control—but she wasn't dead.

He leaned forward suddenly. "I think I'd love to tango," he said, as if he'd given it serious thought.

And probably every woman out there would love to tango with you, too, buddy, she thought.

She had to smile suddenly. "Are you sure you really want to take dance lessons?" she asked him.

"Yes. No." He shrugged. "Doug really wanted me to get into it."

Shannon suddenly felt hesitant about him. She didn't know why—he was so physically impressive that any teacher should be glad to have him, as a challenge, at the least.

A challenge. That was it exactly. Just as he appealed to her, he created a sense of wariness in her, as well. She didn't understand it.

She sat back, smiling, tapping her pencil idly against the table as she looked at him. She spoke casually. "Your brother is a police officer. Are you in the same line of work, Mr. O'Casey?"

"Quinn. Please, call me Quinn. And no, I'm not a cop. Although I was a cop once."

He didn't offer any further details.

"So, what *do* you do?"

"I'm with a charter service down in the Keys."

"Fishing? Diving?"

He smiled slowly. "Yes, both. Why? Are only certain men involved in certain lines of work supposed to take dance lessons?"

She shook her head, annoyed to know that her cheeks were reddening. She stared down at the paper. "No, of course not, and I'm sorry. We just try to tailor a program toward what an individual really wants."

"Well, I guess I just want to be able to dance socially. And I'm not kidding when I say that I can't dance."

Those words were earnest. The dimple in his cheek flashed.

She smiled. "Doug came in with the movement ability of a deeply rooted tree…Quinn." His name rolled strangely on her tongue. "He's made incredible progress."

"Well, he just kind of fell in love with it, huh?"

Her smile deepened, and she nodded. "You don't think you're going to fall in love with it, do you?"

He shrugged, lifting his hands. Large hands, long fingered. Clean and neat, though. Of course. Fishing and diving. He was in the water constantly. Face deeply bronzed, making the blue of his eyes a sharp contrast. "What about you?"

"Pardon?" she said, startled that they had suddenly changed course.

"When did you fall in love with it?"

"When I could walk," she admitted.

"Ah, so you're one of those big competitors," he said.

She shook her head. "No. I'm an instructor."

He arched a brow, and she felt another moment's slight unease as she realized he was assessing her appearance.

"I bet you would make a great competitor."

She shrugged. "I really like what I do."

"I guess competition can be dangerous."

His words sounded casual enough. She felt herself stiffen. "Dangerous? Dancing?"

He shrugged again. "Doug told me someone had a heart attack and died at the last big competition."

She shook her head. "What happened was tragic. But it was an isolated incident. I've certainly never seen anything like it before. We're all shattered, of course…but, no, competition isn't usually dangerous." She was tempted to say more but pulled back, telling herself not to be an absolute idiot. She certainly wasn't going to spill out her own discomfort before a man she'd just met, even if he was Doug's brother. Doug was a student, a promising one, but even he was far from a confident. "I would assume, Mr. O'Casey, that boating and diving are far more dangerous than dancing."

"I wasn't worried," he said. "Just…well, sorry about the loss, of course. And curious."

Obviously, people would be upset. And yes, curious. In the world of dance, Lara had reigned as a queen. Though most people might not have known her name—any more than Shannon might have known that of the leading Nascar racer—such a death still made the newspapers and even a number of news broadcasts. Several stations had been there filming when she had died.

Sure, people were going to be curious.

Gordon had given a speech to her; she had given one to the teachers, and she'd also written up a little notice for the students. She didn't know why she felt annoyed at explaining the situation to this particular man.

"We were all curious," she said evenly. "Lara Trudeau was amazing. She wasn't into alcohol or drugs, prescription or otherwise. None of us knows what happened that day. She was brilliant, and she, and her talent, will be missed. But dancing is hardly dangerous. Obviously, it's a physical activity. But we've had a number of heart patients here for therapy. It's dangerous to sit still and become a couch potato, too." She was suddenly angry, feeling as if she was personally under attack, and didn't understand why. She was about to get up and assure him that she would return Doug's money for the guest pass, but then he spoke.

"Rhythm," he said.

"Pardon?"

"I think I said the wrong thing. I'd like to be able to go to a club like Suede, the one right below you, and not look like a total horse's a—idiot. Salsa, right?"

"They do a lot of salsa. Mambo, samba, merengue… Tuesday nights they have a swing party."

"But they waltz at weddings, right?" He gave the appearance of seriously considering his options.

"Yes."

"Do I have to pick certain dances?"

"No, but it would be nice to know where you'd like to start."

"Where do you generally start?"

She rose. "At the beginning. Come on. If you've no real preferences, we'll do it my way."

"You're going to be my instructor?" He was surprised, but she didn't think he was pleased.

"Yes. Is there a problem?"

"No, I just…Doug said you didn't take new students."

"I don't usually. But the way it works is, unless there's

a problem, the teacher to sign on a new student becomes their regular instructor." She hadn't meant to actually take him as her student, but now...she meant to keep him. There was just something about him that...

A voice in her ear whispered that he was the most arresting man she'd met in a long time. Best-looking, definitely most sensual, man.

Yes, yes, all acknowledged from the start.

But that wasn't the point. It wasn't his appearance, which was, admittedly, imposing.

There was something else.

It was ridiculous that she was feeling so paranoid.

But the man bore watching. That feeling of wariness would not go away.

Maybe.

That was her thought thirty minutes later.

Maybe she hadn't been teaching enough lately. Maybe she couldn't teach and keep an eye on him at the same time. Her patience just wasn't where it should be. There was no chance of anyone stepping in and actually leading him— placing a hand on his arm had assured her of that. It was like setting her fingers on a solid wall. It didn't help that he was stiff, no matter how much she tried to get him to relax.

He actually seemed to be confused between left and right.

They were doing a box step, for God's sake. A simple box step.

"No, Quinn, your left foot goes forward first. The same foot we've used the last twenty-five times." Was her voice showing strain? Once upon a time, she'd been known for her patience.

He hadn't lied when he said he had two left feet.

"We're just making a square—a box. Left foot forward, right side...a box."

"Yeah, right. A box. So how many teachers are there here, actually?"

"Are you afraid that I can't teach you, Mr. O'Casey?"

"No, no, I just wondered. You're doing fine. I was just curious as to how many teachers you have."

"Ben Trudeau is teaching full time now."

"Trudeau?" he said.

"He used to be married to Lara. They've been divorced for several years. He was mainly doing competitions and coaching, but he decided a few months ago that he wanted to take up residence on the beach. He's an excellent teacher."

"He must be devastated."

"We're all devastated, Mr. O'Casey."

"Sorry. I can imagine. She must have been something. So accomplished, and such a friend to everyone here, huh? Doug told me she taught here sometimes."

"She coached," Shannon told him.

"Must be hard for all of you to have the studio open and be teaching already."

"Work goes on."

"So all the teachers have come back?"

"Yes."

"Who are the rest of them?"

"Justin Garcia and Sam Railey, and Jane Ulrich, who teaches your brother, and another woman, Rhianna Markham."

His foot landed hard on hers once again.

"Sorry—I told you I had two left feet," he apologized.

Shannon drew a deep breath. "We do want to get you to where you can converse while you're on the floor, but maybe if you didn't ask so many questions while we were working, it might be better."

"Sorry. Just want to get to know the place, feel a little more comfortable here."

"That's what the practice sessions and parties are for," she murmured.

"Parties?"

"And practice sessions," she said firmly. "Beginners come on Monday, Tuesday and Friday nights, sometimes even the other weeknights if we get busy, and learn more steps in groups. Then you hone those steps with your teacher."

"Do students have to come?"

"Of course not. But individual sessions are expensive. The group sessions are open to all enrolled students. You learn a lot faster and make a lot better use of your money by attending the group classes."

"And the parties? When are they? Are they for all the students?"

"Wednesday nights, eight to ten, and yes, beginners are welcome. You should come."

"I will."

His foot crunched down on hers once again. Hard. She choked back a scream. How much longer? Fifteen more minutes. She wasn't sure she could take it.

She looked around. Jane still hadn't returned from her appointment. Rhianna was working with David Mercutio, husband of Katarina Mercutio, the designer who shared the second floor of the building with them. She was wonderful—specializing in weddings, with one-of-a-kind dresses for both brides and wedding parties. She had also learned the special requirements for ballroom- competition gowns, and had made some truly spectacular dresses. Just as it was great for the studio to be right on top of the club, it was a boon to have Katarina right next to them.

David was a regular who came twice a week to work with Rhianna. He had also known and worked with Lara. He and Rhianna were deep in conversation as they twirled around, working on a tango. She knew they were probably discussing Lara. Sam Railey, however, didn't have a student at the moment. He was putting his CDs in order.

Quinn O'Casey's really large left foot landed on her toe once again.

"Sam!" she called suddenly, breaking away from her partner.

"Yeah?" he looked up.

"Can I borrow you for a minute?"

"Sure."

Shannon headed toward the stereo, waiting for the tango to play out, removed the CD and replaced it with an old classic—Peggy Lee singing "Fever." Sam walked over to partner her as she spoke to her new student. "Right now, you're just trying to get the basic box. But if you think of the steps to the music, it might help you."

Sam led her in the basic steps while she looked at Quinn. She was not at all convinced he was trying very hard.

To her surprise, Sam spoke up. "It looks like a boring dance," he said to Quinn. "But it can be a lot of fun."

The next thing Shannon knew, Sam had taken the initiative. They moved into a grapevine, an underarm spin and a series of pivots. Steps far advanced from anything their new student could begin to accomplish.

"Okay, Sam," she said softly. "We don't want to scare him off."

"Well…he should see what he can learn," Sam replied.

She couldn't argue. They did lots of demonstrations to show their students what they could learn. She just wondered about this particular student.

But Quinn was nodding and looking as if he had suddenly figured something out. He stepped in to take his position with her again. The guy had a great dance hold; he also wore some kind of really great aftershave. He should be a pleasure to teach.

Except that he was always watching.

But weren't students supposed to watch?

Not the way he did, with those piercing blue eyes.

She looked back up into them, reminding herself that she was a teacher, and a good one.

"Listen, feel it, and move your feet. Remember that you're just making a square."

To her amazement, he had it. He finally had it. A box. A simple box. It felt like a miracle.

"Head up," she said softly, almost afraid to push her luck. "Don't look at your feet. It will only mess you up."

His eyes met hers, and he maintained the step and the rhythm. His dimple showed as he smiled, pleased. His hold was just right. There was distance between them, but she was still aware of hot little jolts sweeping through her, despite the lack of real body contact. Not good.

Dance teachers needed to be friendly. Accustomed to contact. The more advanced a student, the closer that contact. She was accustomed to that.

But it had never been like this.

She suddenly wanted the lesson to be over for reasons other than her sore feet.

When they were done, he seemed actually enthused.

"When do I come again?" he asked.

"Whenever you schedule."

"Tomorrow?" he asked.

"You'll have to see Ella, our receptionist."

They were standing near the little elevated office. Ella had already heard. "He can have a two-o'clock."

"I thought I had an appointment with the hotel about blocking out rooms for the Gator Gala?" Shannon said frowning. "And I know I have Dr. Long coming in for his regular class."

"The hotel pushed the meeting to Wednesday," Ella said cheerfully. "And they want you to call them back. Dr. Long isn't in until five-fifteen."

"Two o'clock, then," Shannon said.

"Thanks. I'll see you then."

Their new student departed, and Shannon stared after him.

Jane, returning from the dentist, passed him at the door. "Who the hell was that?" she demanded when she reached Shannon.

"Doug's brother."

"Doug's brother…wow. Look what a few more years are going to do for that guy. Of course, the eyes…shit! Who taught him?"

"I did," Shannon said.

"Oh. And you're keeping him?" She tried to sound light. Shannon hesitated. "Yes."

Sam went dancing by, practicing a Viennese waltz on his own. "Hey," he teased Jane. "You've already got the one brother."

Jane gave him a serious glare. "Yeah, and I also have nasty old Mr. Clinton, ninety-eight, and decaying with each move we make." She looked at Shannon. "I thought you weren't going to take on any new students."

"I wasn't. But you know how it goes."

"You're the manager," Jane reminded her. "You don't have to keep him."

"I know, but that forty-five-minute investment of time felt like ten hours. The guy is a challenge I don't think I can refuse. Hey," she added quickly, teasingly, "careful— your old-timer just walked in."

Jane glanced at her white-haired, smiling student.

Ben had already walked forward to shake his hand. That was studio policy—all employees greeted all students when not otherwise occupied. Courtesy and charm to all students, regardless of sex, age, color, creed or ability.

They were a regular United Nations.

And more. Being in South Florida, gateway to Latin America, they were also a very huggy bunch. People hugged hello and hugged goodbye. Cheek kissing went on continually. It was nice; it was warm, and it was normal behavior for most people who had grown up here.

Mr. Clinton was actually a dear. They all kissed and hugged him hello all the time. He wasn't really decaying, and he wasn't nasty. He was just a little hard-of-hearing, so it sounded as if he was yelling sometimes.

Jane sighed. "Yep, here's my old-timer."

"Jane, he brings you gourmet coffee," Shannon reminded her.

"He's a sweetie, all right."

Jane stared at her. She didn't say anything more. They both knew what she was thinking.

Sure, the old guy was a sweetie. He just wasn't Quinn O'Casey.

Jane forced a smile.

"You are the boss," she murmured lightly, and moved away. "Mr. Clinton, how good to see you. What did you say you wanted to do today. A samba? You're sure you're up to it?"

"You bet, Janie," he assured her with a broad grin. "I got the best pacemaker ever made helping this old ticker. Let's get some action going."

Watching them, Shannon smiled. No, Mr. Clinton wasn't a Quinn O'Casey, but then again...

Just what did Quinn expect to get from the studio?

Suddenly, for no reason that she could explain, she felt a shiver trickle down her spine.

CHAPTER 4

In the afternoon, the beach wasn't so bad, Quinn thought. It was slower. Weekends, it was crazy. If he suddenly heard there had been a run of cab drivers committing suicide on a Friday or Saturday night at the beach, it wouldn't be shocking in the least. Traffic sometimes snarled so badly that a lifetime could pass before a vehicle made it down a block.

But in the afternoon...

Though they were moving into fall, temperatures were still high, but there was a nice breeze coming off the ocean, making the air almost cool. Walking from the studio, which sat between Alton Road and Washington, he passed some of the old Deco buildings and houses that had undergone little or no restoration, appreciating their charm. There were also a number of small businesses, including a coffeehouse that wasn't part of a big chain, a pretty little flower shop, some duplexes, small apartment houses and a few single dwellings. The beach itself was barely three blocks away, and he was tempted to take a quick stroll on the boardwalk and get a real feel for the area.

The stretch of sand facing the bay was dotted with sun

worshipers. A volleyball game was going on, and down a bit, a mother was helping two toddlers build a sand castle. The little girl wore a white eyelet cap, protecting her delicate skin, while just a few feet away, a young couple, both bronzed and beautiful, applied great gobs of something from a tube labeled Mega-Tan to each other's skin. During the week, the beach could be great. He had to admit, the Keys didn't offer huge expanses of beach. Just more privacy.

On the stretch in front of a chic Deco hotel, the bronzed and beautiful were joined by the more mundane. A huge woman wearing a skimpy suit that was totally unsuitable for her ample physique was strolling along with a scrawny man in a Speedo. They were smiling happily, and nodded as they passed him. Quinn offered them a hello and decided that the mind's perception of the self was really what created happiness. The couple looked completely content. More power to them. Who the hell was he to judge? He was walking the beach in dress shoes, chinos and a tailored shirt.

A bit farther down, a group of kids seemed to be dispersing. Gathering towels, chairs and lotion bottles, they were calling out to one another, saying their goodbyes. He kept walking, watching as one by one they all disappeared—except for one little waif who was tall when she stood but slim to the point of boniness. Beyond model slim. She had long brown hair and huge eyes, and as she watched her friends disappear, she suddenly wore a look of loneliness and pain. She looked so lost he was tempted to talk to her, but hell, this was South Beach—she could be anyone, including an undercover cop.

Not old enough.

She heard his footsteps in the sand and swung around, looking straight at him. She sized him up and down, and swallowed.

"Hey, mister, you got a dollar?"

"You a runaway?"

She flushed but said, "Not exactly. I'm eighteen. Honest."

"But you ran away?"

"I left. I've graduated high school. I just haven't been able to find a job. A real job."

"So you're living on the streets."

She actually grinned. "The beach isn't as bad as the streets. Really. If you're going to be homeless, this is the place to be."

"But you've got a home?"

"What are you, a cop?"

"No, just a concerned citizen who doesn't want to see your face in the news. 'Does anyone know this girl? Her body was discovered Saturday night.'"

The girl shook her head vehemently. "I'm careful. You got a dollar or not? I don't need a third degree."

"Hey, wait." He pulled out his wallet and found a five.

She blinked and walked toward him. "What do you want?" she asked uneasily. "I'm not a cheap hooker."

He shook his head. "I just want you to tell me that you're going to buy food, and that you're not a junkie, either."

"Hey, you see any punctures in these arms?" She was wearing a tank top over cutoff jeans, and she spoke with pride as well as conviction.

"Get yourself something to eat, then. And hey, listen. If you do need help, you can get it, you know. Find a cop. The guys on the beach are pretty damned decent, and if not, head for the South Miami station. There's a woman there who is a victims' advocate, and she's an absolute gem. Wait, I'll give you her card."

She looked as if she was going to run with the five at first, but then she waited and even took the card.

"I thought you said you weren't a cop."

"I'm not."

"Kind of overdressed for the beach, aren't you?"

He started to shrug. Her eyes widened. "I'll bet you were at that dance studio."

He didn't answer, and she laughed. "Hey, I'd be there, too, if I had the bucks. God, I love to dance." She flushed again, then wiggled the five in her hand. "Thanks."

"Be careful, huh?"

"Hey, don't I know? Don't worry, I'm tougher than I look. And I know that you can get into a lot more out here than just sea and sand."

She turned and sprinted off, then paused a good thirty feet away and called back to him, "Hey, you're all right, you know? My name is Marnie, by the way." Then, as if she had given away far too much, she turned again, this time running toward the street at full speed.

He watched her go. He hoped she was as tough as she thought.

Miami Beach was a gateway to every vice in the western hemisphere.

He noted the position of the sun in the sky and glanced at his watch. Time to get moving.

He headed back for his car, which was parked over on Alton. He wasn't sure why, but he hadn't wanted to park closer to the studio. He returned to his car, took a look at his watch again and figured he had time. It was a short hop from South Beach to pay a visit to the medical examiner's officer.

The newly revamped and renamed hotel where they were hoping to hold the Gator Gala had called while Shannon was giving Quinn O'Casey his first lesson. When she returned the call, she was happy to learn that she had played hardball with them to just the right degree—they were calling to agree to a per-night room charge that was completely reasonable and would surely help draw northern entrants to the competition, which was planned for the second week in February. Despite the heavy pall that had seemed to hang over her since Lara's death, Shannon was delighted. They would wrap up the deal at their meeting later in the week. She hurried into the main office to tell Gordon.

"Great," he told her, really pleased. "That should make a difference for us. I mean, who wouldn't want to come to Miami Beach in the middle of winter? Especially at such a great price. What about the meals?"

"We're still negotiating," she said.

"What are we negotiating?" Ben Trudeau asked, poking his head in.

"Meals," Shannon told him.

"Ah." Ben was one of those men who was so good-looking he was almost too pretty. Of course, once upon a time, it hadn't seemed that way to Shannon. Once he had been like a god to her—tall, lithe, elegant, able to move with the speed and electric power of lightning or as smoothly as the wind.

He was an incredible dancer and always a striking competitor. His hair was ebony, his eyes dark as ink, and his features classically flawless. He had amazing technical ability and was a showman to boot. For several years he had competed with Lara, but then it had all fallen apart. They'd been divorced for almost five years before her death. In that time, she'd taken a number of championships, working steadily with Jim Burke. Ben, in the meantime, had grabbed any number of best in shows and number ones and cash prizes, but he hadn't gone as far as Lara. He'd changed partners too many times. Now his eyes moved over Shannon as he stood in the doorway.

"It's a waste," he said.

"What?"

"All the time you're spending on business."

"Hey!" Gordon said.

"Well, she should be competing."

Gordon looked at Shannon, a slight smile curving his lips. "She can go back into competition any time she wants."

"Gentlemen, I'm well aware of that. And I don't want to compete."

"You know, that's just silly," Ben said, smoothing back a thatch of hair from his forehead. "You get out there in the Pro-Ams with your students all the time. What's the difference?"

"They're my students."

"Lucky students," Gordon noted, still amused. "You make them look great."

"And I'm really proud of them when they do well. Why can't you two understand that? Everyone isn't ruled by blinding ambition."

She sighed. "Look, since I broke my ankle all those years ago, it's never been the same. I never know when it's going to give, and after too much practice, it hurts like hell. It's not good enough to work as hard as I'd have to if I wanted to compete professionally. The good thing is, I really love to teach. I get my thrills by working with the students."

"Beginners," Ben said, a note of contempt in his voice.

"Everyone is a beginner at some point."

Ben laughed. "Right. So you gonna talk that new student of yours—that tank—into entering the newcomers division at the Gator Gala? That the kind of challenge you're up to?"

"Maybe I *will* talk him into it," she said.

"It's all just an excuse for cowardice," Ben said.

She didn't have a chance to respond. A buzzer sounded on Gordon's desk, and he hit the intercom button.

"Dr. Long is here for his lesson with Shannon," Ella's voice informed them.

"I'm on my way." Before she left, she addressed the two men one last time. "Both of you—I'm happy with what I do. Jane and Rhianna are both young and beautiful and talented. Let's support them, huh?" She glared at both men. Neither responded.

Shannon started out of the office. Ben slipped up behind her, catching her shoulder the minute they were out of the doorway.

"We were good, you know," he reminded her.

"Once."

"You really are afraid, you know. Maybe you're afraid of me."

"Ben, I promise you—I'm not afraid of you."

"We could be really good together again," he whispered huskily.

"Not in this lifetime, Ben," she said sweetly, then edged her shoulder free. "Excuse me. My student is waiting."

"Time has gone by, you know. A lot of it."

"My student is waiting."

"You don't have to hurt us both by being bitter. You could forgive me."

"I forgave you a long time ago, Ben."

"Then don't play so hard to get."

"Are you trying to come on to me again—or do you just want to dance with me?"

"Both?" He laughed with a certain charm, but it just didn't strum the same heartstrings for her it once had.

"I'm sorry. I know this must be amazing to you, but I'm not hateful, bitter or playing hard to get. I'm just not interested."

"You'll be sorry," he said, his voice teasing.

She stopped, staring at him. "Ben, you have a new partner. What's her name, from Broward. Vera Thompson."

He shook his head. "She's okay. She's not the caliber I need."

"Have you told *her* that?" Shannon inquired.

"Of course not. Not yet."

"Why not?"

"You haven't agreed to dance again."

She shook her head. "Ben, if I ever *were* to dance professionally again, it wouldn't be with you."

"Why not?"

She could have told him that the reasons should have been obvious. But then, maybe nothing was as obvious to Ben as it should be.

So she shrugged. And then she couldn't help the reply that came to her lips. "You're just not the caliber I need," she said, and hurried out to meet Richard for his class.

Quinn had already read the police report that had been provided by Doug. He'd read the M.E.'s report, as well, which had provided a stroke of luck. There were eight M.E.s under the direction of the chief, but Anthony Duarte had performed the autopsy on Lara Trudeau.

Just as he had performed the autopsy on Nell Durken.

And though Dixon might not be a ball of fire in the homicide department, Duarte was tops in his field, a man with a natural curiosity that gave him the propensity to go far beyond thorough, even in the most straightforward circumstances.

At the desk, Quinn produced his credentials, though he knew the receptionist and she waved away his wallet as she put through the call to Duarte.

Despite it being close to five, Duarte came down the hall, smiling as he greeted Quinn. "Hey, thought you were heading off on vacation."

"I was."

"What are you doing down here?"

"Right now? Feeling damned lucky to see you."

"Most people don't feel that way—when I'm at work, anyway," Duarte said with a touch of humor.

"Let me rephrase. Since I have to see a medical examiner, I'm glad it's you. You performed the autopsy on Lara Trudeau."

Duarte, a tall, slim black man with the straightest back Quinn had ever seen, arched a graying brow. "You're working an angle on Lara Trudeau?"

"That's surprising, I take it?"

Duarte lifted his shoulders in a shrug. "Nothing surprises me. I've been here far too long. I ruled the death accidental because I sure as hell couldn't find any reason not to. Due to the circumstances, though, Dixon is still doing some work—though nothing more than paperwork, I imagine."

"What do you mean, the circumstances?"

"A healthy woman popped too many nerve pills, swallowed some hard liquor and dropped dead. It isn't a daily occurrence. Not even in Miami." The last was spoken dryly and a little wearily. "Although, in all honesty, the number of people who do die from the misuse of prescriptions and even over-the-counter drugs is a hell of a lot higher than it should be."

"Really?"

"People mix too much stuff. And then they think, like with sleeping pills, hey, if one helps, I could really get a good night's sleep with a bunch of them. As for Lara Trudeau, who the hell knows what she was thinking? Maybe she just thought she was immortal."

"I'm surprised the stuff didn't affect her dancing."

"That too—she must have had a will of steel."

"She dropped dead in front of an audience."

"Not to mention the television cameras. And no one saw anything suspicious."

"There was no sign of…?" Quinn said. Though what the hell there might be a sign of, he didn't know.

"Force? Had someone squeezed open her cheeks to force pills down her throat? Not that I could find. The cops, naturally, checked for prints on her prescription bottle. Not a one to be found."

"Not a single print?" Quinn said with surprise. "Not even hers?"

"She was wearing gloves for her performance."

"And that would normally wipe the entire vial clean?"

"If she was rubbing her fingers around it over and over again, which a nervous person might do."

"Still…"

Duarte shrugged. "I guess it's one of the reasons the cops kept looking. She was famous and apparently not all that nice, so…there might have been any number of people who wanted her dead. Trouble is, they just haven't got anything. There were hundreds of people there. She went out to dance with a smile on her face. No apparent argument with anyone there…well, I'm assuming you've read the report." He stared at Quinn. "She's still here. Want to see her yourself?"

"I thought you'd released her body."

"I did. The funeral home won't be here until sometime tonight. Come on. I'll have her brought out."

They walked down halls that, no matter how clean, still somehow reeked of death. Duarte called an assistant and led Quinn to a small room for the viewing. Loved ones weren't necessarily brought in to see their dearly departed. A camera allowed for them to remain in the more natural atmosphere of the lobby to view the deceased.

She was brought in. Duarte lowered the sheet.

Lara Trudeau had been a beautiful woman. Even in death, her bone structure conveyed a strange elegance. She truly gave the appearance of sleep—until the eye wandered down to the autopsy scars.

Quinn stared at her, circling the gurney on which she lay. Other than the sewn Y incision that marred her chest, there was no sign of any violence. She hadn't even bruised herself when she'd gone down.

"I couldn't find anything but the prescription pills and alcohol. She'd barely eaten, which surely added to the pressure on her heart. That's what killed her—the heart's reaction to drugs and alcohol."

"Like Nell."

Frowning, Duarte stared at him. "Not exactly. No alcohol in Nell. Why, what do you think you're seeing?"

"I don't know."

"Is that why you're on this?"

"Maybe. I found out that Nell Durken had been an amateur dancer and took lessons at the same studio where Lara Trudeau sometimes practiced and coached."

"But the police arrested Nell's husband. And his fingerprints *were* all over the pill bottle. You were the one who followed the guy, right, and gave the police your records on the investigation?"

"Yep."

"Art Durken has been in jail, pending trial, for over a week. He sure as hell wasn't at that competition."

"Yeah, I know."

"So?"

"I don't know. There's just…something. That's all."

"Durken still denying that he murdered his wife?"

"Yes." Quinn met Anthony Duarte's eyes. "Admits he was a womanizing bastard, but swears he didn't kill her."

"You think a dancer is the killer?" Duarte shook his head. "Quinn, the circumstances were odd enough for the police to investigate, but you've got to think about the facts again. Lara Trudeau didn't argue with anyone at that competition, and she walked out on the floor to dance without the least sign of distress. When she fell, she did so in front of a huge audience. The pills she took were prescription, the vial had no prints, and the prescription was written by a physician she'd been seeing for over ten years—and to the best of my knowledge, he wasn't a ballroom dancer."

"Yeah, I know. I read the report. I'm going to pay a visit to Dr. Williams, though I know he was already interviewed and cleared of any wrongdoing."

Duarte grimaced. "If the cops blamed a physician every time a patient abused a prescription, the jails would be spilling over worse than they are now. This is a tough one, Quinn. Strange, and tough. I just don't see where you can go. There's simply no forensic evidence to lead you in any direction. If it is a crime, it's just about the perfect one."

"No crime is perfect."

"We both know a lot of them go unpunished."

"Yeah. And this time, I agree, there's nothing solid to go on. Unless I can find someone who knows something—and that person has to be out there."

"Wish I could be more helpful," Duarte said.

Quinn nodded. "Nell Durken hadn't taken a lesson in the sixth months before she died. With Nell…there was nothing else, either, right? No…grass, speed…anything like that?"

"No, sorry. There were no illegal substances in either woman. Just massive overdoses of prescription medications and, in the Trudeau case, alcohol."

"Well, thanks," Quinn said. "Sorry to take up your time."

Duarte offered him a rueful smile. "You never take up my time. I really believe in the things you read and see on television. The dead can't speak anymore. We have to do their talking for them, but sometimes we're not as good at interpreting as we want to be. If I've missed something, or if I haven't thought to look for something, hell, I want to know."

"Yeah. Thanks."

"You going back to the Keys tonight?" Duarte asked.

"No. I have my boat up at the marina by Nick's, doing some work. I'm still there."

"Maybe I'll see you later. I'm starving—it was a long day. I got busy and forgot to eat. I'm dying for a hamburger."

Quinn nodded, but at the moment, he didn't feel the slightest twinge of hunger. He'd stood through a number of autopsies and he'd never gotten sick or fainted—as some of the biggest, toughest guys he knew had done—but he'd never gotten over a certain abdominal clenching in the presence of a corpse. Time and experience didn't change some things.

Duarte was one of the best of the best. But he could chow down with body parts on the same table. Survival, Quinn thought, in a place where the houses of the dead were as big as they were in Miami-Dade County.

"You'll be around later?" Duarte said.

"Sure," Quinn agreed. It would be a lot later, he knew.

Lara was covered and rolled away by the assistant as the two men started out the door and back down the hall.

A trip to the main station on Kendall was pretty much as worthless as Quinn had suspected. Detective Pete Dixon worked nine to five.

No overtime for Dixon these days.

He said a quick hello to a few old friends and started out. In the parking lot, he ran into Jake Dilessio, with whom he'd worked prior to leaving for Quantico. He wished that Dilessio had been assigned to the Trudeau investigation. He was certain he wouldn't be taking dance lessons if the chips had fallen that way.

"Hey, stranger, haven't seen much of you," Dilessio greeted him. "Seems we're living only a few feet away from one another, too. You're moored at the marina by Nick's, right? Thought you were taking off for the Bahamas."

"I was." Quinn shrugged. "I'm investigating the Trudeau case."

"Trudeau?" Dilessio arched a brow. "Sounds familiar."

"The dancer who died."

"I thought that was ruled accidental. Last I heard, Dixon was just tying up the reports to close the case."

"It *was* ruled accidental."

"But someone thinks it wasn't?"

"Something like that."

"So who are you working for?"

"The word 'work' would imply pay."

"Oh, yeah, that's right. They're calling your brother twinkle-toes on the beat. Not without some envy, I might add. I hear the kid is really good."

"I wouldn't know. I haven't seen him dance yet."

"No?"

"I didn't even know he was dancing until this all came up."

Jake shrugged and nodded. "I saw him not too long ago. He said you'd been really wrapped up in work. Congratulations, by the way. I hear your surveillance reports on Art Durken gave the cops what they needed to arrest him and enough for the D.A.'s office to charge him."

"Not really. If I'd been good enough, she wouldn't be dead."

"How long have you been in this business? You can't blame yourself for all the bad shit that goes down."

"Yeah, I know. But I can't stop it from bugging me, either."

Jake shrugged and said, "That's true. But at least it's better than the shit that goes unpunished."

"I guess you're right. Anyway, the dancer who died was

connected with Doug's studio. I'm doing a little follow-up of my own."

"Well, Dixon is known to show up at Nick's in the evening. No wife, no kids, no kitchen. He eats a hamburger there almost every night. I'm heading home now. In fact, if you're free, I'll buy you dinner."

"If you're buying me dinner, I'm not exactly free, but at least, at Nick's, I'll be cheap. Sounds good to me. Where's your wife? Is she joining us? I saw her when I tied up the other day. That baby's due awful soon, isn't it?"

"Too soon. Three weeks. And she went up to Jacksonville anyway, with a special dispensation from the airline. They wanted her to do some sketches of a homicide suspect."

"I thought that she left forensics and graduated from the academy."

"She did graduate from the academy, but she stayed in forensics. She's one of the best sketch artists in the state, in the country, maybe. They asked her to go, and she thought she could help, so she went."

"You know, you marry a cop, and that's what happens," Quinn said lightly.

"Yeah, I know."

They arrived at Nick's right before six.

It was a great time of the day at the marina. Darkness was falling, coming fast, but the sky over the ocean was in the midst of its last majestic frenzy of color. Magenta, oranges, trails of gold, all sweeping together across the heavens over the shadowed ocean. The breeze at night was cool, pleasant after the heat of the day.

As Jake had suspected, Pete Dixon was there, already on his second cheeseburger, it appeared, since one empty basket was pushed behind the one in front of him.

Quinn pulled out a chair at Dixon's table without being asked, turning it backward and straddling the seat. "Jeez,

Pete, you might want to opt for something green now and then, watch out for the fat and cholesterol once a week, maybe," he said.

Dixon wiped his mouth, looking at Quinn as if he'd just been joined by a barracuda. His eyes, small in the folds of his face, fell on Jake Dilessio next, riddled with pure accusation. "Sit down, Quinn, Jake. Come on, join me. And while you're at it, give me grief about my eating habits."

"Thanks," Jake said, sitting.

"You're close to retirement. You might want to live to enjoy a little of it," Quinn said.

"Like you're a vegetarian or something," Pete muttered.

Quinn grinned. "No, I think I'll have a cheeseburger, too. But just one."

"You brought him here," Pete said to Jake. "Make sure his food goes on your bill."

"I'll even pick up *your* bill," Jake said. "Quinn has a few questions for you."

Pete groaned aloud. He was a big man. His belly jiggled as the sound escaped him. "Hope Nick has some Rolaids back there. Shit. I'm off duty. You had to bring a P.I. here to bug me?"

"Hey, I've got my boat up here," Quinn protested. "This is the most convenient place for me to eat."

"What do you want?" Pete asked him flatly. Before Quinn could answer, he looked at Jake again. "You really picking up my tab? If so, you can order me another beer."

"Sure thing," Jake said, grimacing at Quinn. He looked around and saw one of the waitresses at the next table. "Debbie, when you get a minute…"

The girl turned to him, scratching on her pad. "Pete—another cheeseburger?"

"Funny," Pete said.

"No, but two for Quinn and me, and three Millers," Jake said.

"Coming up." Debbie was young and cheerful, bronzed and wearing tiny white shorts. Pete watched as she walked away.

"Pete, pay attention over here. What's the story on Lara Trudeau?" Quinn asked.

Dixon frowned. "Trudeau? You're here to ask me about that?"

"Yeah. Why?"

"I closed it up today."

"You closed the case already?" Quinn said.

"What case? There is no case. You want to see what happened yourself, the tape is in my office. Come by anytime. She went out on the dance floor smiling like a little lark. Moments later, she drops. A doctor is right there and tries to revive her. The ambulance arrives, and the med techs try to revive her. She gets to the hospital, and she's pronounced dead on arrival. She's turned over to the M.E., who discovers that she did herself in with booze and pills. Or her heart gave in 'cuz of the booze and pills. She ordered a drink at the bar herself—a dozen witnesses will tell you so. And the pills were a prescription from a physician with a flawless reputation. No prints on the vial. Our lady was wearing gloves. Of course, we checked anyway. We questioned waiters and waitresses, judges, dancers and the audience. Dozens of people talked to her. No one saw her argue with anyone. Hell yes, I closed the case. There was no damned case."

Debbie arrived with the three beers as he finished. They thanked her, and she nodded, moving on quickly. It was casual at Nick's, but the place was getting busy, and Debbie seemed to be working the patio area alone.

When she was gone, Quinn asked, "You don't think her death was odd?"

"Odd? You should see my caseload. It's odd that a man shoots his own kid, his wife, and then himself. It's odd that out of the clear blue, a shot rings out in North Miami and a kid in all honors classes falls down dead. Hell, there's odd out there. You bet. But as far as this Trudeau thing goes, what the hell do you want? There's nothing there. So it's odd. So what? Everyone down here is frigging odd. And guess what? It ain't illegal to be odd."

"If I understand the situation," Quinn said evenly, "there were lots of people out there who hated Lara Trudeau."

Pete Dixon stared at him, lifted his beer bottle and took a long swig. "Maybe lots of people hate *you,* Quinn. It's America. It's allowed."

"I'm not dead," Quinn reminded him.

"Yeah, well, hell, you're not in the position we're in at the force, either. People hire you, pay you by the case, and you've got the luxury of lots of time to investigate 'odd' and nasty things. My plate is full with stuff that definitely has murder written all over it. You feel free to spend your time chasing 'odd.' I can't do it."

"Hey, we're all on the same side here," Jake reminded him. "You know, fighting crime. That's the idea."

"Yeah, that's right, and our big man Quinn here comes straight from the FBI. How was it, then, Quinn? What the hell made you leave, anyway? Or did being with the Feds just make you think you could come back and be better than anyone else?"

Quinn might not have expected a lot of help from Dixon, but he hadn't expected total animosity, either. He watched his fingers curl too tightly around his beer bottle, and he forced himself to control his temper.

"You're right, Pete. You've got lots of cases. Right now, I've just got one. If you do think of anything that can help me, I'd appreciate it if you'd let me know."

Maybe he should have spent a little more time with the Bureau shrink—the control thing seemed to work. To his amazement, Pete flushed. Being such a big man, he went very red.

"Yeah, sure." He swallowed more of his beer. "Hell, the whole damned thing was odd, you're right. The oddest thing is, how the hell did she down all that stuff and get out on the floor and dance so damned well, then…drop? She must have been totally oblivious to what she was doing beforehand. Come by and get the tape. Maybe that will help you. Who the hell knows? I looked at it over and over again, and it didn't give me a thing. I gotta go. My brother's kid is playing the saxophone at some dumb school thing." He stood. "Thanks for the meal, Dilessio."

"Sure thing," Jake said.

"He gets discounts here anyway, you know?" Pete said to Quinn. "Married the proprietor's niece. When's that kid due, Dilessio?"

"Soon."

"Hope you have a boy."

"Oh, why?" Jake said.

"'Cause women are trouble. Right from the get-go."

The both stared after him as he walked away toward the parking lot. Then Jake laughed out loud. "Quinn, you've come a long way."

"Oh yeah?"

"For a minute there, I thought you were going to get up and deck him."

Quinn shrugged. "Psychology one-oh-one," he said lightly, except that he had a feeling Jake knew better. "You know, I think he believes there's more there than meets the eye, but he's got the same problem as everyone else."

"And what's that?"

"Figuring out just how 'odd' fits in with illegal. And murder."

"Well, if you need help, I'm around," Jake told him.

"What, you've got a small caseload?"

Jake shook his head, scratching the paper off the beer bottle. "Nope. Murder is murder, though. Whether it's obvious or not. You find something, I'll step on a few toes for you."

"Great. Thanks."

"We're playing poker later, out back in Nick's house, if you want to join us."

"I think I'm going clubbing."

"You're going club hopping?"

"Not hopping. Just clubbing."

"Heading down to Suede?"

"Yep. Want to blow off the poker thing and come with me?"

Jake shook his head. "Someone down there might know me."

"How come?"

"I got called in when a dead hooker was found not far from the place."

"Was that one ever solved?"

"No." Jake looked up at him. "The kid had no track lines, but she managed to overdose."

"So it was, or wasn't, a homicide?"

"I haven't closed the case," Jake said flatly. "Haven't found anything, but I haven't closed the case. I haven't put it into cold cases yet, either. Sometimes, the drug cases are the easiest. The perps are known to the narcotics guys. Not in this instance. They ran the ropes for me on it, checking into every club with a name. No one has come up with anything. She had a name, Sally Grant, and she picked up tricks on the street, no known regular johns. There were no witnesses, no one who could be found who admitted to seeing her in days, just a dead girl with a needle next to her."

"Prints on it?" Quinn asked.

"Her own—but that could have been staged."

"Hell of a lot overdoses going on," Quinn commented.

"The M.E.s will tell you their tables are full of them. Legal substances, illegal substances. But it sure does add up to 'odd,' doesn't it? Two dance students, too much Xanax. One dead hooker, too much heroin. They shouldn't connect. But maybe they do. Hell, maybe dancing is dangerous for your health."

"The prostitute was a dancer?"

"Not that I know of. She was just found not too far from the studio. Not that that necessarily means a damn thing."

"Did they question anyone at the studio, find out if she had ever been in?"

"Yep. None of the teachers had ever seen her."

"Thanks again for the dinner, Jake."

"Keep me informed."

"Will do."

Quinn left Jake at the table and headed for his boat to change. It had been one hell of a long time since he'd been to a club on the beach.

What the hell were people wearing to clubs these days?

CHAPTER 5

"Want to make me look good?"

"Pardon?" Shannon said.

She was definitely off today. First there had been the strange lesson with Quinn O'Casey, which she had wanted to scream through, her patience nonexistent.

Now Richard.

She didn't need to scream when she danced with Richard. He was good. Excellent. A doctor, he had found that dance took his mind off the strain of his day. He wasn't performing brain surgery on a daily basis, but something far more demanding—at least in the eyes of his customers, he had once told her humorously. He was a plastic surgeon. Trusted with looks—the most important thing in the world, to the players in the area. He'd "fixed" or repaired the old, the young, the famous, the rich. He was written up constantly in magazines and had even been touted as the "Botox king of the western world" by one popular publication.

Shannon wasn't sure about his age but assumed he was around forty. He was in great shape, a golf enthusiast when he wasn't in the studio or working. He maintained a great tan, had a full head of almost platinum blond hair and fine gray eyes. He was married, and his wife, a pediatrician, came in now and then, as well, but she wasn't as enamored of dancing as Richard was. She preferred diving and spent most of her free time out on a boat. They seemed to have a perfect relationship. When they could be together, they were. When one had an opportunity that didn't work for the other, they just went their separate ways. Mina Long was petite and, like her husband, fortyish, platinum blond, bronzed and in great shape. The only difference was that she had brown eyes. After all their years of marriage, Shannon thought with some humor, they almost resembled each other.

He was a nice guy, and she enjoyed teaching him. He learned quickly, and in the year since he had been coming to the studio, he had advanced rapidly. But then again, he could afford all the private lessons he wanted. Most people, with more moderate incomes, took one or two private lessons a week and attended group lessons whenever they could.

"Earth to Shannon."

"Oh, sorry. Make you look good? You don't need anyone to make you look good, Richard. In fact, you've gotten so good, I have to admit, I did just drift off in thought. Forgive me. That's not at all a good thing for a teacher to admit."

He smiled. "You're still upset about Lara."

"Of course," she admitted.

"You do know I did everything that I could," he said quietly. "I may be a plastic surgeon, but I was top of my class at med school and spent plenty of time interning in the emergency room."

"Oh, Richard, of course, I know you did everything. It's just still so...sad."

"Yes. We'll all miss her tremendously. I mean, you *will* miss her, right?"

"Of course." Shannon frowned. "Why do you say that?"

"No reason."

They had been waltzing. She stopped near the stereo, frowning as she looked at him.

"Richard, why did you say that?"

"Oh, Lord, now I'm really sorry."

"Richard."

"A little bird told me once—a while ago—that you and Ben Trudeau had been partners and a very hot duo—before Ben married Lara."

"I see."

"You *were* partners, right? I hear you stormed the floor in competitions, that no one even came close to being as good."

"We won a few competitions, but that was ages ago. And I do mean ages."

"Sorry, I shouldn't have said anything."

"Who told you about it?"

"Now, I swear, my lips are sealed."

"It doesn't matter, Richard. It's not like it was a deep, dark secret or anything. I was just curious."

"I told you, my lips are sealed. And hey, you didn't answer my question."

"What question?"

He sighed with a pretense of mock impatience. "Do you want to help me look good?"

"I did answer your question. You do look good."

He shook his head, smiling. "There are some hotshots down from the board. I'm bringing them out to Suede tonight. Would you show up for a few minutes?"

"Richard, I was going to try to head home early. Someone will be down there, though. Rhianna or Jane."

He shook his head. "You're my teacher. We both know that even the top professionals work with their partner over and over again. I look best with you. Show up for one dance and one drink? I'll get you out of there by ten-thirty, I swear it. Please?"

"Richard, don't beg."

"I am begging."

"All right—you tell me what little bird told you about Ben and me, and maybe I'll come."

"That's bribery!"

"You bet," she said, smiling.

"I can't tell you. And I don't fold easy."

"If you want me to show up…"

"Gordon," Richard said.

"Gordon?"

"Yes, I said Gordon, didn't I?"

"Yes…and quickly. You folded like a bad poker hand," she said, laughing.

"Right. So now you have to show up."

"I will, I will," she told him. "Right after I strangle Gordon."

"Why? You just said that it wasn't a deep, dark secret or anything."

"But still…we're not supposed to bring our personal lives into the studio."

Richard let out a snort. "That gets ridiculous, you know."

"It's only professional."

"Not professional—silly," Richard said. "And you're getting that prim look on your face again. I'll let it go, but let's concentrate on something wild and sexy. I want to be known as the salsa king of Miami, not the reigning Botox monarch, okay?"

She laughed.

"We'll give them a show," she promised.

"And, Shannon?"

"What?"

"What happened was terrible. But it wasn't your fault

in any way. We're all stunned, and so sorry, but...please. It's okay to grieve. Lara was tremendously talented, a force.... We'll all miss her, maybe forever. But...well, you've got to move on. It hurts to see you so unhappy."

"I'm fine. It's just...the whole thing was so absurd. I can't believe it. I can't believe Lara would drink on top of drugs before a performance."

"You've got to accept it. It happened. You can't keep questioning fate—you have to let it go, however much you don't want to."

"Thanks. Moving into psychiatry, are you?" she teased.

He put up his hands in mock surrender. "Okay, I quit. Come on, let's play some salsa, huh? I really want to wow 'em tonight."

She walked over to the stereo system. "Salsa it is."

What did they wear to clubs these days?

Next to nothing, it seemed.

It was still early—for clubbing—when Quinn returned to the beach. Luckily it was a weeknight, and he was in time to get a meter right on the street and a seat at the sidewalk café across from Suede and Moonlight Sonata. He sat staring at the Deco building that housed the club and dance studio. He'd watched people arrive for dance classes—taking the stairs up to the second floor at the side of the building—along with the few who were already arriving for a night on the town. Several people had entered the lower level dressed in shorts and T-shirts with lettering that advertised "Suede." Apparently they were employees. In between arrivals, the café was one of those perfect spots for people-watching.

A gothic group cruised by, one girl, two guys, all three with nose rings and enough silver in their ears to weight down a cargo ship. Despite the balmy quality of the weather, they wore dark jeans and long black jackets, along with makeup that left them looking like walking cadavers.

They were followed by an elderly couple, moving very slowly. Harvey, as the wife addressed the man, wasn't holding the bagel bag securely enough, according to Edith, the woman.

Three bathing beauties strolled past him next. One had on a short jacket, which pretended to cover up the expanse of ample breasts displayed by the strings of her bikini top. The jacket, however, ended at her midriff. The bottom of her bathing suit was a thong. She was wearing three-inch heels, as well.

Interesting ensemble.

As night came on, so did more of the bold, the beautiful and the downright ugly.

A doorman came out to guard the entrance to the club.

A lithe Latin girl in see-through white entered with a tall dark man, followed by three obvious rockers, speaking so loudly that their English accents were clearly discernible across the street.

Quinn sipped a mineral water, somewhat amused as he turned a page in the notebook before him—compliments of Doug. His brother was meticulously thorough. This file described the teachers at the studio. Interesting group. He'd started with Gordon Henson, who had bought the business in the early seventies. He no longer taught, but in his day, he had apparently instructed some of the top champions in the world. He still showed up at the studio and did some overseeing of the day-to-day business. He had basically turned things over to Shannon Mackay, though. She had some students but also saw to the running of the studio. She was a native Floridian, born in Winter Haven, moved with her folks to the Miami area when she was three, had graduated from the area's specialized high school, then gone to an arts school in New York City. She was five feet seven inches, one hundred and twenty-five pounds, a green-eyed, dark blond dynamo, with a capacity for pure professionalism. Doug, it seemed, had waxed a little poetic on the last.

That didn't surprise Quinn.

Everyone he had seen in the studio was attractive. Well-dressed, well-groomed. The men wore suits, the women dresses or feminine pants ensembles. The girls were pretty, the men, if not exactly handsome, certainly presentable. But Shannon Mackay was a standout. Features delicate but precise, hair soft in a stunning color of sunlight, and eyes deep, direct and thoughtful. More, she seemed to radiate a sensual energy, her every movement unintentionally seductive, her smile somehow open and secretive in one. Beguiling.

She wore one of the Versace scents—he knew it because his mother loved perfumes and he'd learned the names. Shannon had the ability to touch gently but still steer and manipulate a student as she wanted. At his stage, he stood somewhat awkwardly apart from her when they danced. Close enough, though. She was something. Maybe that was why he had done so badly—it was difficult to concentrate when he was so close to her. Hell, yes, difficult to concentrate, but he just wasn't cut out for dancing. Didn't matter. He wouldn't be taking lessons long.

He wondered idly what he would have felt if he'd met her under different circumstances. Severely piqued interest, at the least. She had a chemistry that instantly aroused interest at an instinctive level. He would have liked to ask her out, listen to her voice, get between the light and shadow of her eyes.

She was as suspect as anyone else in a possible murder, he reminded himself.

A damned sexy suspect.

And yet…what if he'd met her elsewhere? He suddenly found himself pondering his last night with Geneva and wondering what exactly was wrong with him. They'd been together five years, and that night, she had just exploded.

He was never with her, she'd said. Not ever really with her. Not even when they made love. He lived work, breathed work and had become his work. She'd been crying. He had wanted to assure her somehow, but every word she'd said had been true. To others, it had been a perfect relationship. He was FBI; she was an assistant D.A. Tough schedules, the same parties. She teased that she always looked great on his arm; she was bright and beautiful. But somehow, it was true. The work—and the way it didn't always work—had begun to obsess him. He had been able to leave the office but never to let go. His workouts at the gym were no longer exercise but him beating up an enemy he couldn't touch, a vague force that was beating him, creating an inner rage.

Over. Over and done with. He was further disturbed by the knowledge that he hadn't felt any lonelier when she was gone. He had merely felt the strange darkness, the frustration, and, finally, the feeling that he wasn't where he should be, that he was no longer effective. Time to change his life, maybe even come home.

Then there had been the Nell Durken case.

The bastard who had killed her was in jail. Largely because of *his* work, his records, and what he'd given the cops. A killer was caught. He would face trial.

But *was* he the killer?

The question nagged at him, and he gritted his teeth.

Back to the files. The business at hand.

Shannon Mackay. She ran the business, taught, didn't compete. Apparently a broken ankle several years ago had caused her to step out of the arena of professional competition. She'd been at the top of her form, and the trophies she'd won were part of what gave the studio its reputation.

So what had she felt about Lara Trudeau? Doug's files didn't say.

He stared across the street, reflecting on his instructor.

She'd been tense. His questions had made her nervous. Or maybe she was always tense. No…she was on edge, something more than usual.

Rhianna Markham, Jane Ulrich. Both pretty, unmarried, no solid relationships, no children. Rhianna was from Ohio and had a degree from a liberal arts college. Jane had never gone past high school but had worked three years as a dancer at one of the central Florida theme parks before coming south. Both were ambitious, wanted to advance in the professional world. Lara Trudeau would have been their competition.

Of course, every female competitor in the dance world would have been in the same position. Assuming that Lara Trudeau had somehow been helped to her demise, she had done so before a crowd of hundreds—a large percentage of them competitors. He could be barking up the wrong tree entirely.

But he had to start somewhere. If Lara Trudeau had been murdered, it had been by someone with whom she had a close relationship. To have her die the way she did, before a crowd of hundreds, a murderer would have had to plan very carefully. And it certainly did seem odd that a woman who had been a student at the school had died from an eerily similar overdose just weeks before, even if she hadn't been at the studio in some time.

So…

Love. Hate.

The male instructors. Ben Trudeau. The ex-husband. Always a good suspect. Late thirties, tall, attractive, talented, a bit hardened, and, like Lara, growing old for the field of competition. He'd taken a steady teaching job rather than just coaching. Sam Railey, Jane Ulrich's partner, deeply loyal, determined that they would rise to the top—they had come close together, many times. Justin Garcia, salsa specialist, newest teacher at the studio.

Then there was Lara's partner, Jim Burke. Not a full
time teacher at the studio but a coach, as well. Again, a tall,
striking man of thirty, lucky to be chosen to be Lara's partner. Now alone. With Lara, he flew like an eagle. Without
her...he had no partner. He was back to square one. No
matter what his talent, Lara had been the driving force of
the pairs, the true prima donna of the dance floor. Jim
Burke seemed an unlikely candidate as a murderer.

Gordon Henson?

Quinn shook his head. It wasn't difficult finding motives for most of Lara's acquaintances and associates. Gordon had gotten Lara started; he gave her space, taught her
to move. Had she spurned him, rejected him, made fun of
him...threatened him?

He looked across the street again. He had only glanced
through the files on the teachers and he had half a dozen
scenarios already. He hadn't even begun to study the student lists.

It was now beginning to get busier over at Suede. He
checked his watch. After ten. He was surprised to realize
that the waiter at the little café had politely let him sit here,
nursing a water, for so long. He started to rise, then paused,
watching.

Shannon Mackay was coming down the steps from the
side entry to the studio. She had apparently left in a hurry
and rushed halfway down, looking behind her as she did
so.

Then she stopped, took a deep breath and squared her
soldiers.

For a minute she simply stood there. At last she turned
and slowly walked back up. She took out a set of keys and
made quick work of locking the door, then started down
the steps again.

She walked slowly at first. Then, as she neared the bottom, she began rushing again. She reached the sidewalk

and took another deep breath. She stared back up the steps, then shook her head.

The doorman at Suede saw her as she stood on the sidewalk. He called out a greeting, and she swung around, greeting him in turn.

Then she disappeared into the club as he opened the door for her.

Very curious behavior, Quinn thought.

He left the café, making sure to leave a generous tip. He would undoubtedly be wanting his table back in the days to come. He stopped by his car long enough to toss in the files he'd been reading, then headed across the street.

The doorman at Suede was jet-black, a good six-three, and pure muscle. He looked at Quinn, frowned, sized him up and down, and decided to let him pass.

Inside, the music was loud.

The bar was to the rear of the building, the dance floor about ten feet from the entrance. The place advertised live music and lived up to the advertising. The room was handsomely appointed, with the walls painted to imitate a sunset. Floor lighting gave the place just enough illumination to make the tables navigable, while spotlights gave a burst of life to the polished dance floor. A Latin trio was playing, and the beat was fast. Tables surrounded the floor on either side, and despite it being a weeknight, most of the tables were filled, though the place wasn't overcrowded. Scantily clad women on the dance floor gyrated at shocking speeds, some looking good and some not.

Toward the rear of the place, to the left of the bar, he caught sight of Gordon Henson. The thick thatch of white hair on his head was caught in the light, drawing attention to him. Skirting around the dance floor, Quinn saw that his brother was in attendance, along with Bobby Yarborough, one of his classmates from the academy, and Bobby's new wife, or at least, Quinn assumed it was his

wife. He'd never met her. Shannon Mackay was next to
Doug, on her other side a tall man in a white tailored shirt
and sport jacket, who, in turn, was next to a small woman
of about forty, perfectly elegant, but with features so taut
they screamed plastic surgery.

Doug, looking across the floor, saw him and, with some
surprise, called his name. "Quinn!"

Quinn continued across the room, excusing himself
with a quick smile when he nearly collided with a waitress.

"My brother with the two left feet," Doug teased, rising to greet him with a handshake.

"Hey, now, that's not really true," Shannon said, defending him. The words, however, seemed to be a natural reaction; she smiled, but she seemed distracted.

"That's right. You had your first lesson today, so you've
met Shannon and Gordon, and of course, you know
Bobby."

Quinn nodded, reaching out to shake Bobby's hand.
Bobby grinned broadly. "Hey, Quinn. You haven't met my
wife, Giselle."

"Giselle, nice to meet you. Congratulations on your
wedding."

Giselle smiled. "Thank you. It's amazing. I thought it
would never come. Now, I feel as if we've been married
forever."

"Ouch," Bobby said.

She squeezed his arm. "I meant that in the best possible way."

"Hmm," Bobby mused, feigning a frown.

"Quinn, these are the doctors Long," Doug continued.
"Richard and Mina."

He shook hands with the couple. "How nice. Do you
work together?"

The petite blonde laughed. "Good heavens, no. Richard is a dermatologist and plastic surgeon. I'm a lowly, hardworking pediatrician."

"She's far more noble," Richard said, grinning.

"You're the artist," his wife teased back.

His arm, casually around her shoulders as they sat in the expansive booth, tightened affectionately. "We simply thank God we don't work together. That way, we get to enjoy the time we do share."

"Great," Quinn said.

"Here, please, sit," Mina Long said, inching closer to her husband.

"I don't want to crowd you."

"Oh, please, don't worry," Richard said. "We're only here for a few minutes longer. We have to join some other friends across the room. In fact…we were about to dance?" He wasn't looking at his wife but across the table at Shannon.

"That's the music you want?" she asked.

"That's it," he told her.

"Excuse me, then…?"

Bobby and Giselle moved out, allowing Shannon to slip from the booth. She brushed past Quinn, who excused himself, moving backward again to allow her more room.

"Sit, bro," Doug said, as the others slid back in. "So how did you like your lesson?"

"It was…great," Quinn said. He watched as Shannon took the floor with Richard Long. A moment later, they were moving with astonishing grace, taking up the floor, entwined in seemingly impossible ways, and doing it so well that many of the people on the floor moved back, cheering.

"That's salsa?" Quinn said.

"Samba," Gordon told him.

He looked across the table at Mina. "And do you dance, too, Dr. Long?"

"Oh, yes." She laughed pleasantly. "But not like Shannon." She grinned. "Richard and I dance together at social functions, of course. But frankly, he prefers Shannon—and I prefer Sam. Sam Railey. He's my teacher. Two amateurs naturally dance better with two professionals." She leaned closer across the table. "I'm afraid Richard is showing off tonight. We have to join a few of his professional associates in a minute."

"Ah, I see," Quinn said.

She smiled again. It would have been a great smile—if it hadn't appeared that her entire face might shatter. "You *will* see. Wait until you get into it more. Hey, have you seen your brother dance?"

"Believe it or not, I haven't."

Mina Long looked at Doug. "I'm not exactly Jane or Shannon, but we can give your big brother a bit of show, if you like?"

"Absolutely," Doug agreed. "Sorry," he said apologetically to the others again.

"Hey, we might as well dance, too," Bobby told his bride.

"Might as well?" Giselle said with a groan. "See, Bobby, it *is* as if we've been married forever."

Bobby laughed. "Sorry. My beloved wife, would you do me the honor of dancing with me?"

"Good save," Doug muttered, and they all laughed.

"Pretty darned good, yes," Mina agreed, and she took his hand, heading for the dance floor.

"How did you enjoy your lesson?" Gordon Henson asked Quinn.

"You know, quite frankly, I went because Doug bought me the guest passes and he was so into it himself. But I was surprised. I *did* enjoy it," Quinn said, his eyes on his brother and Mina.

His brother, he noted, was good. Bobby and Giselle,

both beginners, weren't as smooth but obviously enjoyed themselves.

"Those two only came in to take some classes before their wedding. They keep coming back," Gordon told him. Then he leaned against the table. "So, what do you do, Mr. O'Casey?"

Quinn didn't have a chance to answer him. A man approached the table, calling out cheerfully, "Gordon! I'll be damned. They actually got you in here?"

The man was tall, dark, good-looking, casually dressed in an open-neck black silk shirt, tan trousers and a dark jacket. His eyes were dark, too, his face deeply bronzed.

"Yeah, they dragged me down," Gordon said, half rising to shake the newcomer's hand.

"Gabe, this is Quinn O'Casey, Doug's brother, a new student. Quinn, meet Gabriel Lopez, entrepreneur extraordinaire! Suede is his club."

"How do you do?" Quinn said, shaking hands with Lopez.

"Great, thanks. And welcome. You ever been in here before?"

Quinn shook his head. "Never. I'm a total novice."

"You'll like it. I get the best musicians, even during the week. We keep up the floor, and our kitchen turns out amazing food."

"So far, so good," Quinn said.

"You haven't been on the dance floor yet?"

Quinn grinned. "No. And you won't see me on it for a very long time, I assure you."

Lopez had slid into the booth next to him. "My friend, you'll be surprised, don't you think, Gordon?"

Gordon nodded. "Dancing gets in your blood. You hear the music, you have to move." He shrugged, staring at the floor. "Maybe you don't get to be a Shannon Mackay right away, but look at Doug. Six months, and he's quite impressive. Most importantly, he's having fun."

"Yeah, he really enjoys it. And hey, what a setup you two have here," Quinn said, including Lopez. "You learn upstairs, you dance downstairs. Couldn't have been planned better."

"True," Gordon agreed. "And it wasn't even planned."

"This wasn't a club before?"

"It's always been a restaurant—with an excuse for a dance floor," Lopez said. He shrugged. "When I came down, a year or so ago now, I saw the potential in the place. The other owners weren't making use of the gold mine they had."

"We have a great relationship," Gordon explained. "We have the same people come in to take care of the floors, and we both get a deal that way."

"They send me their students all the time," Lopez said.

"And we have a place to send our students, so that they have a good time and want to take more lessons," Gordon said, then pointed toward the ceiling. "The other tenant in the building is a designer and costumer. She's great, too. Katarina. When someone is looking for a dress—for a night out on the town, or for a competition—they just go right across the hall. You couldn't get a better setup."

Lopez nodded and stood. "Well, back to business. Welcome, Mr. O'Casey." He cocked his head, smiling. "Are you a cop, too? With your brother and his friends around now, we feel safe all the time."

Quinn shook his head. "No, sorry, I'm not a cop. I'm into boats. Charters, diving, fishing," Quinn said. Absolutely true, just not the whole story.

"Ah, I see. Well, then, you're a lucky man, too. There's nothing in the world like the sea."

"Nothing like it," Quinn agreed.

"Enjoy your night," Lopez said.

"See you, Gabe," Gordon said.

Lopez walked away, toward the kitchen.

"He's a great guy," Gordon said.

"Seems to be," Quinn agreed.

"Hey, you want to see your brother really look good?" Gordon asked. There was a note of pride in his voice.

Quinn looked back to the floor. The couples had all switched around. Doug was dancing with Shannon Mackay, and there were only a few people on the floor now. The music had changed, as had the dance. It was sweeping and incredibly graceful.

"Bolero," Gordon told him briefly.

The dance was beautiful. And Doug *was* good, made all the better by the elegance of his partner.

"I don't think I've ever seen anyone move so…"

"You mean your brother?" Gordon teased.

Quinn shook his head, grinning. "Ms. Mackay."

"She's the best," Gordon said.

"Hey, Quinn, can we slip back in?"

His head jerked up. Bobby and Giselle had returned. Panting. Quinn hadn't realized he had been almost transfixed, watching the dancers.

"You're not doing the bolero?" he asked the pair.

Bobby snorted. "Every time we try it together, we trip each other. I'm actually kind of hopeless."

"You're not!" Giselle protested.

Bobby made a face at Quinn. "You should see her in group class. She subtly—lovingly—tries to make sure she's in front of some other guy all the time."

"I do not. I would never." She shrugged sheepishly at Quinn. "We change partners every few minutes anyway. What good would it do?"

Doug came up to the table, drawing Shannon by the hand. "Well?" he asked Quinn. It was strange. Doug had been totally serious about his suspicions regarding Lara Trudeau's death, but right now, he was like the anxious little kid brother Quinn had known all his life, wanting his approval.

"You two blew me away," he said.

Doug was pleased. "Now it's your turn."

"You're out of your mind," Quinn said, laughing.

"No, no, you'll be fine," Bobby encouraged. "It's a merengue. You can't mess it up."

"Trust me, I can."

"Come on, Mr. O'Casey," Shannon said to him. "It's step, step, step. March, march, march. I know you can do it."

She was extending her elegant hand to him, those eyes of hers directly on his, challenging. It was as if she didn't believe for a second that he had really come for dance lessons.

He shrugged. "All right. If you're all absolutely determined to make me look like a fool…"

"You'll never look like a fool—not with Shannon," Gordon said.

"Doesn't look like they're just doing march, march, march to me," he told her ruefully as they stepped onto the dance floor.

"They are—they're just adding turns."

She was in his arms, showing him the hold. "Just follow my movements. Men always—always—lead in dance," she told him, "but since you haven't done this yet…left, right, left, right…feel the beat?"

He did feel the beat. And more. The searing touch of her eyes, probing his. The subtle movement of her body, erotic along with the music.

"March, march," he said.

"You're doing fine."

"Thanks. And how about you?"

Her brows hiked. "I'm impressed. You really do have a sense of rhythm. We can try some of those arm movements if you want. Just lift them…and I'll turn, then you turn. Merengue is a favorite, because no matter what, it's march, march."

"I'm not wiggling like those guys."

"Because you don't have your Cuban motion yet. You'll get it."

Cuban motion, huh? She certainly had it. The way her hips moved was unbelievable.

He lifted his arms as she had instructed. He was a little too jerky, but she could deal with it.

"Now you," she told him, and he repeated her motion. Step, step, march, march. Okay...

"Was something wrong earlier tonight?" he asked her.

"What?" She frowned.

"I saw you coming down the steps. You looked...uneasy," he said.

"You saw me? You were watching me?" Her tone was level, but he heard a note of outrage. "Are you following me or something, Mr. O'Casey?"

He laughed, keeping the sound light. "No, sorry, and I didn't mean to imply such a thing. I went over to the place across the street for a hamburger before coming here," he said. Okay, so the hamburger was a lie.

"Oh." She flushed. "Sorry. I just... It's an uncomfortable feeling, to think you're being watched."

"No, no...sorry. It's just that...you looked scared."

Maybe women weren't supposed to lead, but she pressed his arms up and moved herself into a turn, shielding her eyes from his for a moment. Facing him again, she said, "Gordon was already down here. I was locking up alone. One of the books fell or something right before I walked out. It startled me."

His hamburger story was a lie, and her falling book story was a lie, as well. Something much bigger had definitely frightened her.

"Unfortunately, Miami deserves its reputation for crime. You do need to be careful if you're locking up alone," he told her.

"The club is open every night. There's a doorman on Thursday through Sunday. We park in the lot in the back, but it's right across from a convenience store. There probably couldn't be a safer place. And there are only three of us in the building—the club, the studio and the design shop. I know everyone."

"But you can't know everyone who comes into the club," he said.

"No, of course not. But still I've always felt safe. Not only that, but I'm tougher than I look."

"Really?" He had to smile.

"Don't doubt it," she told him, and there was definitely a warning in her voice. "Trust me. I can be tough."

"A tough dancer," he mused.

"That's right. I love the studio—and I hate lies."

"Do you, now?" he demanded. He thought that he saw the slightest hint of a flush touch her cheeks before she drew away from him.

"The music has changed. You're not ready for a mambo," she told him.

And turning, she walked away, leaving him on the floor.

CHAPTER 6

Shannon made a point of getting to the studio by nine the following morning. She had agreed to coach Sam and Jane at ten, and at eleven, Gordon wanted to go over more of the Gator Gala figures and plans.

Reaching the studio wasn't difficult—she walked fifty percent of the time. Her house was just a few blocks away—thanks to Gordon.

Years ago, he had found the old place for sale. At that time, the block had been very run-down, and her house had come with horrible plumbing, no central air and the ugliest wallpaper known to man. The carpet could actually cause one to gag.

But the house had been the deal of the century. Small—there were only two bedrooms, and the yard was the size of a postage stamp—but she lived three blocks from the beach, and in the years since she had owned the house, the value had quadrupled. And it was hers. There weren't that many private homes in the area, and she knew she was very lucky to have the space. And she wouldn't have it, if it weren't for Gordon. He'd loaned her the down payment.

Sometimes, when she realized that she'd been in the studio for probably eighty hours in one week, she liked to tell him that he'd gotten his investment back from her in blood and sweat. He told her that of course he had, he wasn't a stupid man.

This morning, though, she was anxious to be in the studio—by the light of day. She was determined to convince herself that she was either overwrought or a little bit crazy—or both.

She climbed the stairs to the front door and waited, then inserted the key in the lock. Hesitantly she pushed the door open, then paused, listening.

Not a thing.

She entered the studio slowly, scoping out the polished wood floor and gazing around the room. Two sides were composed of floor-to-ceiling mirrors. Facing the street, giant picture windows looked out on the day. The "conference room" was to the front, while the reception area and offices lined part of the wall nearest the door. Toward the rear were four doors, the first opening to the instructors' room, the next opening to the men's room, the third to the ladies', and the fourth—with a counter section next to it—leading to the mini-kitchen. A small hallway between the bathrooms led to the rear door, where, just outside, there was a little patio shared by both upstairs establishments. To the left of the rear door was an expanse of wall with a door that led to the storage space. There was also access from the outside, since originally the storage space hadn't come with the studio. Now, all of them had keys to it. Katarina kept a few costume dummies and supplies there, the dance studio kept records and various other items at different times, and while the club actually had much greater space downstairs, they sometimes needed a little extra now and then. There had never been any problems over sharing.

Across the patio were stairs leading up to a newly revamped third floor. Previously, it had pretty much been wasted space, but Gabriel Lopez had gotten permission from the corporate owners of the property to finish it and create an apartment. He and Gordon joked about it all the time—the apartment was terrific, and Gordon was jealous. He wished he'd come up with the idea. He had a great condo farther up on the beach—he just hated driving.

Shannon knew the studio and the building like the back of her hand. And that was why she had been so unnerved the night before.

With everyone else gone and the stereo silent, she had been in her own office, glancing over the student records. They all did their best to keep their students coming. The students were their livelihood. She had an excellent staff— dedicated professionals who were determined to really teach dance and give the clients their money's worth for every minute on the floor—and everyone took responsibility for keeping the students happy. Still, when a student with a regular schedule suddenly became a no-show, something was wrong, and as manager, it was her responsibility to call that person, chat with them and make sure they hadn't been offended in some way.

After Lara's death, she thought she might have to make a number of personal calls and give people the best reassurance she could.

And so she had sat there with the files. Though the building was old, it had been well maintained. The soundproofing down at the club was excellent, and noise from the street never seemed to filter into the studio.

She could have dropped a pin and heard it fall as she worked.

And that was when she'd heard the noise.

A grating.

It had sounded as if it were coming from inside the studio itself.

It was a quick sound. Like nails scraping against a blackboard. Eerie, creepy, quick—gone. Gone so quickly she might have imagined it. Except that she hadn't.

She'd jumped to her feet, dropped the books, and burst out of her office and into the main room. Maybe Gordon had forgotten to lock the doors when he'd left. Or maybe he hadn't forgotten but had just decided he didn't need to bother, since she would be coming down right behind him.

The dance floor was empty. When she walked to the front door, she'd found it locked. She'd wanted to walk through the bathrooms, kitchens, teachers' room and Gordon's office, but she hadn't. For some reason, the silence, and the strangeness of the noise that broke it, had unnerved her too badly. Grabbing her purse and overshirt, she'd sprinted out the door, not at all certain why the noise had made her feel as if she was in imminent danger. She'd been so anxious to get out, she'd nearly forgotten to lock the door and then had forced herself to go back. Silly.

Now she was slightly embarrassed by her reaction.

Especially since it had been seen. Quinn O'Casey had somehow just happened to be having a hamburger across the street. Mr. Twenty Questions, himself.

So what?

The idea made her feel on edge, just as the man himself did. Far too good-looking. Not pretty, though his features were aligned exceptionally well. Just arresting. Two left feet, too tall, arms like steel. He wasn't an ordinary man. He both compelled her and irritated her beyond reason.

He hadn't just happened to be across the street, she was certain.

Either that, or she was paranoid. She had never been paranoid before, but ever since Lara had died, everything seemed to have taken on a new and evil connotation.

You're next.

Those words, spoken when obviously someone would be going up next, should have been entirely innocent.

But she didn't believe they were. Okay, that had to be paranoia. Lara had died. In her warped little mind, she was taking the words to somehow mean that she was supposed to die next.

She gave herself a firm mental shake and walked purposely around the studio as she should have done the night before. Kitchen, bathrooms. Teachers' room, conference room, Gordon's office, her own. She found the books she had dropped and picked them up. Finally she opened the back door and went out, going so far as to check the lock on the outside storage-room door. On a whim, she went back inside, got her keys and opened the door to the storage room.

Everything was in order. Rows of shelves held all kinds of records, a few small appliances, lightbulbs, boxes of material. She moved among the shelves. In the back of the room, she started, freezing for a moment, suddenly convinced she was not alone.

She had merely come face-to-face with one of Katarina's dressmaker's dummies.

"Stupid," she said aloud to herself. Then, turning purposefully, she walked back to the door. Odd, the dressmaker's dummy had given her another wave of unease. She felt that if she turned around, the mannequin was suddenly going to have gotten a face and found movement.

She spun around to look. The dummy stood just as it had, swathed in a spandex body suit with a sweeping skirt. No face. No movement. The mannequin gave that appearance because a huge feathered hat—of a sort that would never be worn on a dance floor—had been tossed on top of its neck.

It was just a dummy, and there didn't seem to be a thing in the room out of place. She exited, closing and locking the door behind her, and returned to the studio.

As she walked through the back hallway, she reminded herself that a person's own mind could be their greatest enemy, and she was letting what had happened to Lara take root in her far too deeply. She couldn't help it. No matter what her personal feelings had been toward Lara at times, she could at least say that she had known her well. Nothing had mattered to Lara more than dance. She might have a drink now and then. She might even take *a* Xanax to steady her nerves. But she would never, never, overindulge to the point of affecting a performance.

A sudden clicking sound caused her to jump, her hand flying to her throat. Then she realized that the front door had opened and closed. Jane was standing in the entry, staring at her with a serious crease furrowed into her brow.

"Hey. What's wrong?"

"Nothing."

"You look as if you've seen a ghost."

"No, no, sorry. I guess I was kind of deep in thought, and you startled me."

"Oh, sorry. I just…opened the door," Jane said.

"I know."

Jane offered her a small smile. "People will be opening and closing the door all day, you know."

"Yep."

Jane walked across the room to her, looking around the studio. "We're alone?"

"Yes. Sam hasn't come in yet."

"He'll be here any minute. He won't be late for a coaching session."

"I'm sure he won't be," Shannon said. She arched a brow to Jane questioningly. She might have jumped when Jane entered, but Jane was definitely acting strangely. "What's up?"

"I don't know. I'm still nervous, I guess."

"Why? Did something happen?"

"To me? No," Jane said.

"Because of Lara."

Jane nodded, looking directly and somberly at her. "You think there was something fishy about it. I know it. I mean, I know you think somebody killed her for some reason. Let's face it, lots of people might have wanted to. We'd both be suspects, you know. Me—she beat me in everything and loved to gloat about it. You—maybe you're entirely circumspect and so blasé that most people don't know, but anyone who goes back several years knows about Ben Trudeau and you."

"Jane, I'm not blasé. It was so long ago that it means nothing."

"You're so professional, to be able to work with Ben."

"I'm not sure I'm all that professional. I simply have no real memory of being attracted to Ben romantically in any way whatsoever. We have different goals and beliefs in life, and…there's just nothing there. Nothing at all. He's a good teacher and an excellent dancer. He should be a competitor, and he should have a great partner. He's that good."

"And she blew him off," Jane said, whispering for some reason. "That's what I mean, Shannon. Anyone might have wanted to kill her. Even Gordon, say."

"Gordon was proud of her. She was a big part of this studio's reputation, since this is where she started and did a lot of coaching."

"And as good as he was to her, she was rude to him."

"People don't usually commit murder simply because someone was rude, Jane," Shannon said. She was actually feeling a little bit ridiculous herself, now that it was daylight and she wasn't alone.

"You say that, but you don't mean it," Jane said.

"I don't know what I feel, exactly," Shannon said. "We've just got to go on and get past this."

"There was so much going on with her," Jane murmured.

"Like what?"

"Well, for one thing, she loved to flaunt the fact that she didn't actually work for the studio, so she wasn't bound to any of that nonfraternization stuff." Jane's voice lowered even more. "You know what I think? I think she just liked to hurt people. Remember how excited I was, pleased with myself, when Doug O'Casey started to learn so much so quickly? Well, Lara knew it. The first coaching session that I arranged for him with her, she seemed to catch on that he was kind of a prize to me, someone very special. She hardly included me in the session at all. And then, later that night, she was dancing with him down at Suede."

"Jane, we all dance with people down at Suede."

"I know, I know, but this was different. It was as if she had her claws in him or something. She looked at me and smiled, and it was like she was gloating, telling me she'd taken over my student."

"Jane, he's still your student."

"Yes, he's my student. But I'd swear she had something going on with him. And not just him. All my students, I think."

"Even old Mr. Clinton?" Shannon said, trying to interject a light note into the conversation.

Jane wasn't amused. "That should be funny—except that Clinton is rich. She was always an angel to him. She knew how to hedge her bets. If she wanted to enter something, she wanted to feel that she had lots of people with money waiting in the wings, in case any of her sponsors fell through."

"Jane, come on, she wasn't having any kind of a thing with Mr. Clinton."

"Maybe not, but I'm willing to bet she would have, if she felt it would further her career."

"She had a great career. Jane, face it, she was good. No, beyond good."

"But she was a witch!"

"She liked to use people, and she liked to jerk their chains. But she's gone now."

Jane nodded, then looked at her again. "I think you should be careful."

"Me? Why?"

"Because too many people know you're convinced that Lara would have never done herself in."

"No one said it was suicide. Just an accidental overdose that caused her heart to stop."

"You don't think it was an accident."

"Neither do you, so it seems."

"But…" Jane paused, her beautiful dark hair sweeping around her delicate, gamine's face as she assured herself once again that they were alone. "People know what you think and feel. You were honest with the police. You've said a few things around her. I think you need to be careful."

You're next.

Shannon forced a smile, refusing to psych herself into a worse state of paranoia. "No matter what anyone thought, Jane, Lara's death was ruled accidental. She's being buried tomorrow. It's over. It's hard, and of course we're not going to forget it right away, but we're going to move on. We have our own lives to live. Okay?"

Jane nodded solemnly, reaching for the hand Shannon offered her, squeezing it.

Then they both jumped a mile when the door opened again.

"What the heck is up with you two?" Sam Railey demanded as he walked in. He frowned at them, then looked over his shoulder.

"What? I have a huge zit on my forehead? Spinach in my teeth?"

Shannon and Jane laughed, looking at each other a bit guiltily.

"Nope, you look great, Sam," Shannon said. "Hey, both of you, get your shoes on. Let's get going. Your CD's over by the stereo, right? When you're ready, go through the whole routine, then we'll break it down. Come on, come on, let's move, before the day gets really busy."

"Yes, ma'am," Sam said. Shaking his head, he started for the teachers' room to get his shoes. "What a tyrant," he muttered, but the words were quite intentionally audible. "Not, gee, Sam, take your time, we'll throw some coffee on and talk a minute or two. Not, good morning, Sam, how are you doing, everything all right? I'll just ask myself, then. Sam, how are you? Not too bad, but somehow, I am getting one mother of a blister on my left heel."

"Shoes, Sam. Chop, chop," Shannon told him.

Giggling, Jane hurried after him to get her own shoes.

Shannon looked around. The day outside was bright and beautiful. Light was pouring in. Sam and Jane were chattering away as they slipped into their smooth shoes.

Everything seemed good, clean, bathed in sun, normal.

It remained so until Gordon came in, informing her that they needed to break any appointments for that evening and cancel their group classes.

Lara Trudeau was being buried Saturday, and that night there was going to be a viewing at the funeral home, and they all had to be there.

"I have to admit," Sam whispered to Shannon, "she looks beautiful. I mean, you know, most of the time when you come to a viewing with an open coffin, the person looks dead. Bad. Stiff. Everyone tries to say that someone looks beautiful, but they don't. But Lara, for real, looks beautiful. Like she's sleeping, huh? She looks young, too. This is so tragic."

Tragic.

Beyond a doubt.

Down on the kneeling pad in front of the coffin, Shannon felt a million emotions rush through her. No, Lara had not been particularly nice. But she had been talented and, more, so full of life that she had exuded energy at every turn. She had entranced her own private world and given dozens who had come after her a height of professionalism and beauty for which to strive.

But not nice.

Sam sighed deeply. "Not that she would ever have been eligible for a community-spirit award."

"Sam!" Shannon nudged him. "You're supposed to sit here and pray for the deceased."

"Think she needs our prayers?" he asked. "Okay, she wasn't Mother Teresa, but she wasn't a murderess or anything. She's probably dancing in the clouds right now. Or maybe...if there is a purgatory, she's there, trying to teach steps to a bunch of dunderheads."

"Sam," Shannon groaned.

"Oh, right, and you're praying that she's sitting on the right hand of God?" he whispered back.

Shannon sighed and gave up. She hadn't been praying. Or maybe she had. It was sad, it was tragic, Lara was gone. And she hoped that her beliefs were right, that there was an afterlife, and that, indeed, Lara was dancing in the clouds. But what she had really discovered was that more and more, with her whole heart, she just didn't believe the ruling of accidental death. Lara had loved life. She had loved the simple act of waking up and living, moving, using the tool of her body to create beautiful, bewitching motion. She simply couldn't have done herself in—not even accidentally.

She rose, Sam taking her elbow to rise with her.

There was a long line behind them. The funeral home

was filled to capacity and beyond. People who had known her, professionals, amateurs and the just plain curious, had come to pay their respects.

She walked over to where Gordon was standing, talking quietly with Gunter Heinrich, one of the champions from Germany. Gunter greeted her with a sad smile and a kiss on the cheek.

"Gunter, you made it here. I'm amazed to see you. This was all arranged so quickly."

Very tall, blond, an elegant man with strong facial features, Gunter shrugged. "I was in the States—Helga and I stayed after the competition on the beach. We're going on—we'd planned on doing the competition in Asheville next week. I was just speaking with Gordon about using the dance studio for some practice sessions next week," Gunter continued. "Are you available for some coaching?"

They were at a wake, she thought, and yet Gunter was scheduling. Maybe she hadn't been to enough wakes. She could hear soft conversation all around her. Maybe that was part of it. Life went on.

"I think so," she murmured.

Mr. Clinton was at the coffin then. Looking grave, he went to his knees, said a little prayer and crossed himself. Jane came up to him as he rose again, slipping an arm around his shoulders. The Longs were there, quietly standing at the back of the room, engaged in conversation with the young couple who had come to learn to dance for their wedding. Rhianna Markham, who had taught the couple, stood with them.

Ben was on the other side of the coffin, standing alone, looking somber, and almost as if he were in another world.

Mary and Judd Bentley, owners of a franchise studio down in South Dade, came up to the coffin and bent down together. They were good people, and good friends. Mary was actually crying—one of the few in attendance doing so.

"You're next."

"What?"

Shannon's attention was drawn sharply back to Gunter.

His brow arched. She hadn't realized how sharply she had spoken, or how loudly. She flushed. "Sorry. I'm afraid I was distracted."

"I was telling Gordon, he has to find the right words to get you out there. You're the best coach we've ever had—and one of the best dancers I've ever seen. If you went back out there, you could be next."

"Oh, I…thanks," she murmured. "That's very sweet. Excuse me, will you?"

She suddenly knew she had to get out of the building, if only for a moment. She turned and started down the center aisle between the rows of chairs. The smell of the multitude of flowers lining the room, set against every available wall, in stands and over the casket itself, was overwhelming. She closed her eyes and nearly crashed into Ella Rodriguez and Justin Garcia as they took their turn heading to kneel down before Lara.

In the antechamber, she moved through a milling crowd. More dancers. She saw one of last year's local salsa champions, a beautiful, petite girl with a body to kill for. She was in black—a tight black dress that hugged her every curve. She was in deep conversation with one of the officers of the national dance association.

Katarina was in the antechamber, looking sedate in a navy suit and apparently saddened by the occasion. But before Shannon could even approach her, another woman stepped in front of her, loudly asking if she could come in for a fitting the following day. When Katarina informed her that she would be attending Lara's funeral, the woman insisted on seeing her Monday.

Shannon lifted a hand to Katarina, then rushed out the front door.

The funeral home Gordon had chosen was almost dead in the center of Miami proper. He'd paid a great deal to buy a plot for Lara in one of the area's oldest cemeteries, Wood-lawn, a beautiful place made more beautiful by the heavy respect that the Latin community paid to their dead.

The street in front of her was busy with traffic racing by. A horn blared. A driver shouted out his window at someone who didn't move fast enough in front of him. There was a convenience store across the street, and a group of teens sat in front of it on the hood of a restored Chevy, chatting, laughing.

The air wasn't exactly fresh and inviting—a burst of exhaust fumes came her way. But she felt better away from the overwhelming scent of the flowers. And away from the strange state of hypocrisy that existed inside.

People exited as she stood there, lifting their hands in solemn salute to her as they headed for the parking lot. Some she knew well, some she had at least seen before, and in some cases, she didn't have any idea who they were. She waved back anyway.

Then, weaving through a group that was leaving, she saw two men on their way in. The brothers O'Casey.

Doug came straight to her, giving her a hug, kissing her cheek. He looked truly distraught. His usually neatly brushed wheat hair was rumpled in front, as if he'd been running his fingers through it. His features were strained.

"This is it, huh?" he said, his voice husky. "This makes it real."

She nodded, touching his cheek, and felt suddenly glad, because here was someone who had really cared about Lara Trudeau, if only as her student and a friend. Except, according to Jane, he might have cared about her as much more.

"It *is* real, Doug, I'm afraid. Very real."

"How does she…look?" he asked.

"This sounds trite, of course, but it's true. She's beautiful. As if she's sleeping," Shannon told him.

He lowered his head. "I'm going in."

He turned and walked toward the door. Quinn remained. Tall, dark, striking in his suit. Watching her. In the shadows of the street, his eyes appeared almost black. Like dual abysses of some deep, dark knowledge that somehow accused her, or saw more than they should.

She crossed her arms over her chest, returning his stare. "It's interesting to see you. You didn't know Lara, did you? Had you ever seen her dance?"

"I came with my brother," he said.

"Ah, I see."

"Do you?" He looked toward the door. "It's interesting to see lots of the people who come to a wake, isn't it? I mean, seriously, how many people are here because they care—and how many are here just to see her and be seen themselves?"

"People often come to see someone well-known," Shannon said. "Gordon didn't specify anywhere that this was to be private. He wanted anyone who wished to see Lara and pay their respects to her talent to feel free to come."

"Noble," Quinn murmured. She couldn't tell if it was in mockery or not.

"Are you going back in?" he asked.

She stared at him and shook her head. "No, I don't think so. I came early with Gordon and Ben to see that everything was set up properly."

"Of course. And then there's the strain of the funeral tomorrow." Again she couldn't pinpoint the tenor of his voice. Was he mocking? Did he somehow see that so much of this was a sham, a performance for Lara or, perhaps, for all of them?

"Do you need a ride home?"

She hesitated. Actually, she did. She had come with Ben, and he and Gordon would be staying to the bitter end.

"Don't worry—I won't fraternize," he told her, definite amusement in his eyes then. "Just give me a minute to go in and pay my own respects."

"It's not necessary."

"I don't mind."

She lifted her head slightly. "Doug is already in there. And you didn't know Lara. So…just what is your intention in going in?"

His lips curled slightly. "Well, to see, of course. And maybe to be seen, as well. Wait for me. I'll be right with you."

He turned and headed for the entrance. She watched him go, wishing that, in the midst of all that was going on— and despite the definite mistrust she felt—she weren't admiring the way his shoulders carried the sleek lines of his suit, or noting again the subdued but rich, evocative scent of aftershave that seemed to linger when he had gone.

Lara was dead and would soon be buried.

She had to admit, she was afraid herself. Afraid of something vague that she knew but couldn't touch.

And Quinn O'Casey?

The man was after something. She just wasn't sure what.

CHAPTER 7

Doug was by the coffin and Quinn decided, for the moment, to let him be. He strode up the aisle and waited off to the side.

People were filling the chairs and lining the walls. Bits and pieces of conversation came to him. One group talked about the weather, and someone chimed in that it was a stroke of genius for Moonlight Sonata to plan the Gator Gala for February, the dead of winter, when everyone would want to be in Florida.

Two others were talking technique, comparing notes on footwork. He was pretty sure that most of the people here were in the world of dance.

Doug remained on his knees before the coffin.

Gordon Henson saw Quinn and lifted a hand in acknowledgment. Jane walked over to Doug, kneeling down beside him.

Ben Trudeau was standing at the coffin, arms crossed over his chest as if he were a sentinel, guarding the remains.

Quinn moved closer, waiting his turn, listening. At last Doug rose, arm in arm with Jane, and the two moved away.

Quinn walked up to the coffin. The woman inside had been beautiful, of course. Now her hair was styled, makeup had been applied. She had been dressed for burial in a sky-blue dance gown with elaborate beadwork on the bodice. Her hands were folded. She held a flower. She really did look as if she were a modern day Sleeping Beauty, awaiting the kiss that would awaken her. Except that it wouldn't come. The telltale autopsy scar was, of course, not visible, and so Lara Trudeau lay like a whirl of grace and motion that had been paused in an eternity of time.

He'd seen the tape of that day. Seen her fly and touch the clouds. Seen her die.

He'd gone to Sunday school every week when he'd been growing up. He still attended church with Doug and his mom now and then. He automatically signed a cross over his chest, bowed his head…

And listened.

Someone was standing with Ben Trudeau by the huge flower urn at the head of the coffin. He recognized the voices—it was that of Gabriel Lopez, the sleek owner of Suede.

"Are you all right, Ben?" Lopez sounded like a true friend, concerned.

"Of course I'm all right. We'd been divorced a long time."

"Still, I didn't know her anywhere near as well, but…she made an impression," Gabriel said.

There was a hesitation. "I guess I never did stop loving her, in a way. Like you love a selfish child. I hated her, too, though, sometimes."

"You might want to be careful what you say," Lopez warned Ben, his voice quiet.

"Why?" Ben demanded.

"Well, the circumstances were pretty strange."

"Oh, jeez, that again. The cops questioned everyone.

They did an autopsy. They studied the tape. The circumstances were strange because Lara was such an idiot for killing herself that way. Accidentally. Idiotically." He sounded angry. "I wish everyone would just stop with this. God knows—we could all point fingers at one another."

"I don't know…is it really over? I heard that Shannon Mackay isn't convinced."

"Shannon doesn't want to face reality. And hey, if someone wanted to start pointing fingers, they could point right at her," Ben said irritably.

"Is everything all right?"

A third voice had joined in. A woman's. Memory clicked. It was Mina Long. *Dr.* Long, the pediatrician.

"Well," Lopez murmured, a trace of humor in his voice, "this *is* a wake."

"Of course, of course. You know, Ben, I meant… You *do* believe Richard did everything he could, don't you? He may be a plastic surgeon, but trust me, he knows CPR and emergency measures."

"Mina, please, of course we know Richard did everything he could," Ben said. "It's just hard to accept that she's really gone. Excuse me, will you? An old partner of mine just walked in. I think I'll say hi."

Ben moved away. "He looks upset," Mina said to Gabriel, concerned.

"Sure he's upset. But I think he sees a chance to find himself a new partner, rather than an old one. Ben hasn't danced professionally in a while now, and he's anxious to get back to it." There was a long sigh. "I've got to get going. I didn't know Lara that well, but the club and the studio have a great relationship, so I wanted to be here. Still, I couldn't close the club, and it's a Friday night. Give Richard my best. How is he holding up, by the way? I know he considered Lara a big part of his success as a dancer."

"Well, of course, his sessions with Lara were important, but I believe Richard knows that Shannon is the one who really taught him. He did admire Lara, though. And being the first one to reach her when it happened… He's all right, though. Good night, Gabriel. We'll be seeing you."

"I count on it," Gabriel assured her, and left.

A woman came up to Mina. "Hello, dear, how are you?"

"Gracie, nice to see you. Sorry for the circumstances, though. And congratulations. I understand that Lara was posthumously awarded the trophy for the night she died, but that you came in second."

"It was a rather hollow victory," the newcomer said. "I wonder why on earth Gordon and Ben chose that dress. She has so many others that would have been…more appropriate. I mean, it was perfect on the dance floor, but in a coffin…it's rather garish, don't you think?"

"I would have chosen that pink gown she wore for her last Viennese waltz," Mina said. "And the delicate little diamonds she wore with it." Mina sighed. "I helped her into it the last time she wore it."

"Really?" the woman named Gracie said, then changed the subject. "We'll be seeing you at the Gator Gala?"

"Of course."

"I've got to find Darrin. You and Richard take care, now."

Mina Long was left standing alone but not for long. She saw Doug standing with Bobby and Giselle, not far away. "Doug, Bobby, Giselle, sweetie. How are you doing?" she called as she walked off.

Quinn didn't hear their replies, distracted when someone knelt next to him. He knew before turning that it was Shannon. He recognized the scent of her cologne.

"Seriously religious, are you?" she asked softly.

"I have been known to go to mass," he replied.

She was staring at the coffin, her expression tense.

"What's wrong?" he asked.

"Well, she *is* dead," Shannon pointed out irritably.

"Yes, but you look a lot more than just sad."

She shook her head. "She shouldn't be dead, that's all. She was only in her thirties. She was stunning. She didn't smoke. She drank power shakes all the time…. She just should not be dead, that's all," Shannon said. "Has everyone seen you yet? Have you seen everyone? I need to get home, but I can call a cab."

"No, I'd be delighted to drive you home. As long as you won't get fired for it or anything."

She cast him a glare. "You know, we're not that ridiculous. It's not a good thing for teachers and students to get too close. It can cause professional difficulties."

"Then again, you have to try to get your students to feel a sense of closeness, right? Dancing is a social activity. The longer you do it, the closer you get."

She rose, saying, "We're hogging the prayer bench."

Then she was gone.

Quinn rose more slowly and found Bobby standing to his side. He offered Quinn an awkward smile. "She was a beautiful woman, huh?"

"You worked with her?"

"Only a few times. Giselle and I wanted a picture-perfect wedding. And we had fun. Doug's the one who got so involved in the dancing." Bobby shrugged. Quinn realized that Bobby didn't know that Doug had not just gotten into dancing, but that he had gotten into Lara Trudeau, as well. Bobby frowned, though, and lowered his voice. "He didn't drag you down here just to get you into dancing, though, did he?"

Quinn shook his head. "But they don't know that at the studio."

"Hey, I wouldn't say anything." He shrugged again. "But I don't know what you're going to find. I was there when it happened. She just dropped."

"I know. I saw the tape today."

"Well, if I can help, I'm there."

"I know. Thanks."

By the time Quinn walked away down the aisle, Shannon Mackay was almost out the front door. He stepped up behind her as she walked out to the street, ready to hail a taxi.

"Sorry. I'm here."

"Look, it's okay. The beach isn't on the way to the Keys."

"I brought a boat up to Coconut Grove. You're only a five-minute detour."

"You can get to the Grove by driving straight south."

"But I like to drive on the causeway out to the beach. Especially at night. All the lights are on. The shadows hide all the city's dirty little secrets. Night on the water is the most beautiful time. Come on. Let me drive you home. It's really no big deal."

"All right, thank you."

She walked along beside him, then stopped suddenly. "How did you know I live on the beach?"

"I didn't. I assumed. I guess because of the studio."

"You assumed?"

"My God, you're suspicious. I figured if you lived somewhere else, you'd tell me so. Just so I could drive you to the right place."

He must have sounded exasperated, because she actually smiled. "I live on the beach. Just a few blocks from the studio."

The night was balmy. As they walked along, however, she shivered slightly.

"Cold? Would you like my jacket?"

"No, thank you. I'm fine."

She spun around suddenly. A couple who had attended the wake was walking behind them. Quinn glanced at them, then at Shannon, arching his brow. "You seem a little jumpy."

"Not at all."

"Okay. If you say so. That's my car."

He hit the clicker, and his Navigator beeped. Stepping ahead, he opened her door. She gave him a brief thanks and climbed in. She was quiet as they left the parking lot, then headed north and east, toward the expressway entrance.

"You really are nervous. You going to feel safe once you get home?" he asked.

"I live in a nice, safe area."

He sniffed. "Sure. I heard they found a dead prostitute near you, not long ago."

She frowned. "Yes, they did, but that was unusual. Most of the people who live and work around there all know one another. She must have gotten in with the wrong element."

"Easy to do on the beach. Face it, South Beach is where people go for action. Sure, for some that means dancing and restaurants, but some people go for the sheer excitement. Some people love alcohol and drugs—like ecstasy. And some of the people there aren't exactly honest. There are big bucks to be made in the drug trade. You know that."

"Of course. But dancers tend to be health freaks."

"Some of your students might not be so dedicated, right?"

"Of course. But Gabriel runs a clean establishment. You can trust me—the cops have checked him out."

"I can imagine. So why are you so jumpy?"

"I'm not jumpy!"

"Hey, you know, you can ask me in for coffee when I drop you off. I can check out the closets and under the beds before I leave."

She stared at him, her emerald eyes bright in the neon glow of the local businesses. "*That* would be fraternizing."

"No, that would be professional courtesy. You teach me to dance, I check out the hidey-holes in your house."

"Gordon doesn't allow any free lessons."

"Not after the customers are sucked in, huh?"

"Sucked in? I resent that. We can give your brother a refund—I told you that."

"But I'm sucked in already," he said.

She turned away from him, looking out the window. "You know, you're right. I forget sometimes how beautiful it is," she said.

Across the water, the skyscrapers of downtown Miami were decked out in their night lights—blues, greens, shades in between. Moonlight glowed down on the water, as well. The breeze was light, the waves small. They lapped gently in a captivating pool of deep color beneath the kaleidoscope of glowing pastels.

"Yeah," he murmured. "The beauty was one of the first things I noticed when I got here."

"You've just moved here?"

"I was born here. I just moved back."

"Where were you before?" she asked. There was a suspicious note in her voice again. It made him smile.

"Northern Virginia. Which is beautiful, too. Virginia has the sea and the mountains and everything between. But this is home. I missed it."

"Did you run a charter service in Virginia, too?"

"What?" He frowned. "Oh, yeah. Boats. I love boats. I can't stay away from a boat very long, or the water. Do you like the water?"

"Sure."

"Do you fish? Dive?"

"I fished when I was kid. And I did some diving in the middle of the state when I was a teenager. I did a few of those dives where you go in with the manatees."

"You didn't like it?"

"I loved it."

"But you don't dive anymore?"

She shrugged. "I don't think I do anything anymore. I've gotten too involved with work."

"But you don't compete."

"I do a lot of coaching. I'm sure I told you—I'm a good teacher." She smiled and added ruefully, "Really good. Come to think of it, I wasn't joking. I really don't have a life other than the studio." She turned back to the window suddenly, as if she had said far more than she intended. She swung back to him. "What an idea, though. A boat would be great."

"You want to go out with me on my boat?"

"Yes. No, not exactly. I wanted to do something special for the group that's registered for the Gator Gala. Let me see, with the teachers and students from the local studios, we'd be talking about a group of about fifty. Can you get a nice boat for an evening out? It doesn't have to be a gourmet meal with a sit-down dinner or anything. In fact, I'd prefer something more casual. A buffet, plastic plates, room for a small dance band, of course. Can you set up something like that?"

"Sure," he said quickly.

"I'll get you some figures…you know, what I can afford to spend. You can arrange it, right? I mean, you really do charters?"

"I can arrange it."

He looked straight ahead as he pulled off on Alton. "Okay, where am I going?"

She directed him. When they pulled up in front of the house she indicated, she frowned.

"What's wrong?"

"I could swear I left the flood light on."

Her porch was dark. He drummed his fingers on the wheel. "I told you, I can look under the beds."

She glanced at him and exited the car quickly on her own, digging into her purse for her keys as she strode up the tiled path and across the porch and the door. The little house was charming, with a bit of the old Spanish style nicely incorporated with some cleaner Deco features.

He followed her. "Really, if something might be wrong, maybe I should look around."

"Come on in," she said.

He did, curious not just about her and what she knew, but about her home, as well. He wondered if he would see her old trophies and pictures of herself dancing, with or without a partner.

Not in the living room, though there was a dance scene above an old coral rock fireplace against the far wall. It was a painting, and the dancers were ballerinas in traditional tutus, floating in a sea of soft blue and pink. It was a beautiful painting, complemented by the warmth of the room. Heavy wood furniture was offset by the lighter colors of the carpeting, draperies and inviting throws tossed over the sofa and love seat, both facing not a television but the fireplace. The floor was light tile, except for the hooked rug before the hearth.

"I can see there's no one hanging around in the living room," she said dryly.

"I figured you'd try to deck me if I went straight into your bedrooms," he told her.

Eyes of green ice swept over him. "You just sized up this place with the same swift once-over you gave me at the studio."

"I gave you a swift once-over?" he queried, feeling a smile as he stepped in farther. "The kitchen?" he asked, striding through the living room.

"The kitchen and dining room are on this side of the hall, behind the living room. The bedrooms and family room are on the other."

He nodded, flicking on the light as he entered the kitchen. Copper pots hung from a rafter above the island workstation in the center. A counter separated the kitchen from the dining room, which was furnished with an antique table, six chairs and a matching hutch.

"Very nice," he commented.

"Glad you approve."

He turned on lights as he went, crossing from the dining room to the family room, where she had an overstuffed sofa, ottoman, recliners, and a television and stereo system. And a closet. He quirked a brow to her before opening the door. There was nothing but an assortment of gowns in plastic bags, tennis rackets and two pool cues.

"I thought you had no life?"

"Not now," she informed him. "I simply don't like to throw things away."

"Are you good?"

"At what?"

"Either pool or tennis."

"No, I suck at both. But I do enjoy them. Or I did. Once."

"All work and no play, you know."

"I never tried to convince you that I wasn't dull."

He brushed past her, heading down the hall to check out the bedrooms. The house was quiet, and the contact between them seemed to scream. He caught her gaze for a moment and wondered if she'd heard it, too.

"Bedroom," he murmured.

"What?" Her eyes widened.

"Bedrooms. I'll check out the bedrooms."

"Yes. Right."

She followed him as he came to the first door. Light flooded the space. It was perhaps twelve feet by fourteen. Not a stick of furniture. The walls were mirrored; the floor was shiny wood. This, he thought, was her own private little studio. Her haven, maybe. He stood, staring, thoughtful.

"There's a closet," she said.

He walked across the room and threw open the closet door. Clothing and tons of shoes. "What did you do? Rob Imelda Marcos?" he asked.

"They're all old dance shoes. I'm hard on them."

"Why do you keep them?"

"Well, some I mean to get fixed. They'd be good again with new soles and heels."

"I see. Interesting."

"Why? I'm a dance teacher. It's a practice floor."

"And you have no other life. But you're three blocks from the studio?"

"I'm three blocks from the ocean, and I wish I had a pool," she said.

"Ah," he murmured. "Well, last room."

He passed by her again, wondering why there could be something almost like open hostility between them at times, then brief encounters where he felt a surge of pure electricity just being near her. Scent, he thought. Or the whisper of gold spun silk against his flesh when his chin and cheek brushed against her hair.

"Bedroom. A real one. With a bed. And look, will you? Great bed—love the canopy. Rug looks as soft as can be…and there, right on the dresser, the computer."

"Everyone has a computer."

"Not in their bedroom."

"I'll bet lots of people keep their computers in their bedrooms."

"Not when they have a whole house."

"Oh, and where do you keep your computer?"

"I'm living on a boat right now. It's in the dining area, by the galley."

"Where did you keep it when you weren't living on a boat?" she demanded. "Or did you live on a boat in Virginia?"

"No, I had an apartment."

"And where was your computer?"

"*Not* in the bedroom. Okay, suppose you did have a life. Suppose you had someone over, and he was the best thing in the world, the greatest lover since Casanova. And there you are, in heaven beneath the canopy, but you've forgotten and left the damned thing on, and right in the throes of a magical moment you hear not how beautiful you are, you hear 'You've got mail.'"

She stared at him with surprise and indignation, but her lips were twitching as well.

"It could happen," he persisted. "Ah, I see. The greatest lover since Casanova hasn't cruised by yet."

"Maybe he has," she informed him.

"You see the problem, then."

"No. I never forget to turn anything off," she said, then spun and started across the hall. "Don't forget the bathrooms. There are two of them, one in there, one on the other side of the studio."

"Sure. As soon as I've looked under the bed."

There was nothing under the bed. Not even dust.

They were small bathrooms; it was a small house. He dutifully checked behind the shower curtains in each. He should have felt as if he was being intrusive. He didn't. He was fascinated, instead, by this strange insight into her intimate life.

"Hey!"

He had opened a medicine cabinet. She was standing behind him, a steaming cup of coffee in her hand.

A cardboard to-go cup.

"Coffee already?" he said. "That was quick."

"It's a state-of-the-art machine. Thanks for making sure the place was secure. However, I don't think there's an intruder hiding in my medicine chest."

"If you're going to search a place, you might as well make sure it's free of aliens, gremlins—you know."

She lowered her head, smiling. "Right. Well, anyway, thanks. I do feel more secure now."

"No problem." He accepted the cup of coffee, studying it. "I guess I'm leaving."

"You're welcome to sugar and milk first."

"Thanks, I like it black."

"Actually, you're welcome to have a seat. I wouldn't want you to spill it on your lap or anything. Get burned, sue the studio, anything like that."

He leaned against the door for a moment, watching her. Those clear bright eyes were on him. She wasn't touching him in any way, but the electricity seemed to sear right through empty space. There was nothing overtly sexual about her; it was all beneath the surface. But in that subtle manner, she was certainly the most sensual creature he'd ever met. He'd done some teasing before. Now just a glance at the bare flesh of her upper arm created mental visions of other parts of her anatomy, equally bare. Libido was kicking in with a sudden vengeance, as it hadn't since before he'd left his teens.

He swallowed his coffee quickly, heedless of whether he burned his mouth or not. He handed the cup back, his eyes locked with hers.

"I'd better go." The depth of his voice was startling to himself, along with its husky tenor. "If I stayed, it would be fraternizing," he said quickly. "Good night."

"Good night, and thank you," she said.

On the porch, he gave himself a serious mental shake and turned back to her. "Do you think…are you nervous because you don't believe Lara Trudeau's death was accidental?"

"I don't know what you're talking about," she said, but her eyes narrowed, and it was almost as if a mask had slipped over her face.

"You think Lara Trudeau was murdered. If you know

something, if you are afraid of something, you've really got to say it, tell the police."

"I talked to the police the day she died," she said flatly. "I never, ever, told anyone I thought Lara had been murdered."

A lie.

Maybe she hadn't said it in so many words, but still...a lie.

"Really? Maybe you should be careful. A lot of people seem convinced you're the main one suggesting Lara didn't pop those pills herself. And if Lara *didn't* just pop those pills—"

"Lara died because she abused a prescription and drank on top of it, Mr. O'Casey. That's what the medical examiner said. And that's all there is to it."

"I'm not the one you need to convince," he said softly. "Make sure you lock your door."

"I always lock my door."

"Good."

He turned and walked to his car, aware that she was still on the porch, watching him.

He turned back. "Now would be a good time to lock it."

She disappeared inside. He could hear the force of it slamming from where he stood on the street.

Smiling, he slid into the driver's seat and twisted his key in the ignition.

Shannon leaned against the door after he had gone. The night had been long. She was so tired it hurt.

She was glad she'd had him in, glad she wouldn't be adding to her ridiculous new paranoia by wondering if someone was hiding in her closet.

And yet...

Damn, he was attractive. She shouldn't find a student so compelling. Maybe she should take a step back. Turn him over to Jane. This was absurd.

Maybe not so absurd. She was twenty-eight. She joked about the fact that she had no life, but…

It was true. She had no life. She saw the same men day after day. Anyone new was a student, and seldom, if ever, had such a student walked into her life.

Most people would think her life was exciting. She danced all day and was guaranteed entry to one of the hottest spots in the city at night. Gabriel was attractive. He'd even asked her out. But Gabriel was a player. He was fun to dance with, and a great man to have as a friend. She would never want anything more with him, though. So this wasn't just a sexual thing, because she did know attractive men.

Just not like this one.

She would never trust a man like Gabriel—he needed too much excitement and variety in his life. And Ben…she had fallen out of love with Ben long ago. He was like a childhood mistake. Sam and Justin were like younger brothers. Sometimes she was mad at them, and sometimes she was proud of them.

It wasn't that no one ever touched her life, or that there weren't possibilities. Just none that had touched her, not in a very long time.

And this man…

Was a liar. He wasn't taking dance lessons just for the hell of it. And he wasn't interested in her just for the hell of it either.

She pushed away from the door. A man like Gabriel was obvious. This guy was more devious.

She suddenly heard something from outside. Like a branch breaking.

She froze against the door, listening. Nothing…no, something. Like footsteps, falling fast and soft, heading from somewhere right by the house out to the street.

And then…

Nothing. She stood there for what felt like forever. She didn't breathe. She didn't move.

And still…

Nothing.

At last she moved away from the door and stared at it. Her throat felt constricted. She tried to reason with herself. If she *had* heard footsteps, they were moving away from the house. And maybe she hadn't really heard steps. There had been a cat out there; it had gotten spooked, and it had run off at high speed. She'd lived in this house for years now. She was in a good neighborhood.

Right. So good she didn't even have an alarm system.

She backed away from her door, staring at it. If she opened it, she was probably an idiot. If she didn't open it just to make sure no one was hanging around the place, she would never get any sleep.

She hesitated for a long time, seconds ticking by, as she stared at the door.

Then she reached for the bolt, slid it, hesitated again and threw the door open.

CHAPTER 8

Back at the marina, Quinn noted the large group of cops still gathered at the patio tables outside Nick's. His brother was among them. He'd thought he was dead tired, ready to call it quits, but on second thought, he headed for the tables.

Dixon wasn't there that night, but Bobby, Giselle and Doug were sitting with Jake Dilessio. Jake greeted him with a wave, drawing out a chair as Quinn approached. At another table, Quinn saw some of the guys he knew who were with narcotics. Waves and casual greetings went around as Quinn sat.

"So, what do you think?" Doug asked. "She looked good, didn't she? Lara, I mean. Even dead. Still beautiful, huh?"

"Yeah, she looked good," Quinn said. His brother had obviously had a few. He looked morose. Okay, so they'd come from a wake. But since Quinn was certain that not even Doug's best friend Bobby knew he'd been sleeping with the deceased, it wasn't like Doug to give himself away like this.

"You've been fraternizing, huh?" Bobby teasingly asked Quinn.

He shrugged. "Not with any intent on the part of Miss Mackay. I'd told her I'd give her a lift, that's all."

"She doesn't know you're a P.I., huh?" Bobby said.

"It's easier to ask questions when people aren't instantly suspicious and defensive," he said.

"Don't worry—I don't intend to mention it," Bobby assured him.

"It's an interesting crowd, isn't it?" Giselle said, smiling. "And it's very strange. You go into the studio, and they're all as friendly as can be. But then, when they come down and dance and have drinks at Suede, you realize that you don't really know any of them. You know, like what they do with their spare time, what makes them tick."

"They don't have spare time," Bobby said. "They dance. The competitors, anyway." He grinned. "You should have been at the championships, Quinn. They change in and out of those outfits in seconds flat. They have to be perfect. There're hairspray cans all over the place. Different shoes, different jewelry. They gush all over each other. Some of them act like they're Gods, and when you listen to them talk, it's as if you walked into a sitcom. Some of them are actually warm and cuddly, as well," he admitted.

"A lot of them are too warm and cuddly." Giselle laughed. "A couple of the gentlemen were a little too impressed with Bobby—if you get my drift."

"If you're talking about sexual orientation," Jake said, leaning forward, half teasing, half serious, "some of the best cops I know are gay."

"I guess," Bobby agreed.

"What are you—homophobic?" Giselle accused.

"Hey! You brought it up."

"Yes, but I'm allowed to. Several of my best friends are of a different persuasion."

"Hey, most of your best friends are my best friends!" Bobby said.

"Trouble in newlywed paradise," Doug moaned. "I gotta take a leak. Stop them if they start to get too crazy, huh?" He rose and walked off, wobbling a little.

"Don't let him drive home," Jake warned Quinn.

"Bobby, he ought to sleep on the boat," Quinn said.

Bobby nodded. "Yeah, I know. He's been kind of weird tonight. A wake isn't any fun, I know, but he's really taking Lara's death to heart. What do you think, Quinn?"

"I haven't had enough time to come to any conclusions," Quinn said. "As far as the actual death went, the M.E. called it as he saw it."

"Hey, O'Casey!" Nick himself stepped out of the bar, bearing the house phone. "Call for you."

"Thanks, Nick."

"Sure thing. Make sure you bring it back in. It'll be the fourth phone I've lost in three months, if you forget," Nick said. "Watch him for me, Jake, huh?"

"Absolutely," Jake promised.

Quinn glared at Jake, shaking his head as he took the receiver. "O'Casey here."

"Hi. I'm sorry to bother you. I had this number in your file, and I accessed it from home. I shouldn't be doing this, calling you like this, taking advantage, but..."

"Shannon?" Quinn said.

"Yes, I'm sorry. I feel like an idiot, but I think there was someone out in my yard. Hanging around the house. I thought maybe you'd know someone who could take a cruise by the house and just look around a little. Or should I just try getting hold of the beach police? You're a cop. What do you think?"

"Shannon, this isn't Doug. It's Quinn."

"Quinn?" Her voice hardened suddenly. "Oh, so you hang around Nick's, too. I thought you weren't a cop?"

"I'm not. They don't require you to be a cop to serve you here. It's a fun place. Have you ever been? No, of course not. I forgot—you don't have a life."

"Funny. Look, never mind. I'm sorry I bothered you. I just thought Doug might have a friend on duty, or…never mind."

Her voice was tight, and she was obviously defensive. He instantly knew what she was thinking. He had just been at her house, just checked it out thoroughly. She was surely thinking that he must think her the most paranoid whiner in the world.

"What happened?" he demanded.

"Nothing."

"So what freaked you out?"

"I…" She hesitated. He thought for a minute that she was going to hang up. He heard a long sigh. "After you left, there was a noise. As if someone had been leaning against the house, listening or something, then ran across the yard. I opened the door—"

"You what?"

"I opened the door."

"Why on earth would you do that?"

"To convince myself there was no one there," she snapped back.

"And?"

"Well, it's dark out, you know."

"Yes, but…?"

"I think someone *had* been there. There was someone moving down the street. Away from the house. Hunched over, in shadow. It's perfectly possible it was just someone walking down the street. And we do have stray cats around here, and it's likely if I'm hearing things, it's one of them. Look, I'm sorry I called. It's just my imagination, I'm certain. A wake tonight, a funeral tomorrow… sorry, really. I'm going to hang up now."

"Don't go to sleep. I'm on my way out."

"No! Don't be ridiculous. It's all right. Really. Don't come back out here."

"I'm on my way," he said, hanging up.

He hit the button to end the call. The three others at the table were staring at him.

"Shannon Mackay. A case of nerves, probably. But I'm going to drive back out. Check things around her place." He set the phone down as he rose. "Bobby, get Doug to sleep on the boat, all right? Jake—"

"I'll see that the phone is returned to the bar," Jake said dryly. "Call if you need anything."

"You bet."

Quinn left them and hurried back to his car.

Shannon paced her living room, swearing to herself, feeling on the one hand like an absolute idiot and then, on the other, wondering how long it would take for Quinn to drive back out to her place.

Why had she opened the door? To assure herself, naturally. She wasn't afraid of the dark—at least, she'd never been afraid of the dark before. She came home late every night of her life, except for Saturdays and Sundays. They were only open mornings on Saturdays, and Sunday the studio was closed. But Monday through Friday, it was usually nearly eleven when she reached her house. She never thought twice about parking her car, hopping out and walking to her door. Sometimes her neighbors were around, walking their dogs in their robes just before bed, throwing out their garbage or recycling, or taking a breather to look at the night sky. It was a friendly area. She had never felt the least threatened before.

With a groan, she sat on the sofa, running her fingers through her hair. This was ridiculous. Lara had died right after a waiter had said to Shannon herself, "You're next."

And since then...

She had once been sane, confident and secure. Life had taken her through a few ups and downs, but she was mature and in charge. She knew she excelled at her chosen profession; she enjoyed the people she worked with; she was meant to take over the reins of the studio. Life was good.

Had been good, even if a little empty.

But then Lara had died.

No, that was just it. She didn't believe that for a minute. Lara *hadn't* just died. And those words... *You're next.* So now...

So now, was it ridiculous to think she was being stalked?

She winced, thinking about her conversation with Jane. Had she let too many people know that, no matter what conclusion the police and the M.E. had come to, she wasn't convinced Lara had brought about her own demise?

There was a noise in the front again. She jumped off the sofa, her heart thundering. She forced herself to walk to the door and stare out the peephole.

She smiled, leaning against the door, actually laughing out loud. Harry—her next-door neighbor's golden retriever—was marking one of the two small palm trees she had recently planted at the front of the walk.

But even as she laughed at herself, a thud against the door brought a scream to her lips.

"Shannon?"

"Idiot, you *are* losing your mind," she whispered to herself, hearing Quinn O'Casey's voice.

"Yes. Hi," she said, unlocking the door and opening it.

"What happened?" he asked sharply. "I heard you scream."

"You knocked," she said ruefully.

"You screamed because I knocked?" he said.

She lowered her head. He must really think she was an idiot.

"Never mind, long story. Hey, you must be sorry Doug bought you those lessons, huh? I swear to you, most dancers are sane."

"I'm here, think you might want to invite me in?"

"Sure, sorry."

He stepped in. "Might as well hear a long story."

"Actually, it's not that long."

"Tell me."

She sighed, suddenly almost as unnerved having him there as she had been when she'd been alone. But for a different reason. Despite the fact that she was wearing a floor-length Victorian nightgown, she felt less dressed than she might have in a bikini. The night was too quiet. He was too close, and the bit of world between them seemed far too intimate.

"It was the dog." She laughed. "I'd better start at the beginning. I guess it's just tonight. The wake and all. It's been a wretched week. Lara wasn't my best friend or anything, but I have known her forever, and her death really was a tragedy. Anyway, I thought I heard something again, so I looked out, and I was just laughing at myself because what I had heard was Harry, the neighbor's dog."

"Big shaggy golden retriever?"

"That's him."

"Anyway, I'd leaned against the door, feeling like an idiot for going into a panic, and then you knocked. You startled me. I screamed. There's absolutely nothing wrong, and I am truly an idiot for having made you come back out here. It's late, you were with friends. I didn't mean to interrupt."

"It's all right. I'm wide-awake. I'll go take a cruise around the house."

"Thanks. Hey, do you want more coffee? Wait, not a

good idea—we'd both be up all night. How about tea? Iced tea? Hot tea?"

He hesitated, looking at her.

"Have you got any microwave popcorn?"

She arched a brow. "I think so."

"Have you got a DVD player?"

"Yes."

"Got a movie you've been wanting to see?"

"Actually, I have dozens of movies. I keep buying them and never watching them."

"Throw in some popcorn, make it iced tea and pick a movie. I'll be back." He started to step back out the door, then popped his head back in. "I guess this would definitely be considered fraternization, huh?"

"I'm afraid so," she agreed.

"I could sit on one side of the room, and you could sit on the other. But then again, I'm just temporary, not really a student."

"Yes, you are. You're taking lessons."

"I'm still so bad surely it can't count."

She laughed. "You're not that bad, and it does count, but I don't intend to tell, and I hope you don't, either. If you're sure you don't mind being a baby-sitter for a few hours."

"Dancer-sitter," he said with a shrug. "And since you probably won't have any toes left after me, I'm sure I can afford the hours."

She hated herself for the thrill of absolute happiness she felt.

Quinn woke, aware of voices on the television and daylight filtering in through the windows in the back. It was a gentle awakening. He didn't move at first, simply opened his eyes.

In a few hours, he would be aching all over. He'd fallen asleep in a sitting position, his head twisted downward at an angle. Shannon was next to him, her head on his lap, her knees tucked to her chest, her arms encircling a throw pillow. Tendrils of golden hair were curled over his trousers, and the warmth of her weight against him was both captivating and arousing. Beyond anything, though, the feel of her against him stirred a sudden sense of memory, of nostalgia. He found himself remaining there, thinking of a time when a wealth of both passion and affection had been so easily his, and he had barely noticed, his mind so consumed with his job. And even when it had all slipped away, he hadn't really noticed, because somewhere inside, he had become deadened. And in the weeks and months that had followed, he hadn't wanted anything more than a brief encounter with the gentler sex, moments of human contact and nothing more. The numbness had remained. He hadn't known how to shake it. He'd been walking through life by rote, wondering where he had lost his senses of humanity and need, and his ability to have fun. Then Nell Durken had been found dead. And the numbness had been pierced with fury and impotence and a need to question every facet of life.

And then had come Shannon Mackay.

He was loath to move her. The softness of her hair against his flesh was like a breath of sweet, fresh air. The sight of her hand dangling over his knee. Fingers elegant, nails manicured, flesh so soft. Just the warmth of her, the weight of her, made him want to stay, drown in these sensations. It was this casual, intimate closeness that had been something so lost to him, something he hadn't known he missed, needed or felt a longing for, somewhere deep within.

She wouldn't be happy, of course, that they had fallen asleep and essentially spent the night together. Definitely fraternization.

At last he rose very carefully. As he moved, she stirred

slightly, seeking the same comfort she had known against him. He quickly put a throw pillow beneath her head, settled her weight and backed away. The Victorian lace of the gown framed her chin, and her hair spilled everywhere, caught by the light, a splendid halo. The fabric was thin, hugging the length of her ultratoned form. She was supple, curvaceous, and swathed in that Victorian purity, she seemed somehow all the more sensual and vulnerable.

It was time for him to get out.

He walked away, found the jacket he had doffed, turned off the television and headed for the front, through the kitchen. He found a notepad and wrote a few quick lines. "Thanks for the popcorn, tea and movie. It's light, and you're locked in. Quinn."

He walked quietly to the front and exited, making sure he hit the button lock, since he didn't have a key. He checked it twice, then headed for his car and drove away.

The cemetery was even more crowded than the funeral home had been. The dance world had come in high numbers: Lara's students, friends, associates and lovers all came to say their final goodbyes. And once again, there were reporters and news cameras and scores of the curious.

Shannon had a seat next to Gordon in the row of folding chairs arranged on the little piece of green carpet before the coffin. As the priest talked about life on earth and life in the sweet promise of eternity, she bowed her head but found her mind wandering. It seemed a terrible shame to her that so many people had come, because others with loved ones in this cemetery tended to the graves, and their tributes of beautiful flower bouquets had ended up strewn across the landscape, kicked around by the unnoticing mob that had come to attend a "celebrity" funeral.

Lara was going into a spot not far from the mausoleum,

surrounded by majestic oaks. A large angel-framed stone
nearby honored a family named Gonzalez, while an elegant marble crypt belonged to Antonio Alfredo Machi-
avelli, who had passed away in the late 1940s.

Birds soared across an amazingly blue and beautiful
sky, not touched by so much as a hint of a cloud. She was
glad Gordon had planned the ceremony early. In a few
hours it would be roasting, whether it was officially autumn or not. Somewhere not far away a bee buzzed. In the
distance, she could hear the barking of a dog. A residen-
tial neighborhood surrounded most of the cemetery. Children played on the lawns nearby; cars impatiently moved
at slower speed limits, and horns honked. Life went on,
even on the outskirts of a cemetery—maybe more so on
the outskirts of a cemetery.

Someone touched her knee. She lifted her head. Ben
Trudeau, grimly passing her a rose to toss onto the coffin.
The service was over.

She stood and walked to the grave site, then threw the
rose in. Gordon took her elbow, and they walked away
from the grave.

"Mr. Henson! Miss Mackay!"

Shannon turned with annoyance to see Ryan Hatfield,
a reporter she particularly disliked from a local paper. He
was tall and skinny and needed a life worse than she did.
When he attended events, he liked to make fun of the amateurs *and* professionals. He'd once written a truly cruel
comment on a less-than-slender couple who'd won an amateur trophy in waltz. She'd furiously—and pointlessly—
tried to explain to him that people were judged on their
steps and the quality of their dance, and that for amateurs,
dance was fun, and it was also excellent exercise. As far as
professionals went, according to him, they were all affected, ridiculous snobs who looked down their noses at
anyone with a new twist to anything. In response, she'd

pointed out the different categories of dance, even the sub-categories. He'd printed her explanation and still made her sound like an affected witch, living in a make-believe world.

"What do you want?" she asked sharply, before Gordon could speak.

"Come on, just a few words," Hatfield said.

"So you can twist them?" she asked.

"Lara was an acknowledged goddess in the world of ballroom dance. How are you feeling?" Ryan demanded, sounding as if he were actually sympathetic.

"How the hell do you think we feel?" she demanded angrily. "She died far too young. It was tragic. What do you think people feel? *Pain.* It's a loss. Now, if you'll excuse us, please?"

"Where are you going? Are you all getting together somewhere? I didn't hear the priest invite the crowd back anywhere," Ryan persisted.

"The wake was open to the public, as the funeral was," Gordon said firmly. "Now it's a private time for those who knew her. Come on, Shannon."

With Gordon's arm around her shoulder, she started for the limousine, but Ryan's words followed her. "Look at that, will you? Ben Trudeau, still standing at the grave. She divorced his ass a long time ago, huh?"

Shannon couldn't remember feeling such deep-seated fury in a long time. She was afraid she was going to lash out, lose control, hurl herself at the reporter with teeth and nails bared, and take out all her concerns, frustrations and, yes, *fears* on the man.

But when she turned, he wasn't alone. Both O'Casey brothers were there, flanking Hatfield, ready to escort him away.

"What on earth are you doing?" the reporter demanded indignantly. "Let me go this minute or I'll go to the police. I'll have you sued until you have to sell the clothes off your back. I have the cops on speed dial."

"I *am* a cop," Doug said flatly.

"Let's go," Gordon said, taking Shannon's arm.

"Go," Quinn said to her.

"Hey, this is like kidnapping or something," Ryan complained.

"They might want to charge you with harrassment," Doug said.

Shannon didn't hear any more. Gordon was moving; he had her arm, so she was moving, too. In another minute, she was in the limo.

Just before the door closed, they were joined by Ben Trudeau. He shook his head as he stared out the window.

"Fucking reporters," he muttered.

"Ben," Gordon admonished quietly.

"There aren't any students around," Ben said distractedly.

"It's still—" Gordon began.

"It's a rat-shit day. Leave him alone, please," Shannon put in.

The limo moved out of the cemetery. Ben looked downward between his hands, then up, letting out a long breath. "It's real. She's really gone. Into the ground. I don't believe it."

Gordon set an arm around his shoulders. "Yeah, it's hard to accept."

You're next.

The memory of the words came to Shannon with a sharp chill. She shivered.

Ben looked past Gordon, who was in the middle. "I'm sorry, Shannon. Are you all right?"

"Of course. I'm fine."

He looked out the window again thoughtfully. "Interesting. That stinking rag writer would have driven us all nuts.

I guess it's a good thing we have one of the county's finest among our students. Doug. You know, though, his brother is the one who saw the guy and went after him first. Are we sure he's not a cop? He's in awful tight with them."

"No, he's not a cop. Maybe he was once, but not anymore," Shannon said.

"He still acts like one," Ben noted.

"What do you mean?" Gordon demanded.

Ben shrugged. "I don't know. He's always…watching. You know, I was at lunch yesterday, and he was in the same café. In the back…"

Gordon shrugged. "I run into people all over town. At the bank, at the movies, wherever."

"Yeah, I guess you're right. Hey, is he coming to this thing?"

"No. I didn't ask any of the students. Only some of the pros Lara worked with, and the people from our building." Gordon pressed a hand to his forehead. "The public had the wake and the funeral. Time to be alone."

The spot he had chosen for the after-funeral tribute was a small place on Lincoln Road where they'd gone many times for special occasions. Gordon had kept the attendance down to about twenty.

They gathered around four tables, and Gordon gave his personal eulogy to Lara. Then Ben spoke, and, to Shannon, his emotions seemed honest. He spoke of their relationship as passionate and sometimes as emotionally violent as the dances she had performed, but said in the end that her spirit was one that had touched them all, and that their loss was tremendous. They would all remember things she had told them—bluntly, at times, but each and every word one that would make them better at their craft, their vocation, the dancing that was not just work but part of their very being.

Shannon was glad to see that the people who attended

included not just friends from the area but all over the country and even from Europe. She agreed again to see Gunter during the week, but broke away when he told her she created the best choreography he'd ever seen and they were all lucky she didn't use it for herself—but she should.

At one point she found herself talking with Christie Castle, five time National Smooth Champion, and now both a coach and a judge at competitions around the world.

"How are you holding up?" Christie asked her. Christie was slender as a reed, about five-five, with huge dark eyes and ink-black hair. Her age was indeterminate, but at ninety, she was still going to be beautiful.

"Fine. It's a shattering event, but Lara and I didn't hang out," Shannon reminded her.

"Gordon says you've been nervous lately." She lowered her voice. "And your receptionist told me that you're convinced there's more going on than we know."

"Ella shouldn't have said anything to you."

"Do you really think Lara might have been murdered?"

Shannon noticed that Christie was whispering. Gordon, Ben, Justin, Sam Railey and several others were right behind them. Shannon thought that Ben turned slightly, as if he were more interested in what they were saying than in the conversation in which he was taking part.

"I don't really think anything," Shannon said.

Christie set a hand on her knee, dark eyes wide with concern. "You look really tired. Are you sleeping all right?"

Last night, ten minutes after the movie had started, Shannon had been sound asleep, but that had been the first time in a week she had really slept.

"Not really. I don't know why. I'm just a little tense."

"You need a dog," Christie said, nodding sagely.

Shannon smiled, looking downward. Christie had Puff, a teacup Yorkie. The little dog went everywhere with her.

In fact, Puff probably had more airline mileage stacked up than most CEOs.

"Christie, I'm gone almost fifteen hours a day. And honestly, if I had a little Puff, and someone was after me…"

"Excuse me, he may be small, but Puff has a killer bark."

"What's that about a killer bark?"

Gabriel Lopez slid into the seat next to Christie. He had a look in his eyes, a flirtatious look. He never actually leered. He had a way of looking at a woman that simply indicated total appreciation and therefore managed not to be offensive.

"Puff, of course," Christie said.

He laughed. "I thought that you were referring to killer cute and meant me."

"Thankfully, Gabriel, neither of us is foolish enough to take you seriously. We're both well aware that you've dated every single celebrity who has ever come to town. And then some," Christie told him.

"Not true!" he protested. With a shrug, he smiled ruefully. "You know, there's an image a club owner needs to keep up."

Ben had apparently tired of the conversation behind them. He slid into the empty chair on Shannon's other side. "You seem to keep it up okay," he assured Gabriel, grinning at his own double entendre.

"And what about you? As charming as Fred Astaire, with women ready to follow your every step." He spoke lightly, but then his face changed slightly. "I'm so sorry, Ben."

"We're all sorry. I guess we have to accept it." Ben stared at Shannon. "God knows we've got the students to set our minds at rest. Doug O'Casey admired Lara, and he's in a position to make sure the police checked out every possibility."

"Ah, yes, the young patrolman," Gabriel murmured. "He watched her like a puppy dog. You could tell he hated it when she danced with others, and he looked as if he'd died and gone to heaven when she danced with him."

"He's a terrific student," Christie said. "She certainly made a difference for him."

"Jane is his instructor, and she's excellent," Shannon put in.

"Yes, but he signed up for a lot of coaching sessions, didn't he?" Christie asked. "I understand he signed up for half the day when Lara was around." She shrugged as she looked at Shannon. "She was still competing and I'm not. That makes a difference to some people."

"Interesting," Ben noted.

"What?" Christie asked him.

"It's so expensive…paying for coaching when you're an amateur. And Doug is just a patrolman. Where do you think he got the money?" Ben mused.

"Dirty cop?" Gabriel said.

"Hey!" Shannon protested.

"Well, he has spent a lot of money at the studio, right?" Ben said.

"Maybe he has family money," she suggested.

"Well, maybe. And now his brother's there. He says he's not a cop, that he runs charters or fishing boats, or something," Ben said.

"Maybe he's a drug lord with a great cover," Gabriel suggested.

"Who's a drug lord?"

They had been joined by Jim Burke, Lara's last partner. He looked like hell. Shannon had the feeling he'd spent the week crying. His hazel eyes were red rimmed. He was in a sleek suit and a subdued blue tailored shirt, but he looked haggard despite the fact that his clothing was immaculate.

"Shannon's new student," Christie said. "Not really—we were just speculating."

"He runs a charter business," Shannon told Jim. She smiled at him. "You all right?"

"Yeah, yeah, I'm doing fine. Feeling a little lost, but... I should be getting ready for Asheville. The competition there. Lara and I were signed up for it. Instead..."

"Take some time," Shannon suggested.

"I can't afford to take too much time," he murmured. "I don't have Lara's deep pockets. I survived on the purses from our winnings most of the time."

"You'll get a new partner," Christie told him.

"Yeah," Ben muttered.

Christie turned to Shannon. "Someone should be cultivating Doug Quinn. I know he's on the police force, but that young man could have a career in professional dance."

"Maybe he likes having a life," Jim muttered.

"And he'd have to go back to making zilch if he wanted to teach, so he could spend time getting the training he'd need," Gabriel pointed out.

"Maybe his drug-dealing brother could help him out," Ben muttered.

Shannon groaned. "Oh, please. Maybe everything is just what it seems. Come on. We're all going to be ripped to shreds in the papers tomorrow—let's not do it to ourselves." She stood. "Excuse me, you all. I think this has been the longest week in history. Christie, you'll be down for at least a week before the Gator Gala, right?" She wanted to kick herself the minute the words were out of her mouth. This was the last tribute to Lara, and she was bringing up business.

"Hey, how about me?" Ben asked her.

"Of course, Ben. We'd love to bring you in to coach," she told him.

Gabriel stood. "You came in the limousine?" he asked her.
"Yes."

"I'll give you a ride home. I need to get to work."

"Great, thanks," she said. She walked around the table, saying her goodbyes, kissing cheeks. Leaving always took a while—they were an affectionate group. It was like leaving an Italian family dinner.

"I'm sorry, I had a lot of goodbyes," she told Gabriel when they at last exited into the late afternoon.

"It's all right. I like following you around," Gabriel said. "Everyone kisses me."

She laughed. "You're so full of it. Everyone walks into your club and kisses you, too."

He shrugged. "It's a good life. I work hard, but it is a good life. Don't you feel that way?"

"Yes, of course. I absolutely love what I do."

"But it doesn't leave room for much else. At least," he teased, "what I do is social."

"Oh, come on. You can't get much more social than dancing."

"But you put up walls. I don't."

She laughed suddenly. "What is this? All of a sudden everyone has decided that they have to be my psychoanalyst. I'm fine."

He arched a brow. "Everyone is telling you this?"

She shook her head, suddenly not wanting to tell him it was her brand-new student—Quinn, the cop's brother, the one they were teasingly suggesting might be a drug lord—who had made a similar observation.

"Never mind. There's my house."

He let out a sound of mock disgust. "I know where your house is."

He pulled up in front and started to get out. For Gabriel, it was natural. A man opened a door for a lady.

"Gabe, I'm fine," she said, reaching for the door handle.

"Hey, you taught me—in dance, a man always leads. I will teach you that, in life, that same man likes to open doors for a lady and walk her to her door."

She laughed. "Okay, Gabe."

He came around and opened the car door, taking her hand in an elaborate show of attention. "If you had any sense, you'd fall madly in love with me. We'd rule the world."

"I have plenty of sense, and that's why I'll never fall madly in love with you. And I don't want the responsibility of ruling the world." She slipped the key into her lock and opened the door, then turned to say goodbye.

"You could still invite me in. We'd be two lonely souls making wild passionate love on a stolen afternoon so that we could go back to our all-business lives with secret memories of what might have been," he said.

"Gabriel, that's the biggest crock I've ever heard."

"Okay, but it would still be fun, huh?"

"I'm sure there are dozens of women out there who would willingly give you an afternoon," she assured him.

"They don't have your body."

"Thanks. I think."

"I've got it. You're already having a secret affair with someone."

"No, I'm afraid not."

"Then come on. My body is pretty good, too."

"Gabriel, you're practically perfect in every way."

"Then why not?"

"You're my friend. I want to keep it that way."

"Okay. Want to go to a movie?"

She burst out laughing again. "You know, that would be fun. Ask me again. But not today. It's just been far too long a week. And, hey, I thought you had to go to work."

"I'd call in sick for you." He sighed. "All right. Spend your lonely Saturday night by yourself."

"Thanks for the ride, Gabriel."

He swept her a little bow and gave her a mocking grin. "Any time. Goodbye. Lock up, now."

She nodded. As he walked down the path to his car, she noted that it had gone from dusky to dark. She wished it was summer. She loved it when the daylight hours extended late.

After closing and locking the door, she hesitated. The shadows had invaded the house. She walked around, turning on all the lights in a sudden flurry. Better.

Ridiculously, she had another creepy feeling. Not creepy enough to make her wish she had invited Gabe in, but uncomfortable.

There was, she thought, absolutely nothing in her house that resembled a weapon. Until recently she had never been afraid in her own home.

The best she could come up with was one of her old tennis rackets. Brandishing it in one hand, she began a methodic check of the house.

Beyond a doubt, it was empty.

She sat down in the back, staring at the TV, despite the fact that it was off. The room was bright. The back windows were large, looking out on her little bit of yard. It was rich with foliage. She suddenly realized that if you were worried about people looking in at you, it wasn't smart to have bright lights on inside, darkness outside and the draperies opened. She jumped up to close the drapes.

As she did so, she thought she saw a flash of movement through the trees.

No.

She *did* see it.

Palms bent, bushes swayed. And a sense of cold deeper than any fear she had ever known coursed through her veins.

* * *

He watched and cursed himself.

Close call.

Close call? No, not really. She wouldn't have come out into the yard. And if she had...?

Pity.

But she was nervous. Really nervous. Why? Because she just didn't believe? The little fool. What the hell did she owe Lara Trudeau? Why should she care?

But she wasn't giving up. Everyone talked about the way Shannon kept insisting that Lara hadn't accidentally done herself in. Was it because she knew Lara?

Or because she knew something else?

He stared at the house for a moment longer. Then he turned, disappearing silently around the back. He knew the house well. There was no alarm. If it was ever necessary...

He paused, looking back.

Let it go, Shannon, he thought.

Let it go.

Or...

You'll be next.

CHAPTER 9

Quinn rubbed his forehead and looked over his notes. Students, teachers, competitors. Possibilities, motives. He had a sheet with the names of everyone who had attended the competition, and there were hundreds of names on it. Many, of course, he had come to know.

He had started a list himself. Similarities, dissimilarities. The death of Nell Durken, the death of Lara Trudeau. Nell, her death classified a homicide. Lara, her death classified an accident, an overdose, self-inflicted.

Two different physicians, both of them respected in their fields, their prescriptions for the tranquilizers perfectly legitimate, proper dosages duly specified. Nell's husband had been caught cheating. His fingerprints had been all over her bottle of pills.

Lara had been drinking as well as pill popping. She had still managed to go out on the dance floor and perform perfectly—until she had dropped. Nell had taken classes at the studio but had quit six months before her death. There had to be a connection, but what? Nell's husband was in jail. And even if someone had killed Lara because she was competition, why would they have killed Nell? Say Ben

Trudeau was the one who'd done Lara in—what on earth would be his connection with Nell? Teachers didn't just off students and make it appear that their husbands had done the deed.

He groaned, having spent the afternoon on a paper chase that went in circles. He glanced at the clock, wishing Gordon Henson and Ben Trudeau hadn't chosen to make their after-service get-together a private one. Someone had a key to this. And it was someone associated with the studio, he was certain.

Water lapped against the boat. He glanced at his watch and noted that the day had gone to dark.

Laughter filtered to him from the restaurant and bar.

Hell, he needed a beer. And maybe his brother or some of the other guys were at Nick's.

His brother, who had gotten him into this.

Impatiently he rose.

He was getting obsessive again.

Doug had better be there, he thought. His brother owed him. Leaving things as they lay, he left the boat.

Shannon stared out the window as time ticked by. Then, at last, she gritted her teeth and arched her back, unknotting her shoulders.

"This is so ridiculous," she said aloud to herself. "Why would anyone run around my yard night after night, staring in?"

If someone really wanted to break in, they would have done so already.

And yet...

She could have sworn that, last night, she had left the porch light on. How had it gotten off?

"Right. Someone broke into my house, touched nothing at all, but turned the porch light off. Sure," she muttered, her words seeming ridiculously loud in the quiet of the house.

She suddenly, and desperately, wanted to get out. She didn't want to be alone, which was absurd. She loved her house, loved her quiet time. Loved nights alone when she worked on steps on her own little dance floor. And, sad as it might seem, she did like those moments when she threw a bag of microwave popcorn in, then caught up on a movie on DVD, since it seemed she never quite made it to a theater.

But not tonight.

On a sudden whim, she raced into the bedroom and quickly changed into more casual attire. She didn't know where she was going, or at least didn't realize where until she got out to her car.

She could have gone to the club. Gabriel would always find her a place, and she might find her friends there. But she wasn't going to the club. A strange idea had actually been brewing in her mind throughout the past several minutes.

There had been so many questions that day. And suppositions. So…

Exactly what was the real story with Quinn O'Casey?

He wasn't a drug lord. She couldn't believe that. Way too far-fetched.

But…

Neither was he what he claimed to be. She was sure of that.

She started to drive, not even sure where Nick's was.

"Wouldn't happen. Would never happen. You can just tell," Doug was saying.

He was sitting across from Bobby. The two of them were alone at the table, remnants of the fish and chips they had eaten pushed to one corner. Doug had an iced tea; Bobby had a beer.

"I don't see why not," Bobby said. "The guy needs a partner." Bobby looked up and saw Quinn coming toward them. "Hey. Are you joining us?"

"Yep." Quinn sat down. A girl named Mollie was working the patio that night. She waved to him. "Miller, please," he called to her. "You're buying," he told Doug.

Doug grimaced. "Sure."

Quinn looked at Bobby. "What wouldn't happen?"

"Shannon. She'd never dance with Ben Trudeau."

"She dances with him at the studio, doesn't she?" Quinn asked.

"Bobby is talking professionally," Doug said.

"She doesn't compete at all, does she?" Quinn asked. Mollie brought his beer, and he gave her a thanks, then stared at the other two.

"No. She did once, though. And according to a few of the conversations I overheard at the wake, she was great. Maybe better than Lara," Bobby told him.

"I watched the tape," Quinn said. "I saw Sam and Jane out there, but no one else from the studio."

"Ben hasn't competed since his last partner got married and decided to have a baby," Doug said. "He's been looking for a new partner for about two years."

"But he's been back at the studio working for a while, too, right?" Quinn asked.

"About a year, I believe," Bobby said.

"So why would Shannon suddenly dance with him now? He wasn't with Lara anymore, anyway," Quinn said.

Bobby looked at Doug. "You never filled him in on Shannon's past, huh?"

"No, he didn't," Quinn said, irritated as he stared at his brother. Doug had gotten him involved. He shouldn't have left out any information that might have been pertinent.

"When she was younger, Shannon was nuts about Ben," Bobby said. "He's the one who found her. She was working some small professional gigs and teaching in a little mom-and-pop place up in the Orlando area. He saw her potential, and whether they started an affair and he brought her down, or he brought her down and then they started an affair, I'm not sure. What we know is really gossip, of course, because I only went for lessons about six months ago—getting ready for Randy's wedding and of course my own—and then I dragged your brother in right after that. But anyway, some of the people there have been taking lessons for years, and they talk. Anyway, one night when I was watching Ben and Shannon do a waltz together, I said something about how incredible they looked together. It was old Mr. Clinton, I think, who said, 'Well hell, they should look great together. They competed together for two years.' Then Shannon had broken her ankle. Lara had been hanging around, and the next thing you knew…well, Shannon needed a lot of therapy, and Ben wasn't about to wait around for her to get better. He started working with Lara. Then…"

"Then they wound up married," Doug said flatly.

Quinn stared at Doug. "Suppose," he said evenly, "something involving foul play did happen to Lara Trudeau. Shannon Mackay might be a prime suspect. Jealousy, passion, anger—the motives are all there."

Doug shook his head. "All you have to do is meet Shannon, speak to her once, and you know she's not a killer."

"The right motives are there, Doug," Quinn said irritably. He didn't think Shannon Mackay could be a killer, either. If she were, she also had to be the best actress in the universe. But then again, murder often proved that all things were possible.

"Hell, everybody had a motive. We all know that," Doug said, sounding a little defensive. "Most women hated Lara—she was gorgeous."

"Wait a minute," Bobby protested. "All women do not hate all other women who are gorgeous."

"You sure?" Doug asked. A slow smile was curving his lips.

"Yes, I'm sure," Bobby said.

"Did Giselle teach you to say that?"

"Bite me," Bobby told him.

"Hey," Quinn protested.

"Okay, seriously?" Bobby said. "She was competition, sure. But they're all competition for each other. Most people don't kill people just because they're in competition with them."

"Ah, but let's see, Jane has gone up against her dozens of times—and lost," Doug said. "Half of the professional dancers out there have gone up against Lara—and lost. That creates hundreds of suspects."

Quinn shook his head. "Whoever did it had to be there that night."

"True," Doug agreed. "And they would have had to figure out how to force all that stuff into her without her protesting, saying anything to anyone…ah, hell. Maybe she did just take too much stuff. I keep thinking that I knew her. Maybe I didn't."

"What about Gordon Henson?" Quinn asked, taking a swig of his beer.

"Lara was kind of a cash cow for Gordon. A prize—even if she could be just as bitchy to him as she was to everyone else," Bobby said.

"Ben could easily have had a motive," Quinn said.

"You bet," Doug agreed, and it sounded as if he was growing angry. "In fact, they argued a lot."

"Really?" Bobby said. "I've never seen *any* of them argue."

"They're not allowed to argue in the studio. But I went back to get coffee one day, and they were both there. Though they shut up when they saw me, I heard him speaking really sharply to her, and she said something like, 'In your dreams, asshole,' to him."

Quinn's chair was facing the pathway that led around

to the patio from the parking lot. Glancing up, he was amazed to see Shannon Mackay—in form-hugging jeans, a tube top and an overshirt—walking tentatively along the trail to the back tables. "I don't believe it," he breathed.

"Why don't you believe it? I'm telling you the truth," Doug said irritably.

He glared at his brother. "No. I don't believe that Shannon Mackay is here. Now."

Both Bobby and Doug swung around. At the same time, she saw them. She looked startled at first, then waved. Bobby waved back, beckoning her over.

She approached the table, smiling. She kissed Doug and Bobby on the cheek, then got to Quinn. Her fingers felt cold and tense on his shoulders. Her lips brushed his face with less than affection. Her smile, he thought, was insincere. Yet her scent, and the way she felt, brushing against him…

"This is a surprise," he said. "A real surprise. I thought your group was all tied up with itself this evening."

She looked intently at him, then shrugged. "I needed to get away. I know too many people on the beach, though, and I'd heard everybody talk about this place, so…"

"So here you are. Running into us," Quinn said flatly.

"Uh, yeah," she murmured.

"Quinn, man, that was rude," Doug said, glaring at him. "Sit down, join us. I mean, I know you're not supposed to hang around with students, but hell you're the boss. And this is definitely a strange occasion, huh?"

"Yeah, I guess it's a strange occasion," she agreed, taking the fourth chair at the table.

"Are you hungry?" Bobby asked her. "The fish is as fresh as it gets. And the burgers are good, too. Or are you a vegetarian? Jane is, right?"

"Jane is a vegetarian. I'm a carnivore. I think a burger sounds great," she said.

"Hey, Mollie!" Bobby started to turn around, but Mollie was already there.

"Hi," she said cheerfully. "What can I get you?"

"Iced tea, please," Shannon said, smiling. "And a hamburger."

"Cheese?"

"Plain, thanks."

"Fries okay? Or would you prefer slaw."

"The fries are wonderful here, too," Doug said.

"Fries."

"You sure you want tea?" Bobby asked her. "You look as if you could use a drink."

She smiled. "I think I could use a lot of drinks. But I drove."

Quinn leaned forward. "Have a drink. You can leave your car here. I can drive you home and get you tomorrow so you can pick it back up."

She was going to say no, he was certain. That would constitute much more than an accidental meeting between a teacher and some students at a restaurant.

"We won't have to talk while I drive," he teased. "I swear, I won't fraternize. Well, unless you fraternize first."

"I can't, I mean I really shouldn't."

"Oh, have the damn beer," Mollie piped in, then grinned. "Sorry, I guess I've worked here too long. I just thought I should solve this thing. Honey, I don't know the situation, but you do look like you need a drink. This one here…" She paused, pointing at Bobby. "He's a newlywed, not dangerous in the least. I'd swear it on a stack of Bibles. And these two…well, if they say they'll get you home safe and sound, they'll do it."

Shannon had looked surprised at first, almost offended. But by the time Mollie finished speaking, she was laughing. "Great. Bring me a beer. Something on draft, and very big."

"You got it," Mollie told her, and moved on.

"I get to pick up the tab, though," Shannon said firmly. "I owe you guys, after this morning."

"After this morning?" Doug said.

"The reporter," Quinn reminded him. "That guy is a real pain in the ass."

"His paper has been sued a dozen times," Shannon assured him. She sat back in her chair, looking around. "Great place," she murmured. "It's so rustic—and nice."

"Dancers are used to white tablecloths and diners in gloves and beaded gowns, huh?" Quinn asked.

"I seldom leave home without my beads, you bet," she said seriously. "I wasn't taking a crack at your special place. I like rustic. I live on the beach. My favorite vacation spot is the islands. This patio is outside, and there are boats and oil and fish all over the place down on the pier, and it's still unbelievably clean. I'm not sure I could manage that."

"Nick is a great guy," Doug said. "He runs a tight ship."

"And it's a big cop hangout, huh?" she said.

She was definitely after something, Quinn decided.

"His niece is a cop. Married to another cop," Bobby said. He stood abruptly, looking uncomfortable. "Thanks very much for dinner, Shannon. I'll let you buy, since we did invest pretty heavily to look good for the wedding."

She grinned. "And you two *did* look good."

"Yeah, we did. Thanks again for dinner. Since I'm still pretty much a newlywed, I've probably hung out long enough. Night, all."

He received a chorus of good-nights in turn, not just from their table, but from others. As he left, Mollie returned with Shannon's meal.

Shannon thanked her and bit in, chewed, then said, "Wow, this is a great burger."

"Naturally," Doug told her. "We wouldn't lie."

"No?" she said, smiling. Doug looked at her gravely and shook his head.

"You nervous to be at your house?" Quinn asked her abruptly.

"Nervous? No," she said quickly.

"Why would she be nervous at her own house?" Doug asked.

"No reason," she assured him.

"Everybody's nervous now and then," Quinn said. "Houses creak. Especially old houses with old floor-boards."

"What's it like living on a boat?" Shannon asked. "You have one up here, right? Isn't that what you said?"

He pointed down to the pier. "She's right there."

"You should see her," Doug said. "Sweetest little thing in the bay."

Quinn glared across the table at his brother.

"I'd love to see your boat," Shannon said.

"Would you?" Quinn murmured. She was nervous, he thought. She wanted company and had actually chosen him. He rose abruptly. "Let me take a look at her first, then—pick up a little."

"Don't be silly. I don't want you to go to any bother," she told him.

"I'll just take a peek and see if the place is presentable. Doug, don't even think about leaving Miss Mackay until I get back."

"Hey, no problem."

Quinn left them at the table, ready to strangle his own brother. Doug had forced him into the game and hadn't given him the full deck.

He hurried down the pier to his boat and jumped aboard, quickly heading into the cabin. The tape of Lara Trudeau's last performance was sitting on the counter between the galley and dining area. His files, with the copies of the autopsy reports on Nell Durken and Lara Trudeau and various other papers, were next it. He quickly stashed them in one of the cabinets by the small desk. Taking a quick look around, he ascertained that he'd left out nothing else incriminating.

Incriminating? Shit! If she'd seen that stuff, she would have been furious.

He went topside again, leaped to the pier and hurried back to Nick's patio. Shannon hadn't lied when she'd said she wasn't a vegetarian—she'd consumed everything on the plate. Apparently she didn't starve herself to stay so perfectly in shape. But then again, in her line of work, she must burn energy by the barrel.

"Am I allowed to see the sacred ground now?" she teased.

"It's still not great, but…hey." He arched a brow. "You're sure you won't be fraternizing if you come to my boat?"

She'd finished her beer, as well. She looked more relaxed than he'd ever seen her. "I'm coming to see if you're capable of arranging the charter I need for my get-together before the Gator Gala."

Doug rose. "If you'll excuse me, I've seen the boat. And I'm on at eight tomorrow morning, which means I try to get into the station by seven. Good night, and, Shannon, thanks for dinner."

"My pleasure, Doug," she said, rising as well.

Quinn realized she had apparently paid the bill in his absence.

"You really didn't have to pick up all our dinners," he told her.

She flashed a smile. "You were really cheap dates, and I was glad of the company. Besides, I didn't pay for *your* dinner. Just a beer. You didn't eat."

He smiled. "I just came out and found those two talking. I ate in."

"You cook?"

"Not a lot, but enough to survive. I'm not bad. And you?"

"I'm pure gourmet."

"Really?"

"No, I'm horrible. But I can manage the basics, like boiling pasta and heating sauce. And hey, can I break a head of lettuce!"

She spoke lightly as they walked along the pier. He glanced at her. It was almost as if a wall had come down.

One beer. And she hadn't really wanted that. He had a feeling she didn't drink very often.

"Lettuce is good," he murmured. "Well, here we are."

She was wearing sneakers and easily leaped the foot that separated the dock from the boat. On deck, she looked around, closing her eyes briefly as she felt the night's breeze. "She's lovely," Shannon said.

"Cabin is that way," he told her, pointing. "Pretty obvious, huh?"

She nodded and turned toward the steps leading down to the cabin.

"Tight, but oddly spacious," she told him.

"There are two bedrooms, one forward, one aft. Galley, as you can see, and the head is there, on the left, right before the master bedroom. She's not all that small, but then again, on a boat, a tour is pretty quick," he said dryly, then switched topics, hoping to surprise her into an honest answer. "You're afraid to be at your house, aren't you?"

"No!" she protested quickly. She turned as if she were inspecting the inside of the cabin. "No, I came home before it was too late." She glanced at him wryly. "I did the inspection thing myself, looking under beds and in closets and all."

"So you just wanted to get out and have some fun?"

"Yes."

"Well, have a seat."

There was a small sofa, which could be used as a sleeper, across from the dining table. She gingerly sat.

"Can I get you something?"

"No, thanks."

"Well, then, excuse me, I'll get myself something."

He walked the few steps into the galley and got a Miller out of the small refrigerator. On second thought, he took two, twisting the top off one and handing it to her.

"Really, I'm fine," she said.

"Really, you need to relax. Forget the last week."

She hesitated, then took the bottle from him. "Thanks," she said, and shrugged. "You're driving."

He sat down next to her, watching her as he sipped his own beer. "So, you do own a pair of jeans."

"Actually, I own several."

"They weren't in your closets."

"You didn't go through my drawers."

"True."

She was downing the beer a little fast, especially for a woman who had originally refused a drink. But it was nice to see her without the guard that was customarily so carefully wrapped around her. Not a guard that repelled—she was warm and friendly with people; he'd seen it. It was a guard that kept something back. He wondered if it would have been there if he'd met her before Lara's death.

Tonight the smiles she flashed were genuine, warm. And despite her casual attire, he didn't think she'd ever been more appealing. The color of her hair was like wheat touched with gold. Her eyes flashed with a true emerald depth. Her skin was pure ivory, barely touched by the sun. Smooth, silken. And that scent she wore…

He should move. He didn't want to. And suddenly he wasn't sure why he should. He was tempted to reach out, smooth back a lock of that golden hair, so he did. She looked at him, startled by the touch.

"Sorry, you look a little lost there."

"Oh, I'm not lost. I know where I'm going," she murmured.

"Why didn't you tell me you'd had a thing with Ben Trudeau?"

She stiffened instantly, looking as if she was about to rise and find her own way home.

"Hey…" He gently laid a hand on her shoulder. "Innocent question."

"Really? And none of your business," she said.

"Sorry. I guess I just heard the talk about it."

"Oh, great, so people are talking about it. It was a long time ago."

"You might have mentioned it."

She stared at him, and her gemstone eyes were hard. "Why should I have mentioned it? It's not as if we've suddenly become deep friends."

He shrugged. "I guess you're right."

"I don't remember you sitting on my couch spilling secrets about your love life," she said.

He smiled, almost laughing. "Shannon, you fell asleep ten minutes after I sat on your couch. By the way, though, I did enjoy the movie."

She blushed, staring across the room. "Sorry. It was nice of you to stay. You're being awfully decent. I really don't want anyone else to know how ridiculously paranoid I've gotten."

"So you *were* nervous at your house. Why?"

She shook her head. "No reason. Well, all right. I thought I saw something moving in the backyard. And being scared of that is kind of ridiculous. There's the neighbor's dog. And we've got cats aplenty in the neighborhood. And now and then a possum or a raccoon. I know I'm being ridiculous. I just can't seem to help it."

"It's all right," he said.

"I'm sorry. I'm probably keeping you from something," she said.

"I offered to drive you home."

"Yes, you did. Still…"

"I'm not married and not involved," he said flatly.

"I didn't ask for that information."

"You said I hadn't told you anything."

"Only because you sounded as if I should have told you about Ben. Why would you think that?"

"No reason, I guess."

She looked at the empty beer in her hand, then at him. "One more. Then I'll sleep like the dead when I get home." She winced. "I'll sleep well, I mean."

He took the empty bottle from her, walked to the galley and got her another. "You're sure?"

"I'm twenty-eight, and I'm sure."

"I don't want you saying I took advantage of you because you'd been drinking."

Her brows arched and she looked down, a little smile teasing at her lips. "You're planning on taking advantage of me?"

"There's nothing planned," he told her. He handed her the new beer and sat next to her. "Okay, sorry, I have to ask. The Ben Trudeau thing is really over?"

She looked irritated. "Years over. I can't believe anyone even brought it up."

"He sounds like a real jackass, but he's working for you. Why?"

She shrugged. "He's good at what he does. I don't hate Ben."

"Did you hate Lara?"

She laughed suddenly. "That would be kind of like hating a bee for having a stinger. I didn't particularly like her. Like I said, we didn't hang out, have lunch or go shopping. But I admired her talent. I even felt sorry for Ben when she broke up with him." She hesitated a minute. "Ben is a really good dancer. Their problems were professional, at first. Ben started getting angry with the way they worked—it was her way or the highway, that kind of thing. The fights spilled over into their marriage, and she walked out. Jim Burke was a perfect partner for Lara. He let her lead. Well, you know, men lead, but…he let her call all the shots, so they worked well together."

"You must have been angry when he walked out on you—all because of a broken ankle."

"I was too young to be really angry. Too naive. He was long gone before I ever realized he'd reached the door. But, like I said, it was ages ago. Whatever our differences, Ben gave me my life, and I love my life. Mostly. He brought me down here. I started working in Gordon's studio, and now I manage the place. I'm the heir apparent to own it, when he decides to retire." She looked at him, grinning. "And now Ben works for me. So…your turn. What about your love life?"

"She left me," he said lightly.

"Why?"

"I was a workaholic."

"But you don't seem to be. Not now. In fact, it seems as if you have tons of leisure time."

He took a long swallow of his own beer. "Not always," he said, not looking at her. "It's slow right now in the Keys, won't pick up until we're closer to real winter. You know, when all the snowbirds fly down."

"Oh, right, of course." She was looking at him, intently. "Were you bitter?"

"Bitter?"

"About being left."

He stared at his bottle. "No…she was right to leave."

"Why?"

"I'd let too many things get in the way. I can get obsessive, I'm afraid."

"An obsessive workaholic," she murmured, still studying him carefully. "But you are here, whiling away the time with a silly woman who's nervous because of a cat in her backyard."

He smiled, and this time took care when he smoothed back the straying tendril of her hair. "I can't think of any place I'd rather be right now, or anyone else I'd rather be with." He was amazed by his own sincerity. Not just because she was beautiful, with the greatest cleavage he'd come across in aeons. Or because of the feel of her hair. Or even the feel of the excitement rising within him. He wanted to have her there, sure, but he also wanted to stand between her and anything that might harm her in any way.

Obsessive?

Oh, yeah, it would be easy to get obsessive over her.

Her eyes remained on his for a long time. It seemed that she was barely breathing. She moistened her lips, and they glistened. Her teeth were tiny and perfect.

"Wow," she murmured, trying to sound light. "That was one hell of a nice statement. Or a very good line."

"Want me to back away?"

"I don't know." He thought her words were honest. Then she seemed to give herself a shake. "I, uh, yes. I guess you should take me home now."

He stood. "No."

She frowned. "I'm sorry?"

"I don't think you should go home."

"Where do you think I *should* go?" she asked.

"I think you should stay here."

She smiled, then laughed out loud. "Now that really *would* be fraternizing."

He shook his head. "No. Not the way I mean it. I'm going to back away. You know, emotionally, socially—even physically. But you should still stay here. If you go home, you'll be afraid. The drinks won't help. I've got a great guest bedroom. There's even a separate head. So you should just stay."

"But…it…I mean…"

"Does anyone check up on you at night?" he asked.

"No."

"Then just stay. Get some sleep. An honest-to-God good night's sleep."

"I slept well last night," she reminded him.

"But was it enough? After this week?"

She still hesitated.

"I bet I even have an extra toothbrush," he offered.

"Maybe you're right," she murmured.

"I have a T-shirt you can sleep in, and I promise I'll stay at my end of the boat. First thing, I'll wake you up. Your car is here, so you can drive yourself home. And just think about this," he added lightly. "No one would ever think anything, should they even recognize your car, because we told Bobby and Doug that I'd be driving you home and your car would be staying here."

"You have a point there."

"Well, that's good."

She looked at him, slightly suspicious again, and bit the bullet. "You were a cop once, weren't you?"

"Yes."

"You weren't fired for anything criminal, were you?"

He laughed. "Hell no." Then he couldn't help himself. "I took part in all my criminal activities before I became a cop."

"Oh yeah?"

"I'm trustworthy. I swear it."

"I know I just thought about that. I've only known you a few days, but I'm choosing to sleep at your place rather than returning to my own—where I'm afraid of what is probably just a cat in the yard."

"Hey, I've already slept at your house."

She laughed. "There you go. True again. Well, then…"

"Well…?"

"Could I have that T-shirt now, please?"

"Absolutely."

Midnight.

He took a cruise by her house again.

The car was gone.

He stared at the front, frowning; then his cell phone rang. Absently he picked it up. "Yes?"

"We've got another problem. No, this one is yours. *You've* got a problem. And you owe me for finding out about this one."

"What do you mean, *I've* got a problem?"

He listened intently.

"So you see what I mean? *You've* got a problem."

Yeah, he had a problem, but still… Half the trouble lately hadn't been caused by him, and he'd coped anyway.

"Don't forget, don't ever forget, that you're in this up to your neck, my friend," he said softly. Very softly.

And then he hung up.

He stared at the house again and felt a rise of fury.

Where the hell was she?

CHAPTER 10

He hadn't been lying down for more than a few seconds when he heard the tap on his cabin door.

Quinn leaped up. As the captain's quarters on a pleasure craft, the cabin was relatively spacious. Still, reaching the door didn't involve much more than getting off the end of the bed.

She was standing just outside. He'd given her one of his T-shirts, and it looked massive on her. It fell almost to mid-thigh. The shoulders and sleeves hung. Even so, the oversize garment somehow managed to cling to her frame. Her face was scrubbed clean, and that ever-present lock of golden hair was falling softly against her cheek.

"Did I wake you?"

He wondered how just the sound of her voice could be so arousing, something that seemed to reach out and tease his flesh. *Did I wake you?* The words woke everything in him. He was sleeping in an old pair of cutoff corduroys. He was grateful he hadn't opted for a light pair of cotton boxers.

He wanted to answer her, but he didn't trust his voice. He managed a "no" that sounded more like a growl.

She simply stood there for a moment, her scent sweeping around him, seeming to touch raw, bare flesh, like the sound of her voice.

"Is there something wrong with me?" she asked at last.

"What?" Was she looking for a psychoanalyst, someone to assure her it was natural to have fears about things going bump in the night?

She smiled, lifting her chin, hair falling back in a cascade his fingers itched to touch. "I was curious, thinking there must be something wrong with me."

He leaned against the doorjamb, braced against himself, doing everything humanly possible to keep from reaching out for her.

"I don't know what you mean."

Her smile deepened. "Why aren't you trying to come on to me?"

Her words stunned him. He stared at her for a long moment, muscles taut and frozen, on fire inside.

"There's nothing wrong with you. You're incredible. You must know that."

"Then…?"

"You've been drinking."

"I'm not drunk."

"You're not your usual reserved self, either."

"I may not be the wildest party-goer in the world, but even for me… It was just three beers. I don't think I should be driving, but well, you know, they may suggest that you don't manipulate heavy machinery while under the influence, but I've never seen, 'Warning! Avoid sex at all costs!' on a beer bottle."

He wasn't sure whether to laugh, send her right back to the other cabin or drag her into his own as swiftly as humanly possible. He chose none of those options and instead folded his arms over his chest as he smiled at her.

Hell.

Who would ever have imagined that he would be standing in his own boat, trying to talk a beautiful woman out of wanting to have sex with him.

"You don't know me very well," he told her, then gave into temptation. He reached out, fingers sliding along the velvet tendril of hair as it caressed the delicate line of her cheek. His thumb stroked the softness there as he looked into her eyes.

You don't know me very well.

When had that stopped him before? How many times had he been out in the last year when it seemed like anyone gave a damn how well they knew each other?

Tonight, it mattered. But why?

Hell, she was twenty-eight. Not a kid, not naive.

But that wasn't what was stopping him. Naive didn't always have to do with knowledge. Her eyes held something deeper. Large, expressive, green and deep as a jungle, usually so careful, so reserved, searching. They held fields of right and wrong, dreams unspent, belief in humanity, art and beauty, truth and honesty. There was something about her that he longed to touch, ached to touch, feared to touch. As if she were fragile. She had never done anything like this before in her life, he knew. Once she had danced, touching the clouds. Then she had broken a bone and never reached into the air the same way again. Ben Trudeau had crushed her, years ago, and she hadn't trusted anyone since. He wasn't sure how he knew all this so well, with such certainty, but he did.

He could step away. He should. He had to, no matter how painful it would be, because it was the right thing to do. But then she spoke again.

"I know you well enough," she told him, the words soft and her eyes openly on his, emerald, sparkling with the strangest glimmer, a hint of tears.

She was still standing at least an inch away. Maybe not

even an inch, but they weren't actually touching. And yet he had never felt so sensually caressed before in his life. Her eyes stroked him. That scent of woman and subtle perfume swirled in the air as if it were tangible, and the warmth she emitted seemed to supplely wrap his flesh, then reach down with a grip of steel to sweep boldly right around his sex.

She wasn't even touching him, he reminded himself.

He should make one last stand. Remind her that she had been drinking.

"Quinn?" she asked tentatively.

Ah, hell. He wasn't that noble.

"Come here," he said softly.

She'd aroused him to the point of pain. He felt almost like a teenage kid in the back of a Chevy. He fought the fury wrestling within, pulled her tight against him. Now they were touching, her breasts crushed to him. He felt her ribs against the muscles of his chest, the flatness of her belly, the flare of her hips, the length of her legs. Her body was wicked, her scent pure sin, and, God help him, he was a sinner.

But he just held her for a moment, his breath hot over the top of her head, his chin brushing the softness of her hair. For a moment, he felt her heart beat. Felt the ragged rise and fall of her breath. Then he pulled away, lifted her chin and touched her lips with his own.

Her lips were wicked, too. Full, sensual. Seducing rather than giving, drawing him into a hot wet duel of tongues that took flight in an instant explosion of teased hunger. Her very kiss evoked visions beyond, hinted of deeper pleasure. How could a mouth that was so taut at times melt into the pure exotic?

They were touching.

The clothing between them was suddenly unbearable.

He drew away, long enough to try the buttons on the shirt, then rip half of them off with total impatience.

Hell. It was his shirt.

Shirt gone.

He couldn't shed his cutoffs fast enough.

Their clothing lay on the floor. Her eyes touched his as she slipped back into his arms.

Immense as a field of emeralds, green fire, alive, not hiding, and yet…

That vulnerability. The look that told him, despite her words, the feel of her flesh, that those things were there. *Something deeper.* A need for honesty, a giving that demanded some kind of honor in the midst of excess and desperation and pure instinctive drive and need.

Then they were really touching. Flesh on flesh. Fire and softness, supple vibrancy and heat. Tongues locked again in some desperate dance. His hands all over her. Breasts full and rounded, waist narrow, hips nicely flaring into a roundness of inspiration. He moved back, not breathing, he was so eager for her mouth. He thanked God that the cabin was small; one step, and he could simply fall against the bed, bringing her down.

Good Lord, but she was erotic, and he was drowning in her. Waves lapped against the boat, rocking them into each other in what began a carnal rhythm. He felt her fingers raking his shoulders, back, chest.

Now he was being touched. Really, really touched.

The length of her rubbed against him, evoking a groan that ground roughly from his lips. She was beneath him, and he was seeking to know everything about her. He was burning in all the fires of both heaven and hell, and glorying in the pain. He tasted the curve of her throat, devoured the fullness of her breasts, reveled in the womanliness of her midriff and abdomen, let passion flow as he brought his attentions ever lower, turned them ever more intimate. Her movements were somehow beyond erotic and passionate. He was half-dying in pure sensuality, and still there seemed to be grace and beauty in every twist and cry. Her fingers dug into his flesh, evoking greater arousal. The taste of her seemed to cause novas to explode in his head. He rose over her, straddled her, met her eyes again, emerald burning in the night. Lips parted, damp, breath coming so quickly, a look of astonished pleasure, almost awe, something that touched manhood, then went beyond ego, the body, and touched his soul. Her arms wrapped around him. Her eyes closed.

"Please," she whispered.

His lips found hers again. Locked in a taste of lava and honey, all that had come before along with all that would come next. His tongue teased, entered, thrust, drove and swept.

His body locked with hers, as well, his sex teasing, entering, thrusting, driving in, deep, deeper. Her legs wound around his hips. The waves lapped at the sides of the boat. The master bunk rocked and within her, he felt as if a tidal wave were sweeping over them, as if the ragged violence of a storm at sea were surging through him, into her, allowing them to touch as no one else ever had.

No one moved quite like a dancer, he discovered.

No one else had such flexibility.

No one could create such a raw sense of instinctive desire and need, nor fulfill it with such shattering finesse.

Their bodies were both sheened in a fine, sweet film of sweat. Muscles flexed, tautened, twisted. Breathing came in a rasp of sound as high as the wind, and sounds, ancient, carnal, came keening from them both. He was aware of her face, her beautiful face, eyes half-closed, lashes sweeping her cheeks. He was aware of the length of her, of himself, and then, of that intimate part of himself, as if everything around him was a wrap of hot, liquid silk, while his true self existed in only one spot, rigid as steel, the only true part of his being.

And then that exploding wave of pleasure, as if the ocean itself had erupted, as if the boat were rocking in a perfect storm, pitching, catapulting, shaking over and over again, and finally, after aeons, drifting into calmer waters, edging into the sand, catching there.

He lay draped over her, pulling her into his arms. His words caressed her forehead as he said, "Miss Mackay, I can assure you, there is absolutely nothing wrong with you. In fact, I don't think I've ever known anyone quite so right in my life."

She twisted slightly, eyes rising to his with that slight glint of vulnerability in them again, a hesitancy now, along with something so soft, trusting and awed that it awoke a new wave of sensation in him. Strange, but that simple look made him want to believe in his own invulnerability and strength.

She didn't speak, only touched his cheek, as if she were seeking words. "You really are quite awesome yourself," she whispered. "And honestly, I'm not drunk."

He smiled. "I know."

She nuzzled against him. "It's been so long…. I didn't even remember."

"It hasn't been that long for me, and there's nothing like you in my memory," he assured her.

She rolled slightly, looking at him a bit skeptically. "Really? Or is that something you say to everyone? I'm usually pretty good at spotting lines. I get to hear quite a lot of them, hanging around at Suede."

He shook his head. "It's not a line. But…there is a bit of a problem."

She drew the sheet up around her, as if his simple statement had brought out something defensive in her once again.

"What?" she murmured.

"I would definitely call this fraternization."

She smiled. "I'm afraid so."

"Can you lose your job?"

"Technically? Yes."

"That's serious."

"Indeed," she said gravely. She touched his face. Ran her fingers down his chest, then lower. She had the most elegant fingers.

Elegant...and talented.

"It's so serious that, well, just in case there are repercussions...I wouldn't mind fraternizing again. So I can really enjoy what I might get in trouble for."

"My dear Miss Mackay," he said very somberly. "We can fraternize all night, if that's what you want."

Her lips curved, her lashes fell, then rose. "That's what I want," she said very softly.

"The way you say it, there's absolutely nothing else I can do but my very best to fulfill your every desire," he assured her.

And when he kissed her again, he felt the rise of the ocean once more, the lapping of the waves, and the sheer, erotic beauty of the power and passion of a storm at sea.

When she first heard the knock on the cabin door, Shannon felt panic set in. She felt almost like a little kid. Caught.

Like Quinn had said, this was definitely fraternization.

At her side, he bounded out of the bunk, found his shorts and slipped them on. He looked back to note the panic in her eyes.

"Hey, it's all right. I do know people who have nothing to do with the studio, and they seldom search the boat when they visit." With a smile, he left her.

Shannon listened intently, but the closed door buffered a lot of sound. After finding the shirt she'd been wearing, she slipped into it, did up the remaining buttons, and went to the door, cracking it just a hair.

"No, I was up most of the night, but knowing what was going on with you, I thought you'd like to hear about it." There was another man in the cabin. Tall, nice looking, well built. He was wearing dockers, a cotton shirt open at the neck and a casual jacket.

Definitely not a uniform, but...

Something about him, his manner, maybe his air of confidence, of intensity, seemed to scream *cop*.

"Of course, and thanks," Quinn said. "Can I meet you on the patio in a few minutes?"

"Yeah."

The visitor left. Quinn turned back toward the cabin, and she opened the door.

"Just a friend of mine. I need to meet with him. You all right?" He smiled, pulling her into his arms. "You looked like the cat who ate the canary. Not all that sorry about eating the canary, either, but scared as hell about getting caught."

She smiled, but she felt uneasy. For some reason, his unknown visitor bothered her more than if it had been Gordon knocking at the door.

"I'm fine. Bright light, daytime."

"And you're glad you stayed?" he queried.

"I told you, I wasn't drunk."

He was tender, cupping her chin, brushing her lips. He was also anxious and in a hurry; she could feel it. Odd. She'd expected him to tell her that since it was Sunday and they'd already been fraternizing...well, she didn't work on Sundays, so...

But he didn't say any such thing.

"I'm not sure how long I'll be. Can I call you later?"

"Sure."

"I have to hop in the shower." He turned toward the tiny head.

"Your friend is a cop, isn't he?" she asked.

He turned slowly, frowning as he looked at her.

"Yes, he is. How did you know?"

"You can just tell."

"He won't be happy to hear he's that obvious."

"Tell him to slump some. His posture is too good."

"You think that will help?"

"Um, no. He just looks like a cop."

Quinn grinned. "Maybe that *is* good."

He slipped into the head and closed the door. She heard the water running and walked back to the other head, wondering if what she was doing was, boatwise, correct. Would she run out of hot water?

Apparently not. She was able to shower. When she stepped out, wrapped in a towel, he was already dressed in jeans and a deep blue polo shirt. He was sliding his wallet into his back pocket.

"I'll talk to you later, right?" he said. He sounded anxious. Either to get going, or he honestly wanted to see her later.

He paused before leaving, hands on her shoulders, eyes doing a sweep of her in the towel.

"You really are beautiful," he said, and his tone was husky. Deep. A grating that touched a lot of newly aroused instincts inside her.

He lingered, as if he honestly would have liked to stay. But then he broke away. "You're all right here alone, right?"

"Of course. I'll be heading home in a few minutes."

He nodded. "I'll talk to you later." He started up the steps, then turned back. "Make yourself at home in the galley, if you want to have coffee before you leave. And hit the lower lock on the cabin door."

"Right." She waved to him, and he went out.

To find out about something important.

Without him there, she felt uncomfortable, standing in

his cabin in a towel. She dressed quickly and was about to head out when she hesitated.

It actually felt strangely pleasant to be trusted alone in his personal space. She had been wondering if she should berate herself, feel some strange sense of having given in to something she shouldn't have. But she couldn't begin to remember a night that had felt so good. She'd probably never had one before.

And as for Quinn…

The more she was with him, the more she wanted to be with him. She liked his grin, his laugh, and he wasn't at all bad on the eyes. She liked the feel of his hands, and, most of all, she liked his quick sense of humor and the dimple when he smiled, the way that he talked.

She also rather liked the feel of being in his personal space, trusted to be alone. She hesitated, then decided that since it was Sunday, and she didn't have to be anywhere, maybe she *would* make some coffee before she left.

The pot and coffee were visible on the counter in the galley. Shannon measured some out and reminded herself that there was something going on with him. All he ever did was ask questions, and yet he denied being a cop. It was illegal, of course, to lie and say that you *were* a cop when you *weren't*, but undercover cops had to lie all the time about their jobs.

But him being an undercover cop didn't make any sense. Surely, she wasn't the only one who thought the circumstances of Lara's death had been suspicious. The police had openly questioned everyone. There had been an autopsy, a case file.

A case file that was now closed. Why not close it? One of the county's best forensic physicians had done the autopsy, they had been told. Human remains didn't lie. Lara's blood had been saturated with prescription drugs and alcohol. There was no denying it.

So…he couldn't be a cop, because the cops had no further interest in the case.

The coffee perked, and she found herself a cup. It was easy to find a small container of milk in the refrigerator, but a search through the cabinets didn't produce any sugar or its substitute, blue or pink, or even off-brand yellow.

"Have some balls, drink it black," she said aloud, as Gordon often did, especially when he had forgotten to buy sugar or cream for the studio.

She made a face. She liked what Rhianna called "evil chemical substitution" in her coffee. Maybe in one of the drawers?

She opened a drawer and found silverware, while another had some kitchen towels. A third drawer held knives and serving pieces. She moved on to the last kitchen drawer.

She didn't find sugar substitute.

She found papers.

Manila files lay atop a stack of receipts and other bits of paper. She hesitated, brows knit, as she stared into the drawer.

She should have closed the drawer, not having found what she wanted.

Except that she just might have found some answers to the mystery of Quinn O'Casey.

And it would have taken a better man—or woman— than she to turn away from what she saw.

Reaching into the drawer, she pulled out the folders. One was labeled Lara Trudeau. The other held the name Nell Durken.

Stunned, she stared at the names for several seconds. Then she set the second folder down to go through Lara's. There was a police report in the front of the folder. Behind it, numerous statements. An autopsy report. Everything.

She set the folder down and picked up the other. It was

organized in the same fashion, but the faces and names were different. Police report, autopsy, pages of statements...the arrest record of Nell's husband.

She heard someone whistling, then footsteps on the pier nearby. She started to shove the folders back into the drawer. They wouldn't go. There was something else in there. She pulled the drawer all the way out and discovered that a videotape was keeping her from stuffing the folders back in and closing the drawer. The tape was labelled with the name of the competition, Lara's name—and "Property of Miami-Dade, Homicide Department."

She adjusted the tape, then the papers, hurriedly putting everything back. She froze and waited, torn between guilt at prying and fury that the man was such a liar.

Fury took precedence.

Along with the fall of her ego, and a geyser of hurt.

Right. She was beautiful. And fascinating.

Humiliation held her at a dead standstill. Yes, she'd come here. Yes, she'd come straight to him. But a man who was pretending an interest in her because he was a lying son of a bitch who was *investigating* her had no right whatsoever to fall so willingly into that kind of intimacy with the person under investigation!

She hoped he was a cop.

She wished fervently that she could get his ass fired!

The sound of the footsteps, and the whistling, went right on by the boat. Whoever was walking by wasn't Quinn O'Casey.

He might come back any minute.

He might not come back for hours.

She gritted her teeth, longing to go through every single thing on the boat—to trash it, as a matter of fact.

A ringing sound stopped her. She paused, listening, then realized with a groan that it was her own cell phone, ringing from her purse.

She quickly dragged it out and surveyed the caller ID. Justin.

She punched in, feeling absurdly guilty over the night before—yes, this had certainly been fraternizing. And now, on top of having done something she should never, ever have done, she had been used. Pathetically.

Because she basically had no life, other than dance.

"Yes?"

She was breathless as she answered the phone.

"Shannon?" Justin said.

"Yes, of course."

"You sound funny."

"Do I? Sorry. I couldn't find the phone at first. Lost it down in the jungle of my purse, you know."

She heard his laughter on the other end. "That's a jungle, all right."

"Mmm. Right. Funny. So, what's up?"

"We were going to go to the beach. Right down the street from your place. We wanted to know if you wanted to come."

"We—who?"

"Just me, Sam, Jane and Rhianna. We've called Ella and Ben but haven't gotten a hold of them yet. Gordon answered the phone half-asleep and said something really nasty to me, like 'eat shit and die,' because I woke him on a Sunday. But you're usually up…so…hey, how about it? Come join your staff for a day of cleansing sun and sand, huh?"

"Oh, wow, Justin, I don't know…it's been a long week."

"So you don't want to see us, uh? I understand."

"No, I'm happy to see you. But—"

"Come on, please? We'll come by and hound your house until you do."

"No!"

"We will. You'll have to call the cops, and then the studio will suffer. There will be more horrible publicity, and your teachers will be in jail."

"Don't come to the house! Give me an hour and I'll join you."

"Really?"

"Yes."

"You swear? This isn't just to blow me off or anything? 'Cause we will come to the house. We're feeling like a lonely group of kids, you know? In need of our fearless leader so we can have some fun with our lives."

"Oh, yeah, sure," she said dryly. "Fun. I'll come—I promise. Just don't come and haunt my house. We can come back…here, if you want, just give me some time right now."

"Sure, cool. We'll be on the public side of the hotel, straight down the street from your place."

"I'll be there."

Shannon clicked off and slowly put the phone back into her purse.

She should go. Because she was far too mature and sane to trash his residence.

Besides, she had discovered what she needed to know.

She had been right all along.

He wasn't what he purported to be.

So just what exactly was he? He'd taken his wallet, so she couldn't check his ID. She could, of course, search his desk, even see if she could get on the computer.

She shook her head, wanting to get out of Nick's parking lot before her car was discovered there. But then she hesitated and turned around, going back to check the desk drawer beneath the computer.

Pens, pencils, erasers, disks, paper…

She opened another drawer, a file drawer. All she needed to see was the header on the first piece of paper.

"Whitelaw and O'Casey, Private Investigations"

There followed an address in Key Largo, phone number, e-mail, and a state of Florida licensing number.

"That son of a bitch!" she said out loud.

She slammed the drawer, burning.

Oh, yeah, the man sure as hell knew how to investigate.

She started to turn away, wondering if she could actually drive with the rage she was feeling.

Then she hesitated, curious, and turned back to the desk. Picking up the phone behind the computer, she dialed the number for the agency. It rang and rang.

What? Did both Quinn and Whitelaw, whoever he was, suck so bad at what they did that they couldn't even afford an answering machine?

It was Sunday. What the hell had she been expecting?

She was startled when the phone was suddenly answered. By a human being.

"Whitelaw and O'Casey."

Her mind went blank.

"Hello? Whitelaw and O'Casey."

"Sorry, sorry—is Mr. O'Casey in?"

"I'm sorry. He's on vacation. Perhaps you'd like to leave a message for Mr. Whitelaw?"

"Ah, no, thanks. I'll call back. It's Mr. O'Casey I need to speak with."

"Are you from the Quantico office? I can reach him if need be."

"No, no, it's a personal matter. Thank you."

She hung up quickly.

Quantico?

He wasn't just a private investigator. He was FBI. Or had been. Maybe not. Lots of people lived in Quantico, Virginia.

That was bull, and she knew it. He either was, or had been, FBI.

Pleasant, laid-back fisherman, diver, charter manager?

Like hell.

All she knew for certain at that moment was that he had used her.

Tears suddenly stung her eyes, and she brushed them away in self-fury. At the steps, she turned back and looked into the cabin.

"I don't know exactly what you are, Mr. O'Casey, except an absolute asshole!"

She left the boat, forgetting to hit the lock, and she didn't look back.

CH**A**PTER 11

"There's probably no association at all," Jake told Quinn, looking bleary as he sipped from a mug of coffee.

They weren't outside on the patio that morning. They were in Nick's kitchen. Nick and his wife were still sleeping.

Jake kept a boat moored at the pier, as well, but in the past months, the rocking of the boat at night had kept his wife, fellow officer Ashley Montague Dilessio, awake, so they'd been sleeping in Ashley's old place at Nick's, an apartment off the side of the restaurant/dwelling.

Quinn was certain that the fact Ashley was away in Jacksonville was wearing on Jake's nerves as much as his schedule was. But despite the fact that he was obviously longing to jump into bed, he was taking the time to bring Quinn up-to-date on the latest.

Another corpse.

"Duarte says it's fresh. He knows his stuff, and I've seen them when they've been in the water awhile. This one hasn't," Jake said. "He probably won't get to the autopsy until tomorrow sometime, but you know him. He's a worker—he was out there when the call came."

"Did he say anything based on the preliminary?" Quinn asked.

"Rich, at a guess. I'll give you my notes with the exact details, but for the moment…Rolex. Necklace with enough gold to sink a ship and a diamond heart with enough carats to make many a woman green with envy."

"Hispanic, Anglo, black, Asian?"

"Or mark here for 'other'—whatever other may be?" Jake asked dryly. "I don't know yet. Dark. Possibly Hispanic. Hell, down here she could have been blond and still Hispanic. Half the South Americans I know look as if they came from Germany. She was dark. Dark hair, dark eyes, deep tan."

"Any sign of a struggle?"

"She was naked, but if she was raped, there aren't any bruises or signs of violence. Just tracks on her arms."

"So she was a junkie?"

"I don't know about a junkie. But she'd done some drugs in her day."

"Did she match up with any recent missing persons reports?" Quinn asked.

"Not so far. All I can say for certain right now is that a young woman's body washed up on the beach. According to Duarte, she probably died last night. She'd been in the water, so she might have been dumped in from a boat. She showed signs of drug abuse, and it's likely she died from an overdose. As soon as I find out more, I'll keep you informed. I still can't figure how the deaths of two women from prescription drugs can tie in with the illegal narcotics scene, but…hell, like you, I think it's odd."

"Odd enough to reopen Lara Trudeau's case?"

Jake winced. "She wasn't my case and it isn't my call. I'll have to bring it to my superiors, and to do that, I'm going to have to give them more than another drug death in the same vicinity. As a county employee, I have a lot of rules and regs to follow. You can get away with a lot that I can't."

"Yeah, but you can call a hell of a lot of shots *I* can't," Quinn reminded him.

Jake shrugged. "The whole damn thing is crazy. It's sad, but true—there's a whole high-flying scene, a lifestyle, on the beach. Drugs flow, no matter what the cops do. Every year, people die of abuse and overdoses, or violence escalated by uppers and downers. It happens. Most cases aren't related. Hell, most of them are random. But anyway, I know your interest. If you want, I'll call you for the autopsy. Duarte won't mind having you there."

"Yeah, I want, thanks."

"You all right? You look as ragged as I feel. Who's down at the boat? Someone I know? Hell, someone you know, at least? I hope."

Quinn angled his head as he stared at his friend sharply. "Someone I know. Let's leave it at that for now, huh?"

"Yep." Jake rose. "I don't know what the hell I'm doing, drinking coffee, when all I want is a shower and bed."

Quinn stood, as well. "You're right—coffee probably isn't the best thing for you to be swilling right now. Thanks. I appreciate you letting me in."

"It may mean nothing."

"It probably does. Thanks anyway."

"You bet. I'll see you tomorrow."

"Hope Ashley gets home."

"She's due in late this afternoon."

"Good. I'll see you later."

Quinn let himself out from the side door, facing the parking lot. He could see Shannon's car was gone.

He'd expected her to leave, hadn't he? After all, he'd had no idea how long he was going to be gone. And the way Shannon felt about being seen with a student...

Fraternizing.

He'd been anxious to talk to Jake, and just as anxious to get him away from the boat, since he hadn't wanted to make her uncomfortable.

And still…

A sense of unease plagued him as he headed back to his boat.

"Now that's bad," Justin said.

They were lying on the sand, the group of them, slicked with lotion, feeling the sun, facing the water.

Justin—who had brought his own beach chair—was doing a lot more people watching than loafing.

"What?" Jane demanded.

Justin pointed. "That is just way too much flesh to be seen."

"Justin, that isn't nice," Rhianna told him.

"You're right. Not nice at all—it's major-league *nasty.*"

"Hey, who told you that you look so great in a bathing suit, anyway?" Jane teased him.

"I may not look great, but I don't look like a beached whale."

Shannon took a look at the woman walking along the shoreline. She was definitely a little large for her suit, but the idea that everyone on the beach looked like a swimsuit model was an invention of the movies and nothing to do with reality.

"Justin, you're being cruel," she told him. "The beach belongs to everyone."

"Yeah, you're picking on women," Jane drawled.

"No, I'm not. There, over there. Look at that old geezer, thinking he's sexy 'cause he's got a package in those skimpy shorts. He's got more skin flapping around than a basset hound."

"Would you stop!" Shannon said.

"I can't. The woman's back. Oh no! She's bending over. I'm blinded by the pure white reflection of her ass."

"Justin…" Rhianna moaned right along with Shannon.

Cruel, Shannon thought, and yet, Justin was funny. He was trying to make them laugh. He wanted the world to get back to normal.

Jane decided to take care of him. She moved her sunglasses down her nose, staring at him. "Since it's so easy to see over your head, Justin, I just got a good view myself."

"Fine, make fun of the poor vertically challenged man," Justin said in mock affront.

"Thank God," Rhianna said, "that at least the cops aren't still crawling all over the place. Those poor guys trudging through the sand in their uniforms and dress shoes."

"The cops?" Shannon said.

"Rhianna," Sam groaned. "We weren't going to say anything, remember?"

Shannon sat up straight, slipping her sunglasses from her nose, staring at them all. "Why were the cops crawling all over the beach?"

"A body washed up," Sam told her. "Someone must have found the corpse at like two or three in the morning. A whole stretch of the beach was closed off until ten or eleven, when they took her away. They were still talking to people until about five or ten minutes before you got here."

"A body?" Shannon said.

"Not a dancer," Justin said quickly.

"How on earth can you know that?" Jane demanded.

Justin sighed. "I heard them talking. She was some kind of ritzy socialite. People who saw her were talking about all the jewelry she had on. Not a stitch of clothing, but tons of jewelry. She had track marks, though. Probably some hot little Latin mama, too into the scene."

"Found with two tons of jewelry," Rhianna mused. "Well, she wasn't killed and then robbed, anyway."

"Who said she was killed?" Jane demanded.

Rhianna sat up, staring at Jane. "What? She accidentally took off all her own clothes and lay down on the beach and died? That's ridiculous."

Yes, ridiculous, Shannon thought, but no more so than the thought that Lara Trudeau would take that many pills when she was dancing. *Knowingly* take them, at any rate.

"Oh, God," Justin groaned. "Read the newspapers. Someone dies every day. We can't take each and every one of them to heart. We're getting over Lara. Let's not start obsessing over a stranger, okay?"

"Do we know that she's a stranger?" Jane asked softly.

Justin sighed. "I don't really know anything," he said. "But come on, think about it. We can't take the woes of the whole world on our shoulders. We're all punch-drunk right now, over Lara and all. We're trying to have a beautiful day."

"Right," Shannon said dryly. "It was rude of that woman to be murdered where we were planning on having fun."

"Definitely murdered, huh?" Jane said.

"Hey, none of us is a cop," Justin said. "We can talk to Doug O'Casey next time he comes in. He should know."

"He's a patrolman—not in homicide," Jane said.

"So? He's got friends. He'll find out the scoop for us," Justin assured her.

Yes, and if he doesn't, his brother can, Shannon thought. His brother, the private eye. Who was apparently there to watch them. All of them.

Why?

And who had hired him?

What did someone else know that they didn't?

Rhianna rose, dusting the sand from her butt. "I think I've had enough of the sun. I'm going to call it quits, guys. See you in the morning."

Jane stood, too. "Justin, thanks for getting us all together. It was a good idea, but I think I'm a little baked, too."

Justin rose with a sigh. "Same here, so…so long."

"I'm going to hang around a while longer," Sam told them. He had laced his hands behind his head to lie back and now looked as if he was caught in the middle of an abdominal exercise. "You should stay, Justin."

"No, he can't—he picked us both up. He has to take us home," Jane told him. "See you tomorrow, Shannon."

She shrugged and waved tiredly. Jane and Sam were the studio's rising stars, willing to work hard. She was just feeling absurdly tired.

Disheartened. Hurt. Crushed, actually. She'd thought she might be acquiring a life with a dynamite guy…and she was just being investigated.

Thoroughly, she thought, with a sense of pained amusement.

"Shannon?" Jane repeated.

"Sure. See you in the morning. Ten-ish."

Jane smiled and waved. Sam lay back in the sand. Shannon remained seated, hugging her knees to her chest, staring out at the waves. She did love the sound of the waves crashing on the sand. She loved the water, the sky, even the salty scent that clung to the air. It seemed bizarre that so much beauty could evoke so much violence.

Suddenly, at her side, Sam gave a deep sigh. "Come on. Let's walk down there."

She started, feeling guilty. She hadn't allowed herself to even form the thought in her head, but she wanted to see where the woman had been found.

"That's morbid, isn't it?" she asked Sam.

"Just natural. Think about it. This isn't far from the studio—not to mention your house." He jumped to his feet and offered her a hand. She stood, and he slipped an arm around her shoulders as they walked down the beach. "We'd all agreed we weren't going to say anything to you, and of course we hoped the cops wouldn't come back."

"Sam, it's sweet of you guys to try to protect me from bad news, but hey, I've got a TV and I do read the paper," she told him.

"No, but Justin was right. You've been so upset about Lara. We wanted you to have a nice, death-free day at the beach. It didn't quite turn out that way, huh?"

She gave him a quick squeeze. "Like I said, it was nice of you guys to try. I'm pretty tough, though, you know."

"Yeah?" He looked at her, a grin curving his lips. "Most of the time, sure. You run a tight ship, you've earned everyone's respect. But a really tough cookie...? I don't know."

"Why do you say that?"

His smile deepened. "I shouldn't encourage you. Because you'd just be new competition for Jane and me. But, if you were really tough, you'd go out there and compete again."

She groaned. "Sam, my ankle will never be what it was."

"Bull. An orthopedist might say that, but it's been years. Your ankle is plenty good."

She was going to ask him to drop it all and leave it dropped, but she didn't have a chance. Sam stopped, causing her to halt along with him. "There."

Actually, there was nothing left "there." The body had been taken away. It had been found on the sand, and there was still an area roped off with crime tape, and some Miami Beach officers hanging around. Two crime-scene specialists were combing the sand inch by inch, and the crime tape was surrounded by the curious. People stared, questioned the cops guarding the area and moved on.

"What are we doing?" Shannon murmured. "It's like slowing down to stare at the scene of an accident."

"But we all do it," he murmured. "People were talking when we first showed up. The kids who stumbled on her first weren't frightened or horrified. They were excited—they kept talking to everyone and anyone. They were celebrities for a day. Weird, huh?"

"Well, thankfully, the poor woman has been taken away," Shannon said.

"Oh, yeah. Can you imagine a corpse lying out on the sand in this heat all day? The kids were talking…. She couldn't have been dead that long, but crabs were already munching on her toes."

"Ugh. Let's go," Shannon said.

She turned, and Sam followed. But as they walked away, she looked back.

Two men were coming through the crowd. Shannon recognized them both. One was Quinn's early-morning visitor.

The other was Quinn.

The first man showed a local cop his ID, then introduced Quinn, who shook hands with the officer. Then both men began to ask questions.

"What's the matter?" Sam asked, stopping.

"Nothing," she said quickly, and kept walking. She didn't know why, but she didn't want Sam seeing their new student at the scene.

"You sure?"

"Yeah, yeah, just a case of the shivers. Let's go."

She quickened her pace. When she had a chance, she glanced back again.

Apparently the men hadn't come alone. They were with a very attractive, very pregnant woman who was carrying a sketch pad. Quinn had an arm around her. He was talking to her softly, and he seemed deeply concerned. She looked up, flashing him a smile. Then she slipped under the crime-scene tape, hunkered down and started to draw.

"What the hell is it?" Sam asked, looking at her with concern.

"Race you to the blankets!" Shannon said, then started to tear down the beach. She was fast, and she knew it. Sam took the bait, flying after her.

When they reached their spot, she sat down first. He followed her, gasping and panting.

"I won," she told him.

Still panting, he stared at her and smiled.

"What?" she demanded.

"Oh, yeah. That ankle is bad. Like hell."

She groaned. "Where's your car?"

"A block from your place."

"Walk me home, then. We can cool off for a while, and then I'll make us something to eat."

There were times when Quinn was definitely glad he was no longer a cop or with the Bureau.

There really were no such things as regular hours, no matter what some schedule said. Of course, for him, life was still that way, but at least he could step back and take time when he wanted.

He'd intended to be doing just that now, he remembered. He should have been on a beach, all right, but a beach in the Bahamas. Cool breezes blowing. An icy brew in his hands. Kids playing in the sand. Calypso music coming from somewhere. Salt eroding the tangle of cobwebs that held all the disillusioned nightmares of his mind.

Then again, had he been in the Bahamas, there wouldn't have been last night on his boat.

And he wouldn't be with Jake and Ashley, wondering what the hell Shannon Mackay had done on his boat after he'd left and staring at a strip of sand where a corpse had washed up from Biscayne Bay.

A fresh one, thank God, as the assistants down at the

M.E.'s office had been saying. Duarte had spent the week so swamped, he wasn't cutting into his newest arrival until the following day. Jake was the head homicide detective on the case, and he'd decided to take another look at the scene in daylight. Quinn had come along, but not until he'd returned to the boat and made a thorough inspection of it, ascertaining that nothing was missing, despite the fact that Shannon had taken the time to make coffee, then left in such haste that she hadn't bothered locking the door. Meanwhile, Ashley had managed to get out on an earlier flight, so Jake had picked her up, and after this quick look at the crime scene, they were going to head over to the morgue. Ashley was going to do a sketch of the woman's face for the paper, hoping to find someone who could identify her.

The cops didn't want a photo of her; they wanted her looking as she would have looked when she was alive.

Ashley had been a rare find for Jake Dilessio—a woman with two loves in her life: art and police work. She never tired. Despite the fact that she was expecting their first child within the month—and looked like she was walking around with a bowling ball under her shirt—she was still intent on work. They were both going to take some time when the baby was born, but until then, as Ashley said with a shrug, what did she have to do except sit around and feel huge? Later, as they drove to the morgue, Quinn couldn't help but ask her if sketching corpses didn't ever give her a queasy stomach, at the least.

"You don't ever get over an unnatural death being horrible," she told Quinn, leaning over the seat to look at him as they drove. "But I've had a great pregnancy. I don't feel ill at all—never had a second of morning sickness. And my work is important. Both Jake and I are creating a better world for the child we're bringing into it." She smiled, glancing at Jake, who was driving. "We can't solve all the ills in the universe, but every little bit helps, right?"

"Ashley, you should be cloned," Quinn told her.

She flashed him a smile. Beautiful and delicate, she could also be tough as nails.

"Thanks." She fell silent, then said, "Whatever the circumstances…you know we're glad to have you back down here, right?" She sounded awkward, but she wasn't the type to pry. "Hey, if Nell Durken hadn't come to you, and you hadn't kept such meticulous records when you tailed her husband, he might have gotten away with it."

"He hasn't gone to trial yet," Quinn reminded her. He frowned. She might not feel queasy, but now, when he thought about the Durken case, *he* did.

They reached the morgue. Jake and Ashley flashed their badges, and an assistant came out to escort them into one of the rooms, where the victim from the beach was brought out.

According to Duarte's initial estimation, she hadn't been dead twenty-four hours yet.

Amazing what the sea and the life within it could do in that time.

And still, certain facts were obvious.

She had been young, beautiful and, apparently, rich. Her nails—on the untouched fingers—were elegantly manicured. What remained of her makeup was expertly applied and apparently long lasting. Her hair was rich, thick, dark, well tendered. High cheekbones graced her face, and, when her mouth was opened, it appeared that her teeth were perfect. Bone structure, muscle tone…everything indicated that she'd had every opportunity in life.

Ashley was already sketching.

The assistant provided gloves, but their cursory inspection provided little additional information, except that they noted the needle tracks in her arms.

"A user…but she hadn't moved beyond her arms," Jake said.

Quinn shook his head. "Her physical condition appears to have been good otherwise."

"She couldn't have been into it long," Jake agreed.

A little while later, Ashley told them that she was finished.

Her sketch wasn't of a smiling, cheerful face but rather one at rest. It was excellent, and far better for a loved one to discover in the newspaper than a photo of what that once-beautiful face had become.

After leaving the morgue, they headed back to the spot where the body had been found. Since the crime-scene detectives were still busy searching the sand, they kept their distance, talking to the patrol officers who had canvassed the area, asking questions.

A delicate matter. The body had actually been found on hotel property, though no one at the hotel recognized Ashley's sketch. Or if they did, they didn't let on.

Jake noted the proximity of the spot where the body had been found to the studio—and to Shannon's house.

He said goodbye to Jake and Ashley, assuring them he would get back to the marina fine, and started walking.

He rang the bell at Shannon's house. He heard movement near the door, apparently someone looking through the peephole, but it wasn't opened.

Then he heard people speaking. Whispering. He leaned his ear against the door.

"What's the matter with you? Why don't you open it?" A man's voice. Quinn recognized it as Sam Railey's.

"It's Sunday—I'm off." Shannon's reply was terse.

He shouldn't have come here, Quinn realized. There was that fraternization thing.

"Well, open the door and tell him that," Sam said.

"No. Just let him go away."

"That guy has a thing for you, I think." Sam sounded teasing.

"He's a student."

"Screw that! He's hardly a student. He won't last. The guy gives new meaning to the term 'two left feet.'"

True but painful, Quinn thought wryly.

"Let's get away from the door," Shannon said.

Great. Thanks for defending me, Quinn thought.

He rang the bell again.

"Oh, for God's sake," Sam muttered.

"All right, all right."

Quinn stepped back just in time. The door flew open.

Shannon stared at him. She didn't simply look angry that he had shown up at her house when a fellow teacher was there.

She looked lethal.

Her emerald-green eyes were harder and icier than he had ever seen them. Her body language was downright hostile. She was stiffer than a concrete pillar.

And she didn't ask him in but left him standing on the porch.

Sam, on the other hand, looked highly amused. "Hey, Quinn," he said cheerfully.

"What do you want, Mr. O'Casey?" Her tone could freeze fire.

"I came by to see how you were." He glanced at Sam. "I knew where Miss Mackay's house was because I dropped her off the other night." He turned to Shannon. "After everything…I was in the neighborhood. I just thought I'd see how you were doing."

"You were just in the neighborhood, were you?" There was saccharine in the query.

Then he knew. Something hit the pit of his stomach like a rock. She'd gone through his place. Well, he'd been a real idiot, leaving her there, with what was in his drawers.

"Are you talking about what happened on the beach? Some kids found a body there," Sam said.

Apparently she hadn't said anything to anyone else yet. That was a relief. Not that his real line of work was a national secret.

"I heard," he said evenly, staring at Shannon.

"Sam and I were on our way out," Shannon said.

"Oh?" She had on a terry cover-up. Sam was in cutoffs. They were both dusted with sand.

"We were?" Sam said. "I thought you were going to cook?"

Shannon glared at him. He stared back, as if really confused. "Well, hell, don't leave our new student out here while we figure this out." He backed away, smiling. "Come in, Quinn. Or Mr. O'Casey. You know, according to the rules, we're supposed to call our students Mr. or Mrs. or Miss all the time. I think those rules must have been written a while ago, because they don't even refer to a possible Ms. We've always gone by first names, though. What do you think?"

"Quinn is just fine," he said, taking advantage of the opportunity Sam afforded him and stepping inside.

He and Shannon needed to talk. Somehow.

"Sam," Shannon said warningly beneath her breath.

"Come on, Shannon, aren't you even curious? Quinn can tell us all about the case."

"You two feel free to chat," she said. By her tone, she didn't mean it at all. "I'm taking a shower. Sam, we *are* going out. Mr. O'Casey, we'd love to invite you, but I'm sure you've heard that we have a studio policy? We don't want anyone feeling we're giving one student more attention than another."

She'd left him little choice. He managed to grin awkwardly.

"Actually, my ride disappeared. I thought I could get a return favor, and you could give me a lift home."

Let her handle that one politically.

"Shannon, let's not be idiotic," Sam pleaded. "Don't you need to talk to Quinn about a charter boat for the Gator Gala, anyway?"

"I don't think Mr. O'Casey has what we're going to need."

"Oh, but I do. Really. And I can get you the best deal in the area," he told her.

She stared back at him. Her eyes were so hard that he could almost hear the word *Liar!* screamed on the air.

"I've been thinking, and I'm not sure we should do business with a student," she said.

"I swear to you, I can give you a charter you won't believe," he said. He leaned a hand against the door frame, and she seemed to understand that, short of having a few honest words right there and then, with Sam present, he wasn't leaving.

"Gordon would want you to hear him out," Sam said pleasantly.

Quinn realized that Sam was actually savoring the situation. He had the look of the devil in his eyes.

"I still need to shower. Sam, if you want, you can rinse off in the guest bath. And, Mr. O'Casey, you can..." Her voice trailed off. He knew exactly what she thought he should be doing with himself. "Have a seat. Wait, if you must."

She spun around, heading for her room.

"Hang tight," Sam said, casting Quinn a sympathetic look. "We'll be ready in a minute."

He, too, disappeared.

Quinn wandered out to the Florida room. It was a day when autumn was becoming more and more obvious—even in Florida. The temperatures were still high, but darkness was coming earlier and earlier.

He leaned against the wall, looking out into the back-

yard, with its rich growth of palms, key limes, shrugs, cro-
tons and more. A stone trail had once cut a swath through
the foliage, but it was largely overgrown now. A gentle
breeze lifted leaves and bent branches.

And yet, as he stared out, he thought that far more than
the breeze was moving in one area of the yard.

He tensed, watching. He had the eerie feeling he was
being watched back.

Lights were on in the house. The shadows of coming
darkness were protecting the yard. And…yes, someone
was there.

He swore, and reached for the knob of the back door.
Nothing happened when he twisted it, and he realized the
door was double bolted.

He twisted the locks with a jerk and threw the door
open with a bang.

Branches snapped, as someone began to run.

Quinn burst out of the house in pursuit.

CHAPTER 12

Gordon Henson appreciated his Sunday afternoons.

Not that he worked all that hard at his studio anymore. He'd banked on grooming Shannon for the job of managing the place, and he'd chosen well. He could actually have retired already, but he had discovered that he didn't want to. In the past few years, he'd actually begun to make money—real money.

But he couldn't do it without his involvement in the studio.

Not to mention the fact that he would never fall out of love with dance. He didn't teach anymore, but he attended the parties and certainly spent time down at the club. A nice lifestyle. He'd been married once, discovered it wasn't for him, and despite the fact that time was passing, he didn't feel the need for a permanent relationship. Rather, he liked the lifestyle on the beach and in the nearby clubs, where just about everything went. There were so many people out there. So many colors, nationalities, heights, weights, creeds, whatever. Even sexual mores. Gordon was open to anything in life.

He loved the studio, the club, his work week.

But he loved his Sundays, too.

Sometimes Sundays meant spending some off time with his employees. He would have Ella Rodriguez plan a picnic at a park, maybe up in Broward, where there was a small pretense of a water park. He also liked to get his teachers up on skates—roller, in-line, or ice—because they helped with movement and balance. Sometimes he used his Sundays very privately, having found an intriguing person to date.

And sometimes, after an eventful week like this one, he liked to sit in his condo and catch up on movies he hadn't seen, or watch an old classic.

Years ago, he'd fallen in love with dance by watching Fred and Ginger, Cyd Charisse, Donald O'Connor, Buddy Ebsen, Gene Kelly, or any one of the men or women who embodied the grace and spirit of dance. Today he'd chosen to watch "Singin' in the Rain." He would never tire of it.

Gene Kelly was moving across the screen with his own particular brand of sheer genius when the phone rang.

He ignored it, letting the machine pick up. When it did, the caller hung up, then rang again. Persistently.

Gordon swore, clicked the hold button on the remote and answered the phone.

"Hello?"

"You got a good thing going there, at that studio."

"Yes?"

"That's it. You got a good thing going at that studio. A really good thing. Remember that. Remember that at all times."

Then the phone went dead in Gordon's hand, and he stared at it, feeling a bead of perspiration break out on his flesh, along with an eerie sense of chill.

"What the hell is going on?" Shannon demanded, bursting out of her room and flying to the back porch.

The door to the yard was open.

It was like inviting the shadows in.

Sam came running up behind her.

"See, look at that. You were so rude, the poor fellow freaked out and ran away."

She shot a furious glare at him. "Sam, something obviously happened out there. Or there was someone out there."

"Then, let's go see, shall we?" He looked at her raised brows and reached out a hand. "What's the matter with you? What are you afraid of?"

"Um, maybe somebody out there with a gun or a knife."

He laughed. "Why on earth would anyone be running around your yard with a gun or a knife?"

"I think there was a body on the beach this morning, and that we all need to be careful," she said sternly.

"Good thing you've got a muscle-bound student to go after things in the dark, huh?" he said slowly.

"Check the front door—let's make sure it's locked before we head out the back," she said.

Through the yard, out to the street, down the street, through another yard.

His elusive prey remained just in front of him.

Finally they hit the beach.

Darkness had crept its fingers over the daylight, so as close as he got, Quinn couldn't quite ascertain the physical makeup of the person he was chasing.

Then, at last, he was almost upon them.

A woman. A small one.

He collided with her body in a tackle, bringing her down into the sand. She didn't scream; her breath escaped her body with a "whooshing" sound. Then he was on top of her, staring down into her face.

Along with making Sam check that the front door was locked, Shannon grabbed her tennis racket. They went out the back. She'd always loved her yard so much. Now, it seemed that every tree, every bush and branch, was hiding something.

"I guess we should look through the foliage?" Sam said.

She shook her head. "If Quinn saw something, someone, out here—which I assume he did—he's chased them out."

"Great. We've checked the front door, we have that lethal tennis racket for protection, and we're just going to stand here?"

She scowled at him.

A rustling sound came from behind them. They both swung around.

It was Mr. Mulligan, who lived next door, with Harry, his retriever.

"Evening, Shannon!" he called out. "Hello there, Sam," he added, since the two men had met before, when Shannon had invited the group over for dinner.

"Hi, Mr. Mulligan," Sam said.

The neighbor smiled at them, then stared at the tennis racket Shannon was holding as if it were a baseball bat.

"You've taken up tennis again? Good for you."

"We think there was someone in the backyard, Mr. Mulligan," Sam said. "A friend is chasing them."

"Here? In this neighborhood?" Mr. Mulligan seemed to think that was unlikely. "Must have been Harry, here." The dog, who loved people far too much ever to be an effective guard dog, trotted over to Shannon.

"Hi, fellow," she said, scratching his ears.

"You know, young lady, I'm right next door, if you ever need help," the older man admonished her.

"I know that, thank you," she said, looking at the man, who—with his wrinkles and bald pate—might have been a hundred and five, in age *and* in weight.

"You just call me any time. Harry, come on in."

The dog trotted obediently back to his master, and they walked back to their own house.

"This is kind of silly," Sam said to Shannon when Mr. Mulligan was out of sight. "Wherever Quinn went, whoever he went after, he's gone, and we don't know where."

"Maybe we should call the police," Shannon murmured.

"Maybe you really did scare the guy off. You *were* awfully rude to him."

"I'm the studio manager, remember? Don't correct me or argue with me in front of students."

"Sorry," Sam said. "Hey! Here he comes. And he's not alone."

Quinn was returning, entering the yard from the sidewalk. He was accompanied by a skinny waif with a cascade of brown hair flowing down her back. She was in jeans and a tank top. Young. Very young. And pretty. With brown eyes that eclipsed her face.

Shannon and Sam just stood, watching.

The girl seemed to be uncomfortable, accompanying Quinn. She was very young, yet it was obvious that she knew him.

Shannon couldn't help staring at him with calculating eyes.

"Shannon, Sam, this is Marnie. Shannon, she's been living in your backyard."

"What?" She focused accusingly on the girl.

"I didn't hurt anything!" the girl said quickly. "I wasn't going to break in or take anything. It's just that it's so overgrown back there.... Some of the trees actually make a little shelter. Honestly, I wasn't going to steal anything."

Shannon thought the girl was telling the truth. "But don't you have a home? Shouldn't you be in school?" she asked.

"Runaway," Sam murmured.

"No, I'm not. Look, my dad died when I was a kid," the girl explained, as if she were now well on her way to old age. "My mother remarried. And he…"

Shannon breathed out a soft expletive, staring at Quinn. "She needs to go to the police. He should be prosecuted!"

"He didn't do anything. Yet," the girl explained. And she did sound as if she were almost one hundred. "You don't understand. My mom was alone a long time. And, like, desperate. And he made her think that…that I was coming on to him. He's not all that old—younger than my mom. And she wants him more than me, and it was just…I had to get out. I graduated from high school last June. I'm over eighteen. It's my right to be out. It's the truth. You can check it all out."

"But you can't…you can't just live in people's yards," Shannon said. She still felt somewhat confused, but sorry, too. There was something about the girl that was defiant; and also truthful. She was like a puppy, thrown out into the cold, determined to adopt the attitude of a Doberman. "Let's go inside," Shannon said. "You can tell us more."

"No," Quinn said firmly.

Shannon stared at him, startled.

"We're going to go see a friend of mine. A cop."

"I don't want you to arrest her," Shannon protested.

"I'm not a cop," Quinn reminded her wearily.

"He's not arresting me," the girl explained, as if she felt obliged to come to Quinn's defense. "He's taking me to some shelter. My, uh, stuff is still in your yard, though."

"Oh." Shannon stared at Quinn again.

"We're going to check out Marnie's story," he said firmly. "Sam, follow what's left of that little trail, and you'll find a book bag. Her things are in it."

"Okay," Sam said, though it was evident he was wondering why he was the one who should look for the book bag, when Marnie was standing right there.

"I'm not going to bolt on you," Marnie said wearily.

"Sam would love to get the book bag for you," Quinn said to her.

"Yeah, sure, I'm going right now," Sam said.

"Quinn…" Shannon murmured. Strange. She'd actually had a few jealous thoughts when she'd first seen him with the girl, but now she felt a protective surge sweep through her. She'd been lucky. She had loving parents who would die before hurting her, and they'd never doubted her word when she'd been growing up. This little waif…

"We're going to the police station," Quinn said firmly. "I have a very good friend who is a victim's advocate. She's wonderful. She'll help Marnie get settled safely."

The girl suddenly smiled, staring at Shannon. "I've seen you dance!" she told her. She flushed. "In fact, that's how I found your yard. I watched you through the windows at the studio. I would trade half my life to move like that."

"You want to dance?"

"More than anything."

"All of our first lessons are free," Shannon said.

The girl stared at Quinn.

He let out a deep sigh. "Tonight, you come and meet my friend, Annie. I'll see to it that you can get to the studio for a lesson. In fact, I'll buy you a guest pass with a bunch of lessons, all right?"

"Really?"

The tiny face lit up. She was more than just pretty. She looked so young, like a child just given the best birthday present in the world.

"Yeah, really." He sounded gruff.

"I don't have a car," Marnie said softly.

"That's the kind of thing Annie can help you with," he explained.

"Actually, I can't even drive."

"Annie will see that you get where you need to go,"

Quinn told her. "Hell, don't worry about it. We'll get you back down here."

Sam returned with the bag. "Here you go," he said, smiling at the girl.

"Thanks." Marnie turned to Shannon. "I know you didn't exactly have me at your place on purpose, but thanks," she said.

"Let's go," Quinn told her.

"Hey, Quinn, how are you going to get her anywhere? I thought you needed a ride," Sam said.

"I'll call a cab." He stared at Shannon. "Well, now, the two of you can have that dinner on your own. Good night. Marnie, let's move. Night, Sam."

He set a hand on Marnie's shoulder, steering her toward the road.

"Why don't we invite both of them to dinner?" Sam whispered to Shannon.

She'd felt the urge herself. But then she'd remembered that Quinn O'Casey was a lying son of a bitch who had used her.

"He needs to get the girl settled," she said firmly.

"She could get settled after dinner."

"No." She sounded sharper than she had intended.

Sam sighed. "Let's see, you have no life. A terrific guy is apparently interested in you. You shove him out like refuse. Don't come to me when you're old and lonely."

She didn't respond.

"Shannon, that guy may not come back."

She turned around. "Oh, he'll be back."

"How can you be so sure?"

Because he's investigating us. Some of us more than others, she thought.

"He'll be back, trust me. Let's just stay in and order a pizza, all right?"

"Shannon…"

She spun on him hard. "I do not want to talk about it. Bring it up one more time, and I will fire your ass!"

He didn't believe it, but the threat fulfilled its purpose.

"No pizza, please. I'm gaining weight. We can order from the sushi place, okay?"

"Fine. But not one more word about Quinn O'Casey, got it?"

"Yes'm, boss, I got it."

They went into the house. Sam was true to his word. They watched a movie and wound up comparing opinions on the leading man. Sam was gay, and they often spent time dissing or admiring various actors.

He left her house at about ten, and she locked the door, glad to be feeling both safe and ridiculous. She *had* been hearing things—because a kid had been living in her backyard. She wondered who Annie was and where she could be found. Because whether Quinn had meant it or not, Shannon intended to make sure Marnie got her dance lessons.

By midnight, she was asleep.

And she slept well, waking in the morning to feel as if it really was over.

Lara was buried.

And that was that.

Quinn's phone rang at six-fifteen in the morning.

It was Jake Dilessio.

"Sonya Marquez Miller, twenty-nine. El Salvadoran by birth, married an older American eight years ago, became an American citizen. She must have cared for him. Even Miller's kids like her. His daughter saw the sketch and called in to identify her. The girl hadn't seen her in almost a year, but Sonya would call and chat now and then. When Gerald Miller died, Sonya went a little crazy, realizing that she was still young. She'd gotten big time into the club scene, partying at a place toward the north end of South Beach most of the time. She lived alone and acquired a lot of acquaintances, but, according to Eva Miller, the step-daughter, no one close. Or not that she knows anything about, anyway."

"Did she ever take dance lessons?" Quinn asked.

"Not that we've discovered so far. The cops have scoured the local hotels and restaurants, and we've found a few places where she liked to eat, shop and party. But not one person ever saw her come in or go out with anyone else. She lived in an apartment on Collins, and the doorman saw her leave her house at about eight o'clock Saturday night. That's the last time we can find anyone who admits to seeing her. Duarte is doing the autopsy in an hour. Show up, if you want. He told me he actually likes having you around."

Quinn thanked him and hung up. Before he could rise and head for the coffeepot and a shower, the phone rang again. It was his brother.

"Hey, bro. You heard about the new body on the beach, right?" Doug asked.

"Yes, Jake Dilessio has the case. I went down with him yesterday, and I'm going to the autopsy this morning."

"Well, that kind of sucks, doesn't it?"

"What? A woman being dead sucks? Hell, yes, it always does."

"No, I'm a cop—you're not. You're invited to the autopsy. I'm not."

"I can get you in if you want."

"Exactly. There's irony for you. No, I'm working, but thanks."

"You *will* make detective."

"Thanks for the vote of confidence. It's just strange sometimes, you know? I wanted you on this, and I'm glad you are, but… Anyway, I don't think this woman has anything to do with Lara, but what do you think?"

"Sure, I have a couple of feelings about things. I feel, like you, that something's not right. Do I have any real leads? Not one."

"It's the studio, I'm telling you. Something is wrong there. We can't see it, because the place looks so benign, but something's going on. Hey, do you have a class scheduled for today?"

"No."

"You should. No, maybe you shouldn't. You need to look a little casual, but make sure you show up tonight."

"For…?"

"Group. Beginners' group class. Seven forty-five. Make sure you're there."

"Do you come to beginners' group? They all talk about you as if you're the next John Travolta—what would you be doing in a beginners' class?"

"Advanced tech is at eight-thirty. I'll be in early for that. I'll see you there."

"I'll be there."

Richard Long was Shannon's first student. He ran in between a face-lift at ten and a tummy tuck in the afternoon. After that, she had Brad and Cindy Gray, a married couple she'd worked with since she had started at Moonlight Sonata. Gunter showed up alone for a coaching session, anxious for help in perfecting his bolero.

She had just finished with Gunter when Gordon stuck his head into her office.

"Hey."

"Hey," she returned.

"How was your Sunday?"

"Great. A couple of us went to the beach." She didn't know why she felt so slimy. That was the truth. "How about you?"

"Great. I spent it alone."

"Didn't want to join us at the beach, huh? You've had it with your 'kids,' is that it?"

"I love you kids, but enough is enough. I wanted to check something with you. Didn't you say you were going to charter a dinner cruise for the local students and teachers taking part in the Gator Gala?"

"Yeah."

"I heard you were going to arrange it through Quinn O'Casey."

She hesitated slightly. "I was."

"Have you talked to him about it yet?"

"Um, not really. I started to think that maybe we shouldn't go through him. He *is* a student."

"Find out what he can do for us. I was just looking over some costs. We don't have to make money doing this our first year, but we can't go into the hole too deeply, either."

"I don't know, Gordon."

"Talk to him. Get some costs. I want to go on the cruise well ahead of the gala. Let the students bond, gear up, you know? Talk to Quinn. Is he scheduled for today?"

"No."

"Maybe I'll give him a call."

"He'll show up."

"I'll call him."

"Gordon, he'll show up."

Gordon hesitated, looking at her. "Confident, aren't you?"

Right. Confident. Why didn't she just tell him that the guy was a private eye?

"I'll call him anyway. Want me to handle this?"

Usually, she would have said no. She liked to handle everything. But this time she hesitated, then said, "Sure. That would be great, Gordon. I hadn't expected to be asked to do so much coaching."

"You got it. I'm on it."

He left. Shannon stared after him, chewing on the nub of a pen. She wondered if she should call Quinn herself anyway. She wanted to find out what had happened with Marnie.

No…she wanted an excuse to see him alone. No Sam, no one else.

Among other things, she wanted to tell him just what she thought about his methods of investigation.

Quinn stood with Jake about three feet back from the table, giving Anthony Duarte room to work. A microphone hung over the corpse, and after the preliminary photographs were taken, Duarte, in slow, clear, well-enunciated words, recorded his observations.

Scrapings were taken from beneath the nails. Duarte noted that there wasn't a single bruise on the woman's body. Her excellent, well-toned physical condition was duly noted, as well. Though it didn't appear that she had been in the water long, there were indications that she had been nibbled on by sea life. Her eyes, he informed the microphone and silent room, were dilated. And there were track marks in her arms, though none were found at other locations on the body.

Vaginal swabs were taken, and Duarte voiced for the microphone that there was no sign of rape or recent intercourse. Her last meal had been a good one: lobster, asparagus, rice, largely undigested.

Duarte's voice seemed to drone after a while as he went through many of the rote, technical aspects of observation as the Y incision was made and organs were removed, weighed, observed, and tissue samples taken. His suspicion that they would discover cardiac arrest due to substance overdose was stated, along with the fact that he would await lab results before final analysis. Duarte was a thorough man.

The brain saw made an eerie sound in the room. The brain was duly weighed, and additional tissue samples were taken.

They had stood silently on the hard floor for hours when Duarte at last stepped back, removing his gloves.

He stepped around the gurney, approaching Jake and Quinn. "Whatever happened to her, it doesn't look like she put up any fight." He shrugged.

"Any chance that she was out with a wild group on a party cruise, got into a state of euphoria and just fell overboard, unnoticed until it was too late?"

"Not unless she managed to die before she plummeted into the water. It's clear she didn't drown. I suspect we'll find she died of cardiac arrest. No, gentlemen, she overdosed, either on her own or with help, and someone with her panicked and tossed her body overboard."

"And then she washed up on the beach," Jake said.

"So she was either helped to her death or died by her own hand, and then she was dumped off a boat," Quinn commented. "But it looks like a case of illegal substances, not overdose by prescription drugs?"

"You saw the tracks," Duarte reminded him.

"But until those lab tests come back, you won't actually know just what was in her," Quinn persisted.

"I'll call Dilessio the minute I get anything. There could be some surprises in the lab work," Duarte said. "I'll have the reports to you by the end of the day, or first thing tomorrow, maybe. We're a bit backed up here. Hell, we're always a bit backed up here. There was a major accident on I-95 this morning. Five people killed, an infant among them. Hell, when will people learn that there's nowhere you have to be in that big a hurry?"

"Thanks. And thanks for letting me hang around," Quinn added.

Duarte managed a grin. "You know, oddly enough, there

are plenty of people out there who would like to witness an autopsy. Not like the line for a pop band, but still… Hell, Quinn, believe it or not, I can remember way back to when you were in the Miami-Dade academy. They were dropping like flies around you. You just turned green. I knew you'd make it big."

"I'm a small-time P.I.," Quinn corrected him.

Duarte arched a brow. It wasn't the time or place to get into the things Quinn had done between then and now.

"I have an infant waiting, gentlemen," Duarte said. "I'll get back to you as soon as possible."

They started out, and Jake's phone rang.

He answered tersely, then a smile split his face.

"I'm having a baby," he said.

"Great, get going."

"No, come with me."

"Ashley doesn't want me in the delivery room!"

"No, and I don't want you in there, either. But apparently she's been there for a while already. You know my wife—she wouldn't take me off duty until the moment it was necessary. The baby should be here within the next two hours, at the most. Come on. Spend some time with the living."

Since Jake sounded cool but looked a little nervous, Quinn decided that he could afford the time. All he had planned for the immediate afternoon was some Internet investigation and a call to Annie about Marnie, a call he could make from the hospital.

When they arrived, he was able to see Ashley for a few minutes. She was having contractions every few minutes, and they were obviously painful, but she managed to grin, and assure her husband that she would never have let it go so far that he wouldn't be able to get there in plenty of time. When the doctor arrived for an examination, Quinn wandered out to the waiting room. A few minutes later, Jake poked his head out to tell him that it was time, and Quinn wished his friend good luck. Then he found a quiet spot and called Annie down in South Miami.

"That girl is precious," Annie told him. "And a smart cookie."

"What about the stepfather?" Quinn asked. "Can anything be done?"

"Not as it stands," Annie told him.

"It's got to mess the kid up—knowing the husband is getting ready to really hit on her, only her own mother thinks she's the guilty one, after the guy."

"She's tough. She'll be all right. I've got some time this afternoon, so I'm going to take her for driving lessons."

"Great. She's situated okay?"

"Sure. I've got her in a home. She misses the beach, though."

"Do you think she'll bolt on you?"

Annie thought for a moment on the other end of the line. "No. She wants to make something out of her life. She knows we're giving her real help."

"Good, then. I'll check in later."

When he hung up, Jake burst out into the waiting room. "It's a girl! I have a daughter." He looked dazed.

Quinn rose, embraced him briefly and told him, "Congratulations."

"They need a few minutes. Then you can come in and see her. She's amazing. Nick is on his way down. In a few hours, this place will be like Grand Central Station."

Jake disappeared, and Quinn waited, as asked.

Fifteen minutes later, he got to hold his friend's daughter.

And she was amazing. A big baby, they told him—a few ounces over nine pounds. But she seemed incredibly tiny. She had been born with curling dark hair, her eyes were immense and blue, and she had a grip like steel. He was

startled to feel a powerful surge of warmth and protec-
tiveness, and as the baby stared up at him, he found himself thinking about Marnie. Jake's daughter would grow up
in a wealth of comfort and love. The innocence in her eyes
would remain.

When he returned the baby to her parents, he departed
thoughtfully. It was amazing to hold an infant in her first
few moments of life.

It made it all the harder to think of the fact that far too
many lives were wasted.

Maybe including his own.

Sam came into Shannon's office at about five.

"Hey, did you see the paper this morning?" he asked.

"No, I didn't even put the news on this morning."

"They ran a picture of the woman they found on the
beach. I heard on the news that she's already been identified."

"Oh? Did we know her?" Shannon asked, feeling a sudden chill.

"I don't think so. She was a Latin American, got into
the U.S. by marrying some rich guy. She got along with
his grown kids, though. One of them identified her this
morning. Sonya Something. The rich old guy died, and she
went wild. Sad, huh?"

"Very sad."

"The old guy finally keels over, she's in the States with
money—and whap!"

"Sam, that's terrible. Sonya what?" she persisted.

"I don't remember. It will be on the news again later. I
didn't recognize her from the sketch in the paper, though."

"How did they know she was murdered? Maybe she
drowned."

"She was found naked on the beach. But she'd been in
the water long enough to get chewed by a few crabs. Plus
she had track marks in her arms."

"How do you know that?"

"I read the paper, and though cause of death isn't certain, the preliminary suspicion is an overdose."

"Maybe she overdosed herself."

"You think she overdosed, took herself to the beach, stripped and managed to make her clothing disappear, and then died?"

Shannon sighed. "Maybe she was out on a boat with a party crowd, did too many drugs, fell into the water and drowned."

He frowned. "How the hell would I know? I was just mentioning it to you because we were there yesterday, and they ran a sketch of her in the paper with what the reporter had been able to find out. Interesting, huh?"

"Sad."

He shrugged. "They found the body of that prostitute not far from there a while back."

She sat back. "This woman wasn't a prostitute, was she?"

"No, unless she was really high-class. She didn't have on any clothing, but she was wearing thousands in jewelry."

"It's horrible. I'm really sorry. And," she added ruefully, "glad she wasn't a student here."

"No, rest assured, I've never seen her. Hey, aren't you going to go eat? Want to go down to the Italian place with me?"

Shannon hesitated, then shook her head. "I'm taking dinner, but I've got a few errands to run. Sorry. I may be a little late, too. I don't have anything scheduled tonight except for going over the books and making sure the papers are in order for the Gator Gala. Do me a favor and let Ella know I may be late getting back."

She rose, grabbed her handbag and started out.

One inner voice was telling her just to let things alone.

But another voice was telling her that she had to take care of a few matters or else explode.

She opted to listen to the second voice.

There were simply far too many dead people shadowing her life these days.

CHAPTER 13

Shannon Mackay walked out on the deck with true purpose, strides long, every inch of her body speaking volumes.

She was really angry.

Quinn wasn't surprised to see she was still furious with him.

He *was* surprised that she was there.

He was sitting at Nick's, where all the regulars had just been treated to drinks in honor of the new baby. He'd opted for a soda himself, since he intended to get to group class, and he was poring over the files on the table in front of him. Somewhere, in either the various police reports or the dossiers on the teachers and clientele of Moonlight Sonata, there had to be a clue.

Shannon searched the crowd, saw him and walked to his table. She didn't wait for an invitation but pulled out the chair opposite from him and sat.

He felt his muscles tighten, and he waited.

"You son of a bitch," she said quietly, evenly. In fact, it was amazing that she could get so much venom into a tone that was so soft.

"You're wrong," he told her.

"Oh, no. I'm not wrong. You are an absolute bastard. In fact, I could go on and on. But I've just come to tell you that, despite your methods, I don't intend to stand in your way, nor have I told anyone at the studio just what you are."

"A bastard?"

"A private eye."

A waitress, Ellen, walked cheerfully up to the table. "What can I get you?" she asked Shannon. "First drink is on the house."

"I'm not drinking, thank you," Shannon said distractedly, staring at Quinn.

"Oh, it doesn't have to be alcohol," Ellen said.

"It's all right. I don't need anything."

Quinn leaned forward. "Have an iced tea, a soda, a coffee. They're celebrating here today."

"Iced tea," Shannon said, then looked at the waitress. "Thank you."

Ellen left. Shannon was too angry to ask what they were celebrating.

"Just keep your distance from me. I'll have Jane or Rhianna take over your lessons. Don't call me, don't come to my house, and stay away from me at the studio."

Quinn leaned back, fighting hard to keep a casual pose. "You're wrong."

"About what? You're not a P.I.? You weren't hired to investigate the people at Moonlight Sonata?"

He stayed silent, staring at her.

"Nice job. You're paid to fraternize."

He shook his head, leaning closer. "No, I'm not making anything on this. It's costing me. I'm looking into it because Doug asked me to."

"That's fine. You keep looking into it. Just stay the hell away from me."

"You're wrong that the one thing has anything to do with the other."

"You were investigating me," she snapped.

"You should be investigated. You might be top of the line in a list of suspects—after Ben Trudeau, the ex-husband. Hey, who would have motive? She stole the man you were living with, your partner. She hit you when you were down." He moved closer and closer, trying to keep his tone low. "You were the best, and you went down completely when Ben left you to dance with Lara, then married her to boot. You even gave up what you loved, competition."

"I never loved competition—I love dance," she grated. "And you are so full of—"

"Iced tea!" Ellen said, arriving back at the table. "They named her Kyra. Kyra Elizabeth," Ellen informed Quinn. "It's a beautiful name."

"She's a beautiful baby," Quinn told Ellen.

"You've seen her already?" Ellen said.

"Yes." He smiled at Ellen. He felt taut, his stomach clenched, and he couldn't think of a thing to say in his defense that Shannon would believe, so he took a certain enjoyment in seeing her try to maintain her temper and refrain from exploding while the waitress remained at their table.

"I'll bet she *is* beautiful, and it's cool that you said that," Ellen informed him. "Most men say all babies look alike—like wrinkly little bald things." She laughed.

"Well, Kyra Elizabeth isn't bald. She came with a head full of curly hair," he said.

"Well, her mother's a beauty, and her dad…he's pretty darned cute, too," Ellen said with a laugh. "Wave if you need me." Then she hurried off to another table.

"Bull!" Shannon enunciated, hard and sharp.

"The baby *is* beautiful."

"*You* are full of bull. The thing with Ben and me ended so long ago, it's ridiculous. And it's so flattering to know that the only reason you were determined to find out whatever you could about me is because I'm so high on your suspect list."

He felt something snap inside him, and he leaned closer. "Whoa, back up here. I drove you home, I checked out your house. *You* came to my boat. I gave you your own cabin. *You* knocked on *my* door. I made a point of suggesting that it might not be a good time."

"I wasn't drunk," she said icily.

"And I wasn't using you," he snapped back. "What, did that whole thing—over so long ago it's ridiculous—warp you so badly that you can't get on with life at all? Take a look at yourself. Is it so impossible that someone could want you? Enjoy your company? Think you're beautiful?"

She stared at him as if she wanted to scream, or simply throw something at him.

"And is what I do so damned bad?" he asked. "I make a legal living. I'm pretty good at what I do, too. Most of the time."

"Oh, I'll give you that. You're good."

"That sounds hostile. However, I'm going to take it as a compliment."

"Being such an ass, you would," she said. "Listen, like I said, I don't intend to give you away."

"Because you think Lara was murdered."

She hesitated. "Yes."

"So quit hating me. Help me."

"I can't help you. I don't have any idea who might have done it. And now I have to leave. Just stay away from me."

"Great. We've discovered that the danger in your yard was a homeless kid, so now I should stay away."

"I was always honest."

"No. You lie to yourself so often you don't know the truth anymore."

She exhaled a long, exasperated sigh. "I have no feelings for Ben Trudeau! No, that's not true. I feel sorry for him. His life isn't working out so well. I can cope with mine, because I love what I do. Ben needs to compete. He needs applause, to win. I hired Ben for the studio because he's good. And I hired Lara whenever I could, too."

He shook his head slowly, looking at her. "You say you don't want to compete, but you're a liar and a coward. And you say that I used you. I didn't. I found out you aren't just some of the greatest eye candy in the world. You're intelligent, thoughtful, fun and a million other wonderful things. But you won't let yourself accept that. Ben Trudeau hurt you a long time ago. And so, for a *ridiculous* amount of time, you've been a coward, afraid of any man who shows an interest."

She issued a sharp expletive and rose, walking away from the table.

Then she turned back, footsteps brisk as she returned. "How is the girl?"

"What?"

"The homeless girl."

"Marnie is fine."

"You'll really get her to the studio?"

"Yes, I'll really get her there. And for your information, I only met her once before, when she was panhandling on the beach. I'm not a child molester."

She flushed. "I didn't suggest that you were."

"You should have seen the way you looked at me that night. And by the way, I'll handle your charter boat for you, as well. I do own two boats—well, I own half of two boats. Dane Whitelaw and I run the investigations, and we also own boats that we rent out. I do fish, and I do dive. And I can give you the best deal you're going to get."

"Gordon will be talking to you about that."

An Important Message from the Editors

Dear Reader,

Because you've chosen to read one of our fine novels, we'd like to say "thank you"! And, as a special way to thank you, we're offering you two more of the books you love so well, and a surprise gift to send you — absolutely FREE!

Please enjoy them with our compliments...

Pam Powers

Peel off Seal and Place Inside...

EDITOR'S FREE GIFT SEAL "THANK YOU"

How to validate your Editor's
"Thank You"
FREE GIFT

1. Peel off gift seal from front cover. Place it in space provided at right. This automatically entitles you to receive 2 FREE BOOKS and a fabulous mystery gift.

2. Send back this card and you'll get 2 brand-new *Suspense* novels. These books have a cover price of $5.99 or more each in the U.S. and $6.99 or more each in Canada, but they are yours to keep absolutely free.

3. There's no catch. You're under no obligation to buy anything. We charge nothing—ZERO—for your first shipment. And you don't have to make any minimum number of purchases— not even one!

4. The fact is, thousands of readers enjoy receiving their books by mail from The Reader Service. They enjoy the convenience of home delivery...they like getting the best new novels at discount prices BEFORE they're available in stores... and they love their Heart to Heart subscriber newsletter featuring author news, special book offers, book reviews and much more!

5. We hope that after receiving your free books you'll want to remain a subscriber. But the choice is yours— to continue or cancel, any time at all! So why not take us up on our invitation, with no risk of any kind. You'll be glad you did!

GET A *Free* MYSTERY GIFT...

SURPRISE MYSTERY GIFT COULD BE YOURS **FREE** AS A SPECIAL "THANK YOU" FROM THE EDITORS

THE EDITOR'S "THANK YOU" FREE GIFTS INCLUDE:

- ▶ Two BRAND-NEW Suspense Novels
- ▶ An exciting surprise gift

YES! I have placed my Editor's "thank you" Free Gifts seal in the space provided at right. Please send me 2 FREE books, and my FREE Mystery Gift. I understand that I am under no obligation to purchase anything further, as explained on the back and opposite page.

PLACE
FREE GIFTS
SEAL
HERE

192 MDL D39R   392 MDL D39S

FIRST NAME	LAST NAME

ADDRESS

APT.#	CITY

STATE / PROV.	ZIP / POSTAL CODE

(ED1-SUS-05) © 1998 MIRA BOOKS

Thank You!

The Reader Service — Here's How It Works:

BUSINESS REPLY MAIL

FIRST-CLASS MAIL   PERMIT NO. 717-003   BUFFALO, NY

POSTAGE WILL BE PAID BY ADDRESSEE

THE READER SERVICE
3010 WALDEN AVE
PO BOX 1341
BUFFALO NY 14240-8571

NO POSTAGE
NECESSARY
IF MAILED
IN THE
UNITED STATES

He folded his arms across his chest. "I won't deal with Gordon."

"It's his studio."

"And I won't dance with Jane or Rhianna. You took me on. You keep me."

"So don't take classes. What do I care?"

"Because I suck?"

"Because you're a jerk!"

She started to walk away, then swung back again.

"Who had the baby?"

"A friend."

"The woman at the beach?"

His eyes narrowed. She had seen him when he had gone to the site where they had found the last body.

"Who else saw me there?" he asked.

She shook her head. "I was with Sam, but he didn't see you."

"Sit down," he told her.

"No!"

"Please."

She inhaled, then sat, perched on the edge of the chair.

"The guy who came on the boat the other day is Jake Dilessio, a homicide cop. His wife is a forensic artist. Cops can get a lot of things P.I.s can't. And Jake is one damned decent guy—he's not threatened when an outsider looks into something. Anyway, I'm happy as hell for Jake and Ashley because they had their first child today. I'm kind of sorry, as well, because they're both going to take time off, and he's been a big help."

She shook her head. "What did the woman on the beach have to do with Lara? She wasn't a student. She was never a student."

He shook his head. "I don't know."

"Then what were you doing there?"

"Trying to figure out why so many women are dying."

He hesitated. "You had a student once, a woman named Nell Durken."

She frowned, and at last the tension in her seemed to dissipate. For this moment, at least, she wasn't ready to rip into him. "Nell was very good. She stopped coming, though. She wanted to put time into making things work with her husband. And then the bastard killed her anyway." She shook her head. "But they got him. The police arrested him. He's facing trial."

He nodded. "Nell hired me. A simple case of following him—she was convinced he was cheating. He was. When she turned up dead, his prints were all over the bottle of pills, and since he was seeing someone, he had definite motive."

"Nell was a lovely woman. She had a lot to offer the world," Shannon murmured.

"Yes, she did."

"If her husband killed her, then…well, then these deaths can't be related," Shannon said. "But it just seems a little too strange that both women might have died the same way and it's a total coincidence."

"Well, that's the point, isn't it? Things *are* a little too strange."

Shannon stood abruptly, as if remembering how angry she was. "I'm working. I have to get back. And as for you, I'll certainly cooperate in any way I can to help you find the truth. But other than that…"

"I know. Keep my distance. Because I know just a little too much about you, right?" His voice had an edge, a sound of bitterness he was surprised to hear himself betray.

"Yes, you've got it," she informed him.

As she started to turn away, he caught her wrist. "There's something you're not telling me. There has to be a reason you were so edgy in your own house."

There *was* something. He could tell. But either she was afraid it was just something minimal or silly, or she was afraid she might give someone else away.

She shook her head. "I don't know anything. I wish I did."

"Maybe that's not a very good wish."

"Why?"

"Maybe people die because they *do* know something," he said.

She pulled her wrist free. "I'm sure I'll be seeing you, Mr. O'Casey."

"Very soon. In a matter of hours."

She frowned.

"Group class," he reminded her pleasantly.

She turned on her heels. Her footsteps clicked in a no-nonsense manner as she walked along the path to the parking lot.

Rhianna was leading the beginners' class. From her office, Shannon could hear her directions.

"Slow, quick, quick, slow. Slow, quick, quick, slow… there you go, Mr. Suarez, look at that, Cuban motion already taking flight. Mr. O'Casey…think box. Just a box. Slow… quick, quick, slow. Think of the way we've been working, fox-trot, rumba. Two very different dances, one smooth, one rhythm, and yet we're still talking box right now. There will always be two aspects involved. The step itself, and then the technique of the step. Belinda, good motion! Just because it's slow, that doesn't mean that it's a stop. Eventually, each step flows into the other. A count doesn't necessarily mean a foot movement but rather a body movement, and though each is distinct, it flows. Feel the music, Mr. O'Casey. Slow, quick, quick, slow…slow, quick, quick, slow."

Shannon stepped outside to watch. All the men—Ben, Justin and Sam—were engaged in private lessons at the moment. Jane didn't have a private, so she was the one assisting Rhianna, who was trying to show the men the proper dance hold so they would one day, be able to lead properly.

Tonight the newcomers group was small. Just the pretty little dressmaker who had started about two weeks ago, Quinn O'Casey and a construction worker, Tito Suarez, who was about to attend his daughter's wedding.

As she stepped out, she heard Mr. Suarez speaking in confusion. "I'm sorry, which of you is being the man?"

"I'm the man right now," Rhianna told him. "Just call me Reggie—that's my name when I play the guy. Jane's guy name is Jason. You'll get used to it. Hey, you should see it when Justin Garcia does his Judy thing when Ben is leading. They're great."

For a moment Shannon leaned against the wall, feeling a brief sense of strange relief. She didn't think she'd heard real laughter in the studio since Lara had died. Tonight it seemed that they might be getting back to normal at last.

Or maybe nothing would ever be normal again.

She caught Quinn's eyes across the room.

You're next.

Why hadn't she told him what the waiter had said to her? Because…it wasn't proof of anything? It might be as silly and paranoid as jumping when a bush moved in her backyard.

But maybe not.

"Small class, huh?"

She nearly jumped a mile. It was just Gordon, standing behind her, speaking softly and glumly.

"Business will pick back up," she said.

"I hope so."

"There's a large group waiting for the advanced class already," she told him.

"I guess you're right. Have we had any cancellations for the Gator Gala?"

"No, not one," she told him.

"Hey, Quinn got us the boat."

She spun around.

Gordon nodded, pleased. "Casual buffet, trip out into Biscayne Bay—he even knew a great band to play for us, and the price is right. Be sure you make the announcement tonight, after advanced. We're going out of Coconut Grove at eight. Everyone should meet at the dock around seven. Tell them that dress is Miami-casual-chic."

"And what the hell is that?" Shannon asked him.

He shrugged. "It means they can wear whatever the hell they want."

He turned to head back for his office. Rhianna announced the end of the group class, and told her students to applaud their partners and themselves. Then Belinda started to chat with Tito. Quinn smiled casually and sauntered over to Jane and Rhianna.

Shannon was amazed to hear her teeth grate as she wondered what investigative techniques he would be using with her staff.

Quinn walked into Gordon's office. "I hear there's some kind of a meeting tonight for the Gator Gala people."

Gordon Henson leaned back in his chair, smiling. "Not a real meeting. Shannon has an advanced class tonight, so a lot of the participants will be here. She's just going to give them a little advice, get them hyped, talk about outfits, shoes, hair—makeup. Your brother will probably stay, though he's heard most of it before."

"Can beginners enter the Gator Gala?"

"Of course." Gordon brightened up, as if his eyes were on the prize. "You interested?"

Hell, no! Quinn thought. But aloud he said, "Maybe. Would it be all right if I hung around for the meeting?"

"Naturally. Hey, I know you feel you don't have much

of an aptitude for this, but believe me, most people are clumsy when they start out."

"Right."

"Your brother looked like a real clod," Gordon said, maybe a little too honestly. "And look at him now."

"Well, I'll hang around. And think about it."

"You'd have a lot of work to do." A lot of work—a lot of classes. More income for the studio. It was the American way, it was what they did.

"I'll give it some thought," Quinn assured him. "Do a little watching."

"Go right ahead. Do that."

Quinn walked back out to where the advanced class was being taught. It was Shannon's class, and they were working on rumba technique. He was amazed to see the individual motions that actually took place in one little step. He was amazed to watch her do it, as well. The twist of the hips, the bend of the knee, how everything combined to become so incredibly fluid that no one watching would realize how complex the motions really were.

She was a good teacher. And she used Doug to demonstrate a lot of what she was saying.

He'd never seen his brother look so damned good.

A twinge of jealousy swept through him and he firmly stomped it down. They were dancing, just dancing. But when dancing looked like that…

Motive…

Jealousy was a major motive for murder. Jealousy, unrequited love, hatred spawned by envy.

She worked with each member of the class. He knew a few of them. The doctors Richard and Mina Long. Gabriel Lopez, owner of the club. His own brother. There was also a much older man, who performed the moves with applaudable finesse. Two other couples, a beautiful younger woman, and a middle-aged woman.

Bobby and Giselle showed up during the class. They stood near Quinn, watching.

"Those are the crème de la crème of the students," Bobby told him. "Katarina and her husband…she's really good. I don't think she's as much in love with dance as she is with showing off her outfits, but hey, whatever works. Richard Long is really good, better than his wife, but they get along amazingly well, anyway. You should see some of the fights between husbands and wives around here— wife accusing husband of not leading right, husband accusing wife of not being able to follow."

"Not us, of course," Giselle said, grinning.

Bobby grimaced. "We don't fight that bad, do we?"

"Let's hope not, we're still newlyweds."

"It looks as if the two of you get along all right," Quinn told them.

"Better than the professionals," Giselle said. "We were here one day when Lara Trudeau and Jim Burke were working. Shannon was coaching. Lara was going on and on about Jim missing the beat, and Shannon told her that Jim was right, she had to actually let him lead."

"And Lara Trudeau just took that?" Quinn said, surprised. From what he had heard about the woman, she wouldn't accept anyone else giving her instruction.

"Oh, no. She said something to Shannon, and Shannon told her that she didn't waste her time with people who didn't think they needed any improvement. She walked off and Lara and Jim got into a big fight. Then they realized that some of the students had arrived and were watching, so Lara went to get Shannon, and everyone started over as if nothing had happened at all."

"Jim must have had some major patience," Quinn said.

"He wanted to compete—she was the best, I guess," Bobby said with a shrug. "I haven't seen him around much, not since she died."

"Was he here a lot?"

"Sure. He knew Shannon could teach. He would come for coaching sessions without Lara."

"The woman was a bitch," Giselle whispered.

The advanced class was over, and Gordon had come out to talk to them about the Gator Gala. Shannon, seeing him in the back of the group, arched her brows.

"I told Gordon I was thinking about entering," he said, not caring that everyone in the room could hear, in response to her unspoken question.

"Oh," she murmured.

"As a beginner. He said there's a beginner category," Quinn told her. He almost laughed aloud at himself. He had sounded defensive. Yes, he thought. *There's a category for people who can't dance. It's the two-left-feet award.*

"Hey, that's great," Sam Railey said. "Our newest student is entering."

The room applauded for him. To his amazement, he felt the dark heat of a flush creeping over his face.

"Maybe," he said.

"Some of you have competed before, some of you haven't," Shannon said, perching on one of the small tables against the wall. "Some things may sound silly, and some may sound fun. I've actually acquired students through the years just because they like the dance outfits, so… Okay, beginners—something dressy is all you really want. And students entering other categories are still free to opt for something simple. Whatever makes you comfortable and works with the dances you've chosen. We have all kinds of catalogues for shoes and clothing, and, of course, we have Katarina right next door, and I can vouch for the beauty of her designs. We'll also have someone to help with hair and makeup. Long hair's best swept up out of the way. There's nothing like throwing your partner off by smacking him in the face with your hair. Makeup should generally be very dark and dramatic—best for pictures and videos. This next is very important. Competitions move fast—always make sure you know where you're supposed to be and when. Be in line or you're disqualified. Your teachers are responsible for you, as well, but try not to torture them too much. Everyone will have an opportunity to see the floor and try it out before the competition begins, and, of course, there will be a professional show at our awards dinner."

Mina Long piped up. "What about shoes?" She hesitated. "Last competition, Lara Trudeau was appalled because I was wearing black shoes. I mean, it was like Joan Crawford in that movie, telling her children there would be no wire coat hangers in the house."

There was laughter after that statement. Uneasy laughter.

Shannon answered casually. "Flesh-colored shoes are best, unless you're doing a cabaret act and need a specific shoe for a specific outfit."

"Black shoes don't go better with a black outfit?" Giselle, seated on the floor with Bobby, asked.

Rhianna, hovering near Shannon, answered. "This may be in opposition to all the fashion advice you've ever heard, but think flesh, think beige. The right shoes are important, because the judges will be looking at your feet. When you're heading out on the town, black heels may look good with your black dress, but in dance, go for the flesh-colored shoes, beige, tan."

"Why?" Mina asked.

"You create a line," Shannon said. "The leg looks longer, movement looks smoother. Check out some of the tapes we have and you'll see. Compare the dancers with 'blending' shoes with those who have color, and you'll see."

"You mean we're going to be judged on our shoes?" Giselle asked.

Shannon shook her head. "No, and of course, there's nothing in the rule books that says you can't buy any dance shoes you want. But take a look at the tapes, and you'll see what Rhianna is saying for yourself. If you don't agree, then you don't agree. There are no laws."

Quinn looked around the room, noting that all the teachers, even Ben, were present. It made sense. They all had students entering the competition. Ben, who had been married to Lara and might have hated her. Jane and Sam, learning to compete together, always losing out. Rhianna, also a competitor. Justin Lopez. Shannon, who had good reason to hate the woman. Then there was Gordon Henson, who had given Lara her start. Jim, who Lara abused, but who needed her for what he craved in life.

Then the students. Gabriel Lopez, who managed the club, and Katarina, who created the clothing. Lots of reasons for hatred, but lots of reasons for need. None of it gelled. Because why would any of them have hated Nell Durken? And what could they have to do with women found dead on the beach with drugs in their systems?

None of it made sense. What *would* make sense would be that none of the deaths were related. Still…

"So thank you all for coming. We'll meet once a week until the competition, just for questions. Don't forget to schedule your private lessons with your teachers, and thanks for coming," Shannon said, rising.

The meeting was over. Students were saying goodbye. Kissing goodbye—everyone here seemed to kiss everyone else goodbye on the cheek. It was like leaving after an Italian wedding.

There was no reason to linger. The teachers were anxious to lock up and go home. In fact, Justin Garcia was out the door along with the students. It was nearly eleven, Quinn realized.

But he had to linger. He stayed behind, avoiding his brother and Bobby as they left. He approached Shannon.

"I can hang around, walk you to your car."

"No, thank you," she said firmly. Coldly. He itched to take hold of her, shake her, tell her she was the best thing that happened to him in ages. In forever. He watched her dance, watched her move, and was afraid for no reason. Still, he felt a rising desperation to be near her.

"Gordon and I will leave together," she lied. Again, that ice in her voice. *You do your thing. And leave me the hell alone.*

"All right, good night, then." He turned to leave, then turned back. "Make sure you let Gordon walk you out."

"Absolutely."

He left. He had no choice.

The last student left. Sam and Jane departed together, discussing the Gator Gala. Rhianna muttered something about having to stop for milk and flew out as if she were being chased by a banshee.

Ella Rodriguez had gone out with her mother for her birthday that night, so Shannon went to the schedule board to make sure that any last-minute appointments had been filled in properly. She looked up to see that Ben, moody and grim, was hovering near the reception area.

"Anything wrong?" she asked him.

He shook his head. "Except that…"

"What?"

"There's a rumor going around that you're going to start working with Jim Burke."

Her brows flew up. "I don't compete anymore. You know that. Who told you that?"

"Gabe. Gabriel Lopez. He said it's the talk down in the club."

"It may be talk, but it's not true." She sighed. "Ben, I don't compete. I don't want to compete. I really like what I do."

He looked away for a minute, then looked back at her. She was surprised by his expression. Ben was very good-looking—suave, dark, with deep, expressive eyes. They were on her intently right now.

"What I was going to say was this—if the rumor was true, I was happy for you. You may think you don't want to compete, but you do. I see your eyes sometimes when other people are on the floor. I see your mind working, and I know that you're calculating steps. I screwed you over once. Big time. I wanted to get ahead too badly myself. You should compete. Not with me—I understand how you feel about me—but with someone. Someone good. And Jim is good. I just wanted to say that you didn't need to try to hide anything like this from me. I would be happy to see you compete with anyone, especially Jim."

She almost fell into the chair behind her, but instead simply stared at him for several long seconds. "Thanks, Ben. Thanks very much. But what you heard is a rumor."

He nodded. "Think about making it not be a rumor," he said, then turned and walked away. "Good night—hey, go ahead and lock up when you leave. Gordon left a few minutes ago."

"Sure, thanks. Good night."

She heard the door close as Ben left.

The music was off. There suddenly seemed to be an eerie silence in the studio.

And she didn't want to be there alone.

She hadn't finished with the schedule, but she didn't care. She wished she hadn't been so surprised by Ben's words that she had let him leave; he would have stayed to walk out with her.

She wished she'd kept Quinn O'Casey around. Why the hell hadn't she?

Because she'd been hurt.

Maybe it was like her dancing. She'd been hurt, so...

Stop, she told herself. Get your purse, get your keys, lock up and leave, rationally.

She left the reception area and started to walk to her office for her purse. It was when she bent down to get it that she heard the noise.

A cranking. A shifting. Something being opened then closed.

She stood very still, trying to tell herself the noise was natural. There was a club on the floor below, after all.

But the noise hadn't come from below. It had come from the second floor.

"Hello," she called.

She forced herself to throw her purse over her shoulder and walk calmly out to the studio area. There was no one there. Nothing had moved, nothing had changed. She felt a ripple along her spine.

Maybe Katarina was working late.

No, she and her husband had gone home directly from the meeting, they'd said good-night to her.

Get out, get out, just get out, a little voice said to her.

She fought the unreasoning sense of fear. Even if someone was around, they probably had a valid reason.

No attempt at logic seemed to help her any. She just wanted to get out, and get out fast. Instinct screamed at her as if she were being chased by a menace she could actually see and touch.

She hurried to the back door, flying out of it, then reminding herself that the noise might not have come from within the studio but from without. She could see no one in the area that led toward the back. The stairs that led to Gabriel Lopez's apartment above seemed swamped in shadow. The door to the storage room was locked.

Even if someone was out here, it could be for a very valid reason.

"Katarina? Hey, Kat, David…are you two here?"

No answer.

She looked at the shadowy stairs leading up to Gabe's place.

"Gabriel?"

Not a whisper sounded from the shadows.

She fled toward the stairs that led down to the rear parking area. As she stepped on the first, the grating sounded again.

From behind her.

She didn't look back but started quickly down.

Footsteps followed.

She started to run.

Her car was only forty feet away, and she had her keys and clicker out as she moved toward it, absolutely certain she was being followed.

She hit the button. Her car clicked a friendly little beeping sound, and the lights went on.

Shannon flew to the driver's door and nearly wrenched it open, then slid into the seat, slamming the door shut instantly.

She hit the locks.

Then she screamed as a tap sounded against the window.

CHAPTER 14

Seated at the table of the galley, legs stretched out on the boothlike seat, Quinn chewed the nub of his pen and stared at his notes. Nell Durken, Lara Trudeau. Dancers with the studio in common. Art Durken in jail, more than a hundred witnesses when Lara died. Two more women found dead from drugs in the area of the studio, neither of them dancers. What could be the connection—or was there one?

He glanced over his list of students and teachers, and realized with a growing headache that motive was not a problem with most of them.

Eliminate. Get rid of the impossible, and whatever was left, however improbable, had to be the truth.

Shit. Who the hell to eliminate?

He started writing another list. Least likely, most likely. Least likely—Justin Garcia. A small burst of pure speed, didn't work with Lara, loved salsa. And probably not her type. Being tall herself, she had apparently liked tall men, though what Quinn knew of her lovers other than Ben Trudeau and his own brother, he didn't know. He wrote down Ben's name and, beneath it, ex-husband still bitter.

Gordon? Which side did he go on?

There was a tap at the cabin door. "Yeah?"

"It's me. I'm here."

He rose, leaning up the steps to open the cabin door and allow his brother to walk down. Doug looked eager. "You've got something?" he asked.

Quinn grimaced. "No."

Doug frowned. "I thought maybe you asked me here because you had something."

"Sit."

"Yes, sir," Doug said, sounding a little irritated.

"Did I interrupt something?" Quinn responded in kind. "You're the one who got me into this."

"Right. I'm sorry," Doug said quickly.

"Who else was Lara seeing? How hot and heavy was your affair? You've got to give me more. I can't get to know all these people overnight."

Doug drummed his fingers on the table, lowered his head for a minute and looked up. "I think she was seeing someone else."

"Was it Ben again?"

"Maybe, I'm not sure. But she was ready to call it off."

"How do you know that?"

"She told me there was something in her life that had to change."

"Why would that be a man?"

"Because she was Lara."

Quinn shook his head and muttered ruefully, "Bring that into a court of law."

Doug sat up straight, giving Quinn his full attention. "You had to know her. She could be the most exquisite person in the world, and she could be cutting and cruel."

"How did you get involved with her, exactly, and when did your involvement with her start?"

"About three months ago."

"Where?"

"Down at the club. We were dancing one night. She'd had a little too much to drink. I suggested I should give her a ride home and maybe stay awhile. I was just playing around, really. I never thought she'd say yes."

"Then?"

"She said no—there was no way she'd take a chance on anyone knowing she was inviting me in. Then, in the same breath, she suggested that she come to my place. And she did. And after that, we saw each other at least once a week. Always at my place. She didn't want anyone to know. I was trying to keep it casual, as if I knew she was a free spirit. But I honestly think she was beginning to care about me. Because, once, I pressed it. I said she didn't work for the studio—we could be a couple if we wanted to be. And she said it wasn't just the studio, that she had a few other problems she needed to solve. And the way she said it, I knew there was someone else. At least one other person."

"Ben?"

Doug shook his head. "Maybe. Someone who was always at the studio, anyway. And I doubt it was Sam, 'cause he's gay, and I doubt it was Justin, because she didn't go for guys who weren't over six feet."

His assumption had been right, Quinn thought.

"Gordon?" he queried.

"Gordon…he's a lot older, but he's still a nice-looking man. Known to go both ways, but I don't know. If they were suddenly a hot ticket, there was no chemistry on the floor."

"What about her partner, Jim Burke?"

"I don't think so."

"Why not?"

Doug stared at him and shrugged. "Lara liked her own strength, but she wasn't attracted to a pushover. Jim did everything she said. I don't see him as a lover for her."

Quinn leaned toward his brother. "There were hundreds

of people there the night she died. Do you remember her having any confrontations?"

Doug hesitated. "Can I get a beer?"

"Help yourself. Just answer me."

Doug walked to the refrigerator and pulled out a bottle of beer. He arched a brow to Quinn, who reached up and caught the Miller his brother tossed his way.

"She had a bit of a confrontation with me."

"Oh?"

"Well, not exactly *with* me. *About* me. She told Jane that she needed to follow, that I knew my stuff and Jane was being too strong, that she needed to let me lead. Under her breath, Jane muttered 'Fuck you, bitch.' Lara heard her and told her that they'd talk about it later. She could be really vicious when she wanted. In a cool, deadly way."

"Yeah, well, she's the dead one. She and Jane were major competition, huh?"

"Rhianna is more the current belle of the studio." As Doug spoke, his cell phone rang. He reached into his pocket with a quick, "'Scuse me."

Quinn looked off. He saw that his brother was glancing furtively at him.

"Yeah, I'm a little busy," Doug said quietly, then listened for a moment.

"I'm not sure," he said next, then glanced at Quinn, looking oddly guilty.

"Who is it?" Quinn mouthed.

For a moment he thought Doug was either going to lie to him or tell him it was none of his business. But Doug covered the mouthpiece of the phone and whispered, "It's Jane."

"Ulrich?" Quinn said.

Doug nodded. "I...uh, I can tell her I can't see her tonight."

"You're not supposed to be seeing her at all, are you?"

"No." No wonder he'd looked so guilty. "You can't say anything," Doug told him quickly. "I mean, she could get fired. Look, I'll just tell her that I can't go over."

"No. Don't. Go over. And don't forget that you're a cop, and don't forget that you dragged me into this."

"Don't forget I'm a cop? You mean, question her."

"Hell yes."

"Doesn't that seem a little…slimy?"

"No. Murder seems a little slimy."

Doug nodded. "You're right."

Quinn shook his head. "You were having an affair with Lara, and she's only been in the ground a few days."

Doug nodded. "I know. But like I said, she was seeing other people, too. She meant something to me, yes. And solving this means a lot to me. I work with Jane. I've worked with her a long time. We're good friends. And she's shaken up right now. It's not so much that we've begun something. She just doesn't want to be alone. You think my spending time with her now is so bad?"

Quinn drummed his fingers on the table. "No, I guess not. But, Doug, if you were so close to Lara, shouldn't you have some idea of who she might have been alone with— if only for a few minutes—at the competition?"

Doug waved a hand in the air. "People move quickly. Before the dinner and competition that night, there was a cocktail hour. People were all milling together. Plus the women instructors had a dressing room, and the men had another, but they were connected by a little outside balcony. So someone having trouble with a tie or a hook or whatever might have slipped out on the balcony and gotten whoever was there to help. And even the pros had some champagne or a cocktail of some kind."

"The glasses from the dressing rooms should have been analyzed," Quinn said, wondering how such a simple procedure had been omitted.

"You have to remember, it looked like a natural death," his brother reminded him. "You don't really think it could have been one of the women, do you?"

"Why not? History has proved that women are certainly capable of murder. And when they do commit murder, they often opt for poison."

"This wasn't poison."

"Drugs act the same way. But what I mean is, no knives, no gunshots, no shows of strength. Silent killers."

"But…Jane? If it were a woman, it would more likely be Shannon. She's the one with the grudge."

"That's true. And if it were just Lara's death, I'd be more inclined to think we should be looking at the fairer sex. But Nell had a connection to the studio, and the circumstances were just too close. And I still don't know if the illegal narcotic deaths were associated or not. My gut reaction says yes, but there's nothing concrete to connect them yet. So I'm suspicious of everyone."

"Even Jane."

"Even Jane. Find out what she takes. If she does drugs. And if she has prescriptions. And if so, find out where she gets them."

"I still feel slimy. But…you're right. I got you into this, and I'm the one who wants to make detective. But you *were* a detective. And when you were with the FBI, you analyzed the ways people acted, their psyches. You've got to have more of a feel for what's going on than I do."

"Nothing but hunches," Quinn told him. "But, hell," he added dryly, "they seem to be just about as good as any other method I learned."

"Should I go now?" Doug asked.

Quinn nodded, then frowned. "She's still on the phone?"

Doug indicated his hand, still tightly clamped over the mouthpiece. Then he moved his hand and spoke into the phone again. "I'm on my way."

On the other end, Jane said something. Something suggestive, Quinn imagined from Doug's reaction.

After Doug left, Quinn stared at his notes.

Coincidence.

Art Durken in jail.

Lara Trudeau dead from the same drug that had killed Nell, combined with alcohol. The prescriptions from different doctors, both with reputations above reproach.

How did the other dead women fit in? Maybe they didn't.

Nell and Lara, both dead by the same drug. Different doctors.

That didn't mean they hadn't gotten more of the drug from different sources.

He glanced at his watch. It was late. Didn't matter. He picked up the phone, intending to call in a few favors.

"Ben!" Shannon exclaimed in relief, reflexively hitting the button to lower the window, then wondering if she should have.

"Shannon, are you all right?" He sounded anxious as he stared in at her.

"I'm fine. Why did you bang on the window like that?"

"Because you came running out of the studio like a bat out of hell."

"Just nerves," she said. But had it just been nerves? Had she imagined the sound of footsteps coming after her?

"Then you're all right?"

"Yes—other than the near heart attack you gave me."

"I'm sorry, really sorry. I thought something was wrong."

She shook her head, then frowned. "Where the hell did you come from, anyway?"

"I'd walked around from the front. I needed a few things

from the convenience store down the street. But my car is back here."

"Oh. You—you didn't go back upstairs, did you?"

"No, I came from the street. Why?"

"I don't know. I thought I heard something."

"Buildings creak. Especially old ones, like ours."

"I suppose," she agreed.

"Want me to follow you home?"

"It's all right."

"I won't get out of my car. I'll just see that you get in your house."

"Sure, fine."

Ben went to his car, and Shannon revved hers into gear. Her house was so close she wondered why she drove.

Because she didn't feel like walking along any shadowy streets right now.

The trip went quickly. As she turned into her own driveway, she saw Ben watching her from his car. She hurried up her walk, opened the door and went in, turning to wave to him before she closed the door.

He waved back, then drove off.

Alone, she leaned against the door and stared around the house. She had left on several lights, but despite that, shadows greeted her.

Silence and shadows.

You're next!

Those two words, spoken to her by a waiter at a competition, where they could have meant anything at all, could have been—must have been—spoken to her by mistake. And yet, they continued to haunt her.

"So just break down already and check yourself into a hospital for the insane," she murmured to herself.

She felt the unbelievable urge to leave home and head for a boat on the marina called the *Twisted Time*.

No.

"Screw this!" she exclaimed aloud with irritation. But once again she found herself going through her house room by room, looking in closets and under the bed, checking out everything, assuring herself that the back door had remained locked and bolted in her absence.

At last she drank a cup of tea and swallowed an Excedrin PM.

After she did, she swore, thinking she would stay up all night long next time, rather than take anything, anything at all, even so much as an aspirin.

It was late when she went to bed, lights blazing in the other rooms, only her own darkened. She would be in shadow and look out to the light. That thought eventually allowed her to close her eyes.

Maybe Christie had been right. Maybe she did need a dog.

She suddenly sat bolt upright, cloaked and chilled by the darkness in her room. Ben had said he'd gone to the convenience store.

For what?

He hadn't been carrying anything, anything at all, when he'd come to her window.

Home again, home again.

She was home again.

Alone. Surely, by now, stretched out in bed, glorious eyes closed, lashes sweetly sweeping her cheeks.

No dog, no alarm, and it wasn't difficult at all to don a pair of gloves and use the key he had to slip inside.

She had no idea how vulnerable she was.

At any time...

Just what the hell did she know?

Nothing, he assured himself.

Except that...

She was listening. Hearing what she shouldn't even be

noticing. Maybe, in time, she would start looking for the source of the noise.

There was more.

He'd overheard her one time too many. He'd seen the way she acted. And now, when he could, he watched her around the studio.

But she'd known something tonight. She'd heard something.

Vague, that was all. She had a vague sense of danger.

He hesitated, thinking how easy it would be to slip in.

But why?

He could take her any time he wanted. If he needed to.

He would really hate to see her dead.

Right now, he would watch. Just watch.

She shouldn't die in her own house. Unless...

No.

There were far better ways. Should it become necessary.

He had been standing on the sidewalk, in the shadows of an elm. But his car wasn't parked far away.

Actually, he tried never to be very far away. Ever. She never even noticed.

Morning was coming.

He would see to it that they were close during the day.

He would watch and wait.

Tonight, he could have touched her.

So close, he could have reached right out and touched her.

He had to remember that. He was always close. Always watching.

And she never knew.

He would always be watching.

Always be close.

Close enough just to reach out...

And touch.

CHAPTER 15

Art Durken entered the jail conference room accompanied by a thirty-something, bulky guard and an older man in a rumpled suit. The older man introduced himself.

"Theodore Smith, Mr. O'Casey. I'm Mr. Durken's attorney, and my client has agreed to see you only in my presence, so if I don't like your questions or attitude, I intend to remind him that he doesn't have to see you at all. Mr. Durken insists on his innocence and is convinced that you may now have a few reasons to believe him—since you requested this meeting."

"I realize Mr. Durken is under no obligation to speak with me," Quinn said. "I appreciate both of you agreeing to the interview."

Smith nodded, looking for all the world like a king granting a subject a special favor, despite his harried appearance. He took a chair on the opposite side of the table, indicating that Art should sit next to him. As Durken did so, Quinn took his own chair.

The burly guard remained in a corner of the room.

Durken was in his early thirties, with sandy hair and

light gray eyes. Slender but wiry, he had a certain charm about him. Apparently that was how he had kept Nell.

And acquired a college senior as a mistress.

"I didn't do it," Durken told him, staring right at him. "I know you were tailing me for Nell, and I know you know exactly what I did with my time in those weeks before she died. But I didn't kill my wife. I swear it."

He looked ill, not at all the same man Quinn had tailed. His hair, so neatly combed in those days, looked ragged, as if he spent his hours running his fingers through it. He had always worn the look of a man who had the world captured between both hands, but now his face was lean, haggard, and there was a sheen of sweat on his upper lip. He might just have looked nervous, like a killer who'd been caught and was ready to deny everything.

But there was something about the way his eyes held Quinn's that seemed to speak of honesty. He didn't start in by scowling, or by accusing Quinn of being the reason he had been arraigned for murder.

"Your fingerprints were all over your wife's pill bottle," Quinn reminded him quietly.

"I handed her the damned thing often enough. And I told her she shouldn't be taking the things. Hell, I even told her that I wasn't worth her having to be on the things. But she had me convinced she knew what she was doing, that she knew when to take them, and that she didn't overdo it. They kept her from mood swings and depression, and fear."

"Let's say you didn't do it, Art," Quinn told him. "Who could have forced her to overdose like that?"

A look of desolation swept over the other man, and he shook his head. "I don't know. You see, the thing of it is…I think Nell was having an affair months ago. She knew…well, she suspected, until she hired you, that I fooled around." He lifted his hands. "I…I did before. And

I think her way of getting even with me might have been to have her own affair. I accused her once, and she told me that she *should* be fooling around, maybe we could stay married that way. It would be messed up as hell, but…she said she loved me and wanted to stay married. Anyway, I went into a big guilt thing, and I wasn't even angry that she was running around, too. I just…you see, I wanted to stay married, too."

"So what happened?"

He shook his head. "It's not in my nature, I guess, to be monogamous. I met Cecily, told her I wasn't married, and you know the rest. Actually," he said, wincing, "I told her that I worked for the CIA, and that's why I was away so much, unable to see her, be with her…and she believed me. I guess you know all that, but…look, I might have been an asshole, a liar and a cheat, but I didn't kill Nell."

"You weren't at all angry, thinking she might have had an affair? You haven't mentioned any of this before. It's not in any of the reports," Quinn pointed out.

"Art, be careful of what you're saying," Smith warned him.

Durken shook his head impatiently. "I didn't mention it before because no one asked me, and…shit, why volunteer that kind of information when I already had a motive and no one wanted to look any further? And while I'm at it, yes, it was always her trust fund that we used for our lifestyle."

"Art, this man can use what you're saying against you in court," Smith warned firmly.

"Was it during the time that your wife was dancing that you thought she was having an affair?" Quinn asked.

Durken looked surprised. "Yes."

"Do you think she was having an affair with a teacher? A fellow student?"

He shrugged. "I never went around the place. Bullshit

dance like that just doesn't appeal to me. She'd asked me to go when she started. I probably should have. Who knows? But, yeah, I suppose she could have had her affair with someone there. We made up big time back then, though. She stopped dancing—and I think she stopped her affair. I didn't press the point, because I didn't want her pressing any points with me. I was guilty as hell, so if she was guilty, too…well, you know."

Durken brightened up suddenly. "I heard about that dancer dying. She died of an overdose, too, huh? Or drugs and booze, something like that." His face fell. "But she died in front of a pack of people, didn't she?"

"Yes, she died before hundreds of people."

Durken looked ill again.

Quinn rose, nodding to Durken's attorney and the guard. "That doesn't mean she wasn't alone with someone before the performance," he said. He pulled out his card, handing it to Durken's attorney. "If there's anything you can think of that might help, could you give me a call?"

He started from the room. Smith called him back. "Mr. Durken is in here because of you, Mr. O'Casey."

"Mr. Durken is in here because his fingerprints were all over the bottle of pills his wife had taken. I merely provided the police with a chronology of his activities prior to his wife's death."

Durken was shaking his head, ignoring his attorney. "I don't care if you got me in here or not—if you can get me out. I'll be thinking. Of anything that can help. Anything at all."

"Thanks," Quinn said.

A guard on the outside opened the door, and Quinn found himself anxious to leave the jail as quickly as possible.

Once outside, he hesitated only a minute, then put through a call to Annie. Though he wasn't scheduled for an appointment himself until the following day, he wanted to get back into the studio.

Marnie was excited.

Dressed in jeans and a polo shirt, she was worried that she didn't really have clothing in which she could move.

"And my shoes," she told Quinn. "My shoes are horrible."

He glanced at her as they drove across the causeway. "I don't think it matters too much—not at first, anyway."

"You sure?"

"We'll find out, won't we?"

She nodded, and he knew she was watching him. "Thanks, by the way," she told him quietly.

"The studio offers a free first class to everyone," he reminded her.

She shook her head, and her long dark hair floated on her shoulders. "I mean, thanks for setting me up with Annie and all. Annie is great. I've been working, you know. At a boutique, right by the shelter. And I can stay at the shelter until I get on my feet. The boutique is great, really cool clothes, and I'll get a fifty percent discount after six months. But you know what? There's an older woman who is a friend of Annie's, and she doesn't have any local family. So Annie's trying to set the two of us up. You know, she'll give me a room, rent free, if I take her to some doctor appointments, buy groceries, take her to church, you know. And if it works out, I can buy the lady's car. Okay, so it's a fifteen-year-old Chevy, but it was never driven anywhere."

"Sounds great," Quinn told her.

"No, it's incredible!" Marnie exclaimed. Then she shook her head again, as if she didn't want to get too sappy. "So, you know, thanks. It's working out well. Better than living in a yard, anyway. Even if it's a pretty decent yard. Besides, the yard was getting a little creepy."

"Creepy? You mean bugs and things?"

She shook her head and said dryly, "No, you live on the street, you learn to live with bugs. No, it was weird sometimes. There was a car that used to cruise by really slowly...then take off. Probably just someone looking for an address."

Tension knotted Quinn's fingers, causing his grip on the steering wheel to tighten. "What car?" he snapped.

"Hey, sorry! I don't know. I didn't get a license number or anything. It was night, dark, you know? It was a car. Maybe beige, maybe gray. Lightish."

"What kind of lightish car?"

"What do you mean? A car—like the kind people drive."

"Big one, little one?"

"Medium."

"Chevy, Ford, Olds, Toyota, Mercedes—what kind of a car?"

"I don't know. I don't have a car, remember? I've never even been shopping for a car. I only know that old Mrs. Marlin's car is a Chevy because Annie told me. It was a medium-size sedan, I guess."

"If you saw it again, would you recognize it?"

She must have felt his tension because she went very stiff herself. She was staring at him, looking a little scared, as if she'd trusted in a mentor who'd turned out to be slightly insane. And yet she still looked as if she wanted to help him.

She shook her head. "I'm sorry. Really."

"How many nights did you see this car?"

"It was only twice—if it was the same car."

"So why did it make things...creepy?"

"I don't know. It just did. Hey, pay attention—you're going to miss the turnoff. I do know how to get to the beach."

They reached the studio. Quinn parked at a meter but told Marnie they would walk around the back, where the teachers, seasoned students and other employees at the building parked.

"Recognize any of them?" he asked, but before she could reply, he knew her answer.

Every flipping car there was gray or beige.

And every single one of them was a sedan.

"Quinn, I'm sorry. They all look alike," she told him, turning her large brown eyes to meet his. "It might have been any one of them."

"Or none," he said.

"Or none," she agreed.

He nodded. "Well, thanks for looking. Let's go on up."

She smiled again. "My first lesson," she breathed happily.

Shannon returned from a meeting to see Marnie out on the floor with Sam Railey. The girl looked like a child getting a Christmas present for the first time. And when she moved, following Sam's instructions on a rumba step, it was with a natural grace.

The girl had caught her eye, but then Shannon looked quickly around, certain Quinn would be there, as well.

He was. By the reception area, with Gordon and Ella, all of them watching the girl.

"You're back," Ella called out to her. "Meeting go well?"

"Yes, everything went perfectly," she said, walking over to join the group. As courtesy required, she forced a note of welcome into her voice as she greeted Quinn.

"Great. You've got a class in fifteen minutes," Ella told her.

"Oh?" Who? she wondered. Quinn wasn't scheduled until the next day.

"Me," he told her, smiling.

"Oh?" she responded, trying not to sound too icy.

"Well, I've decided to enter that Gator thing," he said. "And that means I have a lot to learn in very little time."

"You're really going to enter the Gator Gala?" she asked.

"Why not?" Gordon boomed. "There's a beginners category."

"Gordon, he's had one private lesson!" she said.

"Well, that's the point. I'm going to need a few more," Quinn said.

She nodded. "Fine. Let me get my shoes on."

Trying very hard not to give away her irritation, Shannon went to her office and changed her shoes. Gordon might be delighted that a brand-new student wanted to enter, but she wasn't.

Still it was good for the studio. It would mean lots and lots of classes. Lots and lots of money. Of course, she knew now that he wasn't any poor fishing captain or struggling charter service. Then again, did P.I.s make the big bucks?

Of course, Doug O'Casey felt free to book as many classes as he wanted. On a cop's salary.

There was a light tap on her door. "Hey, Shannon," Ella said softly. "He signed up for this hour."

"Well, he shouldn't have. I just got back," she muttered.

"Gordon was really excited."

"Then Gordon should teach him."

"Shannon, what on earth is the matter?" Ella demanded.

"Nothing. I'll be out in a sec."

Katarina was in the studio, minus her husband David. She was dancing with Ben. They were working on an advanced waltz, with Ben showing her how to create a beautiful arc with her body. "It's easy to forget the body when you're learning the steps," Ben was saying seriously. "But now that you have the routine down, it's time to work the body. Think elegance. We dance together, but you've got to remember your position—your universe."

"And get the hell out of your universe, right?" Katarina said, laughing. "I know what you mean, Ben. I just keep forgetting."

"That's why we'll keep going over it," he said. They waltzed away. Quinn two-left-feet O'Casey was waiting.

She walked over to him and took his hand, leading him to the other side of the floor. Justin Garcia was there, teaching salsa to a pretty young Oriental girl taking her first class. Sam Railey was still with Marnie. Her class was over, but they were talking by the kitchen, where Sam was fixing her a cup of coffee.

There was really nowhere private in the studio, but most of the time the music drowned out any conversation.

"Why are you taking classes at all?" she asked Quinn, leading him to her stash of CDs.

"Because I'm dying to be the Irish salsa sensation of the city," he said dryly.

"Really?"

"Sibling rivalry? Doug has gotten so good, I can't stand it."

"Really."

"It's the best way to be here."

"It's an expensive way to be here."

"True," he agreed. "But if I hang around enough, I can find out all the deep, dark secrets going on around the place."

"Yeah, like our lives are deep, dark secrets," she said dryly. "We don't have lives. That's the sad truth."

"Lara had a life. An active one."

Shannon waited for Justin's salsa to end, then slipped a basic waltz into the player. "Come on," she told him. "Get the count. It's very basic. One, two, three…one, two, three…"

She was amazed to discover that he actually had it.

"Not bad," she told him.

"My mom made me do this one when I was growing up," he admitted. "But you seem really unhappy teaching me. So let's talk."

"Can you talk and keep count?" she asked.

"Yes!"

"Don't bark at me. Lots of times, in the beginning, people need to count. Then they learn to move and converse at the same time."

"Let's see, you know what I am, what I do. So let's start with you. On the day Lara died, did you spend any private time with her?"

Shannon stared at him, realizing that he was far better at dancing than he had let on. Or maybe it was just the waltz. He seemed extremely capable of moving around the floor and grilling her at the same time.

She stared at him hard in return and answered. "No. I got along with her fine. When she came to the studio, I wrote her checks, chatted pleasantly and applauded her triumphs. But we weren't friends, and we didn't go looking for each other's company. So no, I was never alone with her."

"Did you see anyone alone with her?"

She shook her head. "I wouldn't have been watching her."

"So what shook you up so badly that day?"

"Nothing," she said, then stopped, inhaling sharply.

"So you've been lying?"

She shook her head. "No, not lying," she said, and hesitated. "I…I've been pretty angry at you."

"Gee, you're kidding." His eyes were sharp as crystal, cool, distant. He was working now. And he was good at it.

She felt as if she should be ready to spill everything. She reminded herself that he was a P.I., not a cop.

But he had been a cop once. Maybe he'd left in hopes of making more money as a private citizen. She felt as if she was dancing with Eliot Ness.

"Tell me," he persisted. "And tell me, too, why you haven't told me yet."

"Because it isn't really anything," she insisted.

"I'll decide that."

"When Lara was dancing, a waiter came up to me and said, 'You're next.'"

"'You're next'?" Quinn repeated.

"Yes. That's why…well, I'm assuming he just mixed me up with someone else. I wasn't competing, so I couldn't have been next. But that's also why it freaked me out a little. You know…*you're next*. As if I were next…to die. I assumed it's just part of the paranoia I picked up after Lara died."

"You should never assume. You're sure the man was a waiter?"

"He was dressed as a waiter."

"I'll check into it," he told her.

"How are you even going to know what waiters were working that day? Never mind—it's what you do."

The music stopped. Justin slipped a salsa CD back into the machine. Shannon determined to tone her temper down. After all, he wasn't the enemy. He was trying to find the truth.

And that was what she wanted.

"Thank you," she managed to tell him. "If I can find out that the man really was just mixed-up, then I will feel better."

"I'll find out," he said flatly. "And here's the deal—when you think of anything, no matter how silly, you tell me."

"Yes," she said.

"And…" he said firmly.

"And what?"

"My time isn't nearly up. I think I've proved I've got the count on this. What I don't know is any more steps. And why are you arching away like that, trying not to look at me?"

"Because I'm not supposed to look at you in a waltz. There's a way to hold your partner in close contact, but you're not really ready for that yet."

He arched a brow. "Try me," he said softly.

"You're a beginner—two left feet. You said so yourself."

"Not in everything."

She wasn't sure exactly what he meant, if there was an innuendo there, or if he was referring completely to dance.

"Excuse me. I'll get your book and put on a waltz as soon as Justin's disk ends."

She walked away from him, grabbed his new student folder from the bookshelf and headed back over to the stereo system. The salsa ended. She got ready to slip in another waltz.

There was a second between the disks. A split second.

And in that fraction of time, she heard it.

That sound, a scraping, like nails against a blackboard, like metal against metal, like…something moving, opening, closing….

Then the music started again, and Quinn came up behind her.

She turned, frowning. "Did you hear that?"

"What? Something in the music I should have heard?" he asked.

"No…no…like…"

"A car backfired down on the road somewhere," he told her.

She shook her head again.

"What did you hear?" he demanded.

"I don't know. Nothing, really. I guess it was the car." It was broad daylight. The studio was filled with people. The streets below were busy. It could have been anything.

Except she had heard that noise before.

When his lesson ended, she was very surprised to realize that it hadn't been mercilessly painful, and he seemed ruefully pleased himself. Maybe the classes were just a by-product of his work, but he was getting somewhere with them, at least.

He left right after his lesson, taking Marnie with him.

And after he was gone, the day seemed to drag on. She made a point of wandering into every room, studying it. Trying to figure out what might make the noise she kept hearing.

Nothing. She had to make a lame excuse about checking the toilet paper when she ran into Sam as he walked into the men's room while she was on her way out.

"Slow day for you, huh?" he teased.

Then Justin came in. "We never had a lineup like this in here before," he said.

"I was just checking supplies," she said.

Then Gordon entered. "What the hell is this? Grand Central Station?" he demanded. Hands on his hips, eyes narrowed, he looked at her suspiciously.

"I was making sure there was enough toilet paper."

A bushy white brow hiked. "In the men's room? The cleaning lady does that once a week."

"Someone said we were out," she mumbled. Then, both exasperated and embarrassed, she pushed her way out.

Despite her search, she continually found herself listening. And watching Ben. Finally, when she was in the reception area and Ben came to check his schedule, she asked him about the night before.

"Ben?"

"Hmm?"

"Last night…?"

"Yes?"

"You said you'd been at the convenience store."

He looked from the book to her. "Right."

She shook her head. "But you didn't have a bag or anything with you. What did you buy?"

He frowned, staring at her. "Something personal," he said. "And really none of your business."

"Sorry."

"Are you accusing me of having run up here to follow you?"

"No, I was just asking."

He set his hand on her chair and leaned toward her. "Condoms."

"What?"

"If you must know, I was buying condoms. And if you don't believe me, go ask Julio. The little Honduran guy. He was the one working there last night."

She felt a flush cover her cheeks, but it didn't matter. Ben had stepped away from her chair.

"Thanks for the info," she said, rising and pushing past him.

After that, the day became even more tedious, with the tension rising between her and Ben.

That night, a number of the others were going down to the club. Shannon was glad she wasn't going to be leaving the studio alone.

But as she started to close down, she realized Ella was already gone, and the group going clubbing was already on the way down.

She was going to wind up in the studio alone after all.

She ran into her office, grabbed her purse, then froze. There were footsteps coming toward her office.

She swung around, ready to wage battle with her purse.

But it was Gordon. He arched a brow slowly. "What is going on with you, Shannon?"

She lowered her purse but kept it clenched tightly in her hand.

"Shannon?"

His voice seemed low and quiet, and yet his features were tense. He was holding a pen at his side. He seemed to be clutching it very tightly.

Gordon Henson had been her mentor from the beginning. He had given her this job, had given her his trust. He had brought her through the ranks.

He had also been the first to teach and encourage Lara Trudeau.

"Nothing. Nothing is going on." She looked at his pen. He was clicking it open, then clicking it closed. Continuously.

"Hey."

She looked past Gordon. There was someone else in the studio.

Quinn.

"I just wanted to see if Shannon was going down to the club. Or you, Gordon," he said casually. Both of them stared at him. He offered them a slight grin. "Hey, guys, I'm not a ghost. I've been here for a while. I came back to watch the group class."

"I'm going home tonight," Gordon said. "Since you're here, you can walk Shannon out. Ben told me she's been getting a little freaked out at night lately. Good night."

Gordon lifted a hand, waved and left.

"Are you going clubbing tonight?" Quinn asked Shannon.

She shook her head. "I'm really tired. I just want to go home."

"Did you drive?"

"Yes."

"I'll follow you, then."

"Thanks, but you don't have to, not if you want to go to the club."

"Not tonight."

She almost asked him to wait, to let her walk around the studio and try again to find what it was that made that sound.

But she didn't hear it then. And she didn't know how to describe it. And for some reason, she was still disturbed because of what seemed like a strange encounter with Gordon.

She walked out of the studio, locking the door behind her, then paused, listening.

"What's the matter?" he asked.

"Nothing." And there was nothing. Just the sound of the music from down below.

"So…?" he said.

"Let's go," she said with a shrug.

He didn't say a word, just followed her to her car, and when she was in it, slid into the driver's seat of his own Navigator. He followed her to the house, parked and walked up the front door behind her.

"Thanks, thanks a lot," she told him.

"I think I'll sleep on the couch in back," he told her.

"I didn't ask you to."

"I know. I'm telling you that I'm going to."

"What if I don't want you to?"

"Trust me—you want me to," he told her.

He stepped inside, closing and locking the door behind him. And she had to admit, he was right. She *was* glad to have him there.

CHAPTER 16

He cruised by. Easy enough…just cruising. People did it on the beach all the time. Drove around, saw what action was going on.

Except his cruising was a little off the beaten path.

What was it? Had he always had a bit of a thing for her? She moved like liquid. The tilt of her head, the arc of her back, just the reach of her hand, slowly moving to the music…yeah, she was liquid. Elegance in motion.

Had it been that, or…

Or had she always made him a little bit nervous?

Whatever had caused his obsession, she had never known of it.

He suddenly damned his partner, who was causing the trouble now. Strange, but once it started, murder came easy. And he had to admit, his partner had an ungodly finesse….

But his partner could also cause them all to get caught.

Wrong choice of people.

Because, here on the beach, with the garish, shrieking

beat of the night, anything could happen. Rich and poor, they came. Ecstasy flourished—the drug and the feeling it enhanced. New designer drugs hit the streets every night.

People died. They couldn't handle it. Everyone in the world knew it: drugs killed.

But now...

She made him nervous. And she made him angry. Because...

He was obsessed. So if she pushed him too far...

He could solve both his obsession and his problem in one little night.

He was smart. And dangerous.

But she was always watching. And listening.

Hide in plain sight. It was good advice. She could watch and listen, but what could she see?

Lara had known. But Lara had wanted money. She'd actually found the whole thing amusing. Sins weren't sins to Lara Trudeau, not unless they were against her. She had probably dropped dead having no idea of what had happened, or why. Pity. He'd wanted her to know. She shouldn't have pushed the wrong people too far.

He slowed the car as he neared her house.

The Navigator was there.

He swore, feeling his anger—and his obsession—grow.

Jealousy shot through him, like the piercing blade of a knife. He stared at the house, imagining what might be going on inside.

The fury grew.

At last he drove on by, anger now a fierce flame.

It took root, wrapping around his gut like a fist of burning steel. His fingers were so tense around the steering wheel that he jerked the car to the side of the road.

He gave himself a mental shake.

His time would come.

Her time would come.

* * *

There he was, Quinn O'Casey, in her house and heading for the kitchen.

She followed him. "You can't stay here," she informed him.

"What have you got in here?" he asked her, opening a cabinet. "Coffee? No good, I don't want to stay up." He opened the refrigerator.

"You can't stay," she repeated.

"What, not afraid tonight?" he asked her. "Tea," he said. "Hot tea, I guess it's got caffeine, too, but they say it can make you sleep."

She reached for the box of tea bags. "You can't stay."

There was a strange look in his eyes. A bright glimmer of dry amusement. "What? Afraid of me being on your couch? Afraid you won't be able to keep your distance?"

She snatched the box out of his hands. "I guarantee you that I can keep my distance. What you don't understand is this—I can't have your car out in front of my house all night."

"Why? Do your friends—employees—check up on you? Does Gordon make a habit of driving by at night?"

"Of course they don't check up on me. But they drive by occasionally. They stop by in the morning sometimes."

"You're the mother hen, huh?"

"The point is, they may come by."

"I'll move the car," he said.

"Move it where?"

"Out to Alton. People hang out on the beach until the wee hours of the morning. I can leave it there and no one will ever notice."

She couldn't argue with that. But she shook her head. "There's no need for you to stay. I was uneasy, but it turned out that Marnie was living in the yard. Now that she has a home, I'm not afraid anymore."

She was lying. She remained nervous, with no tangible reason, and it was driving her nuts. She wasn't usually such a chicken.

But then, she didn't have a defensive talent to her name. She wasn't a weakling, but she had never shot a gun in her life nor taken a single course in self-defense. She should probably rectify that situation, but everything she had ever said about having no life was true. She spent far too much time at the studio.

She reflected briefly that even Lara Trudeau had allowed herself to have a life.

That didn't matter tonight. He shouldn't be in her house.

Tomorrow, she decided, she was going to go through every room in the studio again. Yes, even the men's room. She was going to find out what that noise was. She was going to find out why she heard not just noises, but footsteps that followed her when she fled the building.

Quinn was watching her. It was almost as if he could read the thoughts running amok in her mind. "I think I should stay," he said firmly.

"But I'm not inviting you!" she said. Then she felt uneasy, wondering just why he was so sure he should stay. "Do you think that I may be in danger?" she demanded.

"Well, let's see, we both know I'm a P.I. working a case. Maybe I think—"

"You *are* a P.I." She cocked her head suddenly.

"Yes, that's been established."

"Couldn't you rig me with a surveillance system?"

"Sure. But they cost. And they take time."

"Tomorrow, maybe?"

"I can do it on Thursday," he told her. "For tonight, I'll move my car." He indicated the box of tea bags in her hands. "I like sugar and milk in mine," he told her, heading for the door. "And lock up while I'm out."

He left the house, and she just stared after him for several seconds. Then she flew to the front door and locked it. Irritably, she threw the box of tea bags on the counter. Then she waited impatiently for him to return.

When he did, she didn't open the door until she saw his face through the peephole.

"Honey, I'm home," he teased. "Where's the tea?"

"I'm exhausted, and I'm going to bed. I'm sure you know how to boil water."

"I do," he told her. "I make a pretty good cup of tea, too. Want one?"

"Thank you, no."

"You don't have to sleep with me just because I make you tea."

"Cute. I don't want tea."

"Still afraid you'll get too tempted with me sleeping out in the Florida room?"

"Not a chance."

"Pity."

"I told you, I don't like liars."

"I never actually lied. But it doesn't matter, not if you're going to be that bitter."

"I still say there's no reason for you to be here."

"Just protecting your interests—in the pursuit of my own. And if there's no chance of you forgiving me, there's no reason for you to be so irritable about me being here."

She shook her head. At least he wasn't coming anywhere near her. He'd done some teasing, but he certainly seemed to have no difficulty keeping his distance.

"You want to sleep on the couch, sleep on the couch," she said at last.

"Good night, then."

"Good night."

She made a good exit, turning, heading straight for her bedroom, then closing and locking the door. She leaned against it for a minute, listening.

She heard him filling the kettle with water and shook her head. Last night, she'd lain awake listening for noises and wondering about Ben.

Tonight she would feel safe.

But she would still lie awake, knowing this man was in her house.

Shannon moved away from the door and went into the bathroom, where she brushed her teeth, she showered, then found a ripped-up flannel nightgown. She put it on, then went back to the door, leaned against it and listened again.

She heard the sound of the television and the drone of his voice. He was on the phone, she thought.

Screw it.

She crawled into bed, reminding herself how angry she was at the way he had used her.

Ah, but he knew how to use a woman well.

She could get up, invite him in and sleep in the real comfort of feeling those arms around her. Feeling…

More. A lot more. Excitement that was raw and seductive and exhilarating. Carnal and lusty and sensual, hot, slick, vibrant…

She turned, slamming a fist into her pillow.

Absolutely not.

Why? It was so much better to lie here, in a cool dry blanket of dignity.

Yes.

No.

She stood up and walked to the door, listening again.

She could still hear him on the phone, thanking someone for taking care of something that would happen tomorrow. She slipped the door open, trying to hear more clearly.

He said goodbye to the person on the other end of the phone as she did so.

"There's still tea in the pot!" he called to her.

She stiffened. "I was just going to ask you to turn the television down a bit."

He turned, seeing her down the length of the hallway. "Really? I thought maybe you were going to come on out and seduce me again." His eyes slid up and down her, taking in the ragged flannel nightgown. "Guess not, huh?"

"Not a chance," she told him solemnly.

She closed the door and went back to bed, swearing.

Later, even as she burned with discomfort, wanting what she refused to allow herself, she began to drift, until finally she fell into a deep refreshing sleep.

Tedium.

Half the work was pure tedium.

There had been dozens of waiters on duty the night of the competition. But thanks to Jake, he had a list of names and phone numbers.

And when he called people, they seemed to think he was a cop, even though he identified himself immediately. At any rate, it worked.

A few of the men he talked to were hesitant at first. He had a feeling that a number of them weren't quite legal. Once they ascertained that he wasn't with INS, they tried to be helpful.

On some of the calls he made, the numbers just rang and rang. On some, he hit answering machines. On some, he hit really sleepy people. Seemed most of the guys worked nights.

He kept dialing, marking off those he had spoken with. The next guy to pick up sounded uneasy. Quinn assured him that he wasn't with INS.

"The waiters didn't help line up the dancers," Miguel Avenaro told him. "The judges do that. They had their clipboards, and their lists of names and schedules, and handled all that themselves."

"Thank you for your time," Quinn told him and hung up.

How many calls had he made? Twenty-something already.

He tried the next name on his list. Manuel Taylor. A true Miami name.

The man who answered spoke English perfectly, no hint of an accent. He listened to Quinn's question.

"Who are you?" he said.

"I'm a private investigator. My name is Quinn O'Casey."

"You're not a cop?"

"No."

"I don't have to speak with you, then, do I?"

"No, you don't. I can have a cop call you," Quinn said.

"They don't think any of the waiters had anything to do with that woman's death, do they?"

"No."

"Then…"

"I'm just trying to find the man who spoke to Miss Mackay and find out who instructed him to do so."

There was silence on the other end.

Then, "It was me," the man said.

In the morning, Quinn was gone. The bottom lock on her front door was in place, though the bolt, which had to be latched from the inside or with a key, had necessarily been left unlocked.

There was coffee waiting in the pot, along with a little note.

Since it seems you're not fond of tea, I made you coffee. See you later. I have a lesson today. Can't wait. Know you can't, either.

"Funny, funny," she muttered.

She poured herself coffee. She leaned against the

counter, feeling a little chill. She hadn't experienced any of the wild, carnal excitement that had teased her memory and stirred her senses. She had gotten a good night's sleep, instead.

She wondered which she might really have needed more.

An edge of hurt came creeping back. He had just been using her, getting to know her, getting close, investigating...

At the same time, he definitely seemed like a decent guy. And decent guys didn't come by all that frequently in life.

Would it be so bad to have another memory of an incredible encounter?

Stop, she warned himself.

She had to teach him today. She didn't want to feel any little electric jolts zapping through her while she danced. And she had a busy day ahead of her. Gunter and Helga, practicing for Asheville. A double appointment with Richard Long, coaching for Jane and Sam, the studio "party" that night, when the students danced with the teachers, practicing the steps they'd learned.

There was a tapping at the door. Still in the ragged flannel nightshirt, she walked to the door and looked through the peephole.

It was Gordon.

Unease filtered through her. She remembered the way he had clicked the pen last night, open, then closed, open, then closed. With such agitation.

Asking her what was wrong with her.

After he'd discovered her prying in the men's room.

She hesitated.

He stood on the step, hands shoved into his pockets, glancing around. He looked at his watch, then pounded on the door again.

"Shannon, what the hell are you doing in there?" he demanded.

It was broad daylight. And it was just Gordon, being impatient. It wasn't the strangest thing in the world that he was there—he had stopped by in the morning many times before over the years. She hesitated a moment longer, then opened the door.

He arched a brow, scanning her attire. "Not out to seduce anyone this morning, huh?" he asked.

She grimaced. "I just woke up."

"Well, take a quick shower and come with me."

"Come where with you?"

"To get something to eat."

"I have a really full schedule today," she said.

"You still have to eat. Don't make your old boss go out alone. I don't want to be alone right now."

"Grab some coffee then—you have to give me a few minutes."

She started back to her bedroom, but as she did, the phone rang.

"Want me to get it?" Gordon asked.

"No, I'm right here." She picked it up, glancing at her watch. Ten o'clock. She really had slept late.

"Hello?"

"It's me, Quinn. Meet me at Nick's in thirty minutes. Can you do it?"

"I have company right now, and a killer schedule today." She winced at her casual use of the word *killer*.

"This is important."

"I was just heading out to eat."

"I've found the waiter."

"Who?"

"The waiter who told you that you'd be next."

"My boss is here," she said. "I'm going out with him."

"Gordon Henson is there? Now?"

"Yes, we're going to lunch. Breakfast. Brunch. Whatever." She glanced at Gordon. He had wandered out to the Florida room as if he were totally uninterested in her conversation. Even so, he could probably hear her.

"Tell him I'm coming to get you both," Quinn said.

"Wait a minute!"

"Just do that. Tell him I'm coming to get you both. That we're going to talk about the trip out on the bay. Tell him that. Make sure he knows I'm on my way over."

"All right. But tell me—"

"Get into your room and lock the door. And make sure he knows I'll be on the doorstep any second."

She felt a chill and lowered her voice, staring out at Gordon, a sinking feeling already seizing her. "It was Gordon, right?" she whispered.

She clutched the phone more tightly.

"Yes, it was Gordon. And he didn't just ask him to say it to you—he tipped him fifty bucks to do it. Hang up, and lock yourself in your room until I get there."

"Right."

She nearly dropped the phone, trying to return it to the base. "That was Quinn," she called out. "He'll be on the doorstep any second. He's going to take us to lunch, discuss the trip this Saturday. I'll be right out!"

She fled into her bedroom, wrenching the door closed, instantly hitting the lock.

For long moments she remained there, her fingers curled around the handle, afraid to let go, even though the lock was in place.

Then she heard Gordon. Walking back from the Florida room.

"Shannon?"

His hand was on the doorknob. She felt it twist beneath her fingers.

# CHAPTER 17

Quinn was in his car in a matter of seconds.

Gordon Henson had paid the waiter to say those words to Shannon. *You're next.* Seconds before Lara fell down dead.

That didn't make him a murderer.

And if he was a murderer, he was of the more devious variety. He would not head to Shannon's house in broad daylight to commit an act of violence.

He wasn't going to hurt her. Especially not now that he knew Quinn was on the way.

Quinn felt as if he was rocketing down US1.

He was amazed he wasn't stopped by a policeman.

I-95 took him to the causeway. He watched the clock on the dashboard. Just a matter of minutes. He must be making record time.

It didn't make sense. What could Gordon Henson possibly gain from the death of Lara Trudeau?

He swore softly. He didn't need to be in such a panic. He hit the digit on his phone that called Shannon's house. Gordon picked up.

"Gordon, hey, it's Quinn."

"Hey there. Thought you'd be here by now. The way Shannon spoke, I though you were just about in the front yard."

"I *am* just about in the front yard."

"Take your time. Shannon isn't ready yet. She must be in the shower."

"I thought we could talk about the cruise."

"So she told me. Looking forward to it. You got us a hell of a deal."

"Right."

He was turning the corner onto her street.

"I'm there," he said, and hung up.

In seconds he was out of the car and running up the path to her house.

Shannon heard the thundering on the door. Heard Gordon walk across the living room to answer it.

Gordon. She couldn't believe it. She'd known him for years; he'd done everything in the world for her. And yet...

She was still standing there by the door, frozen, as time elapsed. Maybe not that much time. Maybe it only felt like it.

Quinn was there. She could let go.

She did. Then she flew to get dressed.

When she came out, both men were seated in the living room. They'd been talking casually, it seemed. Quinn looked as if he didn't have a care in the world.

Gordon only looked hungry.

"I've seen her change outfits five times at a show faster than that," Gordon said, half joking, half aggravated.

"But she's ready now," Quinn said.

"Yes," Shannon said. "I'm ready."

"Well, then, do you mind going to Nick's? There's someone who should be there that I'd kind of like to run into," Quinn said.

"The cop hangout? Sure, I've never been. I'd love to see the place," Gordon agreed, heading for the door. "Maybe we should take two cars. That way Shannon and I can head over to the studio if you have other business during the day," he continued.

"I don't have any business. I'm coming into the studio," Quinn said.

Shannon stared at him, trying to maintain a neutral expression. Had he actually figured out that Gordon had somehow killed Lara? Was he having him arrested? And if not...

"Suit yourself," Gordon said cheerfully.

Quinn seated Shannon in the front seat of the Navigator. She looked at him questioningly, but he didn't say anything as Gordon got in the back, complimenting the car. In fact, as they drove, he seemed laid-back and content, commenting on how nice it was not to be driving but just enjoying the scenery. "It's easy to forget how beautiful it is out here, isn't it?" he said, leaning forward.

"Water, water everywhere," Quinn murmured.

"I hear that Nick's is a nice place. He a friend of yours?"

"I hung around there for years. And a friend of mine, a homicide cop, married Nick's niece. Who is also a cop."

"Cool," Gordon said. "So your brother hangs out there, too?"

"Yes, Doug has always liked the place."

"Maybe we'll run into him," Gordon suggested. He didn't seem worried about fraternization. "Then there's his buddy—the wedding student, Bobby, and his bride, Giselle."

"We won't run into either of them. They're both on duty right now, toeing the line, sticking to their assigned districts," Quinn said. He glanced at Gordon in the mirror. "Doug wants to be homicide eventually."

"Too bad. He could be a pro," Gordon said.

"Maybe he can be both," Quinn said.

Gordon laughed. "You haven't really realized what the world of true pros is like yet, huh? They dance. They dance, and then they dance some more."

"Is Doug really that good?" Quinn asked. He glanced at Shannon.

"I think he could be. He's got a lot going for him," she said.

They had left the causeway and I-95 and were shooting down US1. They would be at Nick's any minute. Gordon didn't seem in the least alarmed.

But why would he have paid a waiter to say such a thing? Shannon wondered.

They parked and got out of the car. Shannon followed Quinn, who immediately headed for the outside patio. Gordon was behind her.

The girl who had waited on them the last time she had been there saw them arrive. Apparently Quinn often wound up in her section, judging by the friendly way she greeted him.

"Welcome back!" she said cheerfully to Shannon, who winced slightly.

"You've been here before, huh?" Gordon said. There was a curious, teasing light in his eyes.

She smiled weakly.

"That friend of yours is in at the bar," the girl told Quinn. "Did you want coffee?"

"All the way round?" Quinn asked, looking at the other two.

"You bet. And orange juice, at least for Shannon and me. You, too, Quinn?" Gordon asked.

"Yeah, great," he said.

They slid into their seats. Before Gordon could ask about Quinn's friend, the man himself came walking out to the patio. Gordon stared at the tall, attractive, Hispanic man coming their way. He squinted slightly, as if trying to remember where he knew him from. Then he said, "Hey! That guy was one of the waiters at the competition. I recognize him."

Shannon inhaled sharply, holding her breath.

Quinn looked intently at Gordon. "That's right. And you *should* recognize him."

Gordon stared at Quinn. The man reached the table.

"Manuel, have a seat," Quinn said.

The man nodded and took a chair, looking a little awkward.

"Manuel, hello. How are you doing? Leaving the hotel business and working here now?" Gordon asked pleasantly. "Or are you two friends?" he asked, looking from Manuel to Quinn.

"Mr. O'Casey asked me to come out," Manuel said.

Coffee and orange juice arrived. "Sir, I brought you fresh coffee, too," she told Manuel cheerfully.

"Thank you," Manuel said.

Gordon waited for her to leave. Then he sat back, crossing his arms over his chest and staring at them all one by one. The biggest accusation in his eyes was for Shannon. "All right. What the hell is going on here?"

"Gordon, right before Lara died," Shannon said, "this man came up to me and said, 'You're next.' You paid him to do that? Why?"

"How the hell did I know Lara was about to drop dead?" Gordon said irritably. "And if you dragged me—and this poor man—out here just to have him as an eyewitness, we can let him go home now. I paid him to go up and talk to you, yes."

"Is it all right if I leave? I'm working a luncheon this afternoon," Manuel said to Quinn.

"Sure. Thanks for coming."

Manuel grinned. "No problem. I'm making pretty big

bucks off your group. I wouldn't mind working a cruise, sometime, though. Call me if you need help."

"Sure thing," Quinn replied.

As soon as Manuel left, Shannon turned to Gordon. "Gordon, why? Why pay someone to say something like that to me?"

"I thought it might slip into your subconscious somewhere," Gordon said. "Remind you that you should be next to dance. Awaken the spark of competition in your soul. Hell, it's no secret that all the rest of us think you should be out there. Wait a minute." He stared at Quinn then. "Hell, I was pretty damned slow there, huh? I think I'm finally getting this. Shannon, you think that someone killed Lara. And since I paid Manuel here to say 'You're next' to you, I must be that person. Great. You think I killed her."

Shannon wanted to crawl beneath a chair. Gordon had never in his life looked so much like a beaten bloodhound.

"Gordon, you don't understand the way those words have haunted me!" she said.

"Lara was my pride and joy. My creation," Gordon said.

"She bit the hand that fed her many a time, too, so I understand," Quinn said.

Gordon shook his head in disgust. "You don't understand. If I were an architect, Lara would have been one of my greatest buildings. We can tease and nit-pick and argue among ourselves, and I'll grant you, she was as impressed with herself as anyone could be, but she was still…family, I guess you'd say. There was a relationship. Good sometimes, aggravating at others. But in a thousand years, I'd never have hurt her. And you?" he told Shannon. "Fine. You want to throw away years of work and an ocean of natural talent, do it. You not competing saves me from any work I might have needed to do in these last few years before retirement." He shook his head in hurt and disgust.

"What, you don't believe me?" he said to Quinn. "Is that why we're here? Have you got the cops lined up to arrest me?"

Quinn shook his head. "No. But when Shannon told me about those words, we had to find out why the waiter came up to her and who told him to."

Gordon sighed, closing his eyes, opening them on Shannon. "So you've been spilling your guts out to this guy, huh?"

"I mentioned a few fears, yes."

"Makes sense," Gordon said.

"Oh?" Shannon murmured.

"Sure. He's a private investigator."

"You knew that?" Shannon said.

"Go through a few channels and you can pull him up on the Internet." Gordon was staring at Quinn. "I shouldn't have been surprised this morning. Finding the waiter was a piece of cake for him." He kept looking at Quinn, but Shannon knew that he was speaking for her benefit. "He had to have his record expunged—he was thrown out his first year of college for drugs and disorderly conduct—but then he made a nice turnaround. A psychology major who became a cop, made it to homicide in record time, then applied to the FBI, where he joined the behavioral science unit—you know, the profilers' division—and then he up and quit and came back here, joining up with a friend who was already in the business."

Shannon stared from Gordon to Quinn. "Everything is available on the damned Net, huh?" Quinn said.

"Hey, you were a civil servant. What do you want?" Gordon said. "Do they serve food around here? I mean, I know you don't trust me, I don't know what to make of you, and Shannon would probably just as soon we both jumped in the bay, but I'm still starving."

"Yes, they serve food," Quinn said, looking around to catch their waitress's eye.

Gordon was hungry. He ordered a breakfast special that included eggs, pancakes, steak, hash browns and toast. Shannon opted for just the last. Quinn stuck with coffee. Which was fine, because Gordon kept trying to get them to help him with the huge platter the waitress set down before him.

Quinn and Shannon were both quiet throughout the meal. Shannon couldn't help feeling a slow boil of anger again when she thought of just how much she hadn't known about Quinn's life. Things he apparently hadn't thought to share, even when insisting on being a protector rather than an investigator.

"Shall we get to the boat?" Gordon said.

"What?" Quinn said.

"The boat. Saturday is almost here. Let me ask this— do you really have a boat?"

Quinn nodded. "She's down in the Keys right now, but I'll have her up here with a crew, the whole bit, by Friday night."

"I need you to speak to the catering company, just to make sure everyone has what they need. And I'm hiring a trio to play—we'll need space for them."

"She'll be just what you need," Quinn assured him. "You can do a walk-through Friday night."

"Great." Gordon threw his napkin down at last. "We need to open up the studio. Are you two ready?"

"I'll get the check," Quinn said.

"Hell, no. I'll get the check. You can put your money toward your entry into the Gator Gala," Gordon told him.

"He's not really entering," Shannon said.

Quinn stared at her, his look suddenly hard and stubborn. "Yes, he really is entering. And I brought you here so I can get the check."

"No, I've got it," Gordon insisted.

Shannon stood. "I'll get the check. Let's just go."

* * *

It was a very busy day. Wednesdays always were. The studio's weekly "party" didn't start until late, but students came all day to brush up and be ready.

Katarina, the designer from next door, was busy, too, making adjustments to costumes for the gala. Gabriel Lopez took a lesson first with Shannon, then one with Jane, and later, he told Quinn, he would be taking a lesson with Rhianna, as well.

"I think it's important," he said. "I run a club, and I ask lots of women to dance to keep the floor moving, keep the wallflowers happy. So I learn from all of them. And the lessons," he said with a grin, "are tax-deductible. It's a deal."

The doctors Long were in, taking a lesson with Justin Garcia as a couple, to work on their salsa, then separating to take individual lessons.

Quinn lounged around, drinking coffee, speaking with the others as they either waited for or finished their sessions. At last it was his turn.

And Shannon was more aloof than ever.

"Gordon is really angry with me," she said, green eyes flashing as she led him through a fox-trot by rote. "He hasn't actually said anything, but I know. I've hurt him really badly."

"I think I'm supposed to be leading," Quinn said.

"You don't know how to lead."

"Right. But you're supposed to be teaching me how."

"Why?" she demanded. "This whole thing is just a joke to you. You think that we're all a bunch of silly prima donnas."

"That's not true," he said, forcefully taking the lead. "I admit, I thought I would hate it. But I don't. And if Gordon is mad, that's the way it goes. What happened to you needed to be checked out. And besides," he added firmly, "who knows? Maybe Gordon is the best actor on earth."

"You think he was lying? That's ridiculous," Shannon protested.

"No, I don't actually think he was lying. I'm just saying it's still a possibility. I wish it wasn't. I wish *someone* could be eliminated."

"I suppose you haven't even eliminated me yet?" she said coolly.

He shrugged. "I don't think you're guilty of anything. Either that, or you really are deserving of an Academy Award."

"Right. And you should have a stack of them," she said. "*Left* foot. Left."

"Why?"

"Because it's the foot you're supposed to be on."

"No, dammit." He stopped dancing. "Why do I deserve that stack of awards?"

"FBI? You might have mentioned that."

"Does it matter? I left the Bureau. I work down here now."

"You should have told me."

"We've never really had an opportunity to talk about our lives, you know. Either one of us."

"What on earth don't you know about me?" she demanded.

"Why you won't compete," he said.

"Oh, God!" she groaned. "That again. I told you. I like to teach. I had an injury."

"You had an injury once."

He stopped speaking, turning to see that Gunter and Helga were doing a fantastic lift. "I don't want to fox-trot. I want to do that."

"You can't even dance."

"I can do that."

She was about to tell him about his left foot again. He didn't give her the chance. Before she could protest, he lifted her, repeating the motion he had just seen, swinging her around his back before he set her on the floor again.

She was flushed, startled, angry—and maybe a little awed.

"Okay, what did I mess up?"

"You didn't give your partner a clue as to what was happening," she snapped.

"But I'm leading. You're supposed to follow. Men lead, women follow. That's the way it is in ballroom dance. No bra burning here."

"That's a cabaret move. People practice it," she muttered.

"Well, there you go. I'm trying to practice my…what? Does it have a name?"

She sighed. "Here in the studio, we call it the pooper-scooper."

"Pooper-scooper?" he said, his brows shooting up. "How…elegant."

"Pooper-scooper just came to mind when we did it the first time. I don't even remember who named it," she said impatiently.

"When we did it the first time?"

"I did it in a piece with Sam for a dinner we had once," she explained impatiently.

"I want to do it for Gator Gala," he insisted.

"You're a beginner. You need to do beginner steps in a long roster of dances. Later—"

"I'll do that. But there are individual routines, right? I want to do a waltz, with a pooper-scooper in it. Look, you know I can do it."

"I know you have the strength. What you need are the skill, balance and coordination."

"Then start teaching me, because I'm going to do it."

"This is really going to cost you."

"Yes." He looked at his watch. "And you're wasting my class time right now."

She stared at him indignantly. "You...asshole!"

"What a way with words. Pooper-scooper. Asshole. Can we work, please?"

For a moment she looked as if she would explode. Then she started in on a waltz, which he thought he knew.

But there was so much he didn't know, he discovered.

And yet, by the end of his forty-five minutes, he actually looked good. Because his partner looked good. And when they choreographed the pooper-scooper into the end of the short routine she planned as they went, there was a spurt of applause.

Quinn looked around to see that the others in the room had stopped to watch them. His brother had arrived, having picked up Marnie, as he had asked him earlier in the day to do. Bobby and Giselle were there, as well, along with a number of the others Quinn was coming to know as regulars.

Gordon walked over to them, laughing. "Hell, you really can teach anyone to dance," he said to Shannon, his tone teasing. He shook Quinn's hand. "Not bad."

"Tell him that he still needs to learn a lot of basics," Shannon said.

"I can tell him anything you want. Doesn't mean it will work with this guy." Gordon seemed to have forgotten the morning. "I see you had Doug bring that girl in again. I understand she's a street kid but over eighteen, an adult. A broke adult."

"Right. I bought her a guest pass that gives her a few lessons," Quinn said.

Gordon nodded. "I'm going to give her a few more. The kid is good—better than you."

"What a surprise," Quinn said dryly.

"I'd thought of that," Shannon said, as she looked at Gordon. "But I was afraid, with the cost of things, that the other students would get mad."

"I can explain it as a community service award," he said. "Not bad, O'Casey. Shannon, Richard Long has signed up for another lesson. He's looking a little irritated over there. Nice guy, but he does like to be a star."

Gordon walked away, and Shannon turned to join Richard. Quinn started off the floor to feel a hand land hard on his back. He turned. Doug was grinning at him. "That was great. You slimy liar. You're good."

"At least I can waltz, thanks to Mom. Listen, let's get out of here. We need to talk."

Ella called to them as they started out of the studio. "Hey, you guys going to be back for the party?"

"Wouldn't miss it," Doug assured her.

Quinn took his brother to the café across the street and chose the front table he'd opted for before. From there, they could see everyone coming and going. Once they had ordered, Quinn filled Doug in on what Shannon had told him, how he'd found Manuel Taylor and had him confront Gordon.

"And Gordon said it was just to get Shannon competing again?" Doug said.

Quinn nodded. "And he was convincing. Thing is, he'd been looking me up, as well. Knew everything about me. My work, at any rate."

"Interesting, but not startling," Doug said. "He's one of those people who really knows his way around the Net. He checks out all the students."

"I wonder why."

"Curiosity, I think. He never tells one student about another, though."

"So how do you know he's into checking up on people?"

"I was in his office talking to him one day. He doesn't hide anything. I happened to see his computer screen, and he'd pulled up the info on Richard Long's practice. He saw me looking and said you could find out practically anything about anybody on the Net."

Quinn sat back. He'd quit smoking a long time ago, but at that moment he really wanted a cigarette. He saw their waitress and ordered another espresso.

"Marnie thinks that a gray or beige car has been cruising by Shannon's house at night," he said.

"Who has a beige or gray car?"

"Everyone in the place, I think."

"I'll get tags tonight, and pull up the owners, makes and models," Doug said.

"Good idea. How's Jane doing?"

"Shaky. She's as convinced as Shannon is that someone killed Lara. Have you heard anything more about the woman they found on the beach?"

"No, but I'll check with Jake later."

"I thought he was taking some time off?" Doug said.

"He is, but I guarantee you, he's still on the phone a few times a day, and if he can't give me anything, he'll direct me to someone who can."

"Like Dixon?" Doug almost spat out the name.

Quinn lifted his hands. "When you hit a guy like Dixon, you just work around him." He leaned forward. "Did you see Gordon hanging around Lara that day? Buying her a drink? Anything?"

"No, the one person I didn't personally see anywhere near her was Gordon. Why?"

"I don't know. Something is still bothering me. It's something Manuel Taylor said, but I can't put my finger on it right now. I'm hoping it will come to me later."

"You done?" Doug said. "I've got my class in about fifteen minutes. Have to put my Latin shoes on."

"You bought special shoes?"

"Of course. You better buy some shoes yourself, bro."

"Right."

"Your pooper-scooper will be even better."

Doug was laughing at him. Quinn shook his head. "Murder, Doug. Come on, we're here to solve a murder."

By party time, Shannon was exhausted, even though she had to admit she'd had a decent night's sleep because of Quinn.

But it had been one hell of a long day.

They started by playing music that ran the gamut of everything they taught. The teachers all danced with the students at first; even Gordon came out on the floor. Then students danced with students, which was usually a time she really enjoyed, watching the more advanced students help out the beginners. Men asked women to dance, and women asked men. Old studio friends chatted, and the more advanced students quizzed the newcomers, making them feel welcome.

In the past, Shannon was aware, many people had considered studios like theirs to be something of a lonely hearts club. She had spent her years as manager trying to make sure that the place wasn't that but that it was instead a warm and hospitable environment where people came to have fun, and where, even if they already had busy and active lives, they met new friends. She thought she had done well. She was, in fact, incredibly proud of the studio. And heartsick that it now seemed to be a place encased in fear and shadow.

After the first set of dances, they had the students sit. Then either she, Gordon or Ben would give a speech about dance. Tonight, she spoke about the awkwardness of first learning to dance. Sam and Jane played a couple coming to their first lesson, with Jane pulling Sam in by the ear. They stepped on one another's feet, argued with each other. Then they improved a little, a little more, and then a little more, until they were whirling around and the room was applauding.

Gordon came and took over the microphone. "Now's the part where a newcomer asks to see a dance."

"Bolero!" Mina Long called out.

"I said a newcomer," Gordon said, laughing.

Shannon was startled when Quinn O'Casey called out, "A waltz. I'd like to see Shannon do a waltz."

"Yeah, Shannon, go, Shannon!" his brother said.

Then an echo went up, as if they were at a football game.

The next thing she knew, Ben was in front of her, reaching out a hand to her, a slight smile on his face.

She accepted his hand, having little other choice.

After all these years, she knew him so well. Knew his lead, every tick of his body. She forgot the audience and was only aware of the music, of how it made her feel, and move.

She was almost startled when it came to an end and she was posed as they had finished their last competition, arched over his knee, her head just above the floor, one leg extended parallel with the length of his body.

The room was alive with applause. She nodded to Ben, rose and went to steal the microphone back from Gordon.

"Let's change pace. Anyone?"

Marnie shouted out, "Samba!"

"Hey, can I be guest teacher?" Gunter called.

"Sure," Shannon told him.

He went to Jane, whirling her out to the floor. Gordon had found the music, and when it started up, Gunter stepped forward, Jane in his arms.

Shannon started clapping, inviting audience participation. The samba was fast, and the pair were well matched, spinning across the floor with perfect motion and speed. Then the music ended and Gunter spun Jane out so she could take an elegant bow.

Then she straightened, and for a minute, pain tensed her features.

Then she doubled over.

"What…?" someone said.

Jane screamed, clutching her abdomen, doubling over, then literally falling to the floor.

"Oh, God! Oh, God, the pain!" she shrieked.

She wasn't acting.

The entire room went still, frozen.

"Ella, call nine-one-one!" Shannon ordered, springing to life, flying over to land on her knees by Jane's side. "What is it? What hurts?"

Gunter was down on his knees, too. Gordon was there, while Ben made sure that the others didn't rush in too close around her.

Jane let out another screech, tightening her hold around her belly. Her dark blond hair spilling on the floor, she turned her huge dark eyes to Shannon.

"Oh, God, help me. Help me. I don't want to die. I don't want to die! Oh, God, I don't want to die like Lara!"

CHAPTER 18

Once he'd ascertained that something was seriously wrong, Quinn was on his feet. Ben Trudeau was doing a good job of holding the others back, but he knew that both Doug and Bobby were behind him, and they were both trained in CPR.

"Let me get to her," Quinn told Shannon, who looked up at him, eyes dazed, features frozen into a mask of concern.

A hand fell on his shoulder. He turned to see that Mina Long was behind him, and her husband was behind her.

"We're actually physicians," she reminded him quietly.

He stepped back. Richard was already down on his knees. He might have been a plastic surgeon, but he obviously remembered the medical basics, as well. His voice was firm but reassuring as he spoke to Jane, and his hands moved with amazing expertise over her abdomen. "It's your stomach, right? And the pain just started?"

Jane seemed to choke on her answer at first, but then she managed to speak past the pain. "There were a few twinges...before. Then...it's like a knife. I'm in agony. It's like I've been...poisoned."

"Poisoned?" The whisper echoed through the crowd like the chorus in an ancient Greek tragedy.

"No, no," Richard told her, his lips twitching in a smile. He looked at his wife, across Jane's body. "Do you think we agree on the possibility of an acute attack of appendicitis?"

Mina smiled at Jane and touched her gently.

Jane moaned. "Appendicitis?" she said.

"I'd say it looks like surgery for you tonight, but we're just minutes from the hospital. You'll be all right," Mina said. She looked up, searching the sea of faces around them. "Ella, you called emergency, right?"

"Yes, the second Shannon told me to," Ella said.

Jane was reaching out, groping. She wanted Shannon. Shannon curled her fingers around Jane's hand.

"You'll come with me? To the hospital, right?" Jane asked breathily.

"Absolutely."

They could already hear the sirens. Within a minute or two, emergency med techs were coming up the front stairs. Questions were asked; vital statistics were taken. Gabe Lopez opened the doors and led the way so that a stretcher could be brought up, and Jane, still moaning, was lifted and brought down the stairs.

Shannon crawled into the back of the ambulance with Jane.

"I'll follow in the car," Quinn told her.

The door was shut, and the sirens blared again.

Quinn realized that not only had everyone in the dance party come down, but people had spilled out from the club. The line waiting for admittance to Suede was also out on the sidewalk. People were talking.

"My God, is she dead?" someone asked.

"A woman was found dead on the beach Sunday," another voice whispered.

Richard Long turned to the crowd. "No, folks, it's all right. Just a case of appendicitis."

Doug pulled out his badge. "There's no danger, just go about your business. Folks, come on, please, break it up."

People began to mill away until only the dance crowd was left.

"I guess the party is over for tonight," Gordon said dryly.

"Ella, you make sure you call us all and tell us how she's doing in the morning," Mr. Clinton said. "Hell, I'll just stop by and see her. Bring her some flowers. Richard, you're sure it's appendicitis?"

"It certainly appears to be, Mr. Clinton."

"You're a plastic surgeon," Clinton reminded him.

"They still made me go to medical school," Richard replied, rolling his eyes with a wink toward his wife. "Mina gets little ones with appendicitis now and then—not frequently, but enough to spot it when she sees it." He slipped an arm around his wife's shoulders. "Shall we go up, change our shoes and get on home? Gordon is right—I'd say the party is over."

"Can someone take me back?" Marnie asked softly.

"Sure, I'll take you," Doug said. He looked at Quinn. "You are going to the hospital, right?"

"Yes."

Quinn realized his brother was looking at him with anxiety.

He had been spending time with Jane, because Jane had been so unnerved.

"Hey, Doug, would you follow them to the hospital? I'll get Marnie back, and then I'll join you there."

Doug gave him a nod of appreciation.

"Come on, Marnie, let's go."

She followed him around back. Quinn paused, staring at all the cars again. There were more colors in back now. The club attendees who could had snagged spaces in back.

As they drove, Marnie said, "You think it's really appendicitis?"

"That's what the doctors said," Quinn replied.

"Why did she scream about being poisoned?"

"Probably because she's in pain."

"Can appendicitis really come on that quickly?"

"I think so, yes. It can be very sudden."

Marnie was quiet for a minute, staring out the window. "You can die from it, can't you?" She sighed softly, then turned to him. "I love it. I love the studio so much. I love dancing so much…but it's a little scary, isn't it? Strange, it's scarier than sleeping on the street."

"Scary, how?"

She shook her head. "People around it…things happen to them."

They reached the shelter where she was staying until Annie could get her squared up with the older woman she was going to assist. Marnie jumped out of the car. "Hey, please don't think I'm a chicken. And please don't stop bringing me to the studio. I want to dance more than anything in the world. And I'm good, honestly, they said so."

"I won't stop bringing you," he promised, thinking that he would keep his word, though he wasn't so sure he wanted her there when he wasn't.

She smiled. "Will you call me, and let me know how Jane is doing?"

"Sure. It's late, though."

"It doesn't matter. The shelter is pretty cool."

"I'll call," he promised.

He watched her enter the shelter, then drove away.

Even Marnie knew it. Something was not right at the studio. In fact, something was very, very wrong.

When he arrived at the hospital, he found that Jane had already been seen in emergency and rushed upstairs for surgery.

The Longs had made the right diagnosis. She had been on the verge of a ruptured appendix. Shannon wasn't alone in the waiting room.

Gordon, Ben, Sam, Justin, Rhianna and Ella were all there. Gordon sat in a chair, his hands folded before him. Sam paced, passing Shannon as they walked the length of the room, turned and walked back again. Ben was fighting with a coin-operated coffee machine, Justin was stretched out on one of the sofas, and Rhianna was half-asleep, draped over Justin and using him as a pillow. Gabriel Lopez was there, and Katarina, but not her husband. They were on one of the waiting room sofas, apparently half-asleep but determined to wait on Jane with the others.

Quinn took a seat by Gordon.

"That was fast," he said.

"She was in a bad way," Gordon said. "And thankfully, there was only one guy with a broken toe in there when we arrived. Hey, they know when they need to move. The guys from fire rescue were great. Shannon said the hospital was ready to take Jane the minute the ambulance pulled in. They had a surgeon all ready to go. They say we caught it in time. She'll only be out of commission for a little while. A matter of weeks, probably. Not too bad."

"Where's my brother?" Quinn asked.

"Down the hall, just outside surgery," Gordon said, staring at him as if he could read something he wanted to know from Quinn's face. Gordon shrugged. Maybe he didn't really want to know. "He seemed really anxious."

"Yeah, anxious," Ben muttered, slamming a fist against the coffee machine. "Why the hell don't these things ever work?" He turned, facing the others. "Just her appendix. That's pretty serious, actually. But around here, it's a relief."

There was a silence in the room then that went beyond exhaustion and worry. Shannon and Sam both went still.

"I think we should cancel the Gator Gala," Shannon said.

"What?" Rhianna said, bolting to an upright position.

"There's been too much trauma," Shannon continued. "Lara…gone. And so close to the studio, that poor woman found on the beach."

"Sadly," Justin said, "there have always been bodies in Miami. You know how many people have been dumped in the water that we'll probably never even know about? And hell—none of us knew that woman. Shannon, we can't take on grief and concern for the whole world."

"We knew Lara. And before that, there was Nell," Shannon said.

"Her husband killed her," Sam said sharply.

"We can't cancel the Gator Gala. We've sunk too much money in it already," Gordon said.

Shannon stared at all of them. "I'm afraid. Afraid that something else is going to happen to someone. Let's be honest, for once. We're all afraid."

Quinn was silent, watching the reactions of the others. Before anyone could speak, the door to the waiting room opened. Richard and Mina Long had arrived.

"Thought you two went home," Ben said.

"We started for home," Mina said.

"But then we decided that we wouldn't sleep until we found out how Jane was doing," Richard explained.

"She's in surgery now," Gordon said.

"We heard."

"You both gave an accurate diagnosis."

"There you go," Richard said lightly. "See, I really did go to medical school." He paused, expecting laughter. None came. "Well, she's going to be fine," he said. "It was actually the best thing in the world that it happened when it did—she was with a crowd, and she got medical attention immediately. If she had been alone, if she had failed to reach a phone and call for help…well, then, it could have been really serious."

"So what's going on?" Mina asked.

"Shannon wants to cancel the Gator Gala," Justin said.

"No!" Richard said, sitting down, but staring at Shannon with a frown. "It's still almost three months away. Jane will be up and kicking by then."

Gabriel Lopez walked over to Shannon, slipping an arm around her shoulders. "*Chiquita,* it will be fine. The way the hospitals do things these days, Jane will be out by tomorrow afternoon."

"I certainly hope not," Mina said.

"Okay, so I'm exaggerating," Gabriel said, winking at Mina.

"Look, Jane carries a lot of the student burden, and she's going to have to be out for a while," Shannon said. "And wasn't she planning something with you, too, Ben? She had a heavy load. It's going to be too much for her."

Ben walked over to Shannon. "*You* can dance with me. You know I'm good."

"Ben, of course you're good. That's not it."

"Jane is going to be all right, but there's nothing suspicious about what happened. And we can cover for her."

"Ben, even if I dance with you, we'll be down one instructor."

"I have an idea," Sam said suddenly. "Marnie. That girl is the most natural dancer I've ever seen in my life. Shannon, seriously, in a few weeks' time, I could turn her into an instructor."

"Sam, think about how hard it is to learn all the steps as one sex. To be certified, she has to learn all the steps for both sexes. There's no way she can do that in time," Shannon said.

Justin shrugged. "When she was a little kid, she said, she took years of ballet, modern and hip-hop. She knows a hell of a lot already."

"She has the natural talent," Rhianna said.

"We'll work with her, right, Justin? Please, don't think about canceling the Gator Gala," Sam said.

Shannon sighed. She stared across the room at Quinn. "What do you think?"

"About the Gator Gala?" he asked, surprised. "I'm the least capable dancer in the room. How would I know what could happen in a few months' time?"

She actually smiled, shaking her head. "Would Marnie want to do it?"

"Are you kidding? That girl would die to come on as a teacher," Rhianna said.

The room fell silent. The word *die* was not a good one at the moment.

"I promised to call her about Jane's condition," Quinn said. "I can ask her."

"Do it," Gordon said. He was staring at Shannon again. "We can't cancel the Gator Gala. We can't. We're in too deep."

Doug came into the waiting room looking haggard but relieved. "They won't let me anywhere near her, but she's going into recovery, and they say she's going to be fine."

There was a collective sigh of relief.

"Sweetheart, we've got to go home," Mina Long said to her husband.

"Right. Well, good night all," Richard said.

Gabriel stood, as well. "There's no need for all of us to be hanging around here, that's for sure."

"Are you going back to the club, Gabe?" Gordon asked.

"Yeah." He shrugged. "I'm not tired. We never close until five."

"I don't remember if I locked up. Check the studio for me?"

"Sure thing."

"You can give me a ride back," Katarina said. "My car is there."

"All right."

"I'm heading home," Gordon said, rising.

"I guess we could all go," Rhianna commented with a yawn.

"I'm staying here awhile. I want to see her when they take her out of recovery," Shannon said.

Ben said, "Then what? Your car is at the studio, too."

"I'll wait around," Quinn said.

"Yeah, well, I was going to hang around, too," Doug told them.

"Were you?" Gordon queried him, looking at Shannon.

"Good night," she said simply.

Gordon nodded. They all began to file on out.

Then they were left alone in the waiting room, Doug, Shannon and Quinn.

"It really was just appendicitis?" Shannon said, sinking into a chair.

Doug sat next to her, taking her hand. "Really. Just appendicitis."

She let out a long sigh and leaned back. Then her head jerked back up, and she stared at Quinn. "What about that woman they found on the beach?"

"There's nothing new," he told her. "I'm expecting to hear anytime."

Quinn pulled his cell phone out and put a call through to Marnie. When he explained that the teachers had suggested she come in and train for a job, her scream of delight was so loud that Quinn had to hold the phone away from his ear.

"I mean, oh, Lord, I'm so sorry about Jane, but…I don't think she'll mind about me, do you? Oh, God, it's like a dream come true. I was on the streets, and now…I'm a dancer." She giggled over the line. "And I don't even have to go to some raunchy dive and dance with a pole. I'm going to be a ballroom instructor. Oh, I could kiss you, all of you, even old Mr. Clinton." Another giggle. "I guess I will be kissing him. You know, the kiss on both cheeks every time someone comes in. Thank you, tell them all thank you, and I'll work so hard they won't believe it. Tell Gordon and Shannon thank you so much!"

"I think Shannon heard you," Quinn said dryly.

"There's a problem," Marnie said suddenly.

"What's that?"

"How am I going to get to and from the studio from here?" She was still talking loudly enough for Shannon and Doug to hear.

"Tell her she can stay at my house. *In* my house, this time," Shannon said.

Quinn stared at her for a moment, then repeated her words to Marnie, who went into another fit of gratitude.

"She won't be sorry. I'll clean the house. I'll cook. I'll do anything!" Marnie said.

Shannon took the phone from Quinn. "Hey, just work at becoming a teacher—that's going to be quite a load. And, work for yourself, too. The world of competition is out there, you know."

Quinn heard Marnie exclaim that she could never be that good. Shannon just shook her head. "Get some sleep, Marnie. You'll need it."

"Thank you, thank you."

"You're welcome. And you're doing us a favor, too." Shannon was smiling as she handed the phone back to Quinn, who managed to calm Marnie down and hang up quickly.

"It's a shame we didn't think of offering her a job to begin with," she murmured, looking at Quinn. "Lots of teachers start out knowing nothing at all and don't have half the natural ability of that girl."

"Fate," Doug said from across the room.

"What?" Both Shannon and Quinn looked at him.

"Sometimes fate is good," he said. "Marnie needed a life, now she's got one. Jane will be all right soon enough, and Marnie will have a job, not just selling clothes, but a real vocation."

A nurse came in then, telling them that they could see Jane briefly.

Quinn decided to remain in the waiting room while Shannon and Doug went in. A while later, his brother came back out.

"There's a chair that becomes a bed," Doug told his brother. "Shannon is going to stay the night."

Quinn nodded, looking at Doug. "You all right?"

Doug nodded. "I'm on first thing in the morning." He shook his head. "Hell, tonight…at first I was terrified. I thought that… It was just too much like déjà vu."

"It was appendicitis," Quinn said.

Doug looked at him. "But there *is* something wrong. You know it now, right? Quinn, I know I dragged you into this, but I was right, wasn't I?"

"Yeah, you were right."

"But I still don't get it. That woman who washed up on the beach…what can she have to do with this?"

"I don't know," Quinn said. "But there's something, and I intend to find out what."

The next morning, Jane awoke moaning. Shannon rushed to her side.

Jane's eyes widened. "You stayed all night?"

"Sure."

"You must be exhausted."

"Actually, the chair was quite comfortable."

Jane tried to smile. She looked at Shannon anxiously. "I'm really all right?"

"You're really all right. You had honest-to-God appendicitis."

Jane tried for a smile.

"Jane, after you fell down, you said you'd been poisoned. Is there some reason why someone would want to poison you?" Shannon asked.

"No, we'd just gotten to talking around the coffeepot, and Mina Long was saying that she can't figure out how Lara could have been dumb enough to take so many pills. The alcohol didn't surprise her—she said she'd seen Lara belt down a few, then go out on stage like it was nothing. I'm trying to remember who was back there at the time…not that it matters now. But Mina said maybe someone had put the pills in her drink or something like that. Then I had coffee, and then I was in agony."

"I see," Shannon told her, suddenly certain she didn't want to drink coffee in the studio ever again.

"Silly, huh?"

"Well, you're all right, and that's what matters."

A look of dismay swept over Jane's face. "They said I just made it. That if my appendix had actually ruptured, I could have died."

"But you're going to be fine."

Jane shook her head. "What about all my students?"

"It will all work out."

"It can't. We don't have enough teachers to go around."

"We're going to bring Marnie in, give her a crash course, and she can take over some of the beginners."

"Marnie?" Jane said, surprised. Then she mulled over the idea. "If someone really works with her… Actually, I didn't know anything at all when I started. There's only one problem."

"What is that?"

"What if the students like her better than me?"

Shannon laughed, squeezing Jane's hand. "We always

have enough students to go around. And anyway, your students love you. It will be fine."

"Maybe," Jane said after a moment.

"Hey, I'll be back later, okay? Your nurse will be coming in any minute, and I've got to take a shower and head to the studio."

"Of course. Thanks for staying."

Shannon hesitated. She had always thought it best not to know things, but at the moment, she couldn't resist. "If I hadn't stayed, someone else would have."

"Who?" Jane said, but she was blushing.

"Doug O'Casey."

"Really?" Jane didn't seem able to prevent her smile.

"Yep."

"Hmm. You know…never mind."

"Do I know what?" Shannon asked a little sharply.

Jane shook her head. "I can't say I'm really going to miss Lara."

"What does that mean?"

"Nothing."

"Jane!"

"Hey, don't harass me. I just had emergency surgery last night."

"Jane?"

"Okay, well, I think I've had one of those 'things' I'm not allowed to have on Doug for a long time. But when he saw Lara…well, he just had a look about him. Now Lara is gone. And he doesn't just think I'm the most wonderful teacher in the world, he…well, like I said, never mind."

Shannon hesitated. "I think you should watch out for everyone right now," she said quietly.

"Doug is a cop."

"I know."

"Then…?"

"I just think we should watch out for everyone."

"Lara was murdered," Jane said firmly. "You know, there are all kinds of top professionals who might have wanted her dead."

Shannon grimaced. "Maybe. But something lately… something about the studio… I keep hearing something, a strange noise. I'm going to do a little prying, find out just what it is."

"Don't be there alone, Shannon. Don't pry when you're alone."

"Hey, the club is right downstairs, Katarina is right next door. But anyway, you just lie low and keep quiet, okay?"

"Yes, ma'am," Jane said. "I don't have any choice, do I?"

"Nope."

Shannon gave her a kiss on the forehead and departed, figuring she could take a cab to her house, then walk to work.

Early.

She would lock herself in, then figure out what in hell was making the noise that was driving her so crazy.

As she left the hospital, she suddenly felt very determined. She was tired of being frightened.

A little prying…

He'd been just about to enter the hospital room when he had heard Shannon's voice.

Flowers in hand, he stepped back, listening.

No, Shannon, you little fool. Don't pry. Don't be an idiot.

As he stood there, listening, he realized that there was no help for it.

Shannon Mackay would look just as beautiful as Lara Trudeau…in a coffin.

She was coming out!

He started to back away, then dropped the flowers and

threaded his way between two nurses and an old lady in a wheelchair. He hurried down the hall. Turning, he could see Shannon.

He didn't wait for the elevator but took the stairs.

Once on the ground, he was furious with himself. What an idiot he'd been. He should have walked right on in and put his flowers down.

He waited until Shannon Mackay was on the street. He watched as she hailed a taxi.

Then he ran back into the hospital, took the elevator and hurried along the hall.

His flowers were still on the floor.

He picked them up, looked in on Jane. She was sleeping again. He walked down the hall and entered a room, dropping the flowers on the table beside an older woman.

"Your lucky day, honey," he told her, then exited the hospital once again.

As he came out into the sun, he remained irritated with himself. Cops always said that killers were bound to mess up somewhere.

He'd been an idiot, running away like that. What the hell had been the matter with him? Like the cops said, he'd fucked up.

No. He could walk in anywhere, any time, and act normally. Shannon had just given him a moment's pause.

He wouldn't mess up again. He was far too good for that.

He would be even more careful, more clever.

When he finally went for her she would never know.

Richard Long's offices were magnificent.

He practiced with another man, Dr. Bertrand Diaz, and between them, they did quite a business. The waiting room was crowded with women when Quinn arrived, and all of them attractive, even if a few did look a little…plastic.

At least Long did plastic well.

He spoke to the receptionist, and with the amount of people in the office, he was surprised to be shown into the doctor's office rather quickly.

Richard Long seemed pleasantly surprised to see him. "I'm sure you're not thinking about surgery, are you, Quinn?" he demanded, half-sitting on the edge of his mahogany desk and folding his arms over his chest with a look of amusement. "So…to what do I owe the pleasure of this visit?"

"I thought you could give me some help."

"Oh?" Long said.

"Well, it occurred to me that you and your wife are physicians."

"Yes?"

"Well, how do you think those drugs got into Lara Trudeau?"

Long stared at him for several seconds, and as he did so, his face began to mottle. "Are you suggesting that *I* would dispense drugs illegally? Never. Lara was not my patient. Nor would I have accepted her as a patient—ever. She would have been far too demanding."

"So how do you think she got all that Xanax into her, then?"

Long's eyes narrowed angrily. "Who the hell are you to be asking? I thought your brother was the cop and that you were a…a fisherman, or something."

"Licensed private investigator, Dr. Long," Quinn told him. What the hell, hiding it hadn't gotten him anywhere. Maybe the truth would serve him better.

"And who hired you?"

"I'm not at liberty to disclose the name of my client."

"Well, I'm sorry, I'm not at liberty to waste any more time with you. I never gave Lara Trudeau a prescription for narcotics. She had her own doctor. Question him."

"I did. I was just curious, thinking you might be able to give me a little help. Now your wife is also—"

"Don't even go there. My wife's reputation is spotless. I can promise you, she wouldn't have given Lara a prescription or supplied her with free samples or anything of the kind!"

"I'm sorry, but let me just ask you this—the day of the competition, did you see Lara alone with anyone at any time?"

"Well, if I'd been there, too, she wouldn't have been alone, right?" Long said sarcastically.

"I think you know what I mean."

"I was busy the day of the competition," Long said. "This is my profession, but dance is my love. I had my own amateur ranking to worry about."

Quinn rose. "I'm sorry I took up your time."

"You could have talked to me at the studio," Long said.

"Well, you know—everyone is at the studio."

"Lara did herself in. That's my professional opinion. Sorry, Quinn. I have patients out there."

"Of course. Sure."

Quinn put his hand on the door handle.

"If anyone spent time with Lara Trudeau, Mr. O'Casey, you might want to look closer to home."

Quinn turned back.

"Most of the students think he was having an affair with her," Long said. "Talk to him. In fact, come to think of it, I think he managed to be alone with her, out on the balcony that joined the dressing rooms, right before she went on stage. And I think they were arguing. Yeah, if you need some help, go to your brother. Ask Doug your questions."

"Thanks, Dr. Long," Quinn managed to say easily.

He exited the office, nodding at the blonde with the fantastic boobs to the left of the waiting room door and the older woman with the tightly stretched face on the right.

Doug!

Dammit. Why did it keep coming back to his brother?

And why the hell wasn't Doug telling him the truth—
all of it?

CH**A**PTER 19

S̲hannon was irritated to reach the studio early—after a very quick shower at her own house—and find out that Gordon was already in. So were Ella and Ben.

Ella was going through the books; Ben was practicing steps by himself, and Gordon was on the phone. When he saw her, he waved her into the office.

"Right, Richard," Gordon said. He grimaced as Shannon took the seat next to his desk. "Richard, I was aware of Mr. O'Casey's profession, yes." A moment's silence as Richard spoke on the other end. "Richard, I'm sure he came to see you for help, not to make an accusation, and of course everyone knows that Mina is beyond reproach." Again silence. "Oh, come now, Richard, you and Mina have to join us on the cruise… As you wish," Gordon said with a sigh. "We'll miss you."

Gordon hung up the phone.

"Richard Long?" Shannon said.

"Totally indignant. O'Casey was over at his office, questioning him."

"Really?"

"Well, you know, the man is a doctor. Doctors can get prescription pills."

"But Lara had a prescription from her own physician," Shannon said.

Gordon shrugged. "At any rate, Dr. Long is pissed off. Says he's not coming on the cruise, and he may just quit taking lessons."

"You didn't try very hard to cajole him," Shannon said. "Want me to call him?"

Gordon shook his head, grinning. "He'll call back any minute. By noon, at the latest. Richard thinks he's Fred Astaire reincarnated. He won't stop coming."

"I hope you're right," Shannon said, rising. "And by the way, Jane seems to be doing all right. I left early, but she was awake."

Gordon nodded. "I stopped in briefly to see her. She said you had just left. I met her doctor. They're going to keep her two or three more days, then she has to lie low at home for a while."

"Maybe I was too panicky last night. I guess she'll be back to teaching in less time than I thought."

Gordon mulled that over. "Whether you were panicky or not, it's kind of a good thing. I think that young lady we're bringing in is going to be quite an asset." He leaned back in his chair, reflecting. "I hope she never changes, though. Her enthusiasm is so wide-eyed, and her energy is so unlimited. She just loves dancing and being here. Lara was like that when I met her. She let it all go to her head, though. She was a champion, but not really a winner."

"I hope it works out well, and I definitely hope she stays sweet—since I said she could live with me," Shannon told him.

"Speak of the devil," Gordon said.

Shannon turned. Marnie was standing hesitantly just outside the door. "Sorry, I didn't mean to interrupt. Quinn dropped me off. With my things. They won't take up much room. I got the impression I needed to get started right away."

"Good call," Shannon said, rising. She smiled, slipping an arm around Marnie's shoulder. "Come on. You'll work with me first. I'm early." She winked. "I'm also the best— and most qualified—instructor."

"Really?" Marnie said.

"Well, in my own mind, anyway," Shannon told her. "Let's get started."

When she moved back into the studio dance floor area, she saw that Quinn had not only brought Marnie, he had stayed. He was in the back by the coffeepot, and Ben had joined him. They seemed to be deep in conversation but broke it off the moment she appeared.

"Coffee, Shannon?" Ben asked.

She hesitated, remembering Jane's words and her earlier decision. But they both appeared to be drinking coffee from the pot.

"Sure, thanks."

"I saw Jane," Ben said.

"You, too? So did Gordon."

Ben laughed. "The hospital is going to be thrilled when they get rid of her—Gordon was just leaving when I arrived. Mr. Clinton showed up with chocolates and flowers. Doug was up to see her, and Gabe and Katarina came together, right when I was leaving. I'm willing to bet that the rest of our group—the teachers, at least—will all show up to check on her."

She smiled. Once that had been the good thing about the studio. They might squabble with one another once in a while, but they were always there for one another, too.

But now...

Now it seemed that a shadow lay over them, that there

was some kind of malady among them that could never quite be cured.

Ben handed her a cup of coffee and said to Marnie, "Hey, kid, do you drink coffee?"

"Of course. I am eighteen," she said.

"Let's hope she keeps it to coffee," Quinn murmured. Marnie made a face at him, but she also looked at him with a certain amount of adoration.

"Quick cup of coffee. We're going to start working," Shannon said.

"Are you? I was hoping to catch you early and get a class in," Quinn said.

"We're not even officially open, Quinn," she said. "Sorry, I—"

"I can start with Marnie," Ben said. "I'm in because I'm restless."

"Yes, but—"

"Don't worry. I'll leave the finer points to you. Marnie has so much to learn, she might as well start some basics with me."

"I really need the help," Quinn said.

"Fine," Shannon told him, unable to come up with another excuse. "Let's go, then."

She usually linked arms with a student to walk across to the stereo and choose a working disk, but she let Quinn O'Casey follow in her wake.

She slid in a fox-trot.

"No, let's work on that waltz."

"You know the waltz—you suck at the fox-trot."

"But we're doing a waltz routine. I'd rather get that right than anything else."

"You can get it right, but if you're going to compete, you need to do the fox-trot."

"You just want to do the fox-trot because you know I hate it." He was grinning.

She sighed. "You need to learn it."

"Why? Do you make everyone learn the fox-trot?"

"We don't *make* people learn anything."

He grinned. "I promise I'll learn the fox-trot. Let's do the waltz today, though. I really want to excel at the pooper-scooper."

"Great."

She put in a waltz and slid into his arms. He really did have this one down.

"You caused some trouble," she told him.

"Only some?"

"Richard Long is refusing to come on the cruise."

"Oh, I bet he'll be there."

"That's what Gordon said. But you went into his office and started accusing him of dispensing drugs illegally."

"Nope."

"You didn't go into his office?"

"Sure. But I just asked him a few questions."

"Great."

"That's what investigators do. Ask questions."

He arched a brow at her. "Yeah, you know, like I did with you. Such an ugly thing."

She shook her head. "You're killing time now, aren't you?"

"Still investigating."

"Me?" she said. "I would have thought you had me down pat by now."

He shook his head. "Not really."

"Oh? And what don't you know?"

"How did you break your ankle?"

She inhaled, shaking her head. "What are you after?"

"The truth."

"I broke my ankle because I wasn't good enough. How's that?"

"Not true."

She let out a sigh. "We were at a competition. I was dancing with Ben at the time, and Lara was dancing with a man named Ronald Yeats. We were all out on the floor during a Viennese waltz and…she crashed, and I went down, too. My ankle was broken."

"So basically, Lara caused all your woes."

"So I murdered her?"

"You didn't, did you?" he said, and his tone was both serious and mocking.

"No," she snapped.

"I didn't think so. But…"

"But what?"

"You're still a coward, you know."

"What are you getting at now?"

He didn't answer her. They'd moved across the floor, following the steps in the routine, and he flipped her up and around in a perfect rendition of the pooper-scooper. Then he spun her into perfect position to take a bow.

She turned to him. "Your mother must be one good dancer."

"She is," he said.

"Are you really planning on dancing at the Gator Gala?" she demanded. She lowered her voice. "Because if all this isn't solved by then…"

"What?"

"Nothing."

"What?"

"I'll be insane, that's what," she admitted.

"The amazing thing is this—okay, I suck at the other dances. But I do want to learn them. It actually feels…great, I guess. To be able to do this. That's the truth."

"Ah," she said.

"And that means?"

"That's the truth, but it's not the whole truth. Why

didn't you mention the FBI? And why did you leave the Bureau? And for that matter, you and Doug seem to have a lot of money. You're not drug smugglers in your spare time, are you?"

He shook his head. "Cops don't make big money, FBI agents don't make big money, and P.I.s just do all right. My father died years ago and left us all trust funds."

"Was he a drug smuggler?" Shannon said, only partially teasing.

"Real estate. He came here when land cost nothing, bought tons of it and made some pretty good money. I try pretty hard not to touch mine. Don't know why, except that I like to make my living on my own. Planning to check out my bank accounts?"

"Maybe. But that would be illegal, wouldn't it?"

He shrugged, and she had the feeling he had the ability to check out just about anything he wanted.

"I'll put the music back on," she murmured, dropping the subject of his finances.

In all, they went through the routine several times. Then they went into the fox-trot, which was just as bad as it had been. Still, as they worked, she realized that she loved teaching him. Loved his rueful smile when he didn't get what she was saying, and the flash in his eyes when something made sense. The scent of him seemed very rich to her, seductive. The feel of his hands on her was magic. She was startled when he suddenly said, "I think I'm way over time. I've got to move on."

They *had* gone over.

She stared at him. "You managed not to answer me before. Why did you leave the FBI?"

He hesitated for a minute. A shield went over his eyes. Then he said, "I made a mistake. A big one."

She stared at him, then shook her head. "You're really something."

"Why?"

"You call me a coward, but you're worse. You made one mistake, so you copped out. You're worse than me."

He stared at her and didn't reply. He walked by, saying something to Marnie and Ben, then departed by the back door.

She followed him, but the door had already closed. Then, as she stood there, hesitant, she heard it.

The grating sound.

She couldn't place it. Was it coming from inside—or outside? Ben turned up the music, and she rushed over, turning down the stereo.

"What are you doing?" he demanded.

"Didn't you hear that?"

"Hear what?" he asked, trying not to sound annoyed.

"That…noise."

"There's noise from all over, Shannon. What noise are you talking about?"

"Never mind," she told him. "When you two are done, let Marnie take a little break, then I'll see what she's learned," Shannon said.

She left them and walked into the ladies' room.

Nothing. And yet…

The noise, she decided, was coming from the rear of the studio. But from where, exactly, and what the hell was it?

Quinn found his brother at Nick's.

Luckily he was alone. He was also looking very worn.

Quinn took the chair opposite him. "You look like death warmed over."

"Yeah, I'm tired," Doug admitted.

"Should you be taking lunch?" Quinn asked.

"Why?"

"Well, you took time off this morning to go by to see Jane."

Doug flushed. "I had to."

"Patrolmen aren't supposed to mess around like that. Your beat is Kendall."

"I only took a few minutes. What's the matter with you? You're coming on like a ball-buster sergeant."

"What were you and Lara fighting about at the competition?" he demanded.

Doug avoided his eyes, looking off in the distance. "Fighting?"

"Yes, fighting. Balcony area, outside the changing rooms."

"I was…angry."

"About what?"

"Her behavior."

"How so?"

"She was…she was drinking more than usual, and really flirting. I thought Katarina was going to deck her once when she made a real play for David."

"You knew she slept around."

"That didn't mean I liked it. She was in rare form that day. Talking about a million places she was going to go." He hesitated. "I'd let her know once that…well, I had told her I might be a cop, but I could take as many lessons, pay for a coach as often as I wanted, because I had a trust fund. That was probably why she got interested in me. But that day, she told me that if I didn't like something, I could just piss off. She'd fool around with anyone she wanted, and she didn't need money—she'd acquired a source for all she needed. I thought she was just talking through the alcohol. I said something to her about that, too, about how much she was drinking. And she told me she could dance no matter what, she was that good, and that I should just piss off."

"And then?" Quinn prompted.

Doug shrugged. "I did. I left her."

"And you didn't see anyone else with her?"

He shook his head. "I went to cool down, to remind myself that I was just in it for the fun, that I'd always known she would never get serious. Then, not too much later, I watched her dance, and I realized she would never really love any guy, because she was too much in love with being Lara Trudeau. Not just dancing. But in being herself, out on the floor, making everyone want her. Or envy her." He took a swallow of iced tea. "Have you found out anything, anything at all?"

Quinn nodded. "Yeah. I found out that if any two people look the most suspicious, it's you and Shannon MacKay." He rose. "Make sure you're back on your beat on time."

Quinn went back to his boat and sat on the deck, going through the files again, looking at his own notes.

Find waiter.

Well, he'd found the waiter. Dead end.

But something was still bothering him. Something Manuel Taylor had said.

He pulled out the sheets with the listing of names Jake had acquired for him, wondering what it was. It eluded him.

He hesitated, then called the man. He got his answering machine, but left a message. "Hey, this is Quinn O'Casey. You said you'd like to work a cruise sometime. How about Saturday night."

He hung up and called down to the Keys, making sure that Dane could still bring up the party boat they owned for Saturday night.

Then he swore to himself.

He'd forgotten all about getting an alarm installed at Shannon's house. Now Marnie would be living there, too, and he didn't want the two women alone without protection.

He swore to himself and pulled out his phone book, then

put through a call, hoping his friends in the area remembered who he was.

Carlos did, and agreed to go out to Shannon's house himself, saying that he could arrive around five-thirty. "An after-hours job," Carlos told him cheerfully.

"Thanks. Really."

"Hey, it's my business," Carlos said. "No problem."

Quinn hung up and pulled out the picture of the woman who had been found dead on Sunday, the drawing that Ashley had done for the paper. Pocketing it, he headed back for the beach.

Late in the afternoon, Shannon finally stopped, smiling at Marnie. "Let's take a real break. Get your things. We'll go to my house and settle you in, grab something to eat."

Marnie nodded, then said, "Hey, are you sure? I mean, I feel like Cinderella, some kind of a fairy-tale princess."

"I'm used to living alone," Shannon admitted. "But we'll manage."

Shannon told Ella to make sure that Gordon—who was in his office with the door closed—knew where she was going. She led Marnie to her car and then drove the short distance to her house. The girl's possessions were truly meager. So far, though, they'd fitted her with some of the used shoes in the studio, and though Shannon and Jane were taller than Marnie, Rhianna was just about her size and had generously seen to it that Marnie took a few of the jeans and shirts she kept in her locker. They would plan a little party for her, Shannon thought, a welcome-to-the-staff party, and everyone could buy her some little thing and she would begin to have real belongings.

"There isn't really an extra bedroom, because I had it made into a studio," Shannon told her. "But we'll fix up some space for you in that closet, and the couch is comfortable. You won't have an actual bedroom, but you'll have a television set, and tons of DVDs and tapes to choose from."

Marnie grinned at her. "Hey, I thought I was lucky when I was living in your yard." She walked in, turned around and said, "Remember, I'm Cinderella. And I mean it. This is like a castle."

"Things were really that bad at home?" Shannon asked her.

Marnie nodded, looking away. She squared her shoulders. "The thing of it is, I'm an adult. I should be able to make it on my own. But once I was out…God, it was harder than I thought it was going to be. I had nothing to start with, I guess."

"Well, now you've got a room, for what it's worth," Shannon told her.

"A lot." Marnie hugged her arms around her thin frame. "If it weren't for you…and Quinn… God, he's really something, isn't he?"

"Oh, yes. He's something," Shannon agreed. What could she say to such hero worship? Especially when he was the best "something" she'd come across herself. Ever.

"I think he's in love with you," Marnie said.

"He's a student," she replied sharply. Too sharply.

Marnie grinned. "Sorry. It's just…don't you ever notice the way he looks at you? Boy, if anyone like that ever looked at me that way, well, I wouldn't be a silly fool and let him get away. Fraternization rule or not."

"I'm going to make tea," Shannon said. "Do you want some?"

"You mean like hot tea?"

"Yes. We've got about forty-five minutes. That's the mealtime. All the teachers make sure to schedule meals around their appointments."

"I know, I know. I got the speech."

Shannon put the water on. Marnie walked down the hall, looking in at the extra bedroom-slash-studio. "Wow."

"I like it," Shannon said when she got back to the kitchen.

"The only thing you're missing is an alarm," Marnie said matter-of-factly.

"There's a dog next door."

"Quinn said something about getting one installed for you. I think he meant to do it today, but after last night, what with Jane and all, I think maybe he forgot." She grinned. "So I bet that means he'll be around tonight."

"Why should he be?"

Shannon crawled up on one of the bar stools that sat at the counter between the kitchen and the family room.

"Because of the car, of course. The car that kind of cruises by your house. I guess maybe he didn't say anything to you. He probably didn't want to freak you out, because, you know, it's probably nothing."

The water boiled. The steam hit Shannon's face. Despite it, she felt a sudden deep, debilitating chill.

Suede hadn't opened for business when Quinn arrived, but the handsome black doorman recognized him and let him in, telling him that he would go find Gabe.

Quinn sat at the bar, sipping a soda water, waiting.

"Hey! It's the new student. I hear you may rival your brother one day," Lopez said pleasantly, taking the chair beside him. "Can I get you something besides the drink? We don't really have a menu, but we've got snacks."

"No, no, thanks. I was hoping you could help me."

"Sure, if I can."

He pulled out the picture of Sonya Marquez Miller. "I was trying to find out if this woman had ever been in the club."

Gabriel Lopez shook his head sadly. "The cops were in

here after she washed up on the beach. I had all my help come out and take a look. I've never seen her. They haven't found out what happened to her, huh?"

"One big overdose," Quinn said.

"I wish I could help." He hesitated. "You know, of course, that weekends down here get wild. And Miami has a little bit of every kind of Mafia known to man—Russian, Italian, Cuban…then there are the Colombians. Hell, someone even told me that we have Haitian drug lords here. And you name a country from Central or South America, and we get their criminal element on the beach. I get every nationality known to man in here on a Friday or Saturday night, and most of them are fine people, just out for fun. And trust me, there are lots of executive types—clean and pure Monday through Friday, nine to five—who do recreational drugs on weekends. But we've kept the club clean. The bartenders and wait staff all know to watch for anyone getting too drunk. We cut them off. And we're known as the toughest club in the district, as far as checking IDs goes."

"Yeah, I've heard. I was just hoping you might have seen her."

"I would have told the cops if I had. Hey, are you going to group class tonight?"

"Not tonight, I'm afraid."

"Well, keep up the dancing. And come back here any time."

"Thanks." He got off the stool.

"You doing some work for your brother?" Lopez asked him.

Quinn turned back.

"I didn't know you were a cop yourself," Lopez explained.

"I'm not," Quinn said. "Private investigator."

"Ah. Well, that's good. Did the woman's family hire you?"

"Can't say," Quinn told him.

"Big secret, huh?"

"Client privilege," Quinn told him. "See you later. Are you going to be on the boat Saturday night?"

"You bet."

"See you then."

He left Suede and went upstairs, where he found that Shannon was at her house. He called and Marnie answered. He told her to tell Shannon not to freak out when the man from the alarm company arrived. "He'll be there any minute."

Marnie went off to talk to Shannon.

"She says we have to go back to work."

"Fine. I'll be there any minute, too, then."

He hung up before there could be any protest.

When he arrived at Shannon's, Carlos Rodriguez was already there, and Shannon was standing at the door, ready to leave.

"Do you know," she told him, "you really need to discuss it with someone when you're ordering something for their house."

"We talked about this. You need an alarm," he told her, and added impatiently, "And I'll pay for it, if that's the problem."

"Trust fund, right?" she said coolly. "Don't be ridiculous. I make a decent income."

She was rigid and entirely aloof. It made him want to grab her and...

He wanted to touch her face. Run his thumb along her cheek, thread his fingers into her hair. Hell. Crush her against him. Every body part he had suddenly came up with a physiological memory of what it was like to be with her.

"I've got to get back. Since you wanted this, you stay here until it's done," she said.

"I intend to stay here," he informed her, noting the grating tone of his own voice.

Marnie gave him a shrug as Shannon started down the walk for her car, then ran to catch up with her.

"Told you," the girl said, and Quinn could hear her. "He's really got a thing for you. Like he's in love with you or something."

"This is what you want, right?"

Quinn jumped. Carlos was in front of him. "What?"

"The system—you want a standard system. Windows and doors, a keypad, and an automatic alarm if they're breeched?"

He nodded, looking after Shannon's car as it drove away down the street.

CHAPTER 20

By the time she drove back home that night, Shannon was exhausted.

She'd intended to get back by the hospital to see Jane, but she never had, because the studio had been so busy.

It amazed her, because she had thought that the death and burial of a major ballroom dance star like Lara Trudeau might have given people pause.

It hadn't.

It seemed that everyone wanted to be at the studio.

One of the important factors in planning the Gator Gala had been encouraging the students to compete, and therefore, to take more classes.

It was working.

On top of that, Jane's attack of appendicitis seemed to have drawn people out of the woodwork. The regulars were all there, and then some.

Gunter and Helga came by, saying they had stopped to see Jane on the way. Christie—who only made an appearance when she was coaching—arrived, as well. Doug showed up and stayed a little while, saying that he was going by the hospital. Bobby Yarborough and Giselle came, saying they had already stopped by the hospital. Both Katarina and David were there. Gabriel was up, bringing a few friends from the club, trying to introduce them to the magical world of dance.

Despite having sworn that he wasn't showing up, Richard Long came, and Mina was with him.

He barely mentioned Quinn, except to note with a certain pleasure that the man wasn't in attendance. Their younger crowd, a number of the high school girls and boys, showed up, as well as some of the newer students. People stayed, chatting after the last class.

Shannon was ready to scream.

She didn't think about noises, or leaving the studio. She wished that she didn't have a new housemate, because Marnie was excited; she had never tired during the day, despite working with each of the teachers in succession. Christie had watched her and given her a number of pointers, then commented to Shannon that they had found someone who could excel.

"She reminds me of Lara, actually," Christie said.

"Her talent, yes," Shannon agreed.

Christie gave a rueful smile. "Certainly not character-wise. Lara always had…well, never mind, it isn't nice to speak ill of the dead. Oh, what the hell. From the time she started, there was something cutthroat about Lara. With Marnie, it's pure love and enthusiasm. Maybe she reminds me more of you. Once."

At that point, Ben had joined in. "Shannon is going to do some dancing with me."

Christie's face lit up. "Really? If you do go back into competition, I'd love to work with the two of you again."

"Maybe," Shannon murmured. She *had* told Ben she would dance with him. And for the first time that night, she felt a spur of excitement. *Yes. Maybe…yes.*

Grudgingly she admitted to herself that if she did indeed

go back into professional competition, Quinn O'Casey would have been the one to stir her into it.

That made her even more tired.

Since Marnie was bubbling all over with enthusiasm, she forced herself not to ask the girl to please just shut up as they drove.

Yet when they reached house and she saw that Quinn's car was still in front, she felt a strange ripple of emotion—one she didn't want to analyze. Could he possibly really care about her? And could she possibly care about him?

"Quinn is still here," Marnie said.

"Yes, well, that's a good thing," she said, realizing that if he hadn't been there, she would have been in trouble—she had left with the alarm man working and her house keys on the counter. "I didn't bring my house key," she reminded Marnie.

"Oh," Marnie said. "And there's an alarm." She grinned. "There's an alarm system on Cinderella's castle now."

When she knocked on her own door, it took him several minutes to answer it. His hair was tousled, and she realized he'd fallen asleep on the soft couch in back. Even the way his hair looked caused electricity to take flight down a path in her spine.

"You ran late," he murmured. But he seemed to have the ability to shake himself to full wakefulness easily enough. "Let me explain the alarm to you." He showed her the keypad, and told her what to punch when she was home and they were both in for the night, and what to punch when she left the house, and what to punch when she wanted the alarm off if she happened to be coming in and out for any reason.

He stood near her, arm over her shoulder as he demonstrated, and she was more tempted than she had ever been in her life just to lean back and rest. She didn't, though. No matter what Marnie had said about the way he looked at her, she wasn't sure she was willing to give her trust so easily.

"Have you got it?" he asked her.

"Yes, I think so."

"Well, the instructions are on the counter, if you have any difficulties."

"Quinn!" Marnie said, throwing herself at him with a childish abandon, hugging him, then letting him free. "It was great, it was so wonderful. Even the coach…what's her name, Shannon?"

"Christie," Shannon said patiently.

"Even Christie said I've real potential."

"That's wonderful." His eyes met Shannon's.

"Can we have some tea?" Marnie asked.

There had been nothing Shannon wanted more than to crawl straight into her bed, but now Quinn's and Marnie's eyes were on her.

"Sure," she said, resigned.

"You'll stay, right, Quinn?" Marnie asked.

"I really need to go."

"Just stay for a cup of tea," Marnie prodded.

"One quick cup of tea," he said, looking at Shannon.

"Have you eaten anything?" Shannon asked. She added, "You did get this alarm in for me. I mean, I owe you."

"No, you don't owe me," he said firmly.

"I'm sorry, I didn't mean it that way," she murmured, wishing she weren't flushing. "Anyway, please go sit down…I'll brew the tea." She smiled. "Marnie can tell you about her day for a while."

He arched a brow, a slow smile curving his lips. He was well aware that Marnie had been talking nonstop.

"All right. Make tea in peace," he said.

He walked toward the back of the house. Marnie stood still for a minute. "Hey, sorry, I should help, huh?"

"No. Go entertain Quinn."

Shannon boiled the water, fixed a pot of English breakfast tea and found some oatmeal bars to set around it. Then she dug around in the refrigerator and found some cheese squares, and decided to add toast points. When she had fixed the tray and was ready to bring it out to the coffee table in front of the couch, she realized that the room was strangely silent.

Marnie was curled into the chair, sound asleep. Quinn was leaning back on the sofa, legs extended on the coffee table.

Sound asleep as well.

As Shannon stood there, Marnie's eyes opened.

"Oh," she murmured. She uncurled herself. "I was talking to him and then I realized he wasn't answering me anymore," she whispered. "I guess we should wake him."

Shannon turned back, putting the tray on the pass-through counter.

"No," she said softly.

"But what do we do?"

"Let him sleep. Come on in the kitchen and drink your tea. We'll sleep in my room."

Marnie leaped up and came around beside Shannon. "You think he'll be all right?"

"He'll be fine." Shannon turned and went into her room for a blanket, then brought it out and swept it over his outstretched legs. "Come on," she said, bringing her fingers to her lips to indicate that they should be quiet.

Marnie nodded and followed Shannon back into the kitchen. They drank their tea, and Marnie went through half the food on the tray. She looked famished.

Well, she'd worked really hard, Shannon thought. And she certainly didn't have any fat stores to draw on.

When she had finished, she seemed to realize that she had inhaled everything. But she didn't apologize, just looked at Shannon a little morosely. "I'll clean up."

"Leave it. We'll get it in the morning. Come on, we'll take turns in the bathroom, then get some sleep."

She was afraid Marnie would want to whisper all night. She didn't. She accepted the new toothbrush and nightgown Shannon gave her with a simple thank-you, then insisted Shannon go first.

At last, way after midnight, they were in bed. Marnie kept carefully to her own side, as if she were afraid to offend her benefactor in any way.

After a minute, she said, "Thank you so much for everything."

There was something in the way she spoke that made Shannon smile, glad in a way she had never imagined.

"It's okay, really."

"Good night. I swear I won't make another sound."

Shannon laughed softly, tousled her guest's long hair and turned her back on her.

Strange. This was not at all the night she would have been having in her dream of dreams.

But at least she felt safe and secure with her house full.

In minutes, she was sound asleep herself.

Jake was still taking time off.

He offered to come into the station, but Quinn flatly refused to let him do so. Jake had a new partner though, a woman named Anna Marino, and she was a blessing—pleased to meet Quinn and happy to help. She was tall for a woman, probably a good five-ten or five-eleven, but she was slim and as wiry as a polecat. She was very pretty, with naturally light hair, vivid blue eyes and classic features. She might well have graced a runway had she not decided to become one of Miami-Dade's finest.

"I'll give you anything I can," she assured Quinn, digging through Jake's files for him. "I wish we had more. That's one of the sad facts of this work. When we have a suspect, modern forensics do wonders for us. But when we haven't got a prayer of a suspect... Here. Here's the old one. Sally Grant." She skimmed the file before handing it to Quinn. "Twenty-two, working the streets, her address is a boardinghouse known to be a little less than reputable but not a drug house, just one of those places that doesn't ask for a lot of background information and doesn't much care what you do in your room as long as the door is closed. Transient, out of Oklahoma, folks dead, one brother found, and he didn't come for the body, he just asked if there was life insurance on her. I found her case one of the saddest. So did Jake. We combed the streets, and narcotics came in on it, too, doing a real rundown on the clubs. No matter how hard we tried, we came up with zilch." She hesitated. "We took up a collection in the department just to get her a decent burial. One of the funeral homes helped out."

Quinn nodded, taking the file and sitting across from Anna. She folded her hands on the desk, watching him. "I'll get the Sonya Miller file. Jake is convinced that these two are associated, though we don't know how. Sonya Miller had money and a family that claimed her. The two women were from totally different social arenas."

"I can see that."

The case of Sally Grant was truly sad. She'd been so young. The photos taken at the scene were truly pathetic. Her eyes were wide-open. She was staring. Long brown hair spilled over the sidewalk, reminding Quinn of Marnie.

He looked up at Anna. "No sign of sexual assault in either case?"

Anna shook her head. "Sally was a hooker—there were enough street people around to assure us on that point. But she hadn't even had any business the night she was killed."

Quinn gave a grim smile as he looked at Anna. "Could have been an accidental death."

She shook her head. "She was found on the sidewalk, with the needle still in her arm. Staged, but staged badly. Where the hell was her stash? Her source for getting the heroin into the needle? It's been called possible homicide, probable homicide and death by misadventure. Call it what you will. She was murdered."

"The two deaths were months apart," Quinn mused.

"Right. Like I said, though, Jake and I are convinced that they're related. I understand that you're investigating the 'accidental' death of the dancer?"

"That's right."

"I wish it had been assigned to Jake and me. But it wasn't. And Dixon closed the case. Though, quite frankly, I'm not sure what correlation Jake or I could have made, either. Your dancer died of prescription drugs and alcohol. There were definitely no street drugs."

"Another woman died recently of a massive overdose of prescription medication," Jake said.

She nodded. "Nell Durken. Husband arrested. Joel Kylie has that case. He said the arrest was easy, you had such great records on the husband."

Quinn winced. "I'm not so sure anymore that the guy is guilty."

Anna looked surprised. "His prints were all over the pill bottle," she reminded him. "What makes you think he's innocent?"

"Well, he says so, for one thing," Quinn told her.

She smiled. "Most murderers claim to be innocent. You know that. You can see a guy pull the trigger, and he'll still look you right in the eye and deny it."

"Like you, I think the two deaths are associated. And I also think they're associated with your drug overdoses."

"There have been other deaths by drug overdose, you know. Even though we've actually cut down on murder cases per capita recently, we're still talking hundreds a year in the general area. You worked here—you know that many go unsolved."

"Sadly, I do know that."

"So what makes *you* think the deaths are all related?"

"Nell was a dance student at Moonlight Sonata. Lara Trudeau was a coach there and got her start there. The beach where Sonya Miller was found is right there, and, according to this report, Sally Grant was found just down the street."

"I don't think our hooker, Sally Grant, took dance lessons. And she would have been thrown out of a club like Suede before her little toe passed the door. Sonya might have been in the place, but we grilled everyone in there as hard as we could, within the limits of the law," Anna assured him. "The other business in the building belongs to a designer, and our hooker couldn't begin to afford her clothing. Patrolmen canvassed the area after both bodies were discovered. Officers spoke with the designer and her husband, and they talked to people at the dance studio, as well."

Quinn stared at her, then paged through the file on Sonya Miller again. An Officer George Banner had spoken with Gordon Henson on Monday and been assured that the woman had not taken classes there at any time, nor did he recognize her as anyone who had ever been around.

Strange, Gordon had never mentioned the fact that the police had been in on Monday.

Gordon had a way of keeping quiet about things, he had realized that the other day at Nick's, when Gordon had revealed all he knew about Quinn.

"Anything else?" Anna asked him.

"After these deaths, narcotics did a sweep of the area clubs," Quinn said. "What happened there?"

"After the first girl was found, we acquired search warrants for Suede and a few other clubs. Ted Healey, in narcotics, told me that when they arrived at Suede, they almost had to force the folks there to look at it. Management said they were welcome to tear the place apart if they wanted to. Suede prides itself on—"

"I know, I know. Controlling alcohol consumption by drivers and putting heavy pressure on their people to make sure that IDs are good," Quinn said.

"Right," Anna agreed, looking at him strangely.

"I know the guy who owns the place," Quinn said. "Hey, you have extra pictures in here, sketches, of your first victim. Can I take one?"

"Absolutely."

"Thanks. For this, and for all your help."

"Hey, if you can find something we didn't, it'll be great." Her eyes darkened for a minute. "Every unnatural death is sad, but you know, you come to live with it. When we found Sally Grant…I don't know. She got to me. Such a kid. And with no one. No one who cared at all. I'd give a lot to see that justice is done for her, even though she's dead and can never know."

"I understand."

"Since you think these deaths are related, as far as your dancer goes, do you have any suspects?" she asked.

He grimaced ruefully. "Too many," he said. *And too few. The two people with the best motive seem to be my brother and the woman I'm falling in love with.*

When he left the station, he returned to the *Twisted Time*. After checking his messages, he discovered that Manuel Taylor hadn't returned his call, so he made another and left another message.

Then, at his desk, he drew a map of the studio and the surrounding blocks.

He looked over his lists, making comparisons, looking for similarities. The only thing in common between the four deaths was proximity to or association with the building that housed Moonlight Sonata.

Someone had to know something.

The same someone, he was certain, who drove by Shannon's house in a gray or beige sedan.

He checked his e-mail.

His brother had come through on one thing. There was a list of plates and cars belonging to everyone who worked at the studio or at the building, or went there on a regular basis.

Elimination time. Shannon—it was unlikely she was casing her own house. Jane—she drove a red Chevy minivan. Rhianna Markham drove a blue Mazda.

Gordon had a beige Lexus. Ben had recently purchased a "pre-owned" gray Mercedes. Old Mr. Clinton owned a "taupe" Audi. Figured. He eliminated Clinton anyway. He went down the list. Gray or beige sedans were owned by Jim Burke, Mina Long, Justin Garcia, Christie Castle, Sam Railey, Gabriel Lopez and four more employees of Suede.

At least his own brother, the one who had definitely argued with Lara Trudeau the day of her death, drove a dark green aging Jaguar.

As he sat there mulling the cars, he finally realized just what Manuel Taylor had said that had bothered him, that he wanted to pursue.

He put through another call, but the man still didn't answer. He left another message, then headed out.

Quinn was gone when Shannon awoke, but he'd left coffee on again. "Schedule me for late afternoon," was the message he left behind that day.

Determined to spend some time at the studio alone in nice bright daylight, Shannon slipped out before Marnie awoke, leaving her a note that she would be back later to pick her up. She hurried to the studio, letting herself in and locking the doors once more before determinedly looking around. She didn't know what she was looking for, but she went so far as to knock on walls, search the area around the toilet stalls, and then, at the end, let herself out the back door into the little hallway-balcony area off the stairs that led down to the back lot, up to Gabe's apartment, and over to Katarina's design shop.

She paused, then opened the door to the storage area. The costume on the dressmaker's dummy still seemed eerie, even in the glare of the light. She noted that the back shelves weren't actually very full and made a mental note that she could move more of the boxes of old paperwork back here, and also that she had lots of her old outfits back here, and some of them were in excellent shape. If she was considering competing again, she should start going through them. As she stood in there, surveying the shelves, she thought she heard someone out in the hallway. Glancing at her watch, she realized that the others would be arriving soon.

Suddenly the light went out.

"Hey!" She turned, not really afraid; it was daytime, after all.

But then the door closed, and the room was plunged into darkness.

"Hey!" she called again, and rushed forward, toward the door, just in time to hear retreating footsteps.

The pitch blackness caused her a moment's disorientation. She plunged into the dressmaker's dummy and struggled with it, trying to keep it upright at first, then trying to maintain her own balance. As she teetered backward, she would have frozen if she could have, because she was suddenly certain she heard the sound of breathing…right next to her ear.

It was right there.

While the footsteps had been outside, even when the light had gone out and the door had closed.

Suddenly the dummy seemed to collide with her. She

fought wildly for her balance, then went crashing down to the floor. Her head struck a shelf, or, she thought rather bizarrely, the shelf struck her.

And as the blackness became complete, she thought that she heard a strange groaning sound, although it might have been issuing from her own lips.

Things were getting out of control, and it was all because of her. What the hell was she doing now, suddenly digging around in the storage room? Should he just have waited? She might have turned around, walked on out.

They all came in.

And they all walked out.

The cops had been through the building. Not because of the studio, but because of the club. They had gone over it with a fine toothed comb and found nothing. Because the club was clean. There was nothing to worry about.

So why had he moved so quickly?

Killers always made a mistake eventually, or so they said. Not true. People definitely got away with murder. So…

Slow down. Calm down.

What did she know?

Too much. Somehow.

She knew too much. Suspected too much. Those beautiful eyes were not as innocent as they looked. But he had known. He had watched. And he had wanted.

And now…

Some things were simply necessary.

All he really had to do was get a grip and remember to act naturally.

Quinn walked in with a handful of flowers, looked around the room and thought that his own bouquet was a bit shabby. But Jane, who was sitting up a little in the hospital bed, smiled radiantly at him.

She might have been in absolute agony on the floor the other night, but she was already glorious again. Her hair was brushed; she was wearing makeup.

"Quinn, hi. This is really nice of you. Thanks for coming by. And thanks for the flowers—they're beautiful," she told him. She reached out, something like a queen awaiting a subject. He realized she was just used to greeting everyone with those double cheek kisses.

He obliged, then sat on the bedside chair.

"You're looking great."

"I'm feeling awfully sore," she said. "But, with the new keyhole surgery," she added, brightening, "at least I'm not going to have one of those really long scars."

"What a relief," he murmured, only slightly amused. She lived off her body—and not in an evil way. He'd started to see more and more of what went on in her world. She was young, and very pretty, and the costumes she wore were often skimpy, exposing the length of her perfect back and toned midriff.

"That sounds petty, doesn't it?" she said with a sigh.

"I'm sorry. I understand."

"Your brother just left," she said.

"Did he? He's supposed to be on the job. He was lucky to get a regular nine-to-five patrol beat."

"He only comes for a minute, just to say good-morning."

He nodded. "So you two are seeing each other?"

"You can't tell anyone," she said, plucking at the sheet nervously.

He smiled. "It might become evident."

"If it reaches that point, I may have to quit." She stared at the sheet, then looked up. "Gordon and Shannon are both willing to look the other way as long as they can, but…then again, maybe Shannon will be more understanding now."

"Oh?"

Jane laughed out loud. "Hey, she hasn't taken on a new student in a long time."

"I thought you were stuck with someone if they fell your way when they came in for their first lesson."

"Not if you're Shannon. She's the manager. She chose to keep you."

"Only because she was investigating me."

Jane smiled again. "Because you're an investigator."

"Everyone knows now, right?"

"Well, to be honest, Doug told me. But Katarina was in yesterday and told me you caused a real flurry, going to Dr. Long's office."

"I see."

"Actually, I can tell you a secret."

"And what is that?"

"I don't think Shannon held on to you to try to find out what you were about," she said with a conspiratorial smile.

"Well, she's not very fond of me at the moment."

"You're wrong, you know."

"Am I?"

"She's very proud. I wasn't around at the time, but Christie told me once that she never let anyone see how it hurt her when Ben decided to dance with Lara, then marry her. Christie said Shannon behaved as if it was the most normal and natural thing in the world, and she held her head high any time she saw them. As if he had meant nothing to her and it was a relief to teach and not have to mess with all the games involved in competition. Well, she does love to teach, of course. But…" Her smile deepened. "Wouldn't it be cool if Doug and I got married, and you married Shannon?"

He had to laugh out loud. "Wow, you two are moving fast."

She wrinkled her nose. "You mean because of his thing with Lara?"

"Uh, frankly, yes."

"Lara knew I liked him. Really liked him. And that I was proud of him as a student. That's why she went after him. I didn't blame Doug. I just kept telling him that I was his teacher, and that…well, we couldn't go out. But after Lara died, I don't know, maybe I realized that life could be short. And who knows? We're an independent studio. No corporate brass can come down on us or anything like that."

"All right, maybe you and Doug have a longer relationship than I realized," he told her. "But I can't say Shannon and I have aeons of experience together. And as I said, I'm not so sure she likes me very much right now."

"That's because she's falling head over heels for you, and she's afraid of herself," Jane said. She grinned deeply. "I know Shannon pretty well. She's different, since you've been around. I have a feeling you two know certain things about each other really well—if you get my drift."

"We'll see. At the moment, Jane, I have two questions for you. You said you were afraid you'd been poisoned when you fell."

She flushed. "Silly, huh? I was just convinced that someone had put something in the coffee because of the chat we'd been having. About Lara. Like how maybe someone might have slipped her some extra pills in a drink or something."

"And who was in on this conversation?"

She grimaced. "Lots of people. The Longs, Mr. Clinton, even one of the new girls—I don't remember her name. Gabe, Katarina…I think David was there. Ben… Doug, and Gordon was nearby, watching the floor. And Sam was near Gordon. Lots of people."

"Did any of them say anything suspicious?"

"Um…David Mercutio, Katarina's husband, he was the one who said you could probably slip pills into a drink."

"Okay, second question. Do you have any idea who might have been alone with Lara at the competition and argued with her? Or even been really friendly?"

Her face darkened.

"I know about my brother," he told her.

She sighed. "Besides Doug...she fought with Jim Burke, her partner. They always fought. There would have been something suspicious if they *hadn't* fought!"

"Anyone else?"

"In the little bar area in front of the actual showroom floor, I saw her talking with Gordon, Ben, Justin...Gabe, both of the Longs, I think. And Shannon."

"Shannon?"

"I told you, there was never a time when you would have known that Shannon had anything against her. I think she bought her a drink. Or maybe not. Maybe she just went up to her to tell her good luck. You can't imagine how busy it is then, how fast everything moves. And remember, Sam and I were in that competition, too."

"Right. You two are really good together, right?"

"Sad to say, maybe we'll have a chance now. We won several times when Lara wasn't there."

He nodded. "One last thing. Do you mind taking a look at a picture?"

She shook her head.

He showed her the sketch of Sally Grant he had gotten from the police file. Jane looked at him right away, shaking her head. "No. I remember when they found her body, though. I mean, actually, I do recognize that picture, because they ran it in the paper. But I never saw her around the studio."

He thanked her and rose.

"Are you going to the studio?"

"Yes, why? Do you need something?"

She shook her head. "You're a good student."

"I have a lot to learn before the Gator Gala."

"Yeah, right."

"I have to keep an eye on people."

"Including Shannon, huh?"

"She is pretty suspicious," he said.

She just grinned, settling into her pillow.

"What the hell are you doing in here? And on the floor?"

Shannon blinked, looking up. Gordon was standing over her.

She sat up, then clutched her wobbling head. "Someone tripped me, bumped me, something."

He arched a brow, looking around. The storeroom was empty.

"What did you do? Walk into a shelf? Oh, I see. You had a major fight with a dressmaker's dummy."

"I came in here, and then there were footsteps in the hall."

"Me," he told her.

"And you turned out the light and closed the door?"

"I thought some idiot had left the light on and the door open. I turned off the light, and closed and locked the door."

"When?"

"Just a few minutes ago. When I went into the studio and found your purse in the office and no you, I came running back out here." He looked concerned. "Are you all right? Hell, we'd better get you to the hospital, if you knocked yourself out."

She looked around the room, noting that, indeed, nothing, no one was there—except for the dressmaker's dummy, down on the floor beside her.

"No one came out?"

"I locked the door from the outside," he told her. "I guess I should have looked in. It just didn't occur to me that you were in here."

She had to be imagining things. It had gone black, and she had panicked. Because, if anyone had been in the room with her, Gordon would have seen him. Or her.

He sighed. "Can you get up?"

"Of course." She rose, only a little unsteadily, to her feet.

"Come on," Gordon said. "Let's go start canceling your lessons for the day."

"No," she protested.

He gave her a stern look. "You probably have one hell of a lump on your head somewhere."

She probed her own skull. She had a lump, but it was a little one.

"I'm okay, Gordon."

"You should—"

"Gordon, I swear to you, I'm okay. And if, during the day, at any time, I feel funny in the least, I swear, I'll let you know. I don't want to go to a hospital, or home, and I sure as hell don't want to cancel my classes."

"But—"

"Really. And, Gordon, don't say a word about this, please?"

"But…?"

"Please? Look, if I'm out of it for any reason, there will just be more talk. And we could wind up having to cancel the Gator Gala."

That gave him pause. He sighed.

"Gordon, not a word. And in turn, I swear I will tell you if I have so much as a headache."

"Deal," he said after a minute.

They walked out into the hall together. Ben was there, just outside the studio's rear door. "What the hell is going on?"

"What?" Shannon asked guiltily.

"Doors open, music blaring…and no one around."

"I was just…" She paused, looking at Gordon. "I was checking on some of my old costumes."

Ben's dark brows arched slowly. "You're really—seriously—considering competing again?"

"Yes."

"With me?"

"Yes, Ben."

"Thank you," he said. She had never heard him sound more humble.

He walked back into the studio, and she and Gordon followed him. Shannon had a feeling it was going to be another long day.

CHAPTER 21

Something was off all day.

Or maybe she was feeling a sense of heightened aware-ness after being hit on the head, however it had happened. Friday was usually slow, but today it was busy.

She spent time training Marnie, as well as her students, after getting Ben to run back to her house to pick up the girl. Richard was peevish, saying that he wanted to learn more lifts, and she wasn't sure he had the ability to do them.

She had a student named Billy that afternoon, one of her regulars, who suffered from cerebral palsy. He tried so hard but continually got frustrated with himself. Still, she respected him for trying, where others might just have given up. She worked with him especially hard, knowing how good the basic movements were for him.

Then there was Quinn.

Unbelievably determined and adept at the waltz, lifting, turning, moving as he should. She wondered how it was possible for him to be so good at the waltz and so horrible at the fox-trot. Students tended to do better at smooth dances and have trouble with rhythm, or do well with rhythm and have a hard time with smooth. She'd never come across anyone who could waltz with the best, then trip over his own feet in a fox-trot. Even tango steps came more naturally to him.

They worked for a while with Rhianna and a student on one side, Justin and Mina Long on the other. It wasn't until the others had gone over to the other side of the room to work rhythm and she moved to the stereo that he said to her, "Any trouble with the alarm system?"

"None whatsoever," she told him. After hesitating, she said stiffly, "Thank you."

"Sure. And thanks for letting me sleep."

"No problem."

She was tempted to tell him about her wild panic in the storeroom that morning. But the more time that passed, the more convinced she was that her imagination had really begun to run wild.

"What?" he demanded. She looked up. He was against the wall, trying to catch her eyes, which were lowered as she stared sightlessly at the floor. She shook her head. "Nothing."

"There's something."

He wasn't going to let up. She turned the tables. "Exactly what mistake did you make with the FBI? What did you do?"

He looked aggravated, as if he was going to tell her to mind her own business.

"I was with profiling."

"Profiling?" She didn't know why she was surprised that that was the root of his issues. Maybe because she'd had a sense that he had shot the wrong person, or someone had died, that something really terrible had happened.

"Yeah, profiling. There was a case in Indiana. I should have been on top of it, but gave an entirely wrong assessment. I was certain the killer had to be late twenties, early thirties, with some kind of a menial day job, maybe even a wife. They arrested a guy who fit our description."

"And?"

"The community let down its guard. The next day, there were two more dead women. The killer left evidence that time—he dropped his wallet. He was fifty, and an executive at a local bank."

"But profiling isn't an exact science. You could only work with what you had."

"Maybe that was the point. I felt that my work was useless. So I came back home, and started working with Dane, an old friend. I figured I couldn't do too much harm on surveillance, that type of thing. I was wrong. I followed a guy named Art Durken, and he wound up killing his wife."

"Nell," Shannon said softly.

"Nell," he agreed. "Kind, pleasant, the type of person who should fill the world. But she wound up dead, and Durken wound up arrested, and now, well, now I'm not at all sure Art is guilty, but I'll be damned if I can figure out who is. Except…"

"Except?"

He stared at her with a shrug. "Well, that's obvious, isn't it? It's someone associated with this studio."

She swallowed hard. "It might not be," she said.

"You don't want it to be," he corrected.

She looked at him again. "Some murders are never solved."

"This one had better be. When Doug talked me into coming here, he told me he was afraid someone else would die. I think he was right."

"Is that what it takes to learn those lifts—lots of long conversation?" Rhianna teased, coming over to them. "Shannon," she asked, "are you going to play anything or can I have a cha-cha?"

"Sure, a cha-cha. Whatever."

Rhianna put in a CD, and moved out to the floor.

"I'll follow you and Marnie back to your house later," Quinn said.

"It will be around ten by then," she told him. As happy as she was to improve someone's life as it seemed they had Marnie's, she suddenly desperately wished she didn't have a roommate.

"It's all right. I'll see you two home."

"I have an alarm now, you know," she reminded him.

"And it's great—once you're inside to be protected by it."

His lesson was over. He gave her the perfunctory and studio-necessary kiss on the cheek, then left.

After that, the day seemed to drag endlessly, even though students kept coming.

At the end of the night, she remembered to announce to the group class that everyone involved with the Gator Gala and who wanted to attend the cruise get-together should be at the marina by seven.

She thought Quinn had forgotten her, but just as they were locking up, he arrived. Since Gordon evidently knew exactly what he did for a living and what he was doing at the studio, it didn't seem to matter that Quinn had come for the precise reason of following her home.

He didn't even get out of his car when they got there. He watched her enter the house with Marnie, waved, and was gone.

So much for his being in love with her.

There was still no word from Manuel Taylor when Quinn reached the *Twisted Time,* though, frankly, he had expected that if the man was going to call him back, he would have called his cell phone.

"No problem. I'm making pretty big bucks off your group," the man had said.

Sure. He'd made money off Gordon, and off Quinn, for showing up to confront Gordon, who had seemed to have such a glib answer.

But the sentence, Quinn was certain, implied more. Someone else in the group had paid the waiter, as well.

But for what?

Did they all tip that well, just for drinks?

He doubted it. He had a feeling someone had tipped Manuel to give Lara Trudeau a drink. A special drink. A drugged drink.

It was late. Still, he tried the hotel and got through to a beverage manager.

The man was no help. He was irritated. Manuel Taylor was supposed to have worked a dinner the night before, but he hadn't shown up.

"Is he usually fairly dependable?"

"Yeah, sure, usually," the beverage manager told Quinn over the phone. "But he was a no-show once before. Went off to Orlando with friends. I told him if he pulled one like that on me again, he'd be fired. He's a good waiter, though. I'm going to be sorry to fire him."

Quinn hung up, aggravated himself.

There was little else he could do that night. He was restless, feeling that he should be at Shannon's house, even though there was an alarm there now, and she wasn't alone.

Nothing to do. He lay in the cabin, awake for hours—events and ideas floating around in his mind like pieces of a puzzle.

Shannon, here, on the *Twisted Time,* not so long ago, a lifetime ago. Wearing his old shirt and framed in the doorway, a silhouette, a shadow of seduction. One night and his world had turned. The boat still seemed to carry the elusive scent of her perfume, permeating his sheets, the cabin, his memory. The sound of her voice echoed in his ears, the dance she practiced between the sheets more hypnotic than the sway of the rumba, as passionate as the steamy encounter of a *pasa doble*.

He was losing it, he told himself.

But he couldn't erase the memory of her coming to his cabin door, and he was chagrined to realize that an eighteen-year-old street waif had seen with clarity the depth of what he had thought was just attraction and arousal. She had touched him once, and now the world revolved around her, both his waking moments and his dreams. He wasn't just after the truth to vindicate himself, but because he had to fix her world and create one in which he could touch her once again. He'd known what it was to care, but never before had he felt that someone had slipped into his skin and was haunting him, flesh and blood. She teased and taunted his dreams. He saw her in the realm of memory, breathed the scent of her, heard her whisper, even above the lapping of the surf against the hull.

Nick's stayed open late on Friday nights. He could hear laughter and conversation from the patio. Men and women, some together, some looking to be together, seeking what could be real, what could be permanent, and others hoping just to get lucky, to get laid. Not that Nick's was really much of a pickup joint. It was usually too full of regulars, married and co-habiting couples, and friends. Sometimes the old jukebox played, and sometimes, on weekends, Nick brought in a band.

Tonight he would be keeping it down. Ashley was home with her new baby. She and Jake had always intended on moving on and buying their own home, but Jake had his boat here, and Ashley's place was a separate apartment, anyway. Plus they had both been too involved with each other and their work to do any house hunting. Nick's reflected that kind of commitment. Not like the places on the beach. Not like Suede....

Searched up and down by the narcotics squads, who had

found nothing. So it was hot, a hot club, a hot pickup place. It was also an establishment that followed the law, crossing the T's and dotting the I's.

But two women had been found nearby, dead. A socialite and a hooker. Illegal substances…not like prescription drugs.

He gave up, dressed and went over to the patio at Nick's. Lots of cops tonight. The old jukebox was playing softly. Dixon was there, eating a cheeseburger.

Inside at the bar, the television was on, though the music from the jukebox drowned out the sound. Quinn ordered a beer, staring at the screen. He froze, his drink halfway to his lips.

There, on the screen, was a picture of Manuel Taylor, and beneath it ran the words, "Caught in the crossfire?"

He rose, walked to the television, turned up the sound.

"Hey!" someone complained.

He ignored the man, turning to stare icily at the protester, and the guy turned away.

The newscaster came back on. "Manuel Taylor was pronounced dead on arrival at Jackson Memorial from a single bullet wound to the head. It's believed that he was an accidental casualty of a gang war currently under way. In other breaking news…"

On Saturdays the studio itself opened for business earlier than on weekdays mornings. Despite the charter that night, plans were no different this Saturday.

Shannon dropped Marnie off, told Ella that she was just hopping over to the hospital, then went to visit Jane, who was both delighted and angry—she was being released the following day with a slew of instructions about what she could and couldn't do until she was healed, which was great, of course, but not in time for her to go out on the boat. "It's not fair," she complained.

"It's not, and I'm sorry. I'd change things if I could," Shannon told her. Jane was restless; she'd been in bed too long. She'd heard all about Marnie's progress, and she was both excited and worried, afraid that the younger girl might end up stealing some of her students.

"We have too many students. None of us can handle so many," Shannon said soothingly. "Besides, pretty soon, you'll be too busy winning competitions everywhere to do much teaching."

"I can't even dance again for weeks," Jane moaned.

Unable to make her friend feel any better, Shannon told her that she would pick her up the following day and get her settled back at home. When Jane told her that she already had a ride arranged, Shannon didn't push the point. She assumed it was going to be Doug O'Casey.

"Watch out for my students tonight, huh?" Jane asked her.

"You bet. I'll keep old Mr. Clinton from flirting."

Jane shot her a dry glance, and Shannon laughed. "Jane, just get better. It's all going to be fine. Just get back on your feet."

Shannon had more paperwork than classwork during the day, since it was time to arrange the group schedule for the following month, and she wanted to read all the notes in the suggestion box and find out what dances the students wanted on the roster.

Gordon wasn't in—he was heading straight down in the afternoon to check out their charter boat and make sure the caterers were ready, that the trio was going to have enough room to set up, and that the dance floor was all it should be.

By three o'clock, the studio had emptied of students, with everyone anxious to get out and get ready, so they could make it to the marina by seven.

Ben was strangely helpful, though, anxious to hang

around and help Shannon close up. Marnie was there, as well, and was the most helpful when it came to clearing up the bits of Saturday doughnuts and croissants left around the room, making sure they wouldn't get bugs over the weekend.

As she locked up, Shannon realized that she was listening for the grating sound, but she didn't hear it.

There wasn't that much for her to do at home, since she had decided to adhere to the casual side of the dress code, wearing a pair of studded jeans and a halter top. Despite Marnie's slimness, Shannon found a cocktail gown that fitted the girl perfectly. She also finally got Marnie to quit thanking her, reminding her that the studio needed her.

"But don't you know how neat that is?" Marnie asked. "I've never actually been needed by anyone before."

They made it to the marina by six. Gordon was already on board and as happy as a clam. He explained the arrangement of tables in the salon area, and introduced Shannon to the caterer and crew. Buffet tables lined the sides of the main salon, surrounding the dance floor. The trio would play in the rear, so they could also be heard on the open deck in back.

Shannon was somewhat surprised that Quinn wasn't around, but Gordon told her that he'd had a few things to do but would be there by seven.

The cruise seemed to have been perfectly planned, and Quinn had definitely come through. The boat was great. Perfect for the fifty or so they would have aboard.

Long before seven, their group started arriving.

The staff of Moonlight Sonata lined the boarding plank from the dock to the boat, greeting their friends and students.

"Leave it to old Mr. Clinton to arrive first," Sam said.

"You know," Shannon teased, "his first name is actually John—not *Old Mister.*"

"Well, I don't call him old Mr. Clinton to his face," Sam protested.

"Oh, my God! He's brought old Mrs. Clinton," Rhianna whispered, watching the older gentleman escort a spry little white-haired lady toward them.

"His wife died years ago," Gordon commented.

"He's found a lady friend, apparently," Ben said.

"I know all about it," Ella whispered. "He lives at a retirement home, you know. And he says that it's great—women outnumber men by two to one, and when you're a man who can dance, you have the pick of the litter at every occasion."

Mr. Clinton introduced his date, a retiree named Lena Mangetti. She seemed charming, and was delighted to be out on the cruise. They headed aboard, and others followed, including the group from their sister studio in Broward. The Longs came with the Beckhams, another couple that attended classes together, and Katarina and David arrived with Gabe, saying that they'd all shared a cab from the beach, since they intended to have more than a few drinks. Christie, who was both a student and a judge, also arrived—with her dog, as usual. She went nowhere without it. And whether the students were canine lovers or not, they all made a fuss over the animal.

It wasn't until the boat was almost ready to go out that Quinn arrived, his brother in tow.

"You almost didn't make it," Shannon said lightly. "Late for what is actually your own party."

He didn't so much as crack a smile, but said, "Well, I'm here now."

Doug gave Quinn a dry gaze and turned to Shannon, shaking his head. "We're both here now. Guess he didn't notice me with him." He was trying to be polite, when Quinn was acting liking a jerk.

Quinn ignored Doug and walked by. Shannon thought, Oh, yeah, he's madly in love. Can't live without me.

She glanced at Doug.

"Don't say anything yet," Doug told her, "but…that waiter was killed. He was caught in some kind of gang war, but Quinn is seeing something else."

"What?" she said incredulously. "Waiter—you mean Manuel Taylor?"

"Don't look so panicky," Doug told her quickly. "He was shot—no overdose of anything. It's got nothing to do with us. It's all right."

It had to be. She had too much to do.

She was shocked, but she couldn't afford to worry about Quinn's state of mind. There was too much going on. As they set sail, there were questions from all quarters. Cocktails were already being served as the boat moved out, but the caterers wanted to know how she wanted the food brought out. Cheese puffs and shrimp balls first? And the trio wanted to know when to play, when to give it a break. She noticed that the Broward and Miami-Dade groups seemed to have chosen opposite sides of the boat, and she wanted to tell the trio that they needed to sing the number from the musical *Oklahoma*, about how "the cowboys and the farmers must be friends," or whatever it was they said exactly. She accepted a glass of champagne herself and went over to sit with Mary and Judd Bentley, who owned the Broward studio.

"Hi, Shannon," Trudy Summers, one of their longtime students said. "Glad you're here. Mary was just talking about how hard it was to dance with her husband."

"Well, it shouldn't be," Judd said, perching atop a table and setting an arm around his wife's shoulders. "It's just that she's a teacher, and she wants to lead all the time, even when we're dancing together."

"Especially when we're dancing together," Mary said, laughing. "Seriously, I do not try to lead."

"You two *will* be dancing together tonight—it's a fun evening," Trudy said.

"Yeah," Judd teased. "It will be a lot of fun. We'll dance out on the deck. We'll do one of those lifts she likes so much."

"Right," Mary said. "He plans on lifting me right overboard, I'm pretty sure."

"Heck, you can swim," Judd said.

"Not a good idea, there's a propeller or something back there," Shannon said lightly. "Trudy, don't forget to mix and mingle. We're all South Florida, you know."

"No problem. Introduce me to some of your guys. Our studio is heavily weighted on the female side. Hey, that guy is really cute—and that one, too." She pointed to Doug and Quinn. "Jane's student. I've seen the younger guy before, but not the other one. Hey, they kind of look alike."

"Brothers," she told Trudy, then couldn't help teasing, "I'll introduce you to Mr. Clinton, if you haven't met him yet. He says that women always outnumber men, two to one," she said with a laugh, and moved on.

She didn't actually sit to eat with anyone, moving from table to table as others helped themselves to the buffet. Dancing went on along with the dinner, but picked up in earnest once the tables were cleared and it began to grow late. They were due to return by midnight.

Gordon and Judd introduced some of their people, who then did one-and-a-half-minute bits of the routines they were going to do at the Gala.

She was startled when Gordon announced that she and Quinn were going to do their waltz, and she was sure Quinn was equally startled, but he rose to the occasion.

She was glad to slip into his arms, feeling that electricity he could so quickly create. But she was troubled by his eyes.

"Are you all right with this?" she asked him.

"With this? Yes," he said simply, and when the music came on, he proved it. The waltz was definitely the man's dance. Dancers, especially beginners, were supportive of one another, but she was surprised by the applause that followed his movements, and the oohs and aahs when they went into their final turn, and he spun and lifted her into the "pooper-scooper."

He smiled; he was charming. When people rushed up, saying they couldn't believe he was a beginner, he said that they should see his fox-trot. He accepted Doug's warm hug and sincere congratulations, but he wasn't really paying attention, not even to his brother. He was watching Gordon, she thought.

She didn't get a chance to stay with him, though, because Judd announced that she and Ben were going to do a bolero. Another surprise.

Ben asked her, "Do you mind?"

"No, let's do it," she told him.

They did, and she had to admit that, as partners, they were good together. Better than good. They excelled.

"Will you really enter as a pro with me at the Gator Gala?" he asked her, hugging her in a brotherly fashion as their number ended and applause sounded.

She squeezed his hand. Something about Ben had changed since Lara's death. She took the microphone herself to announce, "Thank you. Thanks so very much. And here's some news. Ben and I will be entering the professional division at our first ever Gator Gala!"

Ben gave her a look of pure gratitude, but she sidestepped him, anxious to find Quinn. Gordon announced that Judd and Mary would be dancing, followed by more dancing.

Shannon moved toward the aft deck. A few of the students had milled outside, but having heard the announcement, they were now returning to the main salon. She wandered out as they moved in, wondering where Quinn could have gotten to.

She paused, feeling the breeze. The night was beautiful.

The last dance was starting. She hugged her arms around herself and stared at the wake, the foam spewing out from the propeller at the back of the boat. Standing still and silent, she heard the rush of the water and the hum of the engine.

Then, slowly, she became aware of the voices.

Whispers, hushed.

She turned, not sure where the sound was coming from and unable to make out the words.

"...has to stop."

"There is no visible connection!"

"She was too close. They'll see the connection eventually."

"Shannon!" someone called.

She turned back to the door to the salon. Judd was calling to her. Silently she damned him.

Gritting her teeth, she turned to stare out to the rear again, noting the way the water flowed violently from beneath the boat.

She felt a rush of wind and started to turn just as the boat did, starting to head back to the marina.

There was something...someone...

But what, she didn't know.

Suddenly she was flying off the boat, falling toward the water, where it churned violently beneath the giant propeller.

CHAPTER 22

"She fell! She was there a second ago, and then…!" Mr. Clinton called out in horror.

Quinn had been looking for Shannon. He'd wanted to tell her, before they got off the boat, that, to the best of his knowledge, no one but Gordon had known about the lunch meeting he had staged with Manuel Taylor. Maybe the man really had been caught in the crossfire of some gang war, but just in case, Quinn didn't want Shannon alone with Gordon.

Threading his way through a friendly group of Broward students, he had searched the crowd for her but he hadn't been able to find her. Then Clinton had yelled.

The *she* in "She fell!" had to be Shannon.

Panic gripped his heart with fingers of sharp ice.

He pushed past people, heedless of who they were. He practically knocked old Mr. Clinton right out of the way. At first it seemed no one was near the area from which Shannon had disappeared, but by the time he got there, a crowd had already formed.

Tearing across the deck, he plunged into the water.

Someone turned on floodlights; the motor was killed. As he hit the water, chilled by night and depth, he feared to open his eyes not just to the sting of salt but because he was afraid to see a blur of red, if she'd been caught in the propeller.

He scissored himself to the surface, shouting her name.

"Shannon!"

"Here!" she called.

Though the motor had been cut, the boat was now a good distance from them, due to sheer momentum. He could hear the crew lowering lifeboats, so that people could come after them.

"Where?"

"Here!" The word ended with a gurgle. He shot toward the sound of her voice.

"What the hell are you doing?" He swam toward her strongly, then realized that she was treading water with no difficulty, actually pushing away from him when he came close.

His heart was still pounding. Her hair was slicked back from her face, and in the expanse of the night sea, she looked frail and delicate—and defensive.

But all in one piece. She had missed the blades of the propeller.

He fought the frantic urge to reach out for her despite her apparent competence.

"What am I doing?" she repeated incredulously. "I'm just out for a midnight swim."

He reached her in the water. "You fell overboard?"

"I think I was pushed."

"By who?"

"I don't know."

"You didn't see anyone?"

"No."

"How do you know you were pushed? Could you have

been leaning over? We took a bit of a sharp turn—is that when you fell?"

"No. That's when I was pushed."

The seas that night were two to four feet, causing small swells around them. Since she seemed to be doing fine on her own, Quinn made no attempt to reach out for her.

"Mr. Clinton saw you go over, but there was no one else there."

She glared at him but didn't respond, instead swimming toward the lifeboat that was now coming their way.

Gordon was aboard with two of the crew members, Javier Gonzalez and Randy Flores. Quinn knew them both, since Randy was a permanent employee and Javier often worked the cruises. They were ready to help them both aboard. It wasn't cold, but definitely cool, and Shannon shivered as she was helped up. There were blankets on board, and one was quickly wrapped around her. "Are you all right?" Gordon asked Shannon, seeming genuinely anxious about her.

"Either of you hurt?" Javier asked.

"No," Shannon said quickly.

"Fine," Quinn said briefly.

"What the hell were you doing?" Gordon asked Shannon.

To Quinn's amazement, she said, "I don't know. I must have been leaning over too far when the boat veered to head back toward the marina."

"Thank God you didn't hit the propeller," Gordon said vehemently.

"He's right," Suarez said.

Quinn stayed silent. A minute later, they reached the boat, and the anxious captain was there to greet them. Doug helped Shannon from the boat, then assisted his brother, looking at them both in silence.

Shannon quickly assured everyone that she was fine, as her friends, associates and students swept around them.

"I'm so sorry, everyone," she said. "I guess my balance isn't what I thought. You all can remember that when I'm giving you grief when you're dancing."

A little ripple of laughter rose, but despite her words, Quinn knew she was still convinced she had been pushed.

Someone pushed through the crowd. It was Richard Long, and he was carrying take-out cups. "Coffee and brandy, one for our lovely-even-when-wet instructor, and another for the man willing to risk his life to save her. Whoops, wait a minute. He owns the boat we're out on, right? Maybe he's trying to make sure he doesn't get sued." Long spoke teasingly, and laughter rose again.

"Sued? Are you kidding me? I couldn't take the chance that my instructor might drown. I'm just beginning to catch on to the whole dance thing," Quinn said lightly.

"All's well that ends well," Sam said, stepping forward to give Shannon a warm hug.

"Drink the coffee," Ella said. "You're just standing there shivering."

"Coffee sounds great. Thanks, Richard," Shannon said, reaching for a cup.

Once they were docked, Quinn had a few words with the captain, who swore that he hadn't taken any turns too sharply, something Quinn assured him he was already certain of.

When he was ready to debark himself, Quinn saw that Shannon, a bit damp, her clothing still hugging her frame, had taken her place with the rest of the Moonlight Sonata group, saying good-night to everyone. Her trip overboard had become part of a good time, something they would all talk about for years to come.

Quinn had made up his mind. Screw policy.

As the instructors began to say good-night to one another, he came up to her. "We need to talk."

She arched a brow, looking around her, silently reminding him that they were surrounded by her entire staff.

"I need to take Marnie home," she said.

"No, you don't," he said. "Someone else can take her. I can have Doug do it."

A strange expression filtered into her eyes. He thought that she was going to refuse him again, and belligerently. Instead she turned around and called softly to Sam, asking him, "Can you take Marnie home, and—" she hesitated briefly, looking at Quinn "—stay with her tonight?"

Sam looked surprised at first, stared at her, then glanced at Quinn and smiled broadly.

"Sure."

"And stop grinning."

"Absolutely. No grin."

Everyone continued the process of kissing each other good-night, but finally almost everyone had straggled off the dock toward the parking lot.

Gordon lingered, asking Shannon, "You're sure you're okay?"

"Absolutely. Honest, Gordon, I'm sorry I caused such a stir."

"I wouldn't be sorry for that. After it turned out you were okay, the students enjoyed it. Hey, how often have any of them gotten to see you uncoordinated?"

She smiled. "There you go. I was the entertainment."

Sam was still hovering nearby with Marnie, and Doug remained, as well.

"Doug, looks like everything is all right. Go home or…wherever." She smiled knowingly, and he waved, then walked off toward his car. "Sam, quit looking like a two-year-old in training pants. Go ahead and drive Marnie out to the beach."

"Well," Sam murmured.

Marnie gave them each a kiss on the cheek, casting

them a look that was too wise for her years. "Have a good night," she said, preceding Sam along the dock. He shrugged, a smile still hovering on his face, and followed her. With a last, curious look, Gordon left, as well.

Quinn and Shannon turned to each other, both feeling the worse for wear.

Boats knocked against rubber guards at their docks; a bell clanged from somewhere; waves lapped against boats and pilings. From a distance, they could hear the drone of conversation, the sound of a mellow reggae band playing at Nick's.

Quinn stared at Shannon, ready to argue the point as to whether or not she had been pushed, but she shook her head before he could speak. "Stop," she said. "Don't…. Just don't."

He frowned, slowing arching a questioning brow.

God knows who might be around, but she took a step toward him.

Then she slipped her arms around his neck and pressed against him, rising on her toes, the length of her body like a caress, and pressed her lips against his. She tasted like salt, like the sea breeze, like a promise of sweet and decadent sin. He returned her kiss, parting her lips with a ragged and swift hunger, sweeping her mouth with his tongue, deep, returning her initiative with passionate insinuation of what could come. She was trembling in his arms, whether shivering from the touch of the breeze or trembling with anticipation, he wasn't at all certain. Nor did he care. The *Twisted Time* was just yards away. And when her lips parted from his, the words she whispered against his ear were liquid fire. "Don't you ever want to forget it all…just for a few hours, forget it all and…"

His response was so guttural and startling that it evoked an eroticism beyond memory. He drew back, staring at her, cupping her cheek in his hand, a smile slowly taking hold of his lips as tension streaked through him, muscle, sinew, blood and bone.

"Hell, yes," he told her. And he lowered his head, whispering back, "You mean like feeling so desperate that nothing else matters except crawling right into someone? Not time, place, words, anything?"

She nodded, drawing a line down his damp chest. Low. Down to his soggy belt line. Below.

"You're wasting time now," she informed him.

He swept her up into his arms because it seemed the simplest, easiest and fastest move to make at that moment.

His own balance and agility were put to the test when he jumped the distance from the dock to the deck of his boat, but necessity seemed to be the mother of coordination as well as invention.

Balancing her weight, he fumbled in his pocket for his key, then burst into the cabin, banging his elbow and her head as he made his way down the steps into the salon. They were both laughing then.

And then they weren't laughing, they were gasping for breath, heedless of everything else as they struggled to peel away wet clothing and crawl into each other's skin.

Draped over Quinn's bare length, Shannon smiled and then winced. In the heat of the moment, they had wound up on the floor, in the narrow space between the table and the sofa, and she had apparently banged more body parts than she had realized in the process. Now it was awkward trying to rise. She made the attempt to avoid him, but wound up with her knee right in his abdomen.

"Ow!" he groaned.

"Sorry."

He eased to his side, laughing. "Could have been worse. How about I get up first? But what's the urgency?"

"Shower. I'm pure salt."

"I'll come with you."

"We won't fit," she told him.

"We'll make do."

The shower was ridiculously tiny, but the water was steamy and hot, and despite the fact that they barely fit, the rush of warmth brought on by the spray that covered them was delicious. Purely sweet at first. Then purely sensual. Quinn's hand was braced on the Fiberglas wall behind Shannon, and his mouth seemed as hot as the water, moving over her flesh. His wet hair teased against her skin, and she was both breathless and laughing again at the erotic maneuvers he managed in the tiny, tense space. His hands laced around her midriff, and she found herself lifted to stand on the seat of the commode as the sensual movement of his tongue continued down the length of her body. When her knees gave, she was pressed against the Fiberglas herself, aware then of the pounding of water, the rush in her ears, and the force and thrust of his body, bringing her crashing over a brink of sweet forgetfulness and raw abandon once again. Climax shuddered through her with the strength of the rushing water, and she shivered and was held upright only by the power of his body and the smooth shower wall. They stayed there as moments slipped one into another, crushed together, still one, caught in an intimacy that seemed to go beyond any act of love.

At last they stirred, found soap, found shampoo, and, since there really was little choice, washed and soaped various body parts for each other until that too became so intimate and arousing that there was nowhere to go except back where they had been, but this time, when the level of arousal escalated to insanity, Quinn slammed off the showerhead, opened the door and dragged them both back into the cabin, oblivious to the fact that they drenched the floor and sheets.

But there was space…space and limitless comfort, and

here she had the freedom of his body, room to slide and creep and crawl all over him, taste and savor and caress the length of his body, hear the thunder of his heart, the gale wind of his breath, the feel of his arms and hands, know his eyes when he rose over her, drowning in the first slow, excruciating moments as he sank into her with the full force of his body, hunger and being. Then, finally, when it seemed to Shannon that her whole world had rocked and exploded to the highest peaks, she drifted down in comfort and warmth and lay at his side, totally relaxed for what seemed like the first time in forever. Then her mind began working, because it was impossible to turn off her brain, and she felt the first sense of self-defense, because it was frightening to feel so desperately for someone, to want him so badly, not only in such a sexually passionate manner, but in moments of laughter, fear, purpose and just plain existing.

His fingers moved through her hair as he pulled her close, and she was stunned by the first words that left his lips.

"She's right, you know."

"Who?"

"Marnie. I *am* falling in love with you."

She was afraid to reply.

He gripped her harder, pulling her taut to the curve of his body, into something that had surely been a male hold since the beginning of time. She was wrapped in him, and it was good, very good. She wanted to whisper something back, but fear kept her silent.

"Okay," he murmured softly. "Don't reply. Though that is one of those things that kind of demands an answer."

She wasn't facing him, instead lying flush against him, her back to his chest, her rump curved into his hip.

"I think you were pretty incredible."

He laughed. "Always the judge. We're not talking performance level here."

"Cocky, too," she murmured.

He rolled her to face him, and the laughter was gone. His eyes were the deepest, most piercing blue she had ever seen, and his features were striking, strong and taut.

"I don't want to play games anymore. I quit being a student. Screw the friggin' Gator Gala. I want to be with you."

"I'm…I'm…"

"A coward. A chicken."

Anger flickered through her.

"I am not!"

"Then at the least admit you want to take a chance."

She hesitated, uncomfortably aware that he was right. "I want to stay with you until morning. I want to sleep with you over and over again," she said.

"Why?" He smiled. "Other than the fact that we really are great together. Better than the most erotic dance known to man."

She smiled, and then his smile faded, and his words were a promise of everything to come. "Because you are the best waltz I've ever known. The most erotic rumba, the greatest exhilaration, the wildest, most beautiful music."

He kept staring down at her. Then, after a moment, he said, "Okay…so I think you *are* falling in love with me. At least a little bit."

"I *am* falling in love with you," she managed to say. "More than a little bit."

He kissed her again.

She thought later that there was so much they needed to say. So much was happening that she needed to convince him, needed him to see, to understand….

Nothing could be real, nothing could be right…until the trail of corpses shadowing them came to a halt.

But that would have to wait until morning. Because now, more than anything, they needed the night.

CHAPTER 23

"I swear someone pushed me over," Shannon said.

She was more appealing to Quinn than ever, hair fresh washed, dressed in a pair of jeans and a denim shirt borrowed from Ashley Dilessio, sitting at his table on the boat and sipping one last cup of coffee.

He was going with Jake down to the main station.

She was going to go home, check on Marnie, and let Sam have the rest of his Sunday for whatever he wanted to do. Strange, Marnie had been a street kid, but now Shannon didn't even want her left alone during the day.

They'd spent a nice morning taking time for themselves, then having breakfast at Nick's and spending an hour playing with the new baby, Shannon getting to know Ashley, Ashley getting to know Shannon, finding out they were fascinated by each other's professions, quickly becoming friends. They had talked about the case, too. Shannon had expressed her sadness over Manuel Taylor but had been quick to point out that she had overheard Gordon mention him in a group, so his "role" was common knowledge at the studio.

Quinn couldn't help it. He wasn't satisfied with the

possibility that the man's death wasn't connected, so Jake had offered to go down to the station with him, look at the report, then take a ride down to the area of the Grove, where it had happened. But first, he and Shannon had gone back to the boat so Quinn could get ready to go.

"The really strange thing is that right before I went overboard, I heard people whispering."

"Saying what?" he demanded.

She frowned, thinking. "Something about having to stop, about there being no visible connection."

"Connection to what?"

"I have no idea. I was eavesdropping. Well, not really. I was just there and heard pieces of the conversation."

"I'm telling you, everything's connected. I want you to watch out for Gordon, especially. Don't ever be alone around him."

"Gordon has been like a second father to me, you know," she told him.

"I don't care. Watch out for him."

There was a call from topside. "Quinn, you ready?"

"Yeah!" he called back. He gave Shannon a kiss on the top of the head, suddenly loath to leave her, even for a few hours.

"See you later?" he asked.

She nodded. "If Sam doesn't have plans, the three of us will probably head to the beach and get some sun."

"Great." With a wave to her, he headed topside.

"You know," Jake told him, "I'm a big one for hunches myself, but we're beginning to move a little strangely here. Two overdoses by prescription drugs. Two deaths by heroin overdose, both victims found near the studio. But this…okay, so Manuel Taylor was a waiter the day of the competition. But he was in Coconut Grove, not on the beach, when he was killed. And he was shot."

"I know," Quinn said.

"So?"

"I still say everything's related."

Jake shrugged. "All right. Am I driving?"

"Let's take both cars." Jake stared at him, and he shrugged. "I'm heading back out to the beach after we hit the Grove."

At the station, Quinn pored over the report, which had been prepared by Jake's partner, Anna. The woman was thorough. Everything pointed to an innocent man being caught in gang war crossfire.

"I'll make you a copy, then we can head out to the site."

Jake disappeared. The station was staffed on Sunday, but it was still slow. When Quinn's phone rang, it sounded like an alarm going off.

It was Marnie.

"Hey, is Shannon with you?" she asked.

"No, she was heading home."

"She isn't here yet." Marnie sounded a little plaintive. She went into a whisper. "Sam is like a little kid. He wants to go the beach."

"Try her cell. I left before she did. She might still be on the way."

"I just tried her cell. She didn't answer."

"Try her again and leave a message, but I'll drive on out there, okay?"

"Great. Thanks."

He hung up. When Jake returned, Quinn told him he was going to head straight out to the beach. "Shannon's not answering her cell," he explained.

"She could just be out of satellite reach," Jake told him.

"I still feel kind of antsy about this," Quinn said. "Too much happening too fast. This may have nothing in common with the rest—or far too much."

"Want me to follow you?"

Quinn shook his head. "No, I'm probably acting a little panicky. I'm just concerned, I guess."

Jake made no comment on why he might be overly worried. "Call me if you need me."

"Great. Thanks."

As he walked out to his car, Quinn tried dialing Shannon himself.

Her phone rang and rang, and then he heard her voice.

"Shannon! It's Quinn."

"If you'd like to leave a message, I'll get back to you as soon as possible."

He swore. "Dammit, yes, get back to me as soon as possible!"

He pocketed his phone with a growing sense of danger.

Shannon hadn't meant to do anything other than drive straight to her house. She knew that Quinn was worried about her, and that he'd probably come close to insisting that she hang around on the boat until he returned. And he seemed so down on Gordon. She couldn't believe that Gordon could be responsible for the things that had happened, even though she'd had her own brief flights of fear regarding the man. No. Not Gordon.

She hadn't even mentioned the incident in the storeroom to Quinn. In retrospect, the whole thing seemed ridiculous, an instance when panic had caused her problems, so she'd kept quiet.

It took her only minutes to reach the beach. It was getting a little chilly these days for the locals, and they weren't into tourist season yet. But when she reached the turnoff for her house, she found herself driving to the studio.

Sunday. The place would be empty. Katarina wouldn't be working, and there wouldn't be a soul around the studio. No music, no noise. She would only stay a second.

And maybe figure out what the strange sound she kept hearing was.

She parked in back and hurried up the stairs to the outer

hall and balcony. She slipped her key into the lock and entered, carefully locking the door behind her, then walked around the space.

Nothing had changed since they had left yesterday.

Feeling a little foolish, she stood in the center of the dance floor.

Then she heard it again.

The grating sound.

It was coming from the direction of the men's room.

She turned and went into the men's room, checking it out stall by stall. Nothing. And yet, clearer than ever before, she could hear the noise.

She paused, hurried back to her purse and found her key chain with the little container of pepper spray she kept there. So armed, she went out back and stared at the door to the storage room. She should wait. Call someone and tell them about the noise.

But hell, every time she wanted someone to hear it, the noise didn't come. It was undoubtedly nothing.

Maybe they just had a resident rat, or an army of cockroaches.

She slipped the key into the lock and entered, wedging the door open. If there was something in there, she wanted to be ready to run.

Turning the light on, Shannon went in.

Shelves held their multitude of boxes. Katarina's dressmaker's dummy was back up, standing sentinel again. Shannon slowly walked to the back, tiptoeing, listening.

And then she heard it. It was coming from the back wall.

She walked back determinedly, stood and listened. She looked back to the door and then again to the rear of the room.

The room wasn't as deep as it should have been, she realized suddenly.

She went to the shelves and started moving boxes.

* * *

Quinn made it to the house but didn't see Shannon's car.

When she heard him drive up, Marnie came running out, followed by Sam.

"She's not here, I take it?" he said.

Marnie shook her head, leaning in his window, frowning. "What?"

"Why is that woman's picture on your front seat?" she asked.

"What?" he asked, distracted. She pointed. A sketch of Sonya Miller was on top of the file folders stacked on the passenger seat.

"You know her?" he demanded.

"No, I don't know her. But I've seen her go up the back stairs at the studio."

Quinn glared at Sam.

Sam put his hands up. "I've never seen her before. She wasn't a student, Quinn. I swear it! Maybe she went to Suede."

"You're certain you've seen this woman?" Quinn asked Marnie.

"Yes. And she didn't go to the club, she went up the back stairs," Marnie said stubbornly.

He jerked the car into reverse with Marnie still leaning in the window. "I'm going over there. Call the cops."

Marnie moved back just in time.

He shot back out onto the street. He didn't know what the hell it meant, exactly, that Marnie had seen Sonya Miller.

He only knew he felt a sense of urgency unlike any he had ever known before.

Finally she had all the boxes removed from the area of the back wall.

She stepped closer, noticing what looked like either a

crack in the wall or a structural juncture. She pressed it and felt nothing.

She tapped it, and the sound was hollow.

She pressed again, putting weight behind the effort. The wall began to give. She realized she hadn't needed to move the boxes—the shelving was part of a false door.

The door opened. That had been the creaking sound. But opened to what? Maybe she didn't need to know—not now, anyway. It was time to get the hell out. She started to back away, ready to reclose the false door and put the boxes back.

"Ah, Shannon. I knew it was just a matter of time before you got here. Actually, I've been waiting for you."

She opened her mouth to scream and prepared to flee. But before she could do either one, fingers of steel wound around her wrist, jerking her forward.

Quinn raced up the back steps and saw the door to the storage room standing open. He raced to it and looked in just in time to see Shannon heading through the false wall.

For a moment he was stunned into stillness.

Shannon was hiding something at the studio. A sense of illness pervaded him. No, it couldn't be.

But there she was, at the studio, when she had said she was heading straight for the house. No other cars in the lot. No one around, no sound...

Just Shannon, disappearing as he stood.

He hardened himself and flew into action. Behind the false door was a long hallway.

He followed.

She was being jerked along so fast she could barely breathe, much less scream. The pepper spray was in her pocket, but she couldn't get to it because her wrists were being held in such a vise. The hall was narrow. The only light came weakly from the secret doorway back into the storage room.

The hallway ended. She thought she was going to be slammed through a wall, but, like the other, it gave when pressed.

She burst into a room. A narrow room, four feet at best in width, eight feet in length. It was tight and only dimly lit, but when her eyes adjusted, she was able to make out details. At one end were shelves filled with plastic bags that held a white powder. At the other end was a narrow circular stairway that led up.

To Gabriel Lopez's apartment.

Gabriel thrust her away from him, and she saw that he had pulled a gun.

She was terrified into speechlessness at first. Then something kicked in. She stared at the gun, self-preservation telling her to talk, to do anything, say anything, to keep him from shooting her.

"You son of a bitch! Why?"

He shook his head. "Money, *chica,* money. And the life, of course." He gave her a disdainful look. "Dancers! You were the best cover in the world. All your silly little people, awed by the club, always waiting to catch sight of a celebrity. And this building…perfect. Everyone was so pleased with the renovations. When the cops would come by, they met a dressmaker and dancers, and they could check me out and check me out and search the place…and find nothing. Nothing but boxes of costumes and student records."

She had to get out, and she knew it. Taking a chance, she pulled out her key chain.

He lifted the gun, playing with his thumb and finger, showing her how quickly he could cock the weapon. "Drop it."

She didn't dare. She hit the plunger. He ducked, swearing, coughing, choking, wheezing.

But she'd missed his eyes. The gagging fumes of the spray filled the area, and she was trapped, too. Then he was flying toward her. They struggled, but in the end, he had her.

"Let her go. Now."

The voice stunned both of them. Shannon found herself thrust in front of Lopez, coughing from the spray herself, his gun against her temple. Her eyes watered. She blinked and saw that Quinn had come, that he had followed the hallway and found the two of them.

"Let her go, Lopez. Now. I don't want to shoot you. The cops are on the way, and I want you to go to trial. I don't know why you killed Nell Durken, but her husband doesn't deserve a death sentence for what you did."

"You don't know the half of it, buddy. You don't know the half. But the cops aren't here yet. And you're not a cop, just a fuck-up P.I. Get out of the way. I get out of here, and I throw her back to you. That's the way it goes."

Quinn stood his ground, his gun level on Lopez. "Nice little place you've got here, but you'll never get her up the stairs, so it's kind of a trap, isn't it?"

"Not when you get out of the way."

"You'll hear the sirens any minute."

"That's why you'd better move. I'll kill her. And she's such a pretty little thing, huh? I could have taken her for a nice ride. You know, she turned me down all the time. Since she was such a good cover, I had to just smile and take it. But then she went off and slept with a prick like you. Now move!"

Quinn shifted a little.

"Funny thing is, Lopez, I almost thought she was in on it. You know, I came here, saw that false door…you should have thought to close it. Might have taken me and the cops ages to find it. Too bad you didn't think of that."

"Put the gun down and let me out of here."

Shannon was afraid she was going to drop, whether he let her go or not. Her knees were rubber and the pepper spray was burning her eyes. On top of that, she couldn't breathe.

And still, Quinn was standing there.

"I'll shoot her right now!"

"All right, all right, I'm going to put it down."

He started to lower his weapon. Shannon felt the slightest easing of Lopez's hold, but the barrel of the gun was still against her skull.

"Asshole!" Lopez said. "You *both* have to die."

He was going to pull the trigger. This was it. Not even time for her life to flash before her eyes.

The sound of the gunshot was deafening in the small space.

She felt nothing....

Behind her, Lopez crumpled, dragging her to the ground. Only then did she begin to scream when she saw the gaping bullet hole in his head.

She vaguely heard the sirens. Then she felt Quinn's arms around her, heard his voice as if from far, far away.

"Come on, it's over. The cops are here. They'll take it from here."

She couldn't rise on her own; her knees were too wobbly.

But his arms were around her.

And he was going to lead her from the shadows into the light.

CHAPTER 24

"But why did he kill Lara?" Ben demanded.

They were down in Key Largo, guests at Quinn's place, a beautiful home with a pool, right on the water, where he could dock the *Twisted Time*.

There was nothing ostentatious about it, and Shannon loved it. There were three bedrooms; one converted into an office, but it still had a futon that could sleep two. Since the police had requested that the entire studio building be closed for a few days, Gordon had decided that Ella could leave all messages for their students—in case they didn't quite get the concept of crime tape—and since they weren't working, and the entire situation was so traumatic, they should bond together. Thus, these days in the Keys.

Sunday had become something of a blur, with police pouring through the building, Shannon answering the same questions over and over again, Marnie and Sam appearing, first distraught, then relieved, Doug showing up with a pale Jane, freshly out of the hospital, in tow. Shannon had accepted drops for her eyes from the emergency personnel who had arrived but refused the suggestion she be looked at in a hospital. She had insisted she was fine.

Quinn was actually in worse shape. He'd said something about being sorry he'd had to kill Lopez, because there would be so many questions to be answered. She had remembered that he had followed her, *suspected her,* and even though he had saved her life, something had come over her when he bemoaned the death of the man who had been about to kill her, and she had hit him. She had rued the instinctive reaction immediately, but she had done it, and apparently she had a fairly decent hook, because even on Monday, he was still rubbing his jaw. That hadn't, however, interfered with Sunday night, when she had once again slept on the *Twisted Time,* while Sam stayed with Marnie at Shannon's house. That night, more than ever, she had needed to feel alive, and he had been pleased to help her explore every sensation. And, of course, they had talked and talked, before being awakened early the next morning, when Gordon had called with his idea of a studio-group getaway. Quinn had politely suggested his place in the Keys, not the least bit worried about fraternization, and now there they all were.

They headed south and all went out on the boat together. Doug, Ben and Quinn went diving, while Gordon, Sam, Marnie and Rhianna did some fishing, and Shannon mainly lounged around, with Justin, Ella and Jane joining her. Justin worked on his tan and Jane just tried to relax and follow doctor's orders.

On Monday night, they sat around in Quinn's living room, eating dinner. Drapes in the back opened to the pool area, the dock and the bay, a breeze drifted in, along with the smell of the barbecue, and it really did feel like a vacation. Until they started talking and Ben voiced his confusion.

Quinn glanced at Shannon. "Maybe she got too close to him, or maybe she knew too much."

"But…somehow he managed to drug her at the

competition. I mean, he got a hold of prescription drugs to do in two of his victims, and he shot the other two women up with heroin. And," he added, gazing at Doug, "if I've got this right, he also shot Manuel Taylor. Why Taylor?"

"He definitely killed Taylor," Doug said, looking at Quinn.

"Ballistics came back with a positive match. They found the gun that killed Manuel Taylor when they searched Lopez's apartment, and his prints were all over it," he told them. "I imagine Gabriel was afraid Manuel would remember that Gabe had tipped him to make sure Lara got the drink he'd prepared especially for her." He shook his head. "I'm sorry as hell I didn't examine the whole night more thoroughly with Manuel when I talked to him. I was so into the concept that he had told Shannon she was next that it didn't occur to me that he might know more. Anyway, I think Gabe panicked when it came to Manuel, so he shot him."

"And he killed Nell Durken, too?" Ben said, and shook his head, giving Quinn a questioning stare.

"So it seems. At least, Art Durken's attorney is counting on the evidence to get him out of jail," Doug told them.

"But what if Art Durken *did* kill her? What if the murders weren't related? It all seems kind of…I don't know. Weird," Ben persisted.

"Ben," Sam said. "It's over. Let it be."

"I'll bet Lara was having an affair with Gabe Lopez," Gordon said, looking around the room."

"She hadn't been around in months," Ella protested.

"Okay, then maybe…he wanted to start something with her, so he talked to her about it, but she turned him down. He didn't like being turned down. He played the charmer, but he hated Shannon for turning him down, right?" Jane said.

"So he said," Quinn agreed.,

"We're supposed to be bonding, not rehashing this whole thing," Gordon moaned.

"I'm not rehashing," Ben said. "I'm making sure I've got it all straight in my mind. Okay, so maybe that poor little hooker, Sally Grant, scored drugs off Lopez and somehow saw the secret room, so she had to die. Sonya, he probably met in another club, or on the beach, or somewhere, but she, too, was into getting high, found out too much and had to die. Lara wasn't a likely candidate for an overdose of heroin, but…he already knew what he was doing because of Nell Durken. He was probably having an affair with her, then got tired of her or something and decided to kill her. He'd gotten away with killing her by prescription and seeing it nailed on the husband, so he figured he'd do the same thing with Lara. And since she was wearing gloves…it was logical that there were no prints on the bottle. She'd die in front of hundreds of people. No murder, no crime."

"As much as we can figure," Quinn said, "that's about the picture."

"And Manuel," Gordon added dryly. "Manuel was executed purely for purposes of insurance."

"So it appears," Doug said.

Gordon groaned. "My business is going to be in the toilet."

"Gordon, he owned the club, not the studio," Shannon protested.

"Yes, but the club will go right to hell now," Gordon argued.

"Maybe not. Someone else will want to own it—it will have a real reputation now," Sam said. "You know how people love a little bit of the illicit in life."

"It all remains to be seen," Shannon said.

Ben stared across the room at her moodily. "He almost

killed you, Shannon." He shook his head. "In retrospect…
he was always watching you. I think he was worried for a
while that you thought something was going on."

She shook her head. "I didn't think anything at all—
until Lara died, and then…there was the noise. When he
was coming and going through the secret door. Too bad for
him that he didn't come and go more often from his apartment. I'd never have known."

"The point," Doug said, "was that his apartment and the
club itself were free of drugs, just as clean as most of his
employees believed with their whole hearts."

"Most? You think other people were in on it?" Rhianna
said worriedly.

"Maybe," Doug said. "But both homicide and narcotics
are on it. They'll find whatever contacts he had."

"Okay, okay, we're bonding here," Gordon said.
"Please, let's watch a movie or something. Quinn, you got
any good movies?"

Dinner was cleaned up, popcorn was made, and they
settled on *The Lord of the Rings* on the wide-screen TV in
the living room.

Shannon was glad when Quinn tapped her on the shoulder and they slipped away to his room. She had thought it
would be the hardest thing in the world to accept a relationship again, to really live in one. But it wasn't. It was
easy.

The easiest thing in the world just to be with him, and
the most exciting thing in the world just to know that they
could slip away and make love.

But late that night Shannon awoke to find Quinn staring up at the ceiling. He started when she stroked his
cheek.

"What is it?"

"I don't know. Don't you dare hit me again, but I really
wish I hadn't had to kill Lopez. There's too much that's

still going to be up to a jury. Did Lopez kill Nell—or did Art do it?"

"There will be the shadow of a doubt now," Shannon said. There was no lie to tell Quinn, and she knew that his work on behalf of Nell Durken still haunted him.

"Remember how he said, 'You don't know the half of it'?"

She nodded. "I remember everything he said."

"Well, that still bugs me. I don't know the half of it. And I hate like hell to guess."

She was quiet for a minute. "I guess there are some things that will never be solved. There *is* one thing, though."

"And what's that?"

"You saved my life and I'm eternally grateful."

"I'm not so sure. You might have saved mine."

"Because maybe one day you'll be able to cha-cha?"

"Because I've learned that I can't solve everything, but that I can be the best possible person for someone I really love."

She smiled and rolled into his arms, and, for a while, at least, she was certain she made him forget the questions that still plagued him.

"Dear, dear, dear!"

Christie was in the studio a week later, donating an hour of her time to help Marnie. "You're trying to step and turn all in one. They're individual movements. You need to learn to focus if you do want to do all these high-speed turns. Break it down. Step, turn. Heel lead. Step, turn."

Marnie caught Shannon's eye and grimaced. "Dear, dear, dear!" she mouthed.

"Keep working," Shannon ordered. She wondered suddenly how anyone could have allowed a kid like Marnie to live out on the streets, failing to take care of her when she was so young and sweet. But it took all kinds. She was learning that lesson well.

She was awfully grateful to Marnie, too. Quinn, not finding her at home that Sunday, was coming to the studio anyway. But thanks to Marnie recognizing the picture of Sonya Miller, he had come prepared, gun loaded. She had also been able to connect Sonya to both the building, and Gabriel Lopez, since she had witnessed Sonya coming up the back steps.

Shannon watched the pair for a minute, grinned, and headed for her office. Ella had just told her that Quinn was on the phone for her.

She grinned. He was taking his mom out to dinner. He had been feeling really guilty because lately he'd been lax about seeing her or even calling her. Tonight he was going to atone. Doug had explained the family situation to Shannon. Their father was dead, but they had a terrific mother, one who didn't nag but *did* worry. And Quinn had a habit of closing off when he was disturbed or busy, which only worried her more.

"What kind of a son are you? I haven't even met your mom yet—and you've competed!" she had told Doug.

"I had to be a little more confident first," he'd said. "But now…she's going to love it. You'll be surprised. She can dance. Wait until you see her," he had told her with pride.

Shannon picked up the phone in her office. "Hi. So where are you taking her?"

"A new place in North Miami. I probably won't make it back until late. Hey, this restaurant is supposed to be gourmet Scottish cuisine. Have you ever heard of such a thing?"

"No, but it sounds interesting. Steal a menu if you can."

"I'm an ex-cop. I can't steal anything."

She laughed. "Hey, um, do I get to meet Mom soon?"

"Oh, yeah. She's already been hearing all about you."

Shannon smiled. "Hey, listen, have a great dinner."

"Thanks. See you later."

She hung up. When she walked back out, the crowd was beginning to thin. It was close to time for her advanced group, but there were few private lessons on a Monday night. It seemed that Monday was kind of a blah day, no matter what business you were in.

Blah...

Actually, she thought, she enjoyed feeling that there could be blah days again. Or could there? Quinn, she knew, was still uncomfortable about the death of Gabriel Lopez. There was something unfinished, something that didn't quite fit altogether.

You don't know the half of it.

She walked back to the kitchen and poked through the refrigerator. Ben walked back to join her. "What're you up to?"

Sam, with no more classes, had driven Marnie home. Jane had left early, as well. She wasn't working with her students again yet, but she couldn't quite stay away from the studio. Tonight, however, Doug had remained behind. Though he loyally claimed that he wasn't going to dance with anyone but Jane at the Gator Gala, he was taking lessons with Shannon and Rhianna, and not missing any of the group classes. Katarina and David were in, and Richard Long was there, though Mina had gone home, tired from the onslaught of childhood injuries, which always seemed to multiply after a weekend. Gordon had told her earlier that he was leaving by eight because he was the owner and he had good management, so he, too, was gone.

"Hey," Ben repeated. "What are you up to?"

"Champagne. Thought I'd wake up our advanced group a bit."

"Richard just made coffee for that same reason."

Richard came up behind Ben. "Whatever. Champagne sounds good to me."

Mona O'Casey had never remarried, but neither had she fallen into any kind of lifelong depression. Left with an ample income, she had given up her job as a nurse and instead spent her time on a number of charities. She was five-five, slim, with short-cropped silver hair and bright, powder-blue eyes, a little dynamo of energy.

"I was bad, huh?" Quinn said.

Mona smiled. "I guess I know you when you're in your moods. When I can talk to you, naturally, I feel better. But I know you'll always call when you're ready." She sighed softly. "And since you and your brother both insist on dangerous professions, I've learned not to stay awake nights worrying. Besides," she added, "Doug assured me that you were all right, just moody. And," she added, taking a sip of merlot and grinning, "I hear that I'm going to get to see both of you dance very soon."

"Hey, the waltz. I owe it all to you."

She laughed. "Well, thank goodness I taught you something of value."

He took his mother's hand, running his fingers over it. "You taught us both all kind of things of tremendous value. Took me a while to catch on, but Doug was a pretty good kid straight from the start."

Mona grew serious suddenly. "Strange, isn't it, what does and doesn't bother people? Your brother went through everything at the academy, crime scenes, the morgue visits, the tests, and was as stalwart as a tree. But when it comes to his dancing...I would have loved to see him compete, but he didn't want me to watch him. Dancing makes him nervous."

"Heck, I'm afraid for you to see me waltz," he told her.

She looked unhappy for a minute. "Maybe. But nervousness just isn't a good reason to take drugs. I told Doug that."

"Doug?"

"Yes, can you believe it? Your brother got a prescription for that drug himself, just to take the edge off before he dances."

A gut-deep, miserable sensation speared through Quinn. No. Not his brother. Lopez had been the killer.

Lopez had also looked right at him and said, "You don't know the half of it."

His brother had been sleeping with Lara Trudeau.

He'd known something was still wrong with their picture of the crime.

But not Doug. Not his brother.

"What's the matter, dear?"

"Excuse me, Mom, okay?"

He dialed the studio. The machine picked up.

He dialed Shannon's cell phone and was asked to leave a message there, too.

There was no reason to feel that anything was wrong. All sorts of people had been at the studio all week long. Shannon wasn't alone now. Her advanced class would be in progress any minute.

"Quinn, you're scaring me," Mona said.

"I'm sorry. Forgive me just one more minute. I'm going to give Doug a call."

When he got his brother's answering machine, as well, his muscles tightened.

"Mom," he said, standing, "I'll make this up to you, but I've got to go."

She met his eyes. "If you don't call me by midnight, I'll send the cops out after you."

"If I don't call you by midnight, make sure you do."

He threw down some cash and hurried out of the restaurant.

* * *

Shannon set down her glass of champagne, hearing the distant beeping of her phone. "Excuse me, everyone, will you? Advanced class in two minutes, and no champagne, ever again, if anyone blames their lack of balance on it."

She found her cell phone and checked her messages. There was one from Quinn. She called him back and was frustrated when she got the message service. Strange, she should have gotten him at the restaurant. But maybe he had left and was going in and out of coverage areas on the highway.

"Hope all went well with your mom," she said cheerfully. "Call me. We're quiet here, but everything's fine."

She hung up thoughtfully and waited a minute, drumming her fingers on her desk. She started up, but then sat again, grabbing the phone as it rang. "Quinn?"

"Sorry, it's me. Marnie. Just wanted to make sure you were okay."

"I'm fine, why?"

"Quinn called here, said he couldn't get through to you."

"Well, I just left him a message. All is well."

"I'll try to get him back for you again."

"Thanks, Marnie."

She hung up, then frowned. The studio was very quiet except for a waltz playing very softly.

She stood up and left her office. When she reached the dance floor, she came to a dead halt, staring around her.

They were on the floor. All of them. Katarina and David were on top of each other. Richard Long was a few yards in front of her office, facedown. Ben and Rhianna just steps away from him. Doug O'Casey was almost beneath her feet. It looked as if Justin had fallen on his way out of the men's room.

Ella was slumped over the reception desk.

She exhaled in confusion and shock, fear seeping into her. She dropped to her knees, set her fingers against Rhianna's throat and gasped out a sigh of relief.

She could feel Rhianna's pulse.

She rose and spun, anxious to rush to the phone and dial for help.

But she couldn't.

Because one of the fallen had risen.

And for the second time in a little over a week, she was staring down the barrel of a gun.

Quinn got Shannon's message, and while he was listening to it, swearing at the poor reception he got despite the ads the phone company ran all the time, another call beeped through. It was Marnie, telling him that things were fine.

He thanked her and hung up.

But despite her words, and Shannon's, he felt the need to reach the studio quickly.

That was it, wasn't it? The *half* of it. Gabriel Lopez hadn't worked alone.

Doug had been taking a prescription drug for his nerves. The same drug that had killed both Nell Durken and Lara.

"Not my brother!" he swore aloud.

He pushed harder on the gas pedal, swearing at himself for letting his guard down.

He had known it wasn't over.

"You didn't drink your champagne," Richard Long told Shannon. "You should have."

She stared at him. "Richard?"

"You really need to drink your champagne."

"Why are you doing this?"

He sighed. "Well, you see, too many people know that something just isn't right in Denmark, or however the saying goes. I was sweating it big time at first. I was sure Lopez would give me away, but he didn't. Then that damn cop had to come here—sleeping with Lara, for God's sake! And then his big brother, the private eye, showed up. The questioning started all over again. The homicide cop and all his friends, the narc guys. Sooner or later, they're going to come knocking. So, you see, I have to fix things now."

"How can you fix things this way? You know Quinn will come here. And then his friends will come after him—the homicide cops, the narc guys."

"Shannon, I really don't want to hurt you. So drink your champagne. I can't tell you how easy it will be. Like falling asleep."

"Right. And how is all this supposed to have happened?" she asked dryly, gesturing around the room.

He grinned. "The last to arrive will be Mr. Quinn O'Casey. I don't think he knows it, but I wrote Doug a few prescriptions. There's one in his pocket right now. Everyone knows already—whether they admit it or not—that he slept with Lara. So his brother shows up, and knows what Doug has done, so he confronts him on it. Of course Doug's already drugged himself—suicide being the only answer for what he's done—but he has a little juice left and gets into a shoot-out with his big bro. He's the better shot, kills Quinn, and then dies of an overdose, just the way he planned. Everyone in the room dies. I was lucky enough to get tired and leave the class early. Otherwise, I'd have died, too. What a terrible tragedy."

"You're insane," she told him, then wished she hadn't spoken that way, because he was twitching. "Richard, I don't get it. How did you and Lopez...?"

"I introduced Gabe to many of my clients. You can't begin to know how many rich people enjoy their recreational therapy. They never knew he was the supplier. They just knew they could come to his club, leave payment and get their drugs delivered. We both made good money. It started with Nell. She was lonely—and Mina, quite frankly, bores me to tears. Then Nell stepped back. She was going to make up with her husband, who, quite frankly, is a creep. I went to talk to her, we argued…she insulted me. Preferred the creep to me. So I took matters into my own hands. As for Lara…you knew her. What a bitch. First, for fun, she decided to seduce me. Then, for fun, she started following me, and she figured out what I was up to with Lopez. Then she decided she was going to blackmail me, and she taunted me, letting me know she was sleeping with the cop, too. He was younger, she said. So…I had to take care of her. Gabriel got careless with the prostitute and the socialite, so they were his to clean up. I simply got mad—and then even—with Nell. And Lara. Come on, the bitch deserved to die."

"Lara could be a bitch," Shannon agreed placatingly. How much had all those on the floor ingested? How long could they survive?

"You have to understand. This will put an end to everyone saying that something just wasn't right, that Lopez couldn't have done it all."

Shannon jerked around, certain she heard someone rushing up the stairs.

Richard heard it, too. He grabbed her, dragging her down to the floor, the barrel of the gun against her heart.

He burst in and felt as if he had come across the scene of a strange massacre. They were on the floor, all of them, Justin Garcia's body nearly tripping him as he came in. He fell to his knees, checking for a pulse.

Faint, but there.

He rose, carefully moving across the floor.

There was Doug, down like the others.

He thanked God briefly as he checked his brother's throat and found a pulse.

Gun in one hand, he reached for his cell with the other. But before he could hit a single key, a shot exploded, searing across his hand.

His gun flew across the room, and his phone fell to his feet as he instinctively reached for his injured hand, damning himself for his stupid vulnerability.

He turned. Richard Long was halfway up, and it was definitely a moment of déjà vu.

Shannon was in front of him, his gun against her temple.

"The doctor, naturally," he said calmly. "You know, you son of a bitch, I almost suspected my own brother."

"It *was* your brother," Long said.

"Like hell."

"Well, everyone else is going to believe it was your brother. Too bad he's going to shoot you."

"You're a fool. Forensics will come here and figure you out to a T. You'll go up for capital murder. You'll die from lethal injection."

"No, I won't. I have it figured out absolutely logically."

"So why isn't Shannon unconscious on the floor, too?"

"She wouldn't drink her champagne. However, you can get her glass and give it to her, so she can die more easily."

"I am not drinking that champagne!" Shannon said. Quinn met her eyes. She didn't look terrified; she looked furious.

"It will be easier for her. Tell her, Quinn."

Quinn rose slowly, his hands in the air. He flexed his fingers, grateful to realize that the shot had only skimmed his flesh.

"I'll tell her to drink the champagne, Richard," he said evenly, his eyes on Shannon. "But I want something from you. You need to set up your little scene properly, and I'll help you. But I want something from you first."

Richard didn't ease his hold on Shannon.

"What the hell are you talking about, Quinn?" Shannon demanded darkly.

He looked at Richard then. "You let Lara die poetically, and she was the biggest bitch in the world. Shannon has treated you like a king, taught you…face it, she's been great. And as for me, well, I came in off the street and learned something of elegance here."

"So?"

"One waltz," Quinn said. "We get one waltz."

"A waltz? Are you crazy?" Shannon whispered.

"I can shoot you right now!" Richard said.

"Yes, but it won't look right. Let me have my waltz. What have you got to lose?"

Richard still hesitated, then shoved Shannon toward Quinn. She was frowning fiercely as she reached him. He smiled, trying to explain with his eyes. Trying, in seconds, to say that he needed her help. That they had one chance.

"Our routine," he said aloud.

"You're crazy," she told him. Tears stung her eyes. "We're about to die, and you want to waltz?"

"Our routine," he repeated.

She arched a brow to him. He went into a competition position, inviting her to him. She moved into his arms, and they began dance.

Chain steps, turns…promenade, one, two, three, rise and fall…

"Get on with it," Richard said.

"It's our routine," he snapped back.

Aloud, he continued to Shannon, "One, two, three, one, two, three, turn…and pooper-scooper coming up."

At last something registered in her eyes. Knowledge of what he wanted.

Fear that she couldn't follow through.

"Hey, I can do the lifts," he told her. "And you're the dancer—you can do them, too."

"What the hell does it matter?" Long exclaimed.

"One, two, three…now."

Shannon moved around him. He dipped to sweep her up into the lift. He spun.

And she performed magnificently, body flying out with the force of his spin…and slamming hard into Richard Long, forcing him backward, forcing him to fall…then falling, and herself landing hard atop him.

Then Quinn was down, as well, pushing Shannon away, going for Long. The other man rolled, desperate to elude Quinn, to reach the gun that had fallen from his hand when Shannon smashed into him.

Quinn dragged him back. Long lashed out. Quinn slugged him hard, in the jaw, just as Shannon flew across the floor, retrieving both the gun and Quinn's phone, which she handed to him.

Straddled over Long, Quinn dialed 911. "Emergency, major emergency. We need several ambulances, stomach pumps…"

Before he finished talking, they could hear the sirens.

EPILOGUE

The beach was always crazy, that night more so than ever.

Highly publicized, written up in every magazine across the country as "The little contest that could," the Gator Gala—the first-ever competition sponsored by the Moonlight Sonata Dance Studio—was creating pure traffic havoc.

The hotel hosting the gala was booked to overflowing, with people spilling into the neighboring facilities and even beyond. Restaurants thrived. The wicked tale of adultery, narcotics, the wild side, and murder among the elite and famous connected to the studio—which had survived all the ills assailing it—had made the competition taking place that night not notorious, but so fascinating that many of the big names in ballroom dancing had felt that they had to be there to get their share of so much publicity. The more big names that were offered, the more tickets that were sold, the more the prestigious the judges who wanted to be associated with the competition, the more the students who poured in.

It was almost out of control.

And there was more, of course.

Shannon Mackay, who had retired nearly eight years ago, after a broken ankle, was back.

Back in a big way.

She was, quite simply, dazzling. Poetry set to music. Her gown shimmered, exquisitely molding her elegant curves, billowing softly beneath the lights with each movement of her body. She seemed to create such splendor effortlessly, blond hair in a shimmering knot at her nape, studded with jeweled stones to match those on the gown.

Just a stretch of her finger spoke volumes. The tilt of her head, the look in her eyes. She was dance at its most complete, every part of her attuned to the music and the steps. She was lost in the rhythm, and those who watched were lost with her.

It was fairy-tale music, and a fairy tale that was created. She was tall, slim, delicately curved, and her smile was infectious. Her partner was tall, dark, handsome, assured and equally talented. Together they went beyond human belief, sometimes moving in such perfect unison that they appeared almost to be one.

"Lord, she's incredible," Gordon breathed.

"She makes Ben look damned good, too," Sam added.

"Ben can dance," Quinn commented, smiling.

"They complement one another," Rhianna approved. "As dancers, of course," she said quickly, causing Quinn to laugh.

"We were almost as good," Jane said, squeezing Sam's hand.

"Almost," he agreed, smiling.

"I'd say that Marnie and I have a good chance of taking the salsa trophy," Justin said.

Quinn felt another smile coming on. He glanced at Marnie, the street kid, the runaway. She had come into her own. She hadn't made enough yet to afford her own clothes, but with Katarina's help, they had reworked one of Shannon's old Latin dresses, and it would be difficult to point to a figure more perfect than Marnie's at this moment. She had turned nineteen, and it looked as if she had matured far more. Like the others, she had her hair neatly coiled, making the fine lines of her profile more evident, along with the size of her eyes. She smiled back at Quinn. "A very good chance," he told her affectionately.

Perhaps just because of the circumstances of her life, she still tended to be nervous. And Sam still tended to be protective. He had taken a larger apartment, and she had moved into one of his bedrooms. Neither one was allowed to go out unless the man was first approved by the others. They were jokingly considered the "Will and Grace" of the dance world.

"Rhianna, you were striking tonight, too," Gordon said. "You and Doug."

Doug had quit the police force. He had really liked being a cop; he had simply decided that he loved dance more. Besides, with the popularity that had descended upon Moonlight Sonata, they'd been in need of another male teacher. He and Marnie still didn't have the certifications to teach at the higher levels, but they were favorites among the beginners.

"While we're all getting sticky and gooey here," Doug said, "may I compliment your waltz tonight, big brother?"

Quinn laughed. "We came in second. With another partner, Shannon would have won."

"You're a beginner, and you were excellent," Doug said.

"Both my boys were terrific," Mona commented, sliding between them to squeeze their hands.

"Hush. The finale," Gordon commanded.

It almost seemed that Shannon paused in flight, above Ben's head, then alit in his arms, sinking slowly into a perfectly timed stillness.

The applause was deafening.

But after her bows, Quinn saw Shannon searching the room. For him. She flew to him, made another fantastic leap and landed in his arms.

She accepted his congratulations on her performance, and he smiled as he brought her slowly down, kissing her. The act of dancing would always mean more to her than a trophy. And the approval of those who loved her would always mean more than any other judgment.

There were others, of course, from whom she accepted accolades. Her new mother-in-law, her co-workers, her old friends, his old friends, total strangers. But eventually the last of the awards was given out. As expected, she and Ben took the crowning prize of the night, leaving Gordon to boast about the studio. It got a bit ridiculous at times, but even so, it was both gratifying and exhilarating.

But in time they were in their room together, a fantastic suite they'd taken at the hotel, since Shannon had so much to do for the gala that she needed to be on site. Moonlight poured in from the heavens beyond their balcony, and she walked up to him, slipped her arms around him. "I'd never have done it without you."

He gave her a smile. "And I'd never have rejoined the Bureau without your encouragement. And I am good at what I do."

"You're good at everything," she assured him, her eyes searching out his. "You would have taken first for that waltz if I hadn't…well, I back led you, and I shouldn't have."

"I forgot the step. Besides, I won when it mattered."

"I took the trophy with Ben, but I should have taken one with you, too."

He could tell she was anxious. He knew that she had wanted to win far more for Ben than for herself. And she had wanted a win for him.

He cupped her face in his hands. "We won together

once," he told her. "We won together with that silly pooper-scooper—and the most incredible waltz ever mastered by man. Ben may have his trophy, but I get to go home with you, and that's all that matters."

"That was one hell of a pooper-scooper, wasn't it?" she whispered.

"There will never be another like it."

She smiled, moving against him, touching his ear with her whisper. "It's amazing when you know your life is the best applause you'll ever earn. I can't tell you how I love it. It's like my life is a dance I'll never do better with any other partner but you. It requires all kinds of very special moves."

"Leaps and bounds?"

"The most incredible ones."

"Ah, well, you *are* the instructor. Show me."

"Even teachers can learn."

"A dual session. Sounds fascinating."

He swept her up.

And like everything else that night, it was beautiful beyond belief.

They were alive; they were together. Now the years and the world stretched out before them with assurance hard-won, confidence earned, and the dance of time the one they would practice forever.

New York Times bestselling author Heather Graham
takes readers to the edge of their seats with another
spine-tingling dance of death....

KILLING KELLY

Please turn the page for an exciting preview

Available in hardcover
from MIRA Books
March 2005

Prologue

Darkness and Shadows

What was it about the night and the little places where secrets lurked that caused unease to stir in the human heart? It was the unknown, of course. Primeval fear. Something deep within human instinct that all the civilization in the world could not change.

Dr. Dana Sumter knew all about the psyche and the innate responses to stimuli. Yet she didn't like it one bit that it was still dark when she returned, sliding her sleek Mercedes into the driveway. She started to hit the garage door opener, then remembered that she couldn't park in the garage; she was refurbishing the house and the garage was filled with old furniture that would be picked up by a charity organization.

With a sigh, she simply parked. The engine now off, she was suddenly aware of more than the darkness. She heard the sounds of the day dawning. From somewhere far away, the shrill whine of an emergency vehicle's siren mingled with the distant, deep bark of a large dog. There was a clattering and a screeching as alley cats fought somewhere. Then…just whispers in the shadows as the wind picked up slightly, then died down again. The sound was slightly ominous, like a deep, menacing breath…right down her spine.

Dana was irritated to be out at that time of the morning, irritated that she'd agreed to do the crack-of-dawn news show. Why had she? Oh, yes, her ratings had slipped because she'd come down rather hard against a womanizing drunkard. The switchboard at her daily syndicated show had gone off the light beam after that. But still, there had been complaints. A lot of people—men, mainly—calling in to say that she should be shot, or various other colorful phrases, all in the same vein.

She pulled down the visor mirror and studied her features. Good. Maybe her face was a little narrow, a little hard, but basically, for her age, she was sleek, professional, attractive. She lived carefully, didn't smoke, seldom drank and exercised regularly. She gave a little sniff. She'd gotten a lot of flack the time she'd given the overweight housewife the advice to do something about herself. She knew that people had expected her to say that the husband was a louse for ignoring his wife. But on that occasion she'd gone the other way, telling the woman to buy *The South Beach Diet*, or do Atkins, or get thee to a gym! The phones had rung off the hooks with people calling in, raging that women were worthy of love, no matter what their size. She'd done one of her best shows ever after that, saying that being worthy of love didn't make it happen, that both men and women were responsible to keep themselves up.

However, despite the fact that she had definitely improved herself to an even greater degree, she'd still caught Harvey red-handed with a young thing half his age. But at least she'd had the self-respect to follow her own advice! Yes, she'd been swift and brutal. The best lawyers in town had helped her keep what was hers intact. He'd made his pixie mistress into a trophy wife—until the trophy wife discovered that, without Dana, good old Harvey didn't have any money. And suddenly there was Harvey, out in the cold with his dick in his hand.

When asked about her divorce, Dana was cool and calculated, saying that in any marriage there could come a time when both parties simply fell out of love. She forced herself to talk about her ex-husband with affection, as if they were still friends. She had survived the dissolution of her own marriage before the public eye with great esteem, maintaining that, despite the fact that their children were long grown, it was important to be friends for their sakes.

Friends, my ass! She never should have married. Men were all disloyal egoists who used women. She had simply learned to use them back. Even the one fiasco she had endured years ago in weakness was something she had turned to her advantage. And over and over again, at that!

Done with introspection, she opened her car door, ready to head into her house. Yet she was surprised to still feel a faint sense of unease as she sat in the car. She lived in a gorgeous house on a well-lit main street in a very fashionable district of Westchester, New York. And even when it was midnight, or the wee hours of the morning, cars went by constantly. She'd never felt in the least bit of danger, no matter what time she returned to or left her house. But now…

She looked into the rearview mirror, then stepped on the brake, but she saw nothing in the bloodred light created by her action. Still, she waited.

Finally, feeling silly, she got out of the car and walked to her front door. But she couldn't help looking over her shoulder. Then she chided herself. It was ridiculous for a grown woman to be afraid of shadows and the sound of leaves rustling in the summer breeze.

At the front door she paused and looked around again.

This was odd, so odd. She felt the hairs at her nape standing on end. But there was nothing, no one.

Telling herself to stop being an idiot, she slipped her key into the lock and stepped in. There. Nothing. No one had rushed her. She keyed in her number on the alarm pad as she started to close and lock the door. But the door wouldn't close. She frowned, pressing at it. And that was when it burst back in upon her.

For a moment she just stared, stunned, trying to fathom just what…who… Then she opened her mouth to scream as she launched for the alarm pad.

But it was too late.

Several thoughts went through her mind. *It wasn't ridiculous to be wary of shadows, of darkness, of little whispers of danger. She shouldn't have been so mistrusting as to refuse to keep a live-in housekeeper. She should have been more careful about things she said…and did! She should have…*

From somewhere far away she could hear her dog, Muffy barking. Then, with a sudden squeaking sound, the barking was cut off—just as every other noise and sensation faded away.

HEATHER GRAHAM

32074	THE PRESENCE	___ $6.99 U.S.	___ $8.50 CAN.
32010	PICTURE ME DEAD	___ $6.99 U.S.	___ $8.50 CAN.
66892	A SEASON OF MIRACLES	___ $6.99 U.S.	___ $8.50 CAN.
66864	SLOW BURN	___ $5.99 U.S.	___ $6.99 CAN.
66750	HAUNTED	___ $6.99 U.S.	___ $8.50 CAN.
66665	HURRICANE BAY	___ $6.99 U.S.	___ $8.50 CAN.

(limited quantities available)

TOTAL AMOUNT	$ _____
POSTAGE & HANDLING	$ _____
($1.00 FOR 1 BOOK, 50¢ for each additional)	
APPLICABLE TAXES*	$ _____
TOTAL PAYABLE	$ _____

(check or money order—please do not send cash)

To order, complete this form and send it, along with a check or money order for the total above, payable to MIRA Books, to: **In the U.S.:** 3010 Walden Avenue, P.O. Box 9077, Buffalo, NY 14269-9077; **In Canada:** P.O. Box 636, Fort Erie, Ontario, L2A 5X3.

Name: _____

Address: _____ City: _____

State/Prov.: _____ Zip/Postal Code: _____

Account Number (if applicable): _____

075 CSAS

*New York residents remit applicable sales taxes.
*Canadian residents remit applicable GST and provincial taxes.

MIRA®

www.MIRABooks.com

MHG0205BL

THE WORLD'S CLASSICS

MEMOIRS OF A CAVALIER

DANIEL DEFOE was born in London in 1660, the son of
a tallow-chandler. He was educated for the Presbyterian
ministry at Newington Dissenting Academy, but quickly
abandoned this intention. Thereafter he embarked on a
life of several careers and great complexity. He was
captured by Algerian pirates and took part in Monmouth's
Rebellion; his early engagement in commerce ended in
bankruptcy but he later dealt in ship-insurance, wool,
oysters, and linen; he became a secret agent, a political
pamphleteer and was several times arrested. He died 'of a
lethargy' in 1731.

Defoe has been credited with some 500 works, ranging
over politics, economics, history, biography, and crime.
Among his best-known novels are *Robinson Crusoe* (1719),
Moll Flanders (1722), and *Roxana* (1724).

JAMES T. BOULTON is Emeritus Professor and Director
of the Institute for Advanced Research in the Humanities
at the University of Birmingham. He is the editor of
Selected Writings of Daniel Defoe (1975) and General Editor
of the *Letters and Works of D. H. Lawrence*.

JOHN MULLAN is a Fellow of Fitzwilliam College,
Cambridge. He is the author of *Sentiment and Sociability*
(1988).

THE WORLD'S CLASSICS

DANIEL DEFOE

Memoirs of a Cavalier

OR A *Military Journal*

OF

The *WARS* in GERMANY,

AND

The *WARS* in ENGLAND

From the Year 1632, to the Year 1648.
Written Threescore Years ago by an *English* Gentleman,
who served first in the Army of *Gustavus Adolphus,* the
glorious King of *Sweden*, till his Death; and after that,
in the Royal Army of King *Charles* the First, from the
Beginning of the Rebellion, to the End of that War.

Edited by
JAMES T. BOULTON

With a new Introduction by
JOHN MULLAN

Oxford   New York
OXFORD UNIVERSITY PRESS
1991

Oxford University Press, Walton Street, Oxford OX2 6DP

Oxford New York Toronto
Delhi Bombay Calcutta Madras Karachi
Petaling Jaya Singapore Hong Kong Tokyo
Nairobi Dar es Salaam Cape Town
Melbourne Auckland

and associated companies in
Berlin Ibadan

Oxford is a trade mark of Oxford University Press

Chronology © Oxford University Press 1969
Explanatory Notes © Oxford University Press 1972
Introduction and Select Bibliography © John Mullan 1991

First published by Oxford University Press 1972
First issued, with a new introduction, as a World's Classics paperback 1991

British Library Cataloguing in Publication Data
Defoe, Daniel 1660 or 1 –1731
Memoirs of a cavalier, or, A military journal of the wars
in Germany, and the wars in England: from the year 1632
to the year 1648 . . . – (The World's classics).
I. Title II. Boulton, James T. (James Thompson) 1924–   823.5
ISBN 0–19–282710–3

Library of Congress Cataloging in Publication Data
Data available

Printed in Great Britain by
BPCC Hazell Books
Aylesbury, Bucks

CONTENTS

EDITOR'S ACKNOWLEDGEMENTS

I wish to acknowledge the kindness of the following in helping to identify certain historical persons mentioned by Defoe: Dr O. von Feilitzen, Kungliga Biblioteket, Stockholm; Dr Ian Roy, King's College, London; and the Librarians of Newark, Newcastle upon Tyne, Pontefract, the County of Buckinghamshire, and the National Library of Scotland. I am indebted to Miss J. Darden, my research assistant at Hofstra University, New York, and, for devoted secretarial assistance, Miss J. Wootton. For professional advice from the General Editor, the late Professor James Kinsley, I am particularly grateful. Finally no editor of the *Memoirs of a Cavalier* could fail to recognize his debt to the scholarship of the late Arthur W. Secord.

J.T.B.

INTRODUCTION

Modern editions of eighteenth-century texts, such as this one, look different in all sorts of ways from their originals. Some of the differences are apparently small: changes in spelling or printing convention. Others matter more, for the appearance of a book—the way that it presents itself to the world as an object for consumption—did and still can determine how it might be read. In an important respect, this edition of *Memoirs of a Cavalier* advertises itself differently from the first edition, published in 1720. Unlike the work published in Defoe's own lifetime, this edition bears an author's name. What we call '*Memoirs of a Cavalier*, by Daniel Defoe' originally had on its title-page 'MEMOIRS of a CAVALIER: Or a *Military Journal* of the WARS in GERMANY, and the WARS in ENGLAND; From the Year 1632, to the Year 1648. Written Threescore Years ago by an *English* Gentleman, who served first in the Army of *Gustavus Adolphus*, the glorious King of *Sweden*, till his Death; and after that, in the Royal Army of King *Charles* the First, from the Beginning of the Rebellion, to the End of that War'. Many works of fiction, particularly in the eighteenth century, have presented themselves as fortunately discovered journals, manuscripts, or letters. The author of any of these works (Richardson in *Pamela*, Walpole in *The Castle of Otranto*, Mackenzie in *The Man of Feeling*) claims only to be the editor: arranging but not inventing. *Memoirs of a Cavalier* was unusual, though, in that it gave its first readers no clues that it was a recent invention. For more than half a century after its first publication in 1720 it was readily taken as a genuine sample of seventeenth-century autobiography. So why should it now have Defoe's name attached to it, and what difference does that name make to us as readers?

It is important first of all to recognize that the title-page of *Memoirs of a Cavalier* was not unlike the title-page of each of what are now regarded as Defoe's novels. All gave a summary of the events to be narrated, deflating one kind of curiosity ('what will happen?') but provoking another ('how can the book contain and make plausible all *this*?'). So *Moll Flanders* declared itself 'The Fortunes and Misfortunes of the Famous Moll Flanders, &c Who was Born in Newgate, and during a Life of continu'd Variety for Threescore Years, besides her Childhood, was Twelve Year a *Whore*, five times a *Wife* (whereof once to her own Brother) Twelve Year a *Thief*, Eight Year a Transported *Felon* in *Virginia*, at last grew *Rich*, liv'd *Honest*, and died a *Penitent. Written from her own* Memorandums'. All purport to be autobiographical, and are thus guaranteed to be unique and novel. So *Robinson Crusoe* is 'The Life and Strange Surprizing Adventures of Robinson Crusoe'; *Colonel Jack* is proclaimed in its title a 'Remarkable Life . . . a Life of Wonders'. And none have Defoe's name. *Robinson Crusoe* is '*Written by Himself*'; *A Journal of the Plague Year* is 'Written by a *Citizen* who continued all the while in *London*. Never made public before.' Defoe's novels are all fabrications of personal histories, and they are all so keen to mimic authenticity that their author, the writer under whose name they now appear in the bookshop or the library, is always absent. It is not surprising, then, that attributing books to Defoe is usually more of a problem than it is with any other major author of the period (or perhaps any period). It has (rightly) become a more pressing problem since *The Canonisation of Daniel Defoe* by P. N. Furbank and W. R. Owens systematically argued what many scholars had suspected: that over two centuries the list of works attributed to Defoe has grown constantly, but that little (or no) evidence exists for many of the attributions beyond the hunches of the bibliographers.[1] It is now, more than ever, necessary to be sceptical about Defoe's supposed authorship of works previously presumed to be his. So where does this leave the *Memoirs of a Cavalier*?

[1] P. N. Furbank and W. R. Owens, *The Canonisation of Daniel Defoe* (New Haven, Conn.; London, 1988).

Defoe's name was first attached to the *Memoirs* on the title-page of the sixth edition of the work, published by Francis Noble in 1784, though the title-page called it the second edition, and left it unclear as to whether Defoe had been author or merely editor of the work. It declared that the 'Memoirs, Travels, and Adventures of a Cavalier' were 'First published from the original Manuscript, By the late Mr. Daniel Defoe, Author of the Adventures of Robinson Crusoe, And many other Books of Entertainment'.[2] The attribution was not immediately taken up; in fact, the next edition, published in 1792, followed an earlier publisher's supposition that the memoirs were genuine and had been written by Andrew Newport, a Royalist who became a Member of Parliament after the Restoration of Charles II. (In fact, the real Andrew Newport was only a child at the time that the Cavalier was supposed to have been serving with Gustavus Adolphus.) It even changed the book's title to *Memoirs of the Honourable Col. Andrew Newport, a Shropshire Gentleman.* This guess at authorship had first been made by James Lister, the publisher of the second edition of the *Memoirs* in around 1750. In a prefatory note entitled 'The Publisher of the Second Edition, to the READER', Lister recognized what has become an issue for modern bibliographers and critics: ' 'tis a Question, that naturally occurs, *Who is the Author?*' Although Lister has been supposed gullible for believing the *Memoirs* to be genuine, it is clear that he had considered the possibility that it was a work of fiction. Indeed, his rejection of this possibility is phrased in such a way as to suggest that it occurred to many eighteenth-century readers: 'Some have imagin'd the whole to be a Romance; if it be, 'tis a Romance the likest to Truth that I ever read. It has all the Features of Truth'. He even provides himself with an odd escape-clause by declaring that, though the text is evidently not a 'Romance', it would be best 'were all Romance Writers to

[2] *Memoirs, Travels, and Adventures of a Cavalier* (1784).

follow this Author's Example'.[3] It is not fiction; but fiction should be like this.

The next edition, published in Edinburgh in 1759, reprints Lister's preface, approving its attempt to 'vindicate' the work 'against a suspicion of being a Romance'.[4] It also adds its own notes, which explain away some of the Cavalier's historical inconsistencies by asserting that these are only to be found in passages 'which a Reader of Judgment and taste will easily distinguish, have been added and interpolated after the MS was out of the possession of the Author';[5] a cautionary example of the uses to which a confidence in critical judgement can be put. (These passages are said to include the pages on omens, prophecies, and 'providences' which conclude the narrative and which, this Introduction will suggest, form a part of the fiction characteristic of other novels which we believe Defoe to have written.) The work was republished in Edinburgh in 1766, and then in Newark in 1782, this time by a publisher who had decided to avoid the whole problem of attribution by exploiting rather than attempting to clear up the uncertainty over authorship. A new Preface concedes, 'Who the Writer was, it is impossible at this distance of Time, precisely to determine', but only in order to claim that the *Memoirs* are papers which 'came into my Hands many Years since', and that 'a strict Regard has been paid to the Author's own Copy'.[6] No indication is given that this is actually the fourth edition of the work. Instead, we are back to the fiction of the Preface to the first edition: 'valuable Papers' luckily reappearing after all these years.

How did Francis Noble decide, in the edition of 1784, that Daniel Defoe had been the conduit for these memoirs? Surprisingly, he gave his own answer to this question, though it is hardly a very satisfactory one. Three years later, in 1787, Noble published *Daniel Defoe's Voyage Round the World*, a

---

[3] *Memoirs of a Cavalier* (*c.*1750), pp. iii–iv.
[4] *Memoirs of a Cavalier* (1759), p. iv.
[5] Ibid., p. vii.
[6] *Memoirs of a Cavalier* (1782), pp. v–vi.

travel narrative previously published anonymously. Prefaced
to this is a 'Life of the Author', by William Shiells, which talks
of Defoe's 'many works of fancy', but does not include the
Memoirs in its list of these. Noble has added a note to this
'Life' (which is largely cribbed from Cibber's *Lives of the Poets*,
published in 1753). Here he explains that 'Mr. Daniel Defoe
ever chose to conceal his name, and left it to the public to
discover the author . . . he adhered so closely to nature, that
no one had the least suspicion of their being merely invention,
but founded upon real truths'. Added to this is the following:
'P.S. Since the above Mr. Shiells, Mr. Paul Whitehead,
author of a Poem entitled Manners, a Satire, discovered
another work of Mr. De Foe—Memoirs, Travels, and
Adventures of a Cavalier, of which a new edition has been
lately published by F. NOBLE, in three volumes, price nine
shillings bound'.[7] Whitehead had died in 1774, though we
might think it unlikely that Noble would easily use the
reputation of this well-known writer if his claim was merely
invention—merely a bookseller's hype. At most, however, this
only suggests that Defoe's authorship might have been
supposed or rumoured by other writers in the eighteenth
century; and perhaps we will never have less suspect external
evidence.

What is more, it should be recognized that, as the last
clause of the publisher's 'P.S.' indicates, Noble had a
commercial interest in the attribution. At the end of the
Voyage Round the World is a list of 'Novels printed for
F. Noble, No. 324, Holborn'. These include 'De Foe's
Adventures of a Cavalier', along with *Moll Flanders*, *Roxana*,
Captain Singleton, and 'De Foe's History of the Great Plague
in London'. All of them are under Defoe's name—a fact
worth remarking, as none of the other novels listed is given
the dignity of an author. Defoe's name is a commercially
useful property. Noble, who ran a circulating library as well as
being a bookseller, and who specialized in fiction, had

[7] *Daniel De Foe's Voyage Round the World* (1787), 28.

published several of these novels, from the 1740s, without specifying Defoe's authorship. In the 1770s, however, he started attributing works to Defoe in order to license his own rewriting of them. The first was a version of *The Fortunate Mistress* (which we usually call *Roxana*), which appeared as *The history of Mademoiselle de Beleau; or, the new Roxana* in 1775. It is a clumsily bowdlerized version of the text, purportedly 'Published by Mr. Daniel Defoe. And from papers found, since his decease, it appears was greatly altered by himself.' The next year Noble turned the same trick with *Moll Flanders*, retitled *The history of Laetitia Atkins*, which has an Introduction in Defoe's name regretting the previous inclusion of 'many circumstances . . . which, though they were true, upon a more cool reflection, my judgment could not by any means approve. . . . I therefore . . . altered many parts of it, to give it the better reading.'[8] The dead author is made to serve Noble's purposes with that device of which eighteenth-century fiction was so fond: Defoe's texts can be changed because, so the story goes, 'manuscripts of his alteration' have recently been unearthed.

It is not surprising that the published records of perplexity concerning authorship that we have for *Memoirs of a Cavalier* do not exist for, say, *Moll Flanders* or *Roxana*. The now famous fiction of Richardson, Fielding, and Sterne may have seemed to some to have had the status of serious literature (though even these writers were thought by many of their contemporaries to be working in a low or vulgar genre); however, most eighteenth-century fiction had too humble a status to be worth attributing. The puzzle of the *Memoirs* was only worth solving because it might not be mere 'Romance'. It is arguable that Noble began attaching Defoe's name to his novels in the 1770s because 'the Novel' was just beginning to become a confident genre worthy of Defoe's participation; any earlier advocate of this writer's literary merits had relied on his poetry as evidence. To read Fanny Burney's Preface to her

---

[8] *The history of Laetitia Atkins, vulgarly called Moll. Flanders* (1776), p. v.

Evelina, published in 1776, is to encounter an example of a new self-confidence which enables a novelist to be as much ironical as apologetic about the supposed triviality of the genre:

In the republic of letters, there is no member of such inferior rank, or who is so much disdained by his brethren of the quill, as the humble Novelist: nor is his fate less hard in the world at large, since, among the whole class of writers, perhaps not one can be named, of whom the votaries are more numerous, but less respectable.[9]

Nicely, Burney adds in a footnote that, however 'superior the capacities' of Rousseau and Dr Johnson, she has been obliged to 'rank' them too as 'Novelists'. It seems that it was beginning to be possible by the 1770s to mock the aspersions cast upon novelists, and to admire their achievements as much as those of innovators in any other genre. It may well be that Noble is to be trusted because he was a bookseller beginning to realize that novels like Defoe's were worthy of authorship.

All this will indicate that I cannot quite agree with the ringing declaration made by James T. Boulton in his Introduction to the previous Oxford University Press edition of the *Memoirs*: 'The case for Defoe as sole author was finally argued with the authority that rests on full documentary proof by Arthur W. Secord in *Robert Drury's Journal and Other Studies* (1961).'[10] Secord's essay, 'The Origins of Defoe's *Memoirs of a Cavalier*', does prove that the text has been put together from a handful of seventeenth-century historical sources, passages from which it sometimes replicates. It is recommended to any reader who wants to know the precise sources for the stories which make up the *Memoirs*—and therefore to know how much is pure invention. However, Secord's essay does not prove that the end-product is written by Defoe, even if the inventive plagiarism that he charts is a

---

[9] Fanny Burney, *Evelina*, ed. Edward Bloom (Oxford, 1982), 7.

[10] James Boulton (ed.), Introd., *Memoirs of a Cavalier*, by Daniel Defoe (London, 1972), p. viii.

method that Defoe has used elsewhere. But then perhaps proof is not the point; perhaps we should ask ourselves what Defoe's authorship stands for.

It would be usual to say something in an Introduction like this about the life and character of the author—suggesting how the text fits with his career, psychology, or beliefs. Yet even those works which we can confidently attribute to Defoe seem to mock as well as to exploit our need for an author. The first-person voices of his texts leave us to infer—but rarely allow us to know—the attitudes of their inventor. It is characteristic that the nearest thing that Defoe wrote to an autobiography is a piece of special pleading that some commentators have thought similar to the statements of the Quaker woman in *Roxana*: strictly speaking, true; by common standards, wholly misleading.[11] This account of himself, published in 1715, was called *An Appeal to Honour and Justice, Tho' it be of his Worst Enemies. By Daniel Defoe*. It may not let us know who the real Daniel Defoe was, but it tells us something about the conditions of authorship in Grub Street in the early eighteenth century. Much of this account of his life of writing consists of complaints that all sorts of anonymous texts are attributed to him: 'whenever any Piece comes out which is not liked, I am immediately charg'd with being the Author, and very often the first Knowledge I have had of a Books being publish'd, has been from being abus'd for being the Author of it, in some other Pamphlet publish'd in Answer to it.'[12] This can sound disingenuous, of course. The condition of anonymity also allowed for an exercise of ventriloquism which distinguished Defoe's work as a political pamphleteer, and which he was to develop in his late years into what we call his novels. Indeed, it was by using anonymity that Defoe

[11] The plain-dealing Quaker is 'a cunning, as well as an honest Woman': Daniel Defoe, *The Fortunate Mistress* (1928; repr. London, 1974), ii. 134. The capacity of a Quaker to exploit a reputation for plain-speaking in order to deceive is also demonstrated by William Walters in *Captain Singleton*.

[12] Daniel Defoe, *An Appeal to Honour and Justice, Tho' it be of his Worst Enemies. By Daniel Defoe. Being a True Account of his Conduct in Publick Affairs* (1715), 25.

achieved his first big success as a writer with *The Shortest Way with Dissenters* (1702). This mock-tirade against those Protestants, like Defoe himself, who remained outside the Church of England, imitated the intolerance of High-Church Anglicans so well that many did not recognize it as parody. The story of the disturbance that it caused has often been told.[13] Defoe himself was to continue complaining about the reactions, which were a consequence of his own literary ingenuity: "Thus a poor Author has ventur'd to have all Mankind call him Villain, and Traytor to his Country and Friends, for making other People's thoughts speak in his Words'.[14] He is still grumbling more than a dozen years later, in the *Appeal to Honour and Justice*, about the trouble that the pamphlet caused him. It is just the most famous example of the kind of ventriloquism which characterizes his writing, and which also makes it so difficult to decide what he did write.

But if Defoe's *Appeal* might be protesting too much, it does carry a warning for the literary critic: 'My Name has been hackney'd about the Street by the Hawkers, and about the Coffee-Houses by the Politicians, at such a rate, as no Patience could bear. One Man will swear to the Style; another to this or that Expression; another to the Way of Printing; and all so positive, that it is to no purpose to oppose it.'[15] As the complaint implies, the logic of attribution can be self-fulfilling. As Furbank and Owens have shown, once the distinguishing characteristic of an author is supposed to be the ability to adopt any guise, a medley of otherwise unattributed texts start looking like his inventions. Eleven years earlier than the *Appeal* the complaint had been the same: 'My Name's the Hackney Title of the Times.'[16] It is a 'Title'

---

[13] See especially J. R. Moore, *Defoe in the Pillory* (1939; repr. New York, 1973).

[14] From 'A Brief Explanation of a late Pamphlet, Entituled, The Shortest Way with Dissenters', in Daniel Defoe, *A Second Volume of the Writings of the Author of the True-Born Englishman* (1705), 443.

[15] *Appeal*, 46.

[16] Daniel Defoe, *An Elegy on the Author of the True-Born Englishman* (1704), I. 70.

which, after Defoe's death in 1731, continued to be affixed to works not attributed to him in his lifetime: *Memoirs of a Cavalier* is just one of them. The purpose of the rest of this Introduction will be to suggest what this 'Title' stands for.

If an author is often a kind of fiction, then perhaps he or she is a necessary fiction. Defoe protested that, even if a writer stopped writing, antagonistic readers might still 'pretend to indict a Man for every thing they please, as if they had Power to read his Countenance in Letters, and swear to a Stile as they would his Face'.[17] But the would-be escapee from what he calls 'the Clamour of the Pen' is too convenient a role to be beyond suspicion. As Pat Rogers has pointed out, searching for the author of a text was an habitual game for eighteenth-century readers. 'The bibliographical tangles which remain to this day, with their elaborate problems of attribution and publishing history, reflect an authentic piece of Augustan life, as creative artists knew it.'[18] Defoe wrote much that invited those guesses at authorship about which he complained, and to that extent present arguments are a consequence of conditions of publication in the eighteenth century. In fact, in this period it was conventional for authors to remain, at least initially, hidden. *Gulliver's Travels*, *An Essay on Man*, *Pamela*, and *Tristram Shandy* are a few examples of works which first appeared without the names of their authors.

Yet the condition of anonymity was not the same for Defoe as it might have been for Swift, Pope, Richardson, or Sterne. He wrote for money, and never had enough of it not to need to write more. To literary critics it has seemed unfair that Pope should have included him with all the other monstrous specimens of Grub Street in the *Dunciad*; but it was also appropriate. Defoe was a hack, and where he did not have the time to invent, he had to pillage. If Defoe did write *Memoirs of a Cavalier*, it is hardly surprising that it 'has been more

---

[17] Defoe, *An Elegy on the Author* . . . , Preface.
[18] Pat Rogers (ed.), *Defoe: The Critical Heritage* (London, 1972), Introd., 5.

generally considered as history than any other of Defoe's major narratives with the possible exception of the *Journal of the Plague Year*.[19] It had to sound true to sell, and the puzzle of its authorship was a sign of its truth. What we can now see, thanks to Secord's source-hunting, is the artistry of the pillaging. Making history familiar—inventing a narrator who takes possession of the deeds of other men and women—this is Defoe's peculiar kind of achievement.

Memoirs of a Cavalier looks like something better than the fruit of wide reading and polished opportunism. It is a text which deals with a question that Defoe's writings constantly pose: what does a true story sound like? The Preface to the first edition, as if to arouse scepticism, assures the reader of the authenticity of what follows: 'Credit . . . Truth . . . History . . . Facts . . . embellished with Particulars' (pp. 3–4). This is the characteristic lexicon of Defoe-as-reporter, recommending the probability of a narrative to 'all the Men of Sense and Judgment that read it'. We find the same assertiveness (which implicitly credits the reader with stringent standards for truth) in much of his earlier reportage. In his famous account of the great storm of 1703, we have a narrator 'resolv'd to use so much Caution in this Relation as to transmit nothing to Posterity without authentick Vouchers, and such Testimony as no reasonable Man will dispute'.[20] The narrator of *The Storm* has to admit something that remains hidden in the *Memoirs*: that other observers' stories have been used. But the concern with discerning a true story is the same: 'From *Oxfordshire* we have an Account very authentick, and yet unaccountably strange: but the reverend Author of the Story being a Gentleman whose Credit we cannot dispute . . . we give his Letter.'[21] The vocabulary is as tenacious as that of the Preface to the *Memoirs*: 'written by very honest plain and observing Persons . . . We content our selves with relating only the Fact . . . Authentick Particulars . . . the following

[19] Arthur W. Secord, *Robert Drury's Journal and Other Studies* (Urbana, Ill., 1961), 74.
[20] Daniel Defoe, *The Storm* (1704), 33.   [21] Ibid. 87.

plain, but honest Account'. If the 'Title' of Defoe's authorship means anything, it is this obsession with 'factuality'.

This concern with making narratives adequate to the strange, particular, accidental facts of the world characterizes all of Defoe's novels—and in this respect the *Memoirs* is a good candidate for his authorship. 'Realism' is a word that is often used of the novels, but it seems to me a poor word for this type of fiction. Indeed, the end-product is often engagingly unrealistic: narrators like the Cavalier or Robinson Crusoe are so attached to the recording of detail as to be oddly untouched by the experiences they describe. The title-page of *Memoirs of a Cavalier* advertises the unusual and exciting adventures of its narrator, just like *Robinson Crusoe* or *Journal of the Plague Year*; and just like Crusoe or H.F., the Cavalier is often sober, pedantic, and finicky about detail where we might feel that he should be moved or confused. Such narrators are great providers—*in extremis*—of lists, statistics, the barest of facts. But psychological exploration is not really the undertaking of such fiction. The measure of truth is the steady, unblinking eye of the observer. If we are used to the inwardness of much nineteenth-century fiction, the steadiness of Defoe's narrators can be mistaken for artistic limitation. In fact, it is a special achievement.

Each of Defoe's narrators (and, by this criterion, the Cavalier too) is, in a sense, the same narrator: the reporter, the empiricist, the person who must trust his or her eyes and experience. Whatever he wrote, Defoe spoke through a witness. Sometimes it seems plausible to identify this witness as the real historical personage, Daniel Defoe. On closer examination, those texts like the *History of the Union of Great Britain* or *Tour of the Whole Island of Great Britain*, which tell of events and places that Defoe did actually encounter, are also works of plagiarism, invention, and, as Pat Rogers has said, 'special pleading couched as objective annals'.[22] In his *History of the Union*—one of the few prestigious books that Defoe

----

[22] Rogers (ed.), *Critical Heritage*, 28.

wrote, and therefore one of the few that actually bore his
name—he tells his readers that, in the 'Labyrinth of Untrode
Paths' that is history, the only security we have is that 'no Man
can have collected with more Care, nor has had the
Opportunity to Remark with more Advantage, having been
Eye Witness to much of the General Transaction'.[23] We
know now that Defoe was in Scotland, employed as an agent
of the English government, in the year leading up to the
Union of the two countries in 1707. But this does not mean
that we can safely call our 'Eye Witness' Defoe. A wider
reading of his fiction teaches us that the 'Eye Witness' is his
favourite figment. This character is the link from his early
journalism (where the trustworthy reporter often had a
partisan political case to make) to his later novels (imaginative
by managing to sound as if they have not been merely
imagined). Early in Defoe's career as a writer, the narrator of
The Storm (who beguilingly signed himself 'the Ages Humble
Servant') told any potential doubter, 'the Author of this was
an Eye-Witness and Sharer of the Particulars'.[24] Creating an
'Eye-Witness' became his endeavour as a novelist.

The Memoirs has taken history (all those sources) and given
it to a 'Sharer of Particulars'. The Cavalier wanders through
this history and makes it familiar. Everything is witnessed.
Versions of the past which could only ever become coherent
in retrospect are made to seem facts which can be confirmed
by immediate observation. The Cavalier says of the French
King,

Here I saw the King, whose Figure was mean, his Countenance
hollow, and always seemed dejected, and every Way discovering that
Weakness in his Countenance that appeared in his Actions.
If he was ever sprightly and vigorous it was when the Cardinal was
with him; for he depended so much on every Thing he did, that he
was at the utmost Dilemma when he was absent, always timorous,
jealous and irresolute. (p. 22)

[23] Daniel Defoe, The History of the Union of Great Britain (1709), 'Of the
Last Treaty properly called the Union', 1.   [24] The Storm, 83.

What the Cavalier once sees easily becomes what is 'always' the case. Analysis is made into observation; surmise into what can be seen.

> I observed the People degenerated from the ancient glorious Inhabitants, who were generous, brave, and the most valiant of all Nations, to a vicious Baseness of Soul, barbarous, treacherous, jealous and revengeful, lewd and cowardly, intolerably proud and haughty, bigotted to blind, incoherent Devotion, and the grossest of Idolatry. (p. 32.)

How do you 'observe' all of this? A strongly anti-Catholic version of Italy's history is made to sound like a report of what is visible. 'I went to see and not to write' (p. 35), the Cavalier declares—and he does see everything. Understanding and seeing are equivalent; the assertions of credit-worthiness sound the same as those which pepper Defoe's earlier journalism. Narrating one of the crucial battles of the Thirty Years War, the Cavalier tells us, 'I can be more particular in it than other Accounts, having been Eye-witness to every part of it' (p. 87). The *Memoirs* is full of these statements. It is hard to encounter these formulae and not think of Defoe's other particularizing narrators—H.F. with his lists of those dead of the plague, or the narrator of *The Storm*, travelling through Kent counting the fallen trees.

The effect for which Defoe's novels strive is familiarity with unusual events and individuals. The largest patterns of history or providence must be made a matter of personal observation. The Cavalier is driven across Europe mostly by a desire to 'see' what he might otherwise only hear about: 'I resolved, if possible, to see the King of *Sweden*'s Army', he remarks, as an explanation for one of his journeys across Europe (p. 43). As if seeing it will make it exist. He walks through history, easily conversant with kings and generals, talking with Prince Rupert or Charles I, but uncompromised by their errors or prejudices. Thomas De Quincey, discussing the method of such 'forgeries', asked how their pretence of knowledge could ever 'pass for genuine, even with literary men and critics'; his answer seems to me to catch exactly a style common to all of Defoe's 'factual fictions'—a style by which we think we know him:

> How did he accomplish so difficult an end? Simply by inventing such little circumstantiations of any character or incident as seem, by their apparent inertness of effect, to verify themselves . . . To invent, when nothing at all is gained by inventing, there seems no imaginable temptation. It never occurs to us that this very construction of the case, this very inference from such neutral details, was precisely the object which De Foe had in view—was the very thing which he counted on, and by which he meant to profit.[25]

This is what I have called the factuality of Defoe's narratives: a readiness with detail that some readers have found all too pressing in the *Memoirs*; a vaunted willingness to be 'the more particular'.

The narrator who is so full of 'particulars' has a story to tell which had specific religious and political implications in the early eighteenth century. The Cavalier's history is a carefully partisan one, and its bias is certainly consistent with Defoe's authorship. Gustavus Adolphus, in whose army the Cavalier fights, was and remained a Protestant hero—the great seventeenth-century defender of the Reformation. The main source for the part of the *Memoirs* concerning the wars in Germany, William Watt's *The Swedish Intelligencer* (1632), declared him 'the *Caesar* and *Alexander* of our times, that admirably victorious King of *Sweden*'.[26] Throughout Defoe's journal, the *Review*, he is given as the example of a virtuous monarch, motivated by true religiosity and concern for his subjects rather than the love of power and wealth which Defoe thought distinguished most rulers. To any good Protestant, he was God's warrior.

The treatment of the English Civil War in the *Memoirs* is, ideologically speaking, both more awkward and more subtle. The supposed editor of the work refers to its 'Confutation of many Errors in all Writers upon the Subject of our wars in

---

[25] In Rogers (ed.), *Critical Heritage*, 117–18.
[26] William Watts, *The Swedish Intelligencer* (1632), Preface.

England' (p. 3), including the famous history written by the Royalist Earl of Clarendon (another of those texts plundered in the making of the *Memoirs*). As a neat guarantee of the disinterestedness and 'Credit' of its correction of previous histories, he adds that the evidence of the *Memoirs* was withheld from 'a Person who had written a whole Volume in Folio, by Way of Answer to, and Confutation of *Clarendon*'s History', which manages to imply both that ideological debate is beneath those responsible for this text, and that it contains the information to debunk Clarendon's Royalist propaganda. We can see why it might have been useful for the text to have been taken as genuine. If we recognize that it is fiction, it is clear that the very fair-mindedness of the editor and the Cavalier is cleverly partisan by eighteenth-century standards. The Cavalier may have fought for a Stuart king in the 1640s; his narrative fights on the side of Hanoverian Protestants in the 1720s. 'In all his Account he does Justice to his "Enemies", and honours the Merit of those whose Cause he fought against; and many Accounts recorded in his Story, are not to be found even in the best Histories of those Times' (p. 3). To 'honour the Merit' of those who rebelled against their monarch was to imply that they might have had a cause worth fighting for. To describe Charles I as a good man 'who always took the best Measures when he was left to his own Counsel', but was misled by factious priests, was to suggest that his cause might have been flawed.

The trick of all this, of course, is to have a narrator who is of the king's party, and therefore sufficiently in the know to be dependably critical of its undertakings. It is with an imagined sigh of 'Regret' that the Cavalier lists Charles' failings, and manages to damn him with the accent of a sad supporter. Charles would have been a good king if he had not been in the grip of bad advisers. Equally, the Presbyterians amongst Cromwell's forces deserve praise all the more telling because it comes from their enemy. They are represented by the Cavalier as moderate men outflanked by a minority of fanatics 'who aimed at the very Root of the Government'. The message of the concessions that the narrator finds himself making to the cause against which he fights would have been a lesson for Britain in the 1720s: only 'the Revolution Principles' of 1688 (his allegiance to which Defoe boasted of in his *Appeal to Honour and Justice*) could properly bind a monarch and his people. The implication would have been that the so-called Glorious Revolution enabled the triumphant reconciliation of the powers of King and Parliament—those powers disastrously at odds in the *Memoirs*. By having, as if inadvertently, 'advocated for the Enemies', the Cavalier has implied the necessity of that second, but peaceful, rebellion against a despotic (and Catholic) King. The 'Aversion to popular Tumults' which he learns from his adventures must have sounded a good motive for the post-1688 limitation of the monarch's powers.

If the ideological uses of the *Memoirs* seem clear enough, this is not to suggest that the text is entirely confident about how to connect events into a pattern that we might call history. Precisely because the narrator is supposedly close to events, he meets with a difficulty which consistently pre-occupies Defoe's fact-loving reporters. It can be illustrated with a famous episode from *Robinson Crusoe*. When Crusoe notices, in 'astonishment and confusion', that barley is growing on his island, he at first thinks that 'God had miraculously caused this grain to grow', and he weeps 'that such a prodigy of nature should happen on my account'. Eventually, however, he works out natural causes (the seed must have fallen from a bag of chicken feed).

I must confess, my religious thankfulness to God's providence began to abate too, upon the discovering that all this was nothing but what was common; tho' I ought to have been as thankful for so strange and unforseen providence, as if it had been miraculous; for it was really the work of providence to me, that should order or appoint, that 10 or 12 grains should remain unspoiled . . . as if it had been dropt from heaven.[27]

---

[27] Daniel Defoe, *The Life and Strange Surprising Adventures of Robinson Crusoe*, ed. J. Donald Crowley (1972; repr. Oxford, 1981), 78.

The episode can be seen as an attempt to reconcile natural and supernatural explanations. The Cavalier too faces this potential contest of explanations; it is a contest which gives energy to all Defoe's 'novels'. Empiricists like Crusoe (or H.F. or the Cavalier) believe that knowledge should be gained and tested by experience—and that a text which contributes to knowledge is one that accurately reports on the observable world. Yet the observable world of causes and effects (whether historical or physical) is also susceptible to providential explanation. Crusoe is a man who can deduce natural explanations for odd events; but the older Crusoe who tells the story uses the episode of the barley to argue that Providence can work by the ways of nature. The Cavalier also has to try to reconcile different ways of explaining events. The Royalists lost a war because of a series of miscalculations; but perhaps they also lost a war because they were destined to do so. The Cavalier is always at the hinge of history, ready with a political or military explanation of why things happened as they did, and how they might have been otherwise (explanation which is, in fact, the wisdom of historical hindsight). But he is involved in a struggle which God seems to have determined to end in one way. 'Had the King, I say, pushed on his first Design, which he had formed with very good Reason . . . he had turned the Scale of his Affairs' (p. 154): this is typical of his analyses of the unfolding of events. Yet the very paragraph in which it comes ends: 'Providence for our Ruine had otherwise determined it.' Causality itself is subject to larger and stranger rules. The narrator thinks that he sees how events connect, and he is frequently frustrated or amazed at the miscalculations of those who are history's agents. But he also finds himself edged into a kind of fatalism by the recognition that 'Providence' must be deciding what might seem adventitious, or what an informed observer thinks might have turned out otherwise.

Memoirs of a Cavalier never, perhaps, achieves the extraordinary discomfort brought about in *A Journal of the Plague Year* by this oscillation between empirical description and providential speculation. The latter text seems to me a triumph of empiricism's unease about its own limitations, and it would be fanciful to make such large claims for the literary merits of the *Memoirs*. Nevertheless, the shadows of this uncertainty do fall across it. Its narrator is committed to showing how bad advice given to King Charles brings disaster by predictable stages; but then 'Heaven, when the Ruine of a Person or Party is determined, always so infatuates their Counsels, as to make them instrumental to it themselves'.

In fact, this text so much needs to distil the 'Fatality of Circumstances' out from the naturally connected 'Particulars' that it describes, that it attaches to the end of the 'Memoirs' a strange list of 'Providences', in which the 'just Judgment of God' might be clearly seen. This is the list that the Edinburgh edition of 1759 declares to be interpolated, and not without some logic. It is a strange collection of examples of 'the Fatality of Times, Places and Actions'. These are mainly just significant events which happened to have occurred at the same date in different years. The list seems to have little to do with the account that has preceded it. Yet here, finally, is a sign of what we think of as Defoe's authorship. In *Robinson Crusoe* and *A Journal of the Plague Year*, the sense that the turns of the story might be foreordained is made part of the telling of that story; Crusoe and H.F. grasp at omens, and work to distinguish between revelatory prophecies and vain delusions. Crusoe assiduously notes, like the Cavalier, the odd 'concurrences' (events taking place at the same date) that give shape to his wandering life. In *A Journal of the Plague Year*, H.F. recoils from the strange superstitions which grip his fellow Londoners, but still advises anyone who would live through the plague to 'keep his Eye upon the particular Providences which occur at that Time, and look upon them complexly ... he may take them for Intimations from Heaven'.[28]

---

[28] Daniel Defoe, *A Journal of the Plague Year* (1928; repr. London, 1974), 12.

The sense of a life lived as predicted grips Defoe's adventurers. *Memoirs of a Cavalier* begins with the dreams that its narrator's mother had before he was born, evidence that 'some extraordinary Influence affected my Birth'. It is as if the narrator enters a plea against his own illusions of choice or of chance. However, in the *Memoirs*, the discourse of 'Fatality' cannot quite be married to events. It is literally separated out from the reporter's story and tacked on to its end. There it is: just a list of coincidences. It is unsatisfactory and discrepant, and tells us, as *Crusoe* and the *Journal* do more eloquently, that there are shapes to events which escape mere observation.

J. M.

ACKNOWLEDGEMENTS

Thanks to Jeremy Maule, James Raven, and Penny Wilson, and to the staff of the library of Trinity College, Cambridge, where (finally) I found a copy of Francis Noble's (1784) edition of *Memoirs of a Cavalier*.

NOTE ON THE TEXT

Memoirs of a Cavalier was first published in 1720, the only edition to appear in Defoe's lifetime. The present text is that of 1720, printed from a xerox reproduction of the copy in the British Museum. The long 's' of the first edition has been eliminated; obvious errors of the press have been silently corrected.

SELECT BIBLIOGRAPHY

EDITIONS

Memoirs of a Cavalier was first published in London in 1720, and appeared in a further six editions during the eighteenth century: James Lister's (n.d.) in Leeds; in Edinburgh (1759 and 1766); in Newark (1782); Francis Noble's in London (1784); in London (1792). It was reprinted in all the major collections of Defoe's novels: by Sir Walter Scott (1810); Tegg (1840); Hazlitt (1840–3); Bohn (1854–6); Aitken (1895); Maynadier (1903); Blackwell (1927–8). The last of these was reprinted in 1974. The only recent editions have been a facsimile of the 1720 edition, Introd. Malcolm Bosse (1972), and the one edited by James Boulton (London 1972; repr. 1978), from which the text of this edition is taken.

BIBLIOGRAPHY

J. R. Moore, *A Checklist of the Writings of Daniel Defoe* (2nd edn., (Hamden, Conn., 1971), is still the place to start, but users would be well advised to take into account the arguments of P. N. Furbank and W. R. Owens, *The Canonisation of Daniel Defoe* (New Haven, Conn.; London, 1988). Spiro Peterson, *Daniel Defoe a Reference Guide 1731–1924* (Boston, Mass., 1987) is a bibliography (with helpful summaries) of writings about Defoe. For twentieth-century criticism, see John Stoler, *Daniel Defoe: An Annotated Bibliography of Modern Criticism, 1900–1980* (New York, 1984).

BIOGRAPHY, LETTERS, CRITICISM

G. H. Healey (ed.), *The Letters of Daniel Defoe* (Oxford, 1955) contains some fascinating material. The standard life has been for some time J. R. Moore, *Daniel Defoe: Citizen of the Modern World* (Chicago, Ill., 1958); as the title suggests, it puts a (contestable) emphasis on Defoe's modernity. F. Bastian, *Defoe's Early Life* (London, 1981) is to be preferred for the period that it covers but this runs only to 1703. Pat Rogers (ed.), *Defoe: The Critical Heritage* (London, 1972) is a selection of eighteenth- and nineteenth-century reactions to Defoe's writing, and has an excellent Introduction surveying the history of his reputation. For Defoe's treatment by his contemporaries, see also W. L. Payne, 'Defoe in the Pamphlets', *Philological Quarterly*, 52 (1973), 85–96. Whatever the difficulties of attribution, the range of Defoe's various writings is particularly interesting. Readers wishing to sample the variety of genres in which he worked might begin with either (or both, for they scarcely overlap) of two good anthologies: J. T. Boulton (ed.), *Selected Writings of Daniel Defoe* (2nd edn., Cambridge, 1975), and Laura Ann Curtis (ed.), *The Versatile Defoe* (London, 1979). Few of the major critical studies of Defoe's fiction pause to examine *Memoirs of a Cavalier*, but the following are general discussions of his writings which deal with issues also raised by the *Memoirs*: Rodney Baine, *Daniel Defoe and the Supernatural* (Athens, Ga., 1968); J. J. Richetti, *Defoe's Narratives: Situations and Structures* (Oxford, 1975); Geoffrey Sill, *Defoe and the Idea of Fiction* (London, 1983)—an attempt to explain the relationship between his political writing and his fiction; Laura Ann Curtis, *The Elusive Defoe* (London, 1984)—an examination of the variety of voices that Defoe invented for different purposes, journalistic as well as novelistic. Some account of the *Memoirs* is made part of a wider analysis of Defoe's fiction in Maximillian Novak, *Realism, Myth, and History in Defoe's Fiction* (London, 1983) and Michael Boardman, *Defoe and the Uses of Narrative* (New Brunswick, 1983). A thorough description of Defoe's use of original source-material is given by Arthur W. Secord, 'The Origins of Defoe's *Memoirs of a Cavalier*', in *Robert Drury's Journal and Other Studies* (Urbana, Ill., 1961.)

A CHRONOLOGY OF
DANIEL DEFOE

This is based mainly on the detailed 'Chronological Outline' in J. R. Moore's *Daniel Defoe: Citizen of the Modern World* (1958), pp. 345–55.

		Age
1660	Born in London, the son of a tallow-chandler	
1662	Act of Uniformity: Defoe's parents adhered to Presbyterianism	2
1665–6	The Great Plague and the Great Fire of London	5–6
*c.*1671–9	Attended school of the Rev. James Fisher, Dorking, and Dissenting Academy of the Rev. Charles Morton, Newington Green, with intention of entering Presbyterian ministry	*c.*11–19
*c.*1683	Established as Merchant in London	23
1684	Married Mary Tuffley, with dowry of £3,700	24
1685	Took part briefly in Monmouth's Rebellion	25
1685–92	Active in wholesale hosiery trade but dealt also in wine, Maryland tobacco, and other commodities; travelled widely for business purposes in England, probably also on the continent	25–32
1688	Supported Revolution of 1688 by publishing a pamphlet and joining the forces of William of Orange, which were then advancing on London	28
1691	Contributed occasionally to John Dunton's *Athenian Mercury* (1691–7)	30–1
1692	First bankruptcy, for £17,000	32
1697	*An Essay upon Projects*	37

Memoirs of a
Cavalier

THE PREFACE

As an Evidence that 'tis very probable these Memorials were written many Years ago, the Persons now concerned in the Publication, assure the Reader, that they have had them in their Possession finished, as they now·appear, above twenty Years: That they were so long ago found by great Accident, among other valuable Papers in the Closet of an eminent publick Minister, of no less Figure than one of King *William's* Secretaries of State.

As it is not proper to trace them any farther, so neither is there any need to trace them at all, to give Reputation to the Story related, seeing the Actions here mentioned have a sufficient Sanction from all the Histories of the Times to which they relate, with this Addition, that the admirable Manner of relating them, and the wonderful Variety of Incidents, with which they are beautified in the Course of a private Gentleman's Story, add such Delight in the reading, and give such a Lustre, as well to the Accounts themselves, as to the Person who was the Actor; and no Story, we believe, extant in the World, ever came abroad with such Advantages.

It must naturally give some Concern in the reading, that the Name of a Person of so much Gallantry and Honour, and so many Ways valuable to the World, should be lost to the Readers: We assure them no small Labour has been thrown away upon the Enquiry, and all we have been able to arrive to of Discovery in this Affair is, that a *Memorandum* was found with this Manuscript, in these Words, but not signed by any Name, only the two Letters of a Name, which

gives us no Light into the Matter, which Memoir was as
follows.

> *Memorandum*,
> I found this Manuscript among my Father's Writings, and
> I understand that he got them as Plunder, at, or after,
> the Fight at *Worcester*, where he served as Major of ——'s
> Regiment of Horse on the Side of the Parliament.
>
> L.K.

As this has been of no Use but to terminate the Enquiry
after the Person; so, however, it seems most naturally to
give an Authority to the Original of the Work, (*viz.*) that it
was born of a Soldier, and indeed it is thro' every Part,
related with so Soldierly a Stile, and in the very Language
of the Field, that it seems impossible any Thing, but the very
Person who was present in every Action here related, could
be the Relator of them.

The Accounts of Battles, the Sieges, and the several
Actions of which this Work is so full, are all recorded in the
Histories of those Times; such as the great Battle of *Leipsick*,
the Sacking of *Magdeburgh*, the Siege of *Nurembergh*, the
passing the River *Leck* in *Bavaria*; such also as the Battles
of *Keynton*, or *Edge-Hill*; the Battles of *Newberry*, *Marston-
Moor*, and *Naseby*, and the like: They are all, we say,
recorded in other Histories, and written by those who lived
in those Times, and perhaps had good Authority for what
they wrote. But do those Relations give any of the beautiful
Ideas of things formed in this Account? Have they one half
of the Circumstances and Incidents of the Actions themselves, that this Man's Eyes were Witness to, and which his
Memory has thus preserved? He that has read the best
Accounts of those Battles, will be surprized to see the
Particulars of the Story so preserved, so nicely, and so
agreeably describ'd; and will confess what we alledge, that
the Story is inimitably told; and even the great Actions of
the glorious King *GUSTAVUS ADOLPHUS*, receive a
Lustre from this Man's Relations, which the World was

never made sensible of before, and which the present Age has much wanted of late, in Order to give their Affections a Turn in Favour of his late glorious Successor.[1]

In the Story of our own Country's unnatural Wars, he carries on the same Spirit. How effectually does he record the Virtues and glorious Actions of King *Charles* the First, at the same Time that he frequently enters upon the Mistakes of his Majesty's Conduct, and of his Friends, which gave his Enemies all those fatal Advantages against him, which ended in the Overthrow of his Armies, the Loss of his Crown and Life, and the Ruin of the Constitution?

In all his Account he does Justice to his 'Enemies,' and honours the Merit of those whose Cause he fought against; and many Accounts recorded in his Story, are not to be found even in the best Histories of those Times.

What Applause does he give to the Gallantry of Sir *Thomas Fairfax*, to his Modesty, to his Conduct, under which he himself was subdued, and to the Justice he did the King's Troops when they laid down their Arms?

His Description of the *Scots* Troops in the beginning of the War, and the Behaviour of the Party under the Earl of *Holland*, who went over against them, are admirable; and his Censure of their Conduct, who push'd the King upon the Quarrel, and then would not let him fight, is no more than what many of the King's Friends, tho' less knowing (as Soldiers, have often complained of.)

In a Word, this Work is a Confutation of many Errors in all the Writers upon the Subject of our Wars in *England*, and even in that extraordinary History written by the Earl of *Clarendon*;[2] but the Editors were so just, that when near twenty Years ago, a Person who had written a whole Volume in Folio, by Way of Answer to, and Confutation of *Clarendon's* History of the Rebellion, would have borrowed the Clauses in this Account, which clash with that History, and confront it: We say the Editors were so just as to refuse them.

There can be nothing objected against the general Credit

of this Work, seeing its Truth is established upon universal History; and almost all the Facts, especially those of Moment, are confirmed for their general Part by all the Writers of those Times, if they are here embellished with Particulars, which are no where else to be found, that is the Beauty we boast of; and that it is that must recommend this Work to all the Men of Sense and Judgment that read it.

The only Objection we find possible to make against this Work is, that it is not carried on farther; or, as we may say finished, with the finishing the War of the Time; and this we complain of also: But then we complain as a Misfortune to the World, not as a Fault in the Author; for how do we know but that this Author might carry it on, and have another Part finished which might not fall into the same Hands, or may still remain with some of his Family, and which they cannot indeed publish, to make it seem any Thing perfect, for want of the other Part which we have, and which we have now made publick? Nor is it very improbable, but that if any such farther Part is in Being, the publishing these Two Parts may occasion the Proprietors of the Third to let the World see it; and that by such a Discovery, the Name of the Person may also come to be known, which would, no doubt, be a great Satisfaction to the Reader, as well as us.

This, however, must be said, that if the same Author should have written another Part of this Work, and carried it on to the End of those Times; yet as the Residue of those melancholly Days, to the Restoration, were filled with the Intrigues of Government, the Political Management of illegal Power, and the Dissentions and Factions of a People, who were then even in themselves but a *FACTION*, and that there was very little Action in the Field; it is more than probable that our Author, who was a Man of Arms, had little Share in those Things, and might not care to trouble himself with looking at them.

But besides all this, it might happen that he might go abroad again, at that Time, as most of the Gentlemen of

Quality, and who had an Abhorrence for the Power that then govern'd, here did. Nor are we certain that he might live to the End of that Time, so we can give no Account whether he had any Post in the subsequent Actions of that Time.

'Tis enough that we have the Authorities above to recommend this Part to us that is now published; the Relation, we are perswaded, will recommend it self, and nothing more can be needful, because nothing more can invite than the Story it self, which when the Reader enters into, he will find it very hard to get out of, 'till he has gone thro' it.

PART I

IT MAY suffice the Reader, without being very inquisitive
after my Name, that I was born in the County of *SALOP*,
in the Year 1608; under the Government of what Star I was
never Astrologer enough to examine; but the Consequences
of my Life may allow me to suppose some extraordinary
Influence affected my Birth. If there be any thing in Dreams
also, my Mother, who was mighty observant that Way, took
Minutes, which I have since seen in the first Leaf of her
Prayer Book, of several strange Dreams she had while she
was with Child of her second Son, which was myself. Once
she noted that she dreamed she was carried away by a
Regiment of Horse, and delivered in the Fields of a Son,
that as soon as it was born had two Wings came out of its
Back, and in half an Hour's Time flew away from her: And
the very Evening before I was born, she dreamed she was
brought to Bed of a Son, and that all the while she was in
Labour a Man stood under her Window beating on a
Kettle-Drum, which very much discomposed her.

My Father was a Gentleman of a very plentiful Fortune,
having an Estate of above 5000 Pounds *per Annum*, of a
Family nearly allied to several of the principal Nobility, and
lived about six Miles from the Town: And my Mother being
at—on some particular Occasion, was surprized there at a
Friend's House, and brought me very safe into the World.

I was my Father's second Son, and therefore was not
altogether so much slighted as younger Sons of good
Families generally are. But my Father saw something in my

Genius also which particularly pleased him, and so made him take extraordinary Care of my Education.

I was taught therefore, by the best Masters that could be had, every Thing that was needful to accomplish a young Gentleman for the World; and at seventeen Years old my Tutor told my Father an Academick Education was very proper for a Person of Quality, and he thought me very fit for it: So my Father entered me of—College in *Oxford*, where I continued three Years.

A Collegiate Life did not suit me at all, though I loved Books well enough. It was never designed that I should be either a Lawyer, Physician or Divine; and I wrote to my Father, that I thought I had staid there long enough for a Gentleman, and with his Leave I desired to give him a Visit.

During my Stay at *Oxford*, though I passed through the proper Exercises of the House,[1] yet my chief reading was upon History and Geography, as that which pleased my Mind best, and supplied me with Ideas most suitable to my Genius: By one I understood what great Actions had been done in the World; and by the other I understood where they had been done.

My Father readily complied with my Desire of coming home; for besides that he thought, as I did, that three Years time at the University was enough, he also most passionately loved me, and began to think of my settling near him.

At my Arrival I found my self extraordinarily caressed by my Father, and he seemed to take a particular Delight in my Conversation. My Mother, who lived in a perfect Union with him, both in Desires and Affection, received me very passionately: Apartments were provided for me by my self, and Horses and Servants allowed me in particular.

My Father never went a Hunting, an Exercise he was exceeding fond of, but he would have me with him; and it pleased him when he found me like the Sport. I lived thus, in all the Pleasures 'twas possible for me to enjoy, for about a Year more; when going out one Morning with my Father to hunt a Stag, and having had a very hard Chase, and gotten a great Way off from home, we had Leisure enough to ride gently back: And as we returned, my Father took Occasion to enter into a serious Discourse with me concerning the Manner of my settling in the World.

He told me, with a great deal of Passion, that he loved me above all the rest of his Children, and that therefore he intended to do very well for me; that my eldest Brother being already married and settled, he had designed the same for me, and proposed a very advantageous Match for me with a young Lady of very extraordinary Fortune and Merit, and offered to make a Settlement of 2000 *l. per Annum* on me, which he said he would purchase for me without diminishing his paternal Estate.

There was too much Tenderness in this Discourse not to affect me exceedingly. I told him, I would perfectly resign my self unto his Disposal. But, as my Father had, together with his Love for me, a very nice Judgment in his Discourse, he fixed his Eyes very attentively on me; and though my Answer was without the least Reserve, yet he thought he saw some Uneasiness in me at the Proposal, and from thence concluded that my Compliance was rather an Act of Discretion than Inclination; and, that however I seemed so absolutely given up to what he had proposed, yet my Answer was really an Effect of my Obedience rather than my Choice: So he returned very quick upon me, *Look you, Son, though I give you my own Thoughts in the Matter, yet I would have you be very plain with me; for if your own Choice does not agree with mine, I will be your Adviser, but will never impose upon you; and therefore let me know your Mind freely. I don't reckon my self capable, Sir,* said I, with a great deal of respect, *to make so good a Choice for my self as you can for me; and though my Opinion differed from yours, its being your Opinion would reform mine, and my Judgment would as readily comply as my Duty. I gather at least from thence,* said my Father, *that your Designs lay another Way before, however they may comply with mine: And therefore I would know what it was you would have asked of me if I had*

not offered this to you; and you must not deny me your Obed-
ience in this, if you expect I should believe your Readiness in
the other.

Sir, said I, *'twas impossible I should lay out for my self just*
what you have proposed; but if my Inclinations were never so
contrary, though at your Command you shall know them, yet
I declare them to be wholly subjected to your Order: I confess
my Thoughts did not tend towards Marriage or a Settlement;
for though I had no Reason to question your Care of me, yet
I thought a Gentleman ought always to see something of the
World before he confined himself to any part of it: And if I had
been to ask your Consent to any Thing, it should have been to
give me leave to Travel for a short Time, in order [to] *qualifie my*
self to appear at home like a Son to so good a Father.

In what Capacity would you Travel, replied my Father?
You must go abroad either as a private Gentleman, as a
Scholar, or as a Soldier. If it were in the latter Capacity, Sir,
said I, returning pretty quick, *I hope I should not misbehave*
my self; but I am not so determined as not to be ruled by your
Judgment. Truly, replied my Father, *I see no War abroad at*
this Time worth while for a Man to appear in, whether we talk
of the Cause or the Encouragement; and indeed, Son, I am
afraid you need not go far for Adventures of that Nature, for
Times seem to look as if this Part of Europe *would find us*
Work enough. My Father spake then relating to the Quarrel
likely to happen between the King of *England* and the
Spaniard,* for I believe he had no Notions of a Civil War
in his Head.

In short, my Father perceiving my Inclinations very
forward to go abroad, gave me Leave to Travel, upon
Condition I would promise to return in Two Years at
farthest, or sooner, if he sent for me.

While I was at *Oxford* I happened into the Society of a
young Gentleman, of a good Family, but of a low Fortune,
being a younger Brother, and who had indeed instilled into
me the first Desires of going abroad, and who I knew
passionately longed to Travel, but had not sufficient Allow-

---

* Upon the Breach of the Match between the King of *England* and the Infanta of
Spain;[1] and particularly upon the old Quarrel of the King of *Bohemia* and the
Palatinate.

ance to defray his Expences as a Gentleman. We had contracted a very close Friendship, and our Humours being very agreeable to one another, we daily enjoyed the Conversation of Letters. He was of a generous free Temper, without the least Affectation or Deceit, a handsome proper Person, a strong Body, very good Mien, and brave to the last Degree: His Name was *Fielding*,[1] and we called him *Captain*, though it be a very unusual Title in a College; but Fate had some Hand in the Title, for he had certainly the Lines of a Soldier drawn in his Countenance. I imparted to him the Resolutions I had taken, and how I had my Father's Consent to go abroad; and would know his Mind, whether he would go with me: He sent me Word, he would go with all his Heart.

My Father, when he saw him, for I sent for him immediately to come to me, mightily approved my Choice; so we got our Equipage ready, and came away for *London*.

'Twas on the 22nd of *April* 1630, when we embarked at *Dover*, landed in a few Hours at *Calais*, and immediately took Post for *Paris*. I shall not trouble the Reader with a Journal of my Travels, nor with the Description of Places; which every Geographer can do better than I; but these Memoirs being only a Relation of what happened either to our selves, or in our own Knowledge, I shall confine my self to that Part of it.

We had indeed some diverting Passages in our Journey to *Paris*; as first, the Horse my Comrade was upon fell so very lame with a Slip that he could not go, and hardly stand: And the Fellow that rid with us Express, pretended to ride away to a Town five Miles off to get a fresh Horse, and so left us on the Road with one Horse between two of us: We followed as well as we could, but being Strangers, missed the Way, and wandered a great Way out of the Road. Whether the Man performed in reasonable Time, or not, we could not be sure; but if it had not been for an old Priest, we had never found him. We met this Man, by a very good Accident, near a little Village whereof he was Curate: We spoke *Latin* enough just to make him understand us, and he did not speak it much better himself; but he carried us into the Village to his House, gave us Wine and Bread, and entertained us with wonderful Courtesie: After this he sent into the Village, hired a Peasant, and a Horse for my Captain, and sent him to guide us into the Road. At parting he made a great many Compliments to us in *French*, which we could just understand; but the Sum was, to excuse him for a Question he had a mind to ask us. After leave to ask what he pleased, it was, if we wanted any Money for our Journey, and pulled out two Pistoles,[1] which he offered either to give or lend us.

I mention this exceeding Courtesie of the Curate, because, though Civility is very much in Use in *France*, and especially to Strangers, yet 'tis a very unusual thing to have them part with their Money.

We let the Priest know, first, that we did not want Money, and next that we were very sensible of the Obligation he had put upon us; and I told him in particular, if I lived to see him again, I would acknowledge it.

This Accident of our Horse, was, as we afterwards found, of some use to us: We had left our two Servants behind us at *Calais* to bring our Baggage after us, by reason of some Dispute between the Captain of the Pacquet and the Custom-House Officer which could not be adjusted; and we were willing to be at *Paris*: The Fellows followed as fast as they could, and as near as we could learn, in the Time we lost our Way were robbed, and our Portmanteaus opened. They took what they pleased; but as there was no Money there, but Linen and Necessaries, the Loss was not great.

Our Guide carried us to *Amiens*, where we found the Express and our two Servants, who the Express meeting on the Road with a spare Horse, had brought back with him thither.

We took this for a good Omen of our successful Journey, having escaped a Danger which might have been greater to us than it was to our Servants; for the Highway-Men in

France do not always give a Traveller the Civility of bidding him Stand and Deliver his Money, but frequently Fire upon him first, and then take his Money.

We staid one Day at *Amiens*, to adjust this little Disorder, and walked about the Town, and into the great Church, but saw nothing very remarkable there; but going cross a broad Street near the great Church, we saw a Crowd of People gazing at a Mountebank Doctor who made a long Harangue to them with a thousand antick Postures, and gave out Bills this Way, and Boxes of Physick that Way, and had a great Trade, when on a sudden the People raised a Cry,* *Larron*, *Larron*, on the other side the Street, and all the Auditors ran away from Mr. Doctor, to see what the matter was— Among the rest, we went to see; and the case was plain and short enough. Two *English* Gentlemen, and a *Scotch-Man*, Travellers as we were, were standing gazing at this prating Doctor, and one of them catched a Fellow picking his Pocket: The Fellow had got some of his Money, for he dropt two or three Pieces just by him, and had got hold of his Watch; but being surprized, let it slip again: but the Reason of telling this Story, is for the Management of it. This Thief had his Seconds so ready, that as soon as the *English-Man* had seized him, they fell in, pretended to be mighty zealous for the Stranger, takes the Fellow by the Throat, and makes a great Bustle; the Gentleman not doubting but the Man was secured, let go his own Hold of him, and left him to them: The Hubbub was great, and 'twas these Fellows cried *Larron*, *Larron*; but with a Dexterity peculiar to themselves, had let the right Fellow go, and pretended to be all upon one of their own Gang. At last they bring the Man to the Gentleman, to ask him what the Fellow had done? who, when he saw the Person they seized on, presently told them that was not the Man: Then they seemed to be in more Consternation than before, and spread themselves all over the Street, crying *Larron*, *Larron*, pretending to search for the Fellow; and so one one Way, one another, they were all gone, the Noise went over, the

* In English, *Thief*, *Thief*.

Gentlemen stood looking one at another, and the bawling Doctor began to have the Crowd about him again.

This was the first *French* Trick I had the Opportunity of seeing; but I was told they have a great many more as dextrous as this.

We soon got Acquaintance with these Gentlemen, who were going to *Paris* as well as we; so the next Day we made up our Company with them, and were a pretty Troop of five Gentlemen and four Servants.

As we had really no Design to stay long at *Paris*, so indeed, excepting the City it self, there was not much to be seen there. Cardinal *Richlieu*, who was not only a supreme Minister in the Church, but prime Minister in the State, was now made also General of the King's Forces, with a Title never known in *France* before nor since, *viz.* Lieutenant-General *au Place du Roy*,[1] in the King's stead, or as some have since translated it, representing the Person of the King.

Under this Character he pretended to execute all the Royal Powers in the Army without Appeal to the King, or without waiting for Orders: and having parted from *Paris* the Winter before, had now actually begun the War against the Duke of *Savoy*; in the process of which, he restored the Duke of *Mantua*, and having taken *Pignerol* from the Duke, put it into such a state of Defence, as the Duke could never force it out of his hands, and reduced the Duke, rather by Manage[2] and Conduct than by Force, to make Peace without it; so as annexing it to the Crown of *France*, it has ever since been a Thorn in his Foot, that has always made the Peace of *Savoy* lame and precarious: and *France* has since made *Pignerol* one of the strongest Fortresses in the World.

As the Cardinal, with all the Military part of the Court, was in the Field; so the King, to be near him, was gone with the Queen and all the Court, just before I reached *Paris*, to reside at *Lyons*. All these considered, there was nothing to do at *Paris*: the Court looked like a Citizen's House when the Family was all gone into the Country: and I thought the whole City looked very melancholy, compared to all the fine things I had heard of it.

The Queen Mother and her Party were chagrin at the Cardinal, who, tho' he owed his Grandeur to her immediate Favour, was now grown too great any longer to be at the Command of Her Majesty, or indeed in her Interest; and therefore the Queen was under Dissatisfaction, and Her Party looked very much down.

The Protestants were every where disconsolate; for the Losses they had received at *Rochel*, *Nismes*, and *Montpelier*, had reduced them to an absolute Dependence on the King's Will, without all possible hopes of ever recovering themselves, or being so much as in a Condition to take Arms for their Religion; and therefore the wisest of them plainly foresaw their own entire Reduction, as it since came to pass: and I remember vere well, that a Protestant Gentleman told me once, as we were passing from *Orleans* to *Lyons*, That the *English* had ruined them; and therefore, says he, I think the next Occasion the King takes to use us ill, as I know 'twill not be long, before he does, we must all fly over to *England*, where you are bound to maintain us for having helped to turn us out of our own Country. I asked him what he meant by saying the *English* had done it?[1] He returned short upon me; I do not mean, says he, by not relieving *Rochel*, but by helping to ruin *Rochel*, when you and the *Dutch* lent Ships to beat our Fleet, which all the Ships in *France* could not have done without you.

I was too young in the World to be very sensible of this before, and therefore was something startled at the Charge; but when I came to discourse with this Gentleman, I soon saw, the Truth of what he said was undeniable, and have since reflected on it with regret, that the Naval Power of the Protestants, which was then superior to the Royal, would certainly have been the Recovery of all their Fortunes, had it not been unhappily broke by their Brethren of *England* and *Holland*, the former lending seven Men of War, and the latter twenty, for the Destruction of the *Rocheller*'s Fleet;

and by those very Ships the *Rocheller*'s Fleet were actually beaten and destroyed, and they never afterward recovered their Force at Sea, and by consequence sunk under the Siege, which the *English* afterwards in vain attempted to prevent.

These things made the Protestants look very dull, and expected the Ruin of all their Party; which had certainly happened had the Cardinal lived a few Years longer.

We stayed in *Paris* about three Weeks, as well to see the Court, and what Rarities the Place afforded, as by an Occasion which had like to have put a short Period to our Ramble.

Walking one Morning before the Gate of the *Louvre*, with a Design to see the *Swiss* Drawn up, which they always did, and Exercised just before they Relieved the Guards; a Page came up to me, and speaking *English* to me, Sir, says he the Captain must needs have your immediate Assistance. I that had not the knowledge of any Person in *Paris* but my own Companion, whom I called Captain, had no room to question, but it was he that sent for me; and crying out hastily to him, Where, followed the Fellow as fast as 'twas possible: he led me thro' several Passages which I knew not, and at last thro' a Tennis-Court, and into a large Room where three Men, like Gentlemen, were Engaged very briskly, two against one: the Room was very dark, so that I could not easily know them asunder; but being fully possessed with an Opinion before of my Captain's Danger, I ran into the Room with my Sword in my Hand: I had not particularly Engaged any of them, nor so much as made a Pass at any, when I received a very dangerous Thrust in my Thigh, rather occasioned by my hasty running in, than a real Design of the Person; but enraged at the Hurt, without examining who it was hurt me, I threw my self upon him, and run my Sword quite thro' his Body.

The Novelty of the Adventure, and the unexpected Fall of the Man by a Stranger come in no Body knew how, had becalmed the other two, that they really stood gazing at me. By this Time I had discovered that my Captain was not there, and that 'twas some strange Accident brought me thither. I could speak but little *French*, and supposed they could speak no *English*; so I stepped to the Door to see for the Page that brought me thither: but seeing no body there, and the Passage clear, I made off as fast as I could, without speaking a Word; nor did the other two Gentlemen offer to stop me.

But I was in a strange Confusion when coming into those Entries and Passages which the Page led me thro', I could by no means find my way out; at last seeing a Door open that looked through a House into the Street, I went in, and out at the other Door; but then I was at as great a Loss to know where I was, and which was the way to my Lodging. The Wound in my Thigh bled apace, and I could feel the Blood in my Breeches. In this Interval came by a Chair, I called, and went into it, and bid them, as well as I could, go to the *Louvre*; for tho' I knew not the Name of the Street where I lodged, I knew I could find the way to it when I was at the *Bastile*. The Chair-Men went on their own Way, and being stopp'd by a Company of the Guards as they went, set me down till the Souldiers were marched by; when looking out I found I was just at my own Lodging, and the Captain was standing at the Door looking for me; I beckoned him to me, and whispering told him I was very much hurt, but bid him pay the Chairmen, and ask no Questions but come to me.

I made the best of my Way up Stairs, but had lost so much Blood that I had hardly Spirits enough to keep me from swooning till he came in: He was equally concerned with me to see me in such a bloody Condition, and presently called up our Landlord, and he as quickly called in his Neighbours, that I had a Room full of People about me in a quarter of an Hour. But this had like to have been of worse Consequence to me than the other; for by this Time there was great enquiring after the Person who killed a Man at the Tennis-Court. My Landlord was then sensible of his Mistake, and came to me, and told me the Danger I was in, and very honestly offered to convey me to a Friend's of his, where I should be very secure; I thanked him, and suffered my self to be carried at Midnight whither he pleased; he visited me very often till I was well enough to walk about, which was not in less than ten Days, and then we thought fit to be gone, so we took Post for *Orleans*; but when I came upon the Road I found my self in a new Error, for my Wound opened again with riding, and I was in a worse Condition than before, being forced to take up at a little Village on the Road, called   about   Miles from *Orleans*, where there was no Surgeon to be had, but a sorry Country Barber, who nevertheless dressed me as well as he could, and in about a Week more I was able to walk to *Orleans* at three times.[1]

Here I staid till I was quite well, and then took Coach for *Lyons*, and so through *Savoy* into *Italy*.

I spent near two Years Time after this bad beginning in travelling through *Italy*, and to the several Courts of *Rome*, *Naples*, *Venice* and *Vienna*.

When I came to *Lyons* the King was gone from thence to *Grenoble* to meet the Cardinal, but the Queens were both at *Lyons*.

The *French* Affairs seemed at this Time to have but an indifferent Aspect; there was no Life in any Thing but where the Cardinal was, he pushed on every Thing with extraordinary Conduct, and generally with Success; he had taken *Suza* and *Pignerol* from the Duke of *Savoy*, and was preparing to push the Duke even out of all his Dominions.

But in the mean Time every where else Things looked ill; the Troops were ill paid, the Magazines empty, the People mutinous, and a general Disorder seized the Minds of the Court; and the Cardinal, who was the Soul of every Thing, desired this Interview at *Grenoble*, in order to put Things into some better Method.

This politick Minister always ordered Matters so, that if there was Success in any Thing the Glory was his; but if Things miscarried it was all laid upon the King. This Con-

duct was so much the more Nice, as it is the direct contrary
to the Custom in like Cases, where Kings assume the
Glory of all the Success in an Action; and when a Thing
miscarries make themselves easie by sacrificing their Ministers and Favourites to the Complaints and Resentments of
the People; but this accurate refined Statesman got over this
Point.

While we were at *Lyons*, and as I remember, the third
Day after our coming thither, we had like to have been
involved in a State Broil, without knowing where we were;
it was of a *Sunday* in the Evening, the People of *Lyons*, who
had been sorely oppressed in Taxes, and the War in *Italy*
pinching their Trade, began to be very tumultuous; we
found the Day before the Mob got together in great Crouds,
and talked oddly; the King was every where reviled, and
spoken disrespectfully of, and the Magistrates of the City
either winked at, or durst not attempt to meddle, lest they
should provoke the People.

But on *Sunday* Night, about Midnight, we was waked by
a prodigious Noise in the Street; I jumpt out of Bed, and
running to the Window, I saw the Street as full of Mob as
it could hold, some armed with Musquets and Halbards,
marched in very good Order; others in disorderly Crouds,
all shouting and crying out *du Paix*[1] *le Roy*, and the like:
One that led a great Party of this Rabble carried a Loaf of
Bread upon the Top of a Pike, and other lesser Loaves, sig-
nifying the Smallness of their Bread, occasioned by Dearness.

By Morning this Croud was gathered to a great Heighth,
they run roving over the whole City, shut up all the Shops,
and forced all the People to join with them from thence;
they went up to the Castle, and renewing the Clamour, a
strange Consternation seized all the Princes.

They broke open the Doors of the Officers, Collectors of
the new Taxes, and plundered their Houses, and had not the
Persons themselves fled in time they had been very ill
treated.

The Queen Mother, as she was very much displeased to

see such Consequences of the Government, in whose
Management she had no Share, so I suppose she had the
less Concern upon her. However, she came into the Court
of the Castle and shewed her self to the People, gave Money
amongst them, and spoke gently to them; and by a Way
peculiar to her self, and which obliged all she talked with,
she pacified the Mob gradually, sent them home with
Promises of Redress and the like; and so appeased this
Tumult in two Days, by her Prudence, which the Guards in
the Castle had small Mind to meddle with, and if they had,
would, in all Probability, have made the better Side the
worse.

There had been several Seditions of the like Nature in
sundry other Parts of *France*, and the very Army began to
murmur, though not to mutiny, for want of Provisions.

This Sedition at *Lyons* was not quite over when we left
the Place, for, finding the City all in a Broil, we considered
we had no Business there, and what the Consequence of a
popular Tumult might be, we did not see, so we prepared to
be gone. We had not rid above three Miles out of the City
but we were brought as Prisoners of War, by a Party of
Mutineers, who had been abroad upon the Scout, and were
charged with being Messengers sent to the Cardinal for
Forces to reduce the Citizens: With these Pretences they
brought us back in Triumph, and the Queen Mother being
by this Time grown something familiar to them, they carried
us before her.

When they enquired of us who we were, we called our
selves *Scots*; for as the *English* were very much out of Favour
in *France* at this Time, the Peace having been made not
many Months, and not supposed to be very durable, because
particularly displeasing to the People of *England*; so the
Scots were on the other Extreme with the *French*. Nothing
was so much caressed as the *Scots*, and a Man had no more
to do in *France*, if he would be well received there, than to
say he was a *Scotchman*.

When we came before the Queen Mother she seemed to

receive us with some Stiffness at first, and caused her Guards to take us into Custody; but as she was a Lady of most exquisite Politicks, she did this to amuse the Mob, and we were immediately after dismissed; and the Queen her self made a handsome Excuse to us for the Rudeness we had suffered, alledging the Troubles of the Times; and the next Morning we had three Dragoons of the Guards to convoy us out of the Jurisdiction of *Lyons*.

I confess this little Adventure gave me an Aversion to popular Tumults all my Life after, and if nothing else had been in the Cause, would have byassed me to espouse the King's Party in *England*, when our popular Heats carried all before it at home.

But I must say, that when I called to mind since the Address, the Management, the Compliance in shew, and in general the whole Conduct of the Queen Mother with the mutinous People of *Lyons*, and compared it with the Conduct of my unhappy Master the King of *England*, I could not but see that the Queen understood much better than King *Charles*, the Management of Politicks, and the Clamours of the People.

Had this Princess been at the Helm in *England*, she would have prevented all the Calamities of the Civil War here, and yet not have parted with what that good Prince yielded in order to Peace neither; she would have yielded gradually, and then gained upon them gradually; she would have managed them to the Point she had designed them, as she did all Parties in *France*; and none could effectually subject her, but the very Man she had raised to be her principal Support; I mean the Cardinal.

We went from hence to *Grenoble*, and arrived there the same Day that the King and the Cardinal, with the whole Court, went out to view a Body of 6000 *Swiss* Foot, which the Cardinal had wheedled the Cantons to grant to the King to help ruin their Neighbour the Duke of *Savoy*.

The Troops were exceeding fine, well accoutred, brave, clean-limbed, stout Fellows indeed. Here I saw the Cardinal;

there was an Air of Church Gravity in his Habit, but all the Vigor of a General, and the Sprightliness of a vast Genius in his Face; he affected a little Stiffness in his Behaviour, but managed all his Affairs with such Clearness, such Steddiness, and such Application, that it was no Wonder he had such Success in every Undertaking.

Here I saw the King, whose Figure was mean, his Countenance hollow, and always seemed dejected, and every Way discovering that Weakness in his Countenance that appeared in his Actions.

If he was ever sprightly and vigorous it was when the Cardinal was with him; for he depended so much on every Thing he did, that he was at the utmost Dilemma when he was absent, always timorous, jealous and irresolute.

After the Review the Cardinal was absent some Days, having been to wait on the Queen Mother at *Lyons*, where, as it was discoursed, they were at least seemingly reconciled.

I observed while the Cardinal was gone there was no Court, the King was seldom to be seen, very small Attendance given, and no Bustle at the Castle; but as soon as the Cardinal returned the great Councils were assembled, the Coaches of the Ambassadors went every Day to the Castle, and a Face of Business appeared upon the whole Court.

Here the Measures of the Duke of *Savoy*'s Ruine were concerted, and in Order to it the King and the Cardinal put themselves at the Head of the Army, with which they immediately reduced all *Savoy*, took *Chamberry* and the whole Dutchy except *Montmelian*.

The Army that did this was not above 22000 Men, including the *Swiss*, and but indifferent Troops neither, especially the *French* Foot, who compared to the Infantry I have since seen in the *German* and *Swedish* Armies, were not fit to be called Soldiers. On the other hand, considering the *Savoyards* and *Italian* Troops, they were good Troops; but the Cardinal's Conduct made amends for all these Deficiencies.

From hence I went to *Pignerol*, which was then little more

than a single Fortification on the Hill near the Town called
St. *Bride's*; but the Situation of that was very strong: I
mention this because of the prodigious Works since added
to it, by which it has since obtained the Name of the Right
Hand of *France*; they had begun a New Line below the Hill,
and some Works were marked out on the Side of the Town
next the Fort; but the Cardinal afterwards drew the Plan of
the Works with his own Hand, by which it was made one of
the strongest Fortresses in *Europe*.

While I was at *Pignerol* the Governor of *Milan* for the
Spaniards came with an Army and sat down before *Casal*.
The Grand Quarrel and for which the War in this Part of
Italy was begun, was this; the *Spaniards* and *Germans*
pretended to the Dutchy of *Mantua*; the Duke of *Nevers*, a
French Man, had not only a Title to it, but had got Posses-
sion of it, but being ill supported by the *French*, was beaten
out by the *Imperialists*, and after a long Siege the *Germans*
took *Mantua* it self, and drove the poor Duke quite out of the
Country.

The taking of *Mantua* elevated the Spirits of the Duke of
Savoy, and the *Germans* and *Spaniards* being now at more
Leisure, with a compleat Army came to his Assistance, and
formed the Siege of *Montferrat*.

For as the *Spaniards* pushed the Duke of *Mantua*, so the
French by Way of Diversion lay hard upon the Duke of
Savoy; they had seized *Montferrat*, and held it for the Duke
of *Mantua*, and had a strong *French* Garrison under *Thoiras*,
a brave and experienced Commander; and thus Affairs
stood when we came into the *French* Army.

I had no Business there, as a Soldier, but having passed
as a *Scotch* Gentleman with the Mob at *Lyons*, and after with
her Majesty, the Queen Mother, when we obtained the
Guard of her Dragoons; we had also her Majesty's Pass,
with which we came and went where we pleased; and the
Cardinal, who was then not on very good Terms with the
Queen, but willing to keep smooth Water there, when two
or three times our Passes came to be examined, shewed a

more than ordinary Respect to us on that very account, our Passes being from the Queen.

Casal being besieged, as I have observed, began to be in Danger, for the Cardinal, who 'twas thought had formed a Design to ruin *Savoy*, was more intent upon that than upon the Succour of the Duke of *Mantua*; but Necessity calling upon him to deliver so great a Captain as *Thoiras*, and not to let such a Place as *Casal* fall into the Hands of the Enemy, the King, or Cardinal rather, order'd the Duke of *Momorency* and the Mareschal D'*Effiat*, with 10000 Foot and 2000 Horse, to march and joyn the Mareschals *De la Force* and *Schomberg*, who lay already with an Army on the Frontiers of *Genoa*, but too weak to attempt the raising the Siege of *Casal*.

As all Men thought there would be a Battle between the *French* and the *Spaniards*, I could not prevail with my self to lose the Opportunity, and therefore by the Help of the Passes abovementioned, I came to the *French* Army under the Duke of *Momorency*; we marched through the Enemy's Country with great Boldness and no small Hazard, for the Duke of *Savoy* appeared frequently with great Bodies of Horse on the Rear of the Army, and frequently skirmished with our Troops, in one of which I had the Folly, *I can call it no better, for I had no Business there*, to go out and see the Sport, as the *French* Gentlemen called it; I was but a raw Soldier, and did not like the Sport at all, for this Party was surrounded by the Duke of *Savoy*, and almost all killed, for as to Quarter, they neither asked nor gave; I run away very fairly one of the first, and my Companion with me, and by the Goodness of our Horses got out of the Fray, and being not much known in the Army, we came into the Camp an hour or two after, as if we had been only riding abroad for the Air.

This little Rout made the General very cautious, for the *Savoyards* were stronger in Horse by 3 or 4000, and the Army always marched in a Body, and kept their Parties in or very near Hand.

I 'scaped another Rub in this *French* Army about five Days after, which had liked to have made me pay dear for my Curiosity.

The Duke *de Momorency* and the Mareschal *Schomberg* joined their Army above four or five Days after, and immediately, according to the Cardinal's Instructions, put themselves on the March for the Relief of *Casal*.

The Army had marched over a great Plain, with some marshy Grounds on the Right, and the *Po* on the Left, and as the Country was so well discovered that 'twas thought impossible any Mischief should happen, the Generals observed the less Caution. At the End of this Plain was a long Wood, and a Lane or narrow Defile thro' the Middle of it.

Thro' this Pass the Army was to march, and the Van began to file through it about four a Clock; by three Hours Time all the Army was got through, or into the Pass, and the Artillery was just entred when the Duke of *Savoy*, with 4000 Horse and 1500 Dragoons, with every Horse-man a Foot-man behind him; whether he had swam the *Po*, or passed it above at a Bridge, and made a long March after, was not examined, but he came boldly up the Plain and charged our Rear with a great deal of Fury.

Our Artillery was in the Lane, and as it was impossible to turn them about, and make way for the Army, so the Rear was obliged to support themselves, and maintain the Fight for above an Hour and a half.

In this Time we lost abundance of Men, and if it had not been for two Accidents all that Line had been cut off; one was, that the Wood was so near that those Regiments which were disordered presently sheltred themselves in the Wood; the other was, that by this Time the Mareschal *Schomberg*, with the Horse of the Van, began to get back through the Lane, and to make good the Ground from whence the other had been beaten, till at last by this Means it came to almost a pitched Battle.

There were two Regiments of *French* Dragoons who did

excellent Service in this Action, and maintained their Ground till they were almost all killed.

Had the Duke of *Savoy* contented himself with the Defeat of five Regiments on the Right, which he quite broke and drove into the Wood, and with the Slaughter and Havock which he had made among the rest, he had come off with Honour, and might have called it a Victory; but endeavouring to break the whole Party, and carry off some Cannon, the obstinate Resistance of these few Dragoons lost him his Advantages, and held him in play till so many fresh Troops got through the Pass again, as made us too strong for him; and had not Night parted them he had been entirely defeated.

At last finding our Troops encrease and spread themselves on his Flank, he retired and gave over, we had no great Stomach to pursue him neither, tho' some Horse were ordered to follow a little Way.

The Duke lost above a thousand Men, and we almost twice as many, and but for those Dragoons, had lost the whole Rear-guard and half our Cannon. I was in a very sorry Case in this Action too, I was with the Rear in the Regiment of Horse of *Perigoort*, with a Captain of which Regiment I had contracted some Acquaintance; I would have rid off at first, as the Captain desired me, but there was no doing it, for the Cannon was in the Lane, and the Horse and Dragoons of the Van eagerly pressing back through the Lane, must have run me down, or carried me with them: As for the Wood, it was a good Shelter to save ones Life, but was so thick there was no passing it on Horseback.

Our Regiment was one of the first that was broke, and being all in Confusion, with the Duke of *Savoy*'s Men at our Heels, away we ran into the Wood; never was there so much Disorder among a Parcel of Runaways as when we came to this Wood, it was so exceeding bushy and thick at the Bottom there was no entring it, and a Volley of small Shot from a Regiment of *Savoy*'s Dragoons poured in upon us at our breaking into the Wood made terrible Work among our Horses.

For my Part I was got into the Wood, but was forced to quit my Horse, and by that means with a great deal of Difficulty got a little farther in, where there was a little open Place, and being quite spent with labouring among the Bushes, I sat down resolving to take my Fate there, let it be what it would, for I was not able to go any farther; I had twenty or thirty more in the same Condition came to me in less than half an Hour, and here we waited very securely the Success of the Battle, which was as before.

It was no small Relief to those with me to hear the *Savoyards* were beaten, for otherwise they had all been lost; as for me, I confess, I was glad as it was, because of the Danger, but otherwise I cared not much which had the better, for I designed no Service among them.

One Kindness it did me, that I began to consider what I had to do here, and as I could give but a very slender Account of my self for what it was I run all these Risques, so I resolved they should fight it out among themselves, for I would come among them no more.

The Captain with whom, as I noted above, I had contracted some Acquaintance in this Regiment, was killed in this Action, and the *French* had really a great Blow here, though they took Care to conceal it all they could; and I cannot, without smiling, read some of the Histories and Memoirs of this Action, which they are not ashamed to call a Victory.

We marched on to *Saluces*, and the next Day the Duke of *Savoy* presented himself in Batallia on the other Side of a small River giving us a fair Challenge to pass and engage him: We always said in our Camp that the Orders were to fight the Duke of *Savoy* where-ever we met him; but tho' he braved us in our View, we did not care to engage him, but we brought *Saluces* to surrender upon Articles, which the Duke could not relieve without attacking our Camp, which he did not care to do.

The next Morning we had News of the Surrender of *Mantua* to the *Imperial* Army; we heard of it first from the

Duke of *Savoy*'s Cannon, which he fired by way of Rejoycing, and which seemed to make him Amends for the loss of *Saluces*.[1]

As this was a Mortification to the *French*, so it quite damped the Success of the Campaign, for the Duke *de Momorency* imagining that the *Imperial* General would send immediate Assistance to the Marquis *Spinola*, who besieged *Casal*, they call'd frequent Councils of War what Course to take, and at last resolved to halt in *Piedmont*.

A few Days after their Resolutions were changed again, by the News of the Death of the Duke of *Savoy*, *Charles Emanuel*, who died, as some say, agitated with the Extreams of Joy and Grief.

This put our Generals upon considering again, whether they should march to the Relief of *Casal*, but the Chimera of the *Germans* put them by, and so they took up Quarters in *Piedmont*; they took several small Places from the Duke of *Savoy*, making Advantage of the Consternation the Duke's Subjects were in on the Death of their Prince,[2] and spread themselves from the Sea-side to the Banks of the *Po*.

But here an Enemy did that for them which the *Savoyards* could not, for the Plague got into their Quarters and destroyed abundance of People, both of the Army and of the Country.

I thought then it was Time for me to be gone, for I had no manner of Courage for that Risque; and I think verily I was more afraid of being taken sick in a strange Country, than ever I was of being killed in Battle. Upon this Resolution I procured a Pass to go for *Genoa*, and acordingly began my Journey, but was arrested at *Villa Franca* by a slow lingring Fever, which held me about five Days, and then turned to a burning Malignancy, and at last to the Plague:[3] My Friend, the Captain, never left me Night nor Day; and though for four Days more I knew no Body, nor was capable of so much as thinking of my self, yet it pleased God that the Distemper gathered in my Neck, swelled and broke; during the Swelling I was raging mad with the Violence of

Pain, which being so near my Head, swelled that also in Proportion, that my Eyes were swelled up, and for twenty four Hours my Tongue and Mouth; then, as my Servant told me, all the Physicians gave me over, as past all Remedy, but by the good Providence of God the Swelling broke.

The prodigious Collection of Matter which this Swelling discharged, gave me immediate Relief, and I became sensible in less than an Hour's Time; and in two Hours, or thereabouts, fell into a little Slumber which recovered my Spirits, and sensibly revived me. Here I lay by it till the Middle of *September*, my Captain fell sick after me, but recovered quickly; his Man had the Plague, and died in two Days; my Man held it out well.

About the Middle of *September* we heard of a Truce[1] concluded between all Parties, and being unwilling to winter at *Villa Franca*, I got Passes, and though we were both but weak began to travel in Litters for *Milan*.

And here I experienced the Truth of an old *English* Proverb,[2] *That Standers-by see more than the Gamesters.*

The *French*, *Savoyards* and *Spaniards* made this Peace or Truce all for separate and several Grounds, and every one were mistaken.

The *French* yielded to it because they had given over the Relief of *Casal*, and were very much afraid it would fall into the Hands of the Marquiss *Spinola*. The *Savoyards* yielded to it because they were afraid the *French* would winter in *Piedmont*; the *Spaniards* yielded to it because the Duke of *Savoy* being dead, and the Count *de Colalto*, the *Imperial* General, giving no Assistance, and his Army weakened by Sickness and the Fatigues of the Siege, he foresaw he should never take the Town, and wanted but to come off with Honour.

The *French* were mistaken, because really *Spinola* was so weak, that had they marched on into *Montferrat* the *Spaniards* must have raised the Siege; the Duke of *Savoy* was mistaken, because the Plague had so weakened the *French* that they durst not have staid to winter in *Piedmont*; and *Spinola* was mistaken, for tho' he was very slow, if he had staid before the Town one Fortnight longer *Thoiras* the Governour must have surrendred, being brought to the last Extremity.

Of all these Mistakes the *French* had the Advantage, for *Casal* was relieved, the Army had Time to be recruited, and the *French* had the best of it by an early Campaign.

I past through *Montferrat* in my Way to *Milan* just as the Truce was declared, and saw the miserable Remains of the *Spanish* Army, who by Sickness, Fatigue, hard Duty, the Sallies of the Garrison, and such like Consequences, were reduced to less than 2000 Men, and of them above 1000 lay wounded and sick in the Camp.

Here were several Regiments which I saw drawn out to their Arms that could not make up above 70 or 80 Men, Officers and all, and those half starved with Hunger, almost naked, and in a lamentable Condition. From thence I went into the Town, and there Things were still in a worse Condition, the Houses beaten down, the Walls and Works ruined, the Garrison, by continual Duty, reduced from 4500 Men to less than 800, without Clothes, Money, or Provisions. The brave Governour weak with continual Fatigue, and the whole Face of things in a miserable Case.

The *French* Generals had just sent them Thirty Thousand Crowns for present Supply, which heartened them a little, but had not the Truce been made as it was, they must have surrendred upon what Terms the *Spaniards* had pleased to make them.

Never were two Armies in such Fear of one another with so little Cause; the *Spaniards* afraid of the *French* whom the Plague had devoured, and the *French* afraid of the *Spaniards* whom the Siege had almost ruined.

The Grief of this Mistake, together with the Sense of his Master, the *Spaniards*, leaving him without Supplies to compleat the Siege of *Casal*, so affected the Marquess *Spinola* that he died for Grief, and in him fell the last of that rare breed of *Low Country* Soldiers who gave the World so great and just a Character of the *Spanish* Infantry as the best

Soldiers of the World; a Character which we see them so very much degenerated from since, that they hardly deserve the Name of Soldiers.

I tarried at *Milan* the rest of the Winter, both for the Recovery of my Health, and also for Supplies from *England*.

Here it was I first heard the Name of *Gustavus Adolphus*, the King of *Sweden*, who now began his War with the Emperor; and while the King of *France* was at *Lyons*, the League[1] with *Sweden* was made, in which the *French* contributed 1200000 Crowns in Money, and 600000 *per An.* to the Attempt of *Gustavus Adolphus*: About this Time he landed in *Pomerania*, took the Towns of *Stetin*[2] and *Straelsund*, and from thence proceeded in that prodigious Manner, of which I shall have Occasion to be very particular in the Prosecution of these Memoirs.

I had indeed no Thoughts of seeing that King, or his Armies, I had been so roughly handled already that I had given over the Thoughts of appearing among the fighting People, and resolved in the Spring to pursue my Journey to *Venice*, and so for the rest of *Italy*.

Yet I cannot deny, that as every Gazette gave us some Accounts of the Conquests and Victories of this glorious Prince, it prepossessed my Thoughts with secret Wishes of seeing him, but these were so young and unsettled, that I drew no Resolutions from them for a long while after.

About the Middle of *January* I left *Milan* and came to *Genoa*, from thence by Sea to *Leghorn*, then to *Naples*, *Rome* and *Venice*, but saw nothing in *Italy* that gave me any Diversion.

As for what is modern, I saw nothing but Lewdness, private Murthers, stabbing Men at the Corner of a Street, or in the dark, hiring of Bravoes, and the like; all the Diversions here ended in Whoring, Gaming and Sodomy, these were to me the modern Excellencies of *Italy*; and I had no Gust[3] to Antiquities.

'Twas pleasant indeed when I was at *Rome* to say here stood the Capitol, there the Colossus of *Nero*, here was the

Amphitheatre of *Titus*, there the Aqueduct of——here the Forum, there the Catacombs, here the Temple of *Venus*, there of *Jupiter*, here the Pantheon, and the like; but I never designed to write a Book, as much as was useful I kept in my Head; and for the rest, I left it to others.

I observed the People degenerated from the ancient glorious Inhabitants, who were generous, brave, and the most valiant of all Nations, to a vicious Baseness of Soul, barbarous, treacherous, jealous and revengeful, lewd and cowardly, intolerably proud and haughty, bigotted to blind, incoherent Devotion, and the grossest of Idolatry.

Indeed I think the Unsuitableness of the People made the Place unpleasant to me, for there is so little in a Country to recommend it when the People disgrace it, that no Beauties of the Creation can make up for the Want of those Excellencies which suitable Society procure the Defect of; this made *Italy* a very unpleasant Country to me, the People were the Foil to the Place, all manner of hateful Vices reigning in their general Way of living.

I confess I was not very religious my self, and being come abroad into the World young enough, might easily have been drawn into Evils that had recommended themselves with any tolerable Agreeableness to Nature and common Manners; but when Wickedness presented it self full grown in its grossest Freedoms and Liberties, it quite took away all the Gust to Vice that the Devil had furnished me with, and in this I cannot but relate one Scene which passed between no Body but the Devil and my self.

At a certain Town in *Italy*, which shall be nameless, because I won't celebrate the Proficiency of one Place more than another, when I believe the whole Country equally wicked, I was prevailed upon rather than tempted, *a la Courtezan*.

If I should describe the Woman I must give a very mean Character of my own Virtue to say I was allured by any but a Woman of an extraordinary Figure; her Face, Shape, Mein, and Dress, I may, without Vanity, say, the finest that

I ever saw: When I had Admittance into her Apartments, the Riches and Magnificence of them astonished me, the Cupboard or Cabinet of Plate, the Jewels, the Tapestry, and every Thing in Proportion, made me question whether I was not in the Chamber of some Lady of the best Quality;—— but when after some Conversation I found that it was really nothing but a Courtezan, in *English*, a common Street Whore, a Punk of the Trade, I was amazed, and my Inclination to her Person began to cool; her Conversation exceeded, if possible, the best of Quality, and was, I must own, exceeding agreeable; she sung to her Lute, and danced as fine as ever I saw, and thus diverted me two Hours before any Thing else was discoursed of;—but when the vicious Part came on the Stage, I blush to relate the Confusion I was in, and when she made a certain Motion by which I understood she might be made use of, either as a Lady, or as—I was quite Thunder-struck, all the vicious Part of my Thoughts vanished, the Place filled me with Horror, and I was all over Disorder and Distraction.

I began however to recollect where I was, and that in this Country these were People not to be affronted; and though she easily saw the Disorder I was in, she turned it off with admirable Dexterity, began to talk again *a la Gallant*, received me as a Visitant, offered me Sweetmeats and some Wine.

Here I began to be in more Confusion than before, for I concluded she would neither offer me to eat or to drink now *without Poison*, and I was very shy of tasting her Treat, but she scattered this Fear immediately, by readily, and of her own accord, not only tasting but eating freely of every Thing she gave me; whether she perceived my Wariness, or the Reason of it, I know not, I could not help banishing my Suspicion, the obliging Carriage and strange Charm of her Conversation had so much Power of me, that I both eat and drank with her at all Hazards.

When I offered to go, and at parting presented her five Pistoles, I could not prevail with her to take them, when she spoke some *Italian* Proverb which I could not readily understand, but by my Guess it seemed to imply, that *she would not take the Pay, having not obliged me otherwise*: At last I laid the Pieces on her Toilet, and would not receive them again; upon which she obliged me to pass my Word to visit her again, else she would by no Means accept my Present.

I confess I had a strong Inclination to visit her again, and besides thought my self obliged to it in Honour to my Parole; but after some Strife in my Thoughts about it, I resolved to break my Word with her, when going at Vespers one Evening to see their Devotions, I happened to meet this very Lady very devoutly going to her Prayers.

At her coming out of the Church I spoke to her, she paid me her Respects with a *Seignior Inglese*, and some Words she said in *Spanish* smiling, which I did not understand; I cannot say here so clearly as I would be glad I might, that I broke my Word with her; but if I saw her any more I saw nothing of what gave me so much Offence before.

The End of my relating this Story is answered in describing the Manner of their Address, without bringing my self to Confession; if I did any Thing I have some Reason to be ashamed of, it may be a less Crime to conceal it than expose it.

The Particulars related however, may lead the Reader of these Sheets to a View of what gave me a particular Disgust at this pleasant Part of the World, as they pretend to call it, and made me quit the Place sooner than Travellers use to do that come thither to satisfy their Curiosity.

The prodigious stupid Bigottry of the People also was irksome to me; I thought there was something in it very sordid, the entire Empire the Priests have over both the Souls and Bodies of the People, gave me a Specimen of that Meanness of Spirit which is no where else to be seen but in *Italy*, especially in the City of *Rome*.

At *Venice* I perceived it quite different, the Civil Authority having a visible Superiority over the Ecclesiastick; and the Church being more subject there to the State than in any other Part of *Italy*.

For these Reasons I took no Pleasure in filling my Memoirs of *Italy* with Remarks of Places or Things, all the Antiquities and valuable Remains of the *Roman* Nation are done better than I can pretend to by such People who made it more their Business; as for me, I went to see, and not to write, and as little thought then of these Memoirs, as I ill furnished my self to write them.

I left *Italy* in *April*, and taking the Tour of *Bavaria*, though very much out of the Way, I passed through *Munick*, *Passaw*, *Lints*, and at last to *Vienna*.

I came to *Vienna* the 10th of *April* 1631, intending to have gone from thence down the *Danube* into *Hungary*, and by Means of a Pass which I had obtained from the *English* Ambassador[1] at *Constantinople*, I designed to have seen all those great Towns on the *Danube* which were then in the Hands of the *Turks*, and which I had read much of in the History of the War between the *Turks* and the *Germans*; but I was diverted from my Design by the following Occasion.

There had been a long bloody War in the Empire of *Germany* for 12 Years, between the Emperor, the Duke of *Bavaria*, the King of *Spain*, and the Popish Princes and Electors on the one Side, and the Protestant Princes on the other; and both Sides having been exhausted by the War, and even the Catholicks themselves beginning to dislike the growing Power of the House of *Austria*, 'twas thought all Parties were willing to make Peace.

Nay, Things were brought to that Pass that some of the Popish Princes and Electors began to talk of making Alliances with the King of *Sweden*.

Here it is necessary to observe, that the two Dukes of *Mecklenburgh* having been dispossessed of most of their Dominions by the Tyranny of the Emperor *Ferdinand*, and being in danger of losing the rest, earnestly sollicited the King of *Sweden* to come to their Assistance; and that Prince, as he was related to the House of *Mecklenburgh*,[2] and especially as he was willing to lay hold of any Opportunity to break with the Emperor, against whom he had laid up an implacable Prejudice, was very ready and forward to come to their Assistance.

The Reasons of his Quarrel with the Emperor were grounded upon the *Imperialists* concerning themselves in the War of *Poland*, where the Emperor had sent 8000 Foot and 2000 Horse to join the *Polish* Army against the King, and had thereby given some Check to his Arms in that War.

In Pursuance therefore of his Resolution to quarrel with the Emperor, but more particularly at the Instance of the Princes above-named, his *Swedish* Majesty had landed the Year before at *Straelsund* with about 12000 Men, and having joined with some Forces which he had left in *Polish Prussia*, all which did not make 30000 Men, he began a War with the Emperor, the greatest in Event, filled with the most famous Battles, Sieges and extraordinary Actions, including its wonderful Success and happy Conclusion, of any War ever maintained in the World.

The King of *Sweden* had already taken *Stetin*, *Straelsund*, *Rostock*, *Wismar*, and all the strong Places on the *Baltick*, and began to spread himself in *Germany*; he had made a League with the *French*, as I observed in my Story of *Saxony*, he had now made a Treaty[1] with the Duke of *Brandenburg*, and, in short, began to be terrible to the Empire.

In this Conjuncture the Emperor called the General Diet of the Empire to be held at *Ratisbon*, where, as was pretended, all Sides were to treat of Peace and to join Forces to beat the *Swedes* out of the Empire. Here the Emperor, by a most exquisite Management, brought the Affairs of the Diet to a Conclusion, exceedingly to his own Advantage and to the farther Oppression of the Protestants; and in particular, in that the War against the King of *Sweden* was to be carried on in such Manner as that the whole Burthen and Charge would lie on the Protestants themselves, and they be made the Instruments to oppose their best Friends. Other Matters also ended equally to their Disadvantage, as the Methods resolved on to recover the Church-Lands, and to prevent

the Education of the Protestant Clergy; and what remained
was referred to another General Diet to be held at *Frankfort
au Main*, in *August* 1631.

I won't pretend to say the other Protestant Princes of
Germany had never made any Overtures to the King of
Sweden to come to their Assistance, but 'tis plain they had
entred into no League with him; that appears from the
Difficulties which retarded the fixing the Treaties afterward,
both with the Dukes of *Brandenburgh* and *Saxony* which
unhappily occasioned the Ruine of *Magdenburgh*.

But 'tis Plain the *Swede* was resolved on a War with the
Emperor; his *Swedish* Majesty might and indeed could not
but foresee that if he once shewed himself with a sufficient
Force on the Frontiers of the Empire, all the Protestant
Princes would be obliged by their Interest or by his Arms to
fall in with him, and this the Consequence made appear to
be a just Conclusion; for the Electors of *Brandenburgh* and
Saxony were both forced to join with him.

First, They were willing to join with him, at least they
could not find in their Hearts to join with the Emperor, of
whose Power they had such just Apprehensions; they
wished the *Swedes* Success, and would have been very glad
to have had the Work done at another Man's Charge; but
like true *Germans* they were more willing to be saved than to
save themselves, and therefore hung back and stood upon
Terms.

Secondly, They were at last forced to it; the first was forced
to join by the King of *Sweden* himself, who being come so far
was not to be dallied with; and had not the Duke of *Brandenburgh* complied as he did, he had been ruined by the *Swede*;
the *Saxon* was driven into the Arms of the *Swede* by Force,
for Count *Tilly* Ravaging his Country made him comply
with any Terms to be saved from Destruction.

Thus Matters stood at the End of the Diet at *Ratisbon*; the
King of *Sweden* began to see himself leagued against at the
Diet both by Protestant and Papist; and, *as I have often
heard his Majesty say since*, he had resolved to try to force

them off from the Emperor, and to treat them as Enemies equally with the Rest if they did not.

But the Protestants convinced him soon after, that tho' they were tricked into the outward Appearance of a League against him at *Ratisbon*, they had no such Intentions; and by their Ambassadors to him let him know, that they only wanted his powerful Assistance to defend their Councils, when they would soon convince him that they had a due Sense of the Emperor's Designs, and would do their utmost for their Liberty; and these I take to be the first Invitations the King of *Sweden* had to undertake the Protestant Cause as such, and which entitled him to say he fought for the Liberty and Religion of the *German* Nation.

I have had some particular Opportunities to hear these Things from the Mouths of some of the very Princes themselves, and therefore am the forwarder to relate them; and I place them here, because previous to the part I acted on this bloody Scene, 'tis necessary to let the Reader into some Part of the Story, and to shew him in what Manner and on what Occasions this terrible War began.

The Protestants, alarmed at the Usage they had met with at the former Diet, had secretly proposed among themselves to form a general Union or Confederacy, for preventing that Ruin which they saw, unless some speedy Remedies were applied, would be inevitable. The Elector of *Saxony*, the Head of the Protestants, a vigorous and politick Prince, was the first that moved it; and the Landgrave of *Hesse*, a zealous and gallant Prince, being consulted with, it rested a great while between those two, no Method being found practicable to bring it to pass; the Emperor being so powerful in all Parts, that they foresaw the petty Princes would not dare to negotiate an Affair of such a Nature, being surrounded with the *Imperial* Forces, who by their two Generals, *Wallestein* and *Tilly*, kept them in continual Subjection and Terror.

This Dilemma had like to have stifled the Thoughts of the Union as a Thing impracticable, when one *Seigensius*,[1] a *Lutheran* Minister, a Person of great Abilities, and one whom the Elector of *Saxony* made great Use of in Matters of Policy as well as Religion, contrived for them this excellent Expedient.

I had the Honour to be acquainted with this Gentleman while I was at *Leipsick*; it pleased him exceedingly to have been the Contriver of so fine a Structure as the *Conclusions of Leipsick*, and he was glad to be entertained on that Subject; I had the Relation from his own Mouth, when, but very modestly, he told me he thought 'twas an Inspiration darted on a sudden into his Thoughts, when the Duke of *Saxony* calling him into his Closet one Morning, with a Face full of Concern, shaking his Head and looking very earnestly, *What will become of us, Doctor?* said the Duke, *we shall all be undone at* Frankfort au Main. *Why so, please your Highness?* says the Doctor, *Why they will fight with the King of* Sweden *with our Armies and our Money*, says the Duke, *and devour our Friends and our selves, by the help of our Friends and our selves: But what is become of the Confederacy then*, said the Doctor, *which your Highness had so happily framed in your Thoughts, and which the Landgrave of* Hesse *was so pleased with? Become of it*, says the Duke, *'tis a good Thought enough, but 'tis impossible to bring it to pass among so many Members of the Protestant Princes as are to be consulted with, for we neither have Time to treat, nor will half of them dare to negotiate the Matter, the* Imperialists *being quarter'd in their very Bowels. But may not some Expedient be found out*, says the Doctor, *to bring them all together to treat of it in a General Meeting? 'Tis well proposed*, says the Duke, *but in what Town or City shall they assemble where the very Deputies shall not be besieged by* Tilly *or* Wallestein *in* 14 *Days Time, and sacrificed to the Cruelty and Fury of the Emperor* Ferdinand? *Will your Highness be the easier in it*, replies the Doctor, *if a way may be found out to call such an Assembly upon other Causes, at which the Emperor may have no Umbrage, and perhaps gives his Assent? You know the Diet at* Frankfort *is at Hand; 'tis necessary the Protestants should have an Assembly of their own, to prepare Matters for the General Diet, and it may be no difficult Matter to obtain it.* The Duke, surprized with Joy at the Motion, embraced the Doctor with an extraordinary Transport, *Thou hast done it, Doctor*, said he, and immediately caused him to draw a Form of a Letter to the Emperor, which he did with the utmost Dexterity of Style, in which he was a great Master, representing to his *Imperial* Majesty, that in order to put an End to the Troubles of *Germany*, his Majesty would be pleased to permit the Protestant Princes of the Empire to hold a Diet to themselves, to consider of such Matters as they were to treat of at the General Diet, in order to conform themselves to the Will and Pleasure of his *Imperial* Majesty, to drive out Foreigners, and settle a lasting Peace in the Empire; he also insinuated something of their Resolutions unanimously to give their Suffrages in favour of the King of *Hungary* at the Election of a King of the *Romans*, a thing which he knew the Emperor had in his Thought, and would push at with all his Might at the Diet. This Letter was sent, and the Bait so neatly concealed, that the Electors of *Bavaria* and *Mentz*, the King of *Hungary*, and several of the Popish Princes, not foreseeing that the Ruin of them all lay in the bottom of it, foolishly advised the Emperor to consent to it.

In consenting to this the Emperor signed his own Destruction, for here began the Conjunction of the *German* Protestants with the *Swede*, which was the fatalest blow to *Ferdinand*, and which he could never recover.

Accordingly the Diet was held at *Leipsick, Feb.* 8, 1630, where the Protestants agreed on several Heads for their mutual Defence, which were the Grounds of the following War; these were *the Famous Conclusions of Leipsick*, which so alarmed the Emperor and the whole Empire, that to crush it in the Beginning, the Emperor commanded Count *Tilly* immediately to fall upon the Landgrave of *Hesse*, and the Duke of *Saxony*, as the principal Heads of the Union; but it was too late.

The Conclusions were digested into ten Heads;
   1. That since their Sins had brought God's Judgments

upon the whole Protestant Church, they should command Publick Prayers to be made to Almighty God for the diverting the Calamities that attended them.

2. That a Treaty of Peace might be set on Foot, in order to come to a right Understanding with the Catholick Princes.

3. That a Time for such a Treaty being obtained, they should appoint an Assembly of Delegates to meet preparatory to the Treaty.

4. That all their Complaints should be humbly represented to his *Imperial* Majesty, and the Catholick Electors, in order to a peaceable Accommodation.

5. That they claim the Protection of the Emperor, according to the Laws of the Empire, and the present Emperor's solemn Oath and Promise.

6. That they would appoint Deputies who should meet at certain Times to consult of their common Interest, and who should be always empoured to conclude of what should be thought needful for their Safety.

7. That they will raise a competent Force to maintain and defend their Liberties, Rights and Religion.

8. That it is agreeable to the Constitution of the Empire, concluded in the Diet at *Ausburg* to do so.

9. That the arming for their necessary Defence shall by no Means hinder their Obedience to his *Imperial* Majesty, but that they will still continue their Loyalty to him.

10. They agree to Proportion their Forces, which in all amounted to 70000 Men.

The Emperor, exceedingly startled at the Conclusions, issued out a severe Proclamation or Ban against them, which imported much the same Thing as a Declaration of War, and commanded *Tilly* to begin, and immediately to fall on the Duke of *Saxony* with all the Fury imaginable, as I have already observed.

Here began the Flame to break out; for upon the Emperor's Ban, the Protestants send away to the King of *Sweden* for Succour.

His *Swedish* Majesty had already conquered *Mecklenburgh*, and Part of *Pomerania*, and was advancing with his victorious Troops, encreased by the Addition of some Regiments raised in those Parts, in order to carry on the War against the Emperor, having designed to follow up the *Oder* into *Silesia*, and so to push the War home to the Emperor's Hereditary Countries of *Austria* and *Bohemia*, when the first Messengers came to him in this Case; but this changed his Measures, and brought him to the Frontiers of *Brandenburgh*, resolved to answer the Desires of the Protestants: But here the Duke of *Brandenburgh* began to halt, making some Difficulties and demanding Terms which drove the King to use some Extremities with him, and stopt the *Swedes* for a while, who had otherwise been on the Banks of the *Elbe*, as soon as *Tilly* the *Imperial* General had entred *Saxony*, which if they had done, the miserable Destruction of *Magdenburgh* had been prevented, as I observed before.

The King had been invited into the Union, and when he first came back from the Banks of the *Oder* he had accepted it, and was preparing to back it with all his Power.

The Duke of *Saxony* had already a good Army, which he had with infinite Diligence recruited, and mustered them under the Cannon of *Leipsick*. The King of *Sweden* having, by his Ambassador at *Leipsick*, entred into the Union of the Protestants, was advancing victoriously to their Aid, just as Count *Tilly* had enter'd the Duke of *Saxony*'s Dominions. The Fame of the *Swedish* Conquests, and of the Hero who commanded them, shook my Resolution of travelling into *Turkey*, being resolved to see the Conjunction of the Protestants Armies, and before the Fire was broke out too far to take the Advantage of seeing both sides.

While I remained at *Vienna*, uncertain which Way I should proceed, I remember I observed they talked of the King of *Sweden* as a Prince of no Consideration, one that they might let go on and tire himself in *Mecklenbergh*, and thereabout, till they could find Leisure to deal with him, and then might be crushed as they pleased; but as 'tis never safe to despise an Enemy, so this was not an Enemy to be *despised*, as they afterwards found.

As to the Conclusions of *Leipsick*, indeed at first they gave the *Imperial* Court some Uneasiness, but when they found the *Imperial* Armies began to fright the Members out of the Union, and that the several Branches had no considerable Forces on Foot, it was the general Discourse at *Vienna*, that the Union at *Leipsick* only gave the Emperor an Opportunity to crush absolutely the Dukes of *Saxony*, *Brandenburgh*, and the Landgrave of *Hesse*, and they looked upon it as a Thing certain.

I never saw any real Concern in their Faces at *Vienna*, 'till News came to Court that the King of *Sweden* had entered into the Union; but as this made them very uneasie, they began to move the powerfullest Methods possible to divert this Storm; and upon this News *Tilly*[1] was hastened to fall into *Saxony* before this Union could proceed to a Conjunction of Forces. This was certainly a very good Resolution, and no Measure could have been more exactly concerted had not the Diligence of the *Saxons* prevented it.

The gathering of this Storm, which from a Cloud began to spread over the Empire, and from the little Dutchy of *Mecklenburgh* began to threaten all *Germany*, absolutely determined me, as I noted before, as to travelling; and laying aside the Thoughts of *Hungary*, I resolved, if possible, to see the King of *Sweden*'s Army.

I parted from *Vienna* the middle of *May*, and took post for *Great Glogau* in *Silesia*, as if I had purposed to pass into *Poland*, but designing indeed to go down the *Oder* to *Custrin* in the Marquisate of *Brandenburgh*, and so to *Berlin*; but when I came to the Frontiers of *Silesia*, tho' I had Passes I could go no farther, the Guards on all the Frontiers were so strict; so I was obliged to come back into *Bohemia*, and went to *Prague*.

From hence I found I could easily pass through the *Imperial* Provinces to the *Lower Saxony*, and accordingly took Passes for *Hamburgh*, designing however to use them no farther than I found Occasion.

By Virtue of these Passes I got into the *Imperial* Army, under Count *Tilly*, then at the Siege of *Magdenburgh*, *May* the 2d.

I confess I did not foresee the Fate of this City, neither I believe did County *Tilly* himself expect to glut his Fury with so entire a Desolation, much less did the People expect it. I did believe they must capitulate, and I perceived by Discourse in the Army, that *Tilly* would give them but very indifferent Conditions; but it fell out otherwise; the Treaty of Surrender was as it were begun, nay some say concluded, when some of the Out-guards of the *Imperialists* finding the Citizens had abandoned the Guards of the Works, and looked to themselves with less Diligence than usual, they broke in, carried an Half-Moon Sword in Hand with little Resistance; and tho' it was a Surprize on both Sides, the Citizens neither fearing, nor the Army expecting the Occasion, the Garrison, with as much Resolution as could be expected under such a Fright, flew to the Walls, twice beat the *Imperialists* off, but fresh Men coming up, and the Administrator of *Magdenburgh*[1] himself being wounded and taken, the Enemy broke in, took the City by Storm, and entred with such terrible Fury, that without Respect to Age or Condition, they put all the Garrison and Inhabitants, Man, Woman and Child, to the Sword, plundered the City, and when they had done this, set it on Fire.

This Calamity sure was the dreadfullest Sight that ever I saw; the Rage of the *Imperial* Soldiers was most intolerable, and not to be expressed; of 25000, some said 30000 People, there was not a Soul to be seen alive, till the Flames drove those that were hid in Vaults and secret Places to seek Death in the Streets, rather than perish in the Fire: Of these miserable Creatures some were killed too by the furious Soldiers, but at last they saved the Lives of such as came out of their Cellars and Holes, and so about 2000 poor desperate Creatures were left: The exact Number of those that perished in this City could never be known, because those the Soldiers had first butcher'd, the Flames afterwards devour'd.

I was on the other Side the *Elbe* when this dreadful Piece of Butchery was done; the City of *Magdenburgh* had a Sconce or Fort over against it, called the Toll-House, which joined to the City by a very fine Bridge of Boats.

This Fort was taken by the *Imperialists* a few Days before, and having a Mind to see it, and the rather because from thence I could have a very good View of the City, I was gone over *Tilly's* Bridge of Boats to view this Fort; about 10 a Clock in the Morning I perceived they were storming by the firing, and immediately all ran to the Works, I little thought of the taking the City, but imagined it might be some Out-work attacked, for we all expected the City would surrender that Day, or next, and they might have capitulated upon very good Terms.

Being upon the Works of the Fort, on a sudden I heard the dreadfullest Cry raised in the City that can be imagined, 'tis not possible to express the Manner of it, and I could see the Women and Children running about the Streets in a most lamentable Condition.

The City Wall did not run along the Side where the River was with so great a Heighth but we could plainly see the Market-Place and the several Streets which run down to the River: In about an Hour's Time after this first Cry all was Confusion; there was little shooting, the Execution was all cutting of Throats and meer House Murthers; the resolute Garrison, with the brave Baron *Falconberg*, fought it out to the last, and were cut in Pieces, and by this Time the *Imperial* Soldiers having broke open the Gates and entred on all Sides, the Slaughter was very dreadful, we could see the poor People in Crowds driven down the Streets, flying from the Fury of the Soldiers who followed butchering them as fast as they could, and refused Mercy to any Body; 'till driving them to the River's Edge, the desperate Wretches would throw themselves into the River, where Thousands of them perished, especially Women and Children; several

Men that could swim got over to our Side, where the Soldiers not heated with Fight gave them Quarter, and took them up, and I cannot but do this Justice to the *German* Officers in the Fort, they had five small flat Boats, and they gave leave to the Soldiers to go off in them, and get what Booty they could, but charged them not to kill any Body, but take them all Prisoners.

Nor was their Humanity ill rewarded, for the Soldiers wisely avoiding those Places where their Fellows were employed in the butchering the miserable People, rowed to other Places, where Crouds of People stood crying out for help, and expecting to be every Minute either drowned or murdered; of these at sundry Times they fetched over near Six hundred, but took Care to take in none but such as offered them good Pay.

Never was Money or Jewels of greater Service than now, for those that had any Thing of that sort to offer were soonest helped.

There was a Burgher of the Town, who seeing a Boat coming near him, but out of his Call, by the help of a speaking Trumpet, told the Soldiers in it he would give them 20000 Dollers to fetch him off; they rowed close to the Shore, and got him with his Wife and six Children into the Boat, but such Throngs of People got about the Boat that had like to have sunk her, so that the Soldiers were fain to drive a great many out again by main Force, and while they were doing this, some of the Enemies coming down the Street desperately drove them all into the Water.

The Boat however brought the Burgher and his Wife and Children safe, and though they had not all that Wealth about them, yet in Jewels and Money he gave them so much as made all the Fellows very rich.

I cannot pretend to describe the Cruelty of this Day, the Town by five in the Afternoon was all on a Flame; the Wealth consumed was inestimable, and a Loss to the very Conqueror. I think there was little or nothing left but the great Church, and about 100 Houses.

This was a sad Welcome into the Army for me, and gave me a Horror and Aversion to the Emperor's People, as well as to his Cause. I quitted the Camp the third Day after this Execution, while the Fire was hardly out in the City; and from thence getting safe Conduct to pass into the *Palatinate*, I turned out of the Road at a small Village on the *Elbe*, called *Emerfield*, and by Ways and Town I can give but small Account of, having a Boor for our Guide, who we could hardly understand. I arrived at *Leipsick* on the 17th of *May*.

We found the Elector intense upon the strengthening of his Army, but the People, in the greatest Terror imaginable, every Day expecting *Tilly* with the *German* Army, who by his Cruelty at *Magdeburg* was become so dreadful to the Protestants, that they expected no Mercy where-ever he came.

The Emperor's Power was made so formidable to all the Protestants, particularly since the Diet at *Ratisbon* left them in a worse Case than it found them, that they had not only formed the Conclusions of *Leipsick*, which all Men looked on as the Effect of Desperation rather than any probable Means of their Deliverance, but had privately implored the Protection and Assistance of foreign Powers, and particularly the King of *Sweden*, from whom they had Promises of a speedy and powerful Assistance. And truly if the *Swede* had not with a very strong Hand rescued them, all their Conclusions at *Leipsick* had served but to hasten their Ruin. I remember very well when I was in the *Imperial* Army they discoursed with such Contempt of the Forces of the Protestants, that not only the *Imperialists* but the Protestants themselves gave them up as lost: the Emperor had not less than 200000 Men in several Armies on Foot, who most of them were on the back of the Protestants in every Corner. If *Tilly* did but write a threatning Letter to any City or Prince of the Union, they presently submitted, renounced the Conclusions of *Leipsick*, and received *Imperial* Garrisons, as the Cities of *Ulm* and *Memingen*, the Dutchy of *Wirtemberg*, and several others, and almost all *Suaben*.

Only the Duke of *Saxony* and the Landgrave of *Hesse* upheld the drooping Courage of the Protestants, and refused all Terms of Peace; slighted all the Threatnings of the *Imperial* Generals, and the Duke of *Brandenburgh* was brought in afterward almost by Force.

The Duke of *Saxony* mustered his Forces under the Walls of *Leipsick*, and I having returned to *Leipsick* two Days before, saw them pass the Review. The Duke, gallantly mounted, rode through the Ranks, attended by his Field Marshal *Arnheim*, and seemed mighty well pleased with them, and indeed the Troops made a very fine Appearance; but I that had seen *Tilly*'s Army, and his old Weather-beaten Soldiers, whose Discipline and Exercises were so exact, and their Courage so often tried, could not look on the *Saxon* Army without some Concern for them, when I considered who they had to deal with; *Tilly*'s Men were rugged surly Fellows, their Faces had an Air of hardy Courage, mangled with Wounds and Scars, their Armour shewed the Bruises of Musquet Bullets, and the Rust of the Winter Storms; I observed of them their Cloaths were always dirty, but their Arms were clean and bright; they were used to camp in the open Fields, and sleep in the Frosts and Rain; their Horses were strong and hardy like themselves, and well taught their Exercises; the Soldiers knew their Business so exactly that general Orders were enough; every private Man was fit to command, and their Wheelings, Marchings, Counter-marchings and Exercises were done with such Order and Readiness that the distinct Words of Command were hardly of any use among them; they were flushed with Victory, and hardly knew what it was to fly.

There had passed some Messages between *Tilly* and the Duke, and he gave always such ambiguous Answers as he thought might serve to gain Time; but *Tilly* was not to be put off with Words, and drawing his Army towards *Saxony*, sends four Propositions to him to sign, and demands an immediate Reply, the Propositions were positive.

1. To cause his Troops to enter into the Emperor's

Service, and to march in Person with them against the King of *Sweden*.

2. To give the *Imperial* Army Quarters in his Country, and supply them with necessary Provisions.

3. To relinquish the Union of *Leipsick*, and disown the 10 Conclusions.

4. To make Restitution of the Goods and Lands of the Church.

The Duke being pressed by *Tilly*'s Trumpeter for an immediate Answer, sat all Night, and part of the next Day in Council with his Privy Councillors, debating what Reply to give him, which at last was concluded, in short, that he would live and die in Defence of the Protestant Religion, and the Conclusions of *Leipsick*, and bad *Tilly* Defiance.

The Dye being thus cast, he immediately decamped with his whole Army for *Torgau*, fearing that *Tilly* should get there before him, and so prevent his Conjunction with the *Swede*. The Duke had not yet concluded any positive Treaty with the King of *Swedeland*, and the Duke of *Brandenburgh* having made some Difficulty of joining, they both stood on some Niceties till they had like to have ruined themselves all at once.

Brandenburgh had given up the Town of *Spandau* to the King by a former Treaty to secure a Retreat for his Army, and the King was advanced as far as *Frankfort* upon the *Oder*, when on a sudden some small Difficulties arising *Brandenburgh* seems cold in the Matter, and with a sort of Indifference demands to have his Town of *Spandau* restored to him again. *Gustavus Adolphus*, who began presently to imagine the Duke had made his Peace with the Emperor, and so would either be his Enemy, or pretend a Neutrality, generously delivered him his Town of *Spandau*; but immediately turns about, and with his whole Army besieges him in his Capital City of *Berlin*. This brought the Duke to know his Error, and by the Interposition of the Ladies, the Queen of *Sweden* being the Duke's Sister, the Matter was accommodated, and the Duke joined his Forces with the King.

But the Duke of *Saxony* had like to have been undone by this Delay, for the *Imperialists*, under Count *de Furstemburgh*, were entred his Country, and had possessed themselves of *Hall*, and *Tilly* was on his March to join him, as he afterwards did, and ravaging the whole Country laid Siege to *Leipsick* it self; the Duke driven to this Extremity rather flies to the *Swede* than treats with him, and on the second of *September* the Duke's Army joined with the King of *Sweden*.

I had not come to *Leipsick* but to see the Duke of *Saxony*'s Army, and that being marched as I have said for *Torgau*, I had no Business there; but if I had, the approach of *Tilly* and the *Imperial* Army was enough to hasten me away, for I had no Occasion to be besieged there; so on the 27th of *August* I left the Town, as several of the principal Inhabitants had done before, and more would have done had not the Governor published a Proclamation against it; and besides they knew not whether to fly, for all Places were alike exposed, the poor People were under dreadful Apprehensions of a Siege, and of the merciless Usage of the *Imperial* Soldiers, the Example of *Magdeburgh* being fresh before them, the Duke and his Army gone from them, and the Town, though well furnished, but indifferently fortified.

In this Condition I left them, buying up Stores of Provisions, working hard to scour their Moats, set up Palisadoes, repair their Fortifications, and preparing all Things for a Siege; and following the *Saxon* Army to *Torgau*, I continued in the Camp till a few Days before they joined the King of *Sweden*.

I had much ado to persuade my Companion from entring into the Service of the Duke of *Saxony*, one of whose Collonels, with whom we had contracted a particular Acquaintance, offering him a Commission to be Cornet in one of the old Regiments of Horse; but the Difference I had observed between this new Army and *Tilly*'s old Troops had made such an Impression on me, that I confess I had yet no manner of Inclination for the Service; and therefore persuaded him to wait a while till we had seen a little further into Affairs, and particularly till we had seen the *Swedish* Army, which we had heard so much of.

The Difficulties which the Elector Duke of *Saxony* made of joining with the King were made up by a Treaty concluded with the King on the 2d of *September* at *Coswig*, a small Town on the *Elbe*, whither the King's Army was arrived the Night before; for General *Tilly* being now entered into the Duke's Country, had plundered and ruined all the lower part of it, and was now actually besieging the Capital City of *Leipsick*. These Necessities made almost any Conditions easy to him, the greatest Difficulty was that the King of *Sweden* demanded the absolute Command of the Army, which the Duke submitted to with less good Will than he had Reason to do, the King's Experience and Conduct considered.

I had not Patience to attend the Conclusions of their particular Treaties, but as soon as ever the Passage was clear I quitted the *Saxon* Camp, and went to see the *Swedish* Army: I fell in with the Out-guards of the *Swedes* at a little Town called *Beltsig*, on the River *Wersa*, just as they were relieving the Guards, and going to march, and having a Pass from the *English* Ambassador[1] was very well received by the Officer who changed the Guards, and with him I went back into the Army; by nine in the Morning the Army was in full March, the King himself at the Head of them on a gray Pad, and riding from one Brigade to another, ordered the March of every Line himself.

When I saw the *Swedish* Troops, their exact Discipline, their Order, the Modesty and Familiarity of their Officers, and the regular living of the Soldiers, their Camp seemed a well ordered City; the meanest Country Woman with her *Market Ware* was as safe from Violence as in the Streets of *Vienna*: There was no Regiments of Whores and Rags as followed the *Imperialists*; nor any Women in the Camp, but such as being known to the Provosts to be the Wives of the Soldiers, who were necessary for washing Linen, taking Care of the Soldiers Cloaths, and dressing their Victuals.

The Soldiers were well clad, not gay, furnished with excellent Arms, and exceeding careful of them; and though they did not seem so terrible as I thought *Tilly*'s Men did when I first saw them, yet the Figure they made, together with what we had heard of them, made them seem to me invincible: The Discipline and Order of their Marchings, Camping and Exercise was excellent and singular, and which was to be seen in no Armies but the King's, his own Skill, Judgment and Vigilance having added much to the general Conduct of Armies then in use.

As I met the *Swedes* on their March I had no Opportunity to acquaint my self with any Body 'till after the Conjunction of the *Saxon* Army, and then it being but four Days to the great Battle of *Leipsick*, our Acquaintance was but small, saving what fell out accidentally by Conversation.

I met with several Gentlemen in the King's Army who spoke *English* very well, besides that there were 3 Regiments of *Scots* in the Army, the Collonels whereof I found were extraordinarily esteemed by the King, as the Lord *Rea*, Collonel *Lumsdell*, and Sir *John Hepburn*: The latter of these, after I had by an Accident become acquainted with, I found had been for many Years acquainted with my Father, and on that Account I received a great deal of Civility from him, which afterwards grew into a kind of intimate Friendship; he was a compleat Soldier indeed, and for that Reason so well beloved by that gallant King, that he hardly knew how to go about any great Action without him.

It was impossible for me now to restrain my young Comrade from entring into the *Swedish* Service, and indeed every Thing was so inviting that I could not blame him. A Captain in Sir *John Hepburn*'s Regiment had picked Acquaintance with him, and he having as much Gallantry in his Face as real Courage in his Heart, the Captain had persuaded him to take Service, and promised to use his Interest to get him a Company in the *Scotch* Brigade. I had made him promise me not to part from me in my Travels without my Consent, which was the only Obstacle to his Desires of entring in the *Swedish* Pay; and being one Evening in the Captain's Tent with him, and discoursing very freely together, the Captain asked him very short but friendly, and looking earnestly at me, *Is this the Gentleman, Mr.* Fielding, *that has done so much Prejudice to the King of* Sweden's *Service?* I was doubly surprized at the Expression, and at the Collonel, Sir *John Hepburn*, coming at that very Moment into the Tent; the Collonel hearing something of the Question, but knowing nothing of the Reason of it, any more than as I seemed a little to concern my self at it; yet after the Ceremony due to his Character was over, would needs know what I had done to hinder his Majesty's Service. *So much truly*, says the Captain, *that if his Majesty knew it he would think himself very little beholding to him. I am sorry, Sir*, says I, *that I should offend in any Thing, who am but a Stranger; but if you would please to inform me, I would endeavour to alter any Thing in my Behaviour that is prejudicial to any one, much less to his Majesty's Service. I shall take you at your Word, Sir*, says the Captain; *the King of* Sweden, *Sir, has a particular Request to you. I should be glad to know two Things, Sir*, said I, *First, How that can be possible, since I am not known yet to any Man in the Army, much less to his Majesty? And, Secondly, What the Request can be? Why, Sir, his Majesty desires you would not hinder this Gentleman from entring into his Service, who it seems desires nothing more, if he may have your Consent to it. I have too much Honour for his Majesty*, return'd I, *to deny any Thing which he pleases to command me; but methinks 'tis some Hardship, you should make that the King's Order, which 'tis very probable he knows nothing of.* Sir *John Hepburn* took the Case up something gravely, and drinking a Glass of *Leipsick* Beer to the Captain, said, *Come, Captain, don't press these Gentlemen; the King desires no Man's Service but what is purely Voluntier.* So we entred into other Discourse, and the Collonel perceiving by my Talk that I had seen *Tilly*'s Army, was mighty curious in his Questions, and seemed very well satisfied with the Account I gave him.

The next Day the Army having pass'd the *Elbe* at *Wittemberg*, and joyn'd the *Saxon* Army near *Torgau*[1] his Majesty caused both Armies to draw up in Battalia, giving every Brigade the same Post in the Lines as he purposed to fight in: I must do the Memory of that glorious General this Honour, that I never saw an Army drawn up with so much Variety, Order, and exact Regularity since, tho' I have seen many Armies drawn up by some of the greatest Captains of the Age; the Order by which his Men were directed to flank and relieve one another, the Methods of receiving one Body of Men if disordered into another, and rallying one Squadron, without disordering another was so admirable; the Horse every where flank'd, lin'd and defended by the Foot, and the Foot by the Horse, and both by the Cannon, was such, that if those Orders were but as punctually obey'd, 'twere impossible to put an Army so modell'd into any Confusion.

The View being over, and the Troops return'd to their Camps, the Captain with whom we drank the Day before meeting me, told me I must come and sup with him in his Tent, where he would ask my Pardon for the Affront he gave me before. I told him he needed not put himself to the Trouble; I was not affronted at all, that I would do my self the Honour to wait on him, provided he wou'd give me his Word not to speak any more of it as an Affront.

We had not been a quarter of an Hour in his Tent but Sir *John Hepburn* came in again, and addressing to me, told me he was glad to find me there; that he came to the Captain's Tent to enquire how to send to me; and that I must do him the Honour to go with him to wait on the King, who had a Mind to hear the Account I could give him of the *Imperial* Army from my own Mouth. I must confess I was at some Loss in my Mind how to make my Address to his Majesty; but I had heard so much of the conversible Temper of the King, and his particular Sweetness of Humour with the meanest Soldier, that I made no more Difficulty, but having paid my Respects to Collonel *Hepburn*, thank'd

him for the Honour he had done me, and offer'd to rise and
wait upon him: Nay, says the Collonel, we will eat first, for
I find *Gourdon*, which was the Captain's Name, has got
something for Supper, and the King's Order is at seven a
Clock: So we went to Supper, and Sir *John* becoming very
friendly, must know my Name; which, when I had told him,
and of what Place and Family, he rose from his Seat and
embracing me, told me he knew my Father very well, and
had been intimately acquainted with him; and told me several
Passages wherein my Father had particularly obliged him.
After this we went to Supper, and the King's Health being
drank round, the Collonel moved the sooner because he had
a Mind to talk with me; when we were going to the King,
he enquired of me where I had been, and what Occasion
brought me to the Army. I told him the short History of my
Travels, and that I came hither from *Vienna* on purpose to
see the King of *Sweden* and his Army; he ask'd me if there
was any Service he could do me, by which he meant,
whether I desired an Employment; I pretended not to take
him so, but told him the Protection his Acquaintance would
afford me was more than I could have ask'd, since I might
thereby have Opportunity to satisfie my Curiosity, which was
the chief End of my coming abroad. He perceiving by this
that I had no Mind to be a Soldier, told me very kindly I
should command him in any thing; that his Tent and
Equipage, Horses and Servants should always have Orders
to be at my Service: But that as a Piece of Friendship, he
would advise me to retire to some Place distant from the
Army, for that the Army wou'd march to morrow, and the
King was resolved to fight General *Tilly*, and he wou'd not
have me hazard my self; that if I thought fit to take his
Advice, he wou'd have me take that Interval to see the Court
at *Berlin*, whither he would send one of his Servants to wait
on me: His Discourse was too kind not to extort the tenderest
Acknowledgement from me that I was capable of; I told
him his Care of me was so obliging, that I knew not what
Return to make him, but if he pleased to leave me to my

Choice I desired no greater Favour than to trail a Pike under his Command in the ensuing Battle. I can never answer it to your Father, says he, to suffer you to expose your self so far. I told him my Father would certainly acknowledge his Friendship in the Proposal made me; but I believ'd he knew him better than to think he wou'd be well pleas'd with me if I should accept of it; that I was sure my Father would have rod[e] Post 500 Miles to have been at such a Battle under such a General, and it should never be told him that his Son had rod[e] 50 Miles to be out of it: He seem'd to be something concern'd at the Resolution I had taken, and replied very quickly upon me, that he approved very well of my Courage; but, says he, no Man gets any Credit by running upon needless Adventures, nor loses any by shunning Hazards which he has no Order for. 'Tis enough, says he, for a Gentleman to behave well when he is commanded upon any Service; I have had fighting enough, says he, upon these Points of Honour, and I never got any thing but Reproof for it from the King himself. Well, Sir, said I, however if a Man expects to rise by his Valour, he must shew it somewhere; and if I were to have any Command in an Army, I wou'd first try whether I could deserve it; I have never yet seen any Service, and must have my Induction some time or other: I shall never have a better Schoolmaster than your self, nor a better School than such an Army. Well, says Sir *John*, but you may have the same School and the same teaching after this Battle is over; for I must tell you before-hand, this will be a bloody Touch;[1] *Tilly* has a great Army of old Lads that are used to boxing; Fellows with Iron Faces, and 'tis a little too much to engage so hotly the first Entrance into the Wars: You may see our Discipline this Winter, and make your Campaign with us next Summer, when you need not fear but we shall have fighting enough, and you will be better acquainted with Things: We do never put our common Soldiers upon Pitcht Battles the first Campaign, but place our new Men in Garrisons and try them in Parties first. Sir, said I with a little more Freedom,

I believe I shall not make a Trade of the War, and therefore need not serve an Apprenticeship to it: 'Tis a hard Battle where none escapes: If I come off, I hope I shall not disgrace you, and if not, 'twill be some Satisfaction to my Father to hear his Son died fighting, under the Command of Sir *John Hepburn* in the Army of the King of *Sweden*, and I desire no better Epitaph upon my Tomb. Well, says Sir *John*, and by this time we were just come to the King's Quarters, and the Guards calling to us interrupted his Reply; so we went into the Court Yard where the King was lodg'd, which was in an indifferent House of one of the Burghers of *Debien*, and Sir *John* stepping up, met the King coming down some Steps into a large Room which looked over the Town-Wall into a Field where Part of the Artillery was drawn up. Sir *John Hepburn* sent his Man presently to me to come up, which I did; and Sir *John* without any Ceremony carries me directly up to the King, who was leaning on his Elbow in the Window: The King turning about, this is the *English* Gentleman, says Sir *John*, who I told your Majesty had been in the *Imperial* Army. How then did he get hither, says the King, without being taken by the Scouts? At which Question Sir *John* saying nothing; By a Pass, and please your Majesty, from the *English* Ambassador's Secretary at *Vienna*, said I, making a profound Reverence. Have you then been at *Vienna*, says the King? Yes, and please your Majesty, said I; upon which the King folding up a Letter he had in his Hand, seemed much more earnest to talk about *Vienna*, than about *Tilly*: And pray what News had you at *Vienna*? Nothing, Sir, said I, but daily Accounts one in the Neck of another of their own Misfortunes, and your Majesty's Conquests, which makes a very melancholy Court there. But pray, said the King, what is the common Opinion there about these Affairs? The common People are terrified to the last Degree, said I, and when your Majesty took *Frankfort* upon *Oder*, if your Army had march'd but 20 Miles into *Silesia*, half the People wou'd have run out of *Vienna*, and I left them fortifying the City. They need not, reply'd the

King smiling, I have no Design to trouble them, 'tis the Protestant Countries I must be for: Upon this the Duke of *Saxony* entred the Room, and finding the King engag'd, offer'd to retire; but the King beckoning with his Hand call'd to him in *French*, Cousin, says the King, this Gentleman has been travelling and comes from *Vienna*, and so made me repeat what I had said before; at which the King went on with me, and Sir *John Hepburn* informing his Majesty that I spoke high *Dutch*, he changed his Language, and ask'd me in *Dutch* where it was that I saw General *Tilly*'s Army; I told his Majesty at the Siege of *Magdeburgh*. At *Magdeburgh*. said the King shaking his Head, *Tilly* must answer to me one Day for that *City*, and if not to me to a greater King than I: Can you guess what Army he had with him, said the King? He had two Armies with him, said I, but one I suppose will do your Majesty no harm: Two Armies! said the King. Yes Sir, he has one Army of about 26000 Men, said I, and another of above 15000 Whores and their Attendants; at which the King laughed heartily; Ay, ay, says the King, those 15000 do us as much Harm as the 26000; for they eat up the Country, and devour the poor Protestants more than the Men; Well, says the King, do they talk of fighting us? They talk big enough, Sir, said I, but your Majesty has not been so often fought with as beaten in their Discourse. I know not for the Men, says the King, but the old Man is as likely to do it as talk of it, and I hope to try them in a Day or two: The King enquired after that, several Matters of me about the *Low Countries*, the Prince of *Orange*, and of the Court and Affairs in *England*; and Sir *John Hepburn* informing his Majesty that I was the Son of an *English* Gentleman of his Acquaintance, the King had the Goodness to ask him what Care he had taken of me against the Day of Battle. Upon which Sir *John* repeated to him the Discourse we had together by the Way; the King seeming particularly pleased with it, began to take me to Task himself: You *English* Gentlemen, says he, are too forward in the Wars, which makes you leave them too soon again. Your Majesty, reply'd I, makes War in so pleasant a Manner, as makes all the World fond of fighting under your Conduct. Not so pleasant neither, says the King, here's a Man can tell you that sometimes 'tis not very pleasant. I know not much of the Warrior, Sir, said I, nor of the World, but if always to conquer be the Pleasure of the War, your Majesty's Soldiers have all that can be desired. Well, says the King, but however considering all Things, I think you would do well to take the Advice Sir *John Hepburn* has given you. Your Majesty may command me to any Thing, but where your Majesty and so many gallant Gentleman hazard their Lives, mine is not worth mentioning; and I should not dare to tell my Father at my return into *England* that I was in your Majesty's Army, and made so mean a Figure that your Majesty would not permit me to fight under that Royal Standard. Nay, replied the King, I lay no Commands upon you, but you are young. I can never dye, Sir, said I, with more Honour than in your Majesty's Service; I spake this with so much Freedom, and his Majesty was so pleased with it, that he asked me how I would choose to serve, on Horseback or on Foot; I told his Majesty I should be glad to receive any of his Majesty's Commands, but if I had not that Honour I had purpos'd to trail a Pike under Sir *John Hepburn*, who had done me so much Honour as to introduce me into his Majesty's Presence. Do so then, reply'd the King, and turning to Sir *John Hepburn*, said, and pray do you take Care of him; at which overcome with the Goodness of his Discourse I could not answer a Word, but made him a profound Reverence and retired.

The next Day but one, being the Seventh of *September*, before Day the Army march'd from *Dieben* to a large Field[1] about a Mile from *Leipsick*, where we found *Tilly*'s Army in full Battalia in admirable Order, which made a shew both glorious and terrible. *Tilly*, like a fair Gamster, had taken up but one Side of the Plain, and left the other free, and all the Avenues open for the King's Army; nor did he stir to the Charge 'till the King's Army was compleatly drawn up and advanced towards him: He had in his Army 44000 old Soldiers, every Way answerable to what I have said of them before; and I shall only add, a better Army I believe never was so soundly beaten.

The King was not much inferior in Force, being joined with the *Saxons*, who were reckoned 22000 Men, and who drew up on the Left, making a main Battle and two Wings, as the King did on the Right.

The King placed himself at the right Wing of his own Horse; *Gustavus Horn* had the main Battle of the *Swedes*, the Duke of *Saxony* had the main Battle of his own Troops, and General *Arnheim* the right Wing of his Horse.

The second Line of the *Swedes* consisted of the two *Scotch* Brigades, and three *Swedish*, with the *Finland* Horse in the Wings.

In the beginning of the Fight, *Tilly*'s right Wing charg'd with such irresistible Fury upon the Left of the King's Army where the *Saxons* were posted, that nothing could withstand them; the *Saxons* fled amain, and some of them carried the News over the Country that all was lost, and the King's Army overthrown; and indeed it passed for an Oversight with some, that the King did not place some of his old Troops among the *Saxons* who were new raised Men; the *Saxons* lost here near 2000 Men, and hardly ever shew'd their Faces again all the Battle, except some few of their Horse.

I was posted with my Comrade, the Captain, at the Head of three *Scottish* Regiments of Foot, commanded by Sir *John Hepburn*, with express Directions from the Collonel to keep by him: Our Post was in the second Line, as a Reserve to the King of *Sweden*'s main Battle, and which was strange, the main Battle, which consisted of four great Brigades of Foot, were never charged during the whole Fight; and yet we, who had the Reserve, were obliged to endure the whole Weight of the *Imperial* Army; the Occasion was, the right Wing of the *Imperialists* having defeated the *Saxons*, and being eager in the Chace, *Tilly*, who was an old Soldier, and ready to prevent all Mistakes, forbids any Pursuit; let them go, says he, but let us beat the *Swedes*, or we do nothing. Upon this the victorious Troops fall in upon the Flank of the King's Army, which the *Saxons* being fled lay open to them; *Gustavus Horn* commanded the left Wing of the *Swedes*, and having first defeated some Regiments which charged him, falls in upon the Rear of the *Imperial* right Wing, and separates them from the Van, who were advanced a great Way forward in pursuit of the *Saxons*; and having routed the said Rear or Reserve, falls on upon *Tilly's* main Battle, and defeated Part of them, the other Part was gone in Chase of the *Saxons*, and now also returned, fell in upon the Rear of the left Wing of the *Swedes*, charging them in the Flank; for they drew up upon the very Ground which the *Saxons* had quitted. This changed the whole Front, and made the *Swedes* face about to the Left, and make a great Front on their Flank to make this good; our Brigades, who were placed as a Reserve for the main Battle, were by special Order from the King, wheeled about to the Left, and placed for the Right of this new Front to charge the *Imperialists*; they were about 12 Thousand of their best Foot, besides Horse; and flusht with the Execution of the *Saxons*, fell on like Furies: The King by this time had almost defeated the *Imperialist's* left Wing; their Horse with more Haste than good Speed, had charged faster than their Foot could follow, and having broke into the King's first Line, he let them go; where, while the second Line bears the Shock, and bravely resisted them; the King follows them on the Crupper with 13 Troops of Horse, and some Musqueteers, by which being hemm'd in, they were all cut down in a Moment as it were, and the Army never disordered with them. This fatal Blow to the left Wing, gave the King more Leisure to defeat the Foot which followed, and to send some Assistance to *Gustavus Horn* in his left Wing, who had his Hands full with the main Battle of the *Imperialists*.

But those Troops who, as I said, had routed the *Saxons*, being called off from the Pursuit, had charged our Flank, and were now grown very strong, renewed the Battle in a terrible Manner: Here it was I saw our Men go to Wrack; Collonel *Hall*, a brave Soldier, commanded the Rear of the *Swedes* left Wing; he fought like a Lion, but was slain, and most of his Regiment cut off, tho' not unrevenged; for they entirely ruined *Furstemberg*'s Regiment of Foot: Collonel *Cullembach* with his Regiment of Horse, was extreamly overlaid also, and the Collonel and many brave Officers killed, and in short all that Wing was shattered, and in an ill Condition.

In this Juncture came the King, and having seen what Havock the Enemy made of *Cullembach*'s Troops, he comes riding along the Front of our three Brigades, and himself led us on to the Charge; the Collonel of his Guards, the Baron *Dyvel*, was shot dead just as the King had given him some Orders: When the *Scots* advanced, seconded by some Regiments of Horse which the King also sent to the Charge, the bloodiest Fight began that ever Man beheld, for the *Scotish* Brigades giving Fire three Ranks at a Time over one anothers Heads, pour'd in their Shot so thick, that the Enemy were cut down like Grass before a Scyth; and following into the thickest of their Foot with the Clubs of their Musquets, made a most dreadful Slaughter, and yet was there no flying; *Tilly*'s Men might be killed and knocked down, but no Man turned his Back, nor would give an Inch of Ground, but as they were wheel'd, or marched, or retreated by their Officers.

There was a Regiment of Cuirassiers, which stood whole to the last, and fought like Lions, they went ranging over the Field when all their Army was broken, and no Body cared for charging them; they were commanded by Baron *Cronenburgh*, and at last went off from the Battle whole. These were armed in black Armour from Head to Foot, and they carried off their General;[1] about Six a Clock the Field was cleared of the Enemy, except at one Place on the King's Side, where some of them rallied, and though they knew all was lost would take no Quarter, but fought it out to the last

Man, being found dead the next Day in Rank and File as they were drawn up.

I had the good Fortune to receive no Hurt in this Battle, excepting a small Scratch on the side of my Neck by the push of a Pike; but my Friend received a very dangerous Wound when the Battle was as good as over; he had engaged with a *German* Collonel whose Name we could never learn, and having killed his Man, and pressed very close upon him so that he had shot his Horse, the Horse in the fall kept the Collonel down, lying on one of his Legs, upon which he demanded Quarter, which Captain *Feilding* granting, helped him to quit his Horse, and having disarmed him, was bringing him into the Line, when the Regiment of Cuirassiers, which I mentioned, commanded by Baron *Cronenburgh*, came roving over the Field, and with a flying Charge saluted our Front with a Salvo of Carabin-shot, which wounded us a great many Men, and among the rest the Captain received a Shot in his Thigh, which laid him on the Ground, and being separated from the Line, his Prisoner got away with them.

This was the first Service I was in, and indeed I never saw any Fight since maintained with such Gallantry, such desperate Valour, together with such Dexterity of Management, both Sides being composed of Soldiers fully tried, bred to the Wars, expert in every Thing, exact in their Order, and uncapable of Fear, which made the Battle be much more bloody than usual. Sir *John Hepburn*, at my Request, took particular Care of my Comrade, and sent his own Surgeon to look after him; and afterwards when the City of *Leipsick* was retaken, provided him Lodgings there, and came very often to see him; and indeed I was in great Care for him too, the Surgeons being very doubtful of him a great while; for having lain in the Field all Night among the Dead, his Wound, for want of dressing, and with the Extremity of Cold, was in a very ill Condition, and the Pain of it had thrown him into a Fever. 'Twas quite dusk before the Fight ended, especially where the last rallied Troops fought so long, and therefore we durst not break our Order to seek out our Friends, so that 'twas near seven o'Clock the next Morning before we found the Captain, who though very weak by the loss of Blood, had raised himself up, and placed his Back against the Buttock of a dead Horse; I was the first that knew him, and running to him, embraced him with a great deal of Joy: He was not able to speak, but made Signs to let me see he knew me, so we brought him into the Camp, and Sir *John Hepburn*, as I noted before, sent his own Surgeons to look after him.

The Darkness of the Night prevented any Pursuit, and was the only Refuge the Enemy had left; for had there been three Hours more Day-light, ten Thousand more Lives had been lost, for the *Swedes* (and *Saxons* especially) enraged by the Obstinacy of the Enemy, were so thoroughly heated that they would have given Quarter but to few; the Retreat was not sounded 'till seven o'Clock, when the King drew up the whole Army upon the Field of Battle, and gave strict Command that none should stir from their Order;[1] so the Army lay under their Arms all Night, which was another reason why the wounded Soldiers suffered very much by the Cold; for the King, who had a bold Enemy to deal with, was not ignorant what a small Body of desperate Men rallied together might have done in the Darkness of the Night, and therefore he lay in his Coach all Night at the Head of the Line, though it froze very hard.

As soon as the Day began to peep the Trumpets sounded to Horse, and all the Dragoons and Light Horse in the Army were commanded to the Pursuit; the Cuirassiers and some commanded Musqueteers advanced some Miles, if need were, to make good their Retreat, and all the Foot stood to their Arms for a Reserve; but in half an Hour Word was brought to the King, that the Enemy was quite dispersed, upon which Detachments were made out of every Regiment to search among the Dead for any of our Friends that were wounded; and the King himself gave a strict Order, that if any were found wounded and alive among the Enemy none should kill them, but take Care to bring them into the Camp: A Piece of Humanity which saved the Lives of near a Thousand of the Enemies.

This Piece of Service being over, the Enemy's Camp was seized upon, and the Soldiers were permitted to plunder it; all the Cannon, Arms, and Ammunition was secured for the King's Use, the rest was given up to the Soldiers, who found so much Plunder that they had no Reason to quarrel for Shares.

For my share, I was so busie with my wounded Captain that I got nothing but a Sword, which I found just by him when I first saw him; but my Man brought me a very good Horse with a Furniture on him, and one Pistol of extraordinary Workmanship.

I bad him get upon his Back and make the best of the Day for himself, which he did, and I saw him no more till three Days after, when he found me out at *Leipsick* so richly dressed that I hardly knew him; and after making his Excuse for his long Absence, gave me a very pleasant Account where he had been: He told me, that according to my Order being mounted on the Horse he had brought me, he first rid into the Field among the Dead, to get some Clothes suitable to the Equipage of his Horse, and having seized on a laced Coat, a Helmet, a Sword, and an extraordinary good Cane, was resolved to see what was become of the Enemy, and following the Track of the Dragoons, which he could easily do by the Bodies on the Road, he fell in with a small Party of 25 Dragoons, under no Command but a Corporal, making to a Village where some of the Enemies Horse had been quartered; the Dragoons taking him for an Officer by his Horse, desired him to command them, told him the Enemy was very rich, and they doubted not a good Booty: He was a bold brisk Fellow, and told them, with all his Heart; but said he had but one Pistol, the other being broke with firing, so they lent him a pair of Pistols, and a small Piece they had taken, and he led them on. There had been a Regiment of Horse and some Troops of *Crabats*[1] in the Village, but they were fled on the first Notice of the Pursuit, excepting three Troops, and these on Sight of this small Party, supposing them to be only the first of a greater Number, fled in the greatest Confusion imaginable; they took the Village and about 50 Horses, with all the Plunder of the Enemy, and with the Heat of the Service he had spoiled my Horse, he said, for which he had brought me two more; for he passing for the Commander of the Party, had all the Advantage the Custom of War gives an Officer in like Cases.

I was very well pleased with the Relation the Fellow gave me, and laughing at him, *Well, Captain*, said I, *and what Plunder have ye got? Enough to make me a Captain, Sir*, says he, *if you please, and a Troop ready raised too; for the Party of Dragoons are posted in the Village by my Command, till they have farther Orders*. In short, he pulled out 60 or 70 Pieces of Gold, 5 or 6 Watches, 13 or 14 Rings, whereof 2 were diamond Rings, one of which was worth 50 Dollars; Silver as much as his Pockets would hold, besides that he had brought three Horses, two of which were laden with Baggage, and a Boor he had hired to stay with them at *Leipsick* till he had found me out. *But I am afraid Captain*, says I, *you have plundered the Village instead of plundering the Enemy. No indeed not we*, says he, *but the* Crabats *had done it for us, and we light of* [1] *them just as they were carrying it off*. *Well*, said I, *but what will you do with your Men; for when you come to give them Orders, they will know you well enough? No, no*, says he, *I took Care of that; for just now I gave a Soldier five Dollars to carry them News that the Army was marched to* Moersburgh, *and that they should follow thither to the Regiment*.

Having secured his Money in my Lodgings, he asked me if I pleased to see his Horses, and to have one for my self? I told him I would go and see them in the Afternoon; but the Fellow being impatient goes and fetches them: There was three Horses, one whereof was a very good one, and by the Furniture was an Officer's Horse of the *Crabats*, and that my Man would have me accept, for the other he had spoiled, as he said; I was but indifferently horsed before, so I accepted of the Horse, and went down with him to see the rest of his Plunder there; he had got three or four pair of Pistols, two or three Bundles of Officers Linen and Lace, a Field-Bed and a Tent, and several other Things of Value; but at last coming to a small Fardel, and this, says he, I took whole from a *Crabat* running away with it under his Arm, so he brought it up into my Chamber; he had not looked into it, he said, but he understood 'twas some Plunder the Soldiers had made, and finding it heavy took it by Consent; we opened it and found 'twas a Bundle of some Linen, 13 or 14 Pieces of Plate, and in a small Cup three Rings, a fine Necklace of Pearl, and the Value of 100 Rix-dollars[1] in Money. The Fellow was amazed at his own good Fortune, and hardly knew what to do with himself: I bid him go take Care of his other Things, and of his Horses, and come again; so he went and discharged the Boor that waited, and packed up all his Plunder, and came up to me in his old Clothes again. *How now, Captain*, says I, *what have you altered your Equipage already? I am no more ashamed, Sir, of your Livery*, answered he, *than of your Service, and nevertheless your Servant for what I have got by it. Well*, says I to him, *but what will you do now with all your Money? I wish my poor Father had some of it*, says he, *and for the rest I got it for you, Sir, and desire you would take it.* He spoke it with so much Honesty and Freedom that I could not but take it very kindly; but however, I told him I would not take a Farthing from him, as his Master; but I would have him play the good Husband with it now he had such good Fortune to get it: He told me he would take my Directions in every Thing. *Why then*, says I, *I'll tell you what I would advise you to do, turn it all into ready Money, and convey it by Return home into* England, *and follow your self the first Opportunity, and with good Management you may put your self in a good Posture of living with it.* The Fellow, with a sort of Dejection in his Looks, asked me, if he had disobliged me in any Thing?

Why, says I: That I was willing to turn him out of his Service. *No*, George, (that was his Name) says I, *but you may live on this Money without being a Servant. I'd throw it all into the* Elbe, says he, *over* Torgaw *Bridge, rather than leave your Service; and besides*, says he, *can't I save my Money without going from you? I got it in your Service, and I'll never spend it out of your Service, unless you put me away. I hope my Money won't make me the worse Servant, if I thought it would, I'd soon have little enough. Nay*, George, says I, *I shall not oblige you to it, for I am not willing to lose you neither: come then*, says I, *let us put it all together, and see what it will come to*. So he laid it all together on the Table, and by our Computation he had gotten as much Plunder as was worth about 1400 Rix-dollars, besides 3 Horses with their Furniture, a Tent, a Bed, and some wearing Linen. Then he takes the Necklace of Pearl, a very good Watch, a Diamond Ring, and 100 Pieces of Gold, and lays them by themselves, and having according to our best Calculation valued the Things, he put up all the rest, and as I was going to ask him what they were left out for, he takes them up in his Hand, and coming round the Table, told me, that if I did not think him unworthy of my Service and Favour, he begged I would give him leave to make that Present to me; that it was my first thought, his going out; that he had got it all in my Service, and he should think I had no Kindness for him if I should refuse it. I was resolved in my Mind not to take it from him, and yet I could find no Means to resist his Importunity; at last I told him, I would accept of Part of his Present, and that I esteemed his Respect in that as much as the whole; and that I would not have him importune me farther, so I took the Ring and Watch with the Horse and Furniture as before, and made him turn all the rest into Money at *Leipsick*, and not suffering him to wear his Livery, made him put himself into a tolerable Equipage, and taking a young *Leipsicker* into my Service, he attended me as a Gentleman from that Time forward.

The King's Army never entred *Leipsick* but proceeded to

Moersburg, and from thence to *Hall* and so marched on into *Franconia*, while the Duke of *Saxony* employed his Forces in recovering *Leipsick* and the driving the *Imperialists* out of his Country. I continued at *Leipsick* 12 Days, being not willing to leave my Comrade 'till he was recovered; but Sir *John Hepburn* so often importuned me to come into the Army, and sent me Word that the King had very often enquired for me, that at last I consented to go without him; so having made our Appointment where to meet and how to correspond by Letters, I went to wait on Sir *John Hepburn*, who then lay with the King's Army at the City of *Erfurt* in *Saxony*. As I was riding between *Leipsick* and *Hall* I observed my Horse went very aukwardly and uneasy, and sweat very much, though the Weather was cold, and we had rid but very softly; I fancied therefore that the Saddle might hurt the Horse, and calls my new Captain up; *George* say I, I believe this Saddle hurts the Horse; so we alighted and looking under the Saddle found the Back of the Horse extreamly galled; so I bid him take off the Saddle, which he did, and giving the Horse to my young *Leipsicker* to lead, we sat down to see if we could mend it, for there was no Town near us; Says *George*, pointing with his Finger, if you please to cut open the Pannel there, I'll get something to stuff into it which will bear it from the Horse's Back; so while he look'd for something to thrust in, I cut a Hole in the Pannel of the Saddle, and following it with my Finger I felt something hard, which seemed to move up and down; again as I thrust it with my Finger, here's something that should not be here, says I, not yet imagining what afterwards fell out, and calling, run back, bad him put up his Finger; whatever 'tis, says he, 'tis this hurts the Horse, for it bears just on his Back when the Saddle is set on; so we strove to take hold on it, but could not reach it; at last we took the upper Part of the Saddle quite from the Pannel, and there lay a small Silk Purse wrapt in a Piece of Leather, and full of Gold Ducats; thou art born to be rich, *George*, says I to him, here's more Money, we opened the Purse and found in it 438 small Pieces of Gold, there I had a new Skirmish with him whose the Money should be; I told him 'twas his, he told me no, I had accepted of the Horse and Furniture and all that was about him was mine, and solemnly vow'd he wou'd not have a Penny of it: I saw no Remedy but put up the Money for the Present, mended our Saddle, and went on; we lay that Night at *Hall*, and having had such a Booty in the Saddle, I made him search the Saddles of the other two Horses; in one of which, we found Three *French* Crowns, but nothing in the other.

We arrived at *Erfurt* the 28th of *September*, but the Army was removed,[1] and entred into *Franconia*, and at the Siege of *Koningshoven* we came up with them. The first thing I did, was to pay my Civilities to Sir *John Hepburn*, who received me very kindly, but told me withal, that I had not done well to be so long from him; that the King had particularly enquired for me, had commanded him to bring me to him at my return: I told him the Reason of my Stay at *Leipsick*, and how I had left that Place and my Comrade, before he was cured of his Wounds, to wait on him according to his Letters. He told me the King had spoken some Things very obliging about me, and he believed would offer me some Command in the Army, if I thought well to accept of it; I told him I had promised my Father not to take Service in an Army without his Leave; and yet if his Majesty should offer it, I neither knew how to resist it, nor had I an Inclination to any thing more than the Service, and such a Leader; tho' I had much rather have serv'd as a Volunteer at my own Charge, (which as he knew was the Custom of our *English* Gentlemen) than in any Command. He replied, do as you think fit; but some Gentlemen would give 20000 Crowns to stand so fair for Advancement as you do.

The Town of *Koningshoven* capitulated that Day,[2] and Sir *John* was ordered to treat with the Citizens, so I had no farther Discourse with him then; and the Town being taken, the Army immediately advanced down the River *Main*, for the King had his Eye upon *Frankfort* and *Mentz*, two great

Cities, both which he soon became Master of, chiefly by the prodigious Expedition of his March; For within a Month after the Battle, he was in the lower Parts of the Empire, and had passed from the *Elb* to the *Rhine*, an incredible Conquest; had taken all the Strong Cities, the Bishopricks of *Bambergh*, of *Wirtsburgh*, and almost all the Circle of *Franconia*, with Part of *Schawberland*; a Conquest large enough to be seven Year a making by the common Course of Arms.

Business going on thus, the King had not Leisure to think of small Matters, and I being not thoroughly resolved in my Mind, did not press Sir *John* to introduce me; I had wrote to my Father with an Account of my Reception in the Army, the Civilities of Sir *John Hepburn*, the Particulars of the Battle, and had indeed press'd him to give me Leave to serve the King of *Sweden*: To which Particular I waited for an Answer, but the following Occasion determined me before an Answer cou'd possibly reach me.

The King was before the Strong Castle of *Marienburgh*, which commands the City of *Wurtsburgh*; he had taken the *City*, but the Garrison and richer Part of the Burghers were retir'd into the Castle, and trusting to the Strength of the Place, which was thought impregnable, they bad the *Swedes* do their worst; twas well provided with all Things, and a strong Garrison in it; so that the Army indeed expected 'twould be a long Piece of Work. The Castle stood on a high Rock, and on the Steep of the Rock was a Bastion, which defended the only Passage up the Hill into the Castle; the *Scots* were chose out to make this attack, and the King was an Eye Witness of their Gallantry: In the Action Sir *John* was not commanded out, but Sir *James Ramsey* led them on, but I observed that most of the *Scotch* Officers in the other Regiments prepared to serve as Volunteers for the Honour of their Countrymen, and Sir *John Hepburn* led them on: I was resolved to see this Piece of Service, and therefore joined my self to the Volunteers; we were armed with Partizans, and each Man two Pistols at our Belt; it was a Piece of Service that seemed perfectly desperate, the

Advantage of the Hill, the Precipice we were to mount, the height of the Bastion, the resolute Courage and Number of the Garrison, who from a compleat Covert made a terrible Fire upon us, all joined to make the Action hopeless; but the Fury of the *Scots* Musqueteers was not to be abated by any Difficulties; they mounted the Hill, scaled the Works like Madmen, running upon the Enemies Pikes, and after two Hours' desperate Fight in the midst of Fire and Smoke, took it by Storm, and put all the Garrison to the Sword. The Voluntiers did their part, and had their Share of the Loss too, for 13 or 14 were killed out of 37, besides the wounded, among whom I received a Hurt more troublesome than dangerous, by a Thrust of a Halberd into my Arm, which proved a very painful Wound, and I was a great while before it was thoroughly recovered.

The King received us as we drew off at the Foot of the Hill, calling the Soldiers *his brave Scots*, and commending the Officers by Name. The next Morning the Castle was also taken by Storm, and the greatest Booty that ever was found in any one Conquest in the whole War; the Soldiers got here so much Money that they knew not what to do with it and the Plunder they got here and at the Battle of *Leipsick* made them so unruly, that had not the King been the best Master of Discipline in the World they had never been kept in any reasonable Bounds.

The King had taken Notice of our small Party of Voluntiers, and though I thought he had not seen me, yet he sent the next Morning for Sir *John Hepburn*, and asked him if I were not come to the Army? *Yes*, says Sir *John*, *he has been here two or three Days*: And as he was forming an Excuse for not having brought me to wait on his Majesty, says the King interrupting him, *I wonder you would let him thrust himself into such a hot Piece of Service as storming the* Port Graft: *Pray let him know I saw him, and have a very good Account of his Behaviour*. Sir *John* returned with this Account to me, and pressed me to pay my Duty to his Majesty the next Morning; and accordingly, though I had but an ill Night with the Pain of my Wound, I was with him at the Levee in the Castle.

I cannot but give some short Account of the Glory of that Morning; the Castle had been cleared of the dead Bodies of the Enemies, and what was not pillaged by the Soldiers, was placed under a Guard. There was first a Magazine of very good Arms for about 18 or 20000 Foot, and 4000 Horse, a very good Train of Artillery of about 18 Pieces of Battery, 32 brass Field-pieces and four Mortars. The Bishop's Treasure, and other publick Monies not plundered by the Soldiers, was telling out by the Officers, and amounted to 400000 Florins in Money; and the Burghers of the Town in solemn Procession, bareheaded, brought the King three Tun of Gold as a Composition to exempt the City from Plunder. Here was also a Stable of gallant Horses which the King had the Curiosity to go and see.[1]

When the Ceremony of the Burghers was over the King came down into the Castle Court, walked on the Parade (where the great Train of Artillery was placed on their Carriages) and round the Walls, and gave Order for repairing the Bastion that was stormed by the *Scots*; and as at the Entrance of the Parade Sir *John Hepburn* and I made our Reverence to the King, *Ho, Cavalier*, said the King to me, *I am glad to see you*, and so passed forward; I made my bow very low, but his Majesty said no more at that Time.

When the View was over the King went up into the Lodgings, and Sir *John* and I walked in an Anti-Chamber for about a Quarter of an Hour, when one of the Gentlemen of the Bed-Chamber came out to Sir *John*, and told him the King ask'd for him; he staid but a little with the King and came out to me, and told me the King had ordered him to bring me to him.

His Majesty, with a Countenance full of Honour and Goodness interrupted my Compliment, and asked me how I did; at which answering only with a bow, says the King, *I am sorry to see you are hurt, I would have laid my Commands on you not to have shewn your self in so sharp a Piece of Service, if I had known you had been in the Camp. Your Majesty does me too much Honour*, said I, *in your Care of a Life that has yet done nothing to deserve your Favour.* His Majesty was pleased to say something very kind to me relating to my Behaviour in the Battle of *Leipsick*, which I have not Vanity enough to write; at the Conclusion whereof, when I replyed very humbly, that I was not sensible that any Service I had done or could do could possibly merit so much Goodness; he told me he had ordered me a small Testimony of his Esteem, and withal gave me his Hand to kiss: I was now conquered, and with a sort of Surprize, told his Majesty, I found my self so much engaged by his Goodness, as well as my own Inclination, that if his Majesty would please to accept of my Devoir I was resolved to serve in his Army, or wherever he pleased to command me. *Serve me*, says the King, *why so you do, but I must not have you be a Musketeer; a poor Soldier at a Dollar a Week will do that. Pray, Sir* John, says the King, *give him what Commission he desires. No Commission, Sir*, says I, *would please me better than Leave to fight near your Majesty's Person, and to serve you at my own Charge till I am qualified by more Experience to receive your Commands. Why then it shall be so*, said the King, *and I charge you*, Hepburn, says he, *when any Thing offers that is either fit for him, or he desires, that you tell me of it*, and giving me his Hand again to kiss I withdrew.

I was followed before I had passed the Castle-Court by one of the King's Pages, who brought me a Warrant directed to Sir *John Hepburn* to go to the Master of the Horse for an immediate delivery of Things ordered by the King himself for my Account, where being come, the Querry produced me a very good Coach with four Horses, Harness and Equipage, and two very fine Saddle-Horses out of the Stable of the Bishop's Horses, afore-mentioned; with these there was a List for three Servants, and a Warrant to the Steward of the King's Baggage to defray me, my Horses and Servants at the King's Charge till farther Order. I was very much at a Loss how to manage my self in this so strange freedom of so great a Prince, and consulting with Sir *John Hepburn*, I was proposing to him whether it was not proper to go immediately back to pay my Duty to his Majesty and acknowledge his Bounty in the best Terms I could; but while we were resolving to do so, the Guards stood to their Arms, and we saw the King go out at the Gate in his Coach to pass into the City, so we were diverted from it for that Time. I acknowledge the Bounty of the King was very surprising, but I must say it was not so very strange to me when I afterward saw the Course of his Management; Bounty in him was his natural Talent, but he never distributed his Favours but where he thought himself both loved and faithfully served, and when he was so, even the single Actions of his private Soldiers he would take particular Notice of himself, and publickly own, acknowledge and reward them, of which I am obliged to give some Instances.

A private Musqueteer at the storming the Castle of *Wurtzberg*, when all the Detachment was beaten off, stood in the Face of the Enemy and fired his Piece, and though he had 1000 shot made at him, stood unconcerned, and charged his Piece again, and let fly at the Enemy, continuing to do so three Times, at the same Time beckoning with his Hand to his Fellows to come on again, which they did, animated by his Example, and carried the place for the King.

When the Town was taken the King ordered the Regiment to be drawn out, and calling for that Soldier, thanked him before them all for taking the Town for him, gave him 1000 Dollars in Money, and a Commission with his own Hand for a Foot Company, or Leave to go home, which he would; the Soldier took the Commission on his Knees, kissed it, and put it into his Bosom, and told the King, he would never leave his Service as long as he lived.

This Bounty of the King's, timed and suited by his Judgment, was the Reason that he was very well served, intirely beloved, and most punctually obeyed by his Soldiers, who were sure to be cherished and encouraged, if they did well, having the King generally an Eye-witness of their Behaviour.

My Indiscretion rather than Valour had engaged me so far at the Battle of *Leipsick*, that being in the Van of Sir *John Hepburn*'s Brigade, almost three whole Companies of us were separated from our Line, and surrounded by the Enemies Pikes; I cannot but say also that we were disengaged rather by a desperate Charge Sir *John* made with the whole Regiment to fetch us off, than by our own Valour, though we were not wanting to our selves neither, but this Part of the Action being talked of very much to the Advantage of the young *English* Voluntier, and possibly more than I deserved, was the Occasion of all the Distinction the King used me with ever after.

I had by this Time Letters from my Father, in which, though with some Reluctance, he left me at Liberty to enter into Arms if I thought fit, always obliging me to be directed, and, as he said, commanded by Sir *John Hepburn*; at the same Time he wrote to Sir *John Hepburn*, commending his Son's Fortunes, as he called it, to his Care; which Letters Sir *John* shewed the King, unknown to me.

I took Care always to acquaint my Father of every Circumstance, and forgot not to mention his Majesty's extraordinary Favour, which so affected my Father that he obtained a very honourable mention of it in a Letter from King *Charles* to the King of *Sweden*, written by his own Hand.

I had waited on his Majesty with Sir *John Hepburn*, to give him Thanks for his magnificent Present, and was received with his usual Goodness, and after that I was every Day among the Gentlemen of his ordinary Attendance; and if his Majesty went out on a Party, as he would often do, or to view the Country, I always attended him among the Voluntiers of whom a great many always followed him; and he would often call me out, talk with me, send me upon Messages to Towns, to Princes, free Cities, and the like, upon extraordinary Occasions.

The first Piece of Service he put me upon had like to have

embroiled me with one of his favourite Collonels; the King was marching through the *Bergstract*, a low Country on the edge of the *Rhine*, and, as all Men thought, was going to besiege *Heidelberg*, but on a sudden orders a Party of his Guards, with five Companies of *Scots*, to be drawn out; while they were drawing out this Detachment the King calls me to him, *Ho, Cavalier*, says he, *that was his usual Word, you shall command this Party*; and thereupon gives me Orders to march back all Night, and in the Morning, by break of Day, to take Post under the Walls of the Fort of *Oppenheim*, and immediately to entrench my self as well as I could: *Grave Neels*, the Collonel of his Guards, thought himself injured by this Command, but the King took the Matter upon himself, and *Grave Neels* told me very familiarly afterwards, We have such a Master, says he, that no Man can be affronted by: I thought my self wronged, says he, when you commanded my Men over my Head; and for my Life, says he, I knew not which way to be angry.

I executed my Commission so punctually that by break of Day I was set down within Musquet-shot of the Fort, under covert of a little Mount, on which stood a Wind-mill, and had indifferently fortified my self, and at the same Time had posted some of my Men on two other Passes, but at farther Distance from the Fort, so that the Fort was effectually block'd up on the Land-side; in the Afternoon the Enemy sallied on my first Entrenchment, but being covered from their Cannon, and defended by a Ditch which I had drawn cross the Road, they were so well received by my Musqueteers that they retired with the loss of 6 or 7 Men.

The next Day Sir *John Hepburn* was sent with two Brigades of Foot to carry on the Work, and so my Commission ended; the King expressed himself very well pleased with what I had done, and when he was so was never sparing of telling of it, for he used to say that publick Commendations were a great Encouragement to Valour.

While Sir *John Hepburn* lay before the Fort, and was preparing to storm it, the King's Design was to get over the

Rhine, but the *Spaniards* which were in *Oppenheim* had sunk all the Boats they could find; at last the King being informed where some lay that were sunk caused them to be weighed with all the Expedition possible, and in the Night of the 7th of *December* in three Boats passed over his Regiment of Guards, about three Miles above the Town, and as the King thought secure from Danger; but they were no sooner landed and not drawn into Order but they were charged by a Body of *Spanish* Horse, and had not the Darkness given them Opportunity to draw up in the Enclosures in several little Parties, they had been in great Danger of being disordered, but by this Means they lined the Hedges and Lanes so with Musqueteers, that the remainder had Time to draw up in Battalia, and saluted the Horse with their Musquets so that they drew farther off.

The King was very impatient, hearing his Men engaged, having no Boats nor possible Means to get over to help them; at last, about Eleven a Clock at Night the Boats came back, and the King thrust another Regiment into them, and though his Officers dissuaded him, would go over himself with them on Foot, and did so. This was three Months that very Day when the Battle of *Leipsick* was fought, and winter Time too, that the Progress of his Arms had spread from the *Elbe*, where it parts *Saxony* and *Brandenburgh*, to the *Lower Palatinate* and the *Rhine*.

I went over in the Boat with the King, I never saw him in so much Concern in my Life, for he was in Pain for his Men; but before we got on shore the *Spaniards* retired, however the King landed, ordered his Men, and prepared to entrench, but he had not Time; for by that Time the Boats were put off again, the *Spaniards*, not knowing more Troops were landed, and being reinforced from *Oppenheim*, came on again, and charged with great Fury; but all Things were now in Order; and they were readily received and beaten back again: They came on again the third Time, and with repeated Charges attacked us; but at last finding us too strong for them they gave it over. By this Time another

Regiment of Foot was come over, and as soon as Day appeared the King with the three Regiments marched to the Town, which surrendred at the first Summons, and the next Day the Fort yielded to Sir *John Hepburn*.

The Castle at *Oppenheim* held out still with a Garrison of 800 *Spaniards*, and the King leaving 200 *Scots* of Sir *James Ramsey*'s Men in the Town, drew out to attack the Castle; Sir *James Ramsey* being left wounded at *Wurtsburgh* the King gave me the Command of those 200 Men, which were a Regiment, that is to say, all that were left of a Gallant Regiment of 2000 *Scots* which the King brought out of *Sweden* with him, under that Brave Collonel; there was about 30 Officers, who having no Soldiers were yet in Pay, and served as Reformadoes with the Regiment, and were over and above the 200 Men.

The King designed to storm the Castle on the lower side by the Way that leads to *Mentz*, and Sir *John Hepburn* landed from the other Side and marched up to storm on the *Rhine* Port.

My Reformado *Scots* having observed that the Town Port of the Castle was not so well guarded as the rest, all the Eyes of the Garrison being bent towards the King and Sir *John Hepburn*; came running to me, and told me, they believed they could enter the Castle Sword in Hand if I would give them Leave; I told them I durst not give them Orders, my Commission being only to keep and defend the Town; but they being very importunate, I told them they were Voluntiers, and might do what they pleased, that I would lend them 50 Men and draw up the rest to second them, or bring them off, as I saw Occasion, so as I might not hazard the Town; this was as much as they desired, they sallied immediately, and in a trice the Voluntiers scaled the Port, cut in Pieces the Guard and burst open the Gate, at which the 50 entered: finding the Gate won I advanced immediately with 100 Musqueteers more, having locked up all the Gates of the Town but the Castle-Port, and leaving 50 still for a Reserve just at that Gate; the Townsmen too seeing the

Castle as it were taken, run to Arms, and followed me with above 200 Men; the *Spaniards* were knocked down by the *Scots* before they knew what the Matter was, and the King and Sir *John Hepburn* advancing to storm, were surprized, when instead of Resistance, they saw the *Spaniards* throwing themselves over the Walls to avoid the Fury of the *Scots*; few of the Garrison got away, but were either killed or taken, and having cleared the Castle, I set open the Port on the King's Side, and sent his Majesty Word the Castle was his own.[1] The King came on, and entered on Foot, I received him at the Head of the *Scots* Reformadoes, who all saluted him with their Pikes. The King gave them his Hat, and turning about, *Brave* Scots, *Brave* Scots, says he smiling, *you were too quick for me*; then beckoning to me, made me tell him how and in what Manner we had managed the Storm, which he was exceeding well pleased with, but especially at the Caution I had used to bring them off if they had miscarried, and secure the Town.

From hence the Army marched to *Mentz*, which in 4 Days Time capitulated,[2] with the Fort and Citadel, and the City paid his Majesty 300000 Dollars to be exempted from the Fury of the Soldiers; here the King himself drew the Plan of those invincible Fortifications which to this Day makes it one of the strongest Cities in *Germany*.

Friburg, *Koningstien*, *Niustat*, *Keiser-Lautern*, and almost all the *Lower Palatinate*, surrendered at the very Terror of the King of *Sweden*'s Approach, and never suffered the Danger of a Siege.

The King held a most Magnificent Court at *Mentz*, attended by the Landgrave of *Hesse*, with an incredible Number of Princes and Lords of the Empire, with Ambassadors and Residents of Foreign Princes; and here his Majesty staid till *March* when the Queen, with a great Retinue of *Swedish* Nobility came from *Erfurt* to see him. The King attended by a gallant Train of *German* Nobility went to *Frankfort*, and from thence on to *Hoest*, to meet the Queen,[3] where her Majesty arrived *Feb*. 8th.

During the King's stay in these Parts, his Armies were not idle, his Troops on one side under the *Rhinegrave*, a brave and ever-fortunate Commander, and under the Landgrave of *Hesse*, on the other, ranged the Country from *Lorrain* to *Luxemburgh*, and past the *Moselle* on the West, and the *Weser* on the North. Nothing could stand before them, the *Spanish* Army which came to the Relief of the Catholick Electors was every where defeated and beaten quite out of the Country, and the *Lorrain* Army quite ruined; 'twas a most pleasant Court sure as ever was seen, where every Day Expresses arrived of Armies defeated, Towns surrendered, Contributions agreed upon, Parties routed, Prisoners taken, and Princes sending Ambassadours to sue for Truces and Neutralities, to make Submissions and Compositions, and to pay Arrears and Contributions.

Here arrived, *Febr.* 10th, the King of *Bohemia* from *England*, and with him my Lord *Craven*, with a Body of *Dutch Horse*, and a very fine Train of *English* Voluntiers, who immediately, without any stay, marched on to *Hoest* to wait upon his Majesty of *Sweden*, who received him with a great deal of Civility, and was treated at a Noble Collation, by the King and Queen, at *Frankfort*. Never had the Unfortunate King so fair a Prospect of being restored to his Inheritance of the *Palatinate* as at that Time, and had King *James*, his Father-in-Law, had a Soul answerable to the Occasion, it had been effected before, but it was a strange Thing to see him equipped from the *English* Court with one Lord and about 40 or 50 *English Gentlemen* in his Attendance, whereas had the King of *England* now, as 'tis well known he might have done, furnished him with 10 or 12000 *English* Foot, nothing could have hindered him taking a full Possession of his Country; and yet even without that Help did the King of *Sweden* clear almost his whole Country of *Imperialists*, and after his Death, reinstal his Son in the Electorate, but no Thanks to us.

The Lord *Craven* did me the Honour to enquire for me by Name, and his Majesty of *Sweden* did me yet more by presenting me to the King of *Bohemia*, and my Lord *Craven* gave me a Letter from my Father, and speaking something of my Father having served under the Prince of *Orange* in the Famous Battle of *Neuport*,[1] the King smiling returned, *And pray tell him from me his Son has served as well in the warm Battle of* Leipsick.

My Father being very much pleased with the Honour I had received from so great a King, had ordered me to acquaint his Majesty, that if he pleased to accept of their Service he would raise him a Regiment of *English* Horse at his own Charge to be under my Command, and to be sent over into *Holland*; and my Lord *Craven* had Orders from the King of *England* to signify his Consent to the said Levy. I acquainted my old Friend Sir *John Hepburn* with the Contents of the Letter, in order to have his Advice, who being pleased with the Proposal, would have me go to the King immediately with the Letter, but present Service put it off for some Days.

The taking of *Creutznach* was the next Service of any Moment; the King drew out in Person to the Siege of this Town; the Town soon came to a Parly, but the Castle seemed a Work of Difficulty; for its Situation was so strong and so surrounded with Works behind and above one another, that most People thought the King would receive a Check from it; but it was not easy to resist the Resolution of the King of *Sweden*.

He never battered it but with two small Pieces, but having viewed the Works himself, ordered a Mine under the first Ravelin, which being sprung with Success, he commands a storm; I think there was not more commanded Men than Voluntiers, both *English*, *Scots*, *French* and *Germans*: My old Comrade was by this Time recovered of his Wound at *Leipsick*, and made one. The first Body of Voluntiers of about 40, were led on by my Lord *Craven*, and I led the second, among whom were most of the Reformado *Scots* Officers who took the Castle of *Oppenheim*; the first Party was not able to make any Thing of it, the Garrison fought with so much Fury that many of the Voluntier Gentlemen being wounded, and some killed, the rest were beaten off with Loss. The King was in some Passion at his Men, and rated them for running away, as he called it, though they really retreated in good Order, and commanded the Assault to be renewed. 'Twas our Turn to fall on next; our *Scots* Officers not being used to be beaten, advanced immediately, and my Lord *Craven*, with his Voluntiers, pierced in with us, fighting gallantly in the Breach with a Pike in his Hand, and to give him the Honour due to his Bravery, he was with the first on the Top of the Rampart, and gave his Hand to my Comrade, and lifted him up after him; we helped one another up, till at last almost all the Voluntiers had gained the Height of the Ravelin, and maintained it with a great Deal of Resolution, expecting when the commanded Men had gained the same Height to advance upon the Enemy, when one of the Enemies Captains called to my Lord *Craven*, and told him if they might have honourable Terms they would capitulate, which my Lord telling him he would engage for, the Garrison fired no more, and the Captain leaping down from the next Rampart came with my Lord *Craven* into the Camp, where the Conditions were agreed on, and the Castle surrendered.[1]

After the taking of this Town, the King hearing of *Tilly*'s Approach, and how he had beaten *Gustavus Horn*, the King's Field Marshal out of *Bamberg*, began to draw his Forces together, and leaving the Care of his Conquests in these Parts to his Chancellor *Oxenstern*, prepares to advance towards *Bavaria*.

I had taken an Opportunity to wait upon his Majesty with Sir *John Hepburn*, and being about to introduce the Discourse of my Father's Letter, the King told me he had received a Compliment on my account in a Letter from King *Charles*: I told him his Majesty had by his exceeding Generosity bound me and all my Friends to pay their Acknowledgements to him, and that I supposed my Father had obtained such a mention of it from the King of *England* as Gratitude moved him to; that his Majesty's Favour had been shewn in me to a Family both willing and ready to serve him, that I had received some Commands from my Father, which if his Majesty pleased to do me the Honour to accept of, might put me in a Condition to acknowledge his Majesty's Goodness in a Manner more proportioned to the Sense I had of his Favour; and with that I produced my Father's Letter, and read that Clause in it which related to the Regiment of Horse, which was as follows.

I Read with a great deal of Satisfaction the Account you give of the great and extraordinary Conquests of the King of Sweden, *and with more his Majesty's Singular Favour to you, I hope you will be careful to value and deserve so much Honour; I am glad you rather chose to serve as a Voluntier at your own Charge, than to take any Command, which for want of Experience you might misbehave in.*

I have obtained of the King that he will particularly Thank his Majesty of Sweden *for the Honour he has done you, and if his Majesty gives you so much Freedom, I could be glad you should in the humblest Manner thank his Majesty in the Name of an old broken Soldier.*

If you think your self Officer enough to command them, and his Majesty pleased to accept them, I would have you offer to raise his Majesty a Regiment of Horse, which I think I may near compleat in our Neighbourhood with some of your old Acquaintance who are very willing to see the World. If his Majesty gives you the Word, they shall receive his Commands in the Maes, *the King having promised me to give them Arms, and transport them for that Service into* Holland; *and I hope they may do his Majesty such Service as may be for your Honour and the Advantage of his Majesty's Interest and Glory,*

Your loving Father.

'Tis an Offer like a Gentleman and like a Soldier, says the King, *and I'll accept of it on two Conditions; first,* says the King, *that I will pay your Father the Advance Money for the raising the Regiment; and next, that they shall be landed in the*

Weser *or the* Elbe, *for which if the King of* England *will not, I will pay the Passage, for if they land in* Holland, *it may prove very difficult to get them to us when the Army shall be marched out of this Part of the Country.*

I returned this Answer to my Father, and sent my Man *George* into *England* to Order that Regiment, and made him Quarter-Master; I sent blank Commissions for the Officers, signed by the King, to be filled up as my Father should think fit; and when I had the King's Order for the Commissions, the Secretary told me I must go back to the King with them. Accordingly I went back to the King, who opening the Packet, laid all the Commissions but one upon a Table before him, and bad me take them, and keeping that one still in his Hand, *Now*, says he, *you are one of my Soldiers*, and therewith gave me his Commission, as Collonel of Horse in present Pay. I took the Commission kneeling, and humbly thanked his Majesty; *But*, says the King, *there is one Article of War I expect of you more than of others. Your Majesty can expect nothing of me which I shall not willingly comply with*, said I, *as soon as I have the Honour to understand what it is. Why it is*, says the King, *that you shall never fight but when you have Orders; for I shall not be willing to lose my Collonel before I have the Regiment. I shall be ready at all Times*, Sir, returned I, *to obey your Majesty's Orders.*

I sent my Man Express with the King's Answer, and the Commission to my Father, who had the Regiment compleated in less than 2 Months time, and 6 of the Officers with a List of the rest came away to me, who I presented to his Majesty when he lay before *Neurenburg*, where they kissed his Hand.

One of the Captains offered to bring the whole Regiment travelling as private Men into the Army in six Weeks Time, and either to transport their Equipage, or buy it in *Germany*; but 'twas thought impracticable; however, I had so many came in that Manner that I had a compleat Troop always about me, and obtained the King's Order to muster them as a Troop.

On the 8th of *March* the King decampt, and marching up the River *Mayn*, bent his Course directly for *Bavaria*, taking several small Places by the Way, and expecting to engage with *Tilly*, who he thought would dispute his Entrance into *Bavaria*, kept his Army together; but *Tilly* finding himself too weak to encounter him, turned away, and leaving *Bavaria* open to the King, marched into the *Upper Palatinate*. The King finding the Country clear of the *Imperialists*, comes to *Norimberg*, made his Entrance into that City the 21st of *March*, and being nobly treated by the Citizens, he continued his March into *Bavaria*; and on the 26th sat down before *Donawert*: The Town was taken the next Day by Storm, so swift were the Conquests of this invincible Captain. Sir *John Hepburn*, with the *Scots* and the *English* Voluntiers at the Head of them, entred the Town first, and cut all the Garrison to Pieces, except such as escaped over the Bridge.

I had no Share in the Business of *Donawert*, being now among the Horse, but I was posted on the Roads with five Troops of Horse, where we picked up a great many Stragglers of the Garrison, who we made Prisoners of War.

'Tis observable, that this Town of *Donawert* is a very strong Place and well fortified, and yet such Expedition did the King make, and such Resolution did he use in his first Attacks, that he carried the Town without putting himself to the Trouble of formal Approaches; 'twas generally his way when he came before any Town with a Design to besiege it; he never would encamp at a Distance and begin his Trenches a great Way off, but bring his Men immediately within half Musquet-shot of the Place, there getting under the best Cover he could, he would immediately begin his Batteries and Trenches before their Faces; and if there was any Place possible to be attacked, he would fall to storming immediately: By this resolute way of coming on he carried many a Town in the first heat of his Men, which would have held out many Days against a more Regular Siege.

This March of the King broke all *Tilly*'s Measures, for

now was he obliged to face about, and leaving the *Upper Palatinate*, to come to the Assistance of the Duke of *Bavaria*; for the King being 20000 strong, besides 10000 Foot and 4000 Horse and Dragoons which joined him from the *Duringer Wald*, was resolved to ruin the Duke, who lay now open to him, and was the most powerful and inveterate Enemy of the Protestants in the Empire.

Tilly was now joined with the Duke of *Bavaria*, and might together make about 22000 Men, and in Order to keep the *Swedes* out of the Country of *Bavaria*, had planted themselves along the Banks of the River *Lech*, which runs on the Edge of the Duke's Territories; and having fortified the other Side of the River, and planted his Cannon for several Miles at all the convenient Places on the River, resolved to dispute the King's Passage.

I shall be the longer in relating this Account of the *Lech*, being esteemed in those Days as great an Action as any Battle or Siege of that Age, and particularly famous for the Disaster of the gallant old General *Tilly*; and for that I can be more particular in it than other Accounts, having been an Eye-witness to every part of it.

The King being truly informed of the Disposition of the *Bavarian* Army, was once of the Mind to have left the Banks of the *Lech*, have repassed the *Danube*, and so setting down before *Ingolstat*, the Duke's Capital City, by the taking that strong Town to have made his Entrance into *Bavaria*, and the Conquest of such a Fortress, one entire Action; but the Strength of the Place, and the Difficulty of maintaining his Leaguer in an Enemy's Country, while *Tilly* was so strong in the Field, diverted him from that Design; he therefore concluded that *Tilly* was first to be beaten out of the Country, and then the Siege of *Ingolstat* would be the easier.

Whereupon the King resolved to go and view the Situation of the Enemy; his Majesty went out the 2d of *April* with a strong Party of Horse, which I had the Honour to command; we marched as near as we could to the Banks of the

River, not to be too much exposed to the Enemy's Cannon, and having gained a little Height, where the whole Course of the River might be seen, the King halted, and Commanded to draw up. The King alighted, and calling me to him, Examined every Reach and Turning of the River by his Glass, but finding the River run a long and almost a straight Course, he could find no Place which he liked, but at last turning himself North, and looking down the stream, he found the River fetching a long Reach, doubles short upon it self, making a round and very narrow Point, *There's a Point will do our business*, says the King, *and if the Ground be good I'll pass there*, *let* Tilly *do his worst*.

He immediately ordered a small Party of Horse to view the Ground, and to bring him Word particularly how high the Bank was on each Side and at the Point; and he shall have 50 Dollars, says the King, that will bring me Word how deep the Water is. I asked his Majesty Leave to let me go, which he would by no Means allow of; but as the Party was drawing out, a Serjeant of Dragoons[1] told the King, if he pleased to let him go disguised as a Boor, he would bring him an Account of every Thing he desired. The King liked the Motion well enough, and the Fellow being very well acquainted with the Country, puts on a Ploughman's Habit, and went away immediately with a long Pole upon his Shoulder; the Horse lay all this while in the Woods, and the King stood undiscerned by the Enemy on the little Hill aforesaid. The Dragoon with his long Pole comes down boldly to the Bank of the River, and calling to the Centinels which *Tilly* had placed on the other Bank, talked with them, asked them, if they could not help him over the River, and pretended he wanted to come to them; at last being come to the Point, where, as I said, the River makes a short Turn, he stands parlying with them a great while, and sometimes pretending to wade over, he puts his long Pole into the Water, then finding it pretty Shallow he pulls off his Hose and goes in, still thrusting his Pole in before him, till being gotten up to his middle, he could reach beyond him, where it was too deep, and so shaking his Head, comes back again. The Soldiers on the other Side laughing at him, asked him if he could swim? He said, No. Why you Fool you, says one of the Centinels, the Channel of the River is 20 Foot deep. How do you know that? says the Dragoon. Why our Engineer, says he, measured it Yesterday. This was what he wanted, but not yet fully satisfied; Ay but, says he, may be it may not be very broad, and if one of you would wade in to meet me till I could reach you with my Pole, I'd give him half a Ducat to pull me over. The innocent way of his Discourse so deluded the Soldiers, that one of them immediately strips and goes in up to the Shoulders, and our Dragoon goes in on this Side to meet him; but the Stream took the other Soldier away, and he being a good Swimmer, came swimming over to this Side. The Dragoon was then in a great deal of Pain for fear of being discovered, and was once going to kill the Fellow, and make off; but at last resolved to carry on the Humour, and having entertained the Fellow with a Tale of a Tub,[1] about the *Swedes* stealing his Oats, the Fellow being a cold wanted to be gone, and he as willing to be rid of him, pretended to be very sorry he could not get over the River, and so makes off.

By this however he learned both the Depth and Breadth of the Channel, the Bottom and Nature of both Shores, and every Thing the King wanted to know; we could see him from the Hill by our Glasses very plain, and could see the Soldier naked with him: Says the King, he will certainly be discovered and knocked on the Head from the other Side: He is a Fool, says the King, he does not kill the Fellow and run off; but when the Dragoon told his Tale, the King was extremely well satisfied with him, gave him 100 Dollars, and made him a Quarter-master to a Troop of Cuirassiers.

The King having farther examined the Dragoon, he gave him a very distinct Account of the Shore and the Ground on this Side, which he found to be higher than the Enemy's by 10 or 12 Foot, and a hard Gravel.

Hereupon the King resolves to pass there, and in order

to it gives, himself, particular Directions for such a Bridge as I believe never Army passed a River on before nor since.

His Bridge was only loose Plank laid upon large Tressels in the same homely Manner as I have seen Bricklayers raise a low Scaffold to build a Brick Wall; the Tressels were made higher than one another to answer to the River as it become deeper or shallower, and was all framed and fitted before any Appearance was made of attempting to pass.

When all was ready the King brings his Army down to the Bank of the River, and plants his Cannon as the Enemy had done, some here and some there, to amuse them.

At Night *April* 4th, the King commanded about 2000 Men to march to the Point, and to throw up a Trench on either Side, and quite round it with a Battery of six Pieces of Cannon, at each End besides three small Mounts, one at the Point and one of each Side, which had each of them two Pieces upon them. This Work was begun so briskly, and so well carried on, the King firing all the Night from the other Parts of the River, that by Day-light all the Batteries at the new Work were mounted, the Trench lined with 2000 Musqueteers, and all the Utensils of the Bridge lay ready to be put together.

Now the *Imperialists* discovered the Design, but it was too late to hinder it, the Musqueteers in the great Trench, and the five new Batteries, made such continual Fire that the other Bank, which, as before, lay 12 Foot below them, was too hot for the *Imperialists*; whereupon *Tilly*, to be provided for the King at his coming over, falls to work in a Wood right against the Point, and raises a great Battery for 20 Pieces of Cannon, with a Breast-Work, or Line, as near the River as he could, to cover his Men, thinking that when the King had built his Bridge he might easily beat it down with his Cannon.

But the King had doubly prevented him, first by laying his Bridge so low that none of *Tilly*'s Shot could hurt it; for the Bridge lay not above half a Foot above the Water's edge, by which Means the King, who in that shewed himself an excellent Engineer, had secured it from any Batteries to be made within the Land, and the Angle of the Bank secured it from the remoter Batteries, on the other Side, and the continual Fire of the Cannon and small Shot beat the *Imperialists* from their station just against it, they having no Works to cover them.

And in the second Place, to secure his Passage he sent over about 200 Men, and after that 200 more, who had Orders to cast up a large Ravelin on the other Bank, just where he designed to land his Bridge; this was done with such Expedition too, that it was finished before Night, and in a Condition to receive all the Shot of *Tilly*'s great Battery, and effectually covered his Bridge. While this was doing the King on his Side lays over his Bridge. Both Sides wrought hard all Day and all Night, as if the Spade, not the Sword, had been to decide the Controversy, and that he had got the Victory whose Trenches and Batteries were first ready; in the mean while the Cannon and Musquet Bullets flew like Hail, and made the Service so hot, that both Sides had enough to do to make their Men stand to their Work; the King in the hottest of it, animated his Men by his Presence, and *Tilly*, to give him his Due, did the same; for the Execution was so great, and so many Officers killed, General *Attringer* wounded, and two Sergeant Majors killed, that at last *Tilly* himself was obliged to expose himself, and to come up to the very Face of our Line to encourage his Men, and give his necessary Orders.

And here about one a Clock, much about the Time that the King's Bridge and Works were finished, and just as they said he had ordered to fall on upon our Ravelin with 3000 Foot, was the Brave old *Tilly* slain with a Musquet Bullet in the Thigh; he was carried off to *Ingolstat*, and lived some Days after, but died of that Wound the same Day as the King had his Horse shot under him at the Siege of that Town.

We made no question of passing the River here, having brought every Thing so forward, and with such extra-

ordinary Success, but we should have found it a very hot
Piece of Work if *Tilly* had lived one Day more; and if I may
give my Opinion of it, having seen *Tilly's* Battery and Breast-
work, in the Face of which we must have passed the River,
I must say, that whenever we had marched, if *Tilly* had fallen
in with his Horse and Foot, placed in that Trench, the whole
Army would have passed as much Danger *as in the Face of a
strong Town in the storming a Counterscarp*. The King himself, when he saw with what Judgment *Tilly* had prepared
his Works, and what Danger he must have run, would often
say, that Day's Success was every way equal to the Victory
of *Leipsick*.

Tilly being hurt and carried off, as if the Soul of the Army
had been lost, they begun to draw off; the Duke of *Bavaria*
took Horse and rid away as if he had fled out of Battle for his
Life.

The other Generals, with a little more Caution, as well as
Courage, drew off by Degrees, sending their Cannon and
Baggage away first, and leaving some to continue firing on the
Bank of the River to conceal their Retreat; the River preventing any Intelligence, we knew nothing of the Disaster
befallen them; and the King, who looked for Blows, having
finished his Bridge and Ravelin, ordered to run a Line with
Palisadoes to take in more Ground on the Bank of the River,
to cover the first Troops he should send over: This being
finished the same Night, the King sends over a Party of his
Guards to relieve the Men who were in the Ravelin, and
commanded 600 Musqueteers to Man the new line out of
the *Scots* Brigade.

Early in the Morning a small Party of *Scots*, commanded
by one Captain *Forbes*, of my Lord *Reas* Regiment, were
sent out to learn something of the Enemy, the King observing they had not fired all Night; and while this Party were
abroad, the Army stood in Battalia; and my old Friend Sir
John Hepburn, whom of all Men the King most depended
upon for any desperate Service, was ordered to pass the
Bridge with his Brigade, and to draw up without the Line,

with Command to advance as he found the Horse who were to second him came over.

Sir *John* being passed without the Trench, meets Captain *Forbes* with some Prisoners, and the good News of the Enemy's Retreat; he sends him directly to the King, who was by this Time at the Head of his Army, in full Battalia ready to follow his Vanguard, expecting a hot Day's Work of it. Sir *John* sends Messenger after Messenger to the King, intreating him to give him Orders to advance; but the King would not suffer him; for he was ever upon his Guard, and would not venture a Surprize; so the Army continued on this Side the *Lech* all Day, and the next Night. In the Morning the King sent for me, and ordered me to draw out 300 Horse, and a Collonel with 600 Horse, and a Collonel with 800 Dragoons, and ordered us to enter the Wood by 3 Ways, but so as to be able to relieve one another; and then ordered Sir *John Hepburn* with his Brigade to advance to the edge of the Wood to secure our Retreat; and at the same Time commanded another Brigade of Foot to pass the Bridge, if need were, to second Sir *John Hepburn*, so warily did this prudent General proceed.

We advanced with out Horse into the *Bavarian* Camp, which we found forsaken; the plunder of it was inconsiderable, for the exceeding Caution the King had used gave them Time to carry off all their Baggage; we followed them three or four Miles and returned to our Camp.

I confess I was most diverted that Day with viewing the Works which *Tilly* had cast up, and must own again, that had he not been taken off, we had met with as desperate a Piece of Work as ever was attempted. The next Day the rest of the Cavalry came up to us, commanded by *Gustavus Horn*, and the King and the whole Army followed; we advanced through the Heart of *Bavaria*, took *Rain* at the first Summons, and several other small Towns, and sat down before *Ausburg*.[1]

Ausburg, though a Protestant City, had a popish *Bavarian* Garrison in it of above 5000 Men, commanded by a *Fugger* a great Family in *Bavaria*. The Governour had posted several little Parties as out Scouts at the Distance of two Miles and half, or three Miles from the Town. The King, at his coming up to this Town, sends me with my little Troop, and 3 Companies of Dragoons to beat in these out Scouts; the first Party I light on was not above 16 Men, who had made a small Barricado cross the Road, and stood resolutely upon their Guard; I commanded the Dragoons to alight, and open the Barricado, which while they resolutely performed, the 16 Men gave them 2 Volleys of their Musquets, and through the Enclosures made their Retreat to a Turn-pike about a quarter of a Mile farther. We past their first Traverse, and coming up to the Turn-pike, I found it defended by 200 Musqueteers: I prepared to attack them, sending word to the King how strong the Enemy was, and desired some Foot to be sent me. My Dragoons fell on, and tho' the Enemy made a very hot Fire, had beat them from this Post before 200 Foot, which the King had sent me, had come up; being joined with the Foot, I followed the Enemy, who retreated fighting, till they came under the Cannon of a strong Redoubt, where they drew up, and I could see another Body of Foot of about 300 join them out of the Works; upon which I halted, and considering I was in View of the Town, and a great way from the Army, I faced about and began to march off; as we marched I found the Enemy followed, but kept at a Distance, as if they only designed to observe me; I had not marched far, but I heard a Volly of small Shot, answered by 2 or 3 more, which I presently apprehended to be at the Turn-pike, where I had left a small Guard of 26 Men, with a Lieutenant. Immediately I detached 100 Dragoons to relieve my Men, and secure my Retreat, following my self as fast as the Foot could march. The Lieutenant sent me back word the Post was taken by the Enemy, and my Men cut off; upon this I doubled my Pace, and when I came up I found it as the Lieutenant said; for the Post was taken and manned with 300 Musqueteers, and three Troops of Horse; by this Time also I found the Party in my Rear made up towards me, so that I was like to be charged in a narrow Place, both in Front and Rear.

I saw there was no Remedy but with all my Force to fall upon that Party before me, and so to break through before those from the Town could come up with me; wherefore commanding my Dragoons to alight, I ordered them to fall on upon the Foot; their Horse were drawn up in an enclosed Field on one Side of the Road, a great Ditch securing the other Side, so that they thought if I charged the Foot in Front they would fall upon my Flank, while those behind would charge my Rear; and indeed had the other come in Time, they had cut me off; my Dragoons made three fair Charges on their Foot, but were received with so much Resolution, and so brisk a Fire that they were beaten off, and sixteen Men killed: Seeing them so rudely handled, and the Horse ready to fall in, I relieved them with 100 Musqueteers and they renewed the Attack, at the same Time with my Troop of Horse, flanked on both Wings with 50 Musqueteers, I faced their Horse, but did not offer to charge them; the Case grew now desperate, and the Enemy behind were just at my Heels with near 600 Men; the Captain who commanded the Musqueteers who flanked my Horse came up to me, says he, if we do not force this Pass all will be lost; if you will draw out your Troop and 20 of my Foot, and fall in, I'll engage to keep off the Horse with the rest. With all my Heart, says I.

Immediately I wheel'd off my Troop, and a small Party of the Musqueteers followed me, and fell in with the Dragoons and Foot, who seeing the Danger too, as well as I, fought like Mad Men; the Foot at the Turn-pike were not able to hinder our Breaking through, so we made our way out, killing about 150 of them, and put the rest into Confusion.

But now was I in as great a Difficulty as before how to fetch off my brave Captain of Foot, for they charged home upon him; he defended himself with extraordinary Gallantry, having the Benefit of a Piece of a Hedge to cover him; but he lost half his Men, and was just upon the Point of being defeated, when the King, informed by a Soldier that escaped from the Turn-pike, one of 26, had sent a Party of 600 Dragoons to bring me off; these came upon the Spur, and joined with me just as I had broke through the Turn-pike; the Enemy's Foot rallied behind their Horse, and by this Time their other Party was come in, but seeing our Relief they drew off together.

I lost above 100 Men in these Skirmishes, and kill'd them about 180; we secured the Turn-pike, and placed a Company of Foot there with 100 Dragoons, and came back well beaten to the Army. The King, to prevent such uncertain Skirmishes, advanced the next Day in View of the Town, and according to his Custom, sits down with his whole Army within Cannon-shot of their Walls.

The King won this great City by Force of Words, for by two or three Messages and Letters to and from the Citizens, the Town was gained, the Garrison not daring to defend them against their Wills. His Majesty made his publick Entrance into the City on the 14th of *April*, and, receiving the Compliments of the Citizens, advanced immediately to *Ingolstat*, which is accounted, and really is the strongest Town in all these Parts.

The Town had a very strong Garrison in it, and the Duke of *Bavaria* lay entrenched with his Army under the Walls of it, on the other Side of the River. The King, who never loved long Sieges, having viewed the Town, and brought his Army within Musquet-shot of it, called a Council of War, where it was the King's Opinion, in short, that the Town would lose him more than 'twas worth, and therefore he resolved to raise his Siege.

Here the King going to view the Town had his Horse shot with a Cannon-bullet from the Works, which tumbled the King and his Horse over one another, that every Body thought he had been killed, but he received no Hurt at all; that very Minute, as near as could be learnt, General *Tilly* died in the Town of the Shot he received on the Bank of the *Lech* as aforesaid.[1]

I was not in the Camp when the King was hurt, for the King had sent almost all the Horse and Dragoons, under *Gustavus Horn*, to face the Duke of *Bavaria*'s Camp, and after that to plunder the Country, which truly was a Work the Soldiers were very glad of, for it was very seldom they had that Liberty given them, and they made very good use of it when it was; for the Country of *Bavaria* was rich and plentiful, having seen no Enemy before during the whole War.

The Army having left the Siege of *Ingolstat*, proceeds to take in the rest of *Bavaria*; Sir *John Hepburn* with 3 Brigades of Foot, and *Gustavus Horn* with 3000 Horse and Dragoons, went to *Landshut*, and took it the same Day; the Garrison was all Horse, and gave us several Camisadoes at our Approach, in one of which I lost two of my Troops, but when we had beat them into close Quarters, they presently capitulated. The General got a great Sum of Money of the Town besides a great many Presents to the Officers: And from thence the King went on to *Munick*, the Duke of *Bavaria*'s Court; some of the General Officers would fain have had the plundering of the Duke's Palace; but the King was too generous, the City paid him 400000 Dollars; and the Duke's Magazine was there seized, in which was 140 Pieces of Cannon, and small Arms for above 20000 Men. The great Chamber of the Duke's Rarities was preserved by the Kings special Order with a great deal of Care. I expected to have staid here some Time, and to have taken a very exact Account of this curious Laboratory; but being commanded away, I had not Time, and the Fate of the War never gave me Opportunity to see it again.[1]

The *Imperialists* under the Command of Comissary *Osta* had besieged *Bibrach*, an Imperial City not very well fortified, and the Inhabitants being under the *Swede*'s Protection, defended themselves as well as they could, but were in great Danger, and sent several Expresses to the King for Help.

The King immediately detaches a strong Body of Horse and Foot, to relieve *Bibrach*, and would be the Commander himself; I marched among the Horse, but the *Imperialists* saved us the Labour; for the News of the King's coming frighted away *Osta*, that he left *Bibrach*, and hardly looked behind him 'till he got up to the *Bodensee*, on the Confines of *Swisserland*.

At our Return from this Expedition, the King had the first News of *Wallestein*'s Approach, who on the Death of Count *Tilly*, being declared Generalissimo of the Emperor's Forces, had plaid the Tyrant in *Bohemia*, and was now advancing with 60000 Men, as they reported, to relieve the Duke of *Bavaria*.

The King therefore, in order to be in a Posture to receive this great General, resolves to quit *Bavaria*, and to expect him on the Frontiers of *Franconia*; and because he knew the *Norembergers*, for their Kindness to him, would be the first Sacrifice, he resolved to defend that City against him whatever it cost.

Nevertheless he did not leave *Bavaria* without a Defence; but on the one Hand he left Sir *John Bannier* with 10000 Men about *Ausburgh*, and the Duke of *Saxe-Weymar* with another like Army about *Ulme* and *Meningen*, with Orders so to direct their March, as that they might join him upon any Occasion in a few Days.

We encamped about *Noremberg* the Middle of *June*. The Army, after so many Detachments, was not above 19000 Men. The Imperial Army joined with the *Bavarian*, were not so numerous as was reported, but were really 60000 Men. The King, not strong enough to fight yet, as he used to say, was strong enough not to be forced to to fight, formed his Camp so under the Cannon of *Noremberg*, that there was no besieging the Town, but they must besiege him too; and he fortified his Camp in so formidable a Manner, that *Wallestein* never durst attack him. On the 30th of *June*, *Wallestein*'s Troops appeared, and on the 5th of *July*, encamped close by the King, and posted themselves not on the *Bavarian* Side, but between the King and his own Friends of *Schwaben*, and *Frankenland* in order to intercept his Provisions, and, as they thought, to starve him out of his Camp.

Here they lay to see, as it were, who could subsist longest; the King was strong in Horse, for we had full 8000 Horse and Dragoons in the Army, and this gave us great Advantage in the several Skirmishes we had with the Enemy. The Enemy had Possession of the whole Country, and had taken effectual Care to furnish their Army with Provisions; they placed their Guards in such excellent Order, to secure their Convoys, that their Waggons went from Stage to Stage as quiet as in a time of Peace, and were relieved every five Miles by Parties constantly posted on the Road. And thus the Imperial General sat down by us, not doubting but he should force the King either to fight his Way through, on very disadvantageous Terms, or to rise for want of Provisions, and leave the City of *Noremberg* a Prey to his Army; for he had vowed the Destruction of the City, and to make it a second *Magdeburg*.

But the King, who was not to be easily deceived, had countermined all *Wallestein*'s Designs; he had passed his Honour to the *Norembergers*, that he would not leave them, and they had undertaken to Victual his Army, and secure him from Want, which they did so effectually, that he had no Occasion to expose his Troops to any Hazard or Fatigues for Convoys or Forage on any Account whatever.

The City of *Noremberg* is a very rich and populous City; and the King being very sensible of their Danger, had given his Word for their Defence: And when they, being terrified at the Threats of the *Imperialists*, sent their Deputies to beseech the King to take care of them, he sent them Word, he would, and be besieged with them. They on the other Hand laid in such Stores of all Sorts of Provision, both for Men and Horse, that had *Wallestein* lain before it six Months longer, there would have been no Scarcity. Every private House was a Magazine, the Camp was plentifully supplied with all Manner of Provisions, and the Market always full, and as cheap as in Times of Peace. The Magistrates were so careful, and preserved so excellent an Order in the Disposal of all sorts of Provision, that no engrossing[1] of Corn could be practised; for the Prices were every Day directed at the Town-house: And if any Man offered to demand more Money for Corn, than the stated Price, he could not sell, because at the Town Store-house you might buy cheaper. Here are two Instances of good and bad Conduct; the City of *Magdeburgh* had been intreated by the King to settle Funds, and raise Money for their Provision and Security, and to have a sufficient Garrison to defend them, but they made Difficulties, either to raise Men for themselves, or to admit the King's Troops to assist them, for fear of the Charge of maintaining them; and this was the Cause of the City's Ruin.

The City of *Noremberg* open'd their Arms to receive the Assistance proferred by the *Swedes*, and their Purses to defend their Town, and Common Cause, and this was the saving them absolutely from Destruction. The rich Burghers and Magistrates kept open Houses, where the Officers of the Army were always welcome; and the Council of the City took such Care of the Poor, that there was no Complaining nor Disorders in the whole City. There is no doubt but it cost the City a great deal of Money; but I never saw a publick Charge borne with so much Chearfulness, nor managed with so much Prudence and Conduct in my Life. The City fed above 50000 Mouths every Day, including their own Poor, besides themselves; and yet when the King had lain thus 3 Months, and finding his Armies longer in coming up than he expected, asked the Burgrave how their Magazines held out? He answered, they desired his Majesty not to hasten things for them, for they could maintain themselves and him 12 Months longer, if there was Occasion. This Plenty kept both the Army and City in good Health, as well as in good Heart; whereas nothing was to be had of us but Blows; for we fetched nothing from without our Works, nor had no Business without the Line, but to interrupt the Enemy.

The Manner of the King's Encampment deserves a particular Chapter. He was a compleat Surveyor, and a Master in Fortification, not to be outdone by any Body. He had posted his Army in the Suburbs of the Town, and drawn Lines round the whole Circumference, so that he begirt the whole City with his Army; his Works were large, the Ditch deep, flanked with innumerable Bastions, Ravelins, Horn-works, Forts, Redoubts, Batteries and Pallisadoes, the incessant Work of 8000 Men for about 14 Days; besides that the King was adding some thing or other to it every Day; and the very Posture of his Camp was enough to tell a bigger Army than *Wallestein*'s, that he was not to be assaulted in his Trenches.

The King's Design appeared chiefly to be the Preservation of the City; but that was not all: He had three Armies acting abroad in three several Places; *Gustavus Horn* was on the *Mosel*, the Chancellor *Oxenstern* about *Mentz*, *Cologn*, and the *Rhine*, Duke *William* and Duke *Bernard*, together with General *Bannier* in *Bavaria*: And though he designed they should all join him, and had wrote to them all to that purpose, yet he did not hasten them, knowing that while he kept the main Army at Bay about *Noremberg*, they would without Opposition reduce those several Countries they were acting in to his Power. This occasioned his lying longer in the Camp at *Noremberg* than he would have done, and this occasioned his giving the *Imperialists* so many Alarms by his strong Parties of Horse, of which he was well provided, that they might not be able to make any considerable Detachments for the Relief of their Friends: And here he shewed his Mastership in the War; for by this means his Conquests went on as effectually as if he had been abroad himself.

In the mean Time, it was not to be expected two such Armies should lye long so near without some Action; the Imperial Army being Masters of the Field, laid the Country for 20 Miles round *Noremberg* in a manner desolate; what the Inhabitants could carry away had been before secured in such strong Towns as had Garrisons to protect them, and what was left, the hungry *Crabats* devoured, or set on Fire; but sometimes they were met with by our Men, who often paid them home for it. There had passed several small Rencounters between our Parties and theirs; and as it falls out in such Cases, sometimes one Side, sometimes the other, got the better; but I have observed there never was any Party sent out by the King's special Appointment, but always came home with Victory.

The first considerable Attempt, as I remember, was made on a Convoy of Ammunition: The Party sent out was commanded by a *Saxon* Collonel, and consisted of a 1000 Horse, and 500 Dragoons, who burnt above 600 Waggons, loaden with Ammunition and Stores for the Army, besides taking about 2000 Musquets which they brought back to the Army.

The latter end of *July* the King received Advice, that the *Imperialists* had formed a Magazine for Provision at a Town called *Freynstat*, 20 Miles from *Noremberg*. Hither all the Booty and Contributions raised in the *Upper Palatinate*, and Parts adjacent, was brought and laid up as in a Place of Security; a Garrison of 600 Men being placed to defend it; and when a Quantity of Provisions was got together, Convoys were appointed to fetch it off.

The King was resolved, if possible, to take or destroy this Magazine; and sending for Collonel *Dubalt*, a *Swede*, and a Man of extraordinary Conduct, he tells him his Design, and withal, that he must be the Man to put it in Execution, and ordered him to take what Forces he thought convenient. The Collonel, who knew the Town very well, and the Country about it, told his Majesty, he would attempt it with all his Heart; but he was affraid 'twould require some Foot to make the Attack; but we can't stay for that, says the King, you must then take some Dragoons with you, and immediately the King called for me. I was just coming up the Stairs, as the King's Page was come out to enquire for me; so I went immediately in to the King. Here is a Piece of hot Work for you, says the King, *Dubalt* will tell it you; go together and contrive it.

We immediately withdrew, and the Collonel told me the Design, and what the King and he had discoursed; that in his Opinion Foot would be wanted: But the King had declared there was no Time for the Foot to march, and had proposed Dragoons. I told him, I thought Dragoons might do as well; so we agreed to take 1600 Horse and 400 Dragoons. The King, impatient in his Design, came into the Room to us to know what we had resolved on, approved our Measures, gave us Orders immediately; and turning to me, you shall command the Dragoons, says the King, but *Dubalt* must be General in this Case, for he knows the Country. Your Majesty, said I, shall be always served by me in any Figure you please. The King wished us good Speed, and hurried us away the same Afternoon, in order to come to the Place in Time. We marched slowly on because of the Carriages we had with us, and came to *Freynstat* about One a Clock in the Night perfectly undiscover'd; the Guards were so negligent, that we came to the very Port before they had Notice of us, and a Serjeant with 12 Dragoons thrust in upon the Out-Centinels, and killed them without Noise.

Immediately Ladders were placed to the Half-Moon which defended the Gate, which the Dragoons mounted and carried in a trice, about 28 Men being cut in Pieces within. As soon as the Ravelin was taken, they burst open the Gate, at which I entered at the Head of 200 Dragoons, and seized the Drawbridge. By this Time the Town was in Alarm, and the Drums beat to Arms, but it was too late; for by the help of a Petard we broke open the Gate, and entered the Town. The Garrison made an obstinate Fight for about half an Hour, but our Men being all in, and 3 Troops of Horse dismounted coming to our Assistance with their Carabines, the Town was entirely mastered by Three of the Clock, and Guards set to prevent any Body running to give Notice to the Enemy. There were about 200 of the Garrison killed, and the rest taken Prisoners. The Town being thus secured, the Gates were opened, and Collonel *Dubalt* came in with the Horse.

The Guards being set, we entered the Magazine where we found an incredible Quantity of all sorts of Provision. There was 150 Tun of Bread, 8000 Sacks of Meal, 4000 Sacks of Oats, and of other Provisions in Proportion. We caused as much of it as could be loaded to be brought away in such Waggons and Carriages as we found, and set the rest on Fire, Town and all; we staid by it till we saw it past a Possibility of being saved, and then drew off with 800 Waggons, which we found in the Place, most of which we loaded with Bread, Meal and Oats. While we were doing this we sent a Party of Dragoons into the Fields, who met us again as we came out, with above a 1000 Head of Black Cattle, besides Sheep.

Our next Care was to bring this Booty home without meeting with the Enemy; to secure which, the Collonel immediately dispatch'd an Express to the King, to let him know of our Success, and to desire a Detachment might be made to secure our Retreat, being charged with so much Plunder.

And it was no more than Need; for tho' we had used all the Diligence possible to prevent any Notice, yet some body more forward than ordinary, had scap'd away and carried News of it to the *Imperial* Army. The General upon this bad News detaches Major General *Sparr*, with a Body of 6000 Men to cut off our Retreat. The King, who had Notice of this Detachment, marches out in Person with 3000 Men to wait upon General *Sparr*: All this was the Account of one Day; the King met General *Sparr* at the Moment when his Troops were divided, fell upon them, routed one Part of them, and the rest in a few Hours after; killed them a 1000 Men, and took the General Prisoner.

In the Interval of this Action, we came safe to the Camp with our Booty, which was very considerable, and would have supplied our whole Army for a Month. Thus we feasted at the Enemy's Cost, and beat them into the Bargain.

The King gave all the live Cattle to the *Norembergers*, who, tho' they had really no want of Provisions, yet fresh Meat was not so plentiful as such Provisions which were stored up in Vessels and laid by.

After this Skirmish, we had the Country more at Command than before, and daily fetch'd in fresh Provisions and Forage in the Fields.

The two Armies had now lain a long Time in sight of one another, and daily Skirmishes had considerably weakened them;[1] and the King beginning to be impatient, hastened the Advancement of his Friends to join him, in which also they were not backward; but having drawn together their Forces from several Parts, and all joined the Chancellor *Oxenstern*, News came the 15th of *August*, that they were in full March to join us; and being come to a small Town called *Brock*, the King went out of the Camp with about 1000 Horse to view them. I went along with the Horse, and the 21st of *August* saw the Review of all the Armies together, which were 30000 Men in extraordinary Equipage, old Soldiers, and commanded by Officers of the greatest Conduct and Experience in the World. There was the rich Chancellor of *Sweden* who commanded as General, *Gustavus Horn* and *John Bannier*, both *Swedes* and old Generals; Duke *William* and Duke *Bernard* of *Weymar*, the Landgrave of *Hesse Cassel*, the Palatine of *Birkenfelt*, and Abundance of Princes and Lords of the Empire.

The Armies being joined, the King who was now a Match for *Wallestein*, quits his Camp and draws up in Battalia before the *Imperial* Trenches; but the Scene was changed; *Wallestein* was no more able to fight now than the King was before; but keeping within his Trenches, stood upon his Guard. The King coming up close to his Works, plants Batteries, and cannonaded him in his very Camp.

The *Imperialists* finding the King press upon them, retreat into a woody Country about three Leagues, and taking Possession of an old ruin'd Castle, posted their Army behind it.

This old Castle[1] they fortified, and placed a very strong Guard there. The King having viewed the Place, tho' it was a very strong Post, resolved to attack it with the whole right Wing. The Attack was made with a great deal of Order and Resolution, the King leading the first Party on with Sword in Hand, and the Fight was maintained on both Sides with the utmost Gallantry and Obstinacy all the Day and the next Night too; for the Cannon and Musquet never gave over 'till the Morning; but the *Imperialists* having the Advantage of the Hill, of their Works and Batteries, and being continually relieved, and the *Swedes* naked, without Cannon or Works, the Post was maintained; and the King finding it would cost him too much Blood, drew off in the Morning.

This was the famous Fight at *Attembergh*, where the *Imperialists* boasted to have shewn the World the King of *Sweden* was not invincible. They call it the Victory at *Attembergh*; 'tis true, the King failed in his Attempt of carrying their Works, but there was so little of a Victory in it, that the *Imperial* General thought fit not to venture a second Brush, but to draw off their Army as soon as they could to a safer Quarter.[2]

I had no Share in this Attack, very few of the Horse being in the Action; but my Comerade, who was always among the *Scots* Voluntiers was wounded and taken Prisoner by the Enemy. They used him very civilly, and the King and *Wallestein* straining Courtesies with one another, the King released Major General *Sparr* without Ransom, and the *Imperial* General sent home Collonel *Tortenson* a *Swede*, and 16 Voluntier Gentlemen who were taken in the Heat of the Action, among whom my Captain was one.

The King lay 14 Days facing the *Imperial* Army, and using all the Stratagems possible to bring them to a Battle, but to no purpose; during which Time, we had Parties continually out, and very often Skirmishes with the Enemy.

I had a Command of one of these Parties in an Adventure, wherein I got no Booty, nor much Honour. The King had received Advice of a Convoy of Provisions which was to

come to the Enemy's Camp from the *Upper Palatinate*, and
having a great Mind to surprize them, he commanded us to
way-lay them with 1200 Horse, and 800 Dragoons. I had
exact Directions given me of the Way they were to come,
and posting my Horse in a Village a little out of the Road, I
lay with my Dragoons in a Wood, by which they were to
pass by break of Day. The Enemy appeared with their
Convoy, and being very wary, their Out-Scouts discovered
us in the Wood, and fired upon the Centinel I had posted in
a Tree at the Entrance of the Wood. Finding my self discovered, I would have retreated to the Village where my
Horse were posted, but in a Moment the Wood was skirted
with the Enemy's Horse, and a Thousand commanded
Musqueteers advanced to beat me out. In this Pickle I sent
away three Messengers one after another for the Horse, who
were within two Miles of me, to advance to my Relief; but
all my Messengers fell into the Enemy's Hands. 400 of my
Dragoons on foot, whom I had plac'd at a little Distance
before me, stood to their Work, and beat off two Charges of
the Enemy's Foot with some Loss on both Sides: Mean Time
200 of my Men fac'd about, and rushing out of the Wood,
broke through a Party of the Enemy's Horse who stood to
watch our coming out. I confess I was exceedingly surprized
at it, thinking those Fellows had done it to make their
Escape, or else were gone over to the Enemy; and my Men
were so discouraged at it, that they began to look about
which way to run to save themselves, and were just upon the
Point of disbanding to shift for themselves, when one of the
Captains called to me aloud to beat a Parle and Treat. I made
no Answer, but, as if I had not heard him, immediately gave
the Word for all the Captains to come together. The Consultation was but short, for the Musqueteers were advancing
to a third Charge, with Numbers which we were not likely
to deal with. In short, we resolved to beat a Parle, and demand Quarter, for that was all we could expect; when on a
sudden the Body of Horse I had posted in the Village being
directed by the Noise, had advanced to relieve me, if they

saw Occasion, and had met the 200 Dragoons who guided them directly to the Spot where they had broke thro', and all together fell upon the Horse of the Enemy who were posted on that Side, and mastering them before they could be relieved, cut them all to Pieces and brought me off. Under the Shelter of this Party, we made good our Retreat to the Village, but we lost above 300 Men, and were glad to make off from the Village too, for the Enemy were very much too strong for us.

Returning thence towards the Camp, we fell foul with 200 *Crabats* who had been upon the plundering Account: We made our selves some Amends upon them for our former Loss, for we shew'd them no Mercy; but our Misfortunes were not ended, for we had but just dispatch'd those *Crabats* when we fell in with 3000 *Imperial* Horse, who, on the Expectation of the aforesaid Convoy, were sent out to secure them.

All I could do, could not persuade my Men to stand their Ground against this Party; so that finding they would run away in Confusion, I agreed to make off, and facing to the Right, we went over a large Common at full Trot, 'till at last Fear, which always encreases in a Flight, brought us to a plain Flight, the Enemy at our Heels. I must confess I was never so mortified in my Life; 'twas to no Purpose to turn Head, no Man would stand by us, we run for Life, and a great many we left by the Way who were either wounded by the Enemy's Shot, or else could not keep Pace with us.

At last having got over the Common, which was near two Miles, we came to a Lane; one of our Captains, a *Saxon* by Country, and a Gentleman of a good Fortune alighted at the Entrance of the Lane, and with a bold Heart faced about, shot his own Horse, and called his Men to stand by him and defend the Lane. Some of his Men halted, and we rallied about 600 Men which we posted as well as we could, to defend the Pass; but the Enemy charged us with great Fury. The *Saxon* Gentleman, after defending himself with exceed-

ing Gallantry and refusing Quarter, was killed upon the
Spot: A *German* Dragoon as I thought him, gave me a rude
Blow with the Stock of his Piece on the Side of my Head,
and was just going to repeat it, when one of my Men shot
him dead. I was so stunn'd with the Blow, that I knew
nothing; but recovering, I found my self in the Hands of
two of the Enemy's Officers, who offered me Quarter, which
I accepted; and indeed, to give them their due, they used
me very civilly. Thus this whole Party was defeated, and not
above 500 Men got safe to the Army, nor had half the
Number escaped, had not the *Saxon* Captain made so bold a
Stand at the Head of the Lane.

Several other Parties of the King's Army revenged our
Quarrel, and paid them home for it; but I had a particular
Loss in this Defeat, that I never saw the King after; for
tho' his Majesty sent a Trumpet to reclaim us as Prisoners
the very next Day, yet I was not delivered, some Scruple
happening about exchanging, 'till after the Battle of *Lutzen*,
where that Gallant Prince lost his Life.

The Imperial Army rise from their Camp about eight or
ten Days after the King had removed, and I was carried
Prisoner in the Army 'till they sat down to the Siege of
Coburgh Castle,[1] and then was left with other Prisoners of
War, in the Custody of Collonel *Spezuter*, in a small Castle
near the Camp called *Newstad*. Here we continued indifferent well treated, but could learn nothing of what
Action the Armies were upon, 'till the Duke of *Friedland*
having been beaten off from the Castle of *Coburgh*, marched
into *Saxony*, and the Prisoners were sent for into the Camp,
as was said, in order to be exchanged.

I came into the Imperial Leager at the Siege of *Leipsick*,
and within three Days after my coming, the City was
surrendred, and I got Liberty to lodge at my old Quarters
in the Town upon my Parole.

The King of *Sweden* was at the Heels of the *Imperialists*;
for finding *Wallestein* resolved to ruin the Elector of *Saxony*,
the King had recollected as much of his divided Army as he

could, and came upon him just as he was going to besiege *Torgau*.

As it is not my Design to write a History of any more of these Wars than I was actually concerned in, so I shall only note, that upon the King's Approach, *Wallestein* halted, and likewise called all his Troops together; for he apprehended the King would fall on him; and we that were Prisoners, fancied the *Imperial* Soldiers went unwillingly out; for the very Name of the King of *Sweden* was become terrible to them. In short, they drew all the Soldiers of the Garrison they could spare, out of *Leipsick*, sent for *Papenheim* again, who was gone but three Days before with 6000 Men on a private Expedition. On the 16th of *November*, the Armies met on the Plains of *Lutzen*; a long and bloody Battle was fought; the *Imperialists* were entirely routed and beaten, 12000 slain upon the Spot, their Cannon, Baggage and 2000 Prisoners taken, but the King of *Sweden* lost his Life, being killed at the Head of his Troops in the Beginning of the Fight.

It is impossible to describe the Consternation the Death of this conquering King struck into all the Princes of *Germany*; the Grief for him exceeded all Manner of human Sorrow: All People looked upon themselves as ruined and swallowed up; the Inhabitants of two Thirds of all *Germany* put themselves into Mourning for him; when the Ministers mentioned him in their Sermons or Prayers, whole Congregations would burst out into Tears: The Elector of *Saxony* was utterly inconsolable, and would for several Days walk about his Palace like a distracted Man, crying the Saviour of *Germany* was lost, the Refuge of abused Princes was gone; the Soul of the War was dead, and from that Hour was so hopeless of out-living the War, that he sought to make Peace with the Emperor.

Three Days after this mournful Victory, the *Saxons* recovered the Town of *Leipsick* by Stratagem. The Duke of *Saxony*'s Forces lay at *Torgau*, and perceiving the Confusion the *Imperialists* were in at the News of the Overthrow of their Army, they resolved to attempt the Recovery of the Town. They sent about 20 scattering Troopers who pretending themselves to be *Imperialists* fled from the Battle, were let in one by one, and still as they came in, they staid at the Court of Guard in the Port, entertaining the Souldiers with Discourse about the Fight, and how they escaped, and the like; 'till the whole Number being got in at a Watch Word, they fell on the Guard, and cut them all in Pieces; and immediately opening the Gate to three Troops of *Saxon* Horse, the Town was taken in a Moment.

It was a welcome Surprise to me, for I was at Liberty of Course; and the War being now on another Foot, as I thought, and the King dead, I resolved to quit the Service.

I had sent my Man, as I have already noted into *England*, in Order to bring over the Troops my Father had raised for the King of *Sweden*. He executed his Commission so well, that he landed with five Troops at *Embden*, in very good Condition; and Orders were sent them by the King, to join the Duke of *Lunenberg*'s Army; which they did at the Siege of *Boxtude*, in the Lower *Saxony*. Here by long and very sharp Service they were most of them cut off, and though they were several Times recruited, yet I understood there were not three full Troops left.

The Duke of *Saxe-Weymar*, a Gentleman of great Courage, had the Command of the Army after the King's Death, and managed it with so much Prudence, that all things were in as much Order as could be expected, after so great a Loss; for the *Imperialists* were every where beaten, and *Wallestein* never made any Advantage of the King's Death.

I waited on him at *Hailbron*, whither he was gone to meet the great Chancellor of *Sweden*, where I paid him my Respects, and desired he would bestow the Remainder of my Regiment on my Comerade the Captain, which he did with all the Civility and Readiness imaginable: So I took my Leave of him, and prepared to come for *England*.

I shall only note this, that at this Dyet, the Protestant

Princes of the Empire renewed their League[1] with one another, and with the Crown of *Sweden*, and came to several Regulations and Conclusions for the carrying on the War, which they afterwards prosecuted under the Direction of the said Chancellor of *Sweden*. But it was not the Work of a small Difficulty, nor of a short Time; and having been perswaded to continue almost two Years afterwards at *Frankfort*, *Hailbron*, and thereabout, by the particular Friendship of that noble wise Man, and extraordinary Statesman *Axell Oxenstern*, Chancellor of *Sweden*, I had Opportunity to be concerned in, and present at several Treaties of extraordinary Consequence, sufficient for a History, if that were my Design.

Particularly I had the Happiness to be present at, and have some Concern in the Treaty for the restoring the Posterity of the truly noble *Palsgrave* King of *Bohemia*. King *James* of *England* had indeed too much neglected the whole Family; and I may say with Authority enough, from my own Knowledge of Affairs, had nothing been done for them but what was from *England*, that Family had remained desolate and forsaken to this Day.

But that glorious King, whom I can never mention without some Remark of his extraordinary Merit, had left particular Instructions with his Chancellor to rescue the *Palatinate* to its rightful Lord, as a Proof of his Design to restore the Liberty of *Germany*, and reinstate the oppressed Princes who were subjected to the Tyranny of the House of *Austria*.

Pursuant to this Resolution, the Chancellor proceeded very much like a Man of Honour; and tho' the King of *Bohemia* was dead a little before, yet he carefully managed the Treaty, answered the Objections of several Princes, who, in the general Ruin of the Family, had reaped private Advantages, settled the Capitulations for the Quota of Contributions, very much for their Advantage, and fully reinstalled the Prince *Charles* in the Possession of all his Dominions in the *Lower Palatinate*, which afterwards was confirmed to him and his Posterity by the Peace of *West-Phalia*,[1] where all these bloody Wars were finished in a Peace, which has since been the Foundation of the *Protestants* Liberty, and the best Security of the whole Empire.

I spent two Years rather in wandring up and down, than travelling; for tho' I had no Mind to serve, yet I could not find in my Heart to leave *Germany*; and I had obtained some so very close Intimacies with the General Officers, that I was often in the Army, and sometimes they did me the Honour to bring me into their Councils of War.

Particularly, at that eminent Council before the Battle of *Nordlingen*,[2] I was invited to the Council of War, both by Duke *Bernard* of *Weymar*, and by *Gustavus Horn*. They were Generals of equal Worth, and their Courage and Experience had been so well, and so often tried, that more than ordinary Regard was always given to what they said. Duke *Bernard* was indeed the younger Man, and *Gustavus* had served longer under our Great Schoolmaster the King; but 'twas hard to judge which was the better General, since both had Experience enough, and shewn undeniable Proofs both of their Bravery and Conduct.

I am obliged, in the Course of my Relation, so often to mention the great Respect I often received from these great Men, that it makes me sometimes jealous, least the Reader may think I affect it as a Vanity. The Truth is, and I am ready to confess the Honours I received, upon all Occasions, from Persons of such Worth, and who had such an eminent Share in the greatest Action of that Age, very much pleased me; and particularly, as they gave me Occasions to see every thing that was doing on the whole Stage of the War: For being under no Command, but at Liberty to rove about, I could come to no *Swedish* Garrison or Party, but sending my Name to the commanding Officer I could have *the Word* sent me; and if I came into the Army, I was often treated as I was now at this famous Battle of *Nordlingen*.

But I cannot but say, that I always looked upon this particular Respect to be the Effect of more than ordinary

Regard the great King of *Sweden* always shewed me, rather than any Merit of my own; and the Veneration they all had for his Memory, made them continue to shew me all the Marks of a suitable Esteem.

But to return to the Council of War, the great, and indeed the only Question before us was, shall we give Battle to the *Imperialists*, or not? *Gustavus Horn* was against it, and gave, as I thought, the most invincible Arguments against a Battle that Reason could imagine.

First, They were weaker than the Enemy by above 5000 Men.

Secondly, The Cardinal Infant of *Spain*, who was in the *Imperial* Army with 8000 Men, was but there *en Passant*, being going from *Italy* to *Flanders*, to take upon him the Government of the *Low Countries*; and if he saw no Prospect of immediate Action, would be gone in a few Days.

Thirdly, They had two Reinforcements, one of 5000 Men, under the Command of Collonel *Cratz*, and one of 7000 Men under the Rhinegrave, who were just at Hand, the last within three Days March of them: And

Lastly, They had already saved their Honour, in that they had put 600 Foot into the Town of *Nordlingen*, in the Face of the Enemy's Army, and consequently the Town might hold out some Days the longer.

Fate rather than Reason certainly blinded the rest of the Generals against such Arguments as these. Duke *Bernard* and almost all the Generals were for Fighting, alledging, the Affront it would be to the *Swedish* Reputation, to see their Friends in the Town lost before their Faces.

Gustavus Horn stood stiff to his cautious Advice, and was against it; and I thought the Baron *D'Offkirk* treated him a little indecently; for being very warm in the Matter, he told them; *That if* Gustavus Adolphus *had been governed by such cowardly Council, he had never been Conqueror of half* Germany *in two Years. No*, replied old General *Horn*, very smartly, *But he had been now alive to have testified for me, that I was never taken by him for a Coward; and yet* says he, *the King was never for a Victory with a Hazard, when he could have it without.*

I was asked my Opinion, which I would have declined, being in no Commission; but they pressed me to speak. I told them, I was for staying at least till the Rhinegrave came up; who at least might, if Expresses were sent to hasten him, be up with us in 24 Hours. But *Offkirk* could not hold his Passion, and had not he been over-rul'd, he would have almost quarrelled with Marshal *Horn*. Upon which the old General, not to foment him, with a great deal of Mildness stood up, and spoke thus.

Come, Offkirk, says he, *I'll submit my Opinion to you and the Majority of our Fellow-Soldiers: We will fight, but upon my Word we shall have our Hands full.*

The Resolution thus taken, they attacked the *Imperial* Army. I must confess the Councils of this Day seemed as confused as the Resolutions of the Night.

Duke *Bernard* was to lead the Van of the Left Wing, and to post himself upon a Hill which was on the Enemy's Right without their Entrenchments; so that having secured that Post, they might level their Cannon upon the Foot, who stood behind the Lines, and relieved the Town at Pleasure. He marched accordingly by Break of Day, and falling with great Fury upon 8 Regiments of Foot which were posted at the Foot of the Hill, he presently routed them and made himself Master of the Post. Flushed with this Success, he never regards his own concerted Measures of stopping there, and possessing what he had got, but pushes on and falls in with the Main Body of the Enemy's Army.

While this was doing, *Gustavus Horn* attacks another Post on a Hill, where the *Spaniards* had posted and lodged themselves behind some Works they had cast up on the side of the Hill; here they defended themselves with extreme Obstinacy for five Hours, and at last obliged the *Swedes* to give it over with Loss. This extraordinary Gallantry of the *Spaniards* was the saving of the *Imperial* Army; for Duke *Bernard* having all this while resisted the frequent Charges

of the *Imperialists*, and borne the Weight of two Thirds of
their Army, was not able to stand any longer, but sending
one Messenger in the Neck of another to *Gustavus Horn* for
more Foot, he finding he could not carry his Point, had given
it over, and was in full March to second the Duke. But now
'twas too late; for the King of *Hungary* seeing the Duke's
Men as it were wavering, and having Notice of *Horn*'s
wheeling about to second him, falls in with all his Force
upon his Flank, and with his *Hungarian* Hussars, made such
a furious Charge, that the *Swedes* could stand no longer.

The Rout of the Left Wing was so much the more unhappy, as it happened just upon *Gustavus Horn*'s coming up;
for being pushed on with the Enemies at their Heels, they
were driven upon their own Friends, who having no Ground,
to open, and give them way, were trodden down by their
own run-away Brethren. This brought all into the utmost
Confusion. The *Imperialists* cried *Victoria*, and fell into the
Middle of the Infantry with a terrible Slaughter.

I have always observed, 'tis fatal to upbraid an old
experienced Officer with want of Courage. If *Gustavus
Horn* had not been whetted with the Reproaches of the Baron
D'Offkirk, and some of the other General Officers, I believe
it had saved the Lives of a 1000 Men; for when all was thus
lost, several Officers advised him to make a Retreat with
such Regiments as he had yet unbroken; but nothing could
perswade him to stir a Foot: But turning his Flank into a
Front, he saluted the Enemy as they pass'd by him in
Pursuit of the rest, with such terrible Volleys of small Shot,
as cost them the Lives of Abundance of their Men.

The *Imperialists*, eager in the Pursuit, left him unbroken,
till the *Spanish* Brigade came up and charged him: These
he bravely repulsed with a great Slaughter, and after them
a Body of Dragoons; till being laid at on every Side, and
most of his Men killed, the brave old General, with all the
rest who were left, were made Prisoners.

The *Swedes* had a terrible Loss here; for almost all their
Infantry were killed or taken Prisoners. *Gustavus Horn*

refused Quarter several times; and still those that attacked him were cut down by his Men, who fought like Furies, and by the Example of their General, behaved themselves like Lions. But at last, these poor Remains of a Body of the bravest Men in the World were forced to submit. I have heard him say, he had much rather have died than been taken, but that he yielded in Compassion to so many brave Men as were about him; for none of them would take Quarter till he gave his Consent.

I had the worst Share in this Battle that ever I had in any Action of my Life; and that was to be posted among as brave a Body of Horse as any in *Germany*, and yet not be able to succour our own Men; but our Foot were cut in Pieces (as it were) before our Faces; and the Situation of the Ground was such as we could not fall in. All that we were able to do, was to carry off about 2000 of the Foot, who running away in the Rout of the Left Wing, rallied among our Squadrons, and got away with us. Thus we stood till we saw all was lost, and then made the best Retreat we could to save our selves, several Regiments having never charged, nor fired a Shot; for the Foot had so embarassed themselves among the Lines and Works of the Enemy, and in the Vineyards and Mountains, that the Horse were rendered absolutely unserviceable.

The Rhinegrave had made such Expedition to join us, that he reached within three Miles of the Place of Action that Night, and he was a great Safeguard for us in rallying our dispersed Men, who else had fallen into the Enemy's Hands, and in checking the Pursuit of the Enemy.

And indeed, had but any considerable Body of the Foot made an orderly Retreat, it had been very probable they had given the Enemy a Brush that would have turned the Scale of Victory; for our Horse being whole, and in a manner untouched, the Enemy found such a Check in the Pursuit, that 1600 of their forwardest Men following too eagerly, fell in with the Rhinegrave's advanced Troops the next Day, and were cut in Pieces without Mercy.

This gave us some Satisfaction for the Loss, but it was

but small compared to the Ruin of that Day. We lost near 8000 Men upon the Spot, and above 3000 Prisoners, all our Cannon and Baggage, and 120 Colours. I thought I never made so indifferent a Figure in my Life, and so we thought all; to come away, lose our Infantry, our General, and our Honour, and never fight for it. Duke *Bernard* was utterly disconsolate for old *Gustavus Horn*; for he concluded him killed; he tore the Hair from his Head like a mad Man, and telling the Rhinegrave the Story of the Council of War, would reproach himself with not taking his Advice, often repeating it in his Passion, *'Tis I*, said he, *have been the Death of the bravest General* in Germany; would call himself Fool and Boy, and such Names, for not listening to the Reasons of an old experienced Soldier. But when he heard he was alive in the Enemy's Hands, he was the easier, and applied himself to the recruiting his Troops, and the like Business of the War; and it was not long before he paid the *Imperialists* with Interest.

I returned to *Frankfort au Main* after this Action, which happened the 17th of *August* 1634; but the Progress of the *Imperialists* was so great, that there was no staying at *Frankfort*. The Chancellor *Oxenstern* removed to *Magdeburg*, Duke *Bernard* and the Landgrave marched into *Alsatia*, and the *Imperialists* carried all before them, for all the rest of the Campaign: They took *Philipsburgh* by Surprize; they took *Ausburgh* by Famine, *Spire* and *Treves* by Sieges, taking the Elector Prisoner. But this Success did one Piece of Service to the *Swedes*, that it brought the *French* into the War[1] on their Side; for the Elector of *Treves* was their Confederate. The *French* gave the Conduct of the War to Duke *Bernard*. This, though the Duke of *Saxony* fell off, and fought against them, turned the Scale so much in their Favour, that they recovered their Losses, and proved a Terror to all *Germany*. The farther Accounts of the War I refer to the Histories of those Times, which I have since read with a great deal of Delight.

I confess, when I saw the Progress of the *Imperial* Army

after the Battle of *Nordlingen*, and the Duke of *Saxony* turning his Arms against them, I thought their Affairs declining; and giving them over for lost, I left *Frankfort*, and came down the Rhine to *Cologn*, and from thence into *Holland*.

I came to the *Hague* the 8th of *March* 1635, having spent three Years and a half in *Germany* and the greatest Part of it in the *Swedish* Army.

I spent some Time in *Holland* viewing the wonderful Power of Art which I observed in the Fortifications of their Towns, where the very Bastions stand on bottomless Morasses, and yet are as firm as any in the World. There I had the Opportunity to see the *Dutch* Army, and their famous General Prince *Maurice*.[1] 'Tis true, the Men behaved themselves well enough in Action, when they were put to it, but the Prince's way of beating his Enemies without Fighting, was so unlike the Gallantry of my Royal Instructer, that it had no manner of Relish with me. Our way in *Germany* was always to seek out the Enemy and fight him; and, give the *Imperialists* their due, they were seldom hard to be found, but were as free of their Flesh as we were.

Whereas Prince *Maurice* would lye in a Camp till he starved half his Men, if by lying there he could but starve two Thirds of his Enemies; so that indeed the War in *Holland* had more of Fatigues and Hardships in it, and ours had more of Fighting and Blows: Hasty Marches, long and unwholesome Encampments, Winter Parties, Counter-marching, Dodging, and Entrenching, were the Exercises of his Men, and often times killed him more Men with Hunger, Cold, and Diseases, than he could do with Fighting: Not that it required less Courage, but rather more; for a Soldier had at any time rather die in the Field *a la Coup de Mousquet*, than be starved with Hunger, or frozen to Death in the Trenches.

Nor do I think I lessen the Reputation of that Great General; for tis most certain he ruined the *Spaniard* more by spinning the War thus out in Length, than he could possibly have done by a swift Conquest: For had he, *Gustavus* like, with a Torrent of Victory dislodged the *Spaniard* of all the 12 Provinces in 5 Years, whereas he was 40 Years, a beating them out of 7, he had left them rich and strong at Home, and able to keep them in constant Apprehensions of a Return of his Power: Whereas, by the long Continuance of the War, he so broke the very Heart of the *Spanish* Monarchy, so absolutely and irrecoverably impoverished them, that they have ever since languished of the Disease, till they are fallen from the most powerful, to be the most despicable Nation in the World.

The prodigious Charge the King of *Spain* was at in losing the Seven Provinces, broke the very Spirit of the Nation; and that so much, that all the Wealth of their *Peruvian* Mountains have not been able to retrieve it; King *Philip* having often declared, that War, besides his Armada for invading *England*, had cost him 370 Millions of Ducats, and 4000000 of the best Soldiers in *Europe*; whereof, by an unreasonable *Spanish* Obstinacy, above Sixty Thousand lost their Lives before *Ostend*, a Town not worth a sixth Part, either of the Blood or Money it cost in a Siege of three Years; and which at last he had never taken, but that Prince *Maurice* thought it not worth the Charge of defending it any longer.

However, I say, their Way of fighting in *Holland* did not relish with me at all. The Prince lay a long time before a little Fort called *Shenkscans*,[1] which the *Spaniard* took by Surprize, and I thought he might have taken it much sooner. Perhaps it might be my Mistake; but I fancied my Heroe, the King of *Sweden*, would have carried it Sword in Hand, in Half the Time.

However it was, I did not like it; so in the latter End of the Year I came to the *Hague*, and took Shipping for *England*, where I arrived, to the great Satisfaction of my Father and all my Friends.

My Father was then in *London*, and carried me to kiss the King's Hand. His Majesty was pleased to received me very well, and to say a great many very obliging things to my Father upon my Account.

I spent my Time very retired from Court, for I was almost wholly in the Country; and it being so much different from my Genius, which hankered after a warmer Sport than Hunting among our *Welch* Mountains, I could not but be peeping in all the foreign Accounts from *Germany*, to see who and who was together. There I could never hear of a Battle, and the *Germans* being beaten, but I began to wish my self there. But when an Account came of the Progress of *John Bannier*, the *Swedish* General in *Saxony*, and of the constant Victories he had there over the *Saxons*, I could no longer contain my self, but told my Father this Life was very disagreeable to me; that I lost my Time here, and might to much more Advantage go into *Germany*, where I was sure I might make my Fortune upon my own Terms: That, as young as I was, I might have been a General Officer by this Time, if I had not laid down my Commission: That General *Bannier*, or the Marshal *Horn*, had either of them so much Respect for me, that I was sure I might have any thing of them: And that if he pleased to give me Leave, I would go for *Germany* again. My Father was very unwilling to let me go, but seeing me uneasy, told me, that if I was resolv'd, he would oblige me to stay no longer in *England* than the next Spring, and I should have his Consent.

The Winter following began to look very unpleasant upon us in *England*, and my Father used often to sigh at it; and would tell me sometimes, he was afraid we should have no need to send *Englishmen* to fight in *Germany*.

The Cloud that seemed to threaten most was from *Scotland*. My Father, who had made himself Master of the Arguments on both Sides, used to be often saying, he feared there was some about the King who exasperated him too much against the *Scots*, and drove things too high. For my part, I confess I did not much trouble my Head with the Cause; but all my Fear was, they would not fall out, and we should have no Fighting. I have often reflected since, that I ought to have known better, that had seen how the most flourishing Provinces of *Germany* were reduced to the most miserable Condition that ever any Country in the World was, by the Ravagings of Soldiers, and the Calamities of War.

How much soever I was to blame, yet so it was, I had a secret Joy at the News of the King's raising an Army, and nothing could have with-held me from appearing in it; but my Eagerness was anticipated by an Express the King sent to my Father, to know if his Son was in *England*; and my Father having ordered me to carry the Answer my self, I waited upon his Majesty with the Messenger. The King received me with his usual Kindness, and asked me if I was willing to serve him against the *Scots*?

I answered, I was ready to serve him against any that his Majesty thought fit to account his Enemies, and should count it an Honour to receive his Commands. Hereupon his Majesty offered me a Commission. I told him, I supposed there would not be much Time for raising of Men; that if his Majesty pleased I would be at the Rendezvous with as many Gentlemen as I could get together, to serve his Majesty as Voluntiers.

The Truth is, I found all the Regiments of Horse the King designed to raise, were but two, as Regiments; the rest of the Horse were such as the Nobility raised in their several Counties, and commanded them themselves; and, as I had commanded a Regiment of Horse abroad, it looked a little odd to serve with a single Troop at home; and the King took the thing presently. *Indeed 'twill be a Voluntier War*, said the King, *for the Northern Gentry have sent me an Account of above* 4000 *Horse they have already*. I bowed, and told his Majesty I was glad to hear his Subjects were so forward to serve him; so taking his Majesty's Orders to be at *York*[1] by the End of *March*, I returned to my Father.

My Father was very glad I had not taken a Commission, for I know not from what kind of Emulation[2] between the Western and Northern Gentry. The Gentlemen of our Side were not very forward in the Service; their Loyalty to the King in the succeeding Times made it appear it was not from any Disaffection to his Majesty's Interest or Person, or to the Cause; but this however made it difficult for me when I came home, to get any Gentleman of Quality to serve with me, so that I presented my self to his Majesty only as a Voluntier, with eight Gentlemen, and about 36 Countrymen well mounted and armed.

And as it proved, these were enough, for this Expedition ended in an Accommodation with the *Scots*; and they not advancing so much as to their own Borders, we never came to any Action; but the Armies lay in the Counties of *Northumberland* and *Durham*, eat up the Country, and spent the King a vast Sum of Money, and so this War ended, a Pacification[1] was made, and both Sides returned.

The Truth is, I never saw such a despicable Appearance of Men in Arms to begin a War, in my Life; whether it was that I had seen so many braver Armies abroad that prejudiced me against them, or that it really was so; for to me they seemed little better than a Rabble met together to devour, rather than fight for their King and Country. There was indeed a great Appearance of Gentlemen, and those of extraordinary Quality; but their Garb, their Equipages, and their Mein, did not look like War; their Troops were filled with Footmen and Servants, and wretchedly armed, God wot. I believe I might say, without Vanity, one Regiment of *Finland* Horse would have made Sport at beating them all. There were such Crouds of Parsons, (for this was a Church War in particular) that the Camp and Court was full of them; and the King was so eternally besieged with Clergymen of one sort or another, that it gave Offence to the chief of the Nobility.

As was the Appearance, so was the Service; the Army marched to the Borders, and the Head Quarter was at *Berwick* upon *Tweed*; but the *Scots* never appeared, no, not so much as their Scouts; whereupon the King called a Council of War, and there it was resolved to send the Earl

of *Holland* with a Party of Horse into *Scotland*,[1] to learn
some News of the Enemy; and truly the first News he
brought us was, that finding their Army encamped about
Coldingham, 15 Miles from *Berwick*, as soon as he appeared,
the *Scots* drew out a Party to charge him, upon which most
of his Men halted, I don't say run away, but 'twas next
Door to it; for they could not be perswaded to fire their
Pistols, and wheel off like Soldiers, but retreated in such a
disorderly and shameful Manner, that had the Enemy but
had either the Courage or Conduct to have followed them,
it must have certainly ended in the Ruin of the whole Party.

THE SECOND PART

I CONFESS, when I went into Arms at the Beginning of this War, I never troubled my self to examine Sides: I was glad to hear the Drums beat for Soldiers; as if I had been a meer *Swiss*,[1] that had not car'd which Side went up or down, so I had my Pay. I went as eagerly and blindly about my Business, as the meanest Wretch that listed in the Army; nor had I the least compassionate Thought for the Miseries of my native Country, 'till after the Fight at *Edgehill*. I had known as much, and perhaps more than most in the Army, what it was to have an Enemy ranging in the Bowels of a Kingdom; I had seen the most flourishing Provinces of *Germany* reduced to perfect Desarts, and the voracious *Crabats*, with inhuman Barbarity, quenching the Fires of the plundered Villages with the Blood of the Inhabitants. Whether this had hardened me against the natural Tenderness which I afterwards found return upon me, or not, I cannot tell; but I reflected upon my self afterwards with a great deal of Trouble, for the Unconcernedness of my Temper at the approaching Ruin of my native Country.

I was in the first Army at *York*, as I have already noted, and I must confess, had the least Diversion there that ever I found in an Army in my Life; for when I was in *Germany* with the King of *Sweden*, we used to see the King with the General Officers every Morning on Horseback, viewing his Men, his Artillery, his Horses, and always something going forward: Here we saw nothing but Courtiers and Clergymen, Bishops and Parsons, as busy as if the Direction of the War had been in them; the King was seldom seen among us, and never without some of them always about him.

Those few of us that had seen the Wars, and would have made a short End of this for him, began to be very uneasy; and particularly a certain Nobleman took the Freedom to tell the King, that the Clergy would certainly ruin the Expedition; *the Case was this* he would ha' had the King have immediately marched into *Scotland*, and put the Matter to the Trial of a Battle; and he urged it every Day; and the King finding his Reasons very good, would often be of his Opinion; but next Morning he would be of another Mind.

This Gentleman was a Man of Conduct enough, and of unquestioned Courage, and afterwards lost his Life for the King. He saw we had an Army of young stout Fellows, numerous enough; and tho' they had not yet seen much Service, he was for bringing them to Action, that the *Scots* might not have time to strengthen themselves; nor they have time by Idleness and Sotting, *the Bane of Soldiers*, to make themselves unfit for any thing.

I was one Morning in Company with this Gentleman; and as he was a warm Man, and eager in his Discourse, a Pox of these Priests, says he, 'tis for them the King has raised this Army, and put his Friends to a vast Charge; and now we are come, they won't let us fight.

But I was afterwards convinced, the Clergy saw farther into the Matter than we did; they saw the *Scots* had a better Army than we had; bold and ready, commanded by brave Officers; and they foresaw, that if we fought, we should be beaten, and if beaten, they were undone. And 'twas very true, we had all been ruined, if we had engaged.

It is true, when we came to the Pacification which followed, I confess I was of the same Mind the Gentleman had been of; for we had better have fought, and been beaten, than have made so dishonourable a Treaty, without striking a Stroke. This Pacification seems to me to have laid the Scheme of all the Blood and Confusion which followed in the Civil

War; for whatever the King and his Friends might pretend to do by talking big, the *Scots* saw he was to be bullied into any thing, and that when it came to the Push, the Courtiers never cared to bring it to Blows.

I have little or nothing, to say as to Action, in this Mock-Expedition. The King was perswaded at last to march to *Berwick*; and as I have said already, a Party of Horse went out to learn News of the *Scots*, and as soon as they saw them, run away from them, bravely.

This made the *Scots* so insolent, that whereas before they lay encamped behind a River, and never shewed themselves, in a sort of modest Deference to their King, which was the Pretence of not being Aggressors or Invaders, only arming in their own Defence; now, having been invaded by the *English* Troops entring *Scotland*, they had what they wanted: And to shew it was not Fear that restrained them before, but Policy, now they came up in Parties to our very Gates, braving, and facing us every Day.

I had, with more Curiosity than Discretion, put my self as a Voluntier at the Head of one of our Parties of Horse, under my Lord *Holland*, when they went out to discover the Enemy; they went, they said, to see what the *Scots* were a-doing.

We had not marched far, but our Scouts brought Word, they had discovered some Horse, but could not come up to them, because a River parted them. At the Heels of these came another Party of our Men upon the Spur to us, and said the Enemy was behind, which might be true, for ought we knew; but it was so far behind, that no Body could see them; and yet the Country was plain and open for above a Mile before us: Hereupon we made a Halt, and indeed I was afraid 'twould have been an odd Sort of a Halt; for our Men began to look one upon another, as they do in like Cases, when they are going to break; and when the Scouts came galloping in, the Men were in such Disorder, that had but one Man broke away, I am satisfied they had all run for it.

I found my Lord *Holland* did not perceive it; but after

the first Surprize was a little over, I told my Lord what I had observed; and that unless some Course was immediately taken, they would all run at the first Sight of the Enemy. I found he was much concerned at it, and began to consult what Course to take, to prevent it. I confess 'tis a hard Question, how to make Men stand and face an Enemy, when Fear has possessed their Minds with an Inclination to run away: But I'll give that Honour to the Memory of that noble Gentleman, who tho' his Experience in Matters of War was small, having never been in much Service; yet his Courage made amends for it; for I dare say he would not have turned his Horse from an Army of Enemies, nor have saved his Life at the Price of running away for it.

My Lord soon saw, as well as I, the Fright the Men were in, after I had given him a Hint of it; and to encourage them, rode thro' their Ranks, and spoke chearfully to them, and used what Arguments he thought proper to settle their Minds. I remembered a Saying which I had heard old Marshal *Gustavus Horn* speak in *Germany*, If you find your Men faulter, or in Doubt, never suffer them to halt, but keep them advancing; for while they are going forward, it keeps up their Courage.

As soon as I could get Opportunity to speak to him, I gave him this as my Opinion. That's very well, says my Lord, but I am studying, says he, to post them so as that they can't run if they would; and if they stand but once to face the Enemy, I don't fear them afterwards.

While we were discoursing thus, Word was brought, that several Parties of the Enemies were seen on the farther Side of the River, upon which my Lord gave the Word to march, and as we were marching on, my Lord calls out a Lieutenant who had been an old Soldier, with only five Troopers whom he had most Confidence in; and having given him his Lesson, he sends him away; in a Quarter of an Hour, one of the five Troopers comes back galloping and hallowing, and tells us his Lieutenant had with his small Party beaten a Party of 20 of the Enemy's Horse over the River, and had secured the Pass, and desired my Lord would march up to him immediately.

'Tis a strange thing that Mens Spirits should be subjected to such sudden Changes, and capable of so much Alteration from Shadows of things. They were for running before they saw the Enemy; now they are in haste to be led on, and but that in raw Men we are obliged to bear with any thing, the Disorder in both was intolerable.

The Story was a premeditated Sham, and not a Word of Truth in it, invented to raise their Spirits, and cheat them out of their cowardly flegmatick Apprehensions, and my Lord had his End in it; for they were all on Fire to fall on: And I am perswaded, had they been led immediately into a Battle begun to their Hands, they would have laid about them like Furies; for there is nothing like Victory to flush a young Soldier. Thus while the Humour was high, and the Fermentation lasted, away we marched; and passing one of their great Commons which they call *Moors*, we came to the River, as he called it, where our Lieutenant was posted with his four Men; 'twas a little Brook fordable with Ease, and leaving a Guard at the Pass, we advanced to the Top of a small Ascent, from whence we had a fair View of the *Scots* Army, as they lay behind another River larger than the former.

Our Men were posted well enough, behind a small Enclosure, with a narrow Lane in their Front: And my Lord had caused his Dragoons to be placed in the Front to line the Hedges; and in this Posture he stood viewing the Enemy at a Distance. The *Scots* who had some Intelligence of our coming, drew out three small Parties, and sent them by different Ways to observe our Number; and forming a fourth Party, which I guessed to be about 600 Horse, advanced to the Top of the Plain, and drew up to face us, but never offered to attack us.

One of the small Parties making about 100 Men, one third Foot passes upon our Flank in View, but out of reach; and as they marched, shouted at us, which our Men better pleased with that Work than with Fighting, readily enough answered, and would fain have fired at them for the Pleasure of making a Noise; for they were too far off to hit them.

I observed that these Parties had always some Foot with them; and yet if the Horse galloped, or pushed on ever so forward, the Foot were as forward as they, which was an extraordinary Advantage.

Gustavus Adolphus that King of Soldiers, was the first that I have ever observed found the Advantage of mixing small Bodies of Musqueteers among his Horse; and had he had such nimble strong Fellows as these, he would have prized them above all the rest of his Men. These were those they call *Highlanders*; they would run on Foot with their Arms, and all their Acoutrements, and keep very good Order too, and yet keep Pace with the Horse, let them go at what Rate they would. When I saw the Foot thus interlined among the Horse, together with the Way of ordering their flying Parties, it presently occurred to my Mind, that here was some of our old *Scots*, come home out of *Germany*, that had the ordering of Matters; and if so, I knew we were not a Match for them.

Thus we stood facing the Enemy 'till our Scouts brought us Word the whole *Scots* Army was in Motion, and in full march to attack us; and though it was not true, and the Fear of our Men doubled every Object, yet 'twas thought convenient to make our Retreat. The whole Matter was, that the Scouts having informed them what they could, of our Strength; the 600 were ordered to march towards us, and three Regiments of Foot were drawn out to support the Horse.

I know not whether they would have ventured to attack us, at least before their Foot had come up; but whether they would have put it to the Hazard or no, we were resolved not to hazard the Trial, so we drew down to the Pass; and, as retreating looks something like running away, especially when an Enemy is at hand, our Men had much a-do to make their Retreat pass for a March, and not a Flight; and, by their often looking behind them, any Body might know what they would have done if they had been pressed.

I confess, I was heartily ashamed when the *Scots* coming up to the Place where we had been posted, stood and shouted at us. I would have perswaded my Lord to have charged them, and he would have done it with all his Heart, but he saw it was not practicable; so we stood at gaze with them above 2 Hours, by which time their Foot were come up to them, and yet they did not offer to attack us. I never was so ashamed of my self in my Life; we were all dispirited, the *Scots* Gentlemen would come out single, within Shot of our Post, which in a time of War is always accounted a Challenge to any single Gentleman, to come out and exchange a Pistol with them, and no Body would stir; at last our old Lieutenant rides out to meet a *Scotchman* that came pickeering on his Quarter. This Lieutenant was a brave and a strong Fellow, had been a Soldier in the *Low Countries*; and though he was not of any Quality, only a meer Soldier, had his Preferment for his Conduct. He gallops bravely up to his Adversary, and exchanging their Pistols, the Lieutenant's Horse happened to be killed. The *Scotchman* very generously dismounts, and engages him with his Sword, and fairly masters him, and carries him away Prisoner; and I think this Horse was all the Blood was shed in that War.

The Lieutenants Name thus conquered was *English*, and as he was a very stout old Soldier, the Disgrace of it broke his Heart. The *Scotchman* indeed used him very generously; for he treated him in the Camp very courteously, gave him another Horse, and set him at Liberty, *gratis*. But the Man laid it so to Heart, that he never would appear in the Army, but went home to his own Country and died.

I had enough of Party-making, and was quite sick with Indignation at the Cowardise of the Men; and my Lord was in as great a Fret as I, but there was no Remedy; we durst not go about to retreat, for we should have been in such Confusion, that the Enemy must have discovered it: So my Lord resolved to keep the Post, if possible, and send to the King for some Foot. Then were our Men ready to fight with one another who should be the Messenger; and at last when a Lieutenant with 20 Dragoons was dispatched, he told us afterwards he found himself an Hundred strong before he was gotten a Mile from the Place.

In short, as soon as ever the Day declined, and the Dusk of the Evening began to shelter the Designs of the Men, they dropt away from us one by one; and at last in such Numbers, that if we had stayed till the Morning, we had not had 50 Men left, out of 1200 Horse and Dragoons.

When I saw how 'twas, consulting with some of the Officers, we all went to my Lord *Holland*, and pressed him to retreat, before the Enemy should discern the Flight of our Men; so he drew us off, and we came to the Camp the next Morning, in the shamefullest Condition that ever poor Men could do. And this was the End of the worst Expedition ever I made in my Life.

To fight and be beaten, is a Casualty common to a Soldier, and I have since had enough of it; but to run away at the Sight of an Enemy, and neither strike or be stricken, this is the very Shame of the Profession, and no Man that has done it, ought to shew his Face again in the Field, unless Disadvantages of Place or Number make it tolerable, neither of which was our Case.

My Lord *Holland* made another March a few Days after, in hopes to retrieve this Miscarriage; but I had enough of it, so I kept in my Quarters: And though his Men did not desert him as before, yet upon the Appearance of the Enemy, they did not think fit to fight, and came off with but little more Honour than they did before.

There was no need to go out to seek the Enemy after this; for they came, as I have noted, and pitched in Sight of us, and their Parties came up every Day to the very Out-works of *Berwick*; but no Body cared to meddle with them: And in this Posture things stood when the Pacification was agreed on by both Parties; which, like a short Truce, only gave both Sides Breath to prepare for a new War more ridiculously managed than the former. When the Treaty was so near a Conclusion, as that Conversation was admitted on both Sides, I went over to the *Scotch* Camp to satisfy my Curiosity, as many of our *English* Officers did also.[1]

I confess, the Soldiers made a very uncouth Figure, especially the *Highlanders*: The Oddness and Barbarity of their Garb and Arms seemed to have something in it remarkable.

They were generally tall swinging Fellows; their Swords were extravagantly, and I think insignificantly broad, and they carried great wooden Targets large enough to cover the upper part of their Bodies. Their Dress was as antique as the rest; a Cap on their Heads, called by them a Bonnet, long hanging Sleeves behind, and their Doublet, Breeches and Stockings, of a Stuff they called Plaid, striped a-cross red and yellow, with short Cloaks of the same. These Fellows looked, when drawn out, like a Regiment of *Merry Andrews* ready for *Bartholomew* Fair. They are in Companies all of a Name, and therefore call one another only by their Christian Names, as *Jemy*, *Jocky*, that is *John*; and *Sawny*, that is, *Alexander*, and the like. And they scorn to be commanded but by one of their own Clan or Family. They are all Gentlemen, and proud enough to be Kings. The meanest Fellow among them is as tenacious of his Honour, as the best Nobleman in the Country, and they will fight, and cut one another's Throats for every trifling Affront.

But to their own Clans or Lairds, they are the willingest and most obedient Fellows in Nature. Give them their due, were their Skill in Exercises and Discipline proportioned to their Courage, they would make the bravest Soldiers in the World. They are large Bodies, and prodigiously strong; and two Qualities they have above other Nations, *viz.* hardy to endure Hunger, Cold, and Hardships, and wonderfully swift of Foot. The latter is such an Advantage in the Field, that I know none like it; for if they conquer, no Enemy can escape them; and if they run, even the Horse can hardly overtake them. These were some of them, who, as I observed before, went out in Parties with their Horse.

There were three or four Thousand of these in the *Scots* Army, armed only with Swords and Targets; and in their Belts some of them had a Pistol, but no Musquets at that time among them.

But there were also a great many Regiments of disciplined Men, who by their carrying their Arms, looked as if they understood their Business, and by their Faces, that they durst see an Enemy.

I had not been Half an Hour in their Camp, after the Ceremony of giving our Names, and passing their Out-Guards and Main Guard was over, but I was saluted by several of my Acquaintance; and in particular, by one who led the *Scotch* Voluntiers at the Taking the Castle of *Openheim*, of which I have given an Account. They used me with all the Respect they thought due to me, on Account of old Affairs, gave me the Word, and a Sergeant waited upon me whenever I pleased to go abroad.

I continued 12 or 14 Days among them, till the Pacification was concluded; and they were ordered to march home. They spoke very respectfully of the King, but I found were exasperated to the last Degree at Arch-bishop *Laud* and the *English* Bishops, for endeavouring to impose the *Common-Prayer-Book* upon them; and they always talked with the utmost Contempt of our Soldiers and Army. I always waved the Discourse about the Clergy, and the Occasion of the War; but I could not but be too sensible what they said of our Men was true; and by this I perceived they had an universal Intelligence from among us, both of what we were doing, and what sort of People we were that were doing it; and they were mighty desirous of coming to Blows with us. I had an Invitation from their General,[1] but I declined it, lest I should give Offence. I found they accepted the Pacification as a thing not likely to hold, or that they did not design should hold; and that they were resolved to keep their Forces on Foot, notwithstanding the Agreement. Their whole Army was full of brave Officers, Men of as much Experience and Conduct as any in the World; and all Men who know any thing of the War, know good Officers presently make a good Army.

Things being thus huddled up, the *English* came back to *York*, where the Army separated, and the *Scots* went home to encrease theirs; for I easily foresaw, that Peace was the farthest thing from their Thoughts.

The next Year the Flame broke out again, the King draws his Forces down into the North, as before, and Expresses were sent to all the Gentlemen that had Commands, to be at the Place by the 15th of *July*. As I had accepted of no Command in the Army, so I had no Inclination at all to go; for I foresaw there would be nothing but Disgrace attend it. My Father observing such an Alteration in my usual Forwardness, asked me one Day, what was the Matter, that I, who used to be so forward to go into the Army, and so eager to run abroad to fight, now shewed no Inclination to appear when the Service of the King and Country called me to it? I told him, I had as much Zeal as ever for the King's Service, and for the Country too: But he knew a Soldier could not abide to be beaten; and being from thence a little more inquisitive, I told him the Observations I had made in the *Scots* Army, and the People I had conversed with there; and, Sir, says I, assure your self, if the King offers to fight them, he will be beaten; and I don't love to engage, when my Judgement tells me before-hand, I shall be worsted: And as I had foreseen, it came to pass; for the Scots resolving to proceed, never stood upon the Ceremony of Aggression, as before, but on the 20th of *August* they entered *England* with their Army.

However, as my Father desired, I went to the King's Army, which was then at *York*, but not gotten all together: The King himself was at *London*; but upon this News takes Post for the Army, and advancing a Part of his Forces, he posted the Lord *Conway* and Sir *Jacob Astley*, with a Brigade of Foot and some Horse at *Newborn*, upon the River *Tine*, to keep the *Scots* from passing that River.

The *Scots* could have passed the *Tine* without Fighting;

but to let us see that they were able to force their Passage, they fall upon this Body of Men; and notwithstanding all the Advantages of the Place, they beat them from the Post, took their Baggage and two Pieces of Cannon, with some Prisoners. Sir *Jacob Astley* made what Resistance he could; but the *Scots* charged with so much Fury, and being also over-powered, he was soon put into Confusion. Immediately the *Scots* made themselves Masters of *Newcastle*,[1] and the next Day of *Durham*, and laid those two Counties under intolerable Contributions.

Now was the King absolutely ruined; for among his own People the Discontents before were so plain, that had the Clergy had any Forecast, they would never have embroiled him with the *Scots*, till he had fully brought Matters to an Understanding at Home: But the Case was thus: The King, by the good Husbandry of Bishop *Juxon*, his Treasurer, had a Million of ready Money in his Treasury, and upon that Account having no need of a Parliament, had not called one in 12 Years; and perhaps had never called another, if he had not by this unhappy Circumstance been reduced to a Necessity of it; for now this ready Money was spent in two foolish Expeditions, and his Army appeared in a Condition not fit to engage the *Scots*; the Detatchment under Sir *Jacob Astley*, which were of the Flower of his Men, had been routed at *Newborn*, and the Enemy had Possession of two entire Counties.

All Men blamed *Laud* for prompting the King to provoke the *Scots*, a headstrong Nation, and zealous for their own Way of Worship; and *Laud* himself found too late the Consequences of it, both to the whole Cause and to himself; for the *Scots*, whose native Temper is not easily to forgive an Injury, pursued him by their Party in *England*, and never gave it over, till they laid his Head on the Block.

The ruined Country now clamoured in his Majesty's Ears with daily Petitions, and the Gentry of other Neighbour Counties cry out for Peace and a Parliament. The King, embarassed with these Difficulties, and quite empty of

Money, calls a Great Council[1] of the Nobility at *York*, and demands their Advice, which any one could have told him before, would be to call a Parliament.

I cannot, without Regret, look back upon the Misfortune of the King, who, as he was one of the best Princes in his personal Conduct that ever reigned in *England*, had yet some of the greatest Unhappinesses in his Conduct as a King, that ever Prince had, and the whole Course of his Life demonstrated it.

1. An impolitick Honesty. His Enemies called it Obstinacy: But as I was perfectly acquainted with his Temper, I cannot but think it was his Judgment, when he thought he was in the right to adhere to it as a Duty tho' against his Interest.

2. Too much Compliance when he was complying.

No Man but himself would have denied what at some-times he denied, and have granted what at other times he granted; and this Uncertainty of Counsel proceeded from two things.

1. The Heat of the Clergy, to whom he was exceedingly devoted, and for whom indeed he ruined himself.

2. The Wisdom of his Nobility.

Thus when the Counsel of his Priests prevailed, all was Fire and Fury; the *Scots* were Rebels, and must be subdued; and the Parliament's Demands were to be rejected as exorbitant; but whenever the King's Judgment was led by the grave and steady Advice of his Nobility and Counsellors, he was always enclined by them to temperate his Measures between the two Extremes: And had he gone on in such a Temper, he had never met with the Misfortunes which afterward attended him, or had so many Thousands of his Friends lost their Lives and Fortunes in his Service.

I am sure, we that knew what it was to fight for him, and that loved him better than any of the Clergy could pretend to, have had many a Consultation how to bring over our Master from so espousing their Interest, as to ruin himself for it; but 'twas in vain.

I took this Interval, when I sat still and only looked on,

to make these Remarks, because I remember the best Friends the King had were at this time of that Opinion. That 'twas an unaccountable Piece of Indiscretion, to commence a Quarrel with the *Scots*, a poor and obstinate People, for a Ceremony and Book of Church Discipline,[1] at a time when the King stood but upon indifferent Terms with his People at Home.

The Consequence was, it put Arms into the Hands of his Subjects to rebel against him; it embroiled him with his Parliament in *England*, to whom he was fain to stoop in a fatal and unusual Manner to get Money,[2] all his own being spent, and so to buy off the *Scots* whom he cou'd not beat off.

I cannot but give one Instance of the unaccountable Politicks of his Ministers. If they over-ruled this unhappy King to it, with Design to exhaust and impoverish him, they were the worst of Traytors; if not, the grossest of Fools. They prompted the King to equip a Fleet against the *Scots*, and to put on board it 5000 Land Men. Had this been all, the Design had been good, that while the King had faced the Army upon the Borders, these 5000 landing in the Firth of *Edinburgh* might have put that whole Nation into Disorder. But in Order to this, they advise the King to lay out his Money in fitting out the biggest Ships he had, and the Royal Sovereign, the biggest Ship the World had ever seen, which cost him no less than 100000 Pounds was now built, and fitted out for this Voyage.

This was the most incongruous and ridiculous Advice that could be given, and made us all believe we were betrayed, tho' we knew not by whom.

To fit out Ships of 100 Guns to invade *Scotland*, which had not one Man of War in the World, nor any open Confederacy with any Prince or State that had any Fleet! 'twas a most ridiculous thing. An Hundred Sail of *Newcastle* Colliers, to carry the Men with their Stores and Provisions, and ten Frigates of 40 Guns each, had been as good a Fleet as Reason, and the Nature of the thing could ha' made tolerable.

Thus things were carried on, 'till the King, beggar'd by the Mismanagement of his Counsels, and beaten by the *Scots*, was driven to the Necessity of calling a Parliament in *England*.

It is not my Design to enter into the Feuds and Brangles[1] of this Parliament. I have noted, by Observations of their Mistakes, who brought the King to this unhappy Necessity of calling them.

His Majesty had tried Parliaments upon several Occasions before, but never found himself so much embroiled with them but he could send them Home, and there was an End of it; but as he could not avoid Calling these, so they took Care to put him out of a Condition to dismiss them.

The *Scots* Army was now quartered upon the *English*. The Counties, the Gentry, and the Assembly of Lords at *York*, petitioned for a Parliament.

The *Scots* presented their Demands to the King, in which it was observed, that Matters were concerted between them and a Party in *England*; and I confess, when I saw that, I began to think the King in an ill Case; for as the *Scots* pretended Grievances, we thought, the King redressing those Grievances, they could ask no more; and therefore all Men advised the King to grant their full Demands. And whereas the King had not Money to supply the *Scots* in their March home, I know there were several Meetings of Gentlemen with a Design to advance considerable Sums of Money to the King to set him free, and in order to reinstate his Majesty, as before. Not that we ever advised the King to rule without a Parliament, but we were very desirous of putting him out of the Necessity of calling them, at least, just then.

But the Eighth Article[2] of the *Scots* Demands expressly required, That an *English* Parliament might be called to remove all Obstructions of Commerce, and to settle Peace, Religion and Liberty; and in another Article they tell the King, the 24th of *September* being the Time his Majesty appointed for the Meeting of the Peers, will make it too long e'er the Parliament meet.

And in another, That a Parliament was the only Way of settling Peace, and bringing them to his Majesty's Obedience.

When we saw this in the Army, 'twas time to look about. Every body perceived that the *Scots* Army would call an *English* Parliament; and whatever Aversion the King had to it, we all saw he would be obliged to comply with it; and now they all began to see their Error, who advised the King to this *Scotch* War.

While these things were transacting, the Assembly of the Peers meet at *York*; and by their Advice a Treaty was begun with the *Scots*. I had the Honour to be sent with the first Message which was in Writing.

I brought it, attended with a Trumpet, and a Guard of 500 Horse, to the *Scots* Quarters. I was stoped at *Darlington*, and my Errand being known, General *Lesly* sent a *Scots* Major and 50 Horse, to receive me, but would let neither my Trumpet or Guard set Foot within their Quarters. In this Manner, I was conducted to Audience in the Chapter-House at *Durham*, where a Committee of *Scots* Lords who attended the Army, received me very courteously, and gave me their Answer in Writing also.

'Twas in this Answer that they shewed at least to me their Design of embroiling the King with his *English* Subjects; they discoursed very freely with me, and did not order me to withdraw when they debated their private Opinions: They drew up several Answers but did not like them; at last, they gave me one which I did not receive; I thought it was too insolent to be born with, as near as I can remember, it was thus.

The Commissioners of Scotland *attending the Service in the Army, do refuse any Treaty in the City of* York.

One of the Commissioners who treated me with more Distinction than the rest, and discoursed freely with me, gave me an Opportunity to speak more freely of this than I expected.

I told them, if they would return to his Majesty an Answer fit for me to carry, or if they would say they would not treat at all, I would deliver such a Message: But I entreated them to consider the Answer was to their Sovereign, and to whom they made a great Profession of Duty and Respect; and at least they ought to give their Reasons, why they declined a Treaty at *York*; and to name some other Place, or humbly to desire his Majesty to name some other Place: But to send Word they would not treat at *York*, I could deliver no such Message, for when put into *English* it would signify, they would not treat at all.

I used a great many Reasons and Arguments with them on this Head: And at last, with some Difficulty, obtained of them to give the Reason, which was the Earl of *Strafford*'s having the chief Command at *York*, whom they declared their mortal Enemy, he having declared them Rebels in *Ireland*.

With this Answer I returned. I could make no Observation in the short time I was with them; for as I staid but one Night, so I was guarded as a close Prisoner all the while. I saw several of their Officers whom I knew, but they durst not speak to me; and if they would ha' ventured, my Guard would not ha' permitted them.

In this Manner I was conducted out of their Quarters to my own Party again, and having delivered my Message to the King, and told his Majesty the Circumstances, I saw the King receive the Account of the haughty Behaviour of the *Scots* with some Regret; however it was his Majesty's time now to bear, and therefore the *Scots* were comply'd with, and the Treaty appointed at *Rippon*;[1] where, after much Debate, several preliminary Articles were agreed on, as a Cessation of Arms, *Quarters and Bounds to the Armies*, *Subsistence to the* Scots *Army*, and the Residue of the Demands was referred to a Treaty at *London*, &c.

We were all amazed at the Treaty, and I cannot but remember we used to wish much rather we had been suffered to fight;[2] for tho' we had been worsted at first, the Power and Strength of the King's Interest which was not yet tried, must, in fine, ha' been too strong for the *Scots*: Whereas now we saw the King was for complying with any thing, and all his Friends would be ruined.

I confess, I had nothing to fear, and so was not much concerned; but our Predictions soon came to pass: For no sooner was this Parliament called, but Abundance of those who had embroiled their King with his People of both Kingdoms, like the Disciples, when their Master was betrayed to the *Jews, forsook him and fled*;[1] and now Parliament Tyranny began to succeed Church Tyranny, and we Soldiers were glad [to] see it at first: The Bishops trembled, the Judges went to Gaol; the Officers of the Customs were laid hold on; and the Parliament began to lay their Fingers on the great ones, particularly Arch-Bishop *Laud*, and the Earl of *Strafford*.[2] We had no great Concern for the first, but the last was a Man of so much Conduct and Gallantry, and so beloved by the Soldiers and principal Gentry of *England*, that every Body was touched with his Misfortune.

The Parliament now grew mad in their Turn, and as the Prosperity of any Party is the time to shew their Discretion, the Parliament shewed they knew as little where to stop as other People. The King was not in a Condition to deny any thing, and nothing could be demanded but they push'd it. They attainted the Earl of *Strafford*, and thereby made the King cut off his right Hand, to save his left, and yet not save it neither. They obtain another Bill, to empower them to sit during their own Pleasure, and after them, Triennial Parliaments to meet, whether the King call them or no; and Granting this compleated his Majesty's Ruin.

Had the House only regulated the Abuses of the Court, punished evil Counsellors, and restor'd Parliaments to their original and just Powers, all had been well; and the King, tho' he had been more than mortified, had yet reaped the Benefit of future Peace; for now the *Scots* were sent Home, after having eaten up two Counties, and received a prodigious Sum of Money to boot: And the King, tho' too late, goes in Person to *Edinburgh*, and grants them all they could desire, and more than they asked; but in *England*, the Desires of ours were unbounded, and drove at all Extremes.

They threw out the Bishops from sitting in the House, make a Protestation equivalent to the *Scotch* Covenant; and this done, print their Remonstrance.[1] This so provoked the King, that he resolves upon seizing some of the Members,[2] and in an ill Hour enters the House in Person to take them. Thus one imprudent thing on one Hand produced another of the other Hand, 'till the King was obliged to leave them to themselves, for fear of being mobbed into something or other unworthy of himself.

These Proceedings began to alarm the Gentry and Nobility of *England*; for however willing we were to have evil Counsellours removed, and the Government return to a settled and legal Course, according to the happy Constitution of this Nation, and might ha' been forward enough to have owned the King had been misled, and imposed upon to do things which he had rather had not been done; yet it did not follow, that all the Powers and Prerogatives of the Crown should devolve upon the Parliament, and the King in a Manner be deposed, or else sacrificed to the Fury of the Rabble.

The Heats of the House running them thus to all Extremes, and at last to take from the King the Power of the Militia,[3] which indeed was all that was left to make him any thing of a King, put the King upon opposing Force with Force; and thus the Flame of Civil War began.

However backward I was in engaging in the second Year's Expedition against the *Scots*, I was as forward now; for I waited on the King at *York*, where a gallant Company of Gentlemen as ever were seen in *England*, engaged themselves to enter into his Service; and here some of us formed our selves into Troops for the Guard of his Person.

The King having been waited upon by the Gentry of *Yorkshire*, and having told them his Resolution of erecting his Royal Standard, and received from them hearty Assurances of Support; dismisses them, and marches to *Hull*, where lay the Train of Artillery, and all the Arms and

Amunition belonging to the *Northern* Army which had been disbanded. But here the Parliament had been beforehand with his Majesty, so that when he came to *Hull*, he found the Gates shut, and Sir *John Hotham* the Governour upon the Walls, tho' with a great deal of seeming Humility and Protestations of Loyalty to his Person, yet with a positive Denial to admit any of the King's Attendants into the Town. If his Majesty pleased to enter the Town in Person with any reasonable Number of his Houshould, he would submit, but would not be prevailed on to receive the King, as he would be received, with his Forces, tho' those Forces were then but very few.

The King was exceedingly provoked at this Repulse, and indeed it was a great Surprize to us all; for certainly never Prince began a War against the whole Strength of his Kingdom, under the Circumstances that he was in. He had not a Garrison, or a Company of Soldiers in his Pay, not a Stand of Arms, or a Barrel of Powder, a Musquet, Cannon or Mortar, not a Ship of all the Fleet, or Money in his Treasury to procure them; whereas the Parliament had all his Navy, and Ordinance, Stores, Magazines, Arms, Ammunition, and Revenue, in their Keeping. And this I take to be another Defect of the King's Counsel, and a sad Instance of the Distraction of his Affairs; that when he saw how all things were going to wreck, as it was impossible but he should see it, and 'tis plain he did see it, that he should not long enough before it came to Extremities, secure the Navy, Magazines, and Stores of War, in the Hands of his trusty Servants that would have been sure to have preserved them for his Use, at a Time when he wanted them.

It cannot be supposed, but the Gentry of *England*, who generally preserved their Loyalty for their Royal Master, and at last heartily shewed it, were exceedingly discouraged at first, when they saw the Parliament had all the Means of making War in their own Hands, and the King was naked and destitute either of Arms, or Ammunition, or Money to procure them.

Not but that the King, by extraordinary Application, recovered the Disorder the Want of these things had thrown him into, and supplied himself with all things needful.

But my Observation was this, had his Majesty had the Magazines, Navy, and Forts in his own Hand, the Gentry, who wanted but the Prospect of something to encourage them, had come in at first, and the Parliament being unprovided, would have been presently reduced to Reason.

But this was it that baulked the Gentry of *Yorkshire*, who went home again, giving the King good Promises, but never appeard for him, till by raising a good Army in *Shropshire* and *Wales*, he marched towards *London*, and they saw there was a Prospect of their being supported.

In this Condition the King erected his Standard at *Nottingham*, *August* the 22d 1642, and, I confess, I had very melancholy Apprehensions of the King's Affairs; for the Appearance to the Royal Standard was but small. The Affront the King had met with at *Hull*, had baulked and dispirited the Northern Gentry, and the King's Affairs looked with a very dismal Aspect. We had Expresses from *London* of the prodigious Success of the Parliament's Levies, how their Men came in faster than they could entertain them, and that Arms were delivered out to whole Companies listed together, and the like: And all this while the King had not got together a Thousand Foot, and had no Arms for them neither. When the King saw this, he immediately dispatches five several Messengers, whereof one went to the Marquess of *Worcester* into *Wales*; one went to the Queen, then at *Windsor*; one to the Duke of *Newcastle*, then Marquess of *Newcastle*, into the *North*; one into *Scotland*, and one into *France*, where the Queen soon after arrived to raise Money, and buy Arms, and to get what Assistance she could among her own Friends: Nor was her Majesty idle, for she sent over several Ships laden with Arms and Ammunition, with a fine Train of Artillery, and a great many very good Officers; and though one of the first fell into the Hands of the Parliament, with 300 Barrels of Powder and some

Arms, and 150 Gentlemen, yet most of the Gentlemen found Means, one Way or other, to get to us, and most of the Ships the Queen freighted arrived; and at last her Majesty came her self, and brought an extraordinary Supply, both of Men, Money, Arms, &c. with which she joined the King's Forces under the Earl of *Newcastle* in the *North*. Finding his Majesty thus bestirring himself to muster his Friends together, I ask'd him, if he thought it might not be for his Majesty's Service to let me go among my Friends, and his loyal Subjects about *Shrewsbury*? Yes, says the King, smiling, I intend you shall, and I design to go with you my self. I did not understand what the King meant then, and did not think it good Manners to enquire; but the next Day I found all things disposed for a March, and the King on Horseback by Eight of the Clock; when calling me to him, he told me I should go before, and let my Father and all my Friends know, he would be at *Shrewsbury* the *Saturday* following. I left my Equipages, and taking Post with only one Servant, was at my Father's the next Morning by Break of Day. My Father was not surprized at the News of the King's coming at all; for, it seems, he, together with the loyal Gentry of those Parts, had sent particularly to give the King an Invitation to move that Way, which I was not made privy to; with an Account what Encouragement they had there in the Endeavours made for his Interest. In short, the whole Country was entirely for the King, and such was the universal Joy the People shewed when the News of his Majesty's coming down was positively known, that all Manner of Business was laid aside, and the whole Body of the People seemed to be resolved upon the War.

As this gave a new Face to the King's Affairs, so I must own it filled me with Joy; for I was astonished before, when I considered what the King and his Friends were like to be exposed to. The News of the Proceedings of the Parliament, and their powerful Preparations were now no more terrible; the King came at the Time appointed, and having lain at my Father's House one Night, entered *Shrewsbury* in the

Morning. The Acclamations of the People, the Concourse of the Nobility and Gentry about his Person, and the Crouds which now came every Day in to his Standard, were incredible.[1]

The Loyalty of the *English* Gentry was not only worth Notice, but the Power of the Gentry is extraordinary visible in this Matter: The King, in about six Weeks time, which was the most of his Stay at *Shrewsbury*, was supplied with Money, Arms, Ammunition, and a Train of Artillery, and listed a Body of an Army upwards of 20000 Men.

His Majesty seeing the general Alacrity of his People, immediately issued out Commissions, and form'd Regiments of Horse and Foot; and having some experienced Officers about him, together with about 16 who came from *France*, with a Ship loaded with Arms and some Field-pieces which came very seasonably into the *Severn*; the Men were exercised, regularly disciplined, and quartered, and now we began to look like Soldiers. My Father had raised a Regiment of Horse at his own Charge, and compleated them, and the King gave out Arms to them from the Supplies which I mentioned came from Abroad. Another Party of Horse, all brave stout Fellows, and well mounted, came in from *Lancashire*, and the Earl of *Derby* at the Head of them. The *Welchmen* came in by Droves; and so great was the Concourse of People, that the King began to think of Marching, and gave the Command, as well as the Trust of Regulating the Army, to the brave Earl of *Lindsey*, as General of the Foot. The Parliament General being the Earl of *Essex*, two braver men, or two better Officers, were not in the Kingdom; they had both been old Soldiers, and had served together as Voluntiers, in the *Low Country* Wars, under Prince *Maurice*. They had been Comrades and Companions Abroad, and now came to face one another as Enemies in the Field.

Such was the Expedition used by the King and his Friends, in the Levies of this first Army, that notwithstanding the wonderful Expedition the Parliament made, the King was in the Field before them; and now the Gentry in other Parts of the Nation bestirred themselves, and siezed upon, and Garrisoned several considerable Places for the King. In the North, the Earl of *Newcastle* not only Garrisoned the most considerable Places, but even the general Possession of the North was for the King, excepting *Hull*, and some few Places, which the old Lord *Fairfax* had taken up for the Parliament. On the other Hand, entire *Cornwall*, and most of the Western Counties were the King's. The Parliament had their chief Interest in the South and Eastern Part of *England*, as *Kent*, *Surry*, and *Sussex*, *Essex*, *Suffolk*, *Norfolk*, *Cambridge*, *Bedford*, *Huntington*, *Hertford*, *Buckinghamshire*, and the other midland Counties. These were called, or some of them at least, the Associated Counties, and felt little of the War, other than the Charges; but the main Support of the Parliament was the City of *London*. The King made the Seat of his Court at *Oxford*, which he caused to be regularly fortified. The Lord *Say* had been here, and had Possession of the City for the Enemy, and was debating about fortifying it, but came to no Resolution, which was a very great Oversight in them; the Situation of the Place, and the Importance of it, on many Accounts, to the City of *London*, considered; and they would have retrieved this Error afterwards, but then 'twas too late; for the King made it the Head Quarter, and received great Supplies and Assistance from the Wealth of the Colleges, and the Plenty of the neighbouring Country. *Abingdon*, *Wallingford*, *Basing* and *Reading*, were all Garrisoned and fortified as Outworks to defend this as the Center. And thus all *England* became the Theater of Blood, and War was spread into every Corner of the Country, though as yet there was no Stroke struck. I had no Command in this Army; my Father led his own Regiment, and old as he was, would not leave his royal Master, and my elder Brother staid at home to support the Family. As for me, I rode a Voluntier in the royal Troop of Guards, which may very well deserve the Title of a royal Troop; for it was composed of young Gentlemen Sons of the Nobility and some of the prime Gentry of the Nation, and I think not a Person of so mean a Birth or Fortune as my self. We reckoned in this Troop Two and Thirty Lords, or who came afterwards to be such, and Eight and Thirty of younger Sons of the Nobility, five *French* Noblemen, and all the rest Gentlemen of very good Families and Estates.

And that I may give the due to their personal Valour, many of this Troop lived afterwards to have Regiments and Troops under their Command, in the Service of the King; many of them lost their Lives for him, and most of them their Estates: Nor did they behave unworthy of themselves in their first shewing their Faces to the Enemy, as shall be mentioned in its Place.

While the King remained at *Shrewsbury*, his loyal Friends bestirred themselves in several Parts of the Kingdom. *Goring* had secured *Portsmouth*; but being young in Matters of War, and not in Time relieved, though the Marquess of *Hertford* was marching to relieve him, yet he was obliged to quit the Place, and shipped himself for *Holland*, from whence he returned with Relief for the King, and afterwards did very good Service upon all Occasions, and so effectually cleared himself of the Scandal the hasty Surrender of *Portsmouth* had brought upon his Courage.

The chief Power of the King's Forces lay in three Places, in *Cornwall*, in *Yorkshire*, and at *Shrewsbury*: In *Cornwall*, Sir *Ralph Hopton*, afterwards Lord *Hopton*; Sir *Bevil Granvil* and Sir *Nicholas Slamming*, secured all the Country, and afterwards spread themselves over *Devonshire* and *Somersetshire*, took *Exeter* from the Parliament, fortified *Bridgwater*, and *Barnstable*, and beat Sir *William Waller* at the Battle of *Roundway Down*, as I shall touch at more particularly when I come to recite the Part of my own Travels that Way.

In the *North*, the Marquess of *Newcastle* secured all the Country, Garrisoned *York*, *Scarborough*, *Carlisle*, *Newcastle Pomfret*, *Leeds*, and all the considerable Places, and took the Field with a very good Army, though afterwards he proved more unsuccessful than the rest, having the whole Power of a Kingdom at his Back, the *Scots* coming in with an Army to the Assistance of the Parliament; which indeed was the general Turn of the Scale of the War; for had it not been for this *Scots* Army, the King had most certainly reduced the Parliament, at least to good Terms of Peace, in two Years time.

The King was the third Article: His Force at *Shrewsbury* I have noted already; the Alacrity of the Gentry filled him with Hopes, and all his Army with Vigour, and the 8th of *October* 1642, his Majesty gave Orders to march. The Earl of *Essex* had spent above a Month after his leaving *London* (for he went thence the 9th of *September*) in modelling and drawing together his Forces; his Rendezvous was at St. *Albans*, from whence he marched to *Northampton*, *Coventry*, and *Warwick*, and leaving Garrisons in them, he comes on to *Worcester*. Being thus advanced, he possesses *Oxford*, as I noted before, *Banbury*, *Bristol*, *Gloucester*, and *Worcester*, out of all which Places, except *Gloucester*, we drove him back to *London* in a very little while.

Sir *John Biron* had raised a very good Party of 500 Horse, most Gentlemen, for the King, and had possessed *Oxford*; but on the Approach of the Lord *Say* quitted it, being now but an open Town, and retreated to *Worcester*: From whence, on the Approach of *Essex*'s Army, he retreated to the King. And now all things grew ripe for Action, both Parties having secured their Posts, and settled their Schemes of the War, taken their Posts and Places as their Measures and Opportunities directed, the Field was next in their Eye, and the Soldiers began to enquire when they should fight; for as yet there had been little or no Blood drawn, and 'twas not long before they had enough of it; for I believe I may challenge all the Historians in *Europe* to tell me of any War in the World where, in the Space of four Years, there were so many pitched Battles, Sieges, Fights, and Skirmishes, as in this War; we never encamped or entrenched, never fortified the Avenues to our Posts, or lay fenced with Rivers and Defiles; here was no Leaguers in the Field, as at the

Story of *Noremberg*, neither had our Soldiers any Tents, or what they call heavy Baggage. 'Twas the general Maxim of this War, Where is the Enemy? Let us go and fight them: Or, on the other Hand, if the Enemy was coming, what was to be done? Why, what should be done? Draw out into the Fields, and fight them. I cannot say 'twas the Prudence of the Parties, and had the King fought less he had gained more: And I shall remark several times, when the Eagerness of Fighting was the worst Counsel, and proved our Loss. This Benefit however happened in general to the Country, that it made a quick, though a bloody End, of the War, which otherwise had lasted till it might have ruined the whole Nation.

On the 10th of *October* the King's Army was in full March, his Majesty Generalissimo, the Earl of *Lindsey* General of the Foot, Prince *Rupert* General of the Horse; and the first Action in the Field was by Prince *Rupert* and Sir *John Biron*. Sir *John* had brought his Body of 500 Horse, as I noted already, from *Oxford* to *Worcester*; the Lord *Say*, with a strong Party, being in the Neighbourhood of *Oxford*, and expected in the Town, Collonel *Sandys*, a hot Man, and who had more Courage than Judgment, advances with about 1500 Horse and Dragoons, with Design to beat Sir *John Biron* out of *Worcester*, and take Post there for the Parliament.

The King had notice that the Earl of *Essex* designed for *Worcester*, and Prince *Rupert* was ordered to advance with a Body of Horse and Dragoons, to face the Enemy, and bring off Sir *John Biron*. This his Majesty did to amuse[1] the Earl of *Essex*, that he might expect him that Way; whereas the King's Design was to get between the Earl of *Essex*'s Army and the City of *London*; and his Majesty's End was doubly answered; for he not only drew *Essex* on to *Worcester*, where he spent more Time than he needed, but he beat the Party into the Bargain.

I went Voluntier in this Party, and rid in my Father's Regiment; for though we really expected not to see the

Enemy, yet I was tired with lying still. We came to *Worcester* just as Notice was brought to Sir *John Biron*, that a Party of the Enemy was on their March for *Worcester*, upon which the Prince immediately consulting what was to be done, resolves to march the next Morning, and fight them.

The Enemy, who lay at *Pershore*,[1] about eight Miles from *Worcester*, and, as I believe, had no Notice of our March, came on very confidently in the Morning, and found us fairly drawn up to receive them: I must confess this was the bluntest downright Way of making War that ever was seen. The Enemy, who, in all the little Knowledge I had of War ought to have discovered our Numbers, and guessed by our Posture what our Design was, might equally have informed themselves, that we intended to attack them, and so might have secured the Advantage of a Bridge in their Front; but without any Regard to these Methods of Policy, they came on at all Hazards. Upon this Notice, my Father proposed to the Prince, to halt for them, and suffer ourselves to be attacked, since we found them willing to give us the Advantage: The Prince approved of the Advice, so we halted within View of a Bridge, leaving Space enough on our Front for about half the Number of their Forces to pass and draw up; and at the Bridge was posted about 50 Dragoons, with Orders to retire as soon as the Enemy advanced, as if they had been afraid. On the Right of the Road was a Ditch, and a very high Bank behind, where we had placed 300 Dragoons, with Orders to lye flat on their Faces till the Enemy had passed the Bridge, and to let fly among them as soon as our Trumpets sounded a Charge. No Body but Collonel *Sandys* would have been caught in such a Snare; for he might easily have seen, that when he was over the Bridge, there was not Room enough for him to fight in: But the Lord of Hosts was so much in their Mouths, *for that was the Word*[2] *for that Day*, that they took little heed how to conduct the Host of the Lord to their own Advantage.

As we expected, they appeared, beat our Dragoons from

the Bridge, and passed it: We stood firm in one Line with a Reserve, and expected a Charge; but Collonel *Sandys* shewing a great deal more Judgment than we thought he was Master of, extends himself to the Left, finding the Ground too streight, and began to form his Men with a great deal of Readiness and Skill; for by this time he saw our Number was greater than he expected: The Prince perceiving it, and foreseeing that the Stratagem of the Dragoons would be frustrated by this, immediately charges with the Horse, and the Dragoons at the same time standing upon their Feet, poured in their Shot upon those that were passing the Bridge: This Surprize put them into such Disorder, that we had but little Work with them; for though Collonel *Sandys* with the Troops next him sustained the Shock very well, and behaved themselves gallantly enough, yet the Confusion beginning in their Reer, those that had not yet passed the Bridge were kept back by the Fire of the Dragoons, and the rest were easily cut in Pieces. Collonel *Sandys* was mortally wounded and taken Prisoner, and the Crowd was so great, to get back, that many pushed into the Water; and were rather smothered than drowned. Some of them who never came into the Fight, were so frighted, that they never looked behind them, 'till they came to *Pershore*; and as we were afterwards informed, the Life-Guards of the General who had quartered in the Town, left it in Disorder enough, expecting us at the Heels of their Men.

If our Business had been to keep the Parliament Army from coming to *Worcester*, we had a very good Opportunity to have secured the Bridge at *Pershore*; but our Design lay another Way, as I have said, and the King was for drawing *Essex* on to the *Severn*, in hopes to get behind him, which fell out accordingly.

Essex, spurred by this Affront in the Infancy of their Affairs, advances the next Day, and came to *Pershore* time enough to be at the Funeral of some of his Men; and from thence he advances to *Worcester*.

We marched back to *Worcester* extremely pleased with

the good Success of our first Attack; and our Men were so flushed with this little Victory, that it put Vigour into the whole Army. The Enemy lost about 3000 Men, and we carried away near 150 Prisoners, with 500 Horses, some Standards and Arms, and among the Prisoners their Collonel, but he died a little after of his Wounds.

Upon the Approach of the Enemy, *Worcester* was quitted, and the Forces marched back to join the King's Army which lay then at *Bridgnorth*, *Ludlow*, and thereabout. As the King expected, it fell out; *Essex* found so much Work at *Worcester* to settle Parliament Quarters, and secure *Bristol*, *Gloucester*, and *Hereford*, that it gave the King a full Day's March of him; so the King having the Start of him, moves towards *London*; and *Essex*, nettled to be both beaten in Fight, and out-done in Conduct, decamps, and follows the King.

The Parliament, and the *Londoners* too, were in a strange Consternation at this Mistake of their General; and had the King, whose great Misfortune was always to follow precipitant Advices: Had the King, I say, pushed on his first Design, which he had formed with very good Reason, and for which he had been dodging with *Essex* eight or ten Days, *viz.* Of marching directly to *London*, where he had a very great Interest, and where his Friends were not yet oppressed and impoverished, as they were afterwards, he had turned the Scale of his Affairs: And every Man expected it; for the Members began to shift for themselves, Expresses were sent on the Heels of one another to the Earl of *Essex*, to hasten after the King, and if possible to bring him to a Battle. Some of these Letters fell into our Hands, and we might easily discover, that the Parliament were in the last Confusion at the Thoughts of our coming to *London*: Besides this, the City was in a worse Fright than the House, and the great moving[1] Men began to go out of Town. In short, they expected us, and we expected to come, but Providence for our Ruine had otherwise determined it.

Essex, upon News of the King's March, and upon Receipt

of the Parliament's Letters, makes long Marches after us, and on the 23d of *October* reaches the Village of *Keynton* in *Warwickshire*. The King was almost as far as *Banbury*, and there calls a Council of War. Some of the old Officers that foresaw the Advantage the King had, the Concern the City was in, and the vast Addition both to the Reputation of his Forces, and the Encrease of his Interest, it would be, if the King could gain that Point, urged the King to march on to *London*. Prince *Rupert*, and the fresh Collonells pressed for Fighting, told the King, it dispirited their Men to march with the Enemy at their Heels; that the Parliament Army was inferiour to him by 6000 Men, and fatigued with hasty Marching; that their Orders were to fight, he had nothing to do, but to post himself to Advantage, and receive them to their Destruction; that the Action near *Worcester* had let him know how easy it was to deal with a rash Enemy; and that 'twas a Dishonour for him, whose Forces were so much superior, to be pursued by his Subjects in Rebellion. These and the like Arguments prevailed with the King to alter his wiser Measures, and resolve to fight. Nor was this all, when a Resolution of fighting was taken, that Part of the Advice which they who were for fighting gave, as a Reason for their Opinion, was forgot, and instead of halting, and posting our selves to Advantage till the Enemy came up, we were ordered to march back, and meet them.

Nay, so eager was the Prince for fighting, that when from the Top of *Edgehill*, the Enemy's Army was descried in the Bottom between them and the Village of *Keynton*, and that the Enemy had bid us Defiance, by discharging three Cannons, we accepted the Challenge, and answering with two Shot from our Army, we must needs forsake the Advantages of the Hills, which they must have mounted under the Command of our Cannon, and march down to them into the Plain. I confess, I thought here was a great deal more Gallantry than Discretion; for it was plainly taking an Advantage out of our own Hands, and putting it into the Hands of the Enemy. An Enemy that *must fight*, may always be fought with to Advantage. My old Heroe, the Glorious *Gustavus Adolphus*, was as forward to fight as any Man of true Valour mixt with any Policy need to be, or ought to be; but he used to say, *An Enemy reduced to a Necessity of Fighting, is half Beaten.*

'Tis true, we were all but young in the War; the Souldiers hot and forward, and eagerly desired to come to Hands with the Enemy. But I take the more Notice of it here, because the King in this acted against his own Measures: For it was the King himself had laid the Design of getting the Start of *Essex*, and marching to *London*. His Friends had invited him thither, and expected him, and suffered deeply for the Omission; and yet he gave way to these hasty Counsels, and suffered his Judgment to be over-ruled by Majority of Voices; an Error, I say, the Kings of *Sweden* was never guilty of: For if all the Officers at a Council of War were of a different Opinion, yet unless their Reasons mastered his Judgment, their Votes never altered his Measures: But this was the Error of our good, but unfortunate Master, three times in this War, and particularly in two of the greatest Battles of the time, *viz.* this of *Edgehill*, and that of *Naseby*.

The Resolution for Fighting being published in the Army, gave an universal Joy to the Soldiers, who expressed an extraordinary Ardour for Fighting. I remember, my Father talking with me about it, asked me what I Thought of the approaching Battle: I told him, I Thought the King had done very well; for at that time I did not consult the Extent of the Design, and had a mighty Mind, like other rash People, to see it brought to a Day, which made me answer my Father as I did: But said I, Sir, *I Doubt there will be but indifferent Doings on both Sides, between two Armies both made up of fresh Men, that have never seen any Service.* My Father minded little what I spoke of that; but when I seemed pleased that the King had resolved to fight, he looked angrily at me, and told me he was sorry I could see no farther into things. I tell you, says he hastily, *If the King should kill, and take Prisoners, this whole Army, General and all, the Parliament will have the Victory; for we have lost more by slipping this Opportunity of getting into* London, *than we shall ever get by ten Battles.* I saw enough of this afterwards to convince me of the Weight of what my Father said, and so did the King too; but it was then too late, Advantages slipt in War are never recovered.

We were now in a full March to fight the Earl of *Essex*. It was on *Sunday* Morning the 24th of *October*, 1642, fair Weather over Head, but the Ground very heavy and dirty. As soon as we came to the Top of *Edgehill*, we discovered their whole Army. They were not drawn up, having had two Miles to march that Morning; but they were very busy forming their Lines, and posting the Regiments as they came up. Some of their Horse were exceedingly fatigued, having marched 48 Hours together; and had they been suffered to follow us three or four Days March farther, several of their Regiments of Horse would have been quite ruined, and their Foot would have been rendered unserviceable for the present. But we had no Patience.

As soon as our whole Army was come to the Top of the Hill, we were drawn up in Order of Battle: The King's Army made a very fine Appearance; and indeed they were a Body of gallant Men as ever appeared in the Field, and as well furnished at all Points: The Horse exceeding well accoutred, being most of them Gentlemen and Voluntiers; some whole Regiments serving without Pay. Their Horses very good and fit for Service as could be desired. The whole Army were not above 18000 Men, and the Enemy not a 1000 over or under, though we had been told they were not above 12000; but they had been reinforced with 4000 Men from *Northampton*.

The King was with the General, the Earl of *Lindsey*, in the Main Battle; Prince *Rupert* commanded the Right Wing, and the Marquess of *Hertford*, the Lord *Willoughby*, and several other very good Officers, the Left.

The Signal of Battle being given with two Cannon Shot, we marched in Order of Battalia down the Hill, being drawn up in two Lines with Bodies of Reserve; the Enemy advanced to meet us much in the same Form, with this Difference only, that they had placed their Cannon on their Right, and the King had placed ours in the Center, before, or rather between two great Brigades of Foot. Their Cannon began with us first, and did some Mischief among the Dragoons of our left Wing; but our Officers perceiving the Shot took the Men, and missed the Horses, ordered all to alight, and every Man leading his Horse, to advance in the same Order; and this saved our Men, for most of the Enemy's Shot flew over their Heads. Our Cannon made a terrible Execution upon their Foot for a Quarter of an Hour, and put them into great Confusion, till the General obliged them to halt, and changed the Posture of his Front, marching round a small rising Ground by which he avoided the Fury of our Artillery.

By this time the Wings were engaged, the King having given the Signal of Battle, and ordered the Right Wing to fall on. Prince *Rupert* who as is said, commanded that Wing, fell on with such Fury, and pushed the Left Wing of the Parliament Army so effectually, that in a Moment he filled all with Terror and Confusion: Comissary General *Ramsey*, a Scochman, a Low Country Soldier, and an experienced Officer, commanded their Left Wing; and though he did all that an expert Soldier, and a brave Commander could do, yet 'twas to no Purpose; his lines were immediately broken, and all overwhelmed in a trice: Two Regiments of Foot, whether as Part of the Left Wing, or on the Left of the Main Body, I know not, were disordered by their own Horse, and rather trampled to Death by the Horses, than beaten by our Men; but they were so entirely broken and disordered, that I do not remember that ever they made one Volley upon our Men; for their own Horse running away, and falling foul on these Foot, were so vigorously followed by our Men, that the Foot never had a Moment to rally, or look behind them. The Point of the left Wing of Horse were not so soon broken as the rest, and three Regiments of them stood firm for some Time: The dexterous Officers of the other Regiments taking the Opportunity, rallied a great many of their scattered Men behind them, and pieced in some Troops with those Regiments; but after two or three Charges, which a Brigade of our second Line following the Prince, made upon them, they also were broken with the rest.

I remember, that at the great Battle of *Leipsick*, the Right Wing of the *Imperialists* having fallen in upon the *Saxons* with like Fury to this, bore down all before them, and beat the *Saxons* quite out of the Field; upon which the Soldiers cried, *Victoria, Let us follow. No, no*, said the old General *Tilly, let them go, but let us beat the* Swedes *too, and then all's our own*.[1] Had Prince *Rupert* taken this Method, and instead of following the Fugitives, who were dispersed so effectually, that two Regiments would have secured them from rallying; I say, had he fallen in upon the Foot, or wheeled to the Left, and fallen in upon the Rear of the Enemy's Right Wing of Horse, or returned to the Assistance of the Left Wing of our Horse, we had gained the most absolute and compleat Victory that could be; nor had 1000 Men of the Enemy's Army got off: But this Prince, who was full of Fire, and pleased to see the Rout of the Enemy, pursued them quite to the Town of *Keynton*, where indeed he killed Abundance of their Men, *and some Time also was lost in plundering the Baggage:* But in the mean Time, the Glory and Advantage of the Day was lost to the King; for the right Wing of the Parliament Horse could not be so broken. Sir *William Balfour* made a desperate Charge upon the Point of the King's Left; and had it not been for two Regiments of Dragoons who were planted in the Reserve, had routed the whole Wing; for he broke through the first Line, and staggered the second, who advanced to their Assistance, but was so warmly received by those Dragoons, who came seasonably in, and gave their first Fire on Horseback, that his Fury was checked, and having lost a great many Men, was forced to wheel about to his own Men; and had the King had but three Regiments of Horse at hand, to have charged him, he had been routed. The rest of this

Wing kept their Ground, and received the first Fury of the
Enemy with great Firmness; after which, advancing in their
Turn, they were once Masters of the Earl of *Essex*'s Cannon.
And here we lost another Advantage; for if any Foot had
been at hand to support these Horse, they had carried off the
Cannon, or turned it upon the main Battle of the Enemy's
Foot; but the Foot were otherwise engaged. The Horse on
this Side fought with great Obstinacy, and Variety of
Success a great while. Sir *Philip Stapylton*, who commanded
the Guards of the Earl of *Essex*, being engaged with a Party
of our *Shrewsbury* Cavaliers, as we called them, was once in
a fair way to have been cut off by a Brigade of our Foot, who
being advanced to fall on upon the Parliament's main Body,
flanked Sir *Philip*'s Horse in their way, and facing to the
Left, so furiously charged him with their Pikes, that he was
obliged to retire in great Disorder, and with the Loss of a
great many Men and Horses.

All this while the Foot on both Sides were desperately
engaged, and coming close up to the Teêth of one another
with the clubbed Musquet and Push of Pike, fought with
great Resolution, and a terrible Slaughter on both Sides,
giving no Quarter for a great while; and they continued to
do thus, till, as if they were tired, and out of Wind, either
Party seemed willing enough to leave off, and take Breath.
Those which suffered most were that Brigade which had
charged Sir *William Stapylton*'s Horse, who being bravely
engaged in the Front which the Enemy's Foot, were, on the
sudden, charged again in Front and Flank, by Sir *William
Balfour*'s Horse, and disordered, after a very desperate
Defence. Here the King's Standard was taken, the Standard-
bearer, Sir *Edward Varney*, being killed; but it was rescued
again by Captain *Smith*, and brought to the King the same
Night, for which the King Knighted the Captain.

This Brigade of Foot had fought all the Day, and had not
been broken at last, if any Horse had been at Hand to
support them: The Field began to be now clear, both Armies
stood, as it were, gazing at one another, only the King,

having rallied his Foot, seemed inclined to renew the Charge, and began to cannonade them, which they could not return, most of their Cannon being nailed while they were in our Possession, and all the Cannoniers killed or fled, and our Gunners did Execution upon Sir *William Balfour*'s Troops for a good while.

My Father's Regiment being in the Right with the Prince, I saw little of the Fight, but the Rout of the Enemy's Left, and we had as full a Victory there as we could desire, but spent too much Time in it; we killed about 2000 Men in that Part of the Action, and having totally dispersed them, and plundred their Baggage, began to think of our Fellows when 'twas too late to help them. We returned however victorious to the King, just as the Battle was over; the King asked the Prince what News? He told him he could give his Majesty a good Account of the Enemy's Horse; *ay by G—d, says a Gentleman that stood by me, and of their Carts too.* That word was spoken with such a Sense of the Misfortune, and made such an Impression in the whole Army, that it occasioned some ill Blood afterwards among us; and but that the King took up the Business, it had been of ill Consequence; for some Person who had heard the Gentleman speak it, informed the Prince who it was, and the Prince resenting it, spoke something about it in the hearing of the Party when the King was present: The Gentleman not at all surprized, told his Highness openly, he had said the Words; and though he owned he had no Disrespect for his Highness, yet he could not but say, if it had not been so, the Enemy's Army had been better beaten. The Prince replied something very disobliging; upon which the Gentleman came up to the King, and kneeling, humbly besought his Majesty to accept of his Commission, and to give him leave to tell the Prince, that whenever his Highness pleased, he was ready to give him Satisfaction. The Prince was exceedingly provoked, and as he was very passionate, began to talk very oddly, and without all Government of himself: The Gentleman, as bold as he, but much calmer, preserved his Temper, but maintained his

Quarrel; and the King was so concerned, that he was very much out of Humour with the Prince about it. However, his Majesty upon Consideration, soon ended the Dispute, by laying his Commands on them both to speak no more of it for that Day; and refusing the Comission from the Collonel, for he was no less, sent for them both next Morning in private, and made them Friends again.

But to return to our Story, we came back to the King timely enough to put the Earl of *Essex*'s Men out of all Humour of renewing the Fight; and as I observed before, both Parties stood gazing at one another, and our Cannon playing upon them, obliged Sir *William Balfour*'s Horse to wheel off in some Disorder, but they returned us none again; which, as we afterwards understood, was, as I said before, for want of both Powder and Gunners; for the Cannoniers and Firemen were killed, or had quitted their Train in the Fight, when our Horse had Possession of their Artillery; and as they had spiked up some of the Cannon, so they had carryed away 15 Carriages of Powder.

Night coming on, ended all Discourse of more fighting; and the King drew off and marched towards the Hills. I know no other Token of Victory which the Enemy had, than their lying in the Field of Battle all Night, which *they did* for no other Reason, than that having lost their Baggage and Provisions, they had no where to go; and which we *did not*, because we had good Quarters at Hand.

The Number of Prisoners, and of the slain, were not very unequal; the Enemy lost more Men, we most of Quality. Six Thousand Men on both Sides were killed on the Spot, whereof, when our Rolls were examined, we missed 2500. We lost our brave General the old Earl of *Lindsey*, who was wounded and taken Prisoner, and died of his Wounds; Sir *Edward Stradling*, Collonel *Lundsford*, Prisoners; and Sir *Edward Varney*, and a great many Gentlemen of Quality slain. On the other Hand, we carried off Collonel *Essex*, Collonel *Ramsey*, and the Lord St. *John*, who also died of his Wounds; we took five Ammunition Waggons, full of Powder, and brought off about 500 Horse in the Defeat of the Left Wing, with 18 Standards and Colours, and lost 17.

The Slaughter of the Left Wing was so great, and the Flight so effectual, that several of the Officers rid clear away, coasting round, and got to *London*, where they reported, that the Parliament Army was entirely defeated, all lost, killed, or taken, as if none but them were left alive to carry the News. This filled them with Consternation for a while; but when other Messengers followed, all was restored to Quiet again, and the Parliament cried up their Victory, and sufficiently mocked God and their General, with their publick Thanks for it. Truly, as the Fight was a Deliverance to them, they were in the right to give Thanks for it; but as to its being a Victory, neither Side had much to boast of, and they less a great deal than we had.

I got no Hurt in this Fight; and indeed we of the Right Wing had but little fighting; I think I discharged my Pistols but once, and my Carabin twice, for we had more Fatigue than Fight; the Enemy fled, and we had little to do but to follow and kill those we could overtake. I spoiled a good Horse, and got a better from the Enemy in his Room, and came home weary enough. My Father lost his Horse, and in the Fall was bruised in his Thigh by another Horse, treading on him, which disabled him for some Time, and, at his Request, by his Majesty's Consent, I commanded the Regiment in his Absence.

The Enemy received a Recruit of 4000 Men[1] the next Morning; if they had not, I believe they had gone back towards *Worcester*; but, encouraged by that Reinforcement, they called a Council of War, and had a long Debate whether they could attack us again? but notwithstanding their great Victory, they durst not attempt it, though this Addition of Strength made them superiour to us by 3000 Men.

The King indeed expected, that when these Troops joined them they would advance, and we were preparing to receive them at a Village called *Aino*, where the Head Quarter continued three or four Days; and had they really esteemed the first Day's Work a Victory, as they called it, they would have done it, but they thought not good to venture, but march away to *Warwick*, and from thence to *Coventry*. The King, to urge them to venture upon him, and come to a second Battle, sits down before *Banbury*, and takes both Town and Castle, and two entire Regiments of Foot, and one Troop of Horse, quit the Parliament Service, and take up their Arms for the King. This was done almost before their Faces, which was a better Proof of a Victory on our Side, than any they could pretend to. From *Banbury* we marched to *Oxford*; and now all Men saw the Parliament had made a great Mistake, *for they were not always in the right any more than we*, to leave *Oxford* without a Garrison. The King caused new regular Works to be drawn round it, and seven royal Bastions with Ravelins and Out-works, a double Ditch, Counterscarp and Covered Way; all which added to the Advantage of its Situation, made it a formidable Place, and from this Time it became our Place of Arms, and the Center of Affairs on the King's Side.

If the Parliament had the Honour of the Field, the King reaped the Fruits of the Victory; for all this Part of the Country submitted to him: *Essex*'s Army made the best of their Way to *London*, and were but in an ill Condition when they came there, especially their Horse.

The Parliament, sensible of this, and receiving daily Accounts of the Progress we made, began to cool a little in their Temper, abated of their first Rage, and voted an Address for Peace; and sent to the King, to let him know they were desirous to prevent the Effusion of more Blood, and to bring things to an Accommodation, or, as they called it, a *Right Understanding*.

I was now, by the King's particular Favour, summoned to the Councils of War, my Father continuing absent and ill; and now I began to think of the real Grounds, and which was more, of the fatal Issue of this War. I say, I now began it; for I cannot say that I ever rightly stated Matters in my own Mind before, though I had been enough used to Blood, and to see the Destruction of People, sacking of Towns, and plundering the Country; yet 'twas in *Germany*, and among Strangers; but I found a strange secret and unaccountable Sadness upon my Spirits to see this acting in my own native Country. It grieved me to the Heart, even in the Rout of our Enemies, to see the Slaughter of them; and even in the Fight, to hear a Man cry for Quarter in *English*, moved me to a Compassion which I had never been used to; nay, sometimes it looked to me as if some of my own Men had been beaten; and when I heard a Soldier cry, *O God, I am shot*, I looked behind me to see which of my own Troop was fallen. Here I saw my self at the cutting of the Throats of my Friends; and indeed some of my near Relations. My old Comerades and Fellow-soldiers in *Germany* were some *with us*, some *against us*, as their Opinions happened to differ in Religion. For my part, I confess I had not much Religion in me, at that time; but I thought Religion rightly practised on both Sides would have made us all better Friends; and therefore sometimes I began to think, that both the Bishops of our Side, and the Preachers on theirs, made Religion rather *the Pretence* than *the Cause* of the War; and from those Thoughts I vigorously argued it at the Council of War against marching to *Brentford*, while the Address for a Treaty of Peace[1] from the Parliament was in Hand; for I was for taking the Parliament by the Handle which they had given us, and entring into a Negotiation with the Advantage of its being *at their own Request*.

I thought the King had now in his Hands an Opportunity to make an honourable Peace; for this Battle at *Edgehill*, as much as they boasted of the Victory to hearten up their Friends, had sorely weakened their Army, and discouraged their Party too, which in Effect was worse as to their Army. The Horse were particularly in an ill Case, and the Foot greatly diminished; and the Remainder very sickly: But besides this, the Parliament, were greatly alarmed at the Progress we made afterward; and still fearing the King's surprizing them, had sent for the Earl of *Essex* to *London*, to defend them; by which the Country was as it were, deserted and abandoned, and left to be plundered; our Parties over-run all Places at Pleasure. All this while I considered, that whatever the Soldiers of Fortune meant by the War, our Desires were to suppress the exorbitant Power of a Party, to establish our King in his just and legal Rights; but not with a Design to destroy the Constitution of Government, and the Being of Parliament; and therefore I thought now was the Time for Peace, and there were a great many worthy Gentle-men in the Army of my Mind; and, had our Master had Ears to hear us, the War might have had an End here.

This Address for Peace was received by the King at *Maidenhead*, whither this Army was now advanced, and his Majesty returned Answer by Sir *Peter Killegrew*, that he desired nothing more, and would not be wanting on his Part. Upon this the Parliament name Commissioners, and his Majesty excepting against Sir *John Evelyn*, they left him out, and sent others; and desired the King to appoint his Residence near *London*, where the Commissioners might wait upon him. Accordingly the King appointed *Windsor* for the Place of Treaty, and desired the Treaty might be hastened.[1] And thus all things looked with a favourable Aspect, when one unlucky Action knocked it all on the Head, and filled both Parties with more implacable Animosities than they had before, and all Hopes of Peace vanished.

During this Progress of the King's Armies, we were always abroad with the Horse ravaging the Country, and plundering the Roundheads. Prince *Rupert*, a most active vigilant Party-man, and I must own, fitter for such than for a General, was never lying still, and I seldom stayed behind; for our Regiment being very well mounted, he would always send for us, if he had any extraordinary Design in Hand.

One time in particular he had a Design upon *Alisbury*, the Capital of *Buckinghamshire*; indeed our View at first was rather to beat the Enemy out of Town and demolish their Works, and perhaps raise some Contributions on the rich Country round it, than to Garrison the Place, and keep it;

for we wanted no more Garrisons, being Masters of the Field.

The Prince had 2500 Horse with him in this Expedition, but no Foot; the Town had some Foot raised in the Country by Mr. *Hambden*, and two Regiments of the Country Militia, whom we made light of, but we found they stood to their Tackle better than *well enough*. We came very early to the Town, and thought they had no Notice of us; but some false Brother had given them the Alarm and we found them all in Arms, the Hedges without the Town lined with Musqueteers, on that Side in particular where they expected us, and the two Regiments of Foot drawn up in View to support them, with some Horse in the Rear of all.

The Prince willing however to do some thing, caused some of his Horse to alight, and serve as Dragoons; and having broken a Way into the Enclosures, the Horse beat the Foot from behind the Hedges, while the rest who were alighted charged them in the Lane which leads to the Town. Here they had cast up some Works, and fired from their Lines very regularly, considering them as Militia only, the Governour encouraging them by his Example; so that finding without some Foot there would be no good to be done, we gave it over, and drew off; and so *Alisbury* scaped a scouring for that Time.

I cannot deny but these flying Parties of Horse committed great Spoil among the Country People; and sometimes the Prince gave a Liberty to some Cruelties which were not at all for the King's Interest; because it being still upon our own Country, and the King's own Subjects, whom, in all his Declarations, he protested to be careful of. It seemed to contradict all those protestations and Declarations, and served to aggravate and exasperate the Common People; and the King's Enemies made all the Advantages of it that was possible, by crying out of twice as many Extravagancies as were committed.

'Tis true, the King, who naturally abhorred such things, could not restrain his Men, no nor his Generals, so absolutely as he would have done. The War, on his Side, was very much *a la Voluntier*; many Gentlemen served him at their own Charge, and some paid whole Regiments themselves: Sometimes also the King's Affairs were straiter than ordinary, and his Men were not very well paid, and this obliged him to wink at their Excursions upon the Country, though he did not approve of them; and yet I must own, that in those Parts of *England* where the War was hottest, there never was seen that Ruin and Depopulation, Murthers, Ravishments, and Barbarities, which I have seen even among Protestant Armies abroad in *Germany*, and other foreign Parts of the World. And if the Parliament People had seen those things abroad, as I had, they would not have complained.

The most I have seen was plundering the Towns for Provisions, drinking up their Beer, and turning our Horses into their Fields, or Stacks of Corn; and sometimes the Soldiers would be a little rude with the Wenches; but alas! what was this to Count *Tilly*'s Ravages in *Saxony*? Or what was our taking of *Leicester* by Storm, where they cried out of our Barbarities, to the sacking of *New Brandenburgh*, or the taking of *Magdeburgh*? In *Leicester*, of 7 or 8000 People in the Town, 300 were killed; in *Magdeburgh*, of 25000 scarce 2700 were left, and the whole Town burnt to Ashes. I my self, have seen 17 or 18 Villages on Fire in a Day, and the People driven away from their Dwellings, like Herds of Cattle; the Men murthered, the Women stript; and, 7 or 800 of them together, after they had suffered all the Indignities and Abuses of the Soldiers, driven stark naked in the Winter through the great Towns, to seek Shelter and Relief from the Charity of their Enemies. I do not instance these greater Barbarities to justify lesser Actions, which are nevertheless irregular; but, *I do say*, that Circumstances considered, this War was managed with as much Humanity on both Sides as could be expected, especially also considering the Animosity of Parties.

But to Return to the Prince, he had not always the same Success in these Enterprizes, for sometimes we came short home. And I cannot omit one pleasant Adventure which happened to a Party of ours in one of these Excursions into *Buckinghamshire*. The Major of our Regiment was soundly beaten by a Party which, as I may say was led by a Woman; and, if I had not rescued him, I know not but he had been taken Prisoner by a Woman. It seems our Men had besieged some fortified House about *Oxfordshire*, towards *Tame*, and the House being defended by the Lady in her Husband's Absence, she had yielded the House upon a Capitulation; one of the Articles of which was, to march out with all her Servants, Soldiers, and Goods, and to be convey'd to *Tame*: Whether she thought to have gone no farther, or that she reckoned her self safe there, I know not; but my Major, with two Troops of Horse meets with this Lady and her Party, about five Miles from *Tame*, as we were coming back from our defeated Attack of *Alisbury*. We reckoned our selves in an Enemy's Country, and had lived a little at large, or at Discretion, *as 'tis called abroad*; and these two Troops with the Major, were returning to our Detachment from a little Village, where, at a Farmer's House, they had met with some Liquor, and truly some of his Men were so drunk they could but just sit upon their Horses. The Major himself was not much better, and the whole Body were but in a sorry Condition to fight. Upon the Road they meet this Party; the Lady having no Design of Fighting, and being as she thought under the Protection of the Articles, sounds a Parley, and desired to speak with the Officer. The Major *as drunk as he was*, could tell her, that by the Articles she was to be assured no farther than *Tame*, and being now five Miles beyond it, she was a fair Enemy, and therefore demanded to render themselves Prisoners. The Lady seemed surprized, but being sensible she was in the wrong, offered to compound for her Goods, and would have given him 300 l. and, I think, seven or eight Horses: The Major would certainly have taken it, if he had not been drunk; but he refused it, and gave threatening Words to her, blustering in Language which he thought proper to fright a Woman, *viz.* that he would cut them all to Pieces, and give no Quarter, *and the like*. The Lady, who had been more used to the Smell of Powder than he imagined, called some of her Servants to her, and consulting with them what to do, they all unanimously encouraged her to let them fight; told her, it was plain that the Commander was drunk, and all that were with him were rather worse than he, and hardly able to sit their Horses; and that therefore one bold Charge would put them all into Confusion. *In a Word*, she consented, and, as she was a Woman, they desired her to secure her self among the Waggons; but she refused, and told them bravely, she would take her Fate with them. *In short*, she boldly bad my Major Defiance, and that he might do his worst, since she had offered him fair, and he had refused it; her Mind was altered now, and she would give him nothing, and bad his Officer that parlied longer with her, be gone; so the Parly ended. After this, she gave him fair Leave to go back to his Men; but before he could tell his Tale to them, she was at his Heels, with all her Men, and gave him such a home Charge as put his Men into Disorder; and, being too drunk to rally, they were knocked down before they knew what to do with themselves; and, in a few Minutes more, they took to a plain Flight. But what was still worse, the Men, being some of them very drunk, when they came to run for their Lives, fell over one another, and tumbled over their Horses, and made such Work, that a Troop of Women might have beaten them all. In this Pickle, with the Enemy at his Heels, I came in with him, hearing the Noise; when I appeared, the Pursuers retreated, and, seeing what a Condition my People were in, and not knowing the Strength of the Enemy, I contented my self with bringing them off without pursuing the other; nor could I ever hear positively who this Female Captain was, We lost 17 or 18 of our Men, and about 30 Horses; but when the Particulars of the Story were told us, our Major was so laughed at by the whole Army, and laughed at every where, that he was ashamed to shew himself for a Week or a Fortnight after.

But, to return to the King; his Majesty, *as I observed*, was at *Maidenhead* addressed by the Parliament for Peace, and *Windsor* being appointed for the Place of Treaty, the Van of his Army lay at *Colebrook*. In the mean time, whether it were true, or only a Pretence, but it was reported the Parliament General had sent a Body of his Troops, with a Train of Artillery, to *Hammersmith*, in order to fall upon some part of our Army, or to take some advanced Post, which was to the Prejudice of our Men; whereupon the King ordered the Army to march, and, by the Favour of a thick Mist, came within half a Mile of *Brentford* before he was discovered. There were two Regiments of Foot, and about 600 Horse in the Town, of the Enemy's best Troops; these taking the Alarm, posted themselves on the Bridge at the West End of the Town. The King attacked them with a select Detachment of his best Infantry, and they defended themselves with incredible Obstinacy. I must own, I never saw *raw Men*, for they could not have been in Arms above four Months, act like them in my Life. *In short*, there was no forcing these Men; for, though two whole Brigades of our Foot, backed by our Horse, made five several Attacks upon them, they could not break them, and we lost a great many brave Men in that Action. At last, seeing the Obstinacy of these Men, a Party of Horse was ordered to go round from *Osterly*; and, entering the Town on the North Side, where, though the Horse made some Resistance, it was not considerable, the Town was presently taken. I led my Regiment through an Enclosure, and came into the Town nearer to the Bridge than the rest, by which Means I got first into the Town; but I had this Loss by my Expedition, that the Foot charged me before the Body was come up, and pouring in their Shot very furiously, my Men were but in an ill Case, and would not have stood much longer, if the rest of the Horse coming up the Lane had not found them other Employment. When the Horse were thus entered, they immediately dispersed the Enemy's Horse, who fled away towards *London*, and falling in Sword in Hand upon the

Rear of the Foot, who were engaged at the Bridge, they were all cut in Pieces, except about 200, who scorning to ask Quarter, desperately threw themselves into the River of *Thames*, where they were most of them drowned.

The Parliament, and their Party, made a great Outcry at this Attempt; that it was base and treacherous while in a Treaty of Peace; and that the King, having amused them with hearkening to a Treaty, designed to have seized upon their Train of Artillery first, and, after that, to have surprized both the City of *London* and the Parliament. And I have observed since, that our Historians note this Action as contrary to the Laws of Honour and Treaties; though as there was no Cessation of Arms agreed on, nothing is more contrary to the Laws of War than to suggest it.

That it was a very unhappy thing to the King and whole Nation, as it broke off the Hopes of Peace, and was the Occasion of bringing the *Scots* Army in upon us, I readily acknowledge; but that there was any thing dishonourable in it, I cannot allow: For though the Parliament had addressed to the King for Peace, and such Steps were taken in it, as before; yet, as I have said, there was no Proposals made on either Side for a Cessation of Arms; and all the World must allow, that in such Cases the War goes on in the Field, while the Peace goes on in the Cabinet. And if the War goes on, admit the King had designed to surprize the City or Parliament, or all of them, it had been no more than the Custom of War allows, and what they would have done by him, if they could. The Treaty of *Westphalia*,[1] or Peace of *Munster*, which ended the bloody Wars of *Germany*, was a Precedent for this. That Treaty was actually negotiating seven Years, and yet the War went on with all the Vigour and Rancour imaginable, even to the last: Nay, the very Time after the Conclusion of it, but before the News could be brought to the Army, did he that was afterwards King of *Sweden*, *Carolus Gustavus*, take the City of *Prague*, by Surprize, and therein an inestimable Booty. Besides, all the Wars of *Europe* are full of Examples of this Kind; and therefore I cannot see any Reason to blame the King for this Action as to the Fairness of it. Indeed as to the Policy of it, I can say little; but the Case was this, the King had a gallant Army, flushed with Success, and things hitherto had gone on very prosperously, both with his own Army and elsewhere; he had above 35000 Men in his own Army, including his Garrisons left at *Banbury*, *Shrewsbury*, *Worcester*, *Oxford*, *Wallingford*, *Abbingdon*, *Reading*, and Places adjacent. On the other Hand, the Parliament Army came back to *London* in but a very* sorry Condition; for what with their Loss *in their Victory*, *as they called it*, *at* Edgehill, their Sickness, and a hasty March to *London*, they were very much diminished; though at *London* they soon recruited them again. And this Prosperity of the King's Affairs might encourage him to strike this Blow, thinking to bring the Parliament to the better Terms, by the Apprehensions of the superior Strength of the King's Forces.

But *however it was*, the Success did not equally answer the King's Expectation; the vigorous Defence the Troops posted at *Brentford* made as above, gave the Earl of *Essex* Opportunity, with extraordinary Application, to draw his Forces out to *Turnham-Green*; and the exceeding Alacrity of the Enemy was such, that their whole Army appeared with them, making together an Army of 24000 Men, drawn up in View of our Forces, by 8 o' Clock the next Morning. The City Regiments were placed between the regular Troops, and all together offered us Battle, but we were not in a Condition to accept it. The King indeed was sometimes of the Mind to charge them, and once or twice ordered Parties to advance to begin to skirmish; but upon better Advice, altered his Mind; and indeed it was the wisest Counsel to defer the fighting at that Time. The Parliament Generals were as unfixed in their Resolutions on the other Side, as the King: Sometimes they sent out Parties, and then called them back

---

*Note, General *Ludlow*, in his Memoirs, p. 52.[1] says, their Men returned from *Warwick* to *London*, not like Men who had obtained a Victory, but like Men that had been beaten.

again. One strong Party, of near 3000 Men marched off towards *Acton*, with Orders to amuse us on that Side, but were counter-manded. Indeed I was of the Opinion, we might have ventured the Battle; for though the Parliament's Army were more numerous, yet the City Trained-Bands, which made up 4000 of their Foot, were not much esteemed, and the King was a great deal stronger in Horse than they; but the main Reason that hindred the Engagement, was want of Ammunition, which the King having duly weighed, he caused the Carriages and Cannon to draw off first, and then the Foot, the Horse continuing to face the Enemy till all was clear gone, and then we drew off too, and marched to *Kingston*, and the next Day to *Reading*.

Now the King saw his Mistake, in not continuing his March for *London*, instead of Facing about to fight the Enemy at *Edgehill*. And all the Honour we had gained in so many successful Enterprizes lay buried in this shameful Retreat from an Army of Citizens Wives: For, truly that Appearance at *Turnham-Green* was gay, but not great. There was as many Lookers on as Actors; the Crouds of Ladies, 'Prentices and Mob was so great, that when the Parties of our Army advanced, and, as they thought, to Charge, the Coaches, Horsemen, and Croud, that cluttered away, to be out of Harm's way, looked little better than a Rout: And I was perswaded a good home Charge from our Horse would have sent their whole Army after them; but so it was, that this Croud of an Army was to triumph over us, and they did it; for all the Kingdom was carefully informed how their dreadful Looks had frightened us away.

Upon our Retreat, the Parliament resent this Attack, which they called treacherous, and vote no Accommodation; but they considered of it afterwards, and sent six Commissioners to the King with Propositions; but the Change of the Scene of Action changed the Terms of Peace; and now they made Terms like Conquerors, petition him to desert his Army, and return to the Parliament, and the like. Had his Majesty, at the Head of his Army, with the full Reputation they had before, and in the Ebb of their Affairs, rested at *Windsor*, and commenced a Treaty, they had certainly made more reasonable Proposals; but now the Scabbard seemed to be thrown away on both Sides.

The rest of the Winter was spent in strengthening Parties, and Places also in fruitless Treaties of Peace, Messages, Remonstrances, and Paper War on both Sides, and no Action remarkable happened any where that I remember: Yet the King gained Ground every where, and his Forces in the *North* encreased under the Earl of *Newcastle*; also my Lord *Goring*, then only called Collonel *Goring*, arrived from *Holland*, bringing three Ships loaden with Arms and Ammunition, and Notice that the Queen was following with more. *Goring* brought 4000 Barrels of Gunpowder, and 20000 small Arms; all which came very seasonably, for the King was in great want of them, especially the Powder. Upon this Recruit the Earl of *Newcastle* draws down to *York*, and being above 16000 strong, made Sir *Thomas Fairfax* give Ground, and retreat to *Hull*.

Whoever lay still, Prince *Rupert* was always abroad, and I chose to go out with his Highness as often as I had Opportunity; for hitherto he was always successful. About this Time the Prince, being at *Oxford*, I gave him Intelligence of a Party of the Enemy who lived a little at large, too much for good Soldiers, about *Cirencester*: The Prince glad of the News, resolved to attack them, and though it was a wet Season, and the Ways exceeding bad, being in *February*,[1] yet we marched all Night in the Dark, which occasioned the Loss of some Horses and Men too, in Sloughs and Holes, which the Darkness of the Night had suffered them to fall into. We were a very strong Party, being about 3000 Horse and Dragoons, and coming to *Cirencester* very early in the Morning, to our great Satisfaction the Enemy were perfectly surprized, not having the least Notice of our March, which answered our End more Ways than one. However, the Earl of *Stamford*'s Regiment made some Resistance; but the Town having no Works to defend it, saving a slight Breast-

Work at the Entrance of the Road, with a Turn-pike, our Dragoons alighted, and forcing their Way over the Bellies of *Stamford*'s Foot, they beat them from their Defence, and followed them at their Heels into the Town. *Stamford*'s Regiment was entirely cut in Pieces, and several others, to the Number of about 800 Men, and the Town entered without any other Resistance. We took 1200 Prisoners, 3000 Arms, and the County Magazin, which at that [time] was considerable; for there was about 120 Barrels of Powder, and all things in Proportion.

I received the first Hurt I got in this War, at this Action; for having followed the Dragoons, and brought my Regiment within the Barricado which they had gained, a Musquet Bullet struck my Horse just in the Head; and that so effectually, that he fell down as dead as a Stone, all at once. The Fall plunged me into a Puddle of Water, and daubed me; and my Man having brought me another Horse, and cleaned me a little, I was just getting up, when another Bullet strook me on my left Hand, which I had just clapt on the Horse's Mane, to lift my self into the Saddle. The Blow broke one of my Fingers, and bruised my Hand very much, and it proved a very painful Hurt to me. For the present I did not much concern my self about it, but made my Man tye it up close in my Handkerchief, and led up my Men to the Market Place, where we had a very smart Brush with some Musqueteers who were posted in the Church-yard; but our Dragoons soon beat them out there, and the whole Town was then our own. We made no Stay here, but marched back with all our Booty to *Oxford*, for we knew the Enemy were very strong at *Gloucester*, and that way.

Much about the same Time, the Earl of *Northampton*, with a strong Party, set upon *Litchfield*, and took the Town, but could not take the Close; but they beat a Body of 4000 Men coming to the Relief of the Town, under Sir *John Gell* of *Darbyshire* and Sir *William Brereton* of *Cheshire*, and killing 600 of them, dispersed the rest.

Our second Campaign now began to open; the King

marched from *Oxford* to relieve *Reading*, which was besieged
by the Parliament Forces; but Collonel *Fielding*, Lieutenant
Governour, Sir *Arthur Ashton* being wounded, surrendred
to *Essex* before the King could come up; for which he was
tried by Martial Law, and condemned to die; but the King
forbore to execute the Sentence. This was the first Town we
had lost in the War; for still the Success of the King's
Affairs was very encouraging. This bad News however was
over-balanced by an Account brought the King at the same
time, by an Express from *York*, that the Queen had landed
in the *North*, and had brought over a great Magazin of Arms
and Ammunition, besides some Men. Some time after this,
her Majesty marching Southward to meet the King, joined
the Army near *Edgehill*, where the first Battle was fought.
She brought the King 3000 Foot, 1500 Horse and Dragoons,
six Pieces of Cannon, 1500 Barrels of Powder, 12000 small
Arms.

During this Prosperity of the King's Affairs, his Armies
encreased mightily in the Western Counties also. Sir *William
Waller* indeed commanded for the Parliament in those Parts
too, and particularly in *Dorsetshire*, *Hampshire*, and *Berkshire*, where he carried on their Cause but too fast; but
farther West, Sir *Nicholas Flamming*,[1] Sir *Ralph Hopton*,
and Sir *Bevil Greenvil*, had extended the King's Quarters
from *Cornwall* through *Devonshire*, and into *Somersetshire*,
where they took *Exeter*, *Barnstable*, and *Biddiford*; and the
first of these they fortified very well, making it a Place of
Arms for the West, and afterwards it was the Residence of
the Queen.

At last, the Famous Sir *William Waller*, and the King's
Forces met, and came to a pitched Battle, where Sir *William*
lost all his Honour again. This was at *Roundway-down*[2] in
Wiltshire. *Waller* had engaged our *Cornish* Army at *Lansdown*, and in a very obstinate Fight had the better of them,
and made them retreat to the *Devizes*. Sir *William Hopton*
however having a good Body of Foot untouched, sent
Expresses and Messengers one in the Neck of another to the

King for some Horse, and the King being in great Concern for that Army, who were composed of the Flower of the *Cornish* Men, commanded me to march with all possible Secrecy, as well as Expedition, with 1200 Horse and Dragoons from *Oxford*, to join them. We set out in the Depth of the Night, to avoid, if possible, any Intelligence being given of our Rout, and soon joined with the *Cornish* Army, when it was as soon resolved to give Battle to *Waller*; and, give him his due, he was as forward to fight as we. As it is easy to meet when both Sides are willing to be found, Sir *William Waller* met us upon *Roundway-down*, where we had a fair Field on both Sides, and Room enough to draw up our Horse. In a Word, there was little Ceremony to the Work; the Armies joined, and we charged his Horse with so much Resolution, that they quickly fled, and quitted the Field; for we over-matched him in Horse, and this was the entire Destruction of their Army: For their Infantry, which outnumbered ours by 1500, were now at our Mercy; some faint Resistance they made, just enough to give us Occasion to break into their Ranks with our Horse, where we gave Time to our Foot to defeat others that stood to their Work: Upon which they began to disband, and run every Way they could; but our Horse having surrounded them, we made a fearful Havock of them.

We lost not above 200 Men in this Action; *Waller* lost above 4000 killed and taken, and as many dispersed that never returned to their Colours: Those of Foot that escaped got into *Bristol*, and *Waller*, with the poor Remains of his routed Regiments, got to *London*; so that it is plain some run East, and some run West, that is to say, they fled every Way they could.

My going with this Detachment prevented my being at the Siege of *Bristol*,[1] which Prince *Rupert* attacked much about the same Time, and it surrendered in three Days. The Parliament questioned Collonel *Nathaniel Fiures*, the Governor, and had him tried as a Coward by a Court Martial, and condemned to die, but suspended the Execution also, as the King did the Governor of *Reading*. I have often heard Prince *Rupert* say, they did Collonel *Fienns* wrong in that Affair; and that if the Collonel would have summoned him, he would have demanded a Passport of the Parliament, and have come up and convinced the Court, that Collonel *Fienns* had not misbehaved himself; and that he had not a sufficient Garrison to defend a City of that Extent; having not above 1200 Men in the Town, excepting some of *Waller*'s Run-aways, most of whom were unfit for Service, and without Arms; and that the Citizens in general being disaffected to him, and ready on the first Occasion to open the Gates to the King's Forces, it was impossible for him to have kept the City; and *when I had farther informed them*, said the Prince, *of the Measures I had taken for a general Assault the next Day, I am confident I should have convinc'd them, that I had taken the City by Storm, if he had not surrendered.*

The King's Affairs were now in a very good Posture, and three Armies in the North, West, and in the Center, counted in the Musters above 70000 Men, besides small Garrisons and Parties abroad. Several of the Lords, and more of the Commons, began to fall off from the Parliament, and make their Peace with the King; and the Affairs of the Parliament began to look very ill. The City of *London* was their in-exhaustible Support and Magazine, both for Men, Money, and all things necessary; and whenever their Army was out of Order, the Clergy of their Party in but one *Sunday* or two, would preach the young Citizens out of their Shops, the Labourers from their Masters, into the Army, and recruit them on a sudden: And all this was still owing to the Omission I first observed, of not marching to *London*, when it might have been so easily effected.

We had now another, or a fairer Opportunity, than before, but, as ill Use was made of it. The King, as I have observed, was in a very good Posture; he had three large Armies roving at large over the Kingdom. The *Cornish* Army, Victorious and Numerous, had beaten *Waller*, secured and fortified *Exeter*, which the Queen had made her Residence, and was there delivered of a Daughter, the Princess *Henrietta Maria*, afterwards Dutchess of *Orleans*, and Mother of the Dutchess Dowager of *Savoy*, commonly known in the *French* Stile by the Title of *Madam Royal*.[1] They had secured *Salisbury*, *Sherbon* Castle, *Weymouth*, *Winchester*, and *Basing-house*, and commanded the whole Country, except *Bridgewater* and *Taunton*, *Plymouth* and *Linn*; all which Places they held blocked up. The King was also entirely Master of all *Wales*, *Monmouthshire*, *Cheshire*, *Shropshire*, *Staffordshire*, *Worcestershire*, *Oxfordshire*, *Berkshire*, and all the Towns from *Windsor* up the *Thames* to *Cirencester*, except *Reading* and *Henly*; and of the whole *Severn*, except *Gloucester*.

The Earl of *Newcastle* had Garrisons in every strong Place in the *North*, from *Berwick* upon *Tweed*, to *Boston* in *Lincolnshire*, and *Newark* upon *Trent*, *Hull* only excepted, whither the Lord *Fairfax* and his Son Sir *Thomas* were retreated, their Troops being routed and broken, Sir *Thomas Fairfax* his Baggage with his Lady and Servants taken Prisoners, and himself hardly escaping.

And now a great Council of War was held in the King's Quarters, what Enterprize to go upon; and it happened to be the very same Day when the Parliament were in a serious Debate what should become of them, and whose Help they should seek? And indeed they had Cause for it; and had our Counsels been as ready and well grounded as theirs, we had put an End to the War in a Month's time.

In this Council the King proposed the Marching to *London*, to put an End to the Parliament, and encourage his Friends and loyal Subjects in *Kent*, who were ready to rise for him; and shewed us Letters from the Earl of *Newcastle*, wherein he offered to join his Majesty with a Detachment of 4000 Horse, and 8000 Foot, if his Majesty thought fit to march Southward, and yet leave Forces sufficient to guard the *North* from any Invasion. I confess, when I saw the Scheme the King had himself drawn for this Attempt, I felt an unusual Satisfaction in my Mind, from the Hopes that we might bring this War to some tolerable End; for I professed my self on all Occasions heartily weary of Fighting with Friends, Brothers, Neighbours, and Acquaintance: And I made no Question, but this Motion of the King's would effectually bring the Parliament to Reason.

All Men seemed to like the Enterprize but the Earl of *Worcester*, who on particular Views for securing the Country behind, as he called it, proposed the taking in the Town of *Gloucester* and *Hereford* first: He made a long Speech of the Danger of leaving *Massey*, an active, bold Fellow, with a strong Party in the Heart of all the King's Quarters, ready on all Occasions to sally out, and surprize the neighbouring Garrisons, as he had done *Sudley* Castle and others; and of the Ease and Freedom to all those Western Parts, to have them fully cleared of the Enemy. Interest presently backs this Advice, and all those Gentlemen whose Estates lay that way, or whose Friends lived about *Worcester*, *Shrewsbury*, *Bridgnorth*, or the Borders; and who, as they said, had heard the frequent Wishes of the Country to have the City of *Gloucester* reduced, fell in with this Advice, alledging the Consequence it was of for the Commerce of the Country, to have the Navigation of the *Severn* free, which was only interrupted by this one Town from the Sea up to *Shrewsbury* &c.

I opposed this, and so did several others: Prince *Rupert* was vehemently against it; and we both offered, with the Troops of the County, to keep *Gloucester* blocked up during the King's March for *London*, so that *Massey* should not be able to stir.

This Proposal made the Earl of *Worcester*'s Party more eager for the Siege than before; for they had no Mind to a Blockade, which would leave the Country to maintain the Troops all the Summer; and of all Men the Prince did not please them: For he having no extraordinary Character for Discipline, his Company was not much desired even by our Friends. Thus, *in an ill Hour* 'twas resolved to sit down before *Gloucester*. The King had a gallant Army of 28000

Men, whereof 11000 Horse, the finest Body of Gentlemen that ever I saw together in my Life; their Horses without Comparison, and their Equipages the finest and the best in the World, and their Persons *Englishmen*, which I think is enough to say of them.

According to the Resolution taken in the Council of War, the Army marched Westward, and sat down before *Gloucester* the Beginning of *August*. There we spent a Month to the least Purpose that ever Army did; our Men received frequent Affronts from the desperate Sallies of an inconsiderable Enemy. I cannot forbear reflecting on the Misfortunes of this Siege: Our Men were strangely dispirited in all the Assaults they gave upon the Place; there was something looked like Disaster and Mismanagement, and our Men went on with an ill Will, and no Resolution. The King despised the Place, and the King, to carry it Sword in Hand, made no regular Approaches, and the Garrison being desperate, made therefore the greater Slaughter. In this Work our Horse, who were so numerous and so fine, had no Employment: 2000 Horse had been enough for this Business, and the Enemy had no Garrison or Party within fourty Miles of us; so that we had nothing to do but look on with infinite Regret, upon the Losses of our Foot.

The Enemy made frequent and desperate Sallies, in one of which I had my Share. I was posted upon a Parade, or Place of Arms, with Part of my Regiment, and Part of Collonel *Goring*'s Regiment of Horse, in order to support a Body of Foot who were ordered to storm the Point of a Breast-work which the Enemy had raised to defend one of the Avenues to the Town. The Foot were beat off with Loss, as they always were; and *Massey* the Governor, not content to have beaten them from his Works, sallies out with near 400 Men, and falling in upon the Foot as they were rallying under the Cover of our Horse, we put our selves in the best Posture we could to receive them. As *Massey* did not expect, I suppose, to engage with any Horse, he had no Pikes with him, which encouraged us to treat him the more rudely; but as to desperate Men Danger is no Danger, when he found he must clear his Hands of us, before he could dispatch the Foot, he faces up to us, fires but one Volley of his small Shot, and fell to battering us with the Stocks of their Musquets, in such a manner, that one would have thought they had been mad Men.

We at first despised this way of Clubbing us, and charging through them, laid a great many of them upon the Ground; and in repeating our Charge, trampled more of them under our Horses Feet: And wheeling thus continually, beat them off from our Foot, who were just upon the Point of disbanding. Upon this they charged us again with their Fire, and at one Volley killed 33 or 34 Men and Horses; and had they had Pikes with them, I know not what we should have done with them: But at last charging through them again, we divided them; one Part of them being hemmed in between us and our own Foot, were cut in Pieces to a Man; the rest, as I understood afterwards, retreated into the Town, having lost 300 of their Men.

In this last Charge I received a rude Blow from a stout Fellow on Foot, with the But End of his Musquet, which perfectly stunned me, and fetched me off from my Horse; and had not some near me took Care of me, I had been trod to Death by our own Men: But the Fellow being immediately killed, and my Friends finding me alive, had taken me up, and carried me off at some Distance, where I came to my self again, after some time, but knew little of what I did or said that Night. This was the Reason why I say I afterwards understood the Enemy retreated; for I saw no more what they did then; nor indeed was I well of this Blow for all the rest of the Summer, but had frequent Pains in my Head, Dizzinesses and Swimming, that gave me some Fears the Blow had injured the Scull, but it wore off again; nor did it at all hinder my attending my Charge.

This Action, I think, was the only one that looked like a Defeat given the Enemy at this Siege; we killed them near 300 Men, as I have said, and lost about 60 of our Troopers.

All this Time, while the King was harrassing and weakening the best Army he ever saw together during the whole War, the Parliament Generals, or rather Preachers, were recruiting theirs; for the Preachers were better than Drummers to raise Voluntiers, zealously exhorting the *London* Dames to part with their Husbands, and the City to send some of their Trained Bands to join the Army for the Relief of *Gloucester*; and now they began to advance towards us.

The King hearing of the Advance of *Essex*'s Army, who by this time was come to *Alisbury*, had summoned what Forces he had within Call, to join him; and accordingly he received 3000 Foot from *Somersetshire*: And having batter'd the Town for 36 Hours, and made a fair Breach, resolves upon an Assault, if possible, to carry the Town before the Enemy came up. The Assault was begun about Seven in the Evening, and the Men boldly mounted the Breach; but after a very obstinate and bloody Dispute, were beaten out again by the besieged with great Loss.

Being thus often repulsed, and the Earl of *Essex*'s Army approaching, the King calls a Council of War, and proposed to fight *Essex*'s Army. The Officers of the Horse were for fighting; and without doubt we were superior to him both in Number and Goodness of our Horse, but the Foot were not in an equal Condition: And the Collonels of Foot representing to the King the Weakness of their Regiments, and how their Men had been bauked and disheartened at this cursed Siege, the graver Counsel prevailed, and it was resolved to raise the Siege, and retreat towards *Bristol*, till the Army was recruited. Pursuant to this Resolution, the 5th of *September*, the King having before sent away his heavy Cannon and Baggage, raised the Siege, and marched to *Berkley* Castle. The Earl of *Essex* came the next Day to *Birdlip Hills*; and understanding by Messengers from Collonel *Massey*, that the Siege was raised, sends a Recruit of 2500 Men into the City, and followed us himself with a great Body of Horse.

This Body of Horse shewed themselves to us once in a

large Field fit to have entertained them in; and our Scouts having assured us they were not above 4000, and had no Foot with them, the King ordered a Detachment of about the same Number to face them. I desired his Majesty to let us have two Regiments of Dragoons with us, which was then 800 Men in a Regiment, lest there might be some Dragoons among the Enemy, which the King granted; and accordingly we marched, and drew up in View of them. They stood their Ground, having, as they supposed, some Advantage of the manner they were posted in, and expected we would charge them. The King who did us the Honour to command this Party, finding they would not stir, calls me to him, and ordered me with the Dragoons, and my own Regiment, to take a Circuit round by a Village to a certain Lane, where in their Retreat they must have passed, and which opened to a small Common on their Flank, with Orders, if they engaged, to advance and charge them in the Flank. I marched immediately; but though the Country about there was almost all Enclosures, yet their Scouts were so vigilant, that they discovered me, and gave Notice to the Body; upon which their whole Party moved to the Left, as if they intended to charge me, before the King with his Body of Horse could come; but the King was too vigilant to be circumvented so; and therefore his Majesty perceiving this, sends away three Regiments of Horse to second me, and a Messenger before them, to order me to halt, and expect the Enemy, for that he would follow with the whole Body.

But before this Order reached me, I had halted for some time; for, finding my self discovered, and not judging it safe to be entirely cut off from the main Body, I stopt at the Village, and causing my Dragoons to alight, and line a thick Hedge on my Left. I drew up my Horse just at the Entrance into the Village opening to a Common; the Enemy came up on the Trot to charge me, but were saluted with a terrible Fire from the Dragoons out of the Hedge, which killed them near 100 Men. This being a perfect Surprize to them, they halted; and just at that Moment they received Orders from their main Body to retreat; the King at the same time appearing upon some small Heights in their Rear, which obliged them to think of retreating, or coming to a general Battle, which was none of their Design.

I had no Occasion to follow them, not being in a Condition to attack their whole Body; but the Dragoons coming out into the Common, gave them another Volley at a Distance, which reached them effectually; for it killed about 20 of them, and wounded more; but they drew off, and never fired a Shot at us, fearing to be enclosed between two Parties, and so marched away to their General's Quarters, leaving 10 or 12 more of their Fellows killed, and about 180 Horses. Our Men, after the Country Fashion, gave them a Shout at parting, to let them see we knew they were afraid of us.

However, this Relieving of *Gloucester* raised the Spirits as well as the Reputation of the Parliament Forces, and was a great Defeat to us; and from this time things began to look with a melancholy Aspect; for the prosperous Condition of the King's Affairs began to decline. The Opportunities he had let slip, were never to be recovered; and the Parliament, in their former Extremity, having voted an Invitation to the *Scots* to March to their Assistance, we had now new Enemies to encounter; and indeed there began the Ruine of his Majesty's Affairs; for the Earl of *Newcastle*, not able to defend himself against the *Scots* on his Rear, the Earl of *Manchester* in his Front, and Sir *Thomas Fairfax* on his Flank, was every where routed and defeated, and his Forces obliged to quit the Field to the Enemy.

About this Time it was that we first began to hear of one *Oliver Cromwell*, who, like a little Cloud, rose out of the East, and spread first into the North, 'till it shed down a Flood that overwhelmed the three Kingdoms.

He first was a private Captain of Horse, but now commanded a Regiment whom he armed *Cap-a-pee a la Cuirassier*; and joining with the Earl of *Manchester*, the first Action we heard of him, that made him any thing famous, was about *Grantham*,[1] where, with only his own Regiment, he defeated 24 Troops of Horse and Dragoons of the King's Forces: Then at *Gainsborough*, with two Regiments, his own of Horse, and one of Dragoons, where he defeated near 3000 of the Earl of *Newcastle*'s Men, killed Lieutenant General *Cavendish*, Brother to the Earl of *Devonshire*, who commanded them, and relieved *Gainsborough*; and though the whole Army came in to the Rescue, he made good his Retreat to *Lincoln*, with little Loss; and the next Week he defeated Sir *John Henderson*, at *Winsby*, near *Horn Castle*, with sixteen Regiments of Horse and Dragoons, himself having not half that Number, killed the Lord *Widdrington*,[2] Sir *Ingram Hopton*, and several Gentlemen of Quality.

Thus this Firebrand of War began to blaze, and he soon grew a Terror to the North; for Victory attended him like a Page of Honour, and he was scarce ever known to be beaten, during the whole War.

Now we began to reflect again on the Misfortune of our Master's Counsels: Had we marched to *London*, instead of besieging *Gloucester*, we had finished the War with a Stroke. The Parliament's Army was in a most despicable Condition, and had never been recruited, had we not given them a Month's time, which we lingered away at this fatal Town of *Gloucester*:[3] But 'twas too late to reflect; we were a disheartened Army, but we were not beaten yet, nor broken; we had a large Country to recruit in, and we lost no time, but raised Men apace. In the mean time his Majesty, after a short Stay at *Bristol*, makes back again towards *Oxford* with a part of the Foot, and all the Horse.

At *Cirencester* we had a Brush again with *Essex*; that Town owed us a shrewd Turn for having handled them coarsly enough before, when Prince *Rupert* seized the County Magazine. I happened to be in the Town that Night with Sir *Nicholas Crisp*,[4] whose Regiment of Horse quartered there with Collonel *Spencer*, and some Foot; my own Regiment was gone before to *Oxford*. About Ten at Night, a Party of *Essex*'s Men beat up our Quarters by Surprize, just as we had served them before; they fell in with us, just as People were going to Bed, and having beaten the Out-Guards, were gotten into the Middle of the Town, before our Men could get on Horseback. Sir *Nicholas Crisp* hearing the Alarm, gets up, and with some of his Clothes on, and some off, comes into my Chamber: We are all undone, *says he*, the Roundheads are upon us. We had but little time to consult; but being in one of the principal Inns in the Town, we presently ordered the Gates of the Inn to be shut, and sent to all the Inns where our Men were quartered, to do the like, with Orders, if they had any Back-doors, or Ways to get out, to come to us. By this means however we got so much time as to get on Horseback, and so many of our Men came to us by Back-ways, that we had near 300 Horse in the Yards and Places behind the House; and now we began to think of Breaking out by a Lane which led from the back Side of the Inn; but a new Accident determined us another, *though a worse* Way. The Enemy being entered, and our Men cooped up in the Yards of the Inns, Collonel *Spencer* the other Collonel, whose Regiment of Horse lay also in the Town, had got on Horseback before us, and engaged with the Enemy, but being over-powered, retreated fighting, and sends to Sir *Nicholas Crisp* for Help. Sir *Nicholas* moved to see the Distress of his Friend, turning to me, says he *What can we do for him?* I told him, I thought 'twas time to help him, if possible; upon which, opening the Inn Gates, we sallied out in very good Order, about 300 Horse; and several of the Troops from other parts of the Town joining us, we recovered Collonel *Spencer*, and charging home, beat back the Enemy to their main Body: But finding their Foot drawn up in the Church-yard, and several Detachments moving to charge us, we retreated in as good Order as we could. They did not think fit to pursue us, but they took all the Carriages which were under the Convoy of this Party, and loaden with Provisions and Ammunition, and above 500 of our Horse. The Foot shifted away as well as they could: Thus we made off in a shattered Condition towards

Farrington, and so to *Oxford*, and I was very glad my Regiment was not there.

We had small Rest at *Oxford*, or indeed any where else; for the King was marched from thence, and we followed him. I was something uneasy at my Absence from my Regiment, and did not know how the King might resent it, which caused me to ride after them with all Expedition. But the Armies were engaged that very Day at *Newberry*, and I came in too late. I had not behaved my self so as to be suspected of a wilful Shunning the Action; but a Collonel of a Regiment ought to avoid Absence from his Regiment in time of Fight, be the Excuse never so just, as carefully as he would a Surprize in his Quarters. The *Truth is*, 'twas an Error of my own, and owing to two Days Stay I made at the *Bath*, where I met with some Ladies who were my Relations: And this is far from being an Excuse; for if the King had been a *Gustavus Adolphus*, I had certainly received a Check for it.

This Fight was very obstinate, and could our Horse have come to Action as freely as the Foot, the Parliament Army had suffered much more; for we had here a much better Body of Horse than they, and we never failed beating them where the Weight of the Work lay upon the Horse.

Here the City Train-Bands, of which there was two Regiments, and whom we used to despise, fought very well: They lost one of their Collonels,[1] and several Officers in the Action; and I heard our Men say, they behaved themselves as well as any Forces the Parliament had.

The Parliament cried Victory here too, *as they always did*; and indeed where the Foot were concerned they had some Advantage; but our Horse defeated them evidently. The King drew up his Army in Battalia, in Person, and faced them all the next Day, inviting them to renew the Fight; but they had no Stomach to come on again.

It was a kind of a Hedge Fight, for neither Army was drawn out in the Field; if it had, 'twould never have held from six in the Morning to ten at Night: But they fought for Advantages; sometimes one Side had the better, sometimes another. They fought twice through the Town, in at one End, and out at the other; and in the Hedges and Lanes, with exceeding Fury. The King lost the most Men, his Foot having suffered for want of the Succour of their Horse, who on two several Occasions, could not come at them. But the Parliament Foot suffered also, and two Regiments were entirely cut in Pieces, and the King kept the Field.

Essex, the Parliament General, had the Pillage of the dead, and left us to bury them; for while we stood all Day to our Arms, having given them a fair Field to fight us in, their Camp Rabble stript the dead Bodies, and they not daring to venture a second Engagement with us, marched away towards *London*.

The King Lost in this Action the Earls of *Carnarvon* and *Sunderland*, the Lord *Falkland*, a *French* Marquess,[1] and some very gallant Officers, and about 1200 Men. The Earl of *Carnarvon* was brought into an Inn in *Newberry*, where the King came to see him. He had just Life enough to speak to his Majesty, and died in his Presence. The King was exceedingly concerned for him, and was observed to shed Tears at the Sight of it. We were indeed all of us troubled for the Loss of so brave a Gentleman, but the Concern our royal Master discovered, moved us more than ordinary. Every body endeavoured to have the King out of the Room, but he would not stir from the Bed Side, till he see all Hopes of Life was gone.

The indefatigable Industry of the King, his Servants and Friends, continually to supply and recruit his Forces, and to harrass and fatigue the Enemy, was such, that we should still have given a good Account of the War had the *Scots* stood neuter. But bad News came every Day out of the North; as for other Places, Parties were always in Action: Sir *William Waller* and Sir *Ralph Hopton* beat one another by Turns, and Sir *Ralph* had extended the King's Quarters from *Launceston* in *Cornwall* to *Farnham* in *Surry*, where he gave Sir *William Waller* a Rub, and drove him into the Castle.

But in the North, the Storm grew thick, the *Scots* advanced to the Borders, and entered *England* in Confederacy with the Parliament, against their King; for which the Parliament requited them afterwards as they deserved.

Had it not been for this *Scotch* Army, the Parliament had easily been reduced to Terms of Peace: But after this they never made any Proposals fit for the King to receive. Want of Success before had made them differ among themselves: *Essex* and *Waller* could never agree; the Earl of *Manchester* and the Lord *Willoughby* differed to the highest Degree; and the King's Affairs went never the worse for it. But this Storm in the North ruined us all; for the *Scots* prevailed in *Yorkshire*, and being joined with *Fairfax*, *Manchester*, and *Cromwell*, carried all before them; so that the King was obliged to send Prince *Rupert* with a Body of 4000 Horse, to the Assistance of the Earl of *Newcastle*, where that Prince finished the Destruction of the King's Interest, by the rashest and unaccountablest Action in the World, of which I shall speak in its Place.

Another Action of the King's, though in it self no greater a Cause of Offence than the calling the *Scots* into the Nation, gave great Offence in general, and even the King's own Friends disliked it; and was carefully improved by his Enemies to the Disadvantage of the King, and of his Cause.

The Rebels in *Ireland* had, ever since the bloody Massacre of the Protestants, maintained a War against the *English*, and the Earl of *Ormond* was General and Governour for the King. The King finding his Affairs pinch him at home, sends Orders to the Earl of *Ormond* to consent to a Cessation of Arms[1] with the Rebels, and to ship over certain of his Regiments hither to his Majesty's Assistance. *'Tis true*, the *Irish* had deserved to be very ill treated by the *English*; but while the Parliament pressed the King with a cruel and unnatural War at home, and called in an Army out of *Scotland* to support their Quarrel with their King, I could never be convinced, that it was such a dishonourable Action for the King to suspend the Correction of his *Irish* Rebels, 'till he was in a Capacity to do it with Safety to himself; or to delay any farther Assistance to preserve himself at home; and the Troops he recalled being his own, it was no Breach of his Honour to make use of them, since he now wanted them for his own Security, against those who fought against him at home.

But the King was perswaded to make one Step farther; and that, I confess, was unpleasing to us all; and some of his best and most faithful Servants took the Freedom to speak plainly to him of it; and that was bringing some Regiments of the *Irish* themselves over. This cast, as we thought an *Odium* upon our whole Nation, being some of those very Wretches who had dipt their Hands in the innocent Blood of the Protestants, and with unheard of Butcheries, had massacred so many Thousands of *English* in cool Blood.

Abundance of Gentlemen forsook the King upon this Score; and seeing they could not brook the Fighting in Conjunction with this wicked Generation, came into the Declaration of the Parliament, and making Composition for their Estates, lived retired Lives all the rest of the War, or went abroad.

But as Exigences and Necessities oblige us to do things which at other times we would not do, and is, as to Man, some Excuse for such things; so I cannot but think the Guilt and Dishonour of such an Action must lye, very much of it, at least, at their Doors, who drove the King to these Necessities and Distresses by calling in an Army of his own Subjects whom he had not injured, but had complied with them in every thing, to make War upon him without any Provocation.

As to the Quarrel between the King and his Parliament, there may something be said on both Sides; and the King saw Cause himself, to disown and dislike some things he had done, which the Parliament objected against, such as levying Money without Consent of Parliament, Infractions on their Privileges, *and the like*: Here I say, was some room for an Argument at least, and Concessions on both Sides were needful to come to a Peace; but for the *Scots*, all their Demands had been answered, all their Grievances had been redressed, they had made Articles with their Sovereign, and he had performed those Articles; their capital Enemy Episcopacy was abolished; they had not one thing to demand of the King which he had not granted: And therefore they had no more Cause to take up Arms against their Sovereign, than they had against the *Grand Senior*. But it must for ever lye against them as a Brand of Infamy, and as a Reproach on their Whole Nation that, *purchased by the Parliament's Money*, they sold their *Honesty*, and rebelled against their King *for Hire*; and it was not many years before, as I have said already, they were fully paid the Wages of their Unrighteousness, and chastised for their Treachery by the very same People whom they thus basely assisted: Then they would have retrieved it, if it had not been too late.

But I could not but accuse this Age of Injustice and Partiality, who while they reproached the King for his Cessation of Arms with the *Irish* Rebels, and not prosecuting them with the utmost Severity, though he was constrained by the Necessities of the War to do it, could yet, at the same time, justify the *Scots* taking up Arms in a Quarrel they had no Concern in, and against their own King, with whom they had articled and capitulated, and who had so punctually complied with all their Demands, that they had no Claim upon him, no Grievances to be redressed, no Oppression to cry out of, nor could ask any thing of him which he had not granted.

But as no Action in the World is so vile, but the Actors can cover with some specious Pretence, so the *Scots* now passing into *England*, publish a Declaration to justify their Assisting the Parliament: To which I shall only say, in my Opinion, it was no Justification at all; for admit the Parliament's Quarrel had been never so just, it could not be just in them to aid them, because 'twas against their own King too, to whom they had sworn Allegiance, or at least had crowned him; and thereby had recognized his Authority:

For if Male-Administration be, according to *Prynn*'s Doctrine, or according to their own *Buchanan*, a sufficient Reason for Subjects to take up Arms against their Prince, the Breach of his Coronation Oath being supposed to dissolve the Oath of Allegiance, which *however I cannot believe*; yet this can never be extended to make it lawful, that because a King of *England* may, by Male-Administration discharge the Subjects of *England* from their Allegiance, that therefore the Subjects of *Scotland* may take up Arms against the King of *Scotland*, he having not infringed the Compact of Government as to them, and they having nothing to complain of for themselves: Thus I thought their own Arguments were against them, and Heaven seemed to concur with it; for although they did carry the Cause for the *English* Rebels, yet the most of them left their Bones here in the Quarrel.

But what signifies Reason to the Drum and the Trumpet. The Parliament had the supream Argument with those Men, (*viz.*) the Money; and having accordingly advanced a good round Sum, upon Payment of this, (*for the* Scots *would not stir a Foot without it*) they entred *England* on the 15th of *January* 1643[4], with an Army of 12000 Men, under the Command of old *Lesley* now Earl of *Leven*, an old Soldier of great Experience, having been bred to Arms from a Youth in the Service of the Prince of *Orange*.

The *Scots* were no sooner entred *England*, but they were joined by all the Friends to the Parliament Party in the North; and first, Collonel *Grey*, Brother to the Lord *Grey*, joined them with a Regiment of Horse, and several out of *Westmorland* and *Cumberland*, and so they advanced to *Newcastle*, which they summoned to surrender. The Earl of *Newcastle*, who rather saw, than was able to prevent this Storm, was in *Newcastle*, and did his best to defend it; but the *Scots* encreased by this time to above 20000, lay close Siege to the Place, which was but meanly fortified; and having repulsed the Garrison upon several Sallies, and pressing the Place very Close; after a Siege of 12 Days, or thereabouts, they enter the Town Sword in Hand. The Earl of *Newcastle* got away, and afterwards gathered what Forces together he could; but not strong enough to hinder the *Scots* from advancing to *Durham* which he quitted to them, nor to hinder the Conjunction of the *Scots* with the Forces of *Fairfax*, *Manchester*, and *Cromwell*. Whereupon the Earl seeing all things thus going to wreck, he sends his Horse away, and retreats with his Foot into *York*, making all necessary Preparations for a vigorous Defence there, in case he should be attacked, which he was pretty sure of, as indeed afterwards happened. *York* was in a very good Posture of Defence: The Fortifications very regular, and exceeding strong; well furnished with Provisions, and had now a Garrison of 12000 Men in it. The Governour under the Earl of *Newcastle* was Sir *Thomas Glemham*, a good Souldier, and a Gentleman brave enough.

The *Scots*, as I have said, having taken *Durham*, *Tinmouth* Castle and *Sunderland*, and being joined by Sir *Thomas Fairfax*, who had taken *Selby*, resolve, with their united Strength, to besiege *York*; but when they came to view the City, and saw a Plan of the Works, and had Intelligence of the Strength of the Garrison, they sent Expresses to *Manchester* and *Cromwell* for Help, who came on, and join them with 9000, making together about 30000 Men, rather more than less.

Now had the Earl of *Newcastle*'s repeated Messengers convinced the King, that it was absolutely necessary to send some Forces to his Assistance, or else all would be lost in the North. Whereupon Prince *Rupert* was detached with Orders first to go into *Lancashire*, and relieve *Latham-House*, defended by the brave Countess of *Derby*; and then taking all the Forces he could collect in *Cheshire*, *Lancashire*, and *Yorkshire*, to march to relieve *York*.

The Prince marched from *Oxford* with but three Regiments of Horse, and one of Dragoons, making in all about 2800 Men. The Collonels of Horse were Collonel *Charles Goring*, the Lord *Biron*, and my self; the Dragoons were of Collonel *Smith*. In our March we were joined by a Regiment of Horse from *Banbury*, one of Dragoons from *Bristol*, and three Regiments of Horse from *Chester*: So that when we came into *Lancashire*, we were about 5000 Horse and Dragoons. These Horse we received from *Chester*, were those who having been at the Siege of *Nantwich*, were obliged to raise the Siege by Sir *Thomas Fairfax*; and the Foot having yielded, the Horse made good their Retreat to *Chester*, being about 2000; of whom three Regiments now joined us.

We received also 2000 Foot from *West-Chester*, and 2000 more out of *Wales*; and with this Strength we entered *Lancashire*. We had not much time to spend, and a great deal of Work to do.

Bolton and *Leverpool* felt the first Fury[1] of our Prince: At *Bolton* indeed he had some Provocation; for here we were like to be beaten off. When first the Prince came to the Town, he sent a Summons to demand the Town for the King, but received no Answer but from their Guns, commanding the Messenger to keep off at his Peril. They had raised some Works about the Town, and having by their Intelligence, learnt that we had no Artillery, and were only a flying Party, *so they called us*, they contemned the Summons, and shewed themselves upon their Ramparts ready for us. The Prince was resolved to humble them, if possible, and takes up his Quarters close to the Town. In the Evening he orders me to advance with one Regiment of Dragoons, and my Horse to bring them off, if Occasion was, and to post my self as near as possibly I could to the Lines, yet so as not to be discovered; and at the same time having concluded what Part of the Works to fall upon, he draws up his Men on two other Sides, as if he would Storm them there; and on a Signal I was to begin the real Assault on my Side, with my Dragoons. I had got so near the Town with my Dragoons, making them creep upon their Bellies a great way, that we could hear the Soldiers talk on the Walls, that we could hear the Soldiers talk on the Walls, when the Prince believing one Regiment would be too few, sends me Word, that he had ordered a Regiment of Foot to help, and that I should not discover my self till they were come up to me. This broke our Measures; for the March of this Regiment was discovered by the Enemy, and they took the Alarm. Upon this I sent to the Prince, to desire he would put off the Storm for that Night, and I would answer for it the next Day; but the Prince was impatient, and sent Orders we should fall on as soon as the Foot came up to us. The Foot marching out of the Way, missed us, and fell in with a Road that leads to another Part of the Town; and being not able to find us, make an Attack upon the Town themselves; but the Defendants being ready for them, received them very warmly, and beat them off with great Loss. I was at a Loss now what to do; for hearing the Guns, and by the Noise knowing it was an Assault upon the Town, I was very uneasy to have my Share in it; but as I had learnt under the King of *Sweden* punctually to adhere to the Execution of Orders; and my Orders being to lye still till the Foot came up with me; I would not stir if I had been sure to have done never so much Service; but however to satisfy my self, I sent to the Prince to let him know that I continued in the same Place expecting the Foot, and none being yet come, I desired farther Orders. The Prince was a little amazed at this, and finding there must be some Mistake, came galloping away in the Dark to the Place, and drew off the Men, which was no hard Matter, for they were willing enough to give it over.

As for me, the Prince ordered me to come off so privately, as not to be discovered, if possible, which I effectually did; and so we were baulked for that Night. The next Day the Prince fell on upon another Quarter with three Regiments of Foot, but was beaten off with Loss; and the like a third time. At last, the Prince, *resolved to carry it*, doubled his Numbers, and renewing the Attack with fresh Men, the Foot entred the Town over their Works, killing in the first Heat of the Action, all that came in their way; some of the Foot at the same time letting in the Horse; and so the Town was entirely won. There was about 600 of the Enemy killed, and we lost above 400 in all which was owing to the foolish Mistakes we made. Our Men got some Plunder here, which the Parliament made a great Noise about; but it was their due, and they bought it dear enough.

Leverpool did not cost us so much, nor did we get so much by it, the People having sent their Women and Children, and best Goods on board the Ships in the Road; and as we had no Boats to board them with, we could not get at them. Here, as at *Bolton*, the Town and Fort was taken by Storm, and the Garrison were many of them cut in Pieces, which by the way was their own Faults.

Our next Stop was *Latham-House*, which the Countess of *Derby* had gallantly defended above 18 Weeks, against the Parliament Forces; and this Lady not only encouraged her Men by her chearful and noble Maintenance of them, but by Examples of her own undaunted Spirit, exposing her self upon the Walls in the midst of the Enemy's Shot, would be with her Men in the greatest Dangers; and she well deserved our Care of her Person; for the Enemy were prepaired to use her very rudely if she fell into their Hands.

Upon our Approach, the Enemy drew off; and the Prince not only effectually relieved this vigorous Lady, but left her a good Quantity of all Sorts of Ammunition, three great Guns, 500 Arms, and 200 Men, commanded by a Major, as her extraordinary Guard.

Here the Way being now opened, and our Success answering our Expectation, several Bodies of Foot came in to us from *Westmoreland*, and from *Cumberland*; and here it was that the Prince found Means to surprize the Town of *Newcastle upon Tyne*,[1] which was recovered for the King, by the Management of the Mayor of the Town, and some loyal Gentlemen of the County, and a Garrison placed there again for the King.

But our main Design being the Relief of *York*, the Prince advanced that Way a-pace, his Army still increasing; and being joined by the Lord *Goring* from *Richmondshire* with 4000 Horse, which were the same the Earl of *Newcastle* had sent away when he threw himself into *York* with the Infantry. We were now 18000 effective Men, whereof 10000 Horse and Dragoons; so the Prince, full of Hopes, and his Men in good Heart, boldly marched directly for *York*.

The *Scots*, as much surprized at the taking of *Newcastle*, as at the coming of their Enemy, began to enquire which Way they should get home, if they should be beaten; and calling a Council of War, they all agreed to raise the Siege. The Prince, who drew with him a great Train of Carriages charged with Provision and Ammunition, for the Relief of the City, like a wary General, kept at a Distance from the Enemy, and fetching a great Compass about, brings all safe into the City, and enters into *York*[1] himself with all his Army.

No Action of this whole War had gained the Prince so much Honour, or the King's Affairs so much Advantage as this, had the Prince but had the Power to have restrained his Courage after this, and checked his fatal Eagerness for Fighting. Here was a Siege raised, the Reputation of the Enemy justly slurred, a City relieved and furnished, with all things necessary in the Face of an Army superior in Number by near 10000 Men, and commanded by a Triumvirate of Generals *Leven*, *Fairfax* and *Manchester*. Had the Prince but remembered the Proceeding of the great Duke of *Parma* at the Relief of *Paris*,[2] he would have seen the relieving the City was his Business; 'twas the Enemy's Business to fight, if possible, 'twas his to avoid it; for, having delivered the City, and put the Disgrace of raising the Siege upon the Enemy, he had nothing farther to do, but to have waited till he had seen what Course the Enemy would take, and taken his farther Measures from their Motion.

But *the Prince*, a continual Friend to precipitant Counsels, would hear no Advice: I entreated him not to put it to the Hazard; I told him, that he ought to consider if he lost the Day, he lost the Kingdom, and took the Crown off from the King's Head. I put him in mind that it was impossible

those three Generals should continue long together; and
that if they did, they would not agree long in their Counsels:
Which would be as well for us as their separating. 'Twas
plain *Manchester* and *Cromwell* must return to the associated
Counties, who would not suffer them to stay, for fear the
King should attempt them; That he could subsist well
enough, having *York* City and River at his Back; but the
Scots would eat up the Country, make themselves odious,
and dwindle away to nothing, if he would but hold them at
Bay a little; other General Officers were of the same Mind;
but all I could say, or they either, to a Man deaf to any thing
but his own Courage, signified nothing.[1] He would draw
out and fight, there was no perswading him to the contrary,
unless a Man would run the Risque of being upbraided with
being a Coward, and afraid of the Work. The Enemy's Army
lay on a large Common, called *Marston-Moor*, doubtful what
to do: Some were for fighting the Prince, the *Scots* were
against it, being uneasy at having the Garrison of *Newcastle*
at their Backs; but the Prince brought their Councils of
War to a Result; for he let them know, they must fight him,
whether they would or no; for the Prince being, *as before*,
18000 Men, and the Earl of *Newcastle* having joined him
with 8000 Foot out of the City, were marched in Quest of
the Enemy, had entered the Moor in View of their Army,
and began to draw up in Order of Battle; but the Night
coming on, the Armies only viewed each other at a Distance
for that time. We lay all Night upon our Arms, and with the
first of the Day were in Order of Battle; the Enemy was
getting ready, but part of *Manchester*'s Men were not in the
Field, but lay about three Miles off, and made a hasty March
to come up.

The Prince his Army was exceedingly well managed; he
himself commanded the Left Wing, the Earl of *Newcastle*
the Right Wing; and the Lord *Goring*, as General of the
Foot, assisted by Major General *Porter*, and Sir *Charles
Lucas*, led the main Battle. I had prevailed with the Prince,
according to the Method of the King of *Sweden*, to place

some small Bodies of Musqueteers in the Intervals of his Horse, in the Left Wing, but could not prevail upon the Earl of *Newcastle* to do it in the Right; which he afterwards repented. In this Posture we stood facing the Enemy, expecting they would advance to us, which at last they did; and the Prince began the Day by saluting them with his Artillery, which being placed very well, galled them terribly for a Quarter of an Hour; they could not shift their Front, so they advanced the hastier to get within our great Guns, and consequently out of their Danger, which brought the Fight the sooner on.

The Enemy's Army was thus ordered; Sir *Thomas Fairfax* had the Right Wing, in which was the *Scots* Horse, and the Horse of his own and his Father's Army; *Cromwell* led the Left Wing, with his own and the Earl *Manchester*'s Horse, and the three Generals *Lesley*, old *Fairfax*, and *Manchester*, led the main Battle.

The Prince, with our Left Wing, fell on first, and, with his usual Fury, broke, like a Clap of Thunder, into the Right Wing of the *Scots* Horse, led by Sir *Thomas Fairfax*; and, as nothing could stand in his Way, he broke through and through them, and entirely routed them, pursuing them quite out of the Field. Sir *Thomas Fairfax*, with a Regiment of Lances, and about 500 of his own Horse, made good the Ground for some time; but our Musqueteers, which, as I said, were placed among our Horse were such an unlooked for sort of an Article in a Fight among the Horse, that those Lances, which otherwise were brave Fellows, were mowed down with their Shot, and all was put into Confusion. Sir *Thomas Fairfax* was wounded in the Face, his Brother killed, and a great Slaughter was made of the *Scots*, to whom I confess we shewed no Favour at all.

While this was doing on our Left, the Lord *Goring* with the main Battle charged the Enemy's Foot, and particularly one Brigade commanded by Major General *Porter*, being mostly Pikemen, not regarding the Fire of the Enemy, charged with that Fury in a close Body of Pikes, that they overturned all that came in their Way, and breaking into the Middle of the Enemy's Foot, filled all with Terror and Confusion, insomuch that the three Generals thinking all had been lost, fled, and quitted the Field.

But Matters went not so well with that *always Unfortunate* Gentleman the Earl of *Newcastle*, and our Right Wing of Horse; for *Cromwell* charged the Earl of *Newcastle* with a powerful Body of Horse; and though the Earl, and those about him, did what Men could do, and behaved themselves with all possible Gallantry, yet there was no withstanding *Cromwell*'s Horse; but, like Prince *Rupert*, they bore down all before them; and now the Victory was wrung out of our Hands by our own gross Miscarriage; for the Prince, as 'twas his Custom, too eager in the Chase of the Enemy, was gone, and could not be heard of: The Foot in the Center, the Right Wing of the Horse being routed by *Cromwell*, was left, and without the Guard of his Horse; *Cromwell* having routed the Earl of *Newcastle*, and beaten him quite out of the Field, and Sir *Thomas Fairfax* rallying his dispersed Troops, they fall all together upon the Foot. General Lord *Goring*, like himself, fought like a Lion, but, forsaken of his Horse, was hemmed in on all Sides, and overthrown; and an Hour after this, the Prince returning too late to recover his Friends, was obliged with the rest to quit the Field to Conquerors.

This was a fatal Day to the King's Affairs, and the Risque too much for any Man in his Wits to run; we lost 4000 Men on the Spot, 3000 Prisoners, amongst whom was Sir *Charles Lucas*, Major General *Porter*, Major General *Telier*, and about 170 Gentlemen of Quality. We lost all our Baggage, 25 Pieces of Cannon, 300 Carriages, 150 Barrels of Powder, and 10000 Arms.

The Prince got into *York* with the Earl of *Newcastle*, and a great many Gentlemen, and 7 or 8000 of the Men, as well Horse as Foot.

I had but very course Treatment in this Fight; for returning with the Prince from the Pursuit of the Right Wing, and finding all lost, I halted with some other Officers, to consider what to do: At first we were for making our Retreat in a Body, and might have done so well enough, if we had known what had happened, before we saw our selves in the Middle of the Enemy; for Sir *Thomas Fairfax*, who had got together his scattered Troops, and joined by some of the Left Wing, knowing who we were, charged us with great Fury. 'Twas not a Time to think of any thing but getting away, or dying upon the Spot; the Prince kept on in the Front, and Sir *Thomas Fairfax*, by this Charge cut off about three Regiments of us from our Body; but bending his main Strength at the Prince, left us, as it were, behind him, in the Middle of the Field of Battle. We took this for the only Opportunity we could have to get off, and joining together, we made cross the Place of Battle in as good Order as we could, with our Carabines presented. In this Posture we passed by several Bodies of the Enemy's Foot, who stood with their Pikes charged to keep us off; but they had no Occasion, for we had no Design to meddle with them, but to get from them. Thus we made a swift March, and thought our selves pretty secure, but our Work was not done yet; for, on a sudden, we saw our selves under a Necessity of Fighting our Way through a great Body of *Manchester*'s Horse, who came galloping upon us over the Moor. They had as, we suppose, been pursuing some of our broken Troops, which were fled before, and seeing us, they gave us a home Charge. We received them as well as could, but pushed to get through them, which at last we did with a considerable Loss to them. However, we lost so many Men, either killed or separated from us, (for all could not follow the same Way) that of our three Regiments we could not be above 400 Horse together, when we got quite clear, and these were mixt Men, some of one Troop and Regiment, some of another. Not that I believe many of us were killed in the last Attack; for we had plainly the better of the Enemy; but our Design being to get off, some shifted for themselves one Way, and some another, in the best Manner they could, and as their several Fortunes guided them. 400 more of this Body, as I afterwards understood, having broke through the Enemy's Body another Way, kept together, and got into *Pontfract* Castle, and 300 more, made Northward, and to *Skippon*, where the Prince afterwards fetched them off.

Those few of us that were left together, with whom I was, being now pretty clear of Pursuit, halted, and began to enquire who and who we were, and what we should do; and on a short Debate, I proposed we should make to the first Garrison of the King's that we could recover; and that we should keep together, lest the Country People should insult us upon the Roads. With this Resolution we pushed on Westward for *Lancashire*; but our Misfortunes were not yet at an End: We travelled very hard, and got to a Village upon the River *Wharf*, near *Wetherby*. At *Wetherby* there was a Bridge, but we understood that a Party from *Leeds* had secured the Town and the Post, in order to stop the flying Cavaliers; and that 'twould be very hard to get through there; though, as we understood afterwards, there were no Soldiers there but a Guard of the Townsmen. In this Pickle we consulted what Course to take; to stay where we were till Morning, we all concluded would not be safe; some advised to take the Stream with our Horses; but the River, which is deep, and the Current strong, seemed to bid us have a care what we did of that Kind, especially in the Night. We resolved, therefore to refresh our selves and our Horses, *which indeed is more than we did*, and go on till we might come to a Ford or Bridge, where we might get over. Some Guides we had, but they either were foolish or false; for after we had rid eight or nine Miles, they plunged us into a River, at a Place they called a Ford, but 'twas a very ill one; for most of our Horses swam, and seven or eight were lost, but we saved the Men; however, we got all over.

We made bold with our first Convenience to trespass upon the Country for a few Horses, where we could find them, to remount our Men, whose Horses were drowned, and continued our March; but being obliged to refresh our selves at a small Village on the Edge of *Bramham-moor*, we found the Country alarmed by our taking some Horses, and we were no sooner got on Horseback in the Morning, and entering on the Moor, but we understood we were pursued by some Troops of Horse: There was no Remedy but we must pass this Moor; and though our Horses were exceedingly tired, yet we pressed on upon a round Trot, and recovered an enclosed Country on the other Side, where we halted. And here, Necessity putting us upon it, we were obliged to look out for more Horses, for several of our Men were dismounted, and others Horses disabled by carrying double, those who lost their Horses getting up behind them; but we were supplied by our Enemies against their Will.

The Enemy followed us over the Moor, and we having a woody enclosed Country about us, where we were, I observed by their moving, they had lost Sight of us; upon which I proposed concealing our selves till we might judge of their Numbers. We did so, and lying close in a Wood, they past hastily by us, without skirting or searching the Wood, which was what on another Occasion they would not have done. I found they were not above 150 Horse, and considering, that to let them go before us, would be to alarm the Country, and stop our Design; I thought, since we might be able to deal with them, we should not meet with a better Place for it, and told the rest of our Officers my Mind, which all our Party presently, (for we not had Time for a long Debate) agreed to. Immediately upon this I caused two Men to fire their Pistols in the Wood, at two different Places, as far asunder as I could. This I did to give them an Alarm, and amuse them; for being in the Lane, they would otherwise have got through before we had been ready, and I resolved to engage them there, as soon as 'twas possible. After this Alarm, we rushed out of the Wood, with about 100 Horse, and charged them on the Flank in a broad Lane, the Wood being on their Right. Our Passage into the Lane being narrow, gave us some Difficulty in our getting out; but the Surprize of the Charge did our Work; for the

Enemy thinking we had been a Mile or two before, had not the least Thoughts of this Onset, till they heard us in the Wood, and then they who were before could not come back. We broke into the Lane just in the Middle of them, and by that means divided them; and facing to the Left, charged the Rear. First our dismounted Men, which were near 50, lined the Edge of the Wood, and fired with their Carabines upon those which were before, so warmly, that they put them into a great Disorder: Mean while 50 more of our Horse from the farther Part of the Wood shewed themselves in the Lane upon their Front; this put them of the foremost Party into a great Perplexity, and they began to face about, to fall upon us who were engaged in the Rear: But their facing about in a Lane where there was no Room to wheel, and one who understands the Manner of wheeling a Troop of Horse, must imagine, put them into a great Disorder. Our Party in the Head of the Lane taking the Advantage of this Mistake of the Enemy, charged in upon them, and routed them entirely. Some found means to break into the Enclosures on the other Side of the Lane, and get away. About 30 were killed, and about 25 made Prisoners, and 40 very good Horses were taken; all this while not a Man of ours was lost, and not above seven or eight wounded. Those in the Rear behaved themselves better; for they stood our Charge with a great deal of Resolution, and all we could do, could not break them; but at last our Men who had fired on Foot through the Hedges at the other Party, coming to do the like here, there was no standing it any longer. The Rear of them faced about, and retreated out of the Lane, and drew up in the open Field to receive and rally their Fellows. We killed about 17 of them, and followed them to the End of the Lane, but had no mind to have any more fighting than needs must; our Condition at that time not making it proper, the Towns round us being all in the Enemy's Hands, and the Country but indifferently pleased with us; however, we stood facing them till they thought fit to march away. Thus we were supplied with Horses enough to remount our Men, and pursued our first Design of getting into *Lancashire*. As for our Prisoners, we let them go off on Foot.

But the Country being by this time alarmed, and the Rout of our Army every where known, we foresaw Abundance of Difficulties before us; we were not strong enough to venture into any great Towns, and we were too many to be concealed in small ones. Upon this we resolved to halt in a great Wood about three Miles beyond the Place, where we had the last Skirmish, and sent out Scouts to discover the Country, and learn what they could, either of the Enemy, or of our Friends.

Any Body may suppose we had but indifferent Quarters here, either for our selves or for our Horses; but however, we made shift to lye here two Days and one Night. In the interim I took upon me, with two more, to go to *Leeds* to learn some News; we were disguised like Country Ploughmen; the Clothes we got at a Farmer's House, which for that particular Occasion we plundered; and I cannot say no Blood was shed in a Manner too rash, and which I could not have done at another Time; but our Case was desperate, and the People too surly, and shot at us out the Window, wounded one Man and shot a Horse, which we counted as great a Loss to us as a Man, for our Safety depended upon our Horses. Here we got Clothes of all Sorts enough for both Sexes, and thus dressing my self up *a la Paisant*, with a white Cap on my Head, and a Fork on my Shoulder, and one of my Comerades in the Farmer's Wife's Russet Gown and Petticoat, like a Woman; the other with an old Crutch like a lame Man, and all mounted on such Horses as we had taken the Day before from the Country. Away we go to *Leeds* by three several Ways, and agreed to meet upon the Bridge. My pretended Country Woman acted her Part to the Life, though the Party was a Gentleman of good Quality of the Earl of *Worcester*'s Family, and the Cripple did as well he; but I thought my self very awkward in my Dress, which made me very shy, especially among the Soldiers. We passed their Centinels and Guards at *Leeds* unobserved, and put up our Horses at several Houses in the Town, from whence we went up and down to make our Remarks.[1] My Cripple was the fittest to go among the Soldiers, because there was less Danger of being pressed:[2] There he informed himself of the Matters of War, particularly that the Enemy sat down again to the Siege of *York*; that flying Parties were in Pursuit of the Cavaliers; and there he heard that 500 Horse of the Lord *Manchester*'s Men had followed a Party of Cavaliers over *Bramham Moor*; and, that entering a Lane, the Cavaliers, who were 1000 strong, fell upon them, and killed them all but about 50. This, though it was a Lie, was very pleasant to us to hear, knowing it was our Party, because of the other part of the Story, which was thus; that the Cavaliers had taken Possession of such a Wood, where they rallied all the Troops of their flying Army; that they had plundered the Country as they came, taking all the Horses they could get; that they had plundered Goodman *Thompson*'s House, which was the Farmer I mentioned, and killed Man, Woman and Child; and that they were about 2000 strong.

My other Friend in Woman's Clothes got among the good Wives at an Inn, where she set up her Horse, and there she heard the same sad and dreadful Tidings; and that this Party was so strong, none of the neighbouring Garrisons durst stir out; but that they had sent Expresses to *York* for a Party of Horse to come to their Assistance.

I walked up and down the Town, but fancied my self so ill disguised, and so easy to be known, that I cared not to talk with any Body. We met at the Bridge exactly at our Time, and compared our Intelligence, found it answered our End of coming, and that we had nothing to do but to get back to our Men; but my Cripple told me, he would not stir still he bought some Victuals: So away he hops with his Crutch, and buys four or five great Pieces of Bacon, as many of hung Beef, and two or three Loaves; and, borrowing a Sack at the Inn (which I suppose he never restored,) he loads his Horse, and, getting a large Leather

Bottle, he filled that of *Aquavitæ* instead of small Beer; my Woman Comerade did the like. I was uneasy in my Mind, and took no Care but to get out of Town; however, we all came off well enough; but 'twas well for me that I had no Provisions with me, as you will hear presently. We came, as I said, into the Town by several Ways, and so we went out; but about three Miles from the Town we met again exactly where we had agreed: I being about a Quarter of a Mile from the rest, I meets three Country Fellows on Horseback; one had a long Pole on his Shoulder, another a Fork, the third no Weapon at all, that I saw; I gave them the Road very orderly, being habited like one of their Brethren; but one of them stopping short at me, and looking earnestly, calls out, *Hark thee, Friend*, says he, in a broad North Country Tone, *whar hast thou thilk Horse?* I must confess I was in the utmost Confusion at the Question, neither being able to answer the Question, nor to speak in his Tone; so I made as if I did not hear him, and went on. *Na, but ye's not gang soa*, says the Boor, and comes up to me, and takes hold of the Horse's Bridle to stop me; at which, vexed at Heart that I could not tell how to talk to him, I reached him a great Knock on the Pate with my Fork, and fetched him off of his Horse, and then began to mend my Pace. The other Clowns, though it seems they knew not what the Fellow wanted, pursued me, and, finding they had better Heels than I, I saw there was no Remedy but to make use of my Hands, and faced about. The first that came up with me was he that had no Weapons, so I thought I might parley with him; and, speaking as Country like as I could, I asked him what he wanted? *Thou'st knaw that soon*, says *Yorkshire, and Ise but come at thee*. Then keep awa' Man, said I, *or Ise brain thee*. By this Time the third Man came up, and the Parley ended; for he gave me no Words but laid at me with his long Pole, and that with such Fury, that I began to be doubtful of him: I was loath to shoot the Fellow, though I had Pistols under my grey Frock, as well for that the Noise of a Pistol might bring more People in, the Village

being on our Rear; and also because I could not imagine
what the Fellow meant, or would have; but at last finding
he would be too many for me with that long Weapon, and a
hardy strong Fellow, I threw my self off of my Horse, and
running in with him, stabbed my Fork into his Horse; the
Horse being wounded, staggered a while, and then fell
down, and the Booby had not the Sense to get down in time,
but fell with him; upon which, giving him a knock or two
with my Fork, I secured him. The other, by this Time, had
furnished himself with a great Stick out of a Hedge, and,
before I was disingaged from the last Fellow, gave me two
such Blows, that if the last had not missed my Head, and hit
me on the Shoulder, I had ended the Fight and my Life
together. 'Twas time to look about me now, for this was a
mad Man; I defended my self with my Fork, but 'twould
not do; at last, in short, I was forced to Pistol him, and get
on Horseback again, and, with all the Speed I could make
get away to the Wood to our Men.

If my two Fellow Spies had not been behind, I had never
known what was the Meaning of this Quarrel of the three
Countrymen, but my Cripple had all the Particulars; for he
being behind us, as I have already observed, when he came
up to the first Fellow, who began the Fray, he found him
beginning to come to himself; so he gets off, and pretends
to help him, and sets him up upon his Breech, and being a
very merry Fellow, talked to him, *Well and what's the
Matter now*, says he to him, *ah wae's me*, says the Fellow,
I is killed: Not quite Mon, says the Cripple. *O that's a fau
Thief*, says he, and thus they parlied. My Cripple got him
on's Feet, and gave him a Dram of his *Aquavitæ* Bottle,
and made much of him, in order to know what was the
Occasion of the Quarrel. Our disguised Woman pitied the
Fellow too, and together they set him up again upon his
Horse, and then he told him that that Fellow was got upon
one of his Brother's Horses who lived at *Wetherby*: They
said the Cavaliers stole him, but 'twas like such Rogues;
no Mischief could be done in the Country, but 'twas the

poor Cavaliers must bear the Blame, and the like; and thus they jogged on till they came to the Place where the other two lay. The first Fellow they assisted as they had done t'other, and gave him a Dram out of the Leather Bottle; but the last Fellow was past their Care; so they came away: For when they understood that 'twas my Horse, they claimed, they began to be affraid that their own Horses might be known too, and then they had been betraid in a worse Pickle than I, and must have been forced to have done some Mischief or other to have got away.

I had sent out two Troopers to fetch them off, if there was any Occasion; but their Stay was not long, and the two Troopers saw them at a Distance coming towards us, so they returned.

I had enough of going for a Spy, and my Companions had enough of staying in the Wood; for other Intelligences agreed with ours, and all concurred in this, that it was time to be going; however, this Use we made of it, that while the Country thought us so strong we were in the less Danger of being attacked, though in the more of being observed; but all this while we heard nothing of our Friends, till the next Day. We heard Prince *Rupert*, with about 1000 Horse, was at *Skipton*, and from thence marched away to *Westmoreland*.

We concluded now we had two or three Days time good; for, since Messengers were sent to *York* for a Party to suppress us, we must have at least two Days March of them, and therefore all concluded we were to make the best of our Way; early in the Morning therefore we decamped from those dull Quarters; and as we marched through a Village, we found the People very civil to us, and the Women cried out, *God bless them, 'tis pity the Roundheads should make such Woork with such brave Men*, and the like. Finding we were among our Friends, we resolved to halt a little and refresh our selves; and, indeed, the People were very kind to us, gave us Victuals and Drink, and took Care of our Horses. It happened to be my Lot to stop at a House where the good

Woman took a great deal of Pains to provide for us; but I observed the good Man walked about with a Cap upon his Head, and very much out of Order, I took no great Notice of it, being very sleepy, and having asked my Landlady to let me have a Bed, I lay down and slept heartily: When I waked I found my Landlord on another Bed groaning very heavily.

When I came down Stairs, I found my Cripple talking with my Landlady; he was now out of his Disguise, but we called him Cripple still; and the other, who put on the Woman's Clothes, we called Goody *Thompson*. As soon as he saw me, he called me out, *Do you know*, says he *the Man of the House you are quartered in? No, not I*, says I. *No, so I believe, nor they you*, says he, *if they did, the good Wife would not have made you a Posset, and fetched a white Loaf for you. What do you mean*, says I. *Have you seen the Man* says he? *Seen him*, says I, *yes, and heard him too; the Man's Sick, and groans so heavily*, says I, *that I could not lye upon the Bed any longer for him. Why, this is the poor Man*, says he, *that you knocked down with your Fork Yesterday, and I have had all the Story out yonder at the next Door*. I confess it grieved me to have been forced to treat one so roughly who was one of our Friends, but to make some amends, we contrived to give the poor Man his Brother's Horse; and my Cripple told him a formal Story, that he believed the Horse was taken away from the Fellow by some of our Men; and, if he knew him again, if 'twas his Friend's Horse, he should have him. The Man came down upon the News, and I caused six or seven Horses, which were taken at the same time, to be shewn him; he immediately chose the right; so I gave him the Horse, and we pretended a great deal of Sorrow for the Man's Hurt; and that we had not knocked the Fellow on the Head as well as took away the Horse. The Man was so over-joyed at the Revenge he thought was taken on the Fellow, that we heard him groan no more. We ventured to stay all Day at this Town, and the next Night, and got Guides to lead us to *Blackstone Edge*, a Ridge of Mountains which part this Side of *Yorkshire* from *Lancashire*. Early in the Morning we marched, and kept our Scouts very carefully out every Way, who brought us no News for this Day; we kept on all Night, and made our Horses do Penance for that little Rest they had, and the next Morning we passed the Hills, and got into *Lancashire*, to a Town called *Littlebury*; and from thence to *Rochedale*, a little Market-Town. And now we thought our selves safe as to the Pursuit of Enemies from the Side of *York*; our Design was to get to *Bolton*, but all the County was full of the Enemy in flying Parties, and how to get to *Bolton* we knew not. At last we resolved to send a Messenger to *Bolton*; but he came back and told us, he had with lurking and hiding, tried all the Ways that he thought possible, but to no Purpose; for he could not get into the Town. We sent another, and he never returned; and some time after we understood he was taken by the Enemy. At last one got into the Town, but brought us Word, they were tired out with constant Alarms, had been straitly blocked up, and every Day expected a Siege, and therefore advised us either to go Northward, where Prince *Rupert*, and the Lord *Goring* ranged at Liberty; or to get over *Warrington* Bridge, and so secure our Retreat to *Chester*. This double Direction divided our Opinions; I was for getting into *Chester*, both to recruit my self with Horses and with Money, both which I wanted, and to get Refreshment, which we all wanted; but the major Part of our Men were for the North. First they said, there was their General, and 'twas their Duty to the Cause, and the King's Interest obliged us to go where we could do best Service; and there was their Friends, and every Man might hear some News of his own Regiment, for we belonged to several Regiments; besides, all the Towns to the Left of us, were possessed by Sir *William Brereton*, *Warrington* and *Northwich*, Garrisoned by the Enemy, and a strong Party at *Manchester*; so that 'twas very likely we should be beaten and dispersed before we could get to *Chester*. These Reasons, and especially the last, determined us for the North, and we had resolved to

march the next Morning, when other Intelligence brought
us to more speedy Resolutions. We kept our Scouts continually abroad, to bring us Intelligence of the Enemy,
whom we expected on our Backs, and also to keep an Eye
upon the Country; for as we lived upon them something at
large, they were ready enough to do us any ill Turn, as it lay
in their Power.

The first Messenger that came to us, was from our
Friends at *Bolton*, to inform us, that they were preparing at
Manchester to attack us: One of our Parties had been as far
as *Stockport*, on the Edge of *Cheshire*, and was pursued by a
Party of the Enemy, but got off by the Help of the Night.
Thus all things looking black to the South, we had resolved
to march Northward in the Morning, when one of our
Scouts from the Side of *Manchester* assured us, Sir *Thomas
Middleton*, with some of the Parliament Forces, and the
Country Troops, making above 1200 Men, were on their
March to attack us, and would certainly beat up our Quarters
that Night. Upon this Advice we resolved to be gone; and
getting all things in Readiness, we began to march about
two Hours before Night: And having gotten a trusty Fellow
for a Guide, a Fellow that we found was a Friend to our
Side, he put a Project into my Head, which saved us all for
that time; and that was, to give out in the Village, that we
were marched back to *Yorkshire*, resolving to get into
Pontfract Castle; and accordingly he leads us out of the
Town the same way we came in; and taking a Boy with him,
he sends the Boy back just at Night, and bad him say he
saw us go up the Hills at *Blackstone-Edge*; and it happened
very well; for this Party were so sure of us, that they had
placed 400 Men on the Road to the Northward, to intercept
our Retreat that Way, and had left no Way for us, as they
thought, to get away, but back again.

About Ten a Clock at Night, they assaulted our Quarters,
but found we were gone; and being informed which way,
they followed upon the Spur, and travelling all Night, being
Moon-Light, they found themselves the next Day about

15 Miles East, just out of their Way; for we had by the Help of our Guide, turned short at the Foot of the Hills, and through blind, untrodden Paths, and with Difficulty enough, by Noon the next Day, had reached almost 25 Miles North near a Town called *Clithero*. Here we halted in the open Field, and sent out our People to see how things were in the Country. This Part of the Country almost unpassable, and walled round with Hills, was indifferent quiet, and we got some Refreshment for our selves, but very little Horsemeat, and so went on; but we had not marched far before we found our selves discovered; and the 400 Horse sent to lye in wait for us as before, having understood which way we went, followed us hard; and by Letters to some of their Friends at *Preston*, we found we were beset again. Our Guide began now to be out of his Knowledge, and our Scouts brought us Word, the Enemy's Horse was posted before us, and we knew they were in our Rear. In this Exigence, we resolved to divide our small Body, and so amusing them, at least one might get off, if the other miscarried. I took about 80 Horse with me, among which were all that I had of our own Regiment, amounting to above 32, and took the Hills towards *Yorkshire*. Here we met with such unpassable Hills, vast Moors, Rocks, and stony Ways, as lamed all our Horses, and tired our Men; and sometimes I was ready to think we should never be able to get over them, till our Horses failing, and Jack-boots being but indifferent things to travel in, we might be starved before we should find any Road, or Towns, (for Guide we had none) but a Boy who knew but little, and would cry, when we asked him any Questions. I believe neither Men nor Horses ever passed in some Places where we went, and for 20 Hours we saw not a Town nor a House, excepting sometimes from the Top of the Mountains, at a vast Distance. I am perswaded we might have encamped here, if we had had Provisions, till the War had been over, and have met with no Disturbance; and I have often wondered since, how we got into such horrible Places, as much as how got out. That which was worse to

us than all the rest, was, that we knew not where we were going, nor what Part of the Country we should come into, when we came out of those desolate Craggs. At last, after a terrible Fatigue, we began to see the Western Parts of *Yorkshire*, some few Villages, and the Country at a Distance, looked a little like *England*; for I thought before it looked like old *Brennus* Hill,[1] which the *Grisons* call the Grandfather of the *Alps*. We got some Relief in the Villages, which indeed some of us had so much need of, that they were hardly able to sit their Horses, and others were forced to help them off, they were so faint. I never felt so much of the Power of Hunger in my Life; for having not eaten in 30 Hours, I was as ravenous as a Hound; and if I had had a Piece of Horseflesh, I believe I should not have had Patience to have staid Dressing it, but have fallen upon it raw, and have eaten it as greedily as a *Tartar*.

However, I eat very cautiously, having often seen the Danger of Mens eating heartily after long Fasting. Our next Care was to enquire our Way. *Hallifax*, they told us, was on our right; there we durst not think of going; *Skippon* was before us, and there we knew not how it was; for a Body of 3000 Horse, sent out by the Enemy in Pursuit of Prince *Rupert*, had been there but two Days before, and the Country People could not tell us, whether they were gone, or no: And *Manchester*'s Horse, which were sent out after our Party, were then at *Hallifax*, in Quest of us, and afterwards marched into *Cheshire*. In this Distress we would have hired a Guide, but none of the Country People would go with us; for the Roundheads would hang them, they said, when they came there. Upon this I called a Fellow to me, *Harke ye friend*, says I, *dost thee know the Way so as to bring us into* Westmoreland, *and not keep the great Road from* York? *Ay merry*, says he, *I ken the Ways weel enou; and you would go and guide us*, said I, *but that you are afraid the Roundheads will hang you? Indeed would I*, says the Fellow. *Why then*, says I, *thou hadst as good be hanged by a Roundhead as a Cavalier; for if thou wilt not go, I'll hang thee just now. Na*, *and ye serve me soa*, says the Fellow, *Ise ene gang with ye; for I care not for Hanging; and ye'l get me a good Horse, Ise gang and be one of ye, for I'll nere come heame mere.* This pleased us still better, and we mounted the Fellow; for three of our Men died that Night with the extreme Fatigue of the last Service.

Next Morning, when our new Trooper was mounted and cloathed, we hardly knew him; and this Fellow led us by such Ways, such Wildernesses, and yet with such Prudence, keeping the Hills to the left, that we might have the Villages to refresh our selves, that without him, we had certainly either perished in those Mountains, or fallen into the Enemy's Hands. We passed the great Road from *York* so critically as to time, that from one of the Hills he shewed us a Party of the Enemy's Horse, who were then marching into *Westmoreland*. We lay still that Day, finding we were not discovered by them; and our Guide proved the best Scout that we could have had; for he would go out ten Miles at a time, and bring us in all the News of the Country: Here he brought us word, that *York*[1] was surrendered upon Articles, and that *Newcastle*, which had been surprized by the King's Party, was besieged by another Army of *Scots* advanced to help their Brethren.

Along the Edges of those vast Mountains we past with the Help of our Guide, till we came into the Forest of *Swale*; and finding our selves perfectly concealed here, for no Soldier had ever been here all the War, nor perhaps would not, if it had lasted 7 Years; we thought we wanted a few Days Rest, at least for our Horses, so we resolved to halt, and while we did so, we made some Disguises, and sent out some Spies into the Country; but as here were no great Towns, nor no Post Road, we got very little Intelligence. We rested four Days, and then marched again; and indeed having no great Stock of Money about us, and not very free of that we had, four Days was enough for those poor Places to be able to maintain us.

We thought our selves pretty secure now; but our chief

Care was how to get over those terrible Mountains; for having passed the great Road that leads from *York* to *Lancaster*, the Craggs, the farther Northward we looked, look'd still the worse, and our Business was all on the other Side. Our Guide told us, he would bring us out, if we would have Patience, which we were obliged to, and kept on this slow March, till he brought us to *Stanhope*, in the County of *Durham*; where some of *Goring*'s Horse, and two Regiments of Foot, had their Quarters: This was 19 Days from the Battle of *Marston-Moor*. The Prince who was then at *Kendal* in *Westmoreland*, and who had given me over as lost, when he had News of our Arrival, sent an Express to me, to meet him at *Appleby*. I went thither accordingly, and gave him an Account of our Journey, and there I heard the short History of the other Part of our Men, whom we parted from in *Lancashire*. They made the best of their way North; they had two resolute Gentlemen who commanded; and being so closely pursued by the Enemy, that they found themselves under a Necessity of Fighting, they halted, and faced about, expecting the Charge. The Boldness of the Action made the Officer who led the Enemy's Horse (which it seems were the County Horse only) afraid of them; which they perceiving, taking the Advantage of his Fears, bravely advance, and charge them; and, though they were above 200 Horse, they routed them, killed about 30 or 40, got some Horses, and some Money, and pushed on their March Night and Day; but coming near *Lancaster*, they were so way-laid and pursued, that they agreed to separate, and shift every Man for himself; many of them fell into the Enemy's Hands; some were killed attempting to pass through the River *Lune*; some went back again, six or seven got to *Bolton*, and about 18 got safe to Prince *Rupert*.

The Prince was in a better Condition hereabouts than I expected; he and my Lord *Goring*, with the Help of Sir *Marmaduke Langdale*, and the Gentlemen of *Cumberland*, had gotten a Body of 4000 Horse, and about 6000 Foot; they had retaken *Newcastle*, *Tinmouth*, *Durham*, *Stockton*, and several Towns of Consequence from the *Scots*, and might have cut them out Work enough still, if that base People, resolved to engage their whole Interest to ruine their Sovereign, had not sent a second Army of 10000 Men, under the Earl of *Calender*, to help their first. These came and laid Siege to *Newcastle*, but found more vigorous Resistance now than they had done before.

There were in the Town Sir *John Morley*, the Lord *Crawford*, Lord *Rea*, and *Maxwell*, *Scots*; and old Soldiers, who were resolved their Countrymen should buy the Town very dear if they had it; and had it not been for our Disaster at *Marston-Moor*, they had never had it; for *Calender*, finding he was not able to carry the Town, sends to General *Leven* to come from the Siege of *York* to help him.

Mean time the Prince forms a very good Army, and the Lord *Goring*, with 10000 Men shews himself on the Borders of *Scotland*, to try if that might not cause the *Scots* to recal their Forces; and, I am perswaded had he entered *Scotland*, the Parliament of *Scotland* had recalled the Earl of *Calender*, for they had but 5000 Men left in Arms to send against him; but they were loath to venture.

However, this Effect it had, that it called the *Scots* Northward again, and found them Work there for the rest of the Summer, to reduce the several Towns in the Bishoprick of *Durham*.

I found with the Prince the poor Remains of my Regiment, which when joined with those that had been with me, could not all make up three Troops, and but two Captains, three Lieutenants, and one Cornet; the rest were dispersed, killed, or taken Prisoners.

However, with those, which we still called a Regiment, I joined the Prince, and after having done all we could on that Side, the *Scots* being returned from *York*, the Prince returned through *Lancashire* to *Chester*.

The Enemy often appeared and alarmed us, and once fell on one of our Parties, and killed us about a hundred Men; but we were too many for them to pretend to fight us, so we

came to *Bolton*, beat the Troops of the Enemy near *Warring-*
ton, where I got a Cut with a Halbard in my Face, and arrived
at *Chester* the beginning of *August*.

The Parliament, upon their great Success in the North,
thinking the King's Forces quite broken, had sent their
General *Essex* into the West, where the King's Army was
commanded by Prince *Maurice*, Prince *Rupert*'s elder
Brother, but not very strong; and the King being, as they
supposed, by the Absence of Prince *Rupert*, weakened so
much as, that he might be checked by Sir *William Waller*,
who, with 4500 Foot, and 1500 Horse, was at that Time
about *Winchester*, having lately beaten Sir *Ralph Hopton*.
Upon all these Considerations, the Earl of *Essex* marches
Westward.

The Forces in the West being too weak to oppose him,
every thing gives way to him, and all People expected he
would besiege *Exeter*, where the Queen was newly lying in,
and sent a Trumpet to desire he would forbear the City,
while she could be removed; which he did, and passed on
Westward, took *Tiverton*, *Biddeford*, *Barnstable*, *Lanceston*,
relieved *Plymouth*, drove Sir *Richard Greenvil* up into
Cornwall, and followed him thither, but left Prince *Maurice*
behind him with 4000 Men about *Barnstable* and *Exeter*.
The King, in the mean time, marches from *Oxford* into
Worcester, with *Waller* at his Heels; at *Edgehill* his Majesty
turns upon *Waller*, and gave him a Brush, to put him in
mind of the Place; the King goes on to *Worcester*, sends
300 Horse to relieve *Durley* Castle, besieged by the Earl of
Denby, and sending Part of his Forces to *Bristol*, returns to
Oxford.

His Majesty had now firmly resolved to march into the
West, not having yet any Account of our Misfortunes in the
North. *Waller* and *Middleton* way-lay the King at *Cropedy*
Bridge: The King assaults *Middleton* at the Bridge; *Waller*'s
Men were posted with some Cannon to guard a Pass;
Middleton's Men put a Regiment of the King's Foot to the
Rout, and pursued them: *Waller*'s Men, willing to come in

for the Plunder, a thing their General had often used them to, quit their Post at the Pass, and their great Guns, to have Part in the Victory. The King coming in seasonably to the Relief of his Men, routs *Middleton*, and at the same time sends a Party round, who clapt in between Sir *William Waller*'s Men and their great Guns, and secured the Pass and the Cannon too.

The King took three Collonels, besides other Officers, and about 300 Men Prisoners, with eight great Guns, 19 Carriages of Ammunition, and killed about 200 Men.

Waller lost his Reputation in this Fight, and was exceedingly slighted ever after, even by his own Party; but especially by such as were of General *Essex*'s Party, between whom and *Waller* there had been Jealousies and Misunderstandings for some time.

The King, about 8000 strong, marched on to *Bristol*, where Sir *William Hopton* joined him; and from thence he follows *Essex* into *Cornwall*; *Essex* still following *Greenvil*, the King comes to *Exeter*, and joining with Prince *Maurice*, resolves to pursue *Essex*; and now the Earl of *Essex* began to see his Mistake, being cooped up between two Seas, the King's Army in his Rear, the Country his Enemy, and Sir *Richard Greenvil* in his Van.

The King, who always took the best Measures, when he was left to his own Counsel, wisely refuses to engage, though superior in Number, and much stronger in Horse. *Essex* often drew out to fight, but the King fortifies, takes the Passes and Bridges, Plants Cannon, and secures the Country to keep off Provisions, and continually streightens their Quarters, but would not fight.

Now *Essex* sends away to the Parliament for Help, and they write to *Waller*, and *Middleton*, and *Manchester*, to follow, and come up with the King in his Rear; but some were too far off, and could not, as *Manchester* and *Fairfax*; others made no Haste, as having no mind to it, as *Waller* and *Middleton*, and if they had, it had been too late.

At last the Earl of *Essex* finding nothing to be done, and

unwilling to fall into the King's Hands, takes Shipping, and leaves his Army to shift for themselves. The Horse, under Sir *William Balfour*, the best Horse-Officer, and, without Comparison, the bravest in all the Parliament Army, advanced in small Parties, as if to Skirmish, but following in with the whole Body, being 3500 Horse, broke through, and got off. Though this was a Loss to the King's Victory, yet the Foot were now in a Condition so much the worse. Brave old *Skippon* proposed to fight through with the Foot and die, as he called, it, like *English* Men, with Sword in Hand; but the rest of the Officers shook their Heads at it; for, being well paid, they had at present no Occasion for dying.

Seeing it thus, they agreed to treat, and the King grants them Conditions, upon laying down their Arms,[1] to march off free. This was too much; had his Majesty but obliged them upon Oath not to serve again for a certain Time, he had done his Business; but this was not thought of; so they passed free, only disarmed, the Soldiers not being allowed so much as their Swords.

The King gained by this Treaty 40 Pieces of Cannon, all of Brass, 300 Barrels of Gunpowder, 9000 Arms, 8000 Swords, Match and Bullet in Proportion, 200 Waggons, 150 Colours and Standards, all the Bag and Baggage of the Army, and about 1000 of the Men listed in his Army. This was a compleat Victory without Bloodshed; and, had the King but secured the Men from serving but for six Months, it had most effectually answered the Battle of *Marston-Moor*.

As it was, it infused new Life into all his Majesty's Forces and Friends, and retrieved his Affairs very much; but especially it encouraged us in the North, who were more sensible of the Blow received at *Marston-Moor*, and of the Destruction the *Scots* were bringing upon us all.

While I was at *Chester*, we had some small Skirmishes with Sir *William Brereton*. One Morning in particular Sir *William* drew up, and faced us, and one of our Collonels of Horse observing the Enemy to be not, as he thought, above

200, desires Leave of Prince *Rupert* to attack them with the like Number, and accordingly he sallied out with 200 Horse. I stood drawn up without the City with 800 more, ready to bring him off, if he should be put to the worst, which happened accordingly; for, not having discovered neither the Country nor the Enemy as he ought, Sir *William Brereton* drew him into an Ambuscade; so that before he came up with Sir *William*'s Forces, near enough to charge, he finds about 300 Horse in his Rear: Though he was surprized at this, yet, being a Man of a ready Courage, he boldly faces about with 150 of his Men, leaving the other 50 to face Sir *William*. With this small Party, he desperately charges the 300 Horse in his Rear, and putting them into Disorder, breaks through them, and, had there been no greater Force, he had cut them all in Pieces. Flushed with this Success, and loath to desert the 50 Men he had left behind, he faces about again, and charges through them again, and with these two Charges entirely routs them. Sir *William Brereton* finding himself a little disappointed, advances, and falls upon the 50 Men just as the Collonel came up to them; they fought him with a great deal of Bravery, but the Collonel being unfortunately killed in the first Charge, the Men gave Way, and came flying all in Confusion, with the Enemy at their Heels. As soon as I saw this, I advanced, according to my Orders, and the Enemy, as soon as I appeared, gave over the Pursuit. This Gentleman, as I remember, was Collonel *Morough*; we fetched off his Body, and retreated into *Chester*.

The next Morning the Prince drew out of the City with about 1200 Horse and 2000 Foot, and attacked Sir *William Brereton* in his Quarters. The Fight was very sharp for the time, and near 700 Men, on both Sides, were killed; but Sir *William* would not put it to a general Engagement, so the Prince drew off, contenting himself to have insulted him in his Quarters.

We now had received Orders from the King to join him; but I representing to the Prince the Condition of my

Regiment, which was now 100 Men, and, that being within 25 Miles of my Father's House, I might soon recruit it, my Father having got some Men together already, I desired Leave to lye at *Shrewsbury* for a Month, to make up my Men. Accordingly having obtained his Leave, I marched to *Wrexham*, where, in two Days time I got 20 Men, and so on to *Shrewsbury*. I had not been here above 10 Days, but I received an Express to come away with what Recruits I had got together, Prince *Rupert* having positive Orders to meet the King by a certain Day. I had not mounted 100 Men, though I had listed above 200, when these Orders came; but leaving my Father to compleat them for me, I marched with those I had, and came to *Oxford*.

The King, after the Rout of the Parliament Forces in the West, was marched back, took *Barnstable*, *Plympton*, *Lanceston*, *Tiverton*, and several other Places, and left *Plymouth* besieged by Sir *Richard Greenvil*, met with Sir *William Waller* at *Shaftsbury*, and again at *Andover*, and boxed him at both Places, and marched for *Newberry*. Here the King sent for Prince *Rupert* to meet him, who with 3000 Horse made long Marches to join him; but the Parliament having joined their three Armies together, *Manchester* from the North, *Waller* and *Essex*, the Men being cloathed and armed, from the West, had attacked the King, and obliged him to fight the Day, before the Prince came up.

The King had so posted himself, as that he could not be obliged to fight but with Advantage; the Parliament's Forces being superior in Number, and therefore, when they attacked him, he galled them with his Cannon, and declining to come to a general Battle, stood upon the Defensive, expecting Prince *Rupert* with the Horse.[1]

The Parliament's Forces had some Advantage over our Foot, and took the Earl of *Cleveland* Prisoner; but the King, whose Foot were not above one to two, drew his Men under the Cannon of *Dennington* Castle, and having secured his Artillery and Baggage, made a Retreat with his Foot in very good Order, having not lost in all the Fight above 300 Men, and the Parliament as many: We lost five Pieces of Cannon and took two, having repulsed the Earl of *Manchester*'s Men on the North Side of the Town, with considerable Loss.

The King, having lodged his Train of Artillery and Baggage in *Dennington* Castle, marched the next Day for *Oxford*; there we joined him with 3000 Horse, and 2000 Foot. Encouraged with this Reinforcement, the King appears upon the Hills on the North-west of *Newberry*, and faces the Parliament Army. The Parliament having too many Generals as well as Soldiers, they could not agree whether they should fight or no. This was no great Token of the Victory they boasted of; for they were now twice our Number in the whole, and their Foot three for one. The King stood in Battalia all Day, and finding the Parliament Forces had no Stomach to engage him, he drew away his Cannon and Baggage out of *Dennington* Castle, in View of their whole Army, and marched away to *Oxford*.

This was such a false Step of the Parliament's Generals, that all the People cried shame of them: The Parliament appointed a Committee to enquire into it. *Cromwell* accused *Manchester*, and he *Waller*, and so they laid the Fault upon one another. *Waller* would have been glad to have charged it upon *Essex*; but as it happened he was not in the Army, having been taken ill some Days before; but, as it generally is when a Mistake is made, the Actors fall out among themselves, so it was here. No doubt it was as false a Step as that of *Cornwall*, to let the King fetch away his Baggage and Cannon in the Face of three Armies, and never fire a Shot at them.

The King had not above 8000 Foot in his Army, and they above 25000: 'Tis true, the King had 8000 Horse, a fine Body, and much superior to theirs; but the Foot might, with the greatest Ease in the World, have prevented the removing the Cannon, and in three Days time have taken the Castle, with all that was in it.

Those Differences produced their Self-denying Ordinance,[1] and the putting by most of their old Generals, as *Essex*, *Waller*, *Manchester*, and the like; and Sir *Thomas Fairfax*, a terrible Man in the Field, though the mildest of Men out of it, was voted to have the Command of all their Forces, and *Lambert* to take the Command of Sir *Thomas Fairfax*'s Troops in the North, old *Skippon* being Major General.

This Winter was spent on the Enemy's Side in modelling, as they called it, their Army;[2] and, on our Side, in recruiting ours, and some petty Excursions. Amongst the many Addresses, I observed one from *Sussex* or *Surrey*, complaining of the Rudeness of their Soldiers, and particularly of the ravishing of Women, and the murthering of Men; from which I only observed, that there were Disorders among them, as well as among us, only with this Difference, that they, for Reasons I mentioned before, were under Circumstances to prevent it better than the King: But I must do the King's Memory that Justice, that he used all possible Methods, by Punishment of Soldiers, charging, and sometimes entreating, the Gentlemen not to suffer such Disorders and such Violences in their Men; but it was to no Purpose for his Majesty to attempt it, while his Officers, Generals, and Great Men, winked at it; for the Licentiousness of the Soldier is supposed to be approved by the Officer, when it is not corrected.

The Rudeness of the Parliament Soldiers began from the Divisions among their Officers; for, in many Places, the Soldiers grew so out of all Discipline, and so unsufferably rude, that they in particular refused to march when Sir *William Waller* went to *Weymouth*. This had turned to good Account for us, had these cursed *Scots* been out of our way, but they were the Staff of the Party; and now they were daily sollicited to march Southward, which was a very great Affliction to the King, and all his Friends.

One Booty the King got at this time, which was a very seasonable Assistance to his Affairs, (*viz.*) a great Merchant Ship richly laden at *London*, and bound to the *East-Indies*, was, by the Seamen, brought into *Bristol*, and delivered up to the King. Some Merchants in *Bristol* offered the King 40000 l. for her, which his Majesty ordered should be accepted, reserving only 30 great Guns for his own Use.

The Treaty at *Uxbridge* now was begun, and we that had been well beaten in the War, heartily wished the King would come to a Peace; but we all foresaw the Clergy would ruine it all. The Commons were for Presbytery, and would never agree the Bishops should be restored; the King was willinger to comply with any thing than this, and we foresaw it would be so; from whence we used to say among our selves, *That the Clergy was resolved if there should be no Bishop, there should be no King.*

This Treaty at *Uxbridge* was a perfect War between the Men of the Gown, ours was between those of the Sword; and I cannot but take Notice how the Lawyers, Statesmen, and the Clergy of every Side bestirred themselves, rather to hinder than promote the Peace.

There had been a Treaty at *Oxford* some time before, where the Parliament insisting that the King should pass a Bill to abolish Episcopacy, quit the Militia, abandon several of his faithful Servants to be exempted from Pardon, and making several other most extravagant Demands. Nothing was done, but the Treaty broke off, both Parties being rather farther exasperated, than inclined to hearken to Conditions.

However, soon after the Success in the West, his Majesty, to let them see that Victory had not puffed him up so as to make him reject the Peace, sends a Message to the Parliament, to put them in Mind of Messages of like Nature which they had slighted; and to let them know, that notwithstanding he had beaten their Forces, he was yet willing to hearken to a reasonable Proposal for putting an End to the War.

The Parliament pretended the King, in his Message, did not treat with them as a legal Parliament, and so made Hesitations; but after long Debates and Delays they agreed to draw up Propositions for Peace to be sent to the King. As this Message was sent to the Houses about *August*, I think they made it the middle of *November* before they brought the Propositions for Peace; and, when they brought them, they had no Power to enter either upon a Treaty, or so much as Preliminaries for a Treaty, only to deliver the Letter, and receive an Answer.

However, such were the Circumstances of Affairs at this Time, that the King was uneasy to see himself thus treated, and take no Notice of it: The King returned an Answer to the Propositions, and proposed a Treaty by Commissioners which the Parliament appointed.

Three Months more were spent in naming Commissioners. There was much Time spent in this Treaty, but little done; the Commissioners debated chiefly the Article of Religion, and of the Militia; in the latter they were very likely to agree, in the former both Sides seemed too positive. The King would by no Means abandon Episcopacy, nor the Parliament Presbytery; for both in their Opinion were *Jure Divino*.[1]

The Commissioners finding this Point hardest to adjust, went from it to that of the Militia; but the Time spinning out, the King's Commissioners demanded longer Time for the Treaty; the other sent up for Instructions, but the House refused to lengthen out the Time.

This was thought an Insolence upon the King, and gave all good People a Detestation of such haughty Behaviour; and thus the Hopes of Peace vanished,[2] both Sides prepared for War with as much Eagerness as before.

The Parliament was employed at this Time in what they called a Modelling their Army; that is to say, that now the Independent Party beginning to prevail; and, as they outdid all the others in their Resolution of carrying on the War to all Extremities, so they were both the more vigorous and more politick Party in carrying it on.

Indeed the War was after this carried on with greater Annimosity than ever, and the Generals pushed forward with a Vigour, that, as it had something in it unusual, so it told us plainly from this Time, whatever they did before, they now pushed at the Ruine even of Monarchy it self.

All this while also the War went on, and though the Parliament had no settled Army, yet their Regiments and Troops were always in Action; and the Sword was at work in every Part of the Kingdom.

Among an infinite Number of Party Skirmishings and Fights this Winter, one happened which nearly concerned me, which was the Surprize of the Town and Castle of *Shrewsbury*. Collonel *Mitton*, with about 1200 Horse and Foot, having Intelligence with some People in the Town, on a *Sunday* Morning early broke into the Town, and took it, Castle and all. The Loss for the Quality, more than the Number, was very great to the King's Affairs. They took there 15 Pieces of Cannon, Prince *Maurice*'s Magazine of Arms and Ammunition, Prince *Rupert*'s Baggage, above 50 Persons of Quality and Officers: There was not above 8 or 10 Men killed on both Sides; for the Town was surprized, not stormed.[1] I had a particular Loss in this Action; for, all the Men and Horses my Father had got together for the recruiting my Regiment, were here lost and dispersed; and, which was the worse, my Father happening to be then in the Town, was taken Prisoner, and carried to *Beeston* Castle in *Cheshire*.

I was quartered all this Winter at *Banbury*, and went little abroad; nor had we any Action till the latter end of *February*, when I was ordered to march to *Leicester* with Sir *Marmaduke Langdale*, in order, as we thought, to raise a Body of Men in that County and *Staffordshire*, to join the King.

We lay at *Daventry* one Night, and continuing our March to pass the River above *Northampton*, that Town being possessed by the Enemy, we understood a Party of *Northampton* Forces were abroad, and intended to attack us: Accordingly in the Afternoon our Scouts brought us Word, the Enemy were quartered in some Villages on the Road to *Coventry*; our Commander thinking it much better to set upon them in their Quarters, than to wait for them in the

Field, resolves to attack them early in the Morning, before they were aware of it. We refreshed our selves in the Field for that Day, and getting into a great Wood near the Enemy, we stayed there all Night, till almost break of Day, without being discovered.

In the Morning very early we heard the Enemy's Trumpets sound to Horse; this roused us to look abroad; and, sending out a Scout, he brought us Word a Party of the Enemy was at Hand. We were vexed to be so disappointed, but finding their Party small enough to be dealt with, Sir *Marmaduke* ordered me to charge them with 300 Horse and 200 Dragoons, while he at the same Time entered the Town. Accordingly I lay still till they came to the very Skirt of the Wood where I was posted, when I saluted them with a Volley from my Dragoons out of the Wood, and immediately shewed my self with my Horse on their Front, ready to charge them; they appeared not to be surprized, and received our Charge with great Resolution; and, being above 400 Men, they pushed me vigorously in their Turn, putting my Men into some Disorder. In this Extremity I sent to order the Dragoons to charge them in the Flank, which they did with great Bravery, and the other still maintained the Fight with desperate Resolution. There was no want of Courage in our Men on both Sides; but our Dragoons had the Advantage, and at last routed them, and drove them back to the Village. Here Sir *Marmaduke Langdale* had his Hands full too; for my firing had alarmed the Towns adjacent, that when he came into the Town, he found them all in Arms; and, contrary to his Expectation, two Regiments of Foot, with about 500 Horse more. As Sir *Marmaduke* had no Foot, only Horse and Dragoons, this was a Surprize to him; but he caused his Dragoons to enter the Town, and charge the Foot, while his Horse secured the Avenues of the Town.

The Dragoons bravely attacked the Foot, and Sir *Marmaduke* falling in with his Horse, the Fight was obstinate and very bloody, when the Horse that I had routed came flying into the Street of the Village, and my Men at their Heels. Immediately I left the Pursuit, and fell in with all my Force to the Assistance of my Friends, and, after an obstinate Resistance, we routed the whole Party; we killed about 700 Men, took 350, 27 Officers, 100 Arms, all their Baggage, and 200 Horses, and continued our March to *Harborough*, where we halted to refresh our selves.

Between *Harborough* and *Leicester* we met with a Party of 800 Dragoons of the Parliament Forces. They found themselves too few to attack us, and therefore to avoid us, they had gotten into a small Wood; but perceiving themselves discovered, they came boldly out, and placed themselves at the Entrance into a Lane, lining both Sides of the Hedges with their Shot. We immediately attacked them, beat them from their Hedges, beat them into the Wood, and out of the Wood again, and forced them at last to a down right *Run-away*, on Foot, among the Enclosures, where we could not follow them, killed about 100 of them, and took 250 Prisoners, with all their Horses, and came that Night to *Leicester*. When we came to *Leicester*, and had taken up our Quarters, Sir *Marmaduke Langdale* sent for me to sup with him, and told me, that he had a secret Commission in his Pocket, which his Majesty had commanded him not to open 'till he came to *Leicester*; that now he had sent for me to open it together, that we might know what it was we were to do, and to consider how to do it; so pulling out his sealed Orders, we found we were to get what Force we could together, and a certain Number of Carriages with Ammunition which the Governour of *Leicester* was to deliver us, and a certain Quantity of Provision, especially Corn and Salt, and to relieve *Newark*. This Town had been long besieged: The Fortifications of the Place, together with its Situation, had rendered it the strongest Piece in *England*; And, as it was the greatest Pass in *England*, so it was of vast Consequence to the King's Affairs. There was in it a Garrison of brave old rugged Boys, Fellows, that, like Count *Tilly*'s *Germans*, had Iron Faces, and they had defended themselves with extraordinary Bravery a great while, but were reduced to an exceeding Streight for want of Provisions.

Accordingly we received the Ammunition and Provision, and away we went for *Newark*; about *Melton Mowbray*, Collonel *Roseter* set upon us, with above 3000 Men; we were about the same Number, having 2500 Horse, and 800 Dragoons. We had some Foot, but they were still at *Harborough*, and were ordered to come after us.

Roseter, like a brave Officer, as he was, charged us with great Fury, and rather outdid us in Number, while we defended our selves with all the Eagerness we could, and withal gave him to understand we were not so soon to be beaten as he expected. While the Fight continued doubtful; especially on our Side, our People, who had charge of the Carriages and Provisions, began to enclose our Flanks with them, as if we had been marching; which, though it was done without Orders, had two very good Effects, and which did us extraordinary Service. First, it secured us from being charged in the Flank, which *Roseter* had twice attempted; and, Secondly, it secured our Carriages from being plundered, which had spoiled our whole Expedition. Being thus enclosed, we fought with great Security; and though *Roseter* made three desperate Charges upon us, he could never break us. Our Men received him with so much Courage, and kept their Order so well, that the Enemy finding it impossible to force us, gave it over, and left us to pursue our Orders. We did not offer to chase them, but contented enough to have repulsed and beaten them off, and our Business being to relieve *Newark*, we proceeded.

If we are to reckon by the Enemy's usual Method, we got the Victory, because we kept the Field, and had the Pillage of their Dead; but otherwise, neither Side had any great Cause to boast. We lost about 150 Men, and near as many hurt; they left 170 on the Spot, and carried off some. How many they had wounded we could not tell; we got 70 or 80 Horse, which helped to remount some of our Men that had lost theirs in the Fight. We had, however, this Disadvantage, that we were to march on immediately after this Service; the Enemy only to retire to their Quarters, which was but hard by. This was an Injury to our wounded Men, who we were after obliged to leave at *Belvoir* Castle, and from thence we advanced to *Newark*.

Our Business at *Newark* was to relieve the Place, and this we resolved to do, whatever it cost, though, at the same Time, we resolved not to fight, unless we were forced to it. The Town was rather blocked up than besieged; the Garrison was strong, but ill provided; we had sent them word of our coming to them, and our Orders to relieve them, and they proposed some Measures for our doing it. The chief Strength of the Enemy lay on the other Side of the River; but they having also some Notice of our Design, had sent over Forces to strengthen their Leaguer on this Side. The Garrison had often surprized them by Sallies, and indeed had chiefly subsisted for some time by what they brought in on this Manner.

Sir *Marmaduke Langdale*, who was our General for the Expedition, was for a general Attempt to raise the Siege; but I had perswaded him off of that: First, Because if we should be beaten, as might be probable, we then lost the Town. Sir *Marmaduke* briskly replied, *A Soldier ought never to suppose he shall be beaten.* But, *Sir*, says I, *you'll get more Honour by relieving the Town, than by beating them: One will be a Credit to your Conduct, as the other will be to your Courage; and, if you think you can beat them, you may do it afterward, and then if you are mistaken, the Town is nevertheless secured, and half your Victory gained.*

He was prevailed with to adhere to this Advice, and accordingly we appeared before the Town about two Hours before Night. The Horse drew up before the Enemy's Works; the Enemy drew up within their Works, and seeing no Foot, expected when our Dragoons would dismount and attack them. They were in the right to let us attack them, because of the Advantage of their Batteries and Works, if that had been our Design; but, as we intended only to amuse them, this Caution of theirs effected our Design; for, while we thus faced them with our Horse, two Regiments of Foot, which came up to us but the Night before, and was all the Infantry we had, with the Waggons of Provisions, and 500 Dragoons, taking a Compass clean round the Town, posted themselves on the lower Side of the Town by the River. Upon a Signal the Garrison agreed on before, they sallied out at this very Juncture, with all the Men they could spare, and dividing themselves in two Parties, while one Party moved to the Left to meet our Relief, the other Party fell on upon Part of that Body which faced us. We kept in Motion, and upon this Signal advanced to their Works, and our Dragoons fired upon them; and the Horse wheeling and counter-marching often, kept them continually expecting to be attacked. By this Means the Enemy were kept employed, and our Foot with the Waggons, appearing on that Quarter where they were least expected, easily defeated the advanced Guards, and forced that Post, where entring the Leaguer, the other Part of the Garrison, who had sallied that way, came up to them, received the Waggons, and the Dragoons entered with them into the Town. That Party which we faced on the other Side of the Works; knew nothing of what was done till all was over; the Garrison retreated in good Order, and we drew off, having finished what we came for without fighting.

Thus we plentifully stored the Town with all things wanting, and with an Addition of 500 Dragoons to their Garrison; after which we marched away without fighting a Stroke. Our next Orders were to relieve *Pontfract* Castle, another Garrison of the King's, which had been besieged ever since a few Days after the Fight at *Marston-Moor*, by the Lord *Fairfax*, Sir *Thomas Fairfax*, and other Generals in their Turn.

By the Way, we were joined with 800 Horse out of *Derbyshire*, and some Foot, so many as made us, about 4500 Men in all.

Collonel *Forbes*, a *Scotchman*, commanded at the Siege,

in the Absence of the Lord *Fairfax*; the Collonel had sent to my Lord for more Troops, and his Lordship was gathering his Forces to come up to him; but he was pleased to come too late. We came up with the Enemy's Leaguer about Break of Day, and having been discovered by their Scouts, they, with more Courage than Discretion, drew out to meet us. We saw no Reason to avoid them, being stronger in Horse than they; and though we had but a few Foot, we had 1000 Dragoons, which helped us out. We had placed our Horse and Foot throughout in one Line, with two Reserves of Horse, and between every Division of Horse, a Division of Foot, only that on the Extremes of our Wings, there were two Parties of Horse on each Point by themselves, and the Dragoons in the Center, on Foot. Their Foot charged us home, and stood with Push of Pike a great while; but their Horse charging our Horse and Musqueteers, and being closed on the Flanks with those two extended Troops on our Wings, they were presently disordered, and fled out of the Field. The Foot thus deserted, were charged on every Side, and broken. They retreated still fighting, and in good Order, for a while; but the Garrison sallying upon them at the same Time, and being followed close by our Horse, they were scattered, entirely routed, and most of them killed. The Lord *Fairfax* was come with his Horse as far as *Ferribridge*, but the Fight was over; and all he could do was to rally those that fled, and save some of their Carriages, which else had fallen into our Hands. We drew up our little Army in Order of Battle the next Day, expecting the Lord *Fairfax* would have charged us; but his Lordship was so far from any such Thoughts, that he placed a Party of Dragoons, with Orders to fortify the Pass at *Ferribridge*, to prevent our falling upon him in his Retreat, which he needed not have done; for, having raised the Siege of *Pontfract*, our Business was done, we had nothing to say to him, unless we had been strong enough to stay.

We lost not above 30 Men in this Action, and the Enemy 300, with about 150 Prisoners, one Piece of Cannon, all their

Ammunition, 1000 Arms, and most of their Baggage, and Collonel *Lambert* was once taken Prisoner, being wounded, but got off again.

We brought no Relief for the Garrison, but the Opportunity to furnish themselves out of the Country, which they did very plentifully. The Ammunition taken from the Enemy was given to them, which they wanted, and was their Due, for they had siezed it in the Sally they made, before the Enemy was quite defeated.

I cannot omit taking Notice, on all Occasions, how exceeding serviceable this Method was of posting Musqueteers in the Intervals, among the Horse, in all this War: I perswaded our Generals to it, as much as possible, and I never knew a Body of Horse beaten that did so; yet I had great Difficulty to prevail upon our People to believe it, though it was taught me by the greatest General in the World, (viz.) the King of *Sweden*. Prince *Rupert* did it at the Battle *Marston-Moor*; and had the Earl of *Newcastle* not been obstinate against it in his Right Wing, as I observed before, the Day had not been lost. In discoursing this with Sir *Marmaduke Langdale*, I had related several Examples of the Serviceableness of these small Bodies of Firemen, and, with great Difficulty, brought him to agree, telling him, I would be answerable for the Success; but, after the Fight, he told me plainly he saw the Advantage of it, and would never fight otherwise again, if he had any Foot to place. So having relieved these two Places, we hastened, by long Marches, through *Derbyshire*, to join Prince *Rupert* on the Edge of *Shropshire* and *Cheshire*. We found Collonel *Roseter* had followed us at a Distance, ever since the Business at *Melton Mowbray*, but never cared to attack us, and we found he did the like still. Our General would fain have been doing with him again, but we found him too shy. Once we laid a Trap for him at *Dove-Bridge*, between *Derby* and *Burton upon Trent*, the Body being marched two Days before; 300 Dragoons were left to guard the Bridge, as if we were afraid he should fall upon us. Upon this we marched, as I said, on to *Burton*, and, the next Day, fetching a Compass round, came to a Village near *Titbury* Castle, whose Name I forgot, where we lay still expecting our Dragoons would be attacked.

Accordingly the Collonel, strengthned with some Troops of Horse from *Yorkshire*, comes up to the Bridge, and finding some Dragoons posted, advances to charge them: The Dragoons immediately get a Horseback, and run for it, as they were ordered; but the old Lad was not to be caught so; for he halts immediately at the Bridge, and would not come over till he had sent three or four flying Parties abroad, to discover the Country. One of these Parties fell into our Hands, and received but coarse Entertainment. Finding the Plot would not take, we appeared, and drew up in View of the Bridge but he would not stir: So we continued our March into *Cheshire*, where we joined Prince *Rupert*, and Prince *Maurice*, making together a fine Body, being above 8000 Horse and Dragoons.

This was the best and most successful Expedition I was in during this War. 'Twas well concerted, and executed with as much Expedition and Conduct as could be desired, and the Success was answerable to it: And indeed, considering the Season of the Year (for we set out from *Oxford* the latter end of *February*) the Ways bad, and the Season wet, it was a terrible March of above 200 Miles, in continual Action, and continually dodged and observed by a vigilant Enemy, and at a Time when the North was over-run by their Armies, and the *Scots* wanting Employment for their Forces; yet in less than 23 Days, we marched 200 Miles, fought the Enemy in open Field four Times, relieved one Garrison besieged, and raised the Siege of another, and joined our Friends at last in Safety.

The Enemy was in great Pain for Sir *William Brereton* and his Forces, and Expresses rid Night and Day to the *Scots* in the North, and to the Parties in *Lancashire*, to come to his Help. The Prince, who used to be rather too forward to fight than otherwise, could not be perswaded to make use of this Opportunity, but loitered, if I may be allowed to say so, till the *Scots*, with a Brigade of Horse and 2000 Foot, had joined him; and then 'twas not thought proper to engage them.

I took this Opportunity to go to *Shrewsbury* to visit my Father, who was a Prisoner of War there, getting a pass from the Enemy's Governour. They allowed him the Liberty of the Town, and sometimes to go to his own House, upon his Parole, so that his Confinement was not very much to his personal Injury; but this, together with the Charges he had been at in raising the Regiment, and above 20000 l. in Money and Plate, which at several Times he had lent, or given rather, to the King, had reduced our Family to very ill Circumstances; and now they talked of cutting down his Woods.

I had a great deal of Discourse with my Father on this Affair; and finding him extremely concerned, I offered to go to the King, and desire his Leave to go to *London*, and treat about his Composition,[1] or to render my self a Prisoner in his stead, while he went up himself. In this Difficulty I treated with the Governour of the Town, who very civilly offered me his Pass to go for *London*, which I accepted; and waiting on Prince *Rupert*, who was then at *Worcester*, I acquainted him with my Design. The Prince was unwilling I should go to *London*; but told me, he had some Prisoners of the Parliament's Friends in *Cumberland*, and he would get an Exchange for my Father. I told him, if he would give me his Word for it, I knew I might depend upon it, otherwise there was so many of the King's Party in their Hands, that his Majesty was tired with Sollicitations for Exchanges; for we never had a Prisoner but there was ten Offers of Exchanges for him. The Prince told me, I should depend upon him; and he was as good as his Word quickly after.

While the Prince lay at *Worcester* he made an Incursion into *Herefordshire*, and having made some of the Gentlemen Prisoners, brought them to *Worcester*; and though it was an Action which had not been usual, they being Persons not in Arms, yet the like being my Father's Case, who was really not in Commission, nor in any Military Service, having resigned his Regiment three Years before to me, the Prince insisted on exchanging them for such as the Parliament had in Custody in like Circumstances. The Gentlemen seeing no Remedy, sollicited their own Case at the Parliament, and got it passed in their behalf; and by this Means my Father got his Liberty; and, by the Assistance of the Earl of *Denbigh*, got Leave to come to *London* to make a Composition, as a Delinquent, for his Estate. This they charged at 7000 l. but by the Assistance of the same noble Person, he got off for 4000 l. Some Members of the Committee moved very kindly, that my Father should oblige me to quit the King's Service; but that, as a thing which might be out of his Power, was not insisted on.

The Modelling the Parliament Army took them up all this Winter, and we were in great Hopes the Divisions which appeared amongst them might have weakened their Party; but when they voted Sir *Thomas Fairfax* to be General, I confess I was convinced the King's Affairs were lost and desperate. Sir *Thomas*, abating the Zeal of his Party, and the mistaken Opinion of his Cause, was the fittest Man amongst them to undertake the Charge: He was a compleat General, strict in his Discipline, wary in Conduct, fearless in Action, unwearied in the Fatigue of the War, and withal, of a modest, noble, generous Disposition. We all aprehended Danger from him, and heartily wished him of our own Side; and the King was so sensible, though he would not discover it, that when an Account was brought him of the Choice they had made, he replied, *he was sorry for it*; *he had rather it had been any Body than he*.

The first Attempts of this new General and new Army were at *Oxford*, which, by the Neighbourhood of a numerous Garrison in *Abingdon*, began to be very much streightned for Provisions; and the new Forces under *Cromwell* and *Skippon*, one Lieutenant General, the other Major General to *Fairfax*, approaching with a Design to block it up, the King left the

Place, supposing his Absence would draw them away, as it soon did.

The King resolving to leave *Oxford*, marches from thence with all his Forces, the Garrison excepted, with Design to have gone to *Bristol*, but the Plague was in *Bristol*, which altered the Measures, and changed the Course of the King's Designs, so he marched for *Worcester* about the beginning of *June* 1645. The Foot with a Train of 40 Pieces of Cannon, marching into *Worcester*, the Horse stayed behind some time in *Gloucestershire*.

The first Action our Army did, was to raise the Siege of *Chester*; Sir *William Brereton* had besieged it, or rather blocked it up, and when his Majesty came to *Worcester*, he sent Prince *Rupert*, with 4000 Horse and Dragoons, with Orders to join some Foot out of *Wales*, to raise the Siege; but Sir *William* thought fit to withdraw, and not stay for them, and the Town was freed without fighting. The Governour took Care in this Interval to furnish himself with all things necessary for another Siege; and, as for Ammunition and other Necessaries, he was in no Want.

I was sent with a Party into *Staffordshire*, with Design to intercept a Convoy of Stores coming from *London*, for the Use of Sir *William Brereton*; but they having some Notice of the Design, stopt, and went out of the Road to *Burton upon Trent*, and so I missed them; but that we might not come back quite empty, we attacked *Hawkesly* House, and took it, where we got good Booty, and brought 80 Prisoners back to *Worcester*.[1] From *Worcester* the King advanced into *Shropshire*, and took his Head Quarters at *Bridgenorth*. This was a very happy March of the King's, and had his Majesty proceeded, he had certainly cleared the North once more of his Enemies, for the Country was generally for him. At his advancing so far as *Bridgenorth*, Sir *William Brereton* fled up into *Lancashire*; the *Scots* Brigades who were with him retreated into the North, while yet the King was above 40 Miles from them, and all things lay open for Conquest. The new Generals, *Fairfax* and *Cromwell*, lay about *Oxford* preparing as if they would besiege it, and gave the King's Army so much Leisure, that his Majesty might have been at *Newcastle* before they could have been half Way to him. But Heaven, when the Ruine of a Person or Party is determined, always so infatuates their Counsels, as to make them instrumental to it themselves.

The King let slip this great Opportunity, as some thought, intending to break into the Associated Counties, of *Northampton, Cambridge, Norfolk*, where he had some Interests forming. What the Design was, we knew not, but the King turns Eastward, and Marches into *Leicestershire*, and having treated the Country but very indifferently, as having deserved no better of us, laid Siege to *Leicester*.

This was but a short Siege; for the King, resolving not to lose Time, fell on with his great Guns, and having beaten down their Works, our Foot entered, after a vigorous Resistance, and took the Town by Storm. There was some Blood shed here, the Town being carried by Assault; but it was their own Faults; for after the Town was taken, the Soldiers and Townsmen obstinately fought us in the Market-Place; insomuch that the Horse was called to enter the Town to clear the Streets. But this was not all; I was commanded to advance with these Horse, being three Regiments, and to enter the Town; the Foot, who were engaged in the Streets, crying out, *Horse, Horse*. Immediately I advanced to the Gate, for we were drawn up about Musquet Shot from the Works, to have supported our Foot, in Case of a Sally. Having siezed the Gate, I placed a Guard of Horse there, with Orders to let no Body pass in or out, and dividing my Troops, rode up by two Ways towards the Market-Place; the Garrison defending themselves in the Market-Place, and in the Church-yard, with great Obstinancy, killed us a great many Men; but, as soon as our Horse appeared, they demanded Quarter, which our Foot refused them in the first Heat, as is frequent in all Nations, in like Cases; 'till at last, they threw down their Arms, and yielded at Discretion; and then I can testify to the World, that fair Quarter was given them. I am the more particular in this Relation, having been an Eye-witness of the Action, because the King was reproached in all the publick Libels, with which those Times abounded, for having put a great many to Death, and hanged the Committee of the Parliament, and some *Scots*, in cold Blood, which was a notorious Forgery; and as I am sure there was no such thing done, so I must acknowledge I never saw any Inclination in his Majesty to Cruelty, or to act any thing which was not practised by the General Laws of War, and by Men of Honour in all Nations.

But the Matter of Fact, in Respect to the Garrison, was as I have related; and, if they had thrown down their Arms sooner, they had had Mercy sooner; but it was not for a conquering Army, entered a Town by Storm, to offer Conditions of Quarter in the Streets.

Another Circumstance was, that a great many of the Inhabitants, both Men and Women, were killed, which is most true; and the Case was thus: The Inhabitants, to shew their over-forward Zeal to defend the Town, fought in the Breach; nay, the very Women, to the Honour of the *Leicester* Ladies, if they like it, officiously did their Parts; and after the Town was taken, and when, if they had had any Brains in their Zeal, they would have kept their Houses, and been quiet, they fired upon our Men out of their Windows, and from the Tops of their Houses, and threw Tiles upon their Heads; and I had several of my Men wounded so, and 7 or 8 killed. This exasperated us to the last Degree; and, finding one House better manned than ordinary, and many Shot fired at us out of the Windows, I caused my Men to attack it, resolved to make them an Example for the rest; which they did, and breaking open the Doors, they killed all they found there, without Distinction; and I appeal to the World if they were to blame. If the Parliament Committee, or the *Scots* Deputies were here, they ought to have been quiet, since the Town was taken; but they began with us, and, I think, brought it upon themselves. This is the whole Case, so far as came within my Knowledge, for which his Majesty was so much abused.

We took here Collonel *Gray* and Captain *Hacker*, and about 300 Prisoners, and about 300 more were killed.[1] This was the last Day of *May* 1645.

His Majesty having given over *Oxford* for lost, continued here some Days, viewed the Town, ordered the Fortifications to be augmented, and prepares to make it the Seat of War. But the Parliament, rouzed at this Appearance of the King's Army, order their General to raise the Siege of *Oxford*, where the Garrison had, in a Sally, ruined some of their Works, and killed them 150 Men, taking several Prisoners, and carrying them with them into the City; and orders him to march towards *Leicester*, to observe the King.

The King had now a small, but gallant Army, all brave tried Soldiers, and seemed eager to engage the new-modelled Army; and his Majesty, hearing that Sir *Thomas Fairfax* having raised the Siege of *Oxford*, advanced towards him, fairly saves him the Trouble of a long March, and meets him half Way.

The Army lay at *Daventry*, and *Fairfax* at *Towcester*, about 8 Miles off. Here the King sends away 600 Horse, with 3000 Head of Cattle,[2] to relieve his People in *Oxford*; the Cattle he might have spared better than the Men. The King having thus victualled *Oxford*, changes his Resolution of fighting *Fairfax*, to whom *Cromwell* was now joined with 4000 Men,[3] or was within a Day's March, and marches Northward. This was unhappy Counsel, because late given: Had we marched Northward at first, we had done it; but thus it was. Now we marched with a triumphing Enemy at our Heels, and at *Naseby* their advanced Parties attacked our Rear. The King, upon this, alters his Resolution again, and resolves to fight, and at Midnight calls us up at *Harborough* to come to a Council of War. Fate and the King's Opinion determined the Council of War; and 'twas resolved to fight. Accordingly the Van, in which was Prince *Rupert*'s Brigade of Horse, of which my Regiment was a Part, countermarched early in the Morning.

By five a Clock in the Morning,[1] the whole Army, in Order of Battle, began to descry the Enemy from the rising Grounds, about a Mile from *Naseby*, and moved towards them. They were drawn up on a little Ascent in a large Common Fallow Field, in one Line extended from one Side of the Field to the other, the Field something more than a Mile over, our Army in the same Order, in one Line, with the Reserves.

The King led the main Battle of Foot, Prince *Rupert* the Right Wing of the Horse, and Sir *Marmaduke Langdale* the Left. Of the Enemy *Fairfax* and *Skippon* led the Body, *Cromwell* and *Roseter* the Right, and *Ireton* the Left. The Numbers of both Armies so equal, as not to differ 500 Men, save that the King had most Horse by about 1000, and *Fairfax* most Foot by about 500. The Number was in each Army about 18000 Men.

The Armies coming close up, the Wings engaged first. The Prince with his Right Wing charged with his wonted Fury, and drove all the Parliament's Wing of Horse, one Division excepted, clear out of the Field. *Ireton*, who commanded this Wing, give him his due, rallied often, and fought like a Lion; but our Wing bore down all before them, and pursued them with a terrible Execution.

Ireton seeing one Division of his Horse left, repaired to them, and keeping his Ground, fell foul of a Brigade of our Foot, who coming up to the Head of the Line, he like [a] mad Man charges them with his Horse: But they with their Pikes tore him to Pieces; so that this Division was entirely ruined. *Ireton* himself thrust through the Thigh with a Pike, wounded in the Face with a Halberd, was unhorsed and taken Prisoner.

Cromwell, who commanded the Parliament's Right Wing, charged Sir *Marmaduke Langdale* with extraordinary Fury; but he an old tried Soldier, stood firm, and received the Charge with equal Gallantry, exchanging all their Shot,

Carabines and Pistols, and then fell on Sword in Hand. *Roseter* and *Whaley* had the better on the Point of the Wing, and routed two Divisions of Horse, pushing them behind the Reserves, where they rallied, and charged again, but were at last defeated; the rest of the Horse now charged in the Flank retreated fighting, and were pushed behind the Reserves of Foot.

While this was doing, the Foot engaged with equal Fierceness, and for two Hours there was a terrible Fire. The King's Foot backed with gallant Officers, and full of Rage at the Rout of their Horse, bore down the Enemy's Brigade led by *Skippon*. The old Man wounded, bleeding retreats to their Reserves. All the Foot, except the General's Brigade, were thus driven into the Reserves, where their Officers rallied them, and bring them on to a fresh Charge; and here the Horse having driven our Horse about a Quarter of a Mile from the Foot, face about, and fall in on the Rear of the Foot.

Had our Right Wing done thus, the Day had been secured; but Prince *Rupert* according to his Custom, following the flying Enemy, never concerned himself with the Safety of those behind; and yet he returned sooner than he had done in like Cases too. At our Return we found all in Confusion, our Foot broken, all but one Brigade, which though charged in Front, Flank and Rear, could not be broken, till Sir *Thomas Fairfax* himself came up to the Charge with fresh Men, and then they were rather cut in Pieces then beaten; for they stood with their Pikes charged every Way to the last Extremity.

In this Condition, at the Distance of a Quarter of a Mile, we saw the King rallying his Horse, and preparing to renew the Fight; and our Wing of Horse coming up to him, gave him Opportunity to draw up a large Body of Horse, so large, that all the Enemy's Horse facing us, stood still and looked on, but did not think fit to charge us, till their Foot, who had entirely broken our main Battle, were put into Order again, and brought up to us.

The Officers about the King advised his Majesty rather to draw off; for, since our Foot were lost, it would be too much Odds to expose the Horse to the Fury of their whole Army, and would but be sacrificing his best Troops, without any Hopes of Success.

The King, though with great Regret, at the Loss of his Foot, yet seeing there was no other Hope, took this advice, and retreated in good Order to *Harborough*, and from thence to *Leicester*.[1]

This was the Occasion of the Enemy having so great a Number of Prisoners; for the Horse being thus gone off, the Foot had no Means to make their Retreat, and were obliged to yield themselves. Commissary General *Ireton* being taken by a Captain of Foot, makes the Captain his Prisoner, to save his Life, and gives him his Liberty for his Courtesy before.

Cromwell and *Roseter*, with all the Enemy's Horse, followed us as far as *Leicester*, and killed all that they could lay hold on straggling from the Body, but durst not attempt to charge us in a Body. The King expecting the Enemy would come to *Leicester*, removes to *Ashby de la Zouch*, where we had some Time to recollect our selves.

This was the most fatal Action of the whole War; not so much for the Loss of our Cannon, Ammunition, and Baggage, of which the Enemy boasted so much, but as it was impossible for the King ever to retrieve it: The Foot, the best that ever he was Master of, could never be supplied; his Army in the West was exposed to certain Ruin, the North over-run with the *Scots*; *in short*, the Case grew desperate, and the King was once upon the Point of bidding us all disband, and shift for our selves.

We lost in this Fight not above 2000 slain, and the Parliament near as many, but the Prisoners were a great Number; the whole Body of Foot being, as I have said, dispersed, there were 4500 Prisoners, besides 400 Officers, 2000 Horses, 12 Pieces of Cannon, 40 Barrels of Powder, all the King's Baggage, Coaches, most of his Servants, and his

Secretary, with his Cabinet of Letters, of which the Parliament made great Improvement, and, basely enough caused his private Letters between his Majesty and the Queen, her Majesty's Letters to the King, and a great deal of such Stuff to be printed.[1]

After this fatal Blow, being retreated, as I have said, to *Ashby de la Zouch* in *Leicestershire*, the King ordered us to divide; his Majesty, with a Body of Horse, about 3000, went to *Litchfield*, and through *Cheshire* into North *Wales* and Sir *Marmaduke Langdale*, with about 2500 went to *Newark*.

The King remained in *Wales* for several Months; and though the Length of the War had almost drained that Country of Men, yet the King raised a great many Men there, recruited his Horse Regiments, and got together six or seven Regiments of Foot, which seemed to look like the Beginning of a New Army.

I had frequent Discourses with his Majesty in this low Ebb of his Affairs, and he would often wish he had not exposed his Army at *Naseby*. I took the Freedom once to make a Proposition to his Majesty, which if it had taken Effect, I verily believe would have given a new Turn to his Affairs; and that was, at once to slight all his Garrisons in the Kingdom, and give private Orders to all the Soldiers in every Place, to join in Bodies, and meet at two General Rendezvous, which I would have appointed to be, one at *Bristol*, and one at *Westchester*. I demonstrated how easily all the Forces might reach these two Places; and both being strong and wealthy Places, and both Sea-Ports, he would have a free Communication by Sea, with *Ireland*, and with his Friends abroad; and having *Wales* entirely his own, he might yet have an Opportunity to make good Terms for himself, or else have another fair Field with the Enemy.

Upon a fair Calculation of his Troops in several Garrisons and small Bodies dispersed about, I convinced the King, by his own Accounts, that he might have two compleat Armies, each of 25000 Foot, 8000 Horse, and 2000 Dragoons; that the Lord *Goring* and the Lord *Hopton* might Ship all their Forces, and come by Sea in two Tides, and be with him in a shorter Time than the Enemy could follow.

With two such Bodies he might face the Enemy, and make a Day of it; but now his Men were only sacrificed, and eaten up by Piece-meal in a Party-War, and spent their Lives and Estates to do him no Service: That if the Parliament garrisoned the Towns and Castles he should quit, they would lessen their Army, and not dare to see him in the Field; and if they did not, but left them open, then 'twould be no Loss to him, but he might possess them as often as he pleased.[1]

This Advice I pressed with such Arguments, that the King was once going to dispatch Orders for the doing it; but to be irresolute in Counsel, is always the Companion of a declining Fortune; the King was doubtful, and could not resolve till it was too late.

And yet, though the King's Forces were very low, his Majesty was resolved to make one Adventure more, and it was a strange one; for, with but a Handful of Men he made a desperate March, almost 250 Miles in the Middle of the whole Kingdom, compassed about with Armies and Parties innumerable, traversed the Heart of his Enemy's Country, entered their associated Counties, where no Army had ever yet come, and in spight of all their victorious Troops facing and following him, alarmed even *London* it self, and returned safe to *Oxford*.

His Majesty continued in *Wales* from the Battle at *Naseby* till the 5th or 6th *August*, and till he had an Account from all parts of the Progress of his Enemies, and the Posture of his own Affairs.

Here he found, that the Enemy being hard pressed in *Somersetshire* by the Lord *Goring*, and Lord *Hopton*'s Forces, who had taken *Bridgewater*, and distressed *Taunton*, which was now at the Point of Surrender, they had ordered *Fairfax* and *Cromwell*, and the whole Army to march Westward, to relieve the Town; which they did, and *Goring*'s

Troops were worsted, and himself wounded at the Fight at *Langport*.

The *Scots*, who were always the dead Weight upon the King's Affairs, having no more Work to do in the North, were, at the Parliament's Desire, advanced Southward, and then ordered away towards South *Wales*, and were set down to the Siege of *Hereford*. Here this famous *Scotch* Army spent several Months in a fruitless Siege, ill provided of Ammunition, and worse with Money; and having sat near three Months before the Town, and done little but eaten up the Country round them; upon the repeated Accounts of the Progress of the Marquess of *Montrose* in that King-dom, and pressing Instances of their Countrymen, they resolved to raise their Siege, and go home to relieve their Friends.

The King, who was willing to be rid of the *Scots*, upon good Terms; and therefore to hasten them, and least they should pretend to push on the Siege to take the Town first, gives it out, that he was resolved with all his Forces to go into *Scotland*, and join *Montrose*; and so having secured *Scotland*, to renew the War from thence.

And accordingly his Majesty marches Northwards, with a Body of 4000 Horse; and, had the King really done this, and with that Body of Horse marched away, (for he had the Start of all his Enemies, by above a Fortnight's March) he had then had the fairest Opportunity for a general Turn of all his Affairs, that he ever had in all the latter Part of this War: For *Montrose*, a gallant daring Soldier, who from the least Shadow of Force in the farthest Corner of his Country, had, rowling like a Snow Ball, spread all over *Scotland*, was come into the South Parts, and had summoned *Edinburgh*, frighted away their Statesmen, beaten their Soldiers at *Dundee* and other Places, and Letters and Messengers in the Heels of one another, repeated their Cries to their Brethren in *England*, to lay before them the sad Condition of the Country, and to hasten the Army to their Relief. The *Scots* Lords of the Enemy's Party fled to *Berwick*, and the Chancellor of *Scotland* goes himself to General *Lesly*, to press him for help.

In this Extremity of Affairs *Scotland* lay, when we marched out of *Wales*. The *Scots* at the Siege of *Hereford* hearing the King was gone Northward with his Horse, conclude he was gone directly for *Scotland*, and immediately send *Lesly* with 4000 Horse and Foot to follow, but did not yet raise the Siege.

But the King still irresolute, turns away to the Eastward, and comes to *Litchfield*, where he shewed his Resentments[1] at Collonel *Hastings*, for his easy Surrender of *Leicester*.

In this March the Enemy took Heart; we had Troops of Horse on every Side upon us, like Hounds started at a fresh Stag. *Lesly*, with the *Scots*, and a strong Body followed in our Rear, Major General *Points*, Sir *John Gell*, Collonel *Roseter*, and others, in our Way; they pretended to be 10000 Horse, and yet never durst face us. The *Scots* made one Attempt upon a Troop which stayed a little behind, and took some Prisoners; but when a Regiment of our Horse faced them, they retired. At a Village near *Litchfield*, another Party of about 1000 Horse attacked my Regiment; we were on the left of the Army, and, at a little too far a Distance. I happened to be with the King at that time, and my Lieutenant Collonel with me; so that the Major had Charge of the Regiment; he made a very handsome Defence, but sent Messengers for speedy Relief; we were on a March, and therefore all ready, and the King orders me a Regiment of Dragoons and 300 Horse, and the Body halted to bring us off, not knowing how strong the Enemy might be. When I came to the Place I found my Major hard layed to, but fighting like a Lion; the Enemy had broke in upon him in two Places, and had routed one Troop, cutting them off from the Body, and had made them all Prisoners. Upon this I fell in with the 300 Horse, and cleared my Major from a Party who charged him in the Flank; the Dragoons immediately lighting, one Party of them comes up on my Wing, and saluting the Enemy with their Musquets, put them to a stand; the other Party of Dragoons wheeling to the Left, endeavoured to get behind them. The Enemy perceiving they should be over-powered, retreated in as good Order as they could, but left us most of our Prisoners, and about 30 of their own. We lost about 15 of our Men, and the Enemy about 40, chiefly by the Fire of our Dragoons in their Retreat.

In this Posture we continued our March; and though the King halted at *Litchfield*, which was a dangerous Article, having so many of the Enemy's Troops upon his Hands, and this Time gave them Opportunity to get into a Body; yet the *Scots*, with their General *Lesly*, resolving for the North, the rest of the Troops were not able to face us, till having ravaged the Enemy's Country through *Staffordshire*, *Warwick*, *Leicester*, and *Nottinghamshire*, we came to the Leaguer before *Newark*.

The King was once more on the Mind to have gone into *Scotland*, and called a Council of War to that Purpose; but then it was resolved by all Hands, that it would be too late to attempt it; for the *Scots* and Major General *Pointz* were before us, and several strong Bodies of Horse in our Rear; and there was no venturing now, unless any Advantage presented to rout one of those Parties which attended us.

Upon these and like Considerations we resolved for *Newark*; on our Approach the Forces which blocked up that Town drew off, being too weak to oppose us; for the King was now above 5000 Horse and Dragoons, besides 300 Horse and Dragoons he took with him from *Newark*.

We halted at *Newark* to assist the Garrison, or give them Time rather to furnish themselves from the Country with what they wanted, which they were very diligent in doing; for in two Days time they filled a large Island which lies under the Town, between the two Branches of the *Trent*, with Sheep, Oxen, Cows and Horses, an incredible Number; and our Affairs being now something desperate, we were not very nice in our Usage of the Country; for really if it was not with a Resolution, both to punish the Enemy and enrich our selves, no Man can give any rational Account why this desperate Journey was undertaken.

'Tis certain the *Newarkers*, in the Respite they gained by our coming, got above 50000 l. from the Country round them, in Corn, Cattle, Money, and other Plunder.

From hence we broke into *Lincolnshire*, and the King lay at *Belvoir* Castle, and from *Belvoir* Castle to *Stamford*. The Swiftness of our March was a terrible Surprize to the Enemy; for our Van being at a Village on the great Road called *Stilton*, the Country People fled into the Isle of *Ely*, and every Way, as if all was lost. Indeed our Dragoons treated the Country very coarsly; and all our Men in general made themselves rich. Between *Stilton* and *Huntingdon* we had a small Bustle with some of the Association Troops[1] of Horse, but they were soon routed, and fled to *Huntingdon*, where they gave such an Account of us to their Fellows, that they did not think fit to stay for us, but left their Foot to defend themselves as well as they could.

While this was doing in the Van, a Party from *Burleigh* House, near *Stamford*, the Seat of the Earl of *Exeter*, pursued four Troops of our Horse, who straggling towards *Peterborough*, and committing some Disorders there, were surprized before they could get into a Posture of Fighting; and encumbered, as I suppose, with their Plunder, they were entirely routed, lost most of their Horses, and were forced to come away on Foot; but finding themselves in this Condition, they got into a Body in the Enclosures, and in that Posture turning Dragoons, they lined the Hedges, and fired upon the Enemy with their Carabines. This way of Fighting, though not very pleasant to Troopers, put the Enemy's Horse to some Stand, and encouraged our Men to venture into a Village, where the Enemy had secured 40 of their Horse; and boldly charging the Guard, they beat them off and recovered those Horses; the rest made their Retreat good to *Wandsford* Bridge; but we lost near 100 Horses, and about 12 of our Men taken Prisoners.

The next Day the King took *Huntington*; the Foot which

were left in the Town, as I observed by their Horse, had posted themselves at the Foot of the Bridge, and fortified the Pass, with such Things as the Haste and Shortness of the Time would allow; and in this Posture they seemed resolute to defend themselves. I confess, had they in Time planted a good Force here, they might have put a full Stop to our little Army; for the River is large and deep, the Country on the left marshy, full of Drains and Ditches, and unfit for Horse, and we must have either turned back, or took the Right Hand into *Bedfordshire*; but here not being above 400 Foot, and they forsaken of their Horse, the Resistance they made was to no other Purpose than to give us Occasion to knock them in the Head, and plunder the Town.

However, they defended the Bridge, as I have said, and opposed our Passage. I was this Day in the Van, and our Forelorn having entered *Huntington* without any great Resistance till they came to the Bridge, finding it barricaded, they sent me Word; I caused the Troops to halt, and rid up to the Forelorn, to view the Countenance of the Enemy, and found by the Posture they had put themselves in, that they resolved to sell us the Passage as dear as they could.

I sent to the King for some Dragoons, and gave him Account of what I observed of the Enemy, and that I judged them to be 1000 Men; for I could not particularly see their Numbers. Accordingly the King ordered 500 Dragoons to attack the Bridge, commanded by a Major; the Enemy had 200 Musqueteers placed on the Bridge, their Barricade served them for a Breast-work on the Front, and the low Walls on the Bridge served to secure their Flanks: Two Bodies of their Foot were placed on the opposite Banks of the River, and a Reserve stood in the High-way on the Rear. The Number of their Men could not have been better ordered, and they wanted not Courage answerable to the Conduct of the Party. They were commanded by one *Bennet*, a resolute Officer, who stood in the Front of his Men on the Bridge with a Pike in his Hand.

Before we began to fall on, the King ordered to view the River, to see if it was no where passable, or any Boat to be had; but the River being not fordable, and the Boats all secured on the other Side, the Attack was resolved on, and the Dragoons fell on with extraordinary Bravery. The Foot defended themselves obstinately, and beat off our Dragoons twice; and though *Bennet* was killed upon the Spot, and after him his Lieutenant,[1] yet their Officers relieving them with fresh Men, they would certainly have beat us all off, had not a venturous Fellow, one of our Dragoons thrown himself into the River, swum over, and, in the midst of a Shower of Musquet Bullets, cut the Rope which tied a great flat-bottom Boat, and brought her over: With the Help of this Boat, I got over 100 Troopers first, and then their Horses, and then 200 more without their Horses; and with this Party fell in with one of the small Bodies of Foot that were posted on that Side, and having routed them, and after them the Reserve which stood in the Road, I made up to the other Party; they stood their Ground, and having rallied the Run-aways of both the other Parties, charged me with their Pikes, and brought me to a Retreat; but by this time the King had sent over 300 Men more, and they coming up to me, the Foot retreated. Those on the Bridge finding how 'twas and having no Supplies sent them, as before, fainted, and fled; and the Dragoons rushing forward, most of them were killed; about 150 of the Enemy were killed, of which all the Officers at the Bridge, the rest run away.

The Town suffered for it; for our Men left them little of any thing they could carry. Here we halted, and raised Contributions, took Money of the Country, and of the open Towns, to exempt them from Plunder. Twice we faced the Town of *Cambridge*, and several of our Officers advised his Majesty to storm it; but having no Foot, and but 1200 Dragoons, wiser Heads diverted him from it; and, leaving *Cambridge* on the left, we marched to *Wooburn*, in *Bedfordshire*, and our Parties raised Money all over the County quite into *Hertfordshire*, within 5 Miles of St. *Alban*'s.

The swiftness of our March, and Uncertainty which Way we intended, prevented all possible Preparation to oppose us, and we met with no Party able to make Head against us. From *Wooburn* the King went through *Buckingham* to *Oxford*; some of our Men straggling in the Villages for Plunder, were often picked up by the Enemy; but in all this long March we did not loose 200 Men, got an incredible Booty, and brought 6 Waggons loaden with Money, besides 2000 Horses, and 3000 Head of Cattle into *Oxford*.

From *Oxford* his Majesty moves again into *Gloucestershire* having left about 1500 of his Horse at *Oxford*, to scour the Country, and raise Contributions, which they did as far as *Reading*.

Sir *Thomas Fairfax* was returned from taking *Bridgewater*, and was sat down before *Bristol*, in which Prince *Rupert* commanded with a strong Garrison, 2500 Foot and 1000 Horse. We had not Force enough to attempt any thing there; but the *Scots*, who lay still before *Hereford*, were afraid of us, having before parted with all their Horse under Lieutenant General *Lesly*, and but ill stored with Provisions; and, if we came on their Backs, were in a fair way to be starved, or made to buy their Provisions at the Price of their Blood.

His Majesty was sensible of this, and had we had but 10 Regiments of Foot, would certainly have fought the *Scots*; but we had no Foot, or so few as was not worth while to march them. However, the King marched to *Worcester*, and the *Scots* apprehending they should be blocked up, immediately raised the Siege, pretending it was to go help their Brethren in *Scotland*, and away they marched Northwards.

We picked up some of their Stragglers, but they were so poor, had been so ill paid, and so harrassed at the Siege, that they had neither Money nor Clothes; and the poor Soldiers fed upon Apples and Roots, and eat the very green Corn as it grew in the Fields, which reduced them to a very sorry Condition of Health,[1] for they died like People infected with the Plague.

'Twas now debated whether we should yet march for

Scotland, but two Things prevented. 1. The Plague was broke out there, and Multitudes died of it, which made the King backward, and the Men more backward. 2. The Marquess of *Montrose* having routed a whole Brigade of *Lesly*'s best Horse, and carried all before him, wrote to his Majesty, that he did not now want Assistance, but was in Hopes in a few Days to send a Body of Foot into *England*, to his Majesty's Assistance. This over Confidence of his was his Ruine; for, on the contrary, had he earnestly pressed the King to have marched, and fallen in with his Horse, the King had done it, and been absolutely Master of *Scotland* in a Fortnight's time; but *Montrose* was too confident, and defied them all, till at last they got their Forces together, and *Lesly*, with his Horse out of *England*, and worsted him in two or three Encounters, and then never left him till they drove him out of *Scotland*.

While his Majesty stayed at *Worcester* several Messengers came to him from *Cheshire* for Relief, being exceedingly streightened by the Forces of the Parliament: In order to which, the King marched, but *Shrewsbury* being in the Enemy's Hands, he was obliged to go round by *Ludlow*, where he was joined by some Foot out of *Wales*. I took this Opportunity to ask his Majesty's Leave to go by *Shrewsbury* to my Father's, and taking only two Servants, I left the Army two Days before they marched.

This was the most Unsoldier-like Action that ever I was guilty of, to go out of the Army to pay a Visit, when a Time of Action was just at Hand; and, though I protest I had not the least Intimation, no not from my own Thoughts, that the Army would engage, at least before they came to *Chester*, before which I intended to meet them; yet it looked so ill, so like an Excuse, or a Sham of Cowardice, or Disaffection to the Cause, and to my Master's Interest, or something I know not what, that I could not bear to think of it, nor never had the Heart to see the King's Face after it.

From *Ludlow* the King marched to relieve *Chester*; *Poyntz*, who commanded the Parliament's Forces, follows the King, with Design to join with the Forces before *Chester*, under Collonel *Jones*, before the King could come up. To that End *Poyntz* passes through *Shrewsbury* the Day that the King marched from *Ludlow*; yet the King's Forces got the Start of him, and forced him to engage: Had the King engaged him but three Hours sooner, and consequently farther off from *Chester*, he had ruined him; for *Poyntz's* Men not able to stand the Shock of the King's Horse, gave Ground, and would in half an Hour more been beaten out of the Field; but Collonel *Jones*, with a strong Party from the Camp, which was within two Miles, comes up in the Heat of the Action, falls on in the King's Rear, and turned the Scale of the Day: The Body was, after an obstinate Fight defeated, and a great many Gentlemen of Quality killed and taken Prisoners; the Earl of *Litchfield* was of the Number of the former, and 67 Officers of the latter, with 1000 others.

The King with about 500 Horse got into *Chester*,[1] and from thence into *Wales*, whither all that could get away made up to him as fast as they could, but in a bad Condition.[2]

This was the last Stroke they struck, the rest of the War was nothing but taking all his Garrisons from him, one by one, till they finished the War, with the captivating his Person, and then, for want of other Business, fell to fighting with one another.

I was quite disconsolate at the News of this last Action, and the more because I was not there; my Regiment was wholly dispersed, my Lieutenant Collonel, a Gentleman of a good Family, and a near Relation to my Mother, was Prisoner, my Major and three Captains killed, and most of the rest Prisoners.

The King, hopeless of any considerable Party in *Wales*, *Bristol* being surrendered, sends for Prince *Rupert* and Prince *Maurice*, who came to him. With them, and the Lord *Digby*, Sir *Marmaduke Langdale*, and a great Train of Gentlemen, his Majesty marches to *Newark* again, leaves a Thousand Horse with Sir *William Vaughan*, to attempt the

Relief of *Chester*, in doing whereof he was routed the second time by *Jones* and his Men, and entirely dispersed.[1]

The chief Strength the King had in these Parts was at *Newark*, and the Parliament were very earnest with the *Scots* to march Southward, and to lay Siege to *Newark*; and while the Parliament pressed them to it, and they sat still, and delayed it, several Heats began, and some ill blood between them, which afterwards broke out into open War. The *English* reproached the *Scots* with pretending to help them, and really hindering their Affairs. The *Scots* returned, that they come to fight for them, and are left to be starved, and can neither get Money nor Clothes. At last they came to this, the *Scots* will come to the Siege, if the Parliament will send them Money, but not before: However, as People sooner agree in doing ill, than in doing well, they came to Terms, and the *Scots* came with their whole Army to the Siege of *Newark*.

The King, foreseeing the Siege, calls his Friends about him, tells them, he sees his Circumstances are such, that they can help him but little, nor he protect them, and advises them to separate. The Lord *Digby*, with Sir *Marmaduke Langdale*, with a strong Body of Horse, attempt to get into *Scotland*, to join with *Montrose*, who was still in the Highlands, though reduced to a low Ebb; but these Gentlemen are fallen upon on every Side and routed, and at last being totally broken and dispersed, they fly to the Earl of *Derby*'s Protection in the Isle of Man.[2]

Prince *Rupert*, Prince *Maurice*, Collonel *Gerrard*, and above 400 Gentlemen, all Officers of Horse, lay their Commissions down, and siezing upon *Wooton* House for a Retreat, make Proposals to the Parliament to leave the Kingdom, upon their Parole not to return again in Arms against the Parliament,[3] which was accepted, though afterwards the Princes declined it. I sent my Man Post to the Prince to be included in this Treaty, and for Leave for all that would accept of like Conditions, but they had given in the List of their Names, and could not alter it.

This was a sad Time; the poor Remains of the King's Fortunes went every where to wreck; every Garrison of the Enemy was full of the Cavalier Prisoners, and every Garrison the King had was beset with Enemies, either blocked up or besieged. *Goring* and the Lord *Hopton* were the only Remainders of the King's Forces, which kept in a Body, and *Fairfax* was pushing them with all imaginable Vigour with his whole Army, about *Exeter*, and other Parts of *Devonshire* and *Cornwall*.

In this Condition the King left *Newark* in the Night, and got to *Oxford*. The King had in *Oxford* 8000 Men, and the Towns of *Banbury*, *Farrington*, *Dunnington* Castle, and such Places as might have been brought together in 24 Hours, 15 or 20000 Men, with which if he had then resolved to have quitted the Place, and collected the Forces in *Worcester*, *Hereford*, *Lichfield*, *Ashby de la Zouch*, and all the small Castles and Garrisons he had thereabouts, he might have had near 40000 Men, might have beaten the *Scots* from *Newark*, Collonel *Jones* from *Chester*, and all, before *Fairfax* who was in the West, could be able to come to their Relief, and this his Majesty's Friends in North *Wales* had concerted; and, in order to it, Sir *Jacob Ashby* gathered what Forces he could, in our Parts, and attempted to join the King at *Oxford*, and to have proposed it to him; but Sir *Jacob* was entirely routed at *Stow on the Would*, and taken Prisoner, and of 3000 Men not above 600 came to *Oxford*.

All the King's Garrisons dropt one by one; *Hereford* which had stood out against the whole Army of the *Scots* was surprized by six Men and a Lieutenant dressed up for Country Labourers, and a Constable pressed to work, who cut the Guards in Pieces, and let in a Party of the Enemy.[1]

Chester was reduced by Famine, all the Attempts the King made to relieve it being frustrated.

Sir *Thomas Fairfax* routed the Lord *Hopton* at *Torrington*, and drove him to such Extremities, that he was forced up into the farthest Corner of *Cornwall*. The Lord *Hopton* had a gallant Body of Horse with him of nine Brigades, but no Foot; *Fairfax*, a great Army.

Heartless, and tired out with continual ill News, and ill Success, I had frequent Meetings with some Gentlemen, who had escaped from the Rout of Sir *William Vaughan*, and we agreed upon a Meeting at *Worcester* of all the Friends we could get, to see if we could raise a Body fit to do any Service; or, if not, to consider what was to be done. At this Meeting we had almost as many Opinions as People; our Strength appeared too weak to make any Attempt, the Game was too far gone in our Parts to be retrieved; all we could make up did not amount to above 800 Horse.

'Twas unanimously agreed not to go into the Parliament as long as our Royal Master did not give up the Cause; but in all Places, and by all possible Methods, to do him all the Service we could. Some proposed one thing, some another; at last we proposed getting Vessels to carry us to the Isle of *Man* to the Earl of *Derby*, as Sir *Marmaduke Langdale*, Lord *Digby*, and others had done. I did not foresee any Service it would be to the King's Affairs, but I started a Proposal, that marching to *Pembrook* in a Body, we should there sieze upon all the Vessels we could, and embarking our selves, Horses, and what Foot we could get, cross the *Severn* Sea, and land in *Cornwall* to the Assistance of Prince *Charles*, who was in the Army of the Lord *Hopton*, and where only there seemed to be any Possibility of a Chance for the remaining part of our Cause.

This Proposal was not without its Difficulties, as how to get to the Sea-side, and, when there, what Assurance of Shipping. The Enemy, under Major General *Langhorn* had over-run *Wales*, and 'twould be next to impossible to effect it.

We could never carry our Proposal with the whole Assembly; but however, about 200 of us resolved to attempt it, and Meeting being broke up without coming to any Conclusion, we had a private Meeting among our selves to effect it.

We dispatched private Messengers to *Swanzey* and *Pembrook*, and other Places; but they all discouraged us from the Attempt that way, and advised us to go higher towards North *Wales*, where the King's Interest had more Friends, and the Parliament no Forces. Upon this we met, and resolved, and having sent several Messengers that Way, one of my Men provided us two small Vessels in a little Creek near *Harlegh* Castle, in *Merionethshire*. We marched away with what Expedition we could, and embarked in the two Vessels accordingly. It was the worst Voyage sure that ever Man went; for first, we had no Manner of Accommodation for so many People, Hay for our Horses we got none, or very little, but good Store of Oats, which served us for our own Bread as well as Provender for the Horses.

In this Conditions we put off to Sea, and had a fair Wind all the first Night, but early in the Morning a sudden Storm drove us within two or three Leagues of *Ireland*. In this Pickle Sea-Sick, our Horses rouling about upon one another, and our selves stifled for want of Room, no Cabins nor Beds, very cold Weather, and very indifferent Diet, we wished our selves ashore again a thousand times; and yet we were not willing to go on Shore in *Ireland*, if we could help it; for the Rebels having Possession of every Place, that was just having our Throats cut at once. Having rouled about at the Mercy of the Winds all Day, the Storm ceasing in the Evening, we had fair Weather again, but Wind enough, which being large, in two Days and a Night we came upon the Coast of *Cornwall*, and, to our no small Comfort, landed the next Day at St. *Ives* in the County of *Cornwall*.

We rested our selves here, and sent an Express to the Lord *Hopton*, who was then in *Devonshire*, of our Arrival, and desired him to assign us Quarters, and send us his farther Orders. His Lordship expressed a very great Satisfaction at our Arrival, and left it to our own Conduct to join him as we saw convenient.

We were marching to join him, when News came, that

Fairfax had given him an entire Defeat at *Torrington*. This was but the old Story over again; we had been used to ill News a great while, and 'twas the less Surprize to us.

Upon this News we halted at *Bodmin*, till we should hear farther; and it was not long before we saw a Confirmation of the News before our Eyes; for the Lord *Hopton*, with the Remainder of his Horse, which he had brought off at *Torrington* in a very shattered Condition, retreated to *Lanceston*, the first Town in *Cornwall*, and hearing that *Fairfax* pursued him, came on to *Bodmin*. Hither he summoned all the Troops which he had left, which when he had got together, were a fine Body indeed of 5000 Horse, but few Foot but what were at *Pendennis*, *Barnstable*, and other Garrisons; these were commanded by the Lord *Hopton*; the Lord *Goring* had taken shipping for *France*, to get Relief, a few Days before.

Here a Grand Council of War was called, and several things were proposed, but as it always is in Distress, People are most irresolute, so 'twas here: Some were for breaking through by Force, our Number being superiour to the Enemy's Horse. To fight them with their Foot would be Desperation, and ridiculous; and to retreat, would but be to coop up themselves in a narrow Place, where at last they must be forced to fight upon Disadvantage, or yield at Mercy. Others opposed this as a desperate Action, and without Probability of Success; and all were of different Opinions: I confess, when I saw how things were, I saw 'twas a lost Game, and I was for the Opinion of breaking through, and doing it now, while the Country was open and large, and not being forced to it when it must be with more Disadvantage; but nothing was resolved on, and so we retreated before the Enemy. Some small Skirmishes there happened near *Bodmin*, but none that were very considerable.

'Twas the 1st of *March* when we quitted *Bodmin*, and quartered at large at *Columb*, *St. Denis* and *Truro*, and the Enemy took his Quarters at *Bodmin*, posting his Horse at the Passes from *Padstow* on the North, to *War-bridge*

Lestithel and *Foy*, spreading so from Sea to Sea, that now breaking through was impossible. There was no more Room for Counsel; for unless we had Ships to carry us off, we had nothing to do but when we were fallen upon, to defend our selves, and sell Victory as dear as we could to the Enemies.

The Prince of *Wales* seeing the Distress we were in, and loath to fall into the Enemy's Hands, ships himself on board some Vessels at *Falmouth*, with about 400 Lords and Gentlemen; and, as I had no Command here, to oblige my Attendance, I was once going to make one; but my Comerades, whom I had been the principal Occasion of bringing hither, began to take it ill, that I would leave them, and so I resolved we would take our Fate together.

While thus we had nothing before us but a Soldier's Death, a fair Field, and a strong Enemy, and People began to look one upon another: The Soldiers asked how their Officers looked, and the Officers asked how their Soldiers looked, and every Day we expected to be our last, when unexpectedly the Enemy's General sent a Trumpet to *Truro* to my Lord *Hopton* with a very handsom Gentleman-like Offer.

That since the General could not be ignorant of his present Condition, and that the Place he was in could not afford him Subsistance or Defence; and especially considering that the State of our Affairs were such, that if we should escape from thence, we could not remove to our Advantage, he had thought good to let us know, *That if we would deliver up our Horses and Arms, he would, for avoiding the Effusion of Christian Blood, or the putting any unsoldiery Extremities upon us, allow such honourable and safe Conditions, as were rather better than our present Circumstances could demand, and such as should discharge him to all the World, as a Gentleman, as a Soldier, and as a Christian.*

After this followed the Conditions he would give us, which were as follows, (*viz.*) *That all the Soldiery, as well* English *as Foreigners, should have Liberty to go beyond the Seas, or to their own Dwellings, as they pleased; and to such as shall chuse to live at home, Protection for their Liberty, and from all Violence, and plundering of Soldiers, and to give them Bag and Baggage, and all their Goods, except Horses and Arms.*

That for Officers in Commission, and Gentlemen of Quality, he would allow them Horses for themselves and one Servant, or more, suitable to their Quality, and such Arms as are suitable to Gentlemen of such Quality travelling in Times of Peace; and such Officers as would go beyond Sea, should take with them their full Arms and Number of Horses as are allowed in the Army to such Officers.[1]

That all the Troopers should receive on the Delivery of their Horses, 20s. a Man, to carry them home; and the General's Pass and Recommendation to any Gentleman who desires to go to the Parliament to settle the Composition for their Estates.

Lastly, A very honourable Mention of the General, and Offer of their Mediation to the Parliament, to treat him as a Man of Honour, and one who has been tender of the Country, and behaved himself with all the Moderation and Candor that could be expected from an Enemy.

Upon the unexpected Receipt of this Message, a Council of War was called, and the Letter read; no Man offered to speak a Word; the General moved it, but every one was loath to begin.

At last, an old Collonel starts up, and asked the General what he thought might occasion the writing this Letter? The General told him, *he could not tell*; but he could tell he was sure of one thing, that he knew what was not the Occasion of it (*viz.*) That is, not any want of Force in their Army to oblige us to other Terms. Then a Doubt was started, whether the King and Parliament were not in any Treaty, which this Agreement might be prejudicial to.

This occasioned a Letter to my Lord *Fairfax*, wherein our General returning the Civilities, and neither accepting nor refusing his Proposal, put it upon his Honour, whether there was not some Agreement or Concession between his Majesty and the Parliament, in order to a General Peace, which this

Treaty might be prejudicial to, or thereby be prejudicial to us.

The Lord *Fairfax* ingenuously declared, he had heard the King had made some Concessions, and he heartily wished he would make such as would settle the Kingdom in Peace, that *Englishmen* might not wound and destroy one another; *but that he declared he knew of no Treaty commenced, nor any Thing past which could give us the least Shadow of hope for any Advantage in not accepting his Conditions.* At last telling us, *That though he did not insult over our Circumstances, yet if we thought fit, upon any such Supposition, to refuse his Offers, he was not to seek in his Measures.*[1]

And it appeared so, for he immediately advanced his Forlorns, and dispossessed us of two advanced Quarters, and thereby streightened us yet more.

We had now nothing to say, but treat, and our General was so sensible of our Condition, that he returned the Trumpet with a safe Conduct for Commissioners at 12 a Clock that Night; upon which a Cessation of Arms was agreed[2] on, we quitting *Truro* to the Lord *Fairfax*, and he left St. *Allan*'s to us to keep our head Quarter.

The Conditions were soon agreed on, we disbanded nine full Brigades of Horse, and all the Conditions were observed with the most Honour and Care by the Enemy that ever I saw in my Life.

Nor can I omit to make very honourable Mention of this noble Gentleman, though I did not like his Cause; but I never saw a Man of a more pleasant, calm, courteous, down-right, honest Behaviour in my Life; and, for his Courage and personal Bravery in the Field, that we had felt enough of. No Man in the World had more Fire and Fury in him while in Action, or more Temper and Softness out of it. In short, and I cannot do him greater Honour, he exceedingly came near the Character of my Foreign Heroe *Gustavus Adolphus*, and in my Account, is, of all the Soldiers in *Europe*, the fittest to be reckoned in the second Place of Honour to him.

I had particular Occasion to see much of his Temper in all this Action, being one of the Hostages given by our General for the Performance of the Conditions, in which Circumstance the General did me several times the Honour to send to me to dine with him; and was exceedingly pleased to discourse with me about the Passages of the Wars in *Germany*, which I had served in; he having been at the same time in the *Low Countries*, in the Service of Prince *Maurice*; but I observed if at any time my Civilities extended to Commendations of his own Actions, and especially to comparing him to *Gustavus Adolphus*, he would blush like a Woman, and be uneasy, declining the Discourse, and in this he was still more like him.

Let no Man scruple my honourable Mention of this noble Enemy, since no Man can suspect me of favouring the Cause he embarked in, which I served as heartily against as any Man in the Army; but I cannot conceal extraordinary Merit for its being placed in an Enemy.

This was the End of our making War; for now we were all under Parole never to bear Arms against the Parliament; and though some of us did not keep our Word, yet I think a Soldier's Parole ought to be the most sacred in such Case, that a Soldier may be the easier trusted at all Times upon his Word.

For my Part I went home fully contented, since I could do my Royal Master no better Service, that I had come off no worse.

The Enemy going now on in a full Current of Success, and the King reduced to the last Extremity, and *Fairfax*, by long Marches, being come back within five Miles of *Oxford*; his Majesty loath to be cooped up in a Town which could on no Account hold long out, quits the Town in a Disguise, leaving Sir *Thomas Glemham* Governour, and being only attended with Mr. *Ashburnham* and one more,[1] rides away to *Newark* and there fatally committed himself to the Honour and Fidelity of the *Scots*, under General *Leven*.

There had been some little Bickering between the Parliament and the *Scots* Commissioners, concerning the Propositions which the *Scots* were for a Treaty with the King upon, and the Parliament refused it. The Parliament, upon all Proposals of Peace, had formerly invited the King to come and throw himself upon the Honour, Fidelity and Affection of his Parliament; and now the King from *Oxford* offering to come up to *London*, on the Protection of the Parliament for the Safety of his Person, they refused him, and the *Scots* differed from them in it, and were for a personal Treaty.

This, in our Opinion, was the Reason which prompted the King to throw himself upon the Fidelity of the *Scots*, who really by their Infidelity had been the Ruine of all his Affairs, and now, by their perfidious Breach of Honour and Faith with him, will be virtually and mediately the Ruine of his Person.

The *Scots* were, as all the Nation besides them was, surprized at the King's coming among them; the Parliament began very high with them, and send an Order to General *Leven* to send the King to *Warwick* Castle; but he was not so hasty to part with so rich a Prize. As soon as the King came to the General, he signs an Order to Collonel *Ballasis*, the Governour of *Newark*, to surrender it, and immediately the *Scots* decamp homewards, carrying the King in the Camp with them, and marching on, a House was ordered to be provided for the King at *Newcastle*.

And now the Parliament saw their Error, in refusing his Majesty a Personal Treaty, which if they had accepted, (their Army was not yet taught the way of huffing their Masters,) the Kingdom might have been settled in Peace. Upon this the Parliament send to General *Leven* to have his Majesty not *be sent*, which was their first Language, but *be suffered to come to* London, to treat with his Parliament; before it was, *Let the King be sent to* Warwick *Castle*; now 'tis, *To let his Majesty come to* London *to treat with his People.*

But neither one or the other would do with the *Scots*; but

we who knew the *Scots* best, knew that there was *one Thing* would do with them, if the other would not, and that was Money; and therefore our Hearts aked for the King.

The *Scots*, as I said, had retreated to *Newcastle* with the King, and there they quartered their whole Army at large upon the Country; the Parliament voted they had no farther Occasion for the *Scots*,[1] and desired them to go home about their Business. I do not say it was in these Words, but in whatsoever good Words their Messages might be expressed, this and nothing less was the *English* of it. The *Scots* reply, by setting forth their Losses, Damages, and Dues, the Substance of which was, *Pay us our Money, and we will be gone, or else we won't stir.* The Parliament call for an Account of their Demands, which the *Scots* give in, amounting to a Million; but, according to their Custom, and especially finding that the Army under *Fairfax* inclined gradually that Way, fall down to 500000 l. and at last to four; but all the while this is transacting, a separate Treaty is carried on at *London* with the Commissioners of *Scotland*, and afterwards at *Edinburgh*, by which it is given them to understand, that whereas upon Payment of the Money, the *Scots* Army is to march out of *England*, and to give up all the Towns and Garrisons which they hold in this Kingdom, so they are to take it for granted, that 'tis the meaning of the Treaty, that they shall leave the King in the Hands of the *English* Parliament.

To make this go down the better, the *Scotch* Parliament, upon his Majesty's Desire to go with their Army into *Scotland*, send him for Answer, that it cannot be for the Safety of his Majesty or of the State, to come into *Scotland*, not having taken the Covenant, and this was carried in their Parliament but by two Voices.

The *Scots* having refused his coming into *Scotland*, as was concerted between the two Houses, and their Army being to march out of *England*, the delivering up the King became a Consequence of the Thing unavoidable, and of Necessity.

His Majesty thus deserted of those into whose Hands he

had thrown himself, took his Leave[1] of the *Scots* General at *Newcastle*, telling him only, in few Words, this sad Truth, *That he was Bought and Sold.*[2] The Parliament Commissioners received him at *Newcastle* from the *Scots*, and brought him to *Holmby* House, in *Northamptonshire*; from whence, upon the Quarrels and Feuds of Parties, he was fetched by a Party of Horse, commanded by one Cornet *Joyce*, from the Army, upon their mutinous Rendezvous at *Triplow-Heath*; and, after this, suffering many Violences, and Varieties of Circumstances among the Army, was carried to *Hampton-Court*, from whence his Majesty very readily made his Escape; but not having Notice enough to provide effectual Means for his more effectual Deliverance was obliged to deliver himself to Collonel *Hammond* in the Isle of *Wight*. Here, after some very indifferent Usage, the Parliament pursued a farther Treaty with him, and all Points were agreed but two. The entire Abolishing Episcopacy, which the King declared to be against his Conscience, and his Coronation Oath; and the Sale of the Church-Lands, which he declared, being most of them Gifts to God and the Church, by Persons deceased, his Majesty thought could not be alienated without the highest Sacrilege, and if taken from the Uses to which they were appointed by the Wills of the Donors, ought to be restored back to the Heirs and Families of the Persons who bequeathed them.

And these two Articles so stuck with his Majesty, that he ventured his Fortune and Royal Family, and his own Life for them: However, at last, the King condescended so far in these, that the Parliament voted his Majesty's Concessions to be sufficient to settle and establish the Peace of the Nation.

This Vote discovered the bottom of all the Counsels which then prevailed; for the Army, who knew if Peace were once settled, they should be undone, took the Alarm at this, and clubbing together in Committees and Councils, at last brought themselves to a Degree of Hardness above all that ever this Nation saw; for, calling into Question the Proceedings of their Masters who employed them, they immediately fall to Work upon the Parliament, remove Collonel *Hammond*, who had the Charge of the King, and used him honourably, place a new Guard upon him, dismiss the Commissioners, and put a Stop to the Treaty; and, following their Blow, march to *London*, place Regiments of Foot at the Parliament House Door, and, as the Members came up, sieze upon all those whom they had down in a List as Promoters of the Settlement and Treaty, and would not suffer them to sit; but the rest, who being of their own Stamp, are permitted to go on, carry on the Designs of the Army, revive their Votes of Non-Addresses to the King, and then, upon the Army's Petition, to bring all Delinquents to Justice; the Masque was thrown off, the Word all is declared to be meant the King, as well as every Man else they pleased. 'Tis too sad a Story, and too much a Matter of Grief to me, and to all good Men, to renew the Blackness of those Days, when Law and Justice was under the Feet of Power; the Army ruled the Parliament, the private Officers their Generals, the common Soldiers their Officers, and Confusion was in every Part of the Government: In this Hurry they sacrificed their King, and shed the Blood of the *English* Nobility without Mercy.

The History of the Times will supply the Particulars which I omit, being willing to confine my self to my own Accounts and Observations; I was now no more an Actor, but a melancholly Observator of the Misfortunes of the Times. I had given my Parole not to take up Arms against the Parliament, and I saw nothing to invite me to engage on their Side; I saw a World of Confusion in all their Counsels, and I always expected that in a Chain of Distractions, as it generally fals out, the last Link would be Destruction; and though I pretended to no Prophecy, yet the Progress of Affairs have brought it to pass, and I have seen Providence, who suffered, for the Correction of this Nation, the Sword to govern and devour us, has at last brought Destruction *by the Sword*,[1] upon the Head of most of the Party who first drew it.

If together with the brief Account of what Concern I had

in the Active Part of the War, I leave behind me some of my own Remarks and Observations, it may be pertinent enough to my Design, and not unuseful to Prosperity.

1. I observed by the Sequel of Things, that it may be some Excuse to the first Parliament, who began this War, to say that they manifested their Designs were not aimed at the Monarchy, nor their Quarrel at the Person of the King; because, when they had him in their Power, though against his Will, they would have restored both his Person and Dignity as a King, only loading it with such Clogs of the People's Power as they at first pretended to, (*viz.*) the Militia, and Power of naming the great Officers at Court, and the like; which Powers, it was never denied, had been stretched too far in the Beginning of this King's Reign, and several things done illegally, which his Majesty had been sensible of, and was willing to rectify; but they having obtained the Power by Victory, resolved so to secure themselves, as that whenever they laid down their Arms, the King should not be able to do the like again: And thus far they were not to be so much blamed, and we did not, on our own Part, blame them, when they had obtained the Power, for parting with it on good Terms.

But when I have thus far advocated for the Enemies, I must be very free to state the Crimes of this Bloody War, by the Events of it. 'Tis manifest there were among them, from the Beginning, a Party who aimed at the very Root of the Government, and at the very thing which they brought to pass, *viz.* The deposing and murthering of their Sovereign; and, as the Devil is always Master where Mischief is the Work, this Party prevailed, turned the other out of Doors, and over-turned all that little Honesty that might be in the first Beginning of this unhappy Strife.

The Consequence of this was, the Presbyterians saw their Error when it was too late, and then would gladly have joined the Royal Party, to have suppressed this new Leaven, which had infected the Lump; and this is very remarkable, that most of the first Champions of this War, who bore the

Brunt of it; when the King was powerful and prosperous, and when there was nothing to be got by it but Blows, first or last, were so ill used by this Independant powerful Party, who tripped up the Heels of all their Honesty, that they were either forced, by ill Treatment, to take up Arms on our Side, or suppressed and reduced by them. In this the Justice of Providence seemed very conspicuous, that these having pushed all things by Violence against the King, and by Arms and Force brought him to their Will, were at once both robbed of the End, their Church-Government, and punished for drawing their Swords against *their Masters*, by *their own Servants* drawing the Sword against them; and God, in his due Time, punished the others too: And, what was yet farther strange, the Punishment of this Crime of making War against their King, singled out those very Men, both in the Army and in the Parliament, who were the greatest Champions of the Presbyterian Cause in the Council, and in the Field. Some Minutes too of Circumstances I cannot forbear observing, though they are not very material, as to the Fatality and Revolutions of Days and Times.

A *Roman* Catholick Gentleman of *Lancashire*, a very religious Man in his way, who had kept a Calculate of Times, and had observed mightily the Fatality of Times, Places and Actions, being at my Father's House, was discoursing once upon the just Judgment of God in dating his Providences, so as to signify to us his Displeasure at particular Circumstances; and, among an infinite Number of Collections he had made, these were some which I took particular Notice of, and from whence I began to observe the like.

1. That King *Edward* the VIth died the very same Day of the same Month in which he caused the Altar to be taken down, and the Image of the Blessed Virgin in the Cathedral of St. *Paul's*.

2. That *Cranmer* was burnt at *Oxford* the same Day and Month that he gave King *Henry* the VIIIth Advice to Divorce his Queen *Catherine*.

3. That Queen *Elizabeth* died the same Day and Month that she resolved, in her Privy Council, to behead the Queen of Scots.

4. That King *James* died the same Day that he published his Book against *Bellarmine*.

5. That King *Charles*'s long Parliament, which ruined him, began the very same Day and Month which that Parliament began, that at the Request of his Predecessor robbed the *Roman* Church of all her Revenues, and suppressed Abbies and Monasteries.

How just his Calculations were, or how true the Matter of Fact, I cannot tell, but it put me upon the same in several Actions and Successes of this War.

And I found a great many Circumstances, as to Time and Action, which befel both his Majesty and his Parties first.

Then others which befel the Parliament and Presbyterian Faction which raised the War.

Then the Independant Tyranny which succeeded and supplanted the first Party.

Then the *Scots*, who acted on both Sides.

Lastly, The Restoration and Re-establishment of the Loyalty and Religion of our Ancestors.

1. For King *Charles* the First; 'tis observable that the Charge against the Earl of *Strafford*, a thing which his Majesty blamed himself for all the Days of his Life, and at the Moment of his last Suffering, was first read in the Lords House on the 30th of *January*, the same Day of the Month six Year that the King himself was brought to the Block.

2. That the King was carried away Prisoner from *Newark*, by the *Scots*, *May* 10, the same Day six Year that, against his Conscience and Promise, he passed the Bill of Attainder against the loyal noble Earl of *Strafford*.

3. The same Day seven Year that the King entered the House of Commons for the five Members, which all his Friends blamed him for, the same Day the Rump voted

bringing his Majesty to Tryal, after they had set by the Lords for not agreeing to it, which was the 3d of *January* 1648.

4. The 12th of *May* 1646, being the Surrender of *Newark*, the Parliament held a Day of Thanksgiving and Rejoicing, for the Reduction of the King and his Party, and finishing the War, which was the same Day five Year that the Earl of *Strafford* was beheaded.

5. The Battle of *Naseby*, which ruin'd the King's Affairs, and where his Secretary and his Office was taken, was the 14th of *June* the same Day and Month the first Commission was given out by his Majesty to raise Forces.

6. The Queen voted a Traytor by the Parliament the 3d of *May*, the same Day and Month she carried the Jewels into *France*.

7. The same Day the King defeated *Essex* in the West, his Son King *Charles* II. was defeated at *Worcester*.

8. Arch-bishop *Laud*'s House at *Lambeth* assaulted by the Mob, the same Day of the same Month that he advised the King to make War upon the *Scots*.

9. Impeached the 15th of *December* 1640, the same Day Twelve-month that he ordered the Common-Prayer-Book of *Scotland* to be printed, in order to be imposed upon the *Scots*, from which all our Troubles began.

But many more, and more strange, are the critical Junctures of Affairs in the Case of the Enemy, or at least more observed by me.

1. Sir *John Hotham*, who repulsed his Majesty and refused him Admittance into *Hull* before the War, was siezed at *Hull* by the same Parliament for whom he had done it, the same 10th Day of *August* two Years that he drew the first Blood in that War.

2. *Hambden* of *Buckinghamshire* killed the same Day one Year that the Mob Petition from *Bucks* was presented to the King about him, as one of the five Members.

3. Young Captain *Hotham* executed the 1st of *January*,

the same Day that he assisted Sir *Thomas Fairfax* in the first Skirmish with the King's Forces at *Bramham-Moor*.

4. The same Day and Month, being the 6th of *August* 1641, that the Parliament voted to raise an Army against the King, the same Day and Month, *Anno* 1648, the Parliament were assaulted and turned out of Doors by that very Army, and none left to sit but who the Soldiers pleased, which were therefore called the *Rump*.

5. The Earl of *Holland* deserted the King, who had made him General of the Horse, and went over to the Parliament, and the 9th of *March* 1641, carried the Commons reproaching Declaration to the King; and afterwards taking up Arms for the King against the Parliament, was beheaded by them the 9th of *March* 1648, just seven Years after.

6. The Earl of *Holland* was sent to by the King to come to his Assistance and refused, the 11th of *July* 1641, and that very Day seven Years after was taken by the Parliament at *St. Needs*.

7. Collonel *Massey* defended *Gloucester* against the King, and beat him off the 5th of *September* 1643, was after taken by *Cromwell*'s Men fighting for the King, on the 5th of *September* 1651, two or three Days after the Fight at *Worcester*.

8. *Richard Cromwell* resigning because he could not help it, the Parliament voted a free Commonwealth, without a single Person or House of Lords; this was the 25th of *May* 1658; the 25th of *May* 1660 the King landed at *Dover*, and restored the Government of a single Person and House of Lords.

9. *Lambert* was proclaimed a Traytor by the Parliament, *April* the 20th, being the same Day he proposed to *Oliver Cromwell* to take upon him the Title of King.

10. *Monk* being taken Prisoner at *Nantwich* by Sir *Thomas Fairfax*, revolted to the Parliament, the same Day nineteen Years he declared for the King, and thereby restored the Royal Authority.

11. The Parliament voted to approve of Sir *John Hotham*'s

repulsing the King at *Hull*, the 28th of *April* 1642; the 28th of *April* 1660, the Parliament first debated in the House the restoring the King to the Crown.

12. The Agitators of the Army formed themselves into a Cabal, and held their first Meeting to sieze on the King's Person, and take him into their Custody from *Holmby*, the 28th of *April* 1647; the same Day 1660, the Parliament voted the Agitators to be taken into Custody, and committed as many of them as could be found.

13. The Parliament voted the Queen a Traytor for assisting her Husband the King, *May* the 3d 1643; her Son King *Charles* II. was presented with the Votes of Parliament to restore him, and the Present of 50000 l. the 3d of *May* 1660.

14. The same Day the Parliament passed the Act for Recognition of *Oliver Cromwell*, *October* the 13th 1654, *Lambert* broke the Parliament and set up the Army 1659, *October* the 13th.

Some other Observations I have made, which as not so pertinent I forbear to publish, among which I have noted the Fatality of some Days to Parties, as,

The 2d of *September*, the Fight at *Dunbar*; the Fight at *Worcester*; the Oath against a single Person past; *Oliver*'s first Parliament called: For the Enemy.

The 2d of *September*, *Essex* defeated in *Cornwall*; *Oliver* died; City Works demolished: For the King.

The 29th of *May*, Prince *Charles* born; *Leicester* taken by Storm; King *Charles* II. restored: Ditto.

Fatality of Circumstances in this unhappy War, as,

1. The *English* Parliament call in the *Scots*, to invade their King, and are invaded themselves by the same *Scots*, in Defence of the King whose Case, and the Design of the Parliament the *Scots* had mistaken.

2. The *Scots*, who unjustly assisted the Parliament to

conquer their lawful Sovereign, contrary to their Oath of Allegiance, and without any Pretence on the King's Part, are afterwards absolutely conquered and subdued by the same Parliament they assisted.

3. The Parliament, who raised an Army to depose their King, deposed by the very Army they had raised.

4. The Army broke three Parliaments, and are at last broke by a free Parliament and all they had done by the Military Power, undone at once by the Civil.

5. Abundance of the Chief Men, who by their fiery Spirits involved the Nation in a Civil War, and took up Arms against their Prince, first or last met with Ruine or Disgrace from their own Party.

1. Sir *John Hotham* and his Son, who struck the first Stroke, both beheaded or hanged by the Parliament.

2. Major General *Massey* three times taken Prisoner by them, and once wounded at *Worcester*.

3. Major General *Langhorn*. 4. Collonel *Poyer*: And, 5. Collonel *Powell*, changed Sides, and at last taken, could obtain no other Favour than to draw Lots for their Lives; Collonel *Poyer* drew the Dead Lot, and was shot to Death.

6. Earl of *Holland*, who, when the House voted who should be reprieved, Lord *Goring*, who had been their worst Enemy, or the Earl of *Holland*, who, excepting one Offence, had been their constant Servant, voted *Goring* to be spared, and the Earl to die.

7. The Earl of *Essex*, their first General.

8. Sir *William Waller*.

9. Lieutenant General *Ludlow*.

10. The Earl of *Manchester*.

All disgusted and voted out of the Army, though they had stood the first Shock of the War, to make way for the new Model of the Army, and introduce a Party.

In all these Confusions I have observed two great Errors, one of the King, and one of his Friends.

Of the King, that when he was in their Custody, and at

their Mercy, he did not comply with their Propositions of Peace before their Army, for want of Employment, fell into Heats and Mutinies; that he did not at first grant the *Scots* their own Conditions, which, if he had done, he had gone into *Scotland*; and then, if the *English* would have fought the *Scots* for him, he had a Reserve of his loyal Friends, who would have had Room to have fallen in with the *Scots* to his Assistance, who were after dispersed and destroyed in small Parties attempting to serve him.

While his Majesty, remained at *Newcastle*, the Queen wrote to him, perswading him to make Peace upon any Terms; and in Politicks her Majesty's Advice was certainly the best: For, however low he was brought by a Peace, it must have been better than the Condition he was then in.

The Error I mention of the King's Friends was this, that after they saw all was lost, they could not be content to sit still, and reserve themselves for better Fortunes, and wait the happy Time when the Divisions of the Enemy would bring them to certain Ruin; but must hasten their own Miseries by frequent fruitless Risings, in the Face of a victorious Enemy, in small Parties, and I always found these Effects from it.

1. The Enemy, who were always together by the Ears, when they were let alone, were united and reconciled when we gave them any Interruption; as particularly, in the Case of the first Assault the Army made upon them, when Collonel *Pride*, with his Regiment garbled[1] the House, as they called it, at that Time, a fair Opportunity offered; but it was omitted till it was too late: That Insult upon the House had been attempted the Year before, but was hindered by the little Insurrections of the Royal Party, and the sooner they had fallen out, the better.

2. These Risings being desperate, with vast Disadvantages, and always suppressed, ruined all our Friends; the Remnants of the Cavaliers were lessened, the stoutest and most daring were cut off, and the King's Interest exceedingly weakened, there not being less than Thirty Thousand of his

best Friends cut off in the several Attempts made at *Maidstone*, *Colchester*, *Lancashire*, *Pembrook*, *Pontfract*, *Kingston*, *Preston*, *Warrington*, *Worcester*, and other Places. Had these Men all reserved their Fortunes to a Conjunction with the *Scots*, at either of the Invasions they made into this Kingdom, and acted with the Conduct and Courage they were known Masters of, perhaps neither of those *Scots* Armies had been defeated.

But the Impatience of our Friends ruin'd all; for my Part, I had as good a Mind to put my Hand to the Ruine of the Enemy as any of them, but I never saw any tolerable Appearance of a Force able to match the Enemy, and I had no Mind to be beaten, and then hanged. Had we let them alone, they would have fallen into so many Parties and Factions, and so effectually have torn one another to Pieces, that which soever Party had come to us, we should, with them, have been too hard for all the rest.

This was plain by the Course of Things afterwards, when the Independant Army had ruffled the Presbyterian Parliament, the Soldiery of that Party made no Scruple to join us, and would have restored the King with all their Hearts, and many of them did join us at last.

And the Consequence, though late, ended so; for they fell out so many times, *Army* and *Parliament*, *Parliament* and *Army*, and alternately pulled one another down so often, till at last the Presbyterians, who began the War, ended it; and, to be rid of their Enemies, rather than for any Love to the Monarchy, restored King *Charles* the Second, and brought him in on the very Day that they themselves had formerly resolved the Ruine of his Father's Government, being the 29th of *May*, the same Day 20 Year that the private Cabal in *London* concluded their Secret League with the *Scots*, to embroil his Father King *Charles* the First.

been Friends cut off in the several Attempts made at Mark-
now, Colchester, Lancashire, Pembroke, Pontract, Kingston,
Surrey, Warrington, Wocester, and other Places, Had these
Men all reserved their Fortunes to a Conjunction with the
Scots at either of the Invasions they made into this Kingdom,
and acted with the Conduct and Courage they were known
Masters of, perhaps neither of those Scots Armies had been
defeated.

But the Impatience of our Friends ruin'd all; for my Part,
I had as good a Mind to put my Hand to the Ruine of the
Enemy as any of them, but I never saw any tolerable Appearance of a Force able to match the Enemy, and I had no Mind
to be beaten, and then hang'd: Had we let them alone, they
would have fallen into so many Parties and Factions, and so
effectually have torn one another to Pieces, that which
soever Party had come to us, we should, with them, have
been too hard for all the rest.

This was plain by the Course of Things afterwards, when
the Independent Army had ruffled the Presbyterian Parliament; the Soldiery of that Party made no Scruple to join us,
and would have restored the King, with all their Hearts;
and many of them did join us at last.

And the Consequence, though late, ended so; for they fell
out so many ways, Army and Parliament, Parliament and
Army, and alternately pulled one another down so often, till
at last the Presbyterians, who began the War, ended it; and,
to be rid of their Enemies, rather than for any Love to the
Monarchy, restored King Charles the Second, and brought
him in on the very Day that they themselves had formerly
resolved the Ruine of his Father's Government, using the
20th of May, the same Day 20 Year that the private Cabal
in London committed their Secret League with the Scots, to
embroil his Father King Charles the First.

APPENDIX

I. EXTRACTS FROM

The Swedish Intelligencer

The Battell of Leipsich
i. 121–25

Upon the fatall seaventh of *September* therefore being Wednesday, [Tilly] with 44000 brave men, in goodly order of battell first takes the field; which was upon a fayre plaine or heath (about a mile from *Leipsich*) called *Gods Aker*: sayd to be the very same place, wher the Emperor *Charles* the 5 heretofore overthrew the Duke of *Saxony*. *Tilly* like a prudent General, being carefull for all advantages, had placed himselfe upon a little hill thereabouts, (where the place of execution is,) having a wood also to hide his men, and for their retreate . . .

The King of *Sweden* having prepared his Army by prayers unto God, and encouragements to his men the day before, upon the same Wednesday morning before day, he advances from *Dieben* towards the place of battell. His owne Troupes were some 18000: and the Duke of *Saxonie*, together with the Marquis of *Brandenburg* some 20000 or 22000 . . .

Being now ready to come unto the Shocke; the Battels were thus ordered, *Tilly* made choice of the ancient order, to fight in great square bodies, himselfe leading now the right wing, the Duke of *Holsteyn* the left, and the Count of *Furstenburg* the *Battaile*. The King dividing his men into many smaller bodies; takes the right wing to himselfe, committing the left unto the Duke of *Saxonie* and his men: the wings of either battaile, tooke up two *English* miles in length . . . The fight was about 12 a clocke, first begun with their Canon, for that purpose placed before every division. Their roare made the very earth to tremble, and men to groane their last; for two houres together: about which time, the Generall *Tilly* drawing out of the wood, passes by the Kings wing, (which had also gotten one end of the same wood) and set amaine upon the Duke of *Saxonie*. Two charges the *Saxons* endured well enough: but the Enemie having direc-

tion to laye hardest upon the Dukes owne Guards (amongst
whom himselfe fought;) they not able longer to endure it, begin
to give ground a little. The rest of the *Saxons* now perceiving
their Duke, and bravest men thus to retyre, thinke all lost; and
all in confusion away they flie, leaving 3 Canons to the mercy of
the Enemie; and pillaging their owne wagons by the way: that
so they might at least seeme to be Conquerors; in carrying home
spoiles of the warres, though not of their Enemies. Yet all fled
not; for the Lord *Arnheym* (Field-Marshall to the Duke, and an
old Souldier) together with Colonel *Bindauff*, *Done*, and *Vitz-
thimb*, with their 4 Regiments, bravely yet stood unto it. *Steinau*,
a Colonell of Horse, was with 4 Cornets taken prisoner by the
Enemie; who at length perceiving the Kings partie to prevaile,
brake through the Enemie, and assisted his owne side. The
Imperialists now seeing the *Saxons* flying, cry *Victoria*, *Victoria*,
follow, *follow*, *follow*: but the old Lad their Generall quickly
countermaunded that; saying, *Let them goe*, *wee shall overtake
them time enough: but let us beate the* Swede *too*, *and then all*
Germany *is our owne*. In this medlie, *Furstenberg* with his old
Regiment of *Italian* Horse, having charged quite thorow the
Saxons, was now comming upon the *Swedens* backe: which they
perceiving, with such resolution second his charge, and follow
their owne, that they chase him almost an *English* mile from the
place, so utterly cutting off & dispersing the whole Regiment,
that they could not recover it all that battell: and here perchance
himselfe was slaine . . .

   By this time the King having notice of the Duke of *Saxonies*
leaving the field, and that *Tilly* was ready to charge his battaile:
presently drawes out 2000 commaunded Muskettiers of the
brave *Scottish* Nation led by Colonel *Havord*, they having some
2000 horse upon their flancks: to stave off the enemie a while.
The *Scots* ordering themselves in severall small *battagliaes*,
about 6 or 700 in a body, presently now double their rankes,
making their files then but 3 deepe (the discipline of the King of
Sweden being, never to march above 6 deepe) this done, the
formost rancke falling on their knees; the second stooping
forward; and the third rancke standing right up; and all giving
fire together, they powred so much lead at one instant in amongst
the enemies horse, that their ranckes were much broken with
it . . . *Tilly* came, and conjoyned himselfe unto the valiant Baron

of *Cronenberg*. This bold Baron and his Regiment serving in the right wing, had 4 times in those 4 houres, charged the Kings Forces: and hee at last, when no more could be done, bravely carried away his Generall, in the midst of his owne (now flying) Troupes . . .

Had the King had but 3 houres more of day light, scarcely had 1000 Enemies come off alive: but the darkenes which was safest for them to flie, being not so for him to pursue; the joyfull retreate is sounded, and the chace given over for that night.

ii. 11–16

The King thus in possession of the Towne, could not yet thinke himselfe Master of it; so long as the Castle of *Marienburg* (for so is it called) could at pleasure beate it about his eares. This peece is mounted upon so high a hill, as was to be commanded from no other ground: it having the Towne below at the foote of it. And as strongly was it fortified by Art, as advantageously situated by nature. The hill is a maine rocke; whereof one side is craggie and barren, and the other covered with vines: the whole tope of the little mountaine being crowned with the Castle, and with the ditches and out-works of it. Nor wanted here any inward fortifications; 800 or 1000 fighting men, being therein Garrison. And as for victuals, money and Ammunition, *Troy* it selfe was not better provided for its ten yeares siege, then this Fort was . . .

All that night and the next two dayes, did the Ordnance thunder from the Castle; & for as long a time were the garrison kept in continuall Action and Alarmes: a *besieged enemy* being like an *unmade Hawke*, to be *reclaymed* with *watching*. The *Trenches* or *Lines* being finished, the King commands Sir *John Hamilton* and Sir *Iames Ramsye* to fall on with their Regiments: for if a Fort be to be *stormed*, or any desperate peice of service to be set upon; the *Scottish* have hitherto had the honour and the danger, to be the first men that are put upon such a businesse. This *Halfe-moone* therefore upon the vineyards side, right before the bridge (which was over the moate of the Castle) doe the *Scottish* now full resolutely fall upon: the defendants likewise for two houres together (as 'tis said) as stoutly fighting for their worke . . .

An inestimable masse of treasure, which lay hid in a Cave or cleft of the Rocke. The chiefe of the slaine and prisoners, were rifled and stripped by the conquerors: and the Castle for one houre, permitted to the pillage: where an unvaluable booty was obtained by the Souldiers. Here was found about 34 peices of brasse Ordnance; some of which had the *Palsgrave Frederickes* Armes upon them. Many a hundred wayne-load of wine there was: with Ammunition, and some kind of victuals for the Bishops Court, enough (if it would have kept) for 20 yeares provision for such a garrison . . . A Palace it was, for any Prince in *Christendome*: which having beene something defaced by the Cannon, the King caused to be forthwith repaired; and with new fortifications to be made much the stronger. The Towne redeemed itself from pillaging, by the payment of 4 tunne of Gold; or of 300000 *Florens*, as others reckon it: So that the King and his Souldiers, never went so rich away from any place. Here was found a princely stable of goodly Horses; with which the King was very much delighted.

ii. 46–47

Wee left the King lately marching towards *Oppenheim*: where he yet lay, within Canon-shot (almost) of the very walls of it. Summons had already been given unto the towne: which, upon the taking of the Fort, sends out their keyes, and yeelds gladly enough unto his Majesty: and for that they knew him to be a friend unto the Prince Elector their Lord and Master, they receive in a garrison of 200 *Scots* unto them. These 200, were all (or almost all) that were left of Sir *Iames Ramsyes* Regiment: himselfe lay yet at *Wurtsburg* to be cured of his wound, which there (as we told you) he received. Upon an hill, a little above the edge of the towne, was there a large vast Castle with a garrison of 600 or 700 men in it; which yet stood out against the King. There having been 107 boates found under the Towne wall, upon the river; of these the King sends over enow, to fetch *Winckles* Regiment first, and *Hepburnes* after him: with the Cannon, baggage and Cavallery last of all. The streame carrying downe *Hepburn* and *Winckle* something lower then the towne; they upon their landing advance up the hill, to meete the Kings Forces: whom they now saw standing in faire *Battaglia*, ready to give a generall assault upon the Castle. And now those 200 *Scots* that had beene put into the towne at the yeelding of it; fall immediately thereupon to *Storme* the said Castle at the townport which is betwixt the Castle and the Towne. The *Scots* fell in with such a tempest and resolution, that they instantly force the garrison into the inner port; they *Storming* in together with them: so that by that time the King was ready to assault on one side, and *Hepburn* on the other; they meete (to their great admiration,) divers of the garrison that had already leapt over the walls, throwne away their Armes, and crying *Quarter*; as the rest also now did, that had not yet gotten out of the Castle.

ii. 76–82

Upon Thursday Febr. 16. he first sets forward to *Creutzenach* . . . The first view the King tooke of the Towne, was upon the lowest side; and where he had thought to have begun: but that he found so well fortified with Outworkes, Seconds, and Retreats, one worke within another, that he call'd them the *Divels workes*. He quickly discovered, that there was no attempting that way: yea judged by the best souldiours it was, that it could not have beene a businesse of lesse than a fortnight or three weekes time, to have mastered all these works, and so to have come at the Towne. Altering his course therefore, and deviding his little Army into two parts, hee by faire day light brings them on by another side, and lodges them within Musket shot, or 150 pases of the very walles: yea Lieftenant Colonell *George Douglasse* (a brave souldiour then newly come up to the King) having first runne his lines, sets himselfe downe with some three hundred men, (the most of them being the same *Scottish* that had *stormed Oppenheim* Castle even in the very Port. Here lay *Douglasse* all the night following: notwithstanding the place were so hot, that the enemy kill'd him some 47 men, with their shooting upon him; both from the walles, and Port above him . . .

Colonel *Winckle* commanding in Chiefe over the foot; three Captaines of his Regiment with some 350 men, and divers *English* and *French* Gentlemen voluntiers, came first into the breach: among all which, my Lord *Craven*, Lieftenant-Colonell *Talbot*, Master *Robert Marsham* and Master *Henry Wind*, marched in the first File. The Hill was so steepe where they approached, that the enemy by darting downe of Partisans and Halberts, casting downe of great stones, flinging of Fire-brands, and rowling downe of great pieces of Timber, forced the assay-lants unto a retreate . . . The King, (then at the Foote of the Hill) perceiving his men to be beaten off; call them *Pultrons*, and all to be-cowardied them: presently commanding the skaling-ladders to be in another place, set unto the Rampier of the *Ravelin*. And heere his Majesty having taken notice of the valour of my Lord *Craven*, in a familiar and encouraging manner claps him upon the Shoulder, bidding him to goe on againe. The young Lord did so: and was the very first man, that gained up to the top; where he valiantly came to push of pike with the enemy: himself receiving an honorable wound with the thrust of an Halbert in his thigh; which was not found to be dangerous. Those of our *English* Gentlemen before named, behaved themselves right couragiously; being next unto my Lord *Craven*, and in the very heate of the danger. And this was the manner of the fight, for two houres together almost; the defendants bearing themselves like tall Souldiours. At last, the *High-Dutch* being in mutiny with the *Wallons* and *Burgundians*, (who were resolved to defend the place) one of the enemies began to speake of Quarter, and of Termes of yeelding: which the Lord *Craven* (who was still the formest man) wisely apprehending; reaches out his hand unto one of the enemies Captaines, and undertooke upon his honour to bring him to the King. The enemies Muskets hereupon gave over playing.

ii. 142–47

The place resolved upon, was betwixt *Rain* and *Thierhaubten*; just upon a point of land: made so, by the crooking or bending of the River. The ground on the Kings side, was a pikes length higher banckt, and playner withall, then that on *Tillyes*: which was both lower, and wooddy. There was a tryall made first of all, to lay a floate-bridge; but the River would not endure that: for notwithstanding it be not above thirty or forty paces over at the most, yet by reason of the straight course of it, the streame sets very swift and violent.

All the materials being now prepared; the King about nine at night, upon the fourth of *Aprill*, advances some 1000 *Commanded men*, unto the place aforesaid. Two houres after, they begin to worke a *running Trench* round about the crooked banke of the River, that the Muskettiers out of that, might with more security give fire into the Wood on the other side of the River. This *Line* or *Trench*, had a great Battery at each end of it, for halfe and quarter Cannon: together with many lesser *Battereyes* betweene, all along about the *Point*, for the smaller field pieces to play upon. which were every-where intermingled with Muskettiers also. Whilest the Pioners are thus a working, the King in divers other places (both above it and below) gives false fires and Alarms, both with Muskets and smaller fielding peeces, for to amuse the enemy; that till the morning they could not imagine where to find him.

By sixe on the Thursday morning, Aprill 5. was this worke finished, the Cannon mounted, the Arches or Tressels for the bridge, with the planckes and other materialls, all brought; and ready to be laide into the River. These Tressels, were to have great stones or weights tyed unto their legges, to sinke them withall; and were to be no longer, then to reach just unto the bottome of the River, so that the planckes were to lye even almost with the very Water. The longest Tressels were about foure yards long: which were for the channell of the River. By that time it was day-light, General *Tilly* begins to perceive the Kings designe, and falls to worke against him in the Wood: whose Pioners when the King heard chopping downe the trees, he gave order immediately unto his men, to give them a *Salvee* or a *Good morrow* (as he cald it) both with their Cannon and their Muskets. About 8 a clocke the same morning, the King in two small Boats that he had, send over the *Swedes* and *Fins* his Pioners and Carpenters, unto the other side of the River. The designe was, to have them make up a small *Halfe-moone*, with a *Stocket* or *Pallisadoe* unto it: which should both answer that small worke that *Tilly* had made for his Muskettiers to lodge in, almost right before the said point of the River: and to cover the Bridge withall, from the greater shot: which this *Halfe-moone* still latched. The *Fins* and *Swedes* laboured upon the worke, and made good the place; till that about 4 a clock in the afternoone, both it was finished and they relieved.

The King all this while, is diligent in laying over his bridge, and *Tilly* as busie to raise up Batteryes to beate it downe againe. The King himselfe stird not all that night, nor the next day, from the very end of the bridge: nor the King of *Bohemia* from him, for the most part. *Tilly* upon the edge of the thicket, close unto the River, raises up a *Trench* first, to lodge his Muskettiers in, as we told you: and about Musket shot further within the wood, gives order for the making of a very great *Worke*: that if the King should put over his bridge, he might by power of that *Worke*, and by cutting downe of the trees about it; have beene able (at least) to have hindred his further passage. The small and great shot, goe off incessantly on both sides all this while; and they continue thus with extreme hot execution upon one another, till about eleven a clocke at noone the same day. About which time, the General *Altringer* with the shot of a Field-peece (which grased upon his temples) was spoyled and carryed off in the Duke of *Bavariaes* owne Coach . . .

The *Bavarian* Captaines found this so hot a service; that *Tilly* himselfe was enforced to come up to the point, and into the very face of the danger, to give directions: where within halfe an houre after *Altringers* mis-chance; he also received a Musket shot in the thigh a little above the knee, which prooved a mortall wound unto him. This fatall accident of this brave old Generall, did so amaze, not the Common souldiours alone, but the Duke of *Bavaria* himselfe also; (who now staid behind in the groave with the Infantery:) that so soone as ever the sad news was brought unto him, notwithstanding he were *Generalissimo* over the whole Forces; yet he instantly tooke horse upon it, posted with all speed into *Ingolstat*; not staying so much as to give order, either for the continuing of the begun designe, or for the marching away of the army.

Tilly being carryed off, and the Duke gone: the afternoone is spent on the Kings side, as the forenoone had beene; which was with uncessant thunders and volleyes of small and great shot. Among the *Bavarians*, those that understood of the spoyling of their two Generalls, and the flight of the Duke, by degrees and disorder, they one after another retreated from their Charge: whilest others that knew not of it, stoutly maintained the encounter. Little dreamt the King of it all this while: whose men still continue their working. By foure in the afternoone, is the bridge finisht: as 2 houres after, the little *Halfe-moone* and *Pallisadoe* also are, on the other side of the water before the end of the bridge. This done, the Kings owne Company of his *Life-guards* is sent over the bridge, for the manning of the *Halfe-moone*; for feare the enemy should have fallen upon it. In the beginning of the night, other of the *Bavarians* begin to retire, and to draw off their Ordnance; and that in such haste, that they forgot to command off their *Out-guards*, which lay all along upon the side of the River.

The next morning, the King sends over a Partee of some thirty *Scottish* Muskettiers commanded by Captaine *Forbes*, to see what the *Bavarians* were doing in the Wood; for that he had lately heard no more of them. Here could *Forbes* find but two *Horse-Sentryes* upon the edge of the Wood; whom he tooke prisoners: who, when they were brought unto the King, protested that they were ignorant of the retreate of the rest of their fellowes.

But to returne a little backe. The King not knowing of *Tillyes* wounding, or the Dukes fleeing; durst not adventure that evening to put his forces over the bridge: but spends the rest of the night in drawing up his army before it. This being done, order is given unto the Infantery or foote, to march over in the first place: and of all them Sir *Iohn Hepburn* with his *Brigade* was to have the honor of the *Vant-guard*; The King understanding by *Forbes* of this great and unhoped for newes; he alters thereupon all his former intended resolution; commanding the next morning, Aprill sixth, 500 Horse first, and 300 more after them, to passe over into the *Bavarian* forsaken Quarters. The first 500 being advanced thorow the Wood, and into the plaine beyond it; there cut downe a many of the *Bavarian* straglers, that had beene too slow in following of their fellowes. Some other *Swedish* troopes are instantly also commanded towards *Rain*; which though *Tilly* had left reasonably well fortified, yet this former feare amongst his party, made it nothing so resistable to the *Swedish*. They presently entring the Towne, find some wagons, and many horses, ready laden with the enemies goods; which are made good booty: but the Towne paying 30000 dollars to the King, are freed from pillaging. This was the first Towne, that the King tooke in *Bavaria*. There was it understood, that both the Duke of *Bavaria*, and the two wounded Generalls, parted the night before towards *Newburg*; whither they first retired: and from thence with as many of their Army as were then comme to them, unto *Ingolstat*.

To returne to the King and his *Leaguer*. The rest of that Fryday, Aprile sixth, is spent in the marching over of more Horse, and of three *Brigades* of *Infantery*: together with most of the Artillery. The Infantery already marcht over, encampt that night upon the edge of the plaine, a little without the Wood: the rest that were left behind, sitting downe just before the bridge.

And now for that such as are skilled in the Arts of war, will desire to be satisfied with the *reason*, as well as to heare the *successe* of the *Action* (in which oftentimes *Chance* may have as great a share, as *Wisedome*:) we will therefore affoard them a briefe discourse upon the Kings great *Iudgement*, as well as we have done the relation of his fortune.

The reason of the Kings putting over his bridge at this place was, that hee might have the better conveniency, both by flanckering it on either side to defend it from the annoyance of the enemy; and that being as it was, just upon the Point: it could not be touched by *Tillyes* batteryes, which were on each hand of the bridge, though he very often removed his Cannon to that purpose. For notwithstanding *Tilly* had (with as much judgement and advantage as possibly might be) raised his Batteryes, not cloase unto the Rivers side, but at a distance from the banke: yet were all his shot so kept off by the round and sudden shouldering away of the banke of the River at either end, that his Ordnance could not possibly come to beare upon the bridge: but that either the bullets fell short and were latcht by the little *Half-moone*, or hill upon the high banke above the bridge; or else flew quite over the whole leaguer. As for the raising of a Battery right before the face of the point; that could not *Tilly* on the sudden come to doe: for besides that he was hindered by the wood; the fury of the Kings both small and great shot, would at so neere a distance have spoild him as many men, as had adventured upon the service: and the Kings Batteryes being first up, would not suffer *Tilly* to mount any of his Cannon right before him.

And yet for all this, there appeares to be more then a humane direction in it: seeing the King was made constant against all the minds and judgements of his greatest Commanders. For when the day before, he asked the advice of his ablest Generalls; and they, notwithstanding they saw him so farre already engaged in the action, as he could not come off with his honor; had freely (all of them) professed their utter dislike of the designe: yet did the King plainly tell them, that he continued against all their reasons, constant unto his owne purpose. Yea, there appeares not onely a more then humane *direction*, but a *benediction* also, in the easinesse of the attaining of the passage: which very much exceeded all the Kings owne hopes of it. For when the day before he perceived *Tilly* to begin to worke against him; he apprehended so much danger in his owne designe, that should he loose but 2000 men in winning of his passage, he should thinke (as he confessed) that he had made a thrifty purchase of his entrance into *Bavaria*. When the next day (in like manner) that himself being marcht over with the Horse, had with his owne eyes perceived how sufficiently *Tilly* was providing to entertaine him; he blest himselfe for his good successe in it: saying to the King of *Bohemia*, and divers of his Commanders then about him; *That this dayes actions was neere of as great a consequence, as that of Leipsich* . . .

And yet, for all this, had not the King escaped so cheape, as with the lives of two thousand brave men; had not *He* that directed *Davids sling-stone* into *Goliahs* forehead, guided one bullet unto *Altringers* forehead, and another into *Tillyes* thighbone; had not this brave old Count beene thus spoyled, the King had found but an unfriendly well-come into *Bavaria*, from the second and greater *Worke*, which *Tilly* had laboured upon, from sixe in the morning to eleven, but not yet finished. That worke, I meane, which is before mentioned in the wood.

ii. 166–69

About Aprill 27, are *Gustave Horn* and Sir *Iohn Hepburn*, sent with 3000 Horse and 5000 Foote; to take in *Landshut*: a very dainty little Towne upon the River *Iser* (though the glory of it be chiefly in two Streets) some eight *English* miles to the North-East of *Mosburg*. At the first comming of the *Swedish* forces before the walls, one of their Lieftenants of a troope of Horse, with some few others of his Cornet, were shot from an Ambush in the gardens . . .

The Towne paid 100000 Dollars to the King for its ransome; and gave *Gustavus Horn* 20000 besides, for a gratuity . . .

Upon Munday in the forenoone, May 7th, the King shewed himself in faire Battaglia before [Munich]: although by that time he were come within a *Dutch* mile: the Deputies had againe met him, and there presented the towne keyes unto him, with a promise of 300000 Dollars . . .

The next day, the King went to see the Magazine and Armories; where great store of armes and ammunition were found, but no Ordnance; at which the King not a little wondering; espied by and by divers of the carriages; by which he guessed, as the truth was, that the peeces were buried under-ground. These *dead ones* (as he cald them) he caused the Boores with ropes and leavers, to raise up without a miracle. There were 140 faire Peeces of brasse Ordnance; and in one, 30000 pieces of gold, said to be found. Among the rest, were 12 eminent ones; by the Duke called the 12 *Apostles*: though surely the *Apostles* were never such *Sonnes of Thunder*. Some peeces had the *Palsgraves* Armes upon them; which caused the King of *Bohemia* both to sigh and smile, at the sight of them. But the *Kunst-Cammer*, or *Chamber of Rarities*, was the thing that affoorded most entertainment: where the beholders admired rather, then lookt upon, the incomparable varieties and curiosities, both of *Art* and *Nature* . . .

iii. 17–23

The King, towards the 20. of *July*, hearing of a Convoye of *Walensteins*, that was to come out of the nether parts of *Austria* towards his Leaguer: sends out Colonel *Wippenherst*, with a Partee of 800. Horse, and as many Dragooners; to cut off that Convoye. With these 1600 did *Wippenherst* light upon 800. wagons laden with ammunition, and with Gunnes especially: which he destroyed.

About the 27. of *July*, a Partee of *Swedish* Horse, tooke one Captaine *Darmis* prisoner, amongst other Free-booters. He being examined by the King upon his oath, confessed that *Walensteins* great Magazine of victuals was at *Freyenstat*: which was the place appointed for whatsoever came from *Ratisbone*, and the *Upper Palatinate*, untill it were sent for to the Leaguer; which, within 3. or 4. dayes, a strong Convoye was about to goe for. The advantage of this opportunity, the King thought worth the taking: resolving with the first to send either to bring away the provisions, or to destroy that which was to feede his enemies . . .

The leader that the King made choise of to doe the feate, was Colonell *Dubatell*: whom *Walenstein* had lately taken prisoner, and againe released; as we before told you, The Colonel knew the Countrey thereabouts, perfectly well: for it was not farre from thence, that he was taken prisoner. The troopes appointed to goe with him, I find to be 14. Cornets of Horse, some troopes of Dragooners, and 2. Wagons laden with Petards, Storming or Skaling ladders, &c. With these, comes he unto *Karnbergh* first;

2 *Dutch* miles from *Freyenstat*. His season and march he so proportioned, as that he might be before the towne he went unto, before day-light, upon the Munday morning *July* 30. He did so: and found most of the souldiers and townesmen, very securely sleeping: for who would have suspected, that the King of *Swedens* smaller Army, being beseiged as it were, by two greater; durst have presumed to send twenty miles off to surprize *Freyenstat*.

Dubatel, at his first comming before the Towne; surprises some drowsie Sentinells: and hangs 2. Petards upon the Sally-port. These not blowing open the gate, as he expected; he fearing the noyse of their going off, would send in the Alarme into the Towne; claps his skaling ladders to the naked and un-man'd walls; which he mounts and enters. Other Petards being by this time put to worke, had forced open the gate; and made an easie passage that way, for the residue of the *Swedish*. They thus gotten in, cut in pieces those few souldiers, which they found either sleeping or unprovided, upon the next Courts of Guard, and whosoever else, offered to make resistance. Having thus mastered all opposition, they make towards the Towne-Hall; which was the Magazine or Store-house they came thither for. There were in it, at this present, 200000. pound weight of bread; great store of Meale, Corne, salt, and other provisions; sufficient for 2 moneths victuals for *Walensteins* whole Army. For the bringing of all this unto the Emperiall Leaguer, were there 1000 Wagons provided: many of them already prest, and some laden, or, not yet unladen, upon the Market place. Many hundred head both of small and great Catell, were likewise found about the towne: which were to be driven alive unto the Imperiall Army. Of these provisions, the *Swedish* first of all choosing out so much, as they thought themselves well able to carry away: set fire immediately unto the Magazine . . . Twelve hundred Sheepe and Oxen, with 500 horses, they also driving away with them . . .

Some of the Imperial souldiers (it seemes) so soone as the *Swedes* were gotten into the towne; went Post with the newes of it unto *Walenstein*. Which he hearing of; immediately the same day dispatches the Sergeant-Major Generall of his Foot; towards *Freyenstat*: either to save the residue; or to cut off *Dubatell* in his comming home againe. It was Colonell *Sparre* that was now sent . . .

The King of *Sweden* to prevent such a matter, and the better to secure the retreate unto *Dubatel*; goes himselfe out the same day, before *Dubatel* was comme home with a selected Partee of some 2000. commanded men, towards the said *Freyenstat* . . .

Not many charges passed betwixt the King and the enemies Horse; but that the face of the skirmish began to be altered: insomuch that the Imperiall Horse and *Crabats*; were (to be briefe) quite rowted and defeated . . . *Sparre* himself was taken prisoner: 600 of his men, were slaine upon the place: and divers more drowned and buried alive, in the river and moorish places, thorow which they thought to have escaped . . .

After this victory, there (for a while) passed nothing of moment, between the two Armies. The pettier skirmishes betweene commanded Partees abroad, or the continued night-alarmes upon one anothers Camps or Guards at home; I list not to stand upon.

iii. 39–44

Wallenstein perceiving the Kings intention, he the better to assure his Cannon and Ammunition; retired himselfe into the Forest called *Altemberg*: which belongeth unto the Marquesse of *Onspach*. Here could he make use, likewise, of a certaine old Fortresse; which had beene a Lodge, (or some such like thing) in the younger dayes of it. Here, likewise, did he very strongly entrench himselfe; and barricadoed up all the wayes, by cutting downe the trees round about him. The hill was high, and very steepe: craggie withall, and bushie; so that it was an impossible thing (almost) to be taken from an enemy, that had any courage to dispute it . . .

And now began the conflict, for the winning and defending of that old Castle; which proved a medlye of 10 houres long, on both sides. Many a brave Gentleman, here lost his life; many a Cavalier was here wounded: and not a few taken prisoners. The King led on his men, with his sworde drawne in his hand: and the *Swedish*, as if to show the enemy how little they dreaded any thing, that they could doe unto them; and how much they despised danger: exposed themselves all naked unto the enemies shot; having not so much as any one Trench or Earth cast up, to shelter them. In this equipage, runne they close unto the enemies Works and Batteries: stoutly and manfully, fall they upon them; and with the courage of undaunted spirit, doe they rush into the danger. But the Imperialists as full of resolution, made a most stout resistance unto the *Swedish*. For having the advantage, both of the higher ground, of their owne Trenches and Batteries already before hand there cast up: and having the wals of the old Castle to retreate unto, and to shelter their fresh supplies in: they maintained it with extremity confidence . . .

Thus at length, the *Swedes* seeing no good to be done upon it: were enforced to quit the danger; the most of them withdrawing themselves, unto the foote of the Mountaine . . . The *Swedish*, for all their magnanimous undertakings, could not drive the Imperialists to the retreat; or beate up their Quarters: nor could they, much lesse, compell the Kings forces to give it over.

II. EXTRACTS FROM WHITELOCKE'S

Memorials

i. *398*

. . . having several times attempted the taking of Shrewsbury, but failed therein, on the last Lord's-day about twelve hundred horse and foot, under colonel Mitton, marched to Shrewsbury, and unexpectedly entered and surprised the town and castle.

They took there eight knights and baronets, forty colonels, majors, captains, and others of quality, and two hundred others, prisoners, one captain and five soldiers slain, fifteen pieces of ordnance taken, store of arms and ammunition, prince Maurice's magazine, divers carriages, bag and baggage of the prince's.

i. *441*

The king's forces having made their batteries stormed Leicester; those within made stout resistance, but some of them betrayed one of the gates; the women of the town laboured in making up the breaches, and in great danger.

The king's forces having entered the town, had a hot encounter in the market-place; and many of them were slain by shot out of the windows. That they gave no quarter, but hanged some of the committee, and cut others in pieces. Some letters said that the kennels ran down with blood.

That colonel Gray the governor and captain Hacker were wounded and taken prisoners, and very many of the garrison put to the sword, and the town miserably plundered.

Fairfax sent out Ireton with a flying party of horse, who fell upon a party of the king's rear quartered in Naseby town, took many prisoners, some of the prince's lifeguard, and Langdale's brigade.

This gave such an alarm to the whole army, that the king at midnight leaves his own quarters, and for security hastens to Harborough, where the van of his army was quartered, raiseth prince Rupert, and calls a council of war.

There it was resolved (and chiefly by prince Rupert's eagerness, old commanders being much against it) to give battle: and because Fairfax had been so forward, they would no longer stay for him, but seek him out. Fairfax was come from Gilborough to Gilling, and from thence to Naseby, where both armies drawn up in battalia faced each other.

The king commanded the main body of his army, prince Rupert and prince Maurice the right wing, sir Marmaduke Langdale the left, the earl of Lindsey and the lord Ashley the right hand reserve, the lord Bard and sir George L'Isle the left reserve.

Of the parliament's army Fairfax and Skippon commanded the main body, Cromwell the right wing, with whom was Rosseter, and they both came in but a little before the fight: Ireton commanded the left wing, the reserves were brought up by Rainsborough, Hammond, and Pride.

Prince Rupert began, and charged the parliament's left wing with great resolution; Ireton made gallant resistance, but at last was forced to give ground, he himself being run through the thigh with a pike and into the face with a halberd, and his horse shot under him, and himself taken prisoner.

Prince Rupert follows the chase almost to Naseby town, and in his return summoned the train, who made no other answer but by their firelocks; he also visited the carriages, where was good plunder, but his long stay so far from the main body was no small prejudice to the king's army.

In the mean time Cromwell charged furiously on the king's left wing, and got the better, forcing them from the body, and, prosecuting the advantage, quite broke them and their reserve.

During which, the main bodies had charged one another with incredible fierceness, often retreating and rallying, falling in

together with the but-ends of their muskets, and coming to hand blows with their swords.

Langdale's men having been in some discontent before, did not in this fight behave themselves as they used to do in others, as their own party gave it out of them; yet they did their parts, and the rest of the king's army, both horse and foot, performed their duties with great courage and resolution, both commanders and soldiers.

Some of the parliament horse having lingered a while about pillage, and being in some disadvantage, Skippon perceiving it, brought up his foot seasonably to their assistance, and in this charge (as himself related it to me) was shot in the side.

Cromwell coming in with his victorious right wing, they all charged together upon the king, who, unable to endure any longer, got out of the field towards Leicester.

Prince Rupert, who now too late returned from his improvident eager pursuit, seeing the day lost, accompanied them in their flight, leaving a complete victory to the parliamentarians, who had the chase of them for fourteen miles, within two miles of Leicester; and the king finding the pursuit so hot, left that town, and hastes to Litchfield.

This battle was won and lost as that of Marston-Moor, but proved more destructive to the king and his party; and it was exceeding bloody, both armies being very courageous and numerous, and not five hundred odds on either side.

It was fought in a large fallow field, on the north-west side of Naseby, about a mile broad, which space of ground was wholly taken up.

i. 495

Letters from the Scots army before Hereford inform of their proceedings at the leaguer; of their want of money, ammunition, and provisions; that the country will bring in none, and the Scots soldiers feed upon apples, peas, and green wheat, which is unwholesome.

i. 518

. . . the king with about five thousand horse and foot, advanced to relieve Chester; major-general Pointz pursued close after the king, and within two miles of Chester engaged with the king's whole body, was at the first worsted, but made good his ground upon the retreat.

In the meantime colonel Jones, with five hundred horse, and adjutant-general Louthian, came from the leaguer before Chester to the assistance of Pointz, giving notice of their coming by shooting off two great guns; and by that time Pointz had rallied his forces; then Pointz in the front and Jones in the rear charged, and utterly routed the king's whole body.

The king, with about three hundred horse, fled into Chester; and the pursuit was so violent, that he immediately left the town and fled into Wales: the rest of his party were utterly dispersed, killed, and taken.

In the fight and pursuit were slain the lord Bernard, earl of Litchfield, and one other lord, two knights, one colonel, with above four hundred more officers and soldiers.

There were taken prisoners eleven colonels, most of them knights, seven lieutenant-colonels, five majors, about forty other officers, and one thousand common soldiers.

i. 531

Letters from colonel Rossiter, informed that prince Rupert, prince Maurice, col. Gerrard, the lord Hawley, sir Richard Willis, and about four hundred other gentlemen of quality (the meanest whereof was a captain,) had laid down their commissions, deserted the king, and betook themselves to Wotton-house, fourteen miles from Newark, where they stood upon their guard.

They subscribed a declaration, that if they may obtain from the parliament a pass to go beyond sea, they will engage upon their honour and oath never to return to take up arms against the parliament, . . .

i. 549

Letters from colonel Birch informed the particulars of the taking of Hereford:

That he hired six men, and put them in the form of labourers, and a constable with them, with a warrant to bring these men to work in the town; that in the night he lodged these men within three-quarters musket-shot of the town, and an hundred-and-fifty firelocks near them; and himself with the foot and colonel Morgan with the horse came up in the night after them, and cut off all intelligence from coming to the town, so that they were never discovered.

That one night they came too short, but the next night, with careful spies and scouts, they carried on the business; and in the morning, upon letting down the drawbridge, the six countrymen and the constable went with their pickaxes and spades to the bridge;

That the guard beginning to examine them, they killed three of the guard, and kept the rest in play till the firelocks came up to them, and then made it good till the body came up, who entered the town with small loss, and became masters of it.

i. 584–87

Sir Thomas Fairfax sent a summons to the lord Hopton to lay down arms, to prevent effusion of blood . . . A trumpet came with an answer from the lord Hopton to sir Thomas Fairfax's summons, implying a willingness to end the business of the west without more bloodshed, but desires to know whether the king and parliament be not near to a conclusion of a peace; that he, being intrusted, may be careful of the king's honour; . . . Sir Thomas Fairfax and the lord Hopton agreed upon these articles:

That the lord Hopton's army should presently be disbanded, and his horse, arms, and ammunition, artillery, bag and baggage, delivered up to sir Thomas Fairfax.

Officers to have their horses, and troopers 20s. a man, strangers to have passes to go beyond sea, and English to go to their homes.

EXPLANATORY NOTES

ABBREVIATIONS

Ludlow, *Memoirs* *The Memoirs of Edmund Ludlow, 1625–72*, ed. C. H. Firth, 2 vols., 1894.

Swed. Int. *The Swedish Intelligencer*, printed for Nathaniel Butter and Nicolas Bourne, Pt. I, 1632; Pt. II, 1632; Pt. III, 1633.

Whitelocke *Memorials of the English Affairs* by Bulstrode Whitelock(e), new edn., 4 vols., 1853.

PART I

Page 3. (1) *late glorious Successor :* Charles XII of Sweden, killed in action at Frederikshald on 30 November 1718.

(2) *extraordinary History . . . Clarendon :* Edward Hyde's *History of the Rebellion and Civil Wars in England*, Oxford, 1702–4.

Page 8. *House :* a common Oxford term for 'College'. Unlikely to mean Christ Church now particularized as '*the* House'.

Page 10. *Match . . . Spain :* the proposal for a marriage between the Prince of Wales, later Charles I, and Princess Maria, Infanta of Spain, was made in 1617, suspended in 1618, and abortively resumed in 1623. War between England and Spain broke out in 1625 and was not brought to an end until 1630. Meanwhile England also became embroiled with France and attempted to relieve the Huguenots besieged in La Rochelle. Peace with France came in 1629. Consequently, at the time of the Cavalier's conversation—1628/9—it is not obvious what war his father expected to occur in the future 'between the King of England and the Spaniard', or indeed elsewhere in Europe, since England was currently engaged in hostilities.

Page 11. *Fielding :* Defoe possibly derived the name from his extensive reading of the *Swedish Intelligencer*, where (iii. 32) a marginal note reads: 'All this . . . received I from Lieutenant-Colonell *Terret*, Captaine *Feilding*, and Captaine *Legg*, then present in the Action'.

Page 12. *Pistoles :* from *c.* 1600 applied to a Spanish coin (worth 80–90p.), and after 1640 to the *louis d'or* issued by Louis XIII. Defoe probably intended the latter.

Page 14. (1) *Lieutenant-General . . . Roy :* From this point to p. 31 Defoe relies largely on Le Clerc's *Life of Richlieu*, trans. Tom Brown, 1695, i. 330–55.

(2) *Manage :* skilful handling.

Page 15. *English had done it :* cf. Ludlow, *Memoirs*, i. 11–12. (An account of the siege of La Rochelle (1628) is given in a memoir of great interest to Defoe: *Memoirs of the Sieur De Pontis*, trans. Charles Cotton, 1694, i. vii.)

Page 18. *We stayed in Paris* (*p. 16*) . . . *times :* Defoe's interpolation into the material borrowed from Le Clerc.

Page 19. *Paix :* possibly should read '*Pain*'.

Page 28. (1) *The Duke de Momorency* (p. 25). . . . *Saluces*: cf. Le Clerc, op. cit., i. 344–45: 'The Army of Mareschals *de la Force* and *Schomberg* being very much enfeebled by Desertions, and by Sicknesses, required of necessity to be reinforced with a new body of an Army, and the Conduct thereof was given to the Duke of *Montmorency*, and the Marquis *d'Effiat*. It was composed of ten thousand Foot, and a thousand Horse, and to joyn the other Army they were to hazard a battle against the Troops of *Savoy*, commanded by the Prince *Thoiras*. The French being to pass a Defile, the Savoyards staid till all were passed, but the Rear-Guard, which they charged and put them presently into confusion; but the two French Generals having caused some of their Troops to turn back, they defeated the Savoyards, and laid near two thousand Men on the ground. A few days after they took the City of *Saluces*, by composition, which made the Duke of *Savoy* much perplexed. Being come to *Savigliano*, with design to repair the loss by a new Combat, because he was superior in Horse, he received the news of the taking of *Mantua*, which as much rejoyced him as it afflicted the French.'

(2) *This put* . . . *Prince :* cf. Le Clerc, op. cit., i. 345: 'The French Generals having understood the Death of *Charles Emanuel*, deliberated whether they should go to *Casal*, whilst the courage of the Savoyards was abated by the Death of their Prince.'

(3) *Plague :* the attack of the plague suffered by the Cavalier was doubtless prompted by Le Clerc's report (op. cit., i. 355) of the French king's being given over 'for lost without retrieve' from the same cause. But Defoe's long-standing concern with the plague must not be overlooked; it was to lead to his *Journal of the Plague Year* in 1722. The Cavalier suffered from ordinary bubonic plague with the 'bubo' in the neck (see *A Journal of the Plague Year*, World's Classics edition 1990, pp. 76, 200).

Page 29. (1) *a Truce :* Treaty of Regensburg, 13 October 1630.

(2) *Proverb :* first recorded use 1576 (M. P. Tilley, *Dictionary of Proverbs*, 1950, s. 822).

Page 31. (1) *League :* Treaty of Bärwalde, 23 January 1631.

(2) *took* . . . *Stetin :* 20 July 1630.

(3) *Gust :* relish or enjoyment.

Page 35. (1) *English Ambassador :* Sir Peter Wyche (*d.* 1643), ambassador at Constantinople 1627–41.

(2) *related* . . . *Mecklenburgh :* through his grandfather, Gustav Vasa.

Page 36. *Treaty :* on 22 June 1631.

Page 38. *Seigensius :* no person of this name, exercising the influence Defoe ascribes to him, has been traced. The Duke of Saxony did place great confidence in a Lutheran minister—Matthias Hoë von Hoenëgg (1580–1645)—who urged him to defy the Emperor at Leipzig. If Defoe had Hoë in mind it is difficult to explain his use of 'Seigensius' in view of his historical accuracy elsewhere.

Page 43. *Tilly :* he had joined Pappenheim at the siege of Magdeburg in April 1631.

Page 44. *Administrator of Magdenburgh :* Christian William, a prince of the electoral house of Brandenburg (*Swed. Int.*, i. 110).

Page 51. *English Ambassador :* Sir Robert Anstruther.

Page 54. *near Torgau :* actually at Düben on 5 September 1631.

Page 56. *Touch :* trial

Page 59. *Field :* at Breitenfeld.

Page 62. *The next Day* (p. 59). . . . *General :* see App. I, *Swed. Int.*, i. 121–25.

Page 64. *The Darkness . . . Order :* see App. I, *Swed. Int.*, i. 121–25.

Page 65. *Crabats :* obsolete form of Croats or Croatians.

Page 66. *light of :* plundered

Page 67. *Rix-dollars :* silver coins (value 11–23p.) current *c.* 1600–1850 in various European countries.

Page 70. (1) *removed :* Gustavus had marched out of Erfurt on 26 September.
(2) *that Day :* 30 September.

Page 73. *The King was before* (p. 71). . . . *see :* see App. I, *Swed. Int.*, ii. 11–16.

Page 80. (1) *The Castle at Oppenheim* (p. 79). . . . *own :* see App. I, *Swed. Int.*, ii. 46–7.
(2) *capitulated :* on 12 December.
(3) *Queen :* Marie Eleonora actually joined him at Hanau on 22 January 1632.

Page 82. *Neuport :* Prince Maurice of Nassau won one of his most famous victories at Nieuport in July 1600.

Page 83. *The taking of* (p. 82). . . . *surrendered :* see App. I, *Swed. Int.*, ii. 76–82.

Page 88. *Serjeant of Dragoons :* Gustavus in fact made a personal reconnaissance of the situation; he exchanged badinage with Tilly's sentries across the river (M. Roberts, *Gustavus Adolphus*, 1953–8, ii. 700); but the part played by the sergeant is Defoe's invention.

Page 89. *Tale of a Tub :* an apocryphal story.

Page 93. *The King having* (p. 89). . . . *Ausburg :* see App. I, *Swed. Int.*, ii. 142–47.

Page 96. *Here the King . . . aforesaid :* the King narrowly escaped with his life on both 19 and 20 April 1632 at the siege of Ingolstadt; Tilly died in the city on 20th (Roberts, op. cit., ii. 701, 704).

Page 97. *The Army having . . . again :* see App. I, *Swed. Int.*, ii. 166–69.

Page 100. *engrossing :* monopolizing.

Page 105. *The first considerable* (p. 102). . . . *them :* see App. I, *Swed. Int.*, iii. 17–23.

Page 106. (1) *old Castle :* the Alte Feste.
(2) *The Imperialists finding* (p. 105). . . . *Quarter :* see App. I, *Swed. Int.*, iii. 39–44.

Page 178. Siege of Bristol: 23–26 July 1643.

Page 180. delivered of . . . Royal: the daughter was actually named Henrietta Anne (1644–70); her mother was Henrietta Maria (1609–69). Whitelocke had made the same error (i. 205). The Cavalier's knowledge of her later titles is anachronistic.

Page 187. (1) *about Grantham:* on 13 May 1643.

(2) *killed . . . Widdrington:* Defoe here repeats Ludlow's error (*Memoirs*, i. 58). Widdrington's title was not conferred until after the battle of Winceby; he died following the battle of Wigan, 1651.

(3) *Had we marched. . . . of Gloucester:* cf. Whitelocke, i. 213.

(4) *with Sir Nicholas Crisp:* Defoe follows Whitelocke, i. 213–14, in asserting that Crisp was present at this encounter. In fact, though Crisp's regiment was captured to a man at Cirencester on 15 September 1643, he was not with it; he had been involved in a quarrel which led to a duel and was thus absent.

Page 189. one of their Collonels: perhaps 'colonel Tucker' whom Whitelocke mentions (i. 215).

Page 190. a French Marquess: Ludlow is the only contemporary source for this detail (*Memoirs*, i. 56).

Page 191. Cessation of Arms: agreed on 15 September 1643.

Page 196. Bolton . . . first Fury: Defoe follows Whitelocke, i. 275, in giving three events in unhistorical order. The relief of the Countess of Derby at Lathom House (not Rupert's achievement) was nearly simultaneous with the capture of Bolton on 28 May 1644; Liverpool was then taken, followed in July by the seizure of York.

Page 198. surprize . . . Tyne: historically untrue.

Page 199. (1) *fetching . . . York:* cf. Whitelocke, i. 275: 'The prince fetching a compass about with his army got into York.'

(2) *Duke of Parma . . . Paris:* Alessandro Farnese, duke of Parma (1545-92) relieved Paris in 1590.

Page 200. I entreated him not (p. 199) *. . . . nothing:* the Cavalier's wisdom may have derived from Ludlow, *Memoirs*, i. 98–9.

Page 208. (1) *Remarks:* observations.

(2) *pressed:* conscripted into military service.

Page 216. Brennus Hill: perhaps one of the summits (almost permanently covered in snow) near the Brenner Pass; the name is no longer used.

Page 217. York: surrendered on 16 July 1644.

Page 222. laying down their Arms: at Fowey on 1 September 1644. Much of the detail of the King's victory and its consequences derives from Whitelocke, i. 302-3.

Page 224. declining to come . . . Horse: cf. Whitelocke, i. 321.

Page 226. (1) *Self-denying Ordinance:* 'an Ordinance appointing, That no Member of either House, during the Time of this War, shall have or execute any Office or Command, Military or Civil', *Journal of the House of Commons*, 11 December 1644.

(2) *modelling ... their Army:* reforming the organization and discipline of the parliamentary army; the 'New Model Army' was effectively in being by April 1645.

Page 228. (1) *The King would ... Divino:* cf. Whitelocke, i. 390: 'government by bishops was *jure divino* ... the government of the Church by presbyteries was *jure divino.*'

(2) *Hopes of Peace vanished:* negotiations were abandoned on 22 February 1645.

Page 229. *the Surprize of the town ... stormed:* see App. II, Whitelocke, i. 398.

Page 238. *Composition:* the discharging of his liabilities.

Page 240. *we attacked Hawkesly ... Worcester:* cf. Whitelocke, i. 437: 'the king's party took Hawkesley-house ... and carried the garrison, being eighty prisoners, to Worcester.'

Page 243 (1) *Siege to Leicester* (p. 241). ... *killed:* see App. II, Whitelocke i. 441. See also J. Wilshere and S. Green, *The Siege of Leicester—1645* (Leicester, 1970).

(2) *3000 Head of Cattle:* cf. Whitelocke, i. 446.

(3) *Fairfax, to whom ... Men:* cf. Whitelocke, i. 444.

Page 244. *in the Morning:* 14 June 1645.

Page 246. *at Naseby their* (p. 243). ... *Leicester:* see App. II, Whitelocke, i. 446–48.

Page 247. *to be printed:* within a month of the victory at Naseby, *The King's Cabinet Opened, or certain packets of secret letters* was published. A copy of it was probably owned by Defoe; see *The Libraries of Daniel Defoe and Phillip Farewell* ed. H. Heidenreich (Berlin, 1970), item 1420 b.

Page 248. *I took the freedom* (p. 247). ... *pleased:* the source of the Cavalier's wisdom may have been Clarendon, *History*, ix. 42, 67.

Page 250. *showed his Resentments:* by placing Hastings (then Lord Loughborough) under arrest.

Page 252. *Association Troops:* in December 1642 Parliament had ordered groups of counties to associate for mutual defence. One such group was the Eastern Counties Association to which Huntingdonshire and Leicestershire were added in 1643. The troops provided by this Association are referred to here.

Page 254. *They were commanded* (p. 253) .... *Lieutenant:* cf. Whitelocke, i. 500: 'some resistance made at the bridge by captain Bennet with his foot, till he, his lieutenant, and many of his men were slain.'

Page 255 *they were so poor ... Health:* see App. II, Whitelocke, i. 495.

Page 257. (1) *got into Chester:* on 23 September 1645.

(2) *From Ludlow* (p. 256) .... *Condition:* see App. II, Whitelocke, i. 518.

Page 258. (1) *leaves a Thousand* (p. 257) ... *dispersed:* cf. Whitelocke, i. 532–33.

(2) *The Lord Digby ... Man:* cf. Whitelocke, i. 531–32.

(3) *Prince Rupert ... Parliament:* see App. II, Whitelocke, i. 531.

Page 259. *Hereford which had ... Enemy:* see App. II, Whitelocke, i. 549.

Page 264. when unexpectedly the Enemy's General (p. 263) ....*to such Officers:* see App. II, Whitelocke, i. 584–87.

Page 265. (1) *not to seek in his Measures:* not lacking in other action he could take.
(2) *Cessation of Arms was agreed:* on 13 March 1646.

Page 266. quits the Town . . . more: cf. Whitelocke, ii. 13: 'the king was escaped out of Oxford in disguise with Mr. John Ashburnham and one more.' Charles's unnamed companion was his chaplain, Michael Hudson; they left Oxford on 26 April 1646.

Page 268. voted they . . . Scots: cf. Whitelocke, ii. 22.

Page 269. (1) *took his Leave:* on 28 January 1647.
(2) *That he was Bought and Sold:* cf. Whitelocke, ii. 111: 'some reported he used the expression, *that he was bought and sold.*'

Page 270. by the Sword: cf. Matt. 26: 52.

Page 278. garbled: cleansed or purged ('Pride's Purge', December 1648).

GLOSSARY OF MILITARY TERMS

Articles, upon: on conditions

Bastion: a projecting part of a fortification, consisting of an earthwork in the form of an irregular pentagon
battalia, in: in order of battle
breastwork: a defensive parapet of breast height
burgrave: a town governor

Comisado: a night attack
carabine: a fire-arm used by mounted soldiers
counterscarp: the outer wall of a ditch which supports the covered way in a fortified system
crupper, on the: in the rear; close behind
cuirassier: a horse soldier wearing body armour

Fireman: one who uses firearms
flying party: a detachment organized for rapid forays
forelorn: a storming party
furniture: a set of harness and ornamental or defensive trappings for a horse

Halberd: a combination of spear and battle-axe
half-moon: a defensive outwork resembling a bastion with a crescent-shaped gorge
hornwork: an outwork consisting of two demi-bastions connected by a wall and joined to the main work by two parallel wings

Leaguer: a military camp, especially one engaged in a siege; or an investing force
light, to: to dismount
list, to: to enlist

Nail, to: to spike (make unserviceable) a cannon

Parle, to beat a: to call for an informal conference with an enemy, under truce, for the discussion of terms
partizan: an infantry weapon consisting of a long-handled spear, the blade having one or more lateral cutting projections
petard: an explosive device used to breach a wall or gate
pickeer, to: to reconnoitre or scout
piece: a fortified place, or stronghold
port: a gate or gateway of a walled town, or the town itself

Ravelin: an outwork consisting of two embankments which form a salient angle, constructed in front of a fortified position

redoubt: a small defensive position made in a bastion of a permanent fortification

reformado: an officer left without command owing to the reforming of his company; he retained his rank and pay

ride post, to: to ride with post-horses, hence with great haste

Scout, to be upon the: to act as a spy

Trained band: a trained company of citizen soldiery

traverse: a defensive barricade thrown across a line of approach

Yield at discretion, to: to surrender unconditionally

BIOGRAPHICAL INDEX

The page reference records the first appearance of the person named.

Friedland, Duke of: see Wallenstein.

Fugger, Otto-Henri (1592–1644), served under Tilly and Wallenstein; commanded Bavarians at Nördlingen; Imperial Gov. of Augsburg, 93.

Furstenberg, Count de: Egon VIII, Count von Fürstenberg-Heiligenberg (1588–1635), Bavarian Gen. of artillery. *Swed. Int.*, i. 126, records his death at Leipzig; in fact he died at Konstanz, 24 Aug. 1635, 50.

Gell, Sir John (1593–1671), Parl. commander; prominent at capture of Lichfield and battle of Hopton Heath, 1643, 176.

Gerrard, Col.: Sir Charles, 1st Baron Gerard (1618?–94), Roy. Col. of horse, 1643; C.-in-C., South Wales, 1644; laid down king's commission 1645, 258.

Germany, Emperor of: see Ferdinand II.

Glemham, Sir Thomas (d. 1649?), Roy. Gov. of York, later of Oxford, 195.

Goring, Col. Charles: probably brother (1615?–71) to Lord Goring; Col. in Goring's regiment at Langport, 1645; succeeded him as Earl of Norwich, 195.

Goring, Lord: George, Baron Goring, later 2nd Earl of Norwich (1608–57), leading Roy. Gen.; Gov. of Portsmouth; commanded left wing at Marston Moor; Gen. of Horse under Rupert, 1644; after defeat in 1645 fled to continent, 149.

Gourdon, Capt.: not identified, 55.

Granvil [Grenvile], Sir Bevil (1596–1643), Roy. Commander at Bradock Down, 1643; killed at Lansdown, 149.

Grave Neels: see Brahe, Count Nils.

Greenvil [Grenvile], Sir Richard (1600–58), Roy. commander in Ireland, 1641–3, and in south-west of England, 1644–6, 220.

Grey (or Gray), Col: Sir Theophilus Grey, Gov. of Leicester; taken prisoner during siege of the city (see R. Symonds, *Diary of the Marches of the Royal Army during the Great Civil War*, lxxiv (Camden Society, 1859), 178), 194.

Grey, Lord: Henry, Lord Grey (1594–1651), brother of Sir Theophilus; First Commissioner of Leics. Militia, 1642; became Earl of Kent, 1643, 194.

Gustavus Adolphus, (1594–1632) king of Sweden; son of Charles IX and Christina; married Marie Eleonora, sister of Elector of Brandenburg, 1620; killed at Lützen; succeeded by his daughter Christina, 2.

Gustavus Carolus (1622–1600), Charles X of Sweden from 1654, 172.

Hacker, Capt. Francis (d. 1660), Parl. officer captured at Leicester; supervised Charles I's execution; hanged as regicide, 243.

Hall, Col.: Adolf Theodor von Efferen, genannt Hall (d. 1631), officer in Swedish army; killed at Leipzig (*Swed. Int.*, i. 126), 62.

Hambden [Hampden], John (1594–1643), leading opponent of Charles; one of the five members whom King tried to arrest, 1642, 167.

Hammond, Col. Robert (1621–54), Parl. Officer to whom Charles I surrendered on the Isle of Wight, 1647, 269.

Hastings, Col.: Henry 1st Baron Loughborough (d. 1667), Roy. commander at Edgehill, 1642, and at relief of Newark, 1644; Gov. of Leicester, 1645, 250.

Henderson, Sir John, professional soldier, first in Imperialist army, then under Charles; repulsed attack on Newark, 1643; led forces at Winceby; later in service of King of Denmark (at least till 1657), 187.

Henrietta Maria (1609–69), Queen consort of Charles I, 145.

Henrietta. Anne (1644–70), daughter of the preceding, 180.

Henry VIII (1491–1547), King of England, 272.